THE PORTABLE VICTORIAN READER

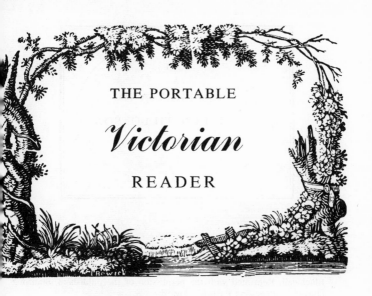

THE PORTABLE

Victorian

READER

Edited with an Introduction by

GORDON S. HAIGHT

Emily Sanford Professor Emeritus

of English Literature,

Yale University

THE VIKING PRESS · NEW YORK

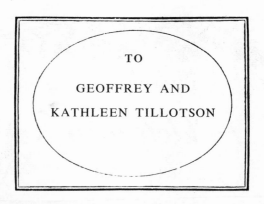

TO

GEOFFREY AND

KATHLEEN TILLOTSON

Acknowledgments:

Stanford University Press and Basil Blackwell: From *The Condition of The Working Class in England* by Friedrich Engels. © 1958 by Basil Blackwell. Reprinted with the permission of the publishers, Stanford University Press and Basil Blackwell.

The decorations in this volume are by Thomas Bewick and Alexander Anderson. They are reproduced from 19th C. sources by courtesy of the Print Collection and the Picture Collection of The New York Public Library and The Graphic Arts Collection of the Yale University Library.

Copyright © 1972 by The Viking Press, Inc.
All rights reserved

First published in 1972 by The Viking Press, Inc.
625 Madison Avenue, New York, N.Y. 10022

Published simultaneously in Canada by
The Macmillan Company of Canada Limited

SBN 670-74598-7 (hardbound)   670-01069-3 (paperbound)
Library of Congress catalog card number: 74-85862

Designed by M. B. Glick

CONTENTS

The Philistines

PART TWO: REFORM

Parliamentary Reform

Elections

The People's Charter

Supply and Demand

Labor Laws

Labor Unions

Prisons

Slavery

Socialism

PART THREE: RELIGION

The Evangelicals

The Tractarians

PART FOUR: EDUCATION

PART FIVE: SCIENCE

Geology

Evolution

PART SIX: HISTORY, THE ARTS, AND LETTERS

INTRODUCTION

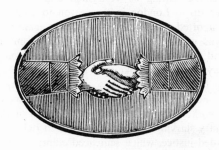

The Victorians

The time is long past when *Victorian* meant everything prudish, sentimental, and conventional. Now that we know more about them, we can see that the surface of respectability the Victorians presented was often only a protective convenience covering feelings and conduct not unlike our own. Under it many of them—some now lying snugly in Westminster Abbey—lived private lives as freely as bearded young rebels today. The beard itself is a Victorian revival, cultivated with the same mingling of exhibitionism and concealment, and in dress clothes the modern youth imitates the fashionable young man of 1870. But in much more fundamental ways the Victorian world offers striking parallels with our own.

The technological revolution the Victorians were born into was in its way as violently disruptive as that of our atomic age. Application of the steam engine to machinery early in the nineteenth century had drawn millions of people from rural cottage and hand loom to work in factories. Even more sharply than ours, their world was divided between "the two nations," the rich and the poor (p. 23 of this volume). The aristocracy

—the titled classes and the landed gentry—still lived in castle, hall, or manor house on rents from vast inherited estates, hunting, visiting, sitting as vestrymen and justices of the peace, going up to London in the season to vote for higher duties on imported corn and stiffer penalties against poachers. In the towns workers lived in unspeakable slums near the factory, and the owner in his spacious house on the hill above, away from the smoke and filth and noise (p. 188). Efforts to form unions or associations to bargain with employers met with brutal opposition. Thousands of unemployed workers demonstrated in the streets of the cities; in the country starving farmhands set fire to ricks and barns. Heavy-handed justice, which sentenced culprits to long terms at hard labor, transportation, or even death, failed to end the violence.

The employers belonged to the great middle class that arose during the Industrial Revolution, when, with the Continent embroiled in the Napoleonic wars and blockaded by her Navy, England made herself the workshop of the world. The two traits that dominated the middle class are the same ones for which the younger generation today repudiates its bourgeois background: materialism and respectability. The merchant or millowner of 1830 had sprung from the working class and, like Dickens's Mr. Bounderby (p. 176), boasted of it. His wealth was tangible evidence of his success in cutthroat competition for trade. He had been too busy to find time for much education; he left reading and artistic affairs to his wife, who, with equally meager intellectual development and plenty of servants, devoted herself to overelaborate dress and cluttered her house with tasteless bric-a-brac. Absorption in possessions and paucity of culture appear in all portraits of the middle class throughout the nineteenth century.

Respectability, the other middle-class characteristic, was not unrelated to materialism. The Calvinism underlying the Puritan ethic regarded wealth as a visible sign of God's approval. To acquire it and to bequeath it to one's children was the duty of an honest businessman. Sound economic principles defined by Adam Smith and Ricardo regulated its acquisition. High moral principles grounded in Protestant religion—with particular stress on the Seventh Commandment—guaranteed the legitimacy of the children who would inherit it. Since sanctity of property demanded sanctity of the marriage bond, commercial honesty and marital fidelity went hand in hand. Failure in either outlawed a man from respectable society.

In *The Mill on the Floss,* George Eliot (1819-1880) shows these traits in a parochial society relatively untouched by industry (p. 128). The Dodsons, while they feel Mr. Tulliver's bankruptcy as a deep disgrace to the family, would not dream of lending him money to prevent it. They "would be frankly hard of speech to inconvenient 'kin,' but would never forsake or ignore them—would not let them want bread, but only require them to eat it with bitter herbs." Describing the Dodsons as "emmet-like," George Eliot still finds something to admire in their simple religion; "we owe much to them," she once said, "for keeping up the sense of respectability, which was the only religion possible to the mass of the English people."[1] The Mayor of Middlemarch, Mr. Vincy, a small ribbon manufacturer, is perhaps less tightly cast in the middle-class pattern. He lives to the top of his income, "keeps a good house," and, without cultural pretensions himself, sends his children to the best schools, hoping to prepare them to step up a little in rank. The great manufacturers like Millbank in *Coningsby* (p. 151) or Rouncewell in *Bleak House,* princes of their class, display the same qualities of honesty, diligence, sobriety, and complacency. In London the City businessmen like Dickens's Veneering (p. 140) or Bounderby (p. 176) are perhaps the harshest caricatures of the parvenu. Trollope's Tappitt and Melmotte supply other examples. Jeames de la Pluche, the footman-made-millionaire in Thackeray's satire on the speculators in railway shares (p. 170), recalls the paper empire of George Hudson, the "Railway King." His wife in her days of glory provided the classic example of cultural inadequacy; on being shown a bust of Marcus Aurelius at

[1] Barbara Stephen, *Emily Davies and Girton College* (London: 1927), p. 183.

Grosvenor House, she said doubtfully, "It ain't the present Markis, is it?"

Thomas Carlyle (1795-1881), the son of peasants, accused the "Working Aristocracy" of Mammonism, lampooning his captain of industry, the textile magnate, as Plugson of St. Dolly Undershot (p. 243), who had conquered cotton but left all of his workers with bare backs. Most critics, however, were themselves of middle-class origin. John Ruskin (1819-1900), son of a wine merchant, suggested sarcastically to the men of Bradford, who had invited him to speak about the design of their new exchange, that they dedicate it to the Goddess of Getting-on (p. 184). Matthew Arnold (1822-1888), the most consistent taunter of the Philistines, the enemies of the children of light, was the grandson of a customs collector and son of a schoolmaster. During a lifetime spent in inspecting schools he observed at first hand the need to spread "knowledge of the best that has been known and thought in the world" in every class of society (p. 490).

The resentment we feel most deeply today in the world of the computer is the same one the poor felt in Victorian times: that *people* should be treated as *things!* Carlyle exclaimed in *Past and Present* (1843):

> We have profoundly forgotten everywhere that *Cash-pay-ment* is not the sole relation of human beings; we think, nothing doubting, that it absolves and liquidates all engage-ments of man. "My starving workers?" answers the rich Mill-owner: "Did I not hire them fairly in the market? Did I not pay them, to the last sixpence, the sum covenanted for? What have I to do with them more?" (p. 160).

In earlier times, when wages could not support a man and his family, they were given relief out of "the poor rate," a tax levied upon the landowners of the parish where they lived. If infirm from sickness or old age, the poor were cared for by the parish in a hospital or poorhouse, probably one surviving from monastic days or established long since by charitable bequest. But the mushroom factory towns had no such means of dealing with poverty, unemployment, or sickness. The New

Poor Law of 1834, in hope of discouraging idleness, gave help to the indigent only in the big new workhouses built for groups of several parishes. Men, women, children, the sick and aged, lunatics and delinquents, were all thrown together in the "great blank barren Union House, as far from old home as the County Jail (the remoteness of which is always its worst punishment for small rural offenders), and in its dietary, and in its lodging, and in its tending of the sick, a much more penal establishment."[2] The Union was bitterly hated by the poor. Dickens catches their feeling truly in old Betty Higden, who would rather die on the road than be "clutched off" to one of the "New Bastilles."

Reform

In 1830 no workers and few millowners sat in Parliament. More than two hundred seats in the House of Commons were filled by the borough-owners without any election. Thackeray does not exaggerate in depicting Sir Pitt Crawley occupying one of his family's seats and voting piously for abolition while he pockets the £1500 a year paid by Mr. Quadroon for the other—"with *carte blanche* on the Slave question."[3] The Duke of Wellington had yielded in 1829 to demands for Catholic Emancipation, eliminating religious tests so that Irish Members could take their seats in Parliament. But against elimination of the pocket boroughs he stood adamant, unmoved by appeals of disenfranchised manufacturers or mobs of starving workers clamoring for relief. When the Tories' control ended at the death of George IV, King William invited Earl Grey to form a Whig government; Lord John Russell brought in the First Reform Bill, and under the threat of creating enough new peers for a majority, it finally passed the House of Lords in 1832 (p. 218).

Though it gave the vote to only one out of six males, the First Reform Bill was the opening wedge of democratic gov-

[2] *Our Mutual Friend*, Part III, Chapter 8.
[3] *Vanity Fair*, Chapter 9.

ernment. Commissions were set up to determine what was needed. The appalling conditions revealed by their reports horrified even the Tory opposition. The huge sprawling towns spawned by the Industrial Revolution were functioning under the same regulations as when they were villages of one or two parishes. Children of six or seven were working in mills twelve hours a day, six days a week, protected only by rules designed in Elizabethan times for apprentices living in a careful master's family. Aghast at these revelations, Parliament overcame its reluctance to meddle with property rights and in 1833 passed the first significant Factory Act. It forbade employment in textile (except silk) factories of any child under nine; limited the work week of those under thirteen to forty-eight hours, with the obligation of attending two hours each day at schools—which did not exist; and limited the work of others under eighteen to ten hours a day. Adults, of course, continued as usual (when they could get it) a twelve-hour day, seventy-two hours a week, for as little as three shillings a day.

Another report described half-naked women working in some mines, young girls crawling on all fours to draw trucks of coal or iron ore through narrow cuttings, children of five or six made to sit solitary in the dark all day long, opening and shutting ventilating doors. In 1842 an act of Parliament forbade the employment of women in the mines or of boys under the age of ten (p. 245). Enforcement of these acts, in either mill or mine, was far from adequate. In other trades child labor was never treated systematically. It was sometimes a family affair; even in mines children often worked beside their parents. But if, like Oliver Twist, they were farmed out to brutal masters, their lot might be desperate. Charles Kingsley's *The Water Babies* (1866) attacked this abuse. Henry Mayhew described many child workers in his *London Labour and the London Poor* (1851), not all of them cruelly treated. For courage in adversity his Watercress Girl (p. 92), sturdily self-reliant, self-employed at the age of eight, confirms the truth of Dickens's little orphan Charley in *Bleak House*.

In 1839 the movement known as Chartism was launched

to persuade Parliament to extend the franchise. The six points of the "People's Charter" demanded manhood suffrage, election by secret ballot, annual Parliaments, payment of Members, abolition of property qualifications for Members, and equal electoral districts. Now that all but the last have been granted, these demands seem mild enough. To us the most surprising of the six points is the ballot. We find it hard to imagine the election of 1832 as an eyewitness describes it (p. 223). Each party set up its own polling booth, to which the qualified electors, well fortified with drink and more durable bribes, had to run the gantlet through jeering lines of the opposite party to record their votes. Everyone knew how a man had voted; and if he opposed his landlord, he might find the lease of his farm withdrawn. In spite of such rank injustice, when the Charter with thousands of signatures was presented to Parliament, neither Whigs nor Tories would accept it. In 1842 it was rejected again. In 1848, with revolutions exploding all over the Continent, almost two million men had signed the Charter. A mob of five hundred thousand gathered, threatening to march with it to Westminster. Faced with two hundred thousand of Wellington's troops and "special constables"—and thanks to a pouring rain—they were dispersed without major combat. It was their last attempt. Improved trade and rising wages in the 1850s relieved the pressure. Yet when the Second Reform Bill in 1867 extended the franchise to almost all males but agricultural workers, and the secret ballot was made law in 1872, the old Chartists could feel that their long campaign had not been fruitless.

Repeal of the Corn Laws in 1846 accounted for some of the improvement in living conditions. For centuries England had had protective duties against the import of corn—i.e., grain of all kinds—to encourage domestic production. In 1815 the landlords secured a law forbidding import of any foreign corn while the domestic price was below 80 shillings a quarter—i.e., eight bushels. In 1839, after the price had reached 77s. 6d., and bread cost more than many could pay, Richard Cobden and John Bright founded the Anti-Corn Law League to agitate for repeal. With Tories again in power and Whig landlords also opposing, there was little prospect of success. But in 1845 a month of continuous rain ruined all the wheat, and a disastrous blight at the same time destroyed the entire potato crop. In Ireland, where the potato was the staple food of the poor, hundreds of thousands died of starvation; those who could escape fled to Liverpool, packing twelve or fifteen to a room in any house they could find. There was nothing to feed them. Yet it was unthinkable to let them die while ships laden with foreign corn lay waiting to enter the ports. Sir Robert Peel, converted to Free Trade by Cobden's arguments and joined by the old Duke of Wellington, who put public welfare above party, forced repeal of the Corn Laws in June 1846.

These measures, long overdue, did not silence the radical reformers. Karl Marx (1818-1883), who had published the *Communist Manifesto* in 1848, came to London in 1850 and lived there the rest of his life, sitting in the British Museum, painstakingly gathering statistics for *Das Kapital,* of which the first volume was published in 1867. He supported himself precariously as correspondent of the New York *Tribune,* sending weekly letters like that on the Ten Hours Bill (p. 254). Ruskin, disillusioned by the Philistines' lack of response to his exhortations for social justice, turned to open attack on their mercantile philosophy in *"Unto This Last"* (p. 296), *The Crown of Wild Olive* (p. 179), *Munera Pulveris,* and *Fors Clavigera.* Under his influence William Morris (1834-1896) set up his highly successful business for the manufacture of furniture, wallpaper, and fabrics by designer-craftsmen, and the production of beautiful books at his Kelmscott Press. His *News from Nowhere* (1891) projected a utopian dream of what English life might be under socialism (p. 300). The Fabian Society, founded in 1883 with Sidney Webb, George Bernard Shaw, and others, rejected the Marxist class struggle for the gradual permeation of socialism into existing political institutions, which has resulted in the present Labour Party. Here too the roots of modern life are found in the intellectual ideas of the Victorians.

Religion

Religion played a smaller role than one might expect in humanitarian reforms. The manufacturing towns contained few parishes. Though contributing generously to support the Mission Society's work from Greenland's icy mountains to India's coral strands, the Church of England showed little concern with what Sam Weller called "flesh-coloured heathen" at home. Among the poor the Dissenters or Nonconformists—Methodists, Independents (Congregationalists), Baptists, and Unitarians—were the most active. The Methodists, founded at Oxford in 1729, had sparked a great revival of religion before their unrestrained enthusiasm stirred such hostility that they were compelled to form a separate church; they were the most numerous sect of Dissenters. The Independents, lacking any central organization, were less influential than their numbers would suggest, and the Baptists were splintered by doctrinal disputes. The Unitarians, descended from the Presbyterian seceders at the Restoration in 1662, were perhaps the most intellectual group, and they supported all the radical reforms.

Within the Church of England the Evangelical party supplied the most active reformers. William Wilberforce, Zachary Macaulay, Henry Thornton, and Hannah More had been among its leaders at the turn of the century. By 1830 the seventh Earl of Shaftesbury (1801-1885) was the dominant figure; it was he who carried to its successful conclusion their long campaign for abolition of slavery in the British colonies (p. 276). Though they shared many goals with the Dissenters, the Evangelicals preferred to work through the Church. They were the Puritans of the Establishment, holding a stern Calvinistic view of man's fallen state and insisting on the experience of conversion. Omnivorous Bible readers, they loved long Gospel sermons and extempore prayers. Like Mrs. Pardiggle in *Bleak House* (p. 111), they went about distributing such tracts as *The Sinner's Friend* to brick-makers, dockworkers, or huntsmen. They would kneel down and pray with a coal miner in a cottage or a drunkard in a railway carriage. They supported the Society for the Promotion of Christian Knowledge, the Society for the Propagation of the Gospel in Foreign Parts, and the Society for the Conversion of the Jews. With eyes turned toward hell-fire, they countenanced no worldly pleasures. Dancing, cards and gambling, theaters, novels, and many less harmful amusements were strictly forbidden. Their most vociferous controversy was waged against violation of the Sabbath. To keep it holy they urged Parliament to outlaw all employment of workers on Sunday. No train or bus should run, no cab be hired, no ship sail, no game be played, no lecture or speech be heard, no museum or library be open. Obviously, these restrictions would fall mostly on the poor, for whom Sunday offered the only chance for rest or culture. They would not inconvenience the rich, whose servants worked harder than ever with weekend entertaining. An Englishman's house was his castle; no law could touch him there, or prevent his driving out on Sunday with coachman and footmen. But the poor had no bus or river boat to take them out for a breath of country air; even at home they would have to eat a cold dinner because the bakehouses were closed. The argument that Sunday amusements would cut into Church attendance was absurd, since nothing could be subtracted from nothing. Dickens ridiculed the injustice of the proposal in *Sunday under Three Heads* (p. 324) in 1836; twenty years later Trollope glanced more gently at it in *Barchester Towers* (p. 330). The bill failed to pass.

Another obsession of the Evangelicals was the suppression of Vice, by which, of course, they meant anything related to sex. When the Crystal Palace was reopened at Sydenham in 1854, a group of Evangelical bishops demanded the installation of fig-leaves on all the nude statues. This early example of that prudery for which the Victorians are now commonly blamed represented not general English opinion, but the prurience of a small, highly organized Evangelical minority.

Dickens has given the trait a name in his description of Mr. Podsnap (p. 148).

One of the organizers of the Evangelical movement was the Reverend Charles Simeon (1759-1836). For many years, as a fellow of King's College and Vicar of Holy Trinity, he worked systematically to inculcate his views among the undergraduates at Cambridge. A bachelor and man of wealth, he established the Simeon Trust to buy up livings, to which young clergymen of approved "seriousness" were appointed. Evidence of his continuing influence can be seen in Samuel Butler's description of "the Sims" in 1858 (p. 335). By then direction of the movement had passed largely into the hands of the Earl of Shaftesbury, an earnest philanthropist who believed that people should be compelled to be good whether they wanted to or not. He supported all the reform measures of his time—not only abolition of slavery, but the humane treatment of the insane, of prisoners and miners and chimney-sweeps, the opening of "ragged schools" for the urchins of the slums, improved housing for the poor, and, of course, the laws enforcing Sabbath observance. Like Simeon, wherever he could exert influence, Shaftesbury urged the preferment of Evangelicals to any position from curate to bishop. In the Church of England, the state church, all bishops are appointed by the Prime Minister. Though there had been some equalization by the Established Church Act of 1836, a few of them still received princely incomes. Since they voted in the House of Lords, their politics were often of greater concern than their religious views. Trollope tells how the fall of the Tory government destroyed Archdeacon Grantly's prospect of a bishopric and brought to Barchester the Evangelical Whig, Bishop Proudie. In the decade 1855-65, during most of which Palmerston was Prime Minister, he had the appointment of twenty-five bishops, and at his death more than half the English bishops were of his nomination, chosen with the advice of Shaftesbury, whose wife was Palmerston's step-daughter. Naturally the Evangelicals were accused of narrow partisanship and were disliked for their holier-than-thou interference with Churchmen of other opinions.

Abhorrence of Roman Catholics, nurtured by patriotic sentiments since the days of the Tudors, stood high among Evangelical aversions. But an interest in the past, stirred perhaps by Scott's novels and Romantic poetry, turned a group of Oxford men toward a very different feeling. They came to view the Church of England as Catholic and Apostolic, free of the corruptions bred in Rome since the Middle Ages, and its bishops as true successors of the Twelve Apostles. In 1833 Parliament proposed to amalgamate the twenty-two Irish bishoprics, which served a small fraction of the population, into twelve, and to use the funds so saved to build schools and even support the Roman Catholic priests, who were doing the real parochial work of the country. John Keble, a fellow of Oriel College and the Professor of Poetry at Oxford, preached an assize sermon denouncing the plan as "national apostasy," and joined with John Henry Newman (1801-1890), Tutor of Oriel and Vicar of St. Mary's, and others to write a series of tracts which they distributed to clerical friends. In the first one Newman called on the bishops to resist the reformers, to proclaim their apostolic descent, to magnify their office. At Oxford the *Tracts for the Times* attracted favorable attention and soon influenced Churchmen everywhere who were unhappy with the Whig reforms. In 1834 a third fellow of Oriel, E. B. Pusey, the Professor of Hebrew, wrote a tract on fasting, of which the title alone kindled Evangelical fears of romanizing, and gave the group the name of Puseyites.

The Tractarian Movement reached its climax in 1841 with the publication of Newman's *Tract 90: Remarks on Certain Passages in the 39 Articles* (p. 360). He argued that the Articles of Religion drawn up in the sixteenth century had been made purposely vague to satisfy the Protestants and at the same time enable the Catholics to subscribe. Passing lightly over the rejection of such doctrines as purgatory and transubstantiation, *Tract 90* seemed to suggest that one might accept the 39 Articles and at the same time hold all the doctrines of the Church of Rome. A great outcry arose. The Heads of Houses moved to censure the tract; the Bishop of Oxford asked

Newman to suppress it and discontinue the series. Newman withdrew to Littlemore near Oxford, where he had built a tiny chapel, and lived a semi-monastic life with a few disciples, pondering his course. When some of them, breaking their promise to him, became Roman Catholics, Newman was unjustly blamed for their defection. He resigned St. Mary's, and two years later was received into the Roman Church. His change of opinion is subtly analyzed in *The History of My Religious Opinions,* originally called *Apologia pro Vita Sua* (p. 346). The Tractarian Movement had become another of Oxford's lost causes.

The Liberals who triumphed over the Tractarians were not a close-knit group but included men of widely varying interests who ranked service to others above theological argument. Their willingness to work with anyone in carrying out Christ's command, "Feed my Sheep," won them the name of the Broad Church Party. They were the ecumenicals of the Victorian age. One leader among them was the Headmaster of Rugby, Dr. Thomas Arnold (1795-1840). An enthusiastic teacher, he exerted a strong influence on the impressible young minds of his boys with weekly sermons inculcating the ideal of the Christian Gentleman (p. 463). Through visits and letters Dr. Arnold followed their careers at Oxford, countering the insidious appeal of Newman's mellifluous discourses with reiteration of his own sturdy faith in the sufficiency of the New Testament. If one of his old pupils—Arthur Hugh Clough, for example—wavered or fell into doubt, the Doctor was always at hand, in the words of his son Matthew, to

> move through the ranks, recall
> The stragglers, refresh the outworn,
> Praise, re-inspire the brave,

in their march

> On, to the City of God.[4]

The expectation of livelier battle against Tractarianism at Oxford, after his appointment to the Regius Professorship of

[4] Matthew Arnold, "Rugby Chapel."

History, was dashed by Dr. Arnold's death in 1840. His spirit survived in men like Arthur Penrhyn Stanley (1815-1881), who had a brilliant academic success at Oxford and carried on the Liberal campaign for many years as Dean of Westminster. Another old Rugby boy, Thomas Hughes (1822-1896), vividly recorded the Doctor's influence in *Tom Brown's School Days* (p. 443) and *Tom Brown at Oxford*.

Thomas Carlyle, the most vigorous and original of those loosely called Liberals, was not a Churchman of any kind. Brought up in strict Scotch Calvinism, he lapsed under the study of German philosophers, especially Kant and Fichte, into a kind of transcendental theism of his own. His distinction between the reality of the divine mind and the appearances which cover it is expressed in the basic metaphor of the tailor retailored in his semi-autobiographical *Sartor Resartus* (1836, p. 368). Nature, man, religions of all kinds are the mere "vesture of the Eternal"; orthodox Christianity is an outworn garment, "Hebrew Old Clothes," to be discarded for any sincere belief in the divine that a man can truly live by in the modern world. We must stop looking for happiness, Carlyle insists, and take up whatever work lies nearest to make the world a truer image of the "Infinite Unnameable." The heroes chosen for his lectures *On Heroes and Hero Worship* (1840) included Odin, Mahomet, Dante, Shakespeare, Dr. Johnson, Robert Burns, Cromwell, and even the arch-enemy Napoleon —not twenty years dead—whose bones were about to be interred in the Invalides. They are a curious group. For Carlyle they have in common the quality of intellect or sincerity, the ability to see through appearances into the open secret of the universe, to reveal its transcendental mysteries (p. 377).

Carlyle's scornful denunciation of the mechanistic laissez-faire doctrines of the Utilitarians turned many earnest young men toward social service. Among them was Frederick Denison Maurice (1805-1872), a Cambridge man, who after a few years as journalist had taken orders and become Chaplain to Lincoln's Inn and Professor of Divinity at the newly founded King's College, London. During the 1848 Chartist uprising a young barrister, John Malcolm Ludlow, persuaded him to collaborate in writing tracts for the workingmen, which they called *Politics for the People*. It soon failed and was replaced by a new penny journal, the *Christian Socialist*. Maurice learned that you can't talk religion to starving men. He helped Ludlow organize workers' co-operatives, labor unions, and the Working Men's College. For a time he was Principal of Queens College, Harley Street, the pioneer venture in higher education for women. Though his writings are of slight literary importance, Maurice's energetic efforts helped to break down the religious barriers between workers and the upper classes.

Another Cambridge man, Charles Kingsley (1819-1875), a hearty, athletic, carnivorous clergyman, completed the trio of Christian Socialists. As incumbent of Eversley, he had been appalled to find that not a single grown-up laborer in that country parish could read or write. The conditions he saw in the sweatshops while working with Maurice in the London slums convinced him that the Church must speak out against social injustice (p. 115). In a fiery "Message of the Church to the Labouring Man" he declared that the Bible proclaims the equality of all men, that it was God's will that they should all "share in the soil and wealth of England." This bold socialism brought Kingsley a rebuke from the Bishop of London and, indirectly, cost Maurice his professorship at King's College. Sharing the Liberal and Evangelical hatred of the Roman Catholic Church, Kingsley was obsessed by its ideal of celibacy, which he attacked in his poems and novels. In a review of Froude's *History of England* in January 1864 Kingsley rashly wrote :

> Truth for its own sake had never been a virtue with the Roman clergy. Father Newman informs us that it need not be, and on the whole ought not to be; that cunning is the weapon which Heaven has given to the saints wherewith to withstand the brute male force of the wicked world which marries and is given in marriage.

Newman naturally objected to the gratuitous slander, and Kingsley made an incomplete and blustering apology. We are indebted to the ensuing controversy for Newman's masterly autobiography, the *Apologia pro Vita Sua* (p. 346).

More damaging to orthodoxy were a number of Liberal writers whose works to many seemed sheer atheism. Perhaps in Carlyle's explanation of how Odin came to be thought a god we hear an early echo of David Friedrich Strauss's *Das Leben Jesu* (1835). Strauss differed from the crude eighteenth-century deists in not denying the existence of a historical Jesus. He simply examined the New Testament critically as if it were any other text to show that its supernatural elements were myths created like other myths by the Messianic expectations of the early disciples. Few Englishmen at this time could read German. Though the blasphemy law (in force since 1698) discouraged most booksellers from issuing such a book, young John Chapman in 1846 published *The Life of Jesus* in three volumes, translated anonymously by a young lady later famous as George Eliot (p. 383). More than any other of that era Strauss's book threw a shadow of doubt over religious thought. Matthew Arnold, John Sterling, Clough, Jowett, Butler, Pater, and many others were troubled by it. For if the Gospel can be reduced to myth, the Savior to an invention of the early church, how could one believe the promise of a future life? Without immortality, what morality? New sanctions must be found which reason could accept. The latter half of the nineteenth century saw many writers—the translator of Strauss among them—earnestly seeking substitutes for their lost faith.

Another challenge to orthodoxy came from within the Church itself. John William Colenso (1814-1883), rector of a country parish in Norfolk, was the author of the textbooks of arithmetic and algebra used in every schoolroom in England —even in the royal nursery. Perhaps in recognition of this he was selected in 1853 to be the first Bishop of Natal. He published that same year his *Village Sermons* with a dedication to Maurice, whom he extolled as his master. The bishops were reluctant to consecrate the disciple of a radical who had been suspected of heresy on the subject of hell-fire until he had affirmed his belief in endless punishment. In Natal

Colenso learned the native language, wrote a Zulu grammar, a Zulu-English dictionary, and a Zulu reader with selections from the Bible and other sources. One day an intelligent young native to whom he was telling the story of Noah and the Flood said, "You don't believe that, do you?" Colenso could not honestly say that he did. He began to study the text and in 1862 published the first volume of *The Pentateuch and the Book of Joshua Critically Examined* (p. 388). It stirred outraged protests. Bishop Gray of Capetown, even then a place with crude ideas of justice, excommunicated Colenso; the Society for the Propagation of the Gospel and the Society for the Promotion of Christian Knowledge, on whose contributions he largely depended, withdrew their support. But the Privy Council in London declared that Gray had no authority over Colenso, who remained Bishop of Natal and continued his honest, if rather ingenuous, Biblical study until his death.

Science

Geology was the first of the physical sciences to collide with the literal interpretation of the Bible. Archbishop Ussher's note, printed in the margin of the King James Version, dated the creation of the world in 4004 B.C. But geologists knew that the rocks they studied could not, except by miracle, have been made in six days of twenty-four hours. Fossils of extinct marine animals found in sedimentary strata on the mountaintops seemed to confirm the story of Noah's Flood, which was calculated to have begun on Sunday, 7 December 2347 B.C., though the water would have had to rise 700 inches a day to cover the Himalayas in the allotted forty. At first the professors of geology at Oxford and Cambridge, who were also clergymen, conceded that the six "days" of Genesis really meant long periods of time, hoping to discover the same sort of universal plan at work in the earth that Newton had demonstrated in the planets. But younger men, ranging farther in research, saw that millions of years were required for the geologic record. In 1830 Charles Lyell produced in the first volume of his *Principles of Geology* massive evidence that annihilated for thoughtful minds belief in a recent and catastrophic explanation of the world (p. 497). It was formed, he believed, by the gradual action of ordinary causes still in operation. Lyell suggested no conflict with Genesis. That problem arose later when the fossil series, more fully explored, showed a long succession of animals, steadily higher in structure, of which it was logical to think man the culmination. Yet, if the earth were created solely for man's use, why had it existed so many eons before man appeared on it?

The "origin of the animated tribes" was the primary theme of *Vestiges of the Natural History of Creation* (1844), an anonymous book that went through many editions. Though never acknowledged in his lifetime, it was the work of a self-educated Scotch publisher, Robert Chambers. Dismissing Genesis lightly, he offered a kind of Lamarckian theory of man's evolution from lower forms of life. Species, he argued, were introduced, not by special creation, but by the same natural process at work today (p. 507). Herbert Spencer in 1852 stated the view more directly in a brief article, "The Development Hypothesis" (p. 513). Estimating the number of species conservatively at not less than ten million, he asked: "Is it most likely that there have been ten millions of special creations? or is it most likely that by continual modifications, due to change of circumstances, the millions of varieties may have been produced, as varieties are being produced still?"

For more than twenty years Charles Darwin (1809-1882) had been patiently collecting evidence to support his hypothesis *On the Origin of Species by Natural Selection, or the Preservation of Favoured Races in the Struggle for Life* (1859). The revolution in modern thought caused by his explanation of the process of evolution is now too familiar to need comment. His argument was presented without rhetorical flourish in the simple, lucid prose that comes only from sincere effort to tell the truth. Though he saw from the first that man must have evolved like other animals, Darwin did not press the implication here (p. 519). Against acrimonious attacks of the orthodox, he was ably defended by Thomas

Henry Huxley (1825-1895), whose crushing rebuttals won him
the name of "Darwin's Bulldog." Like Darwin, Huxley had
studied marine animals during long voyages as a Navy surgeon
in the South Seas, collecting many independent observations
that confirmed the theory of natural selection. Though late
in life he confessed that survival of the fittest was not always
survival of the best,[5] Huxley's vigorous lectures and articles
were a main factor in turning the Victorian mind to the
concept of evolution. His prose, like Darwin's, was admirably
clear and made abstruse scientific details plain for lay readers.
His lecture on protoplasm, "The Physical Basis of Life"
(p. 530), is a good example of his style.

In fields less theoretical Victorian science was developing
ever more complex machinery. In 1851 the first world's fair,
suggested by Prince Albert, and called the Great Exhibition
of the Works of Industry of All Nations, was opened by
Queen Victoria (p. 538). The building itself, covering tall
trees in Hyde Park, was revolutionary. Made almost entirely
of glass supported on interchangeable cast-iron parts, it was
a striking precursor of modern architecture. Within it the most
varied examples of art and industry gathered from all over
the globe offered a dazzling vindication of Free Trade. The
works most highly valued were those with the most elaborate
ornament. Everything tried to look like something else. A
realistic cluster of cast-iron calla lilies spouted gaslight from
every pistil; on the hearth a bronze snake lay stretched across
the bottom of the fender; a kneeling gladiator grasped a real
sword in one hand and with the other held a round tabletop
above his head. Leaves and flowers crawled over every available surface. The displays at the Great Exhibition firmly
established the deplorable taste called mid-Victorian. Even
the machines betrayed the love of excess. Besides the func-
tional loom and spinning machine, the improved McCormick
reaper, the steam locomotive, steam plow, steam fire engine,
steam printing press, steam organ, steam cannon, there were
many useless gadgets like a sportsman's knife with eighty

[5] "An Apologetic Irenicon," *Fortnightly Review*, 58 (November 1892)
p. 568.

blades, or a contrivance with no conceivable purpose, which won a prize simply because it contained seven thousand parts.

Human imagination was working for the machine. In molding the most intractable substances to his use, man seemed to have conquered matter. Other applications of science were advancing toward the conquest of space and time. British railways, after shocking financial scandals, had reached a level of speed and convenience hardly maintained anywhere today (p. 545). The completion of the Suez Canal, spelling the displacement of clipper ship by steamer, cut weeks off the voyage to the East Indies. The penny post, set up in 1840, delivered letters anywhere in Great Britain the day they were mailed; in minutes the telegraph brought news to the printing press; the Atlantic Cable put the Old World in instant communication with the New; the telephone promised easy conversation that would destroy the art of letter-writing. Exulting in progress and the unprecedented prosperity of all classes, the Victorians were in no mood to heed Samuel Butler's warning in *Erewhon* (1872) that the machines threatened to enslave the men who had made them (p. 550).

Education

When Victoria came to the throne in 1837, about half her subjects could not read or write even their own names. One of the reformers' first cries was that the English must be made a "Reading People." Toward this worthy goal both Evangelicals with their Bibles and Utilitarians with a profusion of books for the diffusion of useful knowledge seemed ready to press on together. The parson was traditionally the parish schoolmaster, and except where grammar schools had been endowed, his teaching—if any— was limited to Sunday schools with simple Bible reading and perhaps a little arithmetic. Parliament's proposal of subsidies for existing schools stirred jealous controversy : Dissenters objected to having their children taught by Churchmen, and Churchmen resented any control of government over religious affairs. Elementary education for all was not made compulsory until 1880. Of the endowed schools, Lowood Institution in *Jane Eyre* is an unforgettable sample (p. 399). The picture, drawn by Charlotte Brontë, whose sister had died of tuberculosis in such a school, is undoubtedly colored by resentment; yet the military discipline, the inadequate food, and the excess of gloomy Calvinism must be essentially true. Dickens has an even lower opinion of schools like the Charitable Grinders, whose wretched day pupils were required by the founder's vanity to go through the streets in an outlandish uniform of blue coat and yellow leather trousers. The ignorant Mr. Squeers at Dotheboys Hall in remote Yorkshire keeps unwanted boys out of their parents' way as long as his fees are paid (p. 406). In *David Copperfield* the sadistic Mr. Creakle of Salem House is even more terrifying. For contrast, Dr. Strong, the eccentric old schoolmaster at Canterbury, is made kindly and benevolent; though David once mentions Latin verse, we see little of his actual education there. Paul Dombey at Dr. Blimber's Academy suffers from cramming by Mr. Feeder, B.A., who teaches by rote like a human barrel organ, and Miss Cornelia Blimber, who likes only dead languages, which she digs up like a ghoul. With poor little Tozer, muttering unknown tongues and scraps of Greek or Latin in his sleep, Dicken declares cramming to be worse than ignorance (p. 415). Teachers professionally trained in the new normal (or model) schools Dickens treats more harshly than any. Mr. M'Choakumchild agrees with his employer Mr. Gradgrind that "Facts alone are wanted in life," and that fancy and imagination should be entirely weeded out of education. "If he had only learnt a little less, how infinitely better he might have taught much more !" (p. 419). Bradley Headstone in *Our Mutual Friend* is another and worse product of the normal school training.

There was too little room for fancy in the education that John Stuart Mill got from his Utilitarian father. His toys at the age of three were cards with Greek words and their meanings, and he was soon reading Aesop and the *Anabasis*. Before he was eight he had read six of Plato's *Dialogues*, and he had gone through all the classical Latin authors before the age of twelve. Calculus and the serious study of logic and political economy began at thirteen. During his fourteenth year, which was spent in France, he studied nine hours a day. On his return he served as tutor to his brothers and sisters until at seventeen he was appointed a junior clerk at India House. This rigorous program deprived him of ordinary companionship with other boys and girls. The danger of corruption at school, from which his father protected him, might have been less harmful. He had no friend to confide in when at the age of twenty he suffered a serious nervous breakdown. After a long depression he was saved by his discovery of Wordsworth's poems. In his *Autobiography* (p. 427) he confessed that the habit of analysis instilled in him from infancy had "a tendency to wear away the feelings."

The great Public Schools—Eton, Winchester, Harrow, and the rest—like the Universities, were fixed in the traditional study of the classics. At Rugby, Dr. Arnold, who became headmaster in 1828, added mathematics, modern history, and modern languages. Today Rugby is perhaps best known for the football that developed there (p. 438). In Arnold's time it was his moral influence, exerted chiefly through the Sixth Form, that made the deepest impression on English education. For the rising middle classes in an era of shifting standards his ideal of the Christian Gentleman, combining manliness and integrity with liberal religious belief, though it was not beyond suspicion of priggishness, set a worthy pattern of behavior.

Many Victorians were concerned with the concept of the Gentleman. Thackeray satirized pretenders to it in his *Book of Snobs*, Tennyson praised it in his Arthurian heroes, and Ruskin devoted a chapter to its opposite, Vulgarity, in the final volume of *Modern Painters* (1860). But for Newman the ideal of the Christian Gentleman was not enough. In *The Idea of a University*, his famous definition of a gentleman as "one who never inflicts pain" is elaborated in all its attractive qualities only to be rejected as superficial and inadequate unless centered in true religion (p. 464). The pursuit of knowledge for its own sake, the mere cultivation of the intellect, Newman insists, is quite distinct from the cultivation of Christian virtue, which must be the true aim of education.

Huxley spoke out strongly for science as an essential element in a liberal education, which he believed should equip a man with understanding of the laws of Nature to enable him to play the game of life (p. 470), and train his body and mind to be ready "like a steam engine, to be turned to any kind of work." In reply Matthew Arnold underlined the limitations of this view, arguing that science alone could not give culture—the knowledge of "the best that is known and thought in the world" (p. 490). As a government inspector of schools for forty years, Arnold was painfully aware of the Philistine's indifference to culture, while Huxley, a member of the first London School Board in 1870, realized the ignorance of science in all classes of English society. Of the two, Huxley's is the broader concept, the one aimed at in liberal education today. In *Erewhon* (1872), Samuel Butler, grandson of a famous headmaster of Shrewsbury School, ironically pricked the lack of relevance in the old system; in the "Colleges of Unreason" boys spend the best years of their lives learning a hypothetical language to prepare them to answer questions that will never arise, but are left quite unable to earn their own living. Their most influential teacher is the Professor of Worldly Wisdom, who teaches them to think like other people. He has done most to suppress any kind of originality and flunks students for not writing vaguely enough (p. 479).

History, the Arts, and Letters

History was one of the most popular classes of Victorian literature. Any modern technique of marshaling facts by computer would have been withered by Carlyle's contempt for all machines. To him "the history of the world is but the biography of great men," those Heroes who tower above the rest and point the way. In *The French Revolution* (1837), Danton and Mirabeau are those he most admires, though Napoleon, "our last Great Man," appears briefly to restore law and order with his "whiff of grapeshot" at the end. The ideal of Kingship, once realized in the Middle Ages, in 1774, like Louis XV, lay sick and dying; the new ideal of Democracy was about to begin its stormy reign. Carlyle, making a pioneer study, used what documents he could find. Details gleaned from them, quickened by his poetic imagination, flash into graphic vignettes of action, following one another swiftly as in a modern film. His extraordinary style—abrupt, humorous, satirical, scornful, pathetic—has all the noisy emphasis of Carlyle's own speech (p. 563). He coins descriptive compound epithets to label characters—"Hercules-Mirabeau," "Sea-green Incorruptible Robespierre"—and renders simple statements emphatic by unexpected inversion. Many of these devices were adopted by the creators of the famous *"Time* magazine style," who read Carlyle as freshmen at Yale.

Macaulay was not unaware of Carlyle's achievement. But in beginning his *History of England* in 1839, he looked rather to the novels of Sir Walter Scott, who from the sober accounts of Clarendon and Hume had created his most vivid scenes. Macaulay wanted to combine the pictorial interest of the Waverley novels with sound intellectual history, explaining the history of government as well as of men and arts and manners. The five volumes he completed covered the years 1685-1705.

Macaulay arrays his details like a novelist, touching with pathos episodes like the death of Charles II or the execution of the Duke of Monmouth. Macaulay hardly pretends to be impartial; he is a Whig writing about Whigs, and his comments reflect the Whig's complacency with the material progress of the nineteenth century. His style is direct and clear, advancing perhaps too relentlessly with the oratorical effects and exaggerated contrasts that abound in his speeches. Its interest is maintained by brilliant illustrations rising from his phenomenal memory, and not always documented. Though the accuracy of his facts has often been challenged, no one denies that Macaulay's is the most readable English history of the period.

A close rival is James Anthony Froude's *History of England from the Fall of Wolsey to the Defeat of the Spanish Armada* (1856-1870). Froude had been at the center of the Tractarian controversy, and after Newman became a Roman Catholic, transferred his allegiance to Carlyle. His *History* is a manifest vindication of the English Reformation. He began it in 1852 with an article on Mary Stuart, which showed the strong anti-Catholic bias that was to run throughout the book. A second article portrayed the pirates and buccaneers of the sixteenth century as "indomitable God-fearing men whose life was one great liturgy," laying deep moral foundations for the magnificent harvest of power that England was to reap in the nineteenth.[6] Froude was too bigoted for a historian, and despite arduous labor over the manuscript records, his quotations were sometimes inexact. But his style is always even, showing to the last the fine influence of Newman; it moves swiftly in the dramatic—even melodramatic—scenes for which he is still read with pleasure.

Of the many other Victorian historians, two may be mentioned. Henry Thomas Buckle (1821-1862) was the first to advance an environmental theory. His *History of Civilization in England* (1857-1861), taking issue with Carlyle's Heroes, attributed civilization to conditions like climate and food supply acting on masses of men. William Edward Hartpole Lecky (1838-1903), in his *History of the Rise and Influence of the Spirit of Rationalism in Europe* (1865), written when he was only twenty-seven, attributed the growth of tolerance to decline of belief in the miraculous. His greatest work, *A History of England in the Eighteenth Century* (1878-1890), took up the account where Macaulay left off. Lecky saw history as, "not a series of biographies or accidents, or pictures, but a great organic whole." As he surveyed England's political relations with Ireland, France, and America, his concern was with truth rather than picturesque

Westminster Review, 58 (July 1852), p. 52.

effect. George III, George Washington, and the origins of the slave trade he treated without bias (p. 271).

Sometimes forgotten under the shadow of Evangelical seriousness, a lively strain of humor runs bubbling through the whole Victorian period from Surtees to Max Beerbohm. Dickens, its most popular author and greatest humorist, began *Pickwick Papers* as commentary for a series of comic sporting plates by Seymour, one of the brilliant company of Victorian illustrators, which included Cruikshank, Leech, Doyle, and Tenniel, best remembered for his part in Lewis Carroll's *Alice in Wonderland*. Thackeray was both author and illustrator in *Punch, or the London Charivari*, founded in 1841. "The Snobs of England" and "The Diary of C. Jeames de la Pluche" were first published in its pages. "Punch's Prize Novels," in which Thackeray parodied the absurdities of Bulwer-Lytton, G. P. R. James, Disraeli, and others, mingles riotous humor with shrewd literary criticism. His burlesque of James Fenimore Cooper, "The Stars and Stripes" (p. 570), has some amusing satire of Yankee manners. Upon another of his boyhood favorites, Scott's *Ivanhoe*, Thackeray turns the same critical eye in *Rebecca and Rowena*, his Christmas book for 1849. Whatever seemed hypocritical or pretentious in English life—the Evangelicals' May-Meetings (p. 317) or the glorification of the Great Exhibition (p. 538)—*Punch* neatly deflated. The humorous voice was heard in more serious periodicals too. George Henry Lewes affected a flippant, bantering style in his dramatic reviews for the *Leader;* but these were based on excellent critical principles and marked him, says George Bernard Shaw, as "the most able and brilliant critic between Hazlitt and our own contemporaries."

In all the arts the Victorians' taste seems rather naïve. Sentimental melodrama was their favorite theatrical fare; the oratorios of Handel and Mendelssohn, the most popular music; at the opera Rossini and Bellini reigned. The "New Music" of Wagner was accepted very slowly. George Eliot heard some of his operas at Weimar without being deeply affected, and she shared the general discontent with what was called the "exclusion of melody" in *Lohengrin*. Paintings like Landseer's "The Stag at Bay" or Frith's "Derby Day" were acclaimed by every class. They loved pictures that "told a story." At the Exhibition the outstanding sculpture was Powers's "Greek Slave," a life-size marble wearing nothing but the chains tying her wrists; but it had to be made acceptable by the explanation that she is in a Turkish bazaar, "deprived of her clothing, standing before the licentious gaze of a wealthy Eastern barbarian." Without some such uplifting moral "message" the Philistine felt guilty enjoying any work of art solely for sensual delight in its form or color. Even Ruskin in his celebrated defense of Turner's painting attributed moral principles to its aesthetic qualities, with which they have no connection. In "The Two Boyhoods," Ruskin wrote a lyrical description of the Venice where Giorgione grew up—"A city of marble, did I say? nay, rather a golden city, paved with emerald"—to contrast it with the "square brick pit," dark and narrow, where Turner was born, near Covent Garden market in London. Turner always looked for discarded oranges or cabbage leaves to accent his foregrounds; "anything fishy and muddy" attracted him—black barges, patched sails, and every possible condition of fog, dinginess, smoke, soot, dust, weeds, dunghills, and all the "soilings and stains of every common labour."

Good art for Ruskin could not be separated from good morals, and his writings became increasingly concerned with social criticism —"life trampled out in the slime of the street, crushed to dust amidst the roaring wheel," without joy or faith. This was a darker view than had appeared in earlier volumes of *Modern Painters* in such chapters as that "On Modern Landscape," where he contrasted the clarity of medieval landscape, a very minor part of the old painters' work, with the modern love of clouds, shadow, mystery; the love of mountains came from longing for liberty, the love of darkness, from loss of faith (p. 595). Architecture, too, Ruskin interpreted in moral terms : the glory of Gothic lay in what he (quite mistakenly) imagined to have been the freedom of the medieval workman; those "formless monsters and stern statues, anatomiless and rigid" on the old cathedral front, must not be mocked, "for they are signs of the life and liberty of every workman who struck the stone" (p. 586).

Ruskin's influence on Victorian literature was extensive. Though his didacticism has long been out of fashion, there is sound sense in many of his ideas. The chapter called "The Pathetic Fallacy" (p. 602) is the *locus classicus* of this term in literary criticism. His magnificent prose style, formed—like most great English styles—on the King James Version of the Bible, grew simpler in his later work. The superb purple passages in the first volumes of *Modern Painters* gave way to shorter, stronger sentences that avoided the rhythmical cadences of the earlier books. His style is seen at its finest in "Unto This Last" (p. 296) or in the conversational tone of "Traffic" (p. 179).

Among the numerous revolutions of 1848 was one by a group of young painters, rebelling against the insipid prettiness of academic convention. Holman Hunt and Millais, joined by Rossetti and a few others, resolved to paint directly from nature with the utmost fidelity to detail. They noted Ruskin's approval of the artists before Raphael, who drew everything—leaf or stone or animal or man—with care and clearness; if it was an oak tree, even the acorns were drawn. So they decided to call themselves the Pre-Raphaelite Brotherhood and signed their paintings with the cryptic initials P.R.B. (p. 574). The first attack by the Establishment fell on Millais in 1850, when he showed his "Carpenter's Shop, or Christ in the House of His Parents." Every detail in the scene was rendered with photographic realism : the dirt and shavings on the floor around the workbench, the frost-bite and bunions on the bare feet of the Holy Family, the sweat stains on their workclothes. The painting provoked outrage from every direction. The symbolism—little St. John holding a bowl of water in which to wash the bleeding hand of the young Christ, who has cut his palm on a nail—brought charges of Popery and Puseyism from Evangelicals. When the attacks were renewed in 1851, Ruskin was pursuaded to defend the Pre-Raphaelites, and his championship turned their fortunes.

The Pre-Raphaelites reflect a mid-Victorian trend toward realism which appeared in every genre. In fiction Thackeray, Mrs. Gaskell, Charlotte Brontë, Charles Reade, Trollope, even in the later novels Bulwer-Lytton, turned away from romance to depict the world about them with increasing fidelity. George Eliot in *Adam Bede* (Chapter 17) praised the artists who were "ready to give the loving pains of a life to the faithful representing of commonplace things." Reviewing Volume III of Ruskin's *Modern Painters* for the *Westminster* in 1856, she pointed out :

> The truth of infinite value that he teaches is *realism*—the doctrine that all truth and beauty are to be attained by a humble and faithful study of nature, and not by substituting vague forms, bred by imagination on the mists of feeling, in place of definite, substantial reality. The thorough acceptance of this doctrine would remould our life; and he who teaches its application. . . is a prophet for his generation.

In another article (p. 608) she commented on the disparity between real peasants and those depicted in drama or fiction. English writers, in spite of the censorship exercised by the circulating libraries, were beginning to show the influence of Flaubert and Balzac. Among poets—in the pages of Swinburne—and novelists—in the work of George Moore—the voice of Baudelaire could be heard—not without horror.

French writers were much in Matthew Arnold's mind. His opinion that a critic should strive "to see the object as in itself it really is," first expressed in his lectures *On Translating Homer* (1861), was repeated in "The Function of Criticism at the Present Time" (p. 613), the opening chapter of *Essays in Criticism* (1865). Disinterestedness was the quality Arnold thought most necessary. With its classical tradition France could teach the complacent, provincial Englishmen, who were practical in material affairs but distrustful of ideas, to seek "the best that is known and thought in the world." For Arnold this study of perfection, this "culture," combining beauty and intelligence, sweetness and light, went beyond religion. He preached it in a lucid, urbane prose, shot through with ironic phrases reiterated with devastating force.

In nineteenth-century painting the real pioneers were not the Pre-Raphaelites, looking back toward the Primitives for inspiration, but the French Impressionists. George Moore (1852-1933) had thrust himself among them during the six years he lived in Paris, and on returning to England in 1880 claimed an almost proprietary right in the discovery of Manet and Degas (p. 640). But Whistler (1834-1903), who had worked longer in Paris, brought Impressionism into the London galleries. When his "Falling Rocket. A Nocturne in Black and Gold" at the Grosvenor in 1877 evoked from Ruskin the rash comment that he "never expected to hear a coxcomb ask two hundred guineas for flinging a pot of paint in the public's face," Whistler, relishing the publicity, sued Ruskin for libel. Though the jury awarded him only a farthing in damages and his costs were ruinous, the trial marked the end of Ruskin's domination of English art.

A new aesthetic theory had already been promulgated at Oxford. Unsettled by German rationalism, Walter Pater (1839-1894), tutor of Brasenose College, had decided against taking orders in the Church and was looking for something to replace his lost faith. If a man cannot believe in a future life, what is the best way for him to spend the present one? Pater's *Studies in the History of the Renaissance* (1873) gave his answer. Accepting Arnold's dictum that the aim of criticism is to see the object as it really is, the Aesthete must study the only view he can have of it, his own impressions of art, discriminating and analyzing the pleasure it gives him. This was the opposite of Ruskin's ethical view, and centered on the Renaissance, the period of licentious pleasure Ruskin most abhorred. Pater's famous "Conclusion" (p. 628) expounds an atomic theory of life: all we can know is the impression of single moments, gone while we try to apprehend them.

Not the fruit of experience, but experience itself, is the end. A counted number of pulses only is given to us of a variegated, dramatic life. How may we see in them all that is to be seen in them by the finest senses? How shall we pass most swiftly from point to point, and be present always at the focus where the greatest number of vital forces unite in their purest energy?

To burn always with this hard, gem-like flame, to maintain this ecstasy, is success in life.

This memorable passage may stand as well as any for an example of Pater's prose style: the muted tone, avoiding journalistic color, or what, in his essay "Style" (p. 632) he calls "gipsy phrase"; the simplicity favoring monosyllables and charging ordinary words with profound meaning; the sensitive rhythm, not falling into obvious metrical pattern but making stress reinforce sense; the frugality of the "logically filled space connected always with the delightful sense of difficulty overcome." Though Pater protests that a rich challenging subject is essential to good art, readers are often more fascinated by the technique than what it is communicating. His well-known passage on the "Mona Lisa" (p. 626), describing not the painting but Pater's impressions of it, is, according to Wilde, better than the original.

Oscar Wilde (1856-1900), who came up to Oxford the year after *Studies in the History of the Renaissance* was published, became so enthusiastic an apostle of Art for Art's Sake that Pater withdrew the "Conclusion" from the second edition. Wilde's affectations—long hair, flowers, velvet breeches, and passionate love of blue china—incorporated by W. S. Gilbert into Bunthorne in *Patience,* made the Aesthete widely known. But beneath all the silliness Wilde had some sound critical ideas, far in advance of his time. The dialogue called "The Critic as Artist" (p. 647), glittering with paradox, denies outright any relation between morality and art. Long before the New Critics were born, Wilde declared that the meaning of any work is in the soul of the observer; from the material of actual life the critic creates a new world more true than the real world.

That Oscar Wilde and Carlyle, Macaulay and Pater, Butler and Newman, can all be called Victorians indicates how wide a field the term embraces. Cheap printing and proliferation of the reading public produced such a mass of prose as the world had never seen before. To represent its variety and extent within the compass of a Viking Portable is not easy. Anthologies usually take long extracts from ten or twelve authors, rarely including the novelists, whose reflection of the life of an age is often the most illuminating. Here I have collected briefer passages from some thirty-seven authors, novelists as well as essayists, humorists, scientists, writers on religion and education, writers of leaders for *The Times*, letter writers, even Queen Victoria herself in her Journal. The selections cover the most significant and often conflicting movements of that violently revolutionary period, arranged by subject in an order that provides a new and lively interest to readers of the Victorians.

The text has been taken, when possible, from the earliest edition of each book or article, retaining the original punctuation and spelling except in the case of a few typographical errors. For advice on the historical background, I am obliged to my old friends Lewis P. Curtis, Colgate Professor Emeritus of History at Yale University, and Dudley W. R. Bahlman, Dean of Williams College.

BIOGRAPHICAL LIST OF AUTHORS

ARNOLD, MATTHEW (1822-1888). Poet and critic, served for thirty years as an inspector of schools. From 1857-1867 he was professor of poetry at Oxford, where he developed his conception of culture and criticism.

BODICHON, BARBARA LEIGH SMITH (1827-1891). A founder and benefactor of Girton College, Cambridge, and champion of women's rights, traveled in the United States in 1858, visiting every Southern state but Texas.

BRONTË, CHARLOTTE (1816-1855). Novelist, author of *Jane Eyre* (1847) and *Villette* (1853).

BUTLER, SAMUEL (1835-1902). Novelist and painter; published the satirical *Erewhon* in 1872. During the next dozen years he worked at *The Way of All Flesh*, which was not published until 1903.

CARLYLE, THOMAS (1795-1881). Essayist and historian; made his reputation with *Sartor Resartus* (1836) and *The French Revolution* (1837). The most successful of his courses of lectures was *On Heroes and Hero-Worship* (1840).

CARLYLE, JANE WELSH (1801-1866). One of the most brilliant letter writers of the 19th century; married Thomas Carlyle in 1826.

CHAMBERS, ROBERT (1802-1871). Printer and bookseller in Edinburgh; published his *Vestiges of Creation* anonymously in 1844.

COLENSO, JOHN WILLIAM (1814-1883). Bishop of Natal; stirred violent controversy in 1862 by his *Critical Examination of the Pentateuch,* which challenged literal interpretation of Genesis.

DARWIN, CHARLES ROBERT (1809-1882). Naturalist; gave definite form to the theory of evolution by natural selection in his *Origin of Species* (1859).

DICKENS, CHARLES (1812-1870). Novelist; began his career with newspaper articles collected as *Sketches by Boz* (1836). He described his travels in the United States in *American Notes* (1842).

DISRAELI, BENJAMIN, first Earl of Beaconsfield (1804-1881). Conservative statesman and novelist. *Coningsby, or the New Generation* (1844) and *Sybil, or the Two Nations* (1845), expound his political views before and after the Reform Bill.

ELIOT, GEORGE, pseudonym of Mary Anne Evans (1819-1880). Novelist, author of *Adam Bede* (1859), *The Mill on the Floss* (1860), *Silas Marner* (1861), *Middlemarch* (1871-72), and other novels.

ENGELS, FRIEDRICH (1820-1895). Son of a wealthy German cotton-spinner, he came to Manchester in 1842 and lived there and in London the rest of his life. He was concerned with the

Chartist movement and collaborated with Karl Marx in *The Communist Manifesto* (1848).

FROUDE, JAMES ANTHONY (1818-1894). Historian and man of letters. He came under the influence of Newman at Oxford, but reacted toward skepticism and became a disciple of Carlyle, whose biography he wrote.

GASKELL, ELIZABETH CLEGHORN (1810-1865). A novelist, she was the wife of a Unitarian minister at Manchester, where she observed the condition of the working class depicted in *Mary Barton* (1848) and *North and South* (1855).

HUGHES, THOMAS (1822-1896). Novelist and Christian Socialist, educated under Dr. Thomas Arnold at Rugby, which he describes in *Tom Brown's School Days* (1857), and at Oxford. With John Ludlow and F. D. Maurice he was active in the Christian Socialist movement and helped found the Working Men's College.

HUXLEY, THOMAS HENRY (1825-1895). Biologist and man of letters, whose championship of evolution won him the nickname of "Darwin's Bulldog."

KINGSLEY, CHARLES (1819-1875). Novelist and Christian Socialist, author of *Alton Locke* (1850), *Westward Ho!* (1855), and other novels.

LYELL, SIR CHARLES (1797-1875). Professor of Geology at King's College, London, author of *The Principles of Geology* (1830-33), which substituted a theory of gradual change for the conception of "catastrophic" formation of the earth.

MACAULAY, THOMAS BABINGTON, first Baron Macaulay (1800-1859). Historian, essayist, poet, and statesman.

MARTINEAU, HARRIET (1802-1876). Journalist, novelist, and historian; visited the United States and wrote *Society in America* (1837) and *Retrospect of Western Travel* (1838).

MARX, KARL (1818-1883). German philosopher and political economist; published (with Engels) *The Communist Manifesto* (1848). After being expelled from Germany, he came to London, where he lived the rest of his life.

MAYHEW, HENRY (1812-1887). Journalist, contributed the first of his sketches of *London Labour and the London Poor* (1851) to the *Morning Chronicle*.

MILL, JOHN STUART (1806-1873). Philosopher and political economist; was educated at home by his father, the Utilitarian philosopher. Among his books are *Logic* (1843), *On Liberty* (1859), *The Subjection of Women* (1869), and his *Autobiography* (1873).

MOORE, GEORGE (1852-1933). Novelist and critic; lived in Paris 1873-1880, where he knew some of the Impressionist painters. Of his novels, *Esther Waters* (1894) is the best.

MORRIS, WILLIAM (1834-1896). Poet, painter, printer, designer, and decorator; revived medieval craftsmanship in the arts. Like Ruskin, who strongly influenced him, Morris worked for the improvement of society through socialism.

NEWMAN, JOHN HENRY (1801-1890). Fellow of Oriel college, and leader of the Oxford Movement in the Church of England. In 1845 he became a Roman Catholic and in 1879 was made a cardinal.

PATER, WALTER HORATIO (1839-1894). Critic and essayist, center of the Aesthetic Movement at Oxford. His *Studies in the History of the Renaissance* (1873) and the novel *Marius the Epicurean* (1885) both reflect the new hedonism.

RUSKIN, JOHN (1819-1900). Art critic and writer on social problems. *Modern Painters,* begun as a defense of Turner in 1843, was completed with the fifth volume in 1860.

SMILES, SAMUEL (1812-1904). Author of *Lives of the Engineers* (1861-62) and other biographies. His *Self-Help* (1859), which maintains that perseverance leads to success, was immensely popular.

SPENCER, HERBERT (1820-1903). In his *System of Synthetic Philosophy* he applied the evolutionary principle to life, mind, society, and morality.

STANLEY, ARTHUR PENRHYN (1815-1881). Historian and theological writer, educated at Rugby and Oxford, became Dean of Westminster in 1864.

THACKERAY, WILLIAM MAKEPEACE (1811-1863). Novelist and satirist; was one of the first contributors to *Punch. Vanity Fair* (1847-48), like most of his other novels, was published in monthly numbers.

The Times of London, founded in 1785, was so powerful in forming opinion that it was sometimes referred to as "The Thunderer."

TROLLOPE, ANTHONY (1815-1882). The most prolific of the great Victorians, he wrote nearly fifty novels, of which the Barsetshire series and the Parliamentary series are the most popular.

VICTORIA, QUEEN (1819-1901). Succeeded to the throne in 1837 as Queen of Great Britain and Ireland, and assumed the title Empress of India in 1876.

WILDE, OSCAR (1856-1900). Dramatist, novelist, critic. His aesthetic pose was caricatured by W. S. Gilbert in *Patience.*

SUGGESTIONS FOR FURTHER READING

BRIGGS, ASA. *The Age of Improvement, 1784-1874*. New York: Longmans, Green, 1959.

BURN, W. L. *The Age of Equipoise. A Study of the Mid-Victorian Generation*. New York: Norton, 1964.

CHADWICK, OWEN. *The Victorian Church*. New York: Oxford University Press, 1966.

ELTON, OLIVER. *A Survey of English Literature 1830-1880*. London: St. Martin's Press, 1920. 2 vols.

GILLISPIE, C. C. *Genesis and Geology*. Cambridge, Mass.: Harvard University Press, 1951.

HALEVY, ELIE. *A History of the English People in the Nineteenth Century*, trans. E. I. Watkin and D. A. Barker. London: Ernest Benn, 1949-52. 6 vols. (especially vols. 3, 4).

HOUGHTON, WALTER E. *The Victorian Frame of Mind 1830-1870*. New Haven, Conn.: Yale University Press, 1957.

LEVINE, GEORGE, and MADDEN, WILLIAM. *The Art of Victorian Prose*. New York: Oxford University Press, 1968.

The Oxford History of England, ed. Sir George Clark. New York: Oxford University Press.
Vol. 13, Sir Llewellyn Woodward, *The Age of Reform 1815-1870*, 2nd ed., 1962.
Vol. 14, Sir Robert Ensor, *England 1870-1914*, 1936.

STEVENSON, LIONEL, ed. *Victorian Fiction. A Guide to Research*. Cambridge, Mass.: Harvard University Press, 1964. Separate chapters by authorities on the major novelists and criticism of their work.

TILLOTSON, KATHLEEN. *Novels of the Eighteen-Forties*. New York: Oxford University Press, 1954. The Introduction contains valuable information on methods of publication and the relation of writers and readers.

WALKER, HUGH. *The Literature of the Victorian Era*. Cambridge: Cambridge University Press, 1913.

WEBB, R. K. *Modern England: From the Eighteenth Century to the Present*. New York: Dodd, Mead, 1968.

WILLEY, BASIL. *Nineteenth-Century Studies. Coleridge to Matthew Arnold*. New York: Columbia University Press, 1949.
————. *More Nineteenth-Century Studies. A Group of Honest Doubters*. New York: Columbia University Press, 1956.

YOUNG, G.M., ed. *Early Victorian England, 1835-1865*. New York: Oxford University Press, 1934. Excellent chapters by experts on such subjects as work and wages, homes and habits, town and country life, art, music, drama, etc. The editor's masterly summary, "Portrait of an Age," appears as the final chapter.

PART
ONE

THE VICTORIANS

THE
TWO NATIONS:
THE RICH

An Address to King William

THOMAS BABINGTON MACAULAY

[FROM a letter to his sister]

London June 24. 1831

MY LOVE—

. . . This morning, as I was sitting at breakfast in my dressing-gown, the Times before me, sipping a full bason of tea and eating between whiles of a well-baked loaf, the accompanying note was delivered at my door. Read here enclosure marked A as the Diplomatists say. I send it because I love accuracy; and because I wish to teach you to love it. File this note—(it is from Lord Althorp) with your papers. A hundred years hence people will give ten pounds for it. It will be a relique of famous times.

Well,—having received this note, I was not disobedient to the summons. I attired myself in my drawing-room dress; and at half after twelve was in the House of Commons. We mustered, gradually, about a hundred and eighty members, all of us ministerial. There were a few court-dresses, many official

Here published for the first time by permission of the Master and Fellows of Trinity College, Cambridge, from text supplied by Professor Thomas Pinney.

uniforms; and some members in the uniforms of the regular army or of the local militia. There were many in boots. But the majority were dressed, like me, as for an evening party. Admire, I pray you, for a moment the tact which I showed in dressing myself quite comme il faut without the least instruction. Burdett, who never went up with an address before in his life, was in full court dress. So was Sir Richard Price and Bernal. Admire again, I beseech you, these little touches of narrative. Lord Althorp came in court mourning, Rice, Stanley, Graham, Tennyson, Howick, Baring and Macdonald were blazing with gold lace and white satin. We nicknamed my late colleague Marshal Macdonald.

In came Mr. Speaker with a gown flowered with gold and a long lace ruff. We had prayers; and then Lord Althorp moved that we should adjourn till four and go to the King with our address. The motion was, of course, carried, and we set forth in a train of carriages which reached from Westminster Hall to the Horse Guards, if you know—which I much doubt—where those two places are. Shiel gave me a place in his carriage together with Mr. Perrin and Sir Robert Hart, the successful candidates for Dublin at the late election. We went on at foot's pace, the Speaker preceding us in a huge, old-fashioned, painted, gilded coach, drawn by two immense black horses. The Serjeant with the mace, and the Chaplain went in the Speaker's coach.

At half after one we reached St. James's Palace. The coaches set down their inmates one by one, and we were among the last. In we went—and I was in the inside of a real King's Palace for the first time in my life.

I have seen finer houses. We passed first through a long matted passage with wooden benches, bearing the royal arms, set on both sides. Beef-eaters with their red coats and gold lace stood here and there; and now and then we met a magnificent looking person in a blue suit loaded with dazzling embroidery. At the end of this matted passage was a staircase of stone, not by any means very fine. I have seen finer at several country-seats, and those at the London Club houses beat it all to nothing. Up this stair-case we went and were ushered by two tall yeomen of the guard into a large anti-room. A few good pictures hung around the walls. I caught a glimpse of one of Vandyke's Henrietta-Marias as we passed through. The room was however comfortless. The only furniture consisted of two or three large scarlet benches. The floor was covered with red cloth which looked as if his Majesty was in the habit of riding over it with the whole Royal Hunt. From this antiroom we passed into a reception room, smaller than the antiroom, but still of noble size, with pictures round the walls and a general air of great magnificence in the furniture. We had scarcely assembled here when a large pair of folding-doors at the further end was thrown open, and we advanced, pushing as hard as we could without making a disturbance; and thus we squeezed ourselves into the presence-chamber.

The room is handsome, the walls and cieling covered with gilding and scarlet hangings. On the walls is a picture of the battle of Vittoria, another of the battle of Waterloo, a full-length of George IV by Lawrence, and two or three older pictures which I could not examine on account of the crowd. Fronting us was the throne under a gorgeous canopy. We marched up to it between two court officers in scarlet and gold, bearing halberts. His Majesty was seated in all his glory, wearing an admiral's uniform. Lord Wellesley, in a state of fine preservation looking as if he had just been taken out of a band box, held the white staff at the King's elbow. What a sublime dandy that Marquess Wellesley is! I could see little of the other attendants of the King, by reason of the crowd.

The Speaker read our address. The King bowed at the end of every sentence and at all the peculiarly emphatic words. When the Speaker had done the King turned to one of the Lords in waiting, who handed him a paper containing what he was to say in answer to us. Another presented a pair of spectacles. His Majesty placed them on his royal nose, read a short answer, which you will see in the papers, and bowed us out. The Speaker stept forward and kissed the Sacred Hand of our Gracious Sovereign. Then came the worst part of the show. For we had to walk out backwards, bowing all the way down the presence chamber. You may conceive how two hundred people cooped up pretty close in a room performed this ceremony. We came out with broken shins and broken toes in abundance, vowing—many of us—that we would never do Ko-tou more.

I went only because I wanted to find something to tell you, and if you like to hear about these fine doings I am satisfied. . . .

Ever yours, dearest,
T. B. M.

Old England Before the Reform Bill

GEORGE ELIOT

[FROM *Felix Holt, the Radical*]

1866

Five-and-thirty years ago the glory had not yet departed from the old coach-roads: the great roadside inns were still brilliant with well-polished tankards, the smiling glances of pretty barmaids, and the repartees of jocose ostlers; the mail still announced itself by the merry notes of the horn; the hedge-cutter or the rick-thatcher might still know the exact hour by the unfailing yet otherwise meteoric apparition of the pea-green Tally-ho or the yellow Independent; and elderly gentlemen in pony-chaises, quartering nervously to make way for the rolling swinging swiftness, had not ceased to remark that times were finely changed since they used to see the pack-horses and hear the tinkling of their bells on this very highway.

From the Introduction.

In those days there were pocket boroughs, a Birmingham unrepresented in Parliament and compelled to make strong representations out of it, unrepealed corn-laws, three-and-sixpenny letters, a brawny and many-breeding pauperism, and other departed evils; but there were some pleasant things too, which have also departed. *Non omnia grandior ætas quæ fugiamus habet,* says the wise goddess: you have not the best of it in all things, O youngsters! the elderly man has his enviable memories, and not the least of them is the memory of a long journey in mid-spring or autumn on the outside of a stage-coach. Posterity may be shot, like a bullet through a tube, by atmospheric pressure from Winchester to Newcastle: that is a fine result to have among our hopes; but the slow old-fashioned way of getting from one end of our country to the other is the better thing to have in the memory. The tube-journey can never lend much to picture and narrative; it is as barren as an exclamatory O! Whereas the happy outside passenger seated on the box from the dawn to the gloaming gathered enough stories of English life, enough of English labours in town and country, enough aspects of earth and sky, to make episodes for a modern Odyssey. Suppose only that his journey took him through that central plain, watered at one extremity by the Avon, at the other by the Trent. As the morning silvered the meadows with their long lines of bushy willows marking the watercourses, or burnished the golden corn-ricks clustered near the long roofs of some midland homestead, he saw the full-uddered cows driven from their pasture to the early milking. Perhaps it was the shepherd, head-servant of the farm, who drove them, his sheep-dog following with a heedless unofficial air as of a beadle in undress. The shepherd with a slow and slouching walk, timed by the walk of grazing beasts, moved aside, as if unwillingly, throwing out a monosyllabic hint to his cattle; his glance, accustomed to rest on things very near the earth, seemed to lift itself with difficulty to the coachman. Mail or stage coach for him belonged to that mysterious distant system of things called "Gover'ment," which, whatever it might be, was no business of his, any more than the most out-lying nebula or the coal-sacks of the southern hemisphere: his solar system was the parish; the master's temper and the casualties of lambing-time were his region of storms. He cut his bread and bacon with his pocket-knife, and felt no bitterness except in the matter of pauper labourers and the bad-luck that sent contrarious seasons and the sheep-rot. He and his cows were soon left behind, and the homestead too, with its pond overhung by elder-trees, its untidy kitchen-garden and cone-shaped yew-tree arbour. But everywhere the bushy hedgerows wasted the land with their straggling beauty, shrouded the grassy borders of the pastures with catkined hazels, and tossed their long blackberry branches on the corn-fields. Perhaps they were white with May, or starred with pale pink dogroses; perhaps the urchins were already nutting amongst them, or gathering the plenteous crabs. It was worth the journey only to see those hedgerows, the liberal homes of unmarketable beauty—of the purple-blossomed ruby-berried nightshade, of the wild convolvulus climbing and spreading in tendrilled strength till it made a great curtain of pale-green hearts and white trumpets, of the many-tubed honeysuckle which, in its most delicate fragrance, hid a charm more subtle and penetrating than beauty. Even if it were winter the hedgerows showed their coral, the scarlet haws, the deep-crimson hips, with lingering brown leaves to make a resting-place for the jewels of the hoar-frost. Such hedgerows were often as tall as the labourers' cottages dotted along the lanes, or clustered into a small hamlet, their little dingy windows telling, like thick-filmed eyes, of nothing but the darkness within. The passenger on the coach-box, bowled along above such a hamlet, saw chiefly the roofs of it: probably it turned its back on the road, and seemed to lie away from everything but its own patch of earth and sky, away from the parish church by long fields and green lanes, away from all intercourse except that of tramps. If its face could be seen, it was most likely dirty; but the dirt was Protestant dirt, and the big, bold, gin-breathing tramps were Protestant tramps. There was no sign of superstition near, no crucifix or image to indicate a misguided reverence: the inhabitants were probably so free from superstition that they were in much less awe of the parson than of the overseer. Yet they were saved from the excesses of Protestantism by not knowing how to read, and by the absence of handlooms and mines to be the pioneers of Dissent: they were kept safely in the *via media* of indifference, and could have registered themselves in the census by a big black mark as members of the Church of England.

But there were trim cheerful villages too, with a neat or handsome parsonage and grey church set in the midst; there was the pleasant tinkle of the blacksmith's anvil, the patient cart-horses waiting at his door; the basket-maker peeling his willow wands in the sunshine; the wheelwright putting the last touch to a blue cart with red wheels; here and there a cottage with bright transparent windows showing pots full of blooming balsams or geraniums, and little gardens in front all double daisies or dark wallflowers; at the well, clean and comely women carrying yoked buckets, and towards the free school small Britons dawdling on, and handling their marbles in the pockets of unpatched corduroys adorned with brass buttons. The land around was rich and marly, great corn-stacks stood in the rick-yards—for the rick-burners had not found their way hither; the homesteads were those of rich farmers who paid no rent, or had the rare advantage of a lease, and could afford to keep their corn till prices had risen. The coach would be sure to overtake some of them on their way to their outlying fields or to the market-town, sitting heavily on their well-groomed horses, or weighing down one side of an olive-green gig. They probably thought of the coach with some contempt, as an accommodation for people who had not their own gigs, or who, wanting to travel to London and such distant places, belonged to the trading and less solid part of the nation. The passenger on the box could see that this was the district of protuberant optimists, sure that old England was the best of all possible countries, and that if there were any facts which had not fallen under their own observation, they were facts not worth observing: the district of clean little market-towns without manufactures, of fat livings, an aristocratic clergy, and low poor-rates. But as the day wore on the scene would change: the land would begin to be blackened with coal-pits, the rattle of handlooms to be heard in hamlets and villages. Here were powerful men walking queerly with knees bent outward from squatting in the mine, going home to throw themselves down in their blackened flannel and sleep through the daylight, then rise and spend much of their high wages at the ale-house with their fellows of the Benefit Club; here the pale eager faces of handloom-weavers, men and women, haggard from sitting up late at night to finish the week's work, hardly begun till the Wednesday. Everywhere the cottages and the small children were dirty, for the languid mothers gave their strength to the loom; pious Dissenting women, perhaps, who took life patiently, and thought that salvation depended chiefly on predestination, and not at all on cleanliness. The gables of Dissenting chapels now made a visible sign of religion, and of a meeting-place to counterbalance the ale-house, even in the hamlets; but if a couple of old termagants were seen tearing each other's caps, it was a safe conclusion that, if they had not received the sacraments of the Church, they had not at least given in to schismatic rites, and were free from the errors of Voluntaryism. The breath of the manufacturing town, which made a cloudy day and a red gloom by night on the horizon, diffused itself over all the surrounding country, filling the air with eager unrest. Here was a population not convinced that old England was as good as possible; here were multitudinous men and women aware that their religion was not exactly the religion of their rulers, who might therefore be better than they were, and who, if better, might alter many things which now made the world perhaps more painful than it need be, and certainly more sinful. Yet there were the grey steeples too, and the churchyards, with their grassy mounds and venerable headstones, sleeping in the sunlight; there were broad fields and homesteads, and fine old woods covering a rising ground, or stretching far by the roadside, allowing only peeps at the park and mansion which they shut in from the working-day world. In these midland districts the traveller passed rapidly from one phase of English life to another: after looking down on a village dingy with coal-dust, noisy with the shaking of looms, he might skirt a parish all of fields, high hedges, and deep-rutted lanes; after the coach had rattled over the pavement of a manufacturing town, the scene of riots and trades-union meetings, it would take him in another ten minutes into a rural region, where the neighbourhood of the town was only felt in the advantages of a near market for corn, cheese, and hay, and where men with a considerable banking account were accustomed to say that "they never meddled with politics themselves." The busy scenes of the shuttle and the wheel, of the roaring furnace, of the shaft and the pulley, seemed to make but crowded nests in the midst of the large-spaced, slow-moving life of homesteads and far-away cottages and oak-sheltered parks. Looking at the dwellings scattered amongst the woody flats and the ploughed uplands, under the low grey sky which overhung them with an unchanging stillness as if Time itself were pausing, it was easy for the traveller to conceive that town and country had no pulse in common, except where the handlooms made a far-reaching straggling fringe about the great centres of manufacture; that till the agitation about the Catholics in '29, rural Englishmen had hardly known more of Catholics than of the fossil mammals; and that their notion of Reform was a confused combination of rick-burners, trades-unions, Nottingham riots, and in general whatever required the calling-out of the yeomanry. It was still easier to see that, for the most part, they resisted the rotation of crops and stood by their fallows: and the coachman would perhaps tell how in one parish an innovating farmer, who talked of Sir Humphry Davy, had been fairly driven out by popular dislike, as if he had been a confounded Radical; and how, the parson having one Sunday preached from the words, "Break up your fallow-ground," the people thought he had made the text out of his own head, otherwise it would never have come "so pat" on a matter of business; but when they found it in the Bible at home, some said it was an argument for fallows (else why should the Bible mention fallows?), but a few of the weaker sort were shaken, and thought it was an argument that fallows should be done away with, else the Bible would have said, "Let your fallows lie"; and the next morning the parson had a stroke of apoplexy, which, as coincident with a dispute about fallows, so set the parish against the innovating farmer and the rotation of crops, that he could stand his ground no longer, and transferred his lease.

The coachman was an excellent travelling companion and commentator on the landscape: he could tell the names of sites and persons, and explain the meaning of groups, as well as the shade of Virgil in a more memorable journey; he had as many stories about parishes, and the men and women in them, as the Wanderer in the " Excursion," only his style was different. His view of life had originally been genial, and such as became a man who was well warmed within and without, and held a position of easy, undisputed authority; but the recent initiation of Railways had embittered him: he now, as in a perpetual vision, saw the ruined country strewn with shattered limbs, and regarded Mr Huskisson's death as a proof of God's anger against Stephenson. "Why, every inn on the road would be shut up !" and at that word the coachman looked before him with the blank gaze of one who had driven his coach to the outermost edge of the universe, and saw his leaders plunging into the abyss. Still he would soon relapse from the high prophetic strain to the familiar one of narrative. He knew whose the land was wherever he drove; what noblemen had half-ruined themselves by gambling; who made handsome returns of rent; and who was at daggers-drawn with his eldest son. He perhaps remembered the fathers of actual baronets, and knew stories of their extravagant or stingy housekeeping; whom they had married, whom they had horsewhipped, whether they were particular about preserving their game, and whether they had had much to do with canal companies. About any actual landed proprietor he could also tell whether he was a Reformer or an Anti-Reformer. That was a distinction which had "turned up" in

latter times, and along with it the paradox, very puzzling to
the coachman's mind, that there were men of old family and
large estate who voted for the Bill. He did not grapple with
the paradox; he let it pass, with all the discreetness of an
experienced theologian or learned scholiast, preferring to point
his whip at some object which could raise no questions.

Lord Monmouth after the Reform Bill

BENJAMIN DISRAELI

[FROM *Coningsby; or, the New Generation*]

1844

Towards the end of the session of 1836, the hopes of the
Conservative party were again in the ascendant. The Tadpoles
and the Tapers had infused such enthusiasm into all the
country attorneys, who, in their turn, had so be-deviled
the registration, that it was whispered in the utmost confidence, but as a flagrant truth, that Reaction was at length
'a great fact.' All that was required was the opportunity; but
as the existing parliament was not two years old, and the
government had an excellent working majority, it seemed that
the occasion could scarcely be furnished. Under these circumstances, the backstairs politicians, not content with having
by their premature movements already seriously damaged the
career of their leader, to whom in public they pretended to
be devoted, began weaving again their old intrigues about the
court, and not without effect.

From Book IV, Chapter 3.

It was said that the royal ear lent itself with no marked repugnance to suggestions which might rid the sovereign of ministers, who, after all, were the ministers not of his choice, but of his necessity. But William IV, after two failures in a similar attempt, after his respective embarrassing interviews with Lord Grey and Lord Melbourne, on their return to office in 1832 and 1835, was resolved never to make another move unless it were a checkmate. The king, therefore, listened and smiled, and loved to talk to his favourites of his private feelings and secret hopes; the first outraged, the second cherished; and a little of these revelations of royalty was distilled to great personages, who in their turn spoke hypothetically to their hangers-on of royal dispositions, and possible contingencies, while the hangers-on and go-betweens, in their turn, looked more than they expressed; took county members by the button into a corner, and advised, as friends, the representatives of boroughs to look sharply after the next registration.

Lord Monmouth, who was never greater than in adversity, and whose favourite excitement was to aim at the impossible, had never been more resolved on a dukedom than when the Reform Act deprived him of the twelve votes which he had accumulated to attain that object. While all his companions in discomfiture were bewailing their irretrievable overthrow, Lord Monmouth became almost a convert to the measure, which had furnished his devising and daring mind, palled with prosperity, and satiated with a life of success, with an object, and the stimulating enjoyment of a difficulty.

He had early resolved to appropriate to himself a division of the county in which his chief seat was situate; but what most interested him, because it was most difficult, was the acquisition of one of the new boroughs that was in his vicinity, and in which he possessed considerable property. The borough, however, was a manufacturing town, and returning only one member, it had hitherto sent up to Westminster a radical shopkeeper, one Mr. Jawster Sharp, who had taken what is called 'a leading part' in the town on every 'crisis' that had occurred since 1830; one of those zealous patriots who had

got up penny subscriptions for gold cups to Lord Grey; cries
for the bill, the whole bill, and nothing but the bill; and
public dinners where the victual was devoured before grace
was said; a worthy who makes speeches, passes resolutions,
votes addresses, goes up with deputations, has at all times the
necessary quantity of confidence in the necessary individual;
confidence in Lord Grey; confidence in Lord Durham; confidence in Lord Melbourne: and can also, if necessary, give
three cheers for the King, or three groans for the Queen.

But the days of the genus Jawster Sharp were over in this
borough as well as in many others. He had contrived his
lustre of agitation to feather his nest pretty successfully; by
which he had lost public confidence and gained his private
end. Three hungry Jawster Sharps, his hopeful sons, had all
become commissioners of one thing or another; temporary
appointments with interminable duties; a low-church son-in-
law found himself comfortably seated in a chancellor's living;
and several cousins and nephews were busy in the Excise.
But Jawster Sharp himself was as pure as Cato. He had
always said he would never touch the public money, and he
had kept his word. It was an understood thing that Jawster
Sharp was never to show his face again on the hustings of
Darlford; the Liberal party was determined to be represented
in future by a man of station, substance, character, a true
Reformer, but one who wanted nothing for himself, and therefore might, if needful, get something for them. They were
looking out for such a man, but were in no hurry. The seat
was looked upon as a good thing; a contest certainly, every
place is contested now, but as certainly a large majority. Notwithstanding all this confidence, however, Reaction or Registration, or some other mystification, had produced effects
even in this creature of the Reform Bill, the good Borough
of Darlford. The borough that out of gratitude to Lord Grey
returned a jobbing shopkeeper twice to Parliament as its
representative without a contest, had now a Conservative
Association, with a banker for its chairman, and a brewer for
its vice-president, and four sharp lawyers nibbing their pens,
noting their memorandum-books, and assuring their neigh-

bours, with a consoling and complacent air, that 'Property must tell in the long run.' Whispers also were about, that when the proper time arrived, a Conservative candidate would certainly have the honour of addressing the electors. No name mentioned, but it was not concealed that he was to be of no ordinary calibre; a tried man, a distinguished individual, who had already fought the battle of the constitution, and served his country in eminent posts; honoured by the nation, favoured by his sovereign. These important and encouraging intimations were ably diffused in the columns of the Conservative journal, and in a style which, from its high tone, evidently indicated no ordinary source and no common pen. Indeed, there appeared occasionally in this paper, articles written with such unusual vigour, that the proprietors of the Liberal journal almost felt the necessity of getting some eminent hand down from town to compete with them. It was impossible that they could emanate from the rival Editor. They knew well the length of their brother's tether. Had they been more versant in the periodical literature of the day, they might in this 'slashing' style have caught perhaps a glimpse of the future candidate for their borough, the Right Honourable Nicholas Rigby.

Lord Monmouth, though he had been absent from England since 1832, had obtained from his vigilant correspondent a current knowledge of all that had occurred in the interval: all the hopes, fears, plans, prospects, manœuvres, and machinations; their rise and fall; how some had bloomed, others were blighted; not a shade of reaction that was not represented to him; not the possibility of an adhesion that was not duly reported; he could calculate at Naples at any time, within ten, the result of a dissolution. The season of the year had prevented him crossing the Alps in 1834, and after the general election he was too shrewd a practiser in the political world to be deceived as to the ultimate result. Lord Eskdale, in whose judgment he had more confidence than in that of any individual, had told him from the first that the pear was not ripe; Rigby, who always hedged against his interest by the fulfilment of his prophecy of irremediable discomfiture, was never very sanguine. Indeed, the whole affair was always considered premature by the good judges; and a long time elapsed before Tadpole and Taper recovered their secret influence, or resumed their ostentatious loquacity, or their silent insolence.

The pear, however, was now ripe. Even Lord Eskdale wrote that after the forthcoming registration a bet was safe, and Lord Monmouth had the satisfaction of drawing the Whig Minister at Naples into a cool thousand on the event. Soon after this he returned to England, and determined to pay a visit to Coningsby Castle, feast the county, patronise the borough, diffuse that confidence in the party which his presence never failed to do; so great and so just was the reliance in his unerring powers of calculation and his intrepid pluck. Notwithstanding Schedule A, the prestige of his power had not sensibly diminished, for his essential resources were vast, and his intellect always made the most of his influence.

True, however, to his organisation, Lord Monmouth, even to save his party and gain his dukedom, must not be bored. He, therefore, filled his castle with the most agreeable people from London, and even secured for their diversion a little troop of French comedians. Thus supported, he received his neighbours with all the splendour befitting his immense wealth and great position, and with one charm which even immense wealth and great position cannot command, the most perfect manner in the world. Indeed, Lord Monmouth was one of the most finished gentlemen that ever lived; and as he was good-natured, and for a selfish man even good-humoured, there was rarely a cloud of caprice or ill-temper to prevent his fine manners having their fair play. The country neighbours were all fascinated; they were received with so much dignity and dismissed with so much grace. Nobody would believe a word of the stories against him. Had he lived all his life at Coningsby, fulfilled every duty of a great English nobleman, benefited the county, loaded the inhabitants with favours, he would not have been half so popular as he found himself within a fortnight of his arrival with the worst county reputation conceivable, and every little squire vowing that he would not even leave his name at the Castle to show his respect.

Lord Monmouth, whose contempt for mankind was absolute; not a fluctuating sentiment, not a mournful conviction, ebbing and flowing with circumstances, but a fixed, profound, unalterable instinct; who never loved any one, and never hated any one except his own children; was diverted by his popularity, but he was also gratified by it. At this moment it was a great element of power; he was proud that, with a vicious character, after having treated these people with unprecedented neglect and contumely, he should have won back their golden opinions in a moment by the magic of manner and the splendour of wealth. His experience proved the soundness of his philosophy.

Lord Monmouth worshipped gold, though, if necessary, he could squander it like a caliph. He had even a respect for very rich men; it was his only weakness, the only exception to his general scorn for his species. Wit, power, particular friendship, general popularity, public opinion, beauty, genius, virtue, all these are to be purchased; but it does not follow that you can buy a rich man: you may not be able or willing to spare enough. A person or a thing that you perhaps could not buy, became invested, in the eyes of Lord Monmouth, with a kind of halo amounting almost to sanctity.

As the prey rose to the bait, Lord Monmouth resolved they should be gorged. His banquets were doubled; a ball was announced; a public day fixed; not only the county, but the principal inhabitants of the neighbouring borough, were encouraged to attend; Lord Monmouth wished it, if possible, to be without distinction of party. He had come to reside among his old friends, to live and die where he was born. The Chairman of the Conservative Association and the Vice-President exchanged glances, which would have become Tadpole and Taper; the four attorneys nibbed their pens with increased energy, and vowed that nothing could withstand the influence of the aristocracy 'in the long run.' All went and dined at the Castle; all returned home overpowered by the condescension of the host, the beauty of the ladies, several real Princesses, the splendour of his liveries, the variety of his viands, and the flavour of his wines. It was agreed that at future meetings of the Conservative Association, they should always give 'Lord Monmouth and the House of Lords!' superseding the Duke of Wellington, who was to figure in an after-toast with the Battle of Waterloo.

———•◆•———

Victoria Becomes Queen

QUEEN VICTORIA

[FROM her Journal]

Tuesday, 20th June [1837].—I was awoke at 6 o'clock by Mamma, who told me that the Archbishop of Canterbury and Lord Conyngham were here, and wished to see me. I got out of bed and went into my sitting-room (only in my dressing-gown), and *alone,* and saw them. Lord Conyngham (the Lord Chamberlain) then acquainted me that my poor Uncle, the King, was no more, and had expired at 12 minutes p. 2 this morning, and consequently that I am *Queen.* Lord Conyngham knelt down and kissed my hand, at the same time delivering to me the official announcement of the poor King's demise. The Archbishop then told me that the Queen was desirous that he should come and tell me the details of the last moments of my poor, good Uncle; he said that he had directed his mind to religion, and had died in a perfectly happy, quiet state of mind, and was quite prepared for his death. He added that the King's sufferings at the last were not very

great but that there was a good deal of uneasiness. Lord
Conyngham, whom I charged to express my feelings of con-
dolence and sorrow to the poor Queen, returned directly to
Windsor. I then went to my room and dressed.

Since it has pleased Providence to place me in this station,
I shall do my utmost to fulfil my duty towards my country;
I am very young and perhaps in many, though not in all
things, inexperienced, but I am sure, that very few have more
real good will and more real desire to do what is fit and right
than I have.

Count d'Orsay Calls on Mrs. Carlyle

JANE WELSH CARLYLE

[FROM a letter to her mother]

7 *April* 1839

To-day gone a week the sound of a whirlwind rushed thro'
the street, and there stopt with a prancing of steeds and footman thunder at this door, an equipage, all resplendent with
sky-blue and silver, discoverable thro' the blinds, like a piece
of the Coronation Procession, from whence emanated Count
d'Orsay! ushered in by the small Chorley. Chorley looked
"so much alarmed that he was quite alarming"; his face was
all the colours of the rainbow, the under-jaw of him went zig-
zag; indeed, from head to foot he was all over one universal
quaver, partly, I suppose, from the soul-bewildering honour
of having been borne hither in that chariot of the sun; partly

From *New Letters and Memorials of Jane Welsh Carlyle* (1903),
Volume I, pages 75-77.

from apprehension of the effect which his man of Genius and his man of Fashion were about to produce on one another. Happily it was not one of my nervous days, so that I could contemplate the whole thing from my *prie-Dieu* without being infected by his agitation, and a sight it was to make one think the millennium actually at hand, when the lion and the lamb, and all incompatible things should consort together. Carlyle in his grey plaid suit, and his tub-chair, looking blandly at the Prince of Dandies; and the Prince of Dandies on an opposite chair, all resplendent as a diamond-beetle, looking blandly at *him*. D'Orsay is a really handsome man, after one has heard him speak and found that he has both wit and sense; but at first sight his beauty is of that rather disgusting sort which seems to be like genius, "of no sex." And this impression is greatly helped by the fantastical finery of his dress: sky-blue satin cravat, yards of gold chain, white French gloves, light drab great-coat lined with velvet of the same colour, invisible inexpressibles, skin-coloured and fitting like a glove, etc., etc. All this, as John says, is *"very* absurd"; but his manners are manly and unaffected and he convinces one, shortly, that in the face of all probability he is a devilish clever fellow. Looking at Shelley's bust, he said, "I dislike it very much; there is a sort of faces *who* seem to wish to swallow their chins and this is one of them." He went to Macready after the first performance of *Richelieu*, and Macready asked him, "What would you suggest?" "A little more fulness in your petticoat!" answered d'Orsay. Could contempt for the piece have been more politely expressed? He was no sooner gone than Helen burst into the room to condole with me that Mrs. Welsh had not seen him—such a *"most* beautiful man and most beautiful carriage! The Queen's was no show i' the worl' compared wi' that! Everything was so grand and so preceese! But it will be something for next time."

The Two Nations

BENJAMIN DISRAELI

[FROM *Sybil: or, the Two Nations*]

1845

'It is a community of purpose that constitutes society,' continued the younger stranger; 'without that, men may be drawn into contiguity, but they still continue virtually isolated.'

'And is that their condition in cities?'

'It is their condition everywhere; but in cities that condition is aggravated. A density of population implies a severer struggle for existence, and a consequent repulsion of elements brought into too close contact. In great cities men are brought together by the desire of gain. They are not in a state of co-operation, but of isolation, as to the making of fortunes; and for all the rest they are careless of neighbours. Christianity teaches us to love our neighbour as ourself; modern society acknowledges no neighbour.'

'Well, we live in strange times,' said Egremont, struck by the observation of his companion, and relieving a perplexed spirit by an ordinary exclamation, which often denotes that the mind is more stirred than it cares to acknowledge, or at the moment is able to express.

'When the infant begins to walk, it also thinks that it lives in strange times,' said his companion.

'Your inference?' asked Egremont.

'That society, still in its infancy, is beginning to feel its way.'

'This is a new reign,' said Egremont, 'perhaps it is a new era.'

'I think so,' said the younger stranger.

'I hope so,' said the elder one.

'Well, society may be in its infancy,' said Egremont, slightly

From Book II, Chapter 5.

smiling; 'but, say what you like, our Queen reigns over the greatest nation that ever existed.'

'Which nation?' asked the younger stranger, 'for she reigns over two.'

The stranger paused; Egremont was silent, but looked inquiringly.

'Yes,' resumed the younger stranger after a moment's interval. 'Two nations; between whom there is no intercourse and no sympathy; who are as ignorant of each other's habits, thoughts, and feelings, as if they were dwellers in different zones, or inhabitants of different planets; who are formed by a different breeding, are fed by a different food, are ordered by different manners, and are not governed by the same laws.'

'You speak of——' said Egremont, hesitatingly.

'THE RICH AND THE POOR.'

Unworking Aristocracy

THOMAS CARLYLE

[FROM *Past and Present*]

1843

It is well said, 'Land is the right basis of an Aristocracy'; whoever possesses the Land, he, more emphatically than any other, is the Governor, Viceking of the people on the Land. It is in these days as it was in those of Henry Plantagenet and Abbot Samson; as it will in all days be. The land is *Mother* of us all; nourishes, shelters, gladdens, lovingly enriches us all; in how many ways, from our first wakening to our last sleep on her blessed mother-bosom, does she, as with blessed mother-arms, enfold us all!

From Book III, Chapter 8.

The Hill I first saw the Sun rise over, when the Sun and I and all things were yet in their auroral hour, who can divorce me from it? Mystic, deep as the world's centre, are the roots I have struck into my Native Soil; no *tree* that grows is rooted so. From noblest Patriotism to humblest industrial Mechanism; from highest dying for your country, to lowest quarrying and coal-boring for it, a Nation's Life depends upon its Land. Again and again we have to say, there can be no true Aristocracy but must possess the Land.

Men talk of 'selling' Land. Land, it is true, like Epic Poems and even higher things, in such a trading world, has to be presented in the market for what it will bring, and as we say be 'sold': but the notion of 'selling', for certain bits of metal, the *Iliad* of Homer, how much more the *Land* of the World-Creator, is a ridiculous impossibility! We buy what is saleable of it; nothing more was ever buyable. Who can, or could, sell it to us? Properly speaking, the Land belongs to these two; To the Almighty God; and to all His Children of Men that have ever worked well on it, or that shall ever work well on it. No generation of men can or could, with never such solemnity and effort, sell Land on any other principle: it is not the property of any generation, we say, but that of all the past generations that have worked on it, and of all the future ones that shall work on it. . . .

It is very strange, the degree to which these truisms are forgotten in our days; how, in the ever-whirling chaos of Formulas, we have quietly lost sight of Fact,—which it is so perilous not to keep forever in sight. Fact, if we do not see it, will make us *feel* it by and by!—From much loud controversy, and Corn-Law debating there rises, loud though inarticulate, once more in these years, this very question among others, Who made the Land of England? Who made it, this respectable English Land, wheat-growing, metalliferous, carboniferous, which will let readily hand over head for seventy millions or upwards, as it here lies: who did make it?—'We!' answer the much-*consuming* Aristocracy; 'We!' as they ride in, moist with the sweat of Melton Mowbray. 'It is we that made it; or are the heirs, assigns and representatives of those who did!'—My brothers, You? Everlasting honour to you, then; and Corn-Laws as many as you will, till your own deep stomachs cry Enough, or some voice of Human pity for our famine bids you Hold! Ye are as gods, that can create soil. Soil-creating gods there is no withstanding. They have the might to sell wheat at what price they list; and the right, to all lengths, and famine-lengths,—if they be pitiless infernal gods! Celestial gods, I think, would stop short of the famine-price; but no infernal nor any kind of god can be bidden stop!——Infatuated mortals, into what questions are you driving every thinking man in England?

I say, you did *not* make the Land of England; and, by the possession of it, you *are* bound to furnish guidance and governance to England! That is the law of your position on this God's-Earth; an everlasting act of Heaven's Parliament, not repealable in St. Stephen's or elsewhere! True government and guidance; not no-government and Laissez-faire; how much less, *mis*-government and Corn-Law! ...

The Working Aristocracy; Mill-owners, Manufacturers, Commanders of Working Men: alas, against them also much shall be brought in accusation; much,—and the freest Trade in Corn, total abolition of Tariffs, and uttermost 'Increase of Manufactures' and 'Prosperity of Commerce,' will permanently mend no jot of it. The Working Aristocracy must strike into a new path; must understand that money alone is *not* the representative either of man's success in the world, or of man's duties to man; and reform their own selves from top to bottom, if they wish England reformed. England will not be habitable long, unreformed.

The Working Aristocracy—Yes, but on the threshold of all this, it is again and again to be asked, What of the Idle Aristocracy? Again and again, What shall we say of the Idle Aristocracy, the Owners of the Soil of England; whose recognized function is that of handsomely consuming the rents of England, shooting the partridges of England, and as an agreeable amusement (if the purchase-money and other conveniences serve), dilettante-ing in Parliament and Quarter-Sessions for England? We will say mournfully, in the presence of Heaven and Earth,—that we stand speechless, stupent, and know not what to say! That a class of men entitled to live sumptuously on the marrow of the earth; permitted simply, nay entreated, and as yet entreated in vain, to do nothing at all in return, was never heretofore seen on the face of this Planet. That such a class is transitory, exceptional, and, unless Nature's Laws fall dead, cannot continue. That it has continued now a moderate while; has, for the last fifty years, been rapidly attaining its state of perfection. That it will have to find its duties and do them; or else that it must and will cease to be seen on the face of this Planet, which is a Working one, not an Idle one.

Alas, alas, the Working Aristocracy, admonished by Trades-unions, Chartist conflagrations, above all by their own shrewd sense kept in perpetual communion with the fact of things, will assuredly reform themselves, and a working world still be possible:—but the fate of the Idle Aristocracy, as one reads its horoscope hitherto in Corn-Laws and such like, is an abyss that fills one with despair. Yes, my rosy fox-hunting brothers, a terrible *Hippocratic look* reveals itself (God knows, not to my joy) through those fresh buxom countenances of yours. Through your Corn-Law Majorities, Sliding-Scales, Protecting-Duties, Bribery-Elections, and triumphant Kentish-fire, a thinking eye discerns ghastly images of ruin, too ghastly for words; a handwriting as of MENE, MENE. Men and brothers, on your Sliding-scale you seem sliding, and to have slid,—you little know whither! Good God! did not a French Donothing Aristocracy, hardly above half a century ago, declare in like manner, and in its featherhead believe in like manner, 'We cannot exist, and continue to dress and parade ourselves, on the just rent of the soil of France; but we must have farther payment than rent of the soil, we must be exempted from taxes too,'—we must have a Corn-Law to extend our rent? This was in 1789: in four years more—Did you look into the Tanneries of Meudon, and the long-naked making for themselves breeches of human skins! May the merciful Heavens avert the omen; may we be wiser, that so we be less wretched.

A High Class without duties to do is like a tree planted on precipices; from the roots of which all the earth has been crumbling. Nature owns no man who is not a Martyr withal. Is there a man who pretends to live luxuriously housed up; screened from all work, from want, danger, hardship, the victory over which is what we name work;—he himself to sit serene, amid down-bolsters and appliances, and have all his work and battling done by other men? And such man calls himself a *noble*-man? His fathers worked for him, he says; or successfully gambled for him: here *he* sits; professes, not in sorrow but in pride, that he and his have done no work, time out of mind. It is the law of the land, and is thought to be the law of the Universe, that he, alone of recorded men, shall have no task laid on him, except that of eating his cooked victuals, and not flinging himself out of window. Once more I will say, there was no stranger spectacle ever shown under this Sun. A veritable fact in our England of the Nineteenth Century. His victuals he does eat: but as for keeping in the inside of the window,—have not his friends, like me, enough to do? Truly, looking at his Corn-Laws, Game-Laws, Chandos-Clauses, Bribery-Elections and much else, you do shudder over the tumbling and plunging he makes, held back by the lapels and coatskirts; only a thin fence of window-glass before him,—and in the street mere horrid iron spikes! My sick brother, as in hospital-maladies men do, thou dreamest of Paradises and Eldorados, which are far from thee. 'Cannot I do what I like with my own?' Gracious Heaven, my brother, this that thou seest with those sick eyes is no firm Eldorado, and Corn-Law Paradise of Donothings, but a dream of thy own fevered brain. It is a glass-window, I tell thee, so many stories from the street, where are iron spikes and the law of gravitation!

What is the meaning of nobleness, if this be 'noble'? In a valiant suffering for others, not in a slothful making others suffer for us, did nobleness ever lie. The chief of men is he who stands in the van of men; fronting the peril which frightens back all others; which, if it be not vanquished, will

devour the others. Every noble crown is, and on Earth will
for ever be, a crown of thorns. The Pagan Hercules, why was
he accounted a hero? Because he had slain Nemean Lions,
cleansed Augean Stables, undergone Twelve Labours only not
too heavy for a god. In modern, as in ancient and all societies,
the Aristocracy, they that assume the functions of an Aristocracy, doing them or not, have taken the post of honour;
which is the post of difficulty, the post of danger,—of death,
if the difficulty be not overcome. *Il faut payer de sa vie*. Why
was our life given us, if not that we should manfully give it?
Descend, O Donothing Pomp; quit thy down-cushions; expose
thyself to learn what wretches feel, and how to cure it! The
Czar of Russia became a dusty toiling shipwright; worked
with his axe in the Docks of Saardam; and his aim was small
to thine. Descend thou: undertake this horrid 'living chaos
of Ignorance and Hunger' weltering round thy feet; say, 'I will
heal it, or behold I will die foremost in it.' Such is verily
the law. Everywhere and everywhen a man has to *'pay* with
his life'; to do his work, as a soldier does, at the expense of
life. In no Piepowder earthly Court can you sue an Aristocracy to do its work, at this moment: but in the Higher Court,
which even *it* calls 'Court of Honour,' and which is the Court
of Necessity withal, and the eternal Court of the Universe,
in which all Fact comes to plead, and every Human Soul is
an apparitor,—the Aristocracy is answerable, and even now
answering, *there*. . . .

We write no Chapter on the Corn-Laws, in this place;
the Corn-Laws are too mad to have a Chapter. There is a
certain immorality, when there is not a necessity, in speaking
about things finished; in chopping into small pieces the already
slashed and slain. When the brains are out, why does not
a Solecism die? It is at its own peril if it refuse to die; it
ought to make all conceivable haste to die, and get itself
buried! The trade of Anti-Corn-Law Lecturer in these days,
still an indispensable, is a highly tragic one.

The Corn-Laws will go, and even soon go: would we were
all as sure of the Millennium as they are of going! They go

swiftly in these present months; with an increase of velocity, an ever-deepening, ever-widening sweep of momentum, truly notable. It is at the Aristocracy's own damage and peril, still more than at any other's whatsoever, that the Aristocracy maintains them;—at a damage, say only, as above computed, of a 'hundred thousand pounds an hour'! The Corn-Laws keep all the air hot: fostered by their fever-warmth, much that is evil, but much also, how much that is good and indispensable, is rapidly coming to life among us!

The New Generation

BENJAMIN DISRAELI

[FROM *Coningsby; or, the New Generation*]

1844

Lord Monmouth was sitting in the same dressing-room in which he was first introduced to the reader; on the table were several packets of papers that were open and in course of reference; and he dictated his observations to Monsieur Villebecque, who was writing at his left hand.

Thus were they occupied when Coningsby was ushered into the room.

'You see, Harry,' said Lord Monmouth, 'that I am much occupied to-day, yet the business on which I wish to communicate with you is so pressing that it could not be postponed.' He made a sign to Villebecque, and his secretary instantly retired.

'I was right in pressing your return to England,' continued Lord Monmouth to his grandson, who was a little anxious

From Book VIII, Chapter 3.

as to the impending communication, which he could not in any way anticipate. 'These are not times when young men should be out of sight. Your public career will commence immediately. The Government have resolved on a dissolution. My information is from the highest quarter. You may be astonished, but it is a fact. They are going to dissolve their own House of Commons. Notwithstanding this and the Queen's name, we can beat them; but the race requires the finest jockeying. We can't give a point. Tadpole has been here to me about Darlford; he came specially with a message, I may say an appeal, from one to whom I can refuse nothing; the Government count on the seat, though with the new Registration 'tis nearly a tie. If we had a good candidate we could win. But Rigby won't do. He is too much of the old clique; used up; a hack; besides, a beaten horse. We are assured the name of Coningsby would be a host; there is a considerable section who support the present fellow who will not vote against a Coningsby. They have thought of you as a fit person, and I have approved of the suggestion. You will, therefore, be the candidate for Darlford with my entire sanction and support, and I have no doubt you will be successful. You may be sure I shall spare nothing: and it will be very gratifying to me, after being robbed of all our boroughs, that the only Coningsby who cares to enter Parliament, should nevertheless be able to do so as early as I could fairly desire.'

Coningsby the rival of Mr. Millbank on the hustings of Darlford! Vanquished or victorious, equally a catastrophe! The fierce passions, the gross insults, the hot blood and the cool lies, the ruffianism and the ribaldry, perhaps the domestic discomfiture and mortification, which he was about to be the means of bringing on the roof he loved best in the world, occurred to him with anguish. The countenance of Edith, haughty and mournful as last night, rose to him again. He saw her canvassing for her father, and against him. Madness! And for what was he to make this terrible and costly sacrifice? For his ambition? Not even for that Divinity or Dæmon for which we all immolate so much! Mighty ambition, forsooth, to succeed to the Rigbys! To enter the House of Commons a slave and a tool; to move according to instructions, and to labour for the low designs of petty spirits, without even the consolation of being a dupe. What sympathy could there exist between Coningsby and the 'great Conservative party,' that for ten years in an age of revolution had never promulgated a principle; whose only intelligible and consistent policy seemed to be an attempt, very grateful of course to the feelings of an English Royalist, to revive Irish Puritanism; who when in power in 1835 had used that power only to evince their utter ignorance of Church principles; and who were at this moment, when Coningsby was formally solicited to join their ranks, in open insurrection against the prerogatives of the English Monarchy?

'Do you anticipate then an immediate dissolution, sir?' inquired Coningsby after a moment's pause.

'We must anticipate it; though I think it doubtful. It may be next month; it may be in the autumn; they may tide over another year, as Lord Eskdale thinks, and his opinion always weighs with me. He is very safe. Tadpole believes they will dissolve at once. But whether they dissolve now, or in a month's time, or in the autumn, or next year, our course is clear. We must declare our intentions immediately. We must hoist our flag. Monday next, there is a great Conservative dinner at Darlford. You must attend it; that will be the finest opportunity in the world for you to announce yourself.'

'Don't you think, sir,' said Coningsby, 'that such an announcement would be rather premature? It is, in fact, embarking in a contest which may last a year; perhaps more.'

'What you say is very true,' said Lord Monmouth; 'no doubt it is very troublesome; very disgusting; any canvassing is. But we must take things as we find them. You cannot get into Parliament now in the good old gentlemanlike way; and we ought to be thankful that this interest has been fostered for our purpose.'

Coningsby looked on the carpet, cleared his throat as if about to speak, and then gave something like a sigh.

'I think you had better be off the day after to-morrow,' said Lord Monmouth. 'I have sent instructions to the steward to do all he can in so short a time, for I wish you to entertain the principal people.'

'You are most kind, you are always most kind to me, dear sir,' said Coningsby, in a hesitating tone, and with an air of great embarrassment, 'but, in truth, I have no wish to enter Parliament.'

'What?' said Lord Monmouth.

'I feel that I am not yet sufficiently prepared for so great a responsibility as a seat in the House of Commons,' said Coningsby.

'Responsibility!' said Lord Monmouth, smiling. 'What responsibility is there? How can any one have a more agreeable seat? The only person to whom you are responsible is your own relation, who brings you in. And I don't suppose there can be any difference on any point between us. You are certainly still young; but I was younger by nearly two years when I first went in; and I found no difficulty. There can be no difficulty. All you have got to do is to vote with your party. As for speaking, if you have a talent that way, take my advice; don't be in a hurry. Learn to know the House; learn the House to know you. If a man be discreet, he cannot enter Parliament too soon.'

'It is not exactly that, sir,' said Coningsby.

'Then what is it, my dear Harry? You see to-day I have much to do; yet as your business is pressing, I would not postpone seeing you an hour. I thought you would have been very much gratified.'

'You mentioned that I had nothing to do but to vote with my party, sir,' replied Coningsby. 'You mean, of course, by that term what is understood by the Conservative party.'

'Of course; our friends.'

'I am sorry,' said Coningsby, rather pale, but speaking with firmness, 'I am sorry that I could not support the Conservative party.'

'By——!' exclaimed Lord Monmouth, starting in his seat, 'some woman has got hold of him, and made him a Whig!'

'No, my dear grandfather,' said Coningsby, scarcely able to repress a smile, serious as the interview was becoming, 'nothing of the kind, I assure you. No person can be more anti-Whig.'

'I don't know what you are driving at, sir,' said Lord Monmouth, in a hard, dry tone.

'I wish to be frank, sir,' said Coningsby, 'and am very sensible of your goodness in permitting me to speak to you on the subject. What I mean to say is, that I have for a long time looked upon the Conservative party as a body who have betrayed their trust; more from ignorance, I admit, than from design; yet clearly a body of individuals totally unequal to the exigencies of the epoch, and indeed unconscious of its real character.'

'You mean giving up those Irish corporations?' said Lord Monmouth. 'Well, between ourselves, I am quite of the same opinion. But we must mount higher; we must go to '28 for the real mischief. But what is the use of lamenting the past? Peel is the only man; suited to the times and all that; at least we must say so, and try to believe so; we can't go back. And it is our own fault that we have let the chief power out of the hands of our own order. It was never thought of in the time of your great-grandfather, sir. And if a commoner were for a season permitted to be the nominal Premier to do the detail, there was always a secret committee of great 1688 nobles to give him his instructions.'

'I should be very sorry to see secret committees of great 1688 nobles again,' said Coningsby.

'Then what the devil do you want to see?' said Lord Monmouth.

'Political faith,' said Coningsby, 'instead of political infidelity.'

'Hem!' said Lord Monmouth.

'Before I support Conservative principles,' continued Coningsby, 'I merely wish to be informed what those principles aim to conserve. It would not appear to be the prerogative of the Crown, since the principal portion of a Conservative oration now is an invective against a late royal act which they describe as a Bed-chamber plot. Is it the Church which they wish to conserve? What is a threatened Appropriation Clause against an actual Church Commission in the hands of Parliamentary Laymen? Could the Long Parliament have done worse? Well, then, if it is neither the Crown nor the Church, whose rights and privileges this Conservative party propose to vindicate, is it your House, the House of Lords, whose powers they are prepared to uphold? Is it not notorious that the very man whom you have elected as your leader in that House, declares among his Conservative adherents, that henceforth the assembly that used to furnish those very Committees of great revolution nobles that you mention, is to initiate nothing; and, without a struggle, is to subside into that undisturbed repose which resembles the Imperial tranquillity that secured the frontiers by paying tribute?'

'All this is vastly fine,' said Lord Monmouth; 'but I see no means by which I can attain my object but by supporting Peel. After all, what is the end of all parties and all politics? To gain your object. I want to turn our coronet into a ducal one, and to get your grandmother's barony called out of abeyance in your favour. It is impossible that Peel can refuse me. I have already purchased an ample estate with the view of entailing it on you and your issue. You will make a considerable alliance; you may marry, if you please, Lady Theresa Sydney. I hear the report with pleasure. Count on my at once entering into any arrangement conducive to your happiness.'

'My dear grandfather, you have ever been to me only too kind and generous.'

'To whom should I be kind but to you, my own blood, that has never crossed me, and of whom I have reason to be proud? Yes, Harry, it gratifies me to hear you admired and to learn your success. All I want now is to see you in Parliament. A man should be in Parliament early. There is a sort of stiffness about every man, no matter what may be his talents, who enters Parliament late in life; and now, fortunately, the occasion offers. You will go down on Friday; feed the notabilities well; speak out; praise Peel; abuse O'Connell and the ladies of the Bed-chamber; anathematise all waverers; say a good deal about Ireland; stick to the Irish Registration Bill, that's a good card; and, above all, my dear Harry, don't spare that fellow Millbank. Remember, in turning him out you not only gain a vote for the Conservative cause and our coronet, but you crush my foe. Spare nothing for that object; I count on you, boy.'

'I should grieve to be backward in anything that concerned your interest or your honour, sir,' said Coningsby, with an air of embarrassment.

'I am sure you would, I am sure you would,' said Lord Monmouth, in a tone of some kindness.

'And I feel at this moment,' continued Coningsby, 'that there is no personal sacrifice which I am not prepared to make for them, except one. My interests, my affections, they should not be placed in the balance, if yours, sir, were at stake, though there are circumstances which might involve me in a position of as much mental distress as a man could well endure; but I claim for my convictions, my dear grandfather, a generous tolerance.'

'I can't follow you, sir,' said Lord Monmouth, again in his hard tone. 'Our interests are inseparable, and therefore there can never be any sacrifice of conduct on your part. What you mean by sacrifice of affections, I don't comprehend; but as for your opinions, you have no business to have any other than those I uphold. You are too young to form opinions.'

'I am sure I wish to express them with no unbecoming confidence,' replied Coningsby; 'I have never intruded them on your ear before; but this being an occasion when you yourself said, sir, I was about to commence my public career, I confess I thought it was my duty to be frank; I would not entail on myself long years of mortification by one of those ill-considered entrances into political life which so many public men have cause to deplore.'

'You go with your family, sir, like a gentleman; you are not to consider your opinions, like a philosopher or a political adventurer.'

'Yes, sir,' said Coningsby, with animation, 'but men going with their families like gentlemen, and losing sight of every principle on which the society of this country ought to be established produced the Reform Bill.'

'D—— the Reform Bill!' said Lord Monmouth; if the Duke had not quarrelled with Lord Grey on a Coal Committee, we should never have had the Reform Bill. And Grey would have gone to Ireland.'

'You are in as great peril now as you were in 1830,' said Coningsby.

'No, no, no,' said Lord Monmouth; 'the Tory party is organised now; they will not catch us napping again: these Conservative Associations have done the business.'

'But what are they organised for?' said Coningsby. 'At the best to turn out the Whigs. And when you have turned out the Whigs, what then? You may get your ducal coronet, sir. But a duke now is not so great a man as a baron was but a century back. We cannot struggle against the irresistible stream of circumstances. Power has left our order; this is not an age for factitious aristocracy. As for my grandmother's barony, I should look upon the termination of its abeyance in my favour as the act of my political extinction. What we want, sir, is not to fashion new dukes and furbish up old baronies, but to establish great principles which may maintain the realm and secure the happiness of the people. Let me see authority once more honoured; a solemn reverence again the habit of our lives; let me see property acknowledging, as in the old days of faith, that labour is his twin brother, and that the essence of all tenure is the performance of duty; let results such as these be brought about, and let me participate, however feebly, in the great fulfilment, and public life then indeed becomes a noble career, and a seat in Parliament an enviable distinction.'

'I tell you what it is, Harry,' said Lord Monmouth, very drily, 'members of this family may think as they like, but they must act as I please. You must go down on Friday to Darlford and declare yourself a candidate for the town, or I shall reconsider our mutual positions. I would say, you must go to-morrow; but it is only courteous to Rigby to give him a previous intimation of your movement. And that cannot be done to-day. I sent for Rigby this morning on other business which now occupies me, and find he is out of town.

He will return to-morrow; and will be here at three o'clock, when you can meet him. You will meet him, I doubt not, like a man of sense,' added Lord Monmouth, looking at Coningsby with a glance such as he had never before encountered, 'who is not prepared to sacrifice all the objects of life for the pursuit of some fantastical puerilities.'

His Lordship rang a bell on his table for Villebecque; and to prevent any further conversation, resumed his papers.

The Dedlocks

CHARLES DICKENS

[FROM *Bleak House*]

1852-1853

My Lady Dedlock has returned to her house in town for a few days previous to her departure for Paris, where her ladyship intends to stay some weeks; after which her movements are uncertain. The fashionable intelligence says so, for the comfort of the Parisians, and it knows all fashionable things. To know things otherwise, were to be unfashionable. My Lady Dedlock has been down at what she calls, in familiar conversation, her "place" in Lincolnshire. The waters are out in Lincolnshire. An arch of the bridge in the park has been sapped and sopped away. The adjacent low-lying ground, for half a mile in breadth, is a stagnant river, with melancholy trees for islands in it, and a surface punctured all over, all day long, with falling rain. My Lady Dedlock's "place" has been extremely dreary. The weather, for many a day and night, has been so wet that the trees seem wet through, and

From Chapter 2.

the soft loppings and prunings of the woodman's axe can make no crash or crackle as they fall. The deer, looking soaked, leave quagmires, where they pass. The shot of a rifle loses its sharpness in the moist air, and its smoke moves in a tardy little cloud towards the green rise, coppice-topped, that makes a background for the falling rain. The view from my Lady Dedlock's own windows is alternately a lead-coloured view, and a view in Indian ink. The vases on the stone terrace in the foreground catch the rain all day; and the heavy drops fall, drip, drip, drip, upon the broad flagged pavement, called, from old time, the Ghost's Walk, all night. On Sundays, the little church in the park is mouldy; the oaken pulpit breaks out into a cold sweat; and there is a general smell and taste as of the ancient Dedlocks in their graves. My Lady Dedlock (who is childless), looking out in the early twilight from her boudoir at a keeper's lodge, and seeing the light of a fire upon the latticed panes, and smoke rising from the chimney, and a child, chased by a woman, running out into the rain to meet the shining figure of a wrapped-up man coming through the gate, has been put quite out of temper. My Lady Dedlock says she has been "bored to death."

Therefore my Lady Dedlock has come away from the place in Lincolnshire, and has left it to the rain, and the crows, and the rabbits, and the deer, and the partridges and pheasants. The pictures of the Dedlocks past and gone have seemed to vanish into the damp walls in mere lowness of spirits, as the housekeeper has passed along the old rooms, shutting up the shutters. And when they will next come forth again, the fashionable intelligence—which, like the fiend, is omniscient of the past and present, but not the future—cannot yet undertake to say.

Sir Leicester Dedlock is only a baronet, but there is no mightier baronet than he. His family is as old as the hills, and infinitely more respectable. He has a general opinion that the world might get on without hills, but would be done up without Dedlocks. He would on the whole admit Nature to be a good idea (a little low, perhaps, when not enclosed with a park-fence), but an idea dependent for its execution on

your great county families. He is a gentleman of strict conscience, disdainful of all littleness and meanness, and ready,
on the shortest notice, to die any death you may please to
mention rather than give occasion for the least impeachment
of his integrity. He is an honourable, obstinate, truthful, high-
spirited, intensely prejudiced, perfectly unreasonable man.

Sir Leicester is twenty years, full measure, older than my
Lady. He will never see sixty-five again, nor perhaps sixty-six,
nor yet sixty-seven. He has a twist of the gout now and then,
and walks a little stiffly. He is of a worthy presence, with
his light grey hair and whiskers, his fine shirt-frill, his pure
white waistcoat, and his blue coat with bright buttons always
buttoned. He is ceremonious, stately, most polite on every
occasion to my Lady, and holds her personal attractions in
the highest estimation. His gallantry to my Lady, which has
never changed since he courted her, is the one little touch
of romantic fancy in him.

Indeed, he married her for love. A whisper still goes about,
that she had not even family; howbeit, Sir Leicester had so
much family that perhaps he had enough, and could dispense
with any more. But she had beauty, pride, ambition, insolent
resolve, and sense enough to portion out a legion of fine
ladies. Wealth and station, added to these, soon floated her
upward; and for years, now, my Lady Dedlock has been at
the centre of the fashionable intelligence, and at the top of
the fashionable tree. . . .

[FROM Chapter 12]

All the mirrors in the house are brought into action now:
many of them after a long blank. They reflect handsome faces,
simpering faces, youthful faces, faces of threescore-and-ten
that will not submit to be old; the entire collection of faces
that have come to pass a January week or two at Chesney
Wold, and which the fashionable intelligence, a mighty hunter
before the Lord, hunts with a keen scent, from their breaking
cover at the Court of St. James's to their being run down to
Death. The place in Lincolnshire is all alive. By day, guns

and voices are heard ringing in the woods, horsemen and carriages enliven the park roads, servants and hangers-on pervade the Village and the Dedlock Arms. Seen by night, from distant openings in the trees, the row of windows in the long drawing-room, where my Lady's picture hangs over the great chimney-piece, is like a row of jewels set in a black frame. On Sunday, the chill little church is almost warmed by so much gallant company, and the general flavour of the Dedlock dust is quenched in delicate perfumes.

The brilliant and distinguished circle comprehends within it no contracted amount of education, sense, courage, honour, beauty, and virtue. Yet there is something a little wrong about it, in despite of its immense advantages. What can it be?

Dandyism? There is no King George the Fourth now (more's the pity!) to set the dandy fashion; there are no clear-starched, jack-towel neckcloths, no short-waisted coats, no false calves, no stays. There are no caricatures, now, of effeminate Exquisites so arrayed, swooning in opera-boxes with excess of delight, and being revived by other dainty creatures, poking long-necked scent-bottles at their noses. There is no beau whom it takes four men at once to shake into his buckskins, or who goes to see all the executions, or who is troubled with the self-reproach of having once consumed a pea. But is there Dandyism in the brilliant and distinguished circle notwithstanding, Dandyism of a more mischievous sort, that has got below the surface and is doing less harmless things than jack-towelling itself and stopping its own digestion, to which no rational person need particularly object?

Why, yes. It cannot be disguised. There *are,* at Chesney Wold this January week, some ladies and gentlemen of the newest fashion, who have set up a Dandyism—in Religion, for instance. Who, in mere lackadaisical want of an emotion, have agreed upon a little dandy talk about the Vulgar wanting faith in things in general; meaning, in the things that have been tried and found wanting, as though a low fellow should unaccountably lose faith in a bad shilling, after finding it out! Who would make the Vulgar very picturesque and faith-

ful, by putting back the hands upon the Clock of Time, and
cancelling a few hundred years of history.

There are also ladies and gentlemen of another fashion, not
so new, but very elegant, who have agreed to put a smooth
glaze on the world, and to keep down all its realities. For
whom everything must be languid and pretty. Who have
found out the perpetual stoppage. Who are to rejoice at
nothing, and be sorry for nothing. Who are not to be dis-
turbed by ideas. On whom even the Fine Arts, attending in
powder and walking backward like the Lord Chamberlain,
must array themselves in the milliners' and tailors' patterns
of past generations, and be particularly careful not to be in
earnest, or to receive any impress from the moving age.

Then there is my Lord Boodle, of considerable reputation
with his party, who has known what office is, and who tells
Sir Leicester Dedlock with much gravity, after dinner, that
he really does not see to what the present age is tending. A
debate is not what a debate used to be; the House is not
what the House used to be; even a Cabinet is not what it
formerly was. He perceives with astonishment, that supposing
the present Government to be overthrown, the limited choice
of the Crown, in the formation of a new Ministry, would lie
between Lord Coodle and Sir Thomas Doodle—supposing
it to be impossible for the Duke of Foodle to act with Goodle,
which may be assumed to be the case in consequence of the
breach arising out of that affair with Hoodle. Then, giving
the Home Department and the Leadership of the House of
Commons to Joodle, the Exchequer to Koodle, the Colonies
to Loodle, and the Foreign Office to Moodle, what are you
to do with Noodle? You can't offer him the Presidency of
the Council; that is reserved for Poodle. You can't put him
in the Woods and Forests; that is hardly good enough for
Quoodle. What follows? That the country is shipwrecked,
lost, and gone to pieces (as is made manifest to the Patriotism of Sir Leicester Dedlock), because you can't provide
for Noodle!

On the other hand, the Right Honourable William Buffy,
M.P., contends across the table with some one else, that the

shipwreck of the country—about which there is no doubt; it is only the manner of it that is in question—is attributable to Cuffy. If you had done with Cuffy what you ought to have done when he first came into Parliament, and had prevented him from going over to Duffy, you would have got him into alliance with Fuffy, you would have had with you the weight attaching as a smart debater to Guffy, you would have brought to bear upon the elections the wealth of Huffy, you would have got in for three counties Juffy, Kuffy, and Luffy; and you would have strengthened your administration by the official knowledge and the business habits of Muffy. All this, instead of being as you now are, dependent on the mere caprice of Puffy!

As to this point, and as to some minor topics, there are differences of opinion; but it is perfectly clear to the brilliant and distinguished circle, all round, that nobody is in question but Boodle and his retinue, and Buffy and *his* retinue. These are the great actors for whom the stage is reserved. A People there are, no doubt—a certain large number of supernumeraries, who are to be occasionally addressed, and relied upon for shouts and choruses, as on the theatrical stage; but Boodle and Buffy, their followers and families, their heirs, executors, administrators, and assigns, are the born first-actors, managers, and leaders, and no others can appear upon the scene for ever and ever.

Queen Victoria's Jubilee

[FROM *The Times*, 20 June 1887]

To-day the QUEEN completes the fiftieth year of a reign prosperous and glorious beyond any recorded in the annals of England. To few Sovereigns has it been granted to celebrate the Jubilee of their accession, and among these few we know of no Queen or Empress. In the early morning on the 20th of June, 1837, the ARCHBISHOP of CANTERBURY and the LORD CHAMBERLAIN hastened to Kensington Palace to rouse the young PRINCESS VICTORIA from her sleep and to announce to her that by her uncle's death she had succeeded to the Throne. From that moment onwards the QUEEN has been deeply impressed with the responsibilities of power, and has held her sovereignty to be a sacred trust for the benefit of the peoples under her rule. No constitutional Monarch has shown a more consistent respect for popular liberties or a clearer conception of royal duties. The QUEEN has this week the reward she must prize beyond all else, the spontaneous expression of national enthusiasm. The spectacle, which will culminate in the splendour of to-morrow's Thanksgiving Service in Westminster Abbey, in the Royal Procession through the streets, and in the illuminations of the evening, may well fix the attention, not only of all sorts and conditions of Englishmen, Scotchmen, and Irishmen, but of exalted and eminent personages from all civilized States. The Sovereigns of Europe will be fully represented in the historic scene, and seldom, perhaps, have so many princely visitors assembled to take part in such a ceremony. . . . But the most impressive element in the scene will be the demeanour of the people. Britons, in spite of a confirmed habit of grumbling, look upon their ancient institutions with steadfast affection and reverence, and their attachment to the monarchy has been blended with respect for the character of the QUEEN. Nothing in the rich and various history of the past fifty years is more worthy of record than the purification and refinement of social life and manners to which the influence of the Court has most powerfully contributed. Those who are familiar with the current literature of the early part of the century will most readily acknowledge how vast a change has taken place in the tone in which royalty and royal persons are spoken of. That change is mainly due to the conduct of the QUEEN, in public and in private, since her accession, and to the wisdom of the counsels by which she was long guided. It must ever be remembered that for this and other faithful services the nation owes a deep debt of gratitude to the memory of the PRINCE CONSORT.

If we look back over the half-century which has elapsed since the 20th of June, 1837, we see how stormy were the political waters on which the young SOVEREIGN embarked, and how much she needed the aid of a loyal and devoted adviser. The whirlwind of the Reform agitation left a heaving sea behind it; the struggle for the repeal of the Corn Laws was looming in the near future. There was suffering among the masses, with the menacing spectre of Chartism in the background. Yet if the difficulties were grave, the time was fertile in able and enterprising spirits. In politics, as in everything else, new ideas were at work. It was the good fortune of the QUEEN that at the outset she had in LORD MELBOURNE a faithful servant who piloted her through many anxieties. But among all parties the standard of public life was high, and never, perhaps, had the dignity of Parliament been more solidly established. WELLINGTON'S lofty character was still a tower of strength to the Tories, but PEEL, eminently the statesman of the middle classes, had laid the foundations of his power as a financier and a master of Parliamentary debate. Among the Whigs, after MELBOURNE'S retirement, the long rivalry between RUSSELL and PALMERSTON began, but before it reached its height the opposite party was rent by a great schism. The ablest of the Tories, including MR. GLADSTONE and SIDNEY HERBERT, followed PEEL, and made themselves a separate position in politics; the majority, headed by STANLEY and DISRAELI, held the old Tory camp. Side by side with these party conflicts, there were political privateers, like BROUGHAM and LYNDHURST, survivors of the Anti-Reform Armageddon, and O'CONNELL, with his Irish guerilla party. Political life absorbed ability of the most various kinds—lawyers like FOLLETT and COCKBURN, men of letters like MACAULAY and LYTTON, philanthropists like SHAFTESBURY. The cause of the people of the great manufacturing towns was pleaded with unique power by COBDEN and BRIGHT. As the graver issues were cleared away, the conditions of the conflict were simplified. The Peelites failed to make their mark, when under LORD ABERDEEN they united with the Whigs, and PALMERSTON became the chief of the Liberal party. It was not until after PALMERSTON'S death that MR. GLADSTONE'S right to succeed to the leadership on LORD RUSSELL'S retreat ceased to be questioned, and in like manner MR. DISRAELI'S full recognition was delayed till after LORD DERBY'S retirement. It is needless to touch on the later vicissitudes of the political history of the reign. The prolonged contest for the mastery between MR. GLADSTONE and his great rival enlisted on either side powers not inferior to those of any former generation of statesmen. If the art of political oratory has declined, and if Parliamentary manners have deteriorated, it is not because there is less ability applied to politics than before. In all the political changes of the past half-century, from the Premiership of LORD MELBOURNE to that of LORD SALISBURY, it has been the task of the QUEEN to preserve the neutrality of the CROWN, and that task, by the admission of every man who has held high office, has been faithfully fulfilled.

The names of the eminent men who have been conspicuous in political life since the QUEEN'S accession form a remarkable list, but not more remarkable than the list of those who have done the country service, during the same time, in science, abstract and applied, in commerce and industry, in literature and art, in philosophical speculation, in philanthropic effort, and religious or moral awakening. The new ideas let loose about 1830 were stirring everywhere during the following decade, and when the QUEEN'S reign began science was entering on a series of unparalleled conquests. Bold discovery was

followed up by lucid and eloquent exposition, and the conquests of the thinker were speedily turned to use by the
practical mind. FARADAY and TYNDALL, OWEN and LYELL,
DARWIN and HUXLEY have transformed the popular conceptions of scientific truths. Geology, biology, chemistry, physics
are almost as far in advance of the point reached fifty years
ago as the science of the 18th century was ahead of that of
the middle ages. The scientific spirit has penetrated philosophical speculation; MILL and SPENCER have taken up a
stronger position against the pure metaphysicians than their
forerunners, but the opposite school has been equally active
and aggressive. In another direction science has gained still
more notable victories. The development of railways, steam
navigation, and electricity in its various practical uses is the
work of our own time, and the men who have done that work
are among the ornaments of the Victorian age. The immense
extension of industry and spread of trade could not have been
possible without the aid of science, and inventions like those
of BESSEMER and SIEMENS have added enormously to our
resources. The population has grown with this development,
and vast imports of food are required to make up for the
deficiency in our home supplies. This can only be accomplished
by skilful organization and a highly elaborate system of credit,
of which not the boldest of speculators could have dreamed
in 1837. Yet the nation has not been wholly given up to these
victories over matter. The achievements of the imagination
have been as splendid. The Victorian age can show a record
of brilliant writers that may be fearlessly compared with any
other. The abiding influence of WORDSWORTH in the highest
region of poetry has been conspicuous in bringing out the
true passion of nature. TENNYSON, BROWNING, ARNOLD,
SWINBURNE have shown that, in varying forms, the fire is
kept alive, and in prose writing, especially in fiction, the richness of the English imagination has been abundantly proved.
DICKENS, THACKERAY, and GEORGE ELIOT are among the
highest names in literature, and a host of their contemporaries
and successors have attained a high level of style and power
of depicting character. In historical work the pursuit of truth

has been carried farther than at any former time, and men of great genius, like CARLYLE and MACAULAY, have toiled over the smallest of details. Art, too, has been widely diffused and pursued with ardour, and if the age has produced few painters or sculptors of the very first rank the general excellence of the works produced has cultivated public taste. The same thing may be said of music. The middle classes, and even the working classes, which had no opportunity of appreciating either art or music fifty years ago, cannot now complain that these wholesome enjoyments are monopolized by a fashionable aristocracy. Perhaps the spread of this artistic culture is doing as much to extirpate vice and to brighten the homes of the poor as the admirable efforts of philanthropists. But, as we know, the latter have still a vast task before them. The abolition of slavery was followed up by the measures promoted by LORD SHAFTESBURY for the protection of factory children, and another great enterprise, the encouragement of temperance, has been since carried far by earnest and devoted men. The Church has shaken off the lethargy in which it was formerly sunk and has lent its hand to every good work. If, therefore, our difficulties are on a greater scale than those we had to face when the QUEEN came to the Throne, we may comfort ourselves with the reflection that we have larger forces to bring to our aid and that we are striving to combat them in a higher spirit.

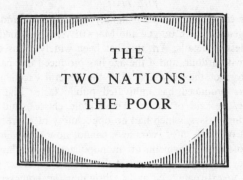

THE
TWO NATIONS:
THE POOR

The Condition of England

THOMAS CARLYLE

[FROM *Past and Present*]

1843

The condition of England, on which many pamphlets are now in the course of publication, and many thoughts unpublished are going on in every reflective head, is justly regarded as one of the most ominous, and withal one of the strangest, ever seen in this world. England is full of wealth, of multifarious produce, supply for human want in every kind; yet England is dying of inanition. With unabated bounty the land of England blooms and grows; waving with yellow harvests; thick-studded with workshops, industrial implements, with fifteen millions of workers, understood to be the strongest, the cunningest and the willingest our Earth ever had; these men are here; the work they have done, the fruit they have realized is here, abundant, exuberant on every hand of us: and behold, some baleful fiat as of Enchantment has gone forth, saying, 'Touch it not, ye workers, ye master-workers, ye master-idlers; none of you can touch it, no man of you

From Book I, Chapter 1.

shall be the better for it; this is enchanted fruit!' On the poor workers such fiat falls first, in its rudest shape; but on the rich master-workers too it falls; neither can the rich master-idlers, nor any richest or highest man escape, but all are like to be brought low with it, and made 'poor' enough, in the money sense or a far fataller one.

Of these successful skilful workers some two millions, it is now counted, sit in Workhouses, Poor-law Prisons; or have 'out-door relief' flung over the wall to them,—the workhouse Bastille being filled to bursting, and the strong Poor-law broken asunder by a stronger. They sit there, these many months now; their hope of deliverance as yet small. In workhouses, pleasantly so-named, because work cannot be done in them. Twelve hundred thousand workers in England alone; their cunning right-hand lamed, lying idle in their sorrowful bosom; their hopes, outlooks, share of this fair world, shut in by narrow walls. They sit there, pent up, as in a kind of horrid enchantment; glad to be imprisoned and enchanted, that they may not perish starved. The picturesque Tourist, in a sunny autumn day, through this bounteous realm of England, describes the Union Workhouse on his path. 'Passing by the Workhouse of St. Ives in Huntingdonshire, on a bright day last autumn,' says the picturesque Tourist, 'I saw sitting on wooden benches, in front of their Bastille and within their ring-wall and its railings, some half-hundred or more of these men. Tall robust figures, young mostly or of middle age; of honest countenance, many of them thoughtful and even intelligent-looking men. They sat there, near by one another; but in a kind of torpor, especially in a silence, which was very striking. In silence: for, alas, what word was to be said? An Earth all lying round, crying, Come and till me, come and reap me;—yet we here sit enchanted! In the eyes and brows of the men hung the gloomiest expression, not of anger, but of grief and shame and manifold inarticulate distress and weariness; they returned my glance with a glance that seemed to say, "Do not look at us. We sit enchanted here, we know not why. The Sun shines and the Earth calls; and, by the governing Powers and Impotences of this England, we are forbidden to obey.

It is impossible, they tell us!" There was something that reminded me of Dante's Hell in the look of all this; and I rode swiftly away.'

So many hundred thousands sit in workhouses: and other hundred thousands have not yet got even workhouses; and in thrifty Scotland itself, in Glasgow or Edinburgh City, in their dark lanes, hidden from all but the eye of God, and of rare Benevolence the minister of God, there are scenes of woe and destitution and desolation, such as, one may hope, the Sun never saw before in the most barbarous regions where men dwelt. Competent witnesses, the brave and humane Dr. Alison, who speaks what he knows, whose noble Healing Art in his charitable hands becomes once more a truly sacred one, report these things for us: these things are not of this year, or of last year, have no reference to our present state of commercial stagnation, but only to the common state. Not in sharp fever-fits, but in chronic gangrene of this kind is Scotland suffering. A Poor-law, any and every Poor-law, it may be observed, is but a temporary measure; an anodyne, not a remedy: Rich and Poor, when once the naked facts of their condition have come into collision, cannot long subsist together on a mere Poor-law. True enough:—and yet, human beings cannot be left to die! Scotland too, till something better come, must have a Poor-law, if Scotland is not to be a byword among the nations. O, what a waste is there; of noble and thrice-noble national virtues; peasant Stoicisms, Heroisms; valiant manful habits, soul of a Nation's worth,—which all the metal of Potosi cannot purchase back; to which the metal of Potosi, and all you can buy with *it*, is dross and dust!

Why dwell on this aspect of the matter? It is too indisputable, not doubtful now to any one. Descend where you will into the lower class, in Town or Country, by what avenue you will, by Factory Inquiries, Agricultural Inquiries, by Revenue Returns, by Mining-Labourer Committees, by opening your own eyes and looking, the same sorrowful result discloses itself: you have to admit that the working body of this rich English Nation has sunk or is fast sinking into a state, to which, all sides of it considered, there was literally never any parallel. At Stockport Assizes—and this too has no reference to the present state of trade, being of date prior to that—a Mother and a Father are arraigned and found guilty of poisoning three of their children, to defraud a 'burial-society of some 3*l.* 8*s.* due on the death of each child: they are arraigned, found guilty; and the official authorities, it is whispered, hint that perhaps the case is not solitary, that perhaps you had better not probe farther into that department of things. This is in the autumn of 1841; the crime itself is of the previous year or season. 'Brutal savages, degraded Irish,' mutters the idle reader of Newspapers; hardly lingering on this incident. Yet it is an incident worth lingering on; the depravity, savagery and degraded Irishism being never so well admitted. In the British land, a human Mother and Father, of white skin and professing the Christian religion, had done this thing; they, with their Irishism and necessity and savagery, had been driven to do it. Such instances are like the highest mountain apex emerged into view; under which lies a whole mountain region and land, not yet emerged. A human Mother and Father had said to themselves, What shall we do to escape starvation? We are deep sunk here, in our dark cellar; and help is far.—Yes, in the Ugolino Hunger-tower stern things happen; best-loved little Gaddo fallen dead on his Father's knees!—The Stockport Mother and Father think and hint: Our poor little starveling Tom, who cries all day for victuals, who will see only evil and not good in this world: if he were out of misery at once; he well dead, and the rest of us perhaps kept alive? It is thought, and hinted; at last it is done. And now Tom being killed, and all spent and eaten, Is it poor little starveling Jack that must go, or poor little starveling Will?—What an iniquity of ways and means!

In starved sieged cities, in the uttermost doomed ruin of old Jerusalem fallen under the wrath of God, it was prophesied and said, 'The hands of the pitiful women have sodden their own children.' The stern Hebrew imagination could conceive no blacker gulf of wretchedness; that was the ultimatum of degraded god-punished man. And we here, in modern England, exuberant with supply of all kinds, besieged by nothing if it

be not by invisible Enchantments, are we reaching that?——
How come these things? Wherefore are they, wherefore should
they be?

Nor are they of the St. Ives workhouses, of the Glasgow
lanes, and Stockport cellars, the only unblessed among us.
This successful industry of England, with its plethoric wealth,
has as yet made nobody rich; it is an enchanted wealth, and
belongs yet to nobody. We might ask, Which of us has it
enriched? We can spend thousands where we once spent
hundreds; but can purchase nothing good with them. In Poor
and Rich, instead of noble thrift and plenty, there is idle
luxury alternating with mean scarcity and inability. We have
sumptuous garnitures for our Life, but have forgotten to *live*
in the middle of them. It is an enchanted wealth; no man of
us can yet touch it. The class of men who feel that they are
truly better off by means of it, let them give us their name!

Many men eat finer cookery, drink dearer liquors,—with
what advantage they can report, and their Doctors can: but
in the heart of them, if we go out of the dyspeptic stomach,
what increase of blessedness is there? Are they better, beautifuller, stronger, braver? Are they even what they call 'happier?'
Do they look with satisfaction on more things and human
faces in this God's-Earth; do more things and human
faces look with satisfaction on them? Not so. Human faces
gloom discordantly, disloyally on one another. Things, if it
be not mere cotton and iron things, are growing disobedient
to man. The Master Worker is enchanted, for the present,
like his Workhouse Workman; clamours, in vain hitherto, for
a very simple sort of 'Liberty': the liberty 'to buy where
he finds it cheapest, to sell where he finds it dearest.' With
guineas jingling in every pocket, he was no whit richer; but
now, the very guineas threatening to vanish, he feels that he
is poor indeed. Poor Master Worker! And the Master Un-
worker, is not he in a still fataller situation? Pausing amid
his game-preserves, with awful eye,—as he well may! Coercing
fifty-pound tenants; coercing, bribing, cajoling; doing what
he likes with his own. His mouth full of loud futilities, and

arguments to prove the excellence of his Corn-law; and in his heart the blackest misgiving, a desperate half-consciousness that his excellent Corn-law is *in*defensible, that his loud arguments for it are of a kind to strike men too literally *dumb*.

To whom, then, is this wealth of England wealth? Who is it that it blesses; makes happier, wiser, beautifuller, in any way better? Who has got hold of it, to make it fetch and carry for him, like a true servant, not like a false mock-servant; to do him any real service whatsoever? As yet no one. We have more riches than any Nation ever had before; we have less good of them than any Nation ever had before. Our successful industry is hitherto unsuccessful; a strange success, if we stop here! In the midst of plethoric plenty, the people perish; with gold walls, and full barns, no man feels himself safe or satisfied. Workers, Master Workers, Unworkers, all men, come to a pause; stand fixed, and cannot farther. Fatal paralysis spreading inwards, from the extremities, in St. Ives workhouses, in Stockport cellars, through all limbs, as if towards the heart itself. Have we actually got enchanted, then; accursed by some god?—

Midas longed for gold, and insulted the Olympians. He got gold, so that whatsoever he touched became gold—and he, with his long ears, was little the better for it. Midas had misjudged the celestial music-tones; Midas had insulted Apollo and the gods: the gods gave him his wish, and a pair of long ears, which also were a good appendage to it. What a truth in these old Fables!

A Liberal Landlord

GEORGE ELIOT

[FROM *Middlemarch*]

1870-1871

Mr Brooke . . . said that he would step into the carriage
and go with Dorothea as far as Dagley's, to speak about the
small delinquent who had been caught with the leveret.
Dorothea renewed the subject of the estate as they drove
along, but Mr Brooke, not being taken unawares, got the
talk under his own control.

"Chettam, now," he replied; "he finds fault with me, my
dear; but I should not preserve my game if it were not for
Chettam, and he can't say that *that* expense is for the sake
of the tenants, you know. It's a little against my feeling:—
poaching, now, if you come to look into it—I have often
thought of getting up the subject. Not long ago, Flavell, the
Methodist preacher, was brought up for knocking down a
hare that came across his path when he and his wife were
walking out together. He was pretty quick, and knocked it
on the neck."

"That was very brutal, I think," said Dorothea.

"Well, now, it seemed rather black to me, I confess, in a
Methodist preacher, you know. And Johnson said, 'You may
judge what a hypo*crite* he is.' And upon my word, I thought
Flavell looked very little like 'the highest style of man'—as
somebody calls the Christian—Young, the poet Young, I think
—you know Young? Well, now, Flavell in his shabby black
gaiters, pleading that he thought the Lord had sent him and
his wife a good dinner, and he had a right to knock it down,
though not a mighty hunter before the Lord, as Nimrod

From Chapter 39.

was—I assure you it was rather comic: Fielding would have made something of it—or Scott, now—Scott might have worked it up. But really, when I came to think of it, I couldn't help liking that the fellow should have a bit of hare to say grace over. It's all a matter of prejudice—prejudice with the law on its side, you know—about the stick and the gaiters, and so on. However, it doesn't do to reason about things; and law is law. But I got Johnson to be quiet, and I hushed the matter up. I doubt whether Chettam would not have been more severe, and yet he comes down on me as if I were the hardest man in the county. But here we are at Dagley's."

Mr Brooke got down at a farmyard-gate, and Dorothea drove on. It is wonderful how much uglier things will look when we only suspect that we are blamed for them. Even our own persons in the glass are apt to change their aspect for us after we have heard some frank remark on their less admirable points; and on the other hand it is astonishing how pleasantly conscience takes our encroachments on those who never complain or have nobody to complain for them. Dagley's homestead never before looked so dismal to Mr Brooke as it did to-day, with his mind thus sore about the fault-finding of the "Trumpet," echoed by Sir James.

It is true that an observer, under that softening influence of the fine arts which makes other people's hardships pictur-esque, might have been delighted with this homestead called Freeman's End: the old house had dormer-windows in the dark-red roof, two of the chimneys were choked with ivy, the large porch was blocked up with bundles of sticks, and half the windows were closed with grey worm-eaten shutters about which the jasmine-boughs grew in wild luxuriance; the mouldering garden wall with hollyhocks peeping over it was a perfect study of highly-mingled subdued colour, and there was an aged goat (kept doubtless on interesting superstitious grounds) lying against the open back-kitchen door. The mossy thatch of the cow-shed, the broken grey barn-doors, the pauper labourers in ragged breeches who had nearly finished unloading a waggon of corn into the barn ready for early thrashing; the scanty dairy of cows being tethered for milking and leaving one half of the shed in brown emptiness; the very pigs and white ducks seeming to wander about the uneven neglected yard as if in low spirits from feeding on a too meagre quality of rinsings—all these objects under the quiet light of a sky marbled with high clouds would have made a sort of picture which we have all paused over as a "charming bit," touching other sensibilities than those which are stirred by the depression of the agricultural interest, with the sad lack of farming capital, as seen constantly in the newspapers of that time. But these troublesome associations were just now strongly present to Mr Brooke, and spoiled the scene for him. Mr Dagley himself made a figure in the landscape, carrying a pitchfork and wearing his milking-hat—a very old beaver flattened in front. His coat and breeches were the best he had, and he would not have been wearing them on this week-day occasion if he had not been to market and returned later than usual, having given himself the rare treat of dining at the public table of the Blue Bull. How he came to fall into this extravagance would perhaps be matter of wonderment to himself on the morrow; but before dinner something in the state of the country, a slight pause in the harvest before the Far Dips were cut, the stories about the new King and the numerous handbills on the walls, had seemed to warrant a little recklessness. It was a maxim about Middlemarch, and regarded as self-evident, that good meat should have good drink, which last Dagley interpreted as plenty of table ale well followed up by rum-and-water. These liquors have so far truth in them that they were not false enough to make poor Dagley seem merry: they only made his discontent less tongue-tied than usual. He had also taken too much in the shape of muddy political talk, a stimulant dangerously disturbing to his farming conservatism, which consisted in holding that whatever is, is bad, and any change is likely to be worse. He was flushed, and his eyes had a decidedly quarrelsome stare as he stood still grasping his pitchfork, while the landlord approached with his easy shuffling walk, one hand in his trouser-pocket and the other swinging round a thin walking-stick.

"Dagley, my good fellow," began, Mr. Brooke, conscious that he was going to be very friendly about the boy.

"Oh, ay, I'm a good feller, am I? Thank ye, sir, thank ye," said Dagley, with a loud snarling irony which made Fag the sheep-dog stir from his seat and prick his ears; but seeing Monk enter the yard after some outside loitering, Fag seated himself again in an attitude of observation. "I'm glad to hear I'm a good feller."

Mr Brooke reflected that it was market-day, and that his worthy tenant had probably been dining, but saw no reason why he should not go on, since he could take the precaution of repeating what he had to say to Mrs Dagley.

"Your little lad Jacob has been caught killing a leveret, Dagley: I have told Johnson to lock him up in the empty stable an hour or two, just to frighten him, you know. But he will be brought home by-and-by, before night: and you'll just look after him, will you, and give him a reprimand, you know?"

"No, I woon't: I'll be dee'd if I'll leather my boy to please you or anybody else, not if you was twenty landlords istid o' one, and that a bad un."

Dagley's words were loud enough to summon his wife to the back-kitchen door—the only entrance ever used, and one always open except in bad weather—and Mr Brooke, saying soothingly, "Well, well, I'll speak to your wife—I didn't mean beating, you know," turned to walk to the house. But Dagley, only the more inclined to "have his say" with a gentleman who walked away from him, followed at once, with Fag slouching at his heels and sullenly evading some small and probably charitable advances on the part of Monk.

"How do you do, Mrs Dagley?" said Mr Brooke, making some haste. "I came to tell you about your boy: I don't want you to give him the stick, you know." He was careful to speak quite plainly this time.

Overworked Mrs Dagley—a thin, worn woman, from whose life pleasure had so entirely vanished that she had not even any Sunday clothes which could give her satisfaction in preparing for church—had already had a misunderstanding with her husband since he had come home, and was in low spirits, expecting the worst. But her husband was beforehand in answering.

"No, nor he woon't hev the stick, whether you want it or no," pursued Dagley, throwing out his voice, as if he wanted it to hit hard. "You've got no call to come an' talk about sticks o' these primises, as you woon't give a stick tow'rt mending. Go to Middlemarch to ax for *your* charrickter."

"You'd far better hold your tongue, Dagley," said the wife, "and not kick your own trough over. When a man as is father of a family has been an' spent money at market and made himself the worse for liquor, he's done enough mischief for one day. But I should like to know what my boy's done, sir."

"Niver do you mind what he's done," said Dagley, more fiercely, "it's my business to speak, an' not yourn. An' I wull speak, too. I'll hev my say—supper or no. An' what I say is, as I've lived upo' your ground from my father and grandfather afore me, an' hev dropped our money into't, an' me an' my children might lie an' rot on the ground for top-dressin' as we can't find the money to buy, if the King wasn't to put a stop."

"My good fellow, you're drunk, you know," said Mr Brooke, confidentially but not judiciously. "Another day, another day," he added, turning as if to go.

But Dagley immediately fronted him, and Fag at his heels growled low, as his master's voice grew louder and more insulting, while Monk also drew close in silent dignified watch. The labourers on the waggon were pausing to listen, and it seemed wiser to be quite passive than to attempt a ridiculous flight pursued by a bawling man.

"I'm no more drunk nor you are, nor so much," said Dagley. "I can carry my liquor, an' I know what I meean. An' I meean as the King 'ull put a stop to't, for them say it as knows it, as there's to be a Rinform, and them landlords as never done the right thing by their tenants 'ull be treated i' that way as they'll hev to scuttle off. An' there's them i' Middlemarch knows what the Rinform is—an' as knows who'll hev to scuttle. Says they, 'I know who *your* landlord is.' 'An' ' says I, 'I hope you're the better for knowin' him, I arn't.' Says they, 'He's a close-fisted un.' 'Ay, ay,' says I. 'He's a man for the Rinform,' says they. That's what they says. An' I made out what the Rinform were—an' it were to send you an' your likes a-scuttlin'; an' w' pretty strong-smellin' things too. An' you may do as you like now, for I'm none afeard on you. An' you'd better let my boy aloan, an' look to yoursen, afore the Rinform has got upo' your back. That's what I'n got to say," concluded Mr Dagley, striking his fork into the ground with a firmness which proved inconvenient as he tried to draw it up again.

At this last action Monk began to bark loudly, and it was a moment for Mr Brooke to escape. He walked out of the yard as quickly as he could, in some amazement at the novelty of his situation. He had never been insulted on his own land before, and had been inclined to regard himself as a general favourite (we are all apt to do so, when we think of our own amiability more than of what other people are likely to want of us). When he had quarrelled with Caleb Garth twelve years before he had thought that the tenants would be pleased at the landlord's taking everything into his own hands.

Some who follow the narrative of his experience may wonder at the midnight darkness of Mr Dagley; but nothing was easier in those times than for an hereditary farmer of his grade to be ignorant, in spite somehow of having a rector in the twin parish who was a gentleman to the backbone, a curate nearer at hand who preached more learnedly than the rector, a landlord who had gone into everything, especially fine art and social improvement, and all the lights of Middlemarch only three miles off. As to the facility with which mortals escape knowledge, try an average acquaintance in the intellectual blaze of London, and consider what that eligible person for a dinner-party would have been if he had learned scant skill in "summing" from the parish-clerk of Tipton, and read a chapter in the Bible with immense difficulty, because such names as Isaiah or Apollos remained unmanageable after twice spelling. Poor Dagley read a few verses sometimes on a Sunday evening, and the world was at least not darker to him than it had been before. Some things he knew thoroughly, namely, the slovenly habits of farming, and the awkwardness of weather, stock and crops, at Freeman's End—so called apparently by way of sarcasm, to imply that a man was free to quit it if he chose, but that there was no earthly "beyond" open to him.

———◆◆◆———

Slums in Manchester

FRIEDRICH ENGELS

[FROM *The Condition of the Working-Class in England in 1844*]

1845

The whole of this built-up area is commonly called Manchester, and contains about 400,000 people. This is probably an underestimate rather than an exaggeration. Owing to the curious lay-out of the town it is quite possible for someone to live for years in Manchester and to travel daily to and from his work without ever seeing a working-class quarter or coming into contact with an artisan. He who visits Manchester simply on business or for pleasure need never see the slums, mainly because the working-class districts and the middle-class districts are quite distinct. This division is due partly to deliberate policy and partly to instinctive and tacit agreement between the two social groups. In those areas where the two social groups happen to come into contact with each other the middle classes sanctimoniously ignore the existence of their

Translated and edited by W. O. Henderson and W. H. Chaloner (New York: Macmillan, 1958); from pages 54-73.

less fortunate neighbours. In the centre of Manchester there is a fairly large commercial district, which is about half a mile long and half a mile broad. This district is almost entirely given over to offices and warehouses. Nearly the whole of this district has no permanent residents and is deserted at night, when only policemen patrol its dark, narrow thoroughfares with their bull's eye lanterns. This district is intersected by certain main streets which carry an enormous volume of traffic. The lower floors of the buildings are occupied by shops of dazzling splendour. A few of the upper stories on these premises are used as dwellings and the streets present a relatively busy appearance until late in the evening. Around this commercial quarter there is a belt of built-up areas on the average one and a half miles in width, which is occupied entirely by working-class dwellings. This area of worker's houses includes all Manchester proper, except the centre, all Salford and Hulme, an important part of Pendleton and Chorlton, two-thirds of Ardwick and certain small areas of Cheetham Hill and Broughton. Beyond this belt of working-class houses or dwellings lie the districts inhabited by the middle classes and the upper classes. The former are to be found in regularly laid out streets near the working-class districts—in Chorlton and in the remoter parts of Cheetham Hill. The villas of the upper classes are surrounded by gardens and lie in the higher and remoter parts of Chorlton and Ardwick or on the breezy heights of Cheetham Hill, Broughton and Pendleton. The upper classes enjoy healthy country air and live in luxurious and comfortable dwellings which are linked to the centre of Manchester by omnibuses which run every fifteen or thirty minutes. To such an extent has the convenience of the rich been considered in the planning of Manchester that these plutocrats can travel from their houses to their places of business in the centre of the town by the shortest routes, which run entirely through working-class districts, without even realising how close they are to the misery and filth which lie on both sides of the road. This is because the main streets which run from the Exchange in all directions out of the town are occupied almost uninterruptedly on both sides by shops, which are kept by members of the lower middle classes. . . .

I will now give a description of the working-class districts of Manchester. The first of them is the Old Town, which lies between the northern limit of the commercial quarter and the River Irk. Here even the better streets, such as Todd Street, Long Millgate, Withy Grove and Shudehill, are narrow and tortuous. The houses are dirty, old and tumble-down. The side streets have been built in a disgraceful fashion. If one enters the district near the 'Old Church' and goes down Long Millgate, one sees immediately on the right-hand side a row of antiquated houses where not a single front wall is standing upright. This is a remnant of the old Manchester of the days before the town became industrialised. The original inhabitants and their children have left for better houses in other districts, while the houses in Long Millgate, which no longer satisfied them, were left to a tribe of workers containing a strong Irish element. Here one is really and truly in a district which is quite obviously given over entirely to the working classes, because even the shopkeepers and the publicans of Long Millgate make no effort to give their establishments a semblance of cleanliness. The condition of this street may be deplorable, but it is by no means as bad as the alleys and courts which lie behind it, and which can be approached only by covered passages so narrow that two people cannot pass. Anyone who has never visited these courts and alleys can have no idea of the fantastic way in which the houses have been packed together in disorderly confusion in impudent defiance of all reasonable principles of town planning. And the fault lies not merely in the survival of old property from earlier periods in Manchester's history. Only in quite modern times has the policy of cramming as many houses as possible on to such space as was not utilised in earlier periods reached its climax. The result is that today not an inch of space remains between the houses and any further building is now physically impossible . . . .

To the right and left a number of covered passages from Long Millgate give access to several courts. On reaching them one meets with a degree of dirt and revolting filth, the like of which is not to be found elsewhere. The worst courts are those leading down to the Irk, which contain unquestionably the most dreadful dwellings I have ever seen. In one of these courts, just at the entrance where the covered passage ends, there is a privy without a door. This privy is so dirty that the inhabitants of the court can only enter or leave the court if they are prepared to wade through puddles of stale urine and excrement. Anyone who wishes to confirm this description should go to the first court on the bank of the Irk above Ducie Bridge. Several tanneries are situated on the bank of the river and they fill the neighbourhood with the stench of animal putrefaction. The only way of getting to the courts below Ducie Bridge is by going down flights of narrow dirty steps and one can only reach the houses by treading over heaps of dirt and filth. The first court below Ducie Bridge is called Allen's Court. At the time of the cholera [1832] this court was in such a disgraceful state that the sanitary inspectors [of the local Board of Health] evacuated the inhabitants. The court was then swept and fumigated with chlorine. . . . At the bottom the Irk flows, or rather, stagnates. It is a narrow, coal-black, stinking river full of filth and rubbish which it deposits on the more low-lying right bank. In dry weather this bank presents the spectacle of a series of the most revolting blackish-green puddles of slime from the depths of which bubbles of miasmatic gases constantly rise and create a stench which is unbearable even to those standing on the bridge forty or fifty feet above the level of the water. Moreover, the flow of the river is continually interrupted by numerous high weirs, behind which large quantities of slime and refuse collect and putrefy. Above Ducie Bridge there are some tall tannery buildings, and further up there are dye-works, bone mills and gasworks. All the filth, both liquid and solid, discharged by these works finds its way into the River Irk, which also receives the contents of the adjacent sewers and privies. The nature of the filth deposited by this river may well be imagined. If one looks at the heaps of garbage below Ducie Bridge one can gauge the extent to which accumulated dirt, filth and decay permeates the courts on the steep left bank of the river. The houses are packed very closely together and since the bank of the river is very steep it is possible to see a part of every house. All of them have been blackened by soot, all of them are crumbling with age and all have broken window-panes and window-frames. In the background there are old factory buildings which look like barracks. On the opposite, low-lying bank of the river, one sees a long row of houses and factories. The second house is a roofless ruin, filled with refuse, and the third is built in such a low situation that the ground floor is uninhabitable and has neither doors nor windows. In the background one sees the paupers' cemetery, and the stations of the railways to Liverpool and Leeds. Behind these buildings is situated the workhouse, Manchester's "Poor Law Bastille." The workhouse is built on a hill and from behind its high walls and battlements seems to threaten the whole adjacent working-class quarter like a fortress. . . .

The recently constructed extension of the Leeds railway which crosses the Irk at this point has swept away some of these courts and alleys, but it has thrown open to public gaze some of the others. So it comes about that there is to be found immediately under the railway bridge a court which is even filthier and more revolting than all the others. This is simply because it was formerly so hidden and secluded that it could only be reached with considerable difficulty [but is now exposed to the human eye]. I thought I knew this district well, but even I would never have found it had not the railway viaduct made a breach in the slums at this point. One walks along a very rough path on the river bank, in between clothes-posts and washing lines, to reach a chaotic group of little, one-storied, one-roomed cabins. Most of them have earth floors, and working, living and sleeping all take place in the one room. In such a hole, barely six feet long and five feet wide, I saw two beds—and what beds and bedding!—which filled the room, except for the fireplace and the doorstep. Several of these huts, as far as I could see, were completely empty, although the door was open and the inhabitants were leaning against the door posts. In front of the doors filth and garbage abounded. I could not see the pavement, but from time to time I felt it was there because my feet scraped it. This whole collection of cattle sheds for human beings was surrounded on two sides by houses and a factory and on a third side by the river. [It was possible to get to this slum by only two routes.] One was the narrow path along the river bank, while the other was a narrow gateway which led to another human rabbit warren which was nearly as badly built and was nearly in such a bad condition as the one I have just described. . . .

This, then, is the Old Town of Manchester. On re-reading my description of the Old Town I must admit that, far from having exaggerated anything, I have not written vividly enough to impress the reader with the filth and dilapidation of a district which is quite unfit for human habitation. The shameful lay-out of the Old Town has made it impossible for the wretched inhabitants to enjoy cleanliness, fresh air, and good health. And such a district of at least twenty to thirty thousand inhabitants lies in the very centre of the second city in England, the most important factory town in the world. It is here that one can see how little space human beings need to move about in, how little air—and what air!—they need to breathe in order to exist, and how few of the decencies of civilisation are really necessary in order to survive. It is true that this is the *Old Town* and Manchester people stress this when their attention is drawn to the revolting character of this hell upon earth. But that is no defence. . . . No hovel is so wretched but it will find a worker to rent it because he is too poor to pay for better accommodation. But the middle classes salve their consciences by arguing that this state of affairs obtains only in the Old Town. Let us therefore see what the New Town has to offer. . . .

The area crossed by the railway to Birmingham has the most houses and is therefore the worst part of the district. Here the River Medlock flows with endless twists and turns through a valley which may be compared with that of the

Irk. From its entry into Manchester to its confluence with the Irwell, this coal-black, stagnant, stinking river is lined on both sides by a broad belt of factories and workers' dwellings. The cottages are all in a sorry state. The banks of the Medlock like those of the Irk are generally steep and the buildings run down to the very edge of the river. The . . . most disgusting spot of all is one . . . called Little Ireland. It lies in a fairly deep natural depression on a bend of the river and is completely surrounded by tall factories or high banks and embankments covered with buildings. Here lie two groups of about two hundred cottages, most of which are built on the back-to-back principle. Some four thousand people, mostly Irish, inhabit this slum. The cottages are very small, old and dirty, while the streets are uneven, partly unpaved, not properly drained and full of ruts. Heaps of refuse, offal and sickening filth are everywhere interspersed with pools of stagnant liquid. The atmosphere is polluted by the stench and is darkened by the thick smoke of a dozen factory chimneys. A horde of ragged women and children swarm about the streets and they are just as dirty as the pigs which wallow happily on the heaps of garbage and in the pools of filth. In short, this horrid little slum affords as hateful and repulsive a spectacle as the worst courts to be found on the banks of the Irk. The inhabitants live in dilapidated cottages, the windows of which are broken and patched with oilskin. The doors and the door posts are broken and rotten. The creatures who inhabit these dwellings and even their dark, wet cellars, and who live confined amidst all this filth and foul air—which cannot be dissipated because of the surrounding lofty buildings—must surely have sunk to the lowest level of humanity. That is the conclusion that must surely be drawn even by any visitor who examines the slum from the outside, without entering any of the dwellings. But his feelings of horror would be intensified if he were to discover that on the average twenty people live in each of these little houses, which at the moment consist of two rooms, an attic and a cellar. One privy—and that usually inaccessible—is shared by about one hundred and twenty people. In spite of all the warnings of the doctors and in spite of the alarm caused to the health authorities by the condition of Little Ireland during the cholera epidemic, the condition of this slum is practically the same in this year of grace 1844 as it was in 1831.

———◆———

Child Labor in the Mines

FRIEDRICH ENGELS

[FROM *The Condition of the Working-Class in England in 1844*]

1845

We turn now to the coal and ironstone mines which are the most important branches of mining in England. . . . Children of 4, 5 and 7 years work in coal and ironstone mines, where very similar methods of extraction are used. But most of the children are over 8 years of age. They carry the loosened coal or ironstone from the face either to the underground tramway or to the bottom of the shaft. Their services are also used to open and shut the ventilation doors which divide the various parts of a mine, so as to allow the passage of men, carts and tubs. The smallest children are usually given the task of minding the doors. They have to sit alone for 12 hours every day in a narrow, dark passage which is generally damp. They are not even given enough to do to save them from the idle boredom which gradually turns them into stupid animals. The transport of coal and ironstone, on the other hand, is very heavy work, because these minerals are moved about in fairly large tubs which have no wheels. The tubs have to be hauled over the bumpy ground of the

Translated and edited by W. O. Henderson and W. H. Chaloner (New York: Macmillan, 1958); from pages 277-84.

underground passages, often through wet clay or even water. Sometimes the tubs have to be hauled up steep inclines and are brought through passages which are so narrow that the workers have to crawl on their hands and knees. The older boys and girls have to perform this heavy work. Sometimes one of the older youths has to handle the tub by himself, but sometimes the work is given to two younger children one of whom pushes and the other pulls. The actual hewing of the coal or ironstone is done by grown men or by physically well-developed youths of 16 or more. This also is very exhausting work. The normal working day in the mines is between 11 and 12 hours, but may often be longer. In Scotland miners work up to 14 hours a day. Double shifts are frequently worked, and this means that all miners are frequently at work for 24, or even 26, hours without coming to the surface. There are rarely any set times for meals, so that the hungry miners take their meals when they can. . . .

All the children and young people employed in hauling coal and ironstone complain of being very tired. Not even in a factory where the most intensive methods of securing output are employed do we find the workers driven to the same limits of physical endurance as they are in the mines. Every page of the report to which we have referred gives chapter and verse for this assertion. It is a very common occurrence for children to come home from the mine so exhausted that they throw themselves on to the stone floor in front of the fire. They cannot keep awake even to eat a morsel of food. Their parents have to wash them and put them to bed while they are still asleep. Sometimes the children actually fall asleep on the way home and are eventually discovered by their parents late at night. It appears to be the almost universal practice of these children to stay in bed most of Sunday in an attempt to recover from the exertions of the previous week's work. Only a few go to church or Sunday school. The teachers at these schools complain that their pupils are very tired and listless. . . .

The miners rarely if ever go to church. All the clergy complain of the shocking ignorance of the miners on religious matters. Their abysmal lack of knowledge concerning both religious and secular affairs could be illustrated by even more striking examples than those already given to show the ignorance of the factory workers. Only when they swear do the miners show any acquaintance with religion. Their standards of morality are undermined by the very nature of their work. To such an extent are they overworked that it is inevitable that they should take to drink. In the dark loneliness of the mines men, women and children work in great heat and the majority of them take off most (if not all) of their clothes. You can imagine the consequences for yourself. There are more illegitimate children in the mining districts than elsewhere, and this is in itself sufficient evidence of what these half-savage creatures are doing when they get below ground. But it suggests that sexual irregularities have not degenerated into large-scale prostitution in the mining districts as they have in the big cities.

The Rural Town of Marney

BENJAMIN DISRAELI

[FROM *Sybil; or, the Two Nations*]

1845

The situation of the rural town of Marney was one of the most delightful easily to be imagined. In a spreading dale, contiguous to the margin of a clear and lively stream, surrounded by meadows and gardens, and backed by lofty hills, undulating and richly wooded, the traveller on the opposite

From Book II, Chapter 3.

heights of the dale would often stop to admire the merry
prospect that recalled to him the traditional epithet of his
country.

Beautiful illusion! For behind that laughing landscape, penury and disease fed upon the vitals of a miserable population.

The contrast between the interior of the town and its
external aspect was as striking as it was full of pain. With the
exception of the dull high street, which had the usual characteristics of a small agricultural market town, some sombre
mansions, a dingy inn, and a petty bourse, Marney mainly
consisted of a variety of narrow and crowded lanes formed
by cottages built of rubble, or unhewn stones without cement,
and, from age or badness of the material, looking as if they
could scarcely hold together. The gaping chinks admitted
every blast; the leaning chimneys had lost half their original
height; the rotten rafters were evidently misplaced; while in
many instances the thatch, yawning in some parts to admit
the wind and wet, and in all utterly unfit for its original purpose of giving protection from the weather, looked more like
the top of a dunghill than a cottage. Before the doors of these
dwellings, and often surrounding them, ran open drains full of
animal and vegetable refuse, decomposing into disease, or
sometimes in their imperfect course filling foul pits or spreading into stagnant pools, while a concentrated solution of every
species of dissolving filth was allowed to soak through, and
thoroughly impregnate, the walls and ground adjoining.

These wretched tenements seldom consisted of more than
two rooms, in one of which the whole family, however
numerous, were obliged to sleep, without distinction of age,
or sex, or suffering. With the water streaming down the walls,
the light distinguished through the roof, with no hearth even
in winter, the virtuous mother in the sacred pangs of child-
birth gives forth another victim to our thoughtless civilization;
surrounded by three generations whose inevitable presence is
more painful than her sufferings in that hour of travail; while
the father of her coming child, in another corner of the sordid
chamber, lies stricken by that typhus which his contaminating
dwelling has breathed into his veins, and for whose next prey

is perhaps destined his new-born child. These swarming walls had neither windows nor doors sufficient to keep out the weather, or admit the sun, or supply the means of ventilation; the humid and putrid roof of thatch exhaling malaria like all other decaying vegetable matter. The dwelling-rooms were neither boarded nor paved; and whether it were that some were situate in low and damp places, occasionally flooded by the river, and usually much below the level of the road; or that the springs, as was often the case, would burst through the mud floor; the ground was at no time better than so much clay, while sometimes you might see little channels cut from the centre under the doorways to carry off the water, the door itself removed from its hinges: a resting-place for infancy in its deluged home. These hovels were in many instances not provided with the commonest conveniences of the rudest police;[1] contiguous to every door might be observed the dung-heap on which every kind of filth was accumulated, for the purpose of being disposed of for manure, so that, when the poor man opened his narrow habitation in the hope of refreshing it with the breeze of summer, he was met with a mixture of gases from reeking dunghills.

This town of Marney was a metropolis of agricultural labour, for the proprietors of the neighbourhood having for the last half-century acted on the system of destroying the cottages on their estates, in order to become exempted from the maintenance of the population, the expelled people had flocked to Marney, where, during the war, a manufactory had afforded them some relief, though its wheels had long ceased to disturb the waters of the Mar.

Deprived of this resource, they had again gradually spread themselves over that land which had, as it were, rejected them; and obtained from its churlish breast a niggardly subsistence. Their re-entrance into the surrounding parishes was viewed with great suspicion; their renewed settlement opposed by every ingenious contrivance; those who availed themselves of their labour were careful that they should not become dwellers on the soil; and though, from the excessive competi-

[1]Civilization.

tion, there were few districts in the kingdom where the rate of wages was more depressed, those who were fortunate enough to obtain the scant remuneration, had, in addition to their toil, to endure, each morn and even, a weary journey before they could reach the scene of their labour, or return to the squalid hovel which profaned the name of home. To that home, over which malaria hovered, and round whose shivering hearth were clustered other guests beside the exhausted family of toil—Fever, in every form, pale Consumption, exhausting Synochus, and trembling Ague—returned after cultivating the broad fields of merry England, the bold British peasant, returned to encounter the worst of diseases, with a frame the least qualified to oppose them; a frame that, subdued by toil, was never sustained by animal food; drenched by the tempest, could not change its dripping rags; and was indebted for its scanty fuel to the windfalls of the woods.

The eyes of this unhappy race might have been raised to the solitary spire that sprang up in the midst of them, the bearer of present consolation, the harbinger of future equality; but Holy Church at Marney had forgotten her sacred mission. We have introduced the reader to the vicar, an orderly man, who deemed he did his duty if he preached each week two sermons, and enforced humility on his congregation, and gratitude for the blessings of this life. The high street and some neighbouring gentry were the staple of his hearers. Lord and Lady Marney came, attended by Captain Grouse, every Sunday morning, with commendable regularity, and were ushered into the invisible interior of a vast pew, that occupied half of the gallery, was lined with crimson damask, and furnished with easy chairs, and, for those who chose them, well-padded stools of prayer. The people of Marney took refuge in conventicles, which abounded; little plain buildings of pale brick with the names painted on them, of Sion, Bethel, Bethesda; names of a distant land, and the language of a persecuted and ancient race; yet such is the mysterious power of their divine quality, breathing consolation in the nineteenth century to the harassed forms and the harrowed souls of a Saxon peasantry.

But, however devoted to his flock might have been the Vicar of Marney, his exertions for their well-being, under any circumstances, must have been mainly limited to spiritual consolation. Married, and a father, he received for his labours the small tithes of the parish, which secured to him an income by no means equal to that of a superior banker's clerk, or the cook of a great loanmonger. The great tithes of Marney, which might be counted by thousands, swelled the vast rental which was drawn from this district by the fortunate earls that bore its name.

The Men Who Are Eaten

CHARLES KINGSLEY

[FROM *Alton Locke*]

1850

About eight o'clock the next morning I started forth with my guide, the shoemaker, over as desolate a country as men can well conceive. Not a house was to be seen for miles, except the knot of hovels which we had left, and here and there a great lump of farm-buildings, with its yard of yellow stacks. Beneath our feet the earth was iron, and the sky iron above our heads. Dark curdled clouds, "which had built up everywhere an under-roof of doleful grey," swept on before the bitter northern wind, which whistled through the low leafless hedges and rotting wattles, and crisped the dark sodden leaves of the scattered hollies, almost the only trees in sight.

We trudged on, over wide stubbles, with innumerable weeds;

From Chapter 28.

over wide fallows, in which the deserted ploughs stood frozen fast; then over clover and grass, burnt black with frost; then over a field of turnips, where we passed a large fold of hurdles, within which some hundred sheep stood, with their heads turned from the cutting best. All was dreary, idle, silent; no sound or sign of human beings. One wondered where the people lived who cultivated so vast a tract of civilised, over-peopled, nineteenth-century England. As we came up to the fold, two little boys hailed us from the inside—two little wretches with blue noses and white cheeks, scarecrows of rags and patches, their feet peeping through bursten shoes twice too big for them, who seemed to have shared between them a ragged pair of worsted gloves, and cowered among the sheep, under the shelter of a hurdle, crying and inarticulate with cold.

"What's the matter, boys?"

"Turmits is froze, and us can't turn the handle of the cutter. Do ye gie us a turn, please!"

We scrambled over the hurdles, and gave the miserable little creatures the benefit of ten minutes' labour. They seemed too small for such exertion: their little hands were purple with chilblains, and they were so sorefooted they could scarce-ly limp. I was surprised to find them at least three years older than their size and looks denoted, and still more surprised, too, to find that their salary for all this bitter exposure to the elements—such as I believe I could not have endured two days running—was the vast sum of one shilling a week each, Sundays included. "They didn't never go to school, nor to church nether, except just now and then, sometimes—they had to mind the shep."

I went on, sickened with the contrast between the highly bred, over-fed, fat, thick-woolled animals, with their troughs of turnips and malt-dust, and their racks of rich clover-hay, and their little pent-house of rock-salt, having nothing to do but to eat and sleep, and eat again, and the little half-starved shivering animals who were their slaves. Man the master of the brutes? Bah! As society is now, the brutes are the masters—the horse, the sheep the bullock, is the master, and the labourer is their slave. "Oh! but the brutes are eaten!" Well; the horses at least are not eaten—they live, like landlords, till they die. And those who are eaten, are certainly not eaten by their human servants. The sheep they fat, another kills, to parody Shelley; and, after all, is not the labourer, as well as the sheep, eaten by you, my dear Society? —devoured body and soul, not the less really because you are longer about the meal, there being an old prejudice against cannibalism, and also against murder—except after the Riot Act has been read.

"What!" shriek the insulted respectabilities, "have we not paid him his wages weekly, and has he not lived upon them?" Yes; and have you not given your sheep and horses their daily wages, and have they not lived on them? You wanted to work them; and they could not work, you know, unless they were alive. But here lies your iniquity: you gave the labourer nothing but his daily food—not even his lodgings; the pigs were not stinted of their wash to pay for their sty-room, the man was; and his wages, thanks to your competitive system, were beaten down deliberately and conscientiously (for was it not according to political economy, and the laws thereof?) to the minimum on which he could or would work, without the hope or the possibility of saving a farthing. You know how to invest your capital profitably, dear Society, and to save money over and above your income of daily comforts; but what has he saved?—what is he profited by all those years of labour? He has kept body and soul together—perhaps he could have done that without you or your help. But his wages are used up every Saturday night. When he stops working, you have in your pocket the whole real profits of his nearly fifty years' labour, and he has nothing. And then you say that you have not eaten him! You know, in your heart of hearts, that you have. . . .

With some such thoughts I walked across the open down, toward a circular camp, the earthwork, probably, of some old British town. Inside it, some thousand or so of labouring people were swarming restlessly round a single large block of stone, some relic of Druid times, on which a tall man stood, his dark figure thrown out in bold relief against the dreary sky. As we pushed through the crowd, I was struck with the wan, haggard look of all faces; their lack-lustre eyes and drooping lips, stooping shoulders, heavy, dragging steps, gave them a crushed, dogged air, which was infinitely painful, and bespoke a grade of misery more habitual and degrading than that of the excitable and passionate artisan.

There were many women among them, talking shrilly, and looking even more pinched and wan than the men. I remarked, also, that many of the crowd carried heavy sticks, pitchforks, and other tools which might be used as fearful weapons— an ugly sign, which I ought to have heeded betimes.

They glared with sullen curiosity at me and my Londoner's clothes, as, with no small feeling of self-importance, I pushed my way to the foot of the stone. The man who stood on it seemed to have been speaking some time. His words, like all I heard that day, were utterly devoid of anything like eloquence or imagination—a dull string of somewhat incoherent complaints, which derived their force only from the intense earnestness, which attested their truthfulness. As far as I can recollect, I will give the substance of what I heard. But, indeed, I heard nothing but what has been bandied about from newspaper to newspaper for years—confessed by all parties, deplored by all parties, but never an attempt made to remedy it.

—"The farmers makes slaves on us. I can't hear no difference between a Christian and a nigger, except they flogs the niggers and starves the Christians; and I don't know which I'd choose. I served Farmer —— seven year, off and on, and arter harvest he tells me he's no more work for me, nor my boy nether, acause he's getting too big for him, so he gets a little 'un instead, and we does nothing; and my boy lies about, getting into bad ways, like hundreds more; and then we goes to board, and they bids us go and look for work; and we goes up next part to London. I couldn't get none; they'd enough to do, they said, to employ their own; and we begs our way home, and goes into the Union; and they turns us out again in two or three days, and promises us work again, and gives us two days' gravel-pecking, and then says they has no more

for us; and we was sore pinched, and laid a-bed all day;
then next board-day we goes to 'em and they gives us one
day more—and that threw us off another week, and then
next board-day we goes into the Union again for three days,
and gets sent out again: and so I've been starving one-half of
the time, and they putting us off and on o' purpose like that;
and I'll bear it no longer, and that's what I says."

———◆◆◆———

A Village Workhouse in 1830

GEORGE ELIOT

[FROM *Scenes of Clerical Life:* "Amos Barton"]

1857

At eleven o'clock, Mr Barton walked forth in cape and boa,
with the sleet driving in his face, to read prayers at the workhouse, euphuistically called the "College." The College was
a huge square stone building, standing on the best apology
for an elevation of ground that could be seen for about ten
miles round Shepperton. A flat ugly district this; depressing
enough to look at even on the brightest days. The roads are
black with coal-dust, the brick houses dingy with smoke; and
at that time—the time of handloom weavers—every other
cottage had a loom at its window, where you might see a pale,
sickly-looking man or woman pressing a narrow chest against
a board, and doing a sort of tread-mill work with legs and
arms. A troublesome district for a clergyman; at least to one
who, like Amos Barton, understood the "cure of souls" in
something more than an official sense; for over and above
the rustic stupidity furnished by the farm-labourers, the

From Chapter 2.

miners brought obstreperous animalism, and the weavers an acrid Radicalism and Dissent. Indeed, Mrs Hackit often observed that the colliers, who many of them earned better wages than Mr Barton, "passed their time in doing nothing but swilling ale and smoking, like the beasts that perish" (speaking, we may presume, in a remotely analogical sense); and in some of the alehouse corners the drink was flavoured by a dingy kind of infidelity, something like rinsings of Tom Paine in ditch-water. A certain amount of religious excitement created by the popular preaching of Mr Parry, Amos's predecessor, had nearly died out, and the religious life of Shepperton was falling back towards low-water mark. Here, you perceive, was a terrible stronghold of Satan; and you may well pity the Rev. Amos Barton, who had to stand single-handed and summon it to surrender. We read, indeed, that the walls of Jericho fell down before the sound of trumpets; but we nowhere hear that those trumpets were hoarse and feeble. Doubtless they were trumpets that gave forth clear ringing tones, and sent a mighty vibration through brick and mortar. But the oratory of the Rev. Amos resembled rather a Belgian railway-horn, which shows praiseworthy intentions inadequately fulfilled. He often missed the right note both in public and private exhortation, and got a little angry in consequence. For though Amos thought himself strong, he did not *feel* himself strong. Nature had given him the opinion, but not the sensation. Without that opinion he would probably never have worn cambric bands, but would have been an excellent cabinetmaker and deacon of an Independent church, as his father was before him (he was not a shoemaker, as Mr Pilgrim had reported). He might then have sniffed long and loud in the corner of his pew in Gun Street Chapel; he might have indulged in halting rhetoric at prayer-meetings, and have spoken faulty English in private life; and these little infirmities would not have prevented him, honest faithful man that he was, from being a shining light in the dissenting circle of Bridgeport. A tallow dip, of the long-eight description, is an excellent thing in the kitchen candlestick, and Betty's nose and eye are not sensitive to the difference between it and the finest wax; it is only when you stick it in the silver candle-stick, and introduce it into the drawing-room, that it seems plebeian, dim, and ineffectual. Alas for the worthy man who, like that candle, gets himself into the wrong place! It is only the very largest souls who will be able to appreciate and pity him—who will discern and love sincerity of purpose amid all the bungling feebleness of achievement.

But now Amos Barton has made his way through the sleet as far as the College, has thrown off his hat, cape, and boa, and is reading in the dreary stone-floored dining-room, a por-tion of the morning service to the inmates seated on the benches before him. Remember, the New Poor-law had not yet come into operation, and Mr Barton was not acting as paid chaplain of the Union, but as the pastor who had the cure of all souls in his parish, pauper as well as other. After the prayers he always addressed to them a short discourse on some subject suggested by the lesson for the day, striving if by this means some edifying matter might find its way into the pauper mind and conscience—perhaps a task as trying as you could well imagine to the faith and patience of any honest clergyman. For, on the very first bench, these were the faces on which his eye had to rest, watching whether there was any stirring under the stagnant surface.

Right in front of him—probably because he was stone-deaf, and it was deemed more edifying to hear nothing at a short distance than at a long one—sat "Old Maxum," as he was familiarly called, his real patronymic remaining a mystery to most persons. A fine philological sense discerns in this cog-nomen an indication that the pauper patriarch had once been considered pithy and sententious in his speech; but now the weight of ninety-five years lay heavy on his tongue as well as in his ears, and he sat before the clergyman with protruded chin, and munching mouth, and eyes that seemed to look at emptiness.

Next to him sat Poll Fodge—known to the magistracy of her county as Mary Higgins—a one-eyed woman, with a scarred and seamy face, the most notorious rebel in the work-house, said to have once thrown her broth over the master's coat-tails, and who, in spite of nature's apparent safeguards against that contingency, had contributed to the perpetuation of the Fodge characteristics in the person of a small boy, who was behaving naughtily on one of the back benches. Miss Fodge fixed her one sore eye on Mr Barton with a sort of hardy defiance.

Beyond this member of the softer sex, at the end of the bench, sat "Silly Jim," a young man afflicted with hydrocephalus, who rolled his head from side to side, and gazed at the point of his nose. These were the supporters of Old Maxum on his right.

On his left sat Mr Fitchett, a tall fellow, who had once been a footman in the Oldinport family, and in that giddy elevation had enunciated a contemptuous opinion of boiled beef, which had been traditionally handed down in Shepperton as the direct cause of his ultimate reduction to pauper commons. His calves were now shrunken, and his hair was grey without the aid of powder; but he still carried his chin as if he were conscious of a stiff cravat; he set his dilapidated hat on with a knowing inclination towards the left ear; and when he was on field-work, he carted and uncarted the manure with a sort of flunkey grace, the ghost of that jaunty demeanour with which he used to usher in my lady's morning visitors. The flunkey nature was nowhere completely subdued but in his stomach, and he still divided society into gentry, gentry's flunkeys, and the people who provided for them. A clergyman without a flunkey was an anomaly, belonging to neither of these classes. Mr Fitchett had an irrepressible tendency to drowsiness under spiritual instruction, and in the recurrent regularity with which he dozed off until he nodded and awaked himself, he looked not unlike a piece of mechanism, ingeniously contrived for measuring the length of Mr Barton's discourse.

Perfectly wide-awake, on the contrary, was his left-hand neighbour, Mrs Brick, one of those hard undying old women, to whom age seems to have given a network of wrinkles, as a coat of magic armour against the attacks of winters, warm or cold. The point on which Mrs Brick was still sensitive—

the theme on which you might possibly excite her hope and fear—was snuff. It seemed to be an embalming powder, helping her soul to do the office of salt.

And now, eke out an audience of which this front benchful was a sample, with a certain number of refractory children, over whom Mr Spratt, the master of the workhouse, exercised an irate surveillance, and I think you will admit that the university-taught clergymen, whose office it is to bring home the gospel to a handful of such souls, has a sufficiently hard task. For, to have any chance of success, short of miraculous intervention, he must bring his geographical, chronological, exegetical mind pretty nearly to the pauper point of view, or of no view; he must have some approximate conception of the mode in which the doctrines that have so much vitality in the plenum of his own brain will comport themselves *in vacuo*—that is to say, in a brain that is neither geographical, chronological, nor exegetical. It is a flexible imagination that can take such a leap as that, and an adroit tongue that can adapt its speech to so unfamiliar a position. The Rev. Amos Barton had neither that flexible imagination, nor that adroit tongue. He talked of Israel and its sins, of chosen vessels, of the Paschal lamb, of blood as a medium of reconciliation; and he strove in this way to convey religious truth within reach of the Fodge and Fitchett mind. This very morning, the first lesson was the twelfth chapter of Exodus, and Mr Barton's exposition turned on unleavened bread. Nothing in the world more suited to the simple understanding than instruction through familiar types and symbols! But there is always this danger attending it, that the interest or comprehension of your hearers may stop short precisely at the point where your spiritual interpretation begins. And Mr Barton this morning succeeded in carrying the pauper imagination to the dough-tub, but unfortunately was not able to carry it upwards from that well-known object to the unknown truths which it was intended to shadow forth.

Alas! a natural incapacity for teaching, finished by keeping "terms" at Cambridge, where there are able mathematicians, and butter is sold by the yard, is not apparently the medium through which Christian doctrine will distil as welcome dew on withered souls.

And so, while the sleet outside was turning to unquestionable snow, and the stony dining-room looked darker and drearier, and Mr Fitchett was nodding his lowest, and Mr Spratt was boxing the boys' ears with a constant *rinforzando,* as he felt more keenly the approach of dinner-time, Mr Barton wound up his exhortation with something of the February chill at his heart as well as his feet. Mr Fitchett, thoroughly roused now the instruction was at an end, obsequiously and gracefully advanced to help Mr Barton in putting on his cape, while Mrs Brick rubbed her withered forefinger round and round her little shoe-shaped snuff-box, vainly seeking for the fraction of a pinch. I can't help thinking that if Mr Barton had shaken into that little box a small portion of Scotch high-dried, he might have produced something more like an amiable emotion in Mrs Brick's mind than anything she had felt under his morning's exposition of the unleavened bread. But our good Amos laboured under a deficiency of small tact as well as of small cash; and when he observed the action of the old woman's forefinger, he said, in his brusque way, "So your snuff is all gone, eh?"

Mrs Brick's eyes twinkled with the visionary hope that the parson might be intending to replenish her box, at least mediately, through the present of a small copper.

"Ah, well! you'll soon be going where there is no more snuff. You'll be in need of mercy then. You must remember that you may have to seek for mercy and not find it, just as you're seeking for snuff."

At the first sentence of this admonition, the twinkle subsided from Mrs Brick's eyes. The lid of her box went "click!" and her heart was shut up at the same moment.

But now Mr Barton's attention was called for by Mr Spratt, who was dragging a small and unwilling boy from the rear. Mr Spratt was a small-featured, small-statured man, with a remarkable power of language, mitigated by hesitation, who piqued himself on expressing unexceptionable sentiments in unexceptionable language on all occasions.

"Mr Barton, sir—aw—aw—excuse my trespassing on your time—aw—to beg that you will administer a rebuke to this boy; he is—aw—aw—most inveterate in ill-behaviour during service-time."

The inveterate culprit was a boy of seven, vainly contending against "candles" at his nose by feeble sniffing. But no sooner had Mr Spratt uttered his impeachment, than Miss Fodge rushed forward and placed herself between Mr Barton and the accused.

"That's *my* child, Muster Barton," she exclaimed, further manifesting her maternal instincts by applying her apron to her offspring's nose. "He's al'ys a-findin' faut wi' him, an' a-poundin' him for nothin'. Let him goo an' eat his roost goose as is a-smellin' up in our noses while we're a-swallering them greasy broth, an' let my boy allooan."

Mr Spratt's small eyes flashed, and he was in danger of uttering sentiments not unexceptionable before the clergyman; but Mr Barton, foreseeing that a prolongation of this episode would not be to edification, said "Silence!" in his severest tones.

"Let me hear no abuse. Your boy is not likely to behave well, if you set him the example of being saucy." Then stooping down to Master Fodge, and taking him by the shoulder, "Do you like being beaten?"

"No-a."

"Then what a silly boy you are to be naughty. If you were not naughty, you wouldn't be beaten. But if you are naughty, God will be angry, as well as Mr Spratt; and God can burn you for ever. That will be worse than being beaten."

Master Fodge's countenance was neither affirmative nor negative of this proposition.

"But," continued Mr Barton, "if you will be a good boy, God will love you, and you will grow up to be a good man. Now, let me hear next Thursday that you have been a good boy."

Master Fodge had no distinct vision of the benefit that would accrue to him from this change of courses. But Mr Barton, being aware that Miss Fodge had touched on a delicate sub-

ject in alluding to the roast goose, was determined to witness
no more polemics between her and Mr Spratt, so, saying good
morning to the latter, he hastily left the College.

A London Workhouse in 1850

CHARLES DICKENS

[FROM "A Walk in a Workhouse"]

A few Sundays ago, I formed one of the congregation
assembled in the chapel of a large metropolitan Workhouse.
With the exception of the clergyman and clerk, and a very
few officials, there were none but paupers present. The children sat in the galleries; the women in the body of the chapel,
and in one of the side aisles; the men in the remaining aisle.
The service was decorously performed, though the sermon
might have been much better adapted to the comprehension
and to the circumstances of the hearers. The usual supplica-
tions were offered, with more than the usual significancy in
such a place, for the fatherless children and widows, for all
sick persons and young children, for all that were desolate
and oppressed, for the comforting and helping of the weak-
hearted, for the raising-up of them that had fallen; for all that
were in danger, necessity, and tribulation. The prayers of the
congregation were desired "for several persons in the various
wards dangerously ill"; and others who were recovering returned their thanks to Heaven.

Among this congregation were some evil-looking young wom-
en, and beetle-browed young men; but not many—perhaps
that kind of characters kept away. Generally, the faces (those
of the children excepted) were depressed and subdued, and
wanted colour. Aged people were there, in every variety.

From *Household Words*, 25 May 1850.

Mumbling, blear-eyed, spectacled, stupid, deaf, lame; vacantly winking in the gleams of sun that now and then crept in through the open doors, from the paved yard; shading their listening ears or blinking eyes with their withered hands; poring over their books, leering at nothing, going to sleep, crouching and drooping in corners. There were weird old women, all skeleton within, all bonnet and cloak without, continually wiping their eyes with dirty dusters of pocket-handkerchiefs; and there were ugly old crones, both male and female, with a ghastly kind of contentment upon them which was not at all comforting to see. Upon the whole, it was the dragon, Pauperism, in a very weak and impotent condition; toothless, fangless, drawing his breath heavily enough, and hardly worth chaining up.

When the service was over, I walked with the humane and conscientious gentleman whose duty it was to take that walk, that Sunday morning, through the little world of poverty enclosed within the workhouse walls. It was inhabited by a population of some fifteen hundred or two thousand paupers, ranging from the infant newly born or not yet come into the pauper world to the old man dying on his bed.

In a room opening from a squalid yard, where a number of listless women were lounging to and fro, trying to get warm in the ineffectual sunshine of the tardy May morning,—in the "Itch-Ward," not to compromise the truth,—a woman, such as HOGARTH has often drawn, was hurriedly getting on her gown before a dusty fire. She was the nurse, or wardswoman, of that insalubrious department—herself a pauper—flabby, raw-boned, untidy—unpromising and coarse of aspect as need be. But on being spoken to about the patients whom she had in charge, she turned round, with her shabby gown half on, half off, and fell a-crying with all her might. Not for show, not querulously, not in any mawkish sentiment, but in the deep grief and affliction of her heart; turning away her dishevelled head; sobbing most bitterly, wringing her hands, and letting fall abundance of great tears, that choked her utterance. What was the matter with the nurse of the itch-ward? Oh, "the dropped child" was dead! Oh, the child that was found in the street, and she had brought up ever since, had died an hour ago, and see where the little creature lay, beneath this cloth! The dear, the pretty dear!

The dropped child seemed too small and poor a thing for Death to be in earnest with, but Death had taken it; and already its diminutive form was neatly washed, composed, and stretched as if in sleep upon a box. I thought I heard a voice from Heaven saying, It shall be well for thee, O nurse of the itch-ward, when some less gentle pauper does those offices to thy cold form, that such as the dropped child are the angels who behold my Father's face!

In another room were several ugly old women crouching, witch-like, round a hearth, and chattering and nodding, after the manner of the monkeys. "All well here? And enough to eat?" A general chattering and chuckling; at last an answer from a volunteer. "Oh, yes, gentleman! Bless you gentleman! Lord bless the parish of St. So-and-So! It feed the hungry, sir, and give drink to the thusty, and it warm them which is cold, so it do, and good luck to the parish of St. So-and-So, and thankee gentleman!" Elsewhere, a party of pauper nurses were at dinner. "How do *you* get on?" "Oh, pretty well, sir! We works hard, and we lives hard—like the sodgers!"

In another room, a kind of purgatory or place of transition, six or eight noisy madwomen were gathered together, under the superintendence of one sane attendant. Among them was a girl of two or three and twenty, very prettily dressed, of most respectable appearance, and good manners, who had been brought in from the house where she had lived as domestic servant (having, I suppose, no friends), on account of being subject to epileptic fits, and requiring to be removed under the influence of a very bad one. She was by no means of the same stuff, or the same breeding, or the same experience, or in the same state of mind, as those by whom she was surrounded; and she pathetically complained that the daily association and the nightly noise made her worse, and was driving her mad— which was perfectly evident. The case was noted for enquiry and redress, but she said she had already been there for some weeks.

If this girl had stolen her mistress's watch, I do not hesitate to say she would, in all probability, have been infinitely better off. . . . We have come to this absurd, this dangerous, this monstrous pass, that the dishonest felon is, in respect of cleanliness, order, diet, and accommodation, better provided for, and taken care of, than the honest pauper.

And this conveys no special imputation on the workhouse of the parish of St. So-and-So, where, on the contrary, I saw many things to commend. It was very agreeable, recollecting that most infamous and atrocious enormity committed at Tooting,—an enormity which, a hundred years hence, will still be vividly remembered in the byways of English life, and which has done more to engender a gloomy discontent and suspicion among many thousands of the people than all the Chartist leaders could have done in all their lives,—to find the pauper children in this workhouse looking robust and well, and apparently the objects of very great care. In the Infant School—a large, light, airy room at the top of the building—the little creatures, being at dinner, and eating their potatoes heartily, were not cowed by the presence of strange visitors, but stretched out their small hands to be shaken, with a very pleasant confidence. And it was comfortable to see two mangy pauper rocking-horses rampant in a corner. In the girls' school, where the dinner was also in progress, everything bore a cheerful and healthy aspect. The meal was over in the boys' school, by the time of our arrival there, and the room was not yet quite rearranged; but the boys were roaming unrestrained about a large and airy yard, as any other schoolboys might have done. Some of them had been drawing large ships upon the schoolroom wall; and if they had a mast with shrouds and stays set up for practice (as they have in the Middlesex House of Correction), it would be so much the better. At present, if a boy should feel a strong impulse upon him to learn the art of going aloft, he could only gratify it, I presume, as the men and women paupers gratify their aspirations after better board and lodging, by smashing as many workhouse windows as possible, and being promoted to prison.

In one place, the Newgate of the Workhouse, a company of boys and youths were locked up in a yard alone; their day-room being a kind of kennel where the casual poor used formerly to be littered down at night. Divers of them had been there some long time. "Are they never going away?" was the natural enquiry. "Most of them are crippled, in some form or other," said the wardsman, "and not fit for anything." They slunk about, like dispirited wolves or hyaenas; and made a pounce at their food when it was served out, much as those animals do. The big-headed idiot shuffling his feet along the pavement, in the sunlight outside, was a more agreeable object every way.

Groves of babies in arms; groves of mothers and other sick women in bed; groves of lunatics; jungles of men in stone-paved down-stairs day-rooms, waiting for their dinners; longer and longer groves of old people, in up-stairs Infirmary wards, wearing out life, God knows how—this was the scenery through which the walk lay, for two hours. In some of these latter chambers there were pictures stuck against the wall, and a neat display of crockery and pewter on a kind of sideboard; now and then it was a treat to see a plant or two; in almost every ward there was a cat.

In all of these Long Walks of aged and infirm, some old people were bedridden, and had been for a long time; some were sitting on their beds half naked; some dying in their beds; some out of bed, and sitting at a table near the fire. A sullen or lethargic indifference to what was asked, a blunted sensibility to everything but warmth and food, a moody absence of complaint as being of no use, a dogged silence and resentful desire to be left alone again, I thought were generally apparent. On our walking into the midst of one of these dreary perspectives of old men, nearly the following little dialogue took place, the nurse not being immediately at hand:—

"All well here?"

No answer. An old man in a Scotch cap sitting among others on a form at the table, eating out of a tin porringer, pushes back his cap a little to look at us, claps it down on his forehead again with the palm of his hand, and goes on eating.

"All well here?" (repeated).

No answer. Another old man sitting on his bed, paralytically peeling a boiled potato, lifts his head and stares.

"Enough to eat?"

No answer. Another old man, in bed, turns himself and coughs.

"How are *you* to-day?" To the last old man.

That old man says nothing; but another old man, a tall old man of very good address, speaking with perfect correctness, comes forward from somewhere, and volunteers an answer. The reply almost always proceeds from a volunteer, and not from the person looked at or spoken to.

"We are very old, sir," in a mild, distinct voice. "We can't expect to be well, most of us."

"Are you comfortable?"

"I have no complaint to make, sir." With a half shake of his head, a half shrug of his shoulders, and a kind of apologetic smile.

"Enough to eat?"

"Why, sir, I have but a poor appetite," with the same air as before; "and yet I get through my allowance very easily."

"But," showing a porringer with a Sunday dinner in it, "here is a portion of mutton and three potatoes. You can't starve on that?"

"Oh, dear, no, sir," with the same apologetic air. "Not starve."

"What do you want?"

"We have very little bread, sir. It's an exceedingly small quantity of bread."

The nurse, who is now rubbing her hands at the questioner's elbow, interferes with, "It ain't much raly, sir. You see they've only six ounces a day, and when they've took their breakfast, there *can* only be a little left for night, sir."

Another old man, hitherto invisible, rises out of his bedclothes, as out of a grave, and looks on.

"You have tea at night?" The questioner is still addressing the well-spoken old man.

"Yes, sir, we have tea at night."

"And you save what bread you can from the morning, to eat with it?"

"Yes, sir—if we can save any."

"And you want more to eat with it?"

"Yes, sir." With a very anxious face.

The questioner, in the kindness of his heart, appears a little discomposed, and changes the subject.

"What has become of the old man who used to lie in that bed in the corner?"

The nurse don't remember what old man is referred to. There has been such a many old men. The well-spoken old man is doubtful. The spectral old man who has come to life in bed says, "Billy Stevens." Another old man who has previously had his head in the fireplace pipes out:—

"Charley Walters."

Something like a feeble interest is awakened. I suppose Charley Walters had conversation in him.

"He's dead," says the piping old man.

Another old man, with one eye screwed up, hastily displaces the piping old man, and says:—

"Yes! Charley Walters died in that bed, and—and—"

"Billy Stevens," persists the spectral old man.

"No, no! and Johnny Rogers died in that bed, and—and —they're both on 'em dead—and Sam'l Bowyer" (this seems very extraordinary to him), "he went out!"

With this he subsides, and all the old men (having had quite enough of it) subside, and the spectral old man goes into his grave again, and takes the shade of Billy Stevens with him.

As we turn to go out at the door, another previously invisible old man, a hoarse old man in a flannel gown, is standing there, as if he had just come up through the floor.

"I beg your pardon, sir, could I take the liberty of saying a word?"

"Yes; what is it?"

"I am greatly better in my health, sir; but what I want to get me quite round," with his hand on his throat, "is a little fresh air, sir. It has always done my complaint so much good, sir. The regular leave for going out comes round so seldom, that if the gentlemen, next Friday, would give me leave to go out walking, now and then—for only an hour or so, sir!—"

Who could wonder, looking through those weary vistas of bed and infirmity, that it should do him good to meet with some other scenes, and assure himself that there was something else on earth? Who could help wondering why the old men lived on as they did; what grasp they had on life; what crumbs of interest or occupation they could pick up from its bare board; whether Charley Walters had ever described to them the days when he kept company with some old pauper woman in the bud, or Billy Stevens ever told them of the time when he was a dweller in the far-off foreign land called Home!

The morsel of burnt child, lying in another room, so patiently, in bed, wrapped in lint, and looking steadfastly at us with his bright quiet eyes when we spoke to him kindly, looked as if the knowledge of these things, and of all the tender things there are to think about, might have been in his mind—as if he thought, with us, that there was a fellow-feeling in the pauper nurses which appeared to make them more kind to their charges than the race of common nurses in the hospitals—as if he mused upon the Future of some older children lying around him in the same place, and thought it best, perhaps, all things considered, that he should die—as if he knew, without fear, of those many coffins, made and unmade, piled up in the store below, and of his unknown friend, "the dropped child," calm upon the box-lid covered with a cloth. But there was something wistful and appealing, too, in his tiny face, as if, in the midst of all the hard necessities and incongruities he pondered on, he pleaded, in behalf of the helpless and the aged poor, for a little more liberty—and a little more bread.

A Watercress Girl

HENRY MAYHEW

[FROM *London Labour and the London Poor*]

1851

The little watercress girl who gave me the following statement, although only eight years of age, had entirely lost all
childish ways, and was, indeed, in thoughts and manner, a
woman. There was something cruelly pathetic in hearing this
infant, so young that her features had scarcely formed themselves, talking of the bitterest struggles of life, with the calm
earnestness of one who had endured them all. I did not know
how to talk with her. At first I treated her as a child, speaking
on childish subjects; so that I might, by being familiar with
her, remove all shyness, and get her to narrate her life freely.
I asked her about her toys and her games with her companions; but the look of amazement that answered me soon
put an end to any attempt at fun on my part. I then talked
to her about the parks, and whether she ever went to them.
"The parks!" she replied in wonder, "where are they?" I
explained to her, telling her that they were large open places
with green grass and tall trees, where beautiful carriages drove
about, and people walked for pleasure, and children played.
Her eyes brightened up a little as I spoke; and she asked,
half doubtingly, "Would they let such as me go there—just
to look?" All her knowledge seemed to begin and end with
watercresses, and what they fetched. . . . When some hot
dinner was offered to her, she would not touch it, because,
if she eat too much, "it made her sick," she said; "and she
wasn't used to meat, only on a Sunday."

The poor child, although the weather was severe, was
dressed in a thin cotton gown, with a threadbare shawl
wrapped round her shoulders. She wore no covering to her

From Volume I, pages 157-58.

head, and the long rusty hair stood out in all directions. When she walked she shuffled along, for fear that the large carpet slippers that served her for shoes should slip off her feet.

"I go about the streets with watercreases, crying, 'Four bunches a penny, watercreases.' I am just eight years old— that's all, and I've a big sister, and a brother and a sister younger than I am. On and off, I've been very near a twelve-month in the streets. Before that, I had to take care of a baby for my aunt. No, it wasn't heavy—it was only two months old; but I minded it for ever such a time—till it could walk. It was a very nice little baby, not a very pretty one; but, if I touched it under the chin, it would laugh. Before I had the baby, I used to help mother, who was in the fur trade; and, if there was any slits in the fur, I'd sew them up. My mother learned me to needle-work and to knit when I was about five. I used to go to school, too; but I wasn't there long. I've forgot all about it now, it's such a time ago; and mother took me away because the master whacked me, though the missus use'n't to never touch me. I didn't like him at all. What do you think? he hit me three times, ever so hard, across the face with his cane, and made me go dancing down-stairs; and when mother saw the marks on my cheek, she went to blow him up, but she couldn't see him—he was afraid. That's why I left school.

"The creases is so bad now, that I haven't been out with 'em for three days. They're so cold, people won't buy 'em; for when I goes up to them, they say, 'They'll freeze our bellies.' Besides, in the market, they won't sell a ha'penny handful now—they're ris to a penny and tuppence. In summer there's lots, and 'most as cheap as dirt, but I have to be down at Farringdon-market between four and five, or else I can't get any creases, because every one almost—especially the Irish— is selling them, and they're picked up so quick. . . . We children never play down there, 'cos we're thinking of our living. No; people never pities me in the street—excepting one gentleman, and he says, says he, 'What do you do out so soon in the morning?' but he gave me nothink—he only walked away.

"It's very cold before winter comes on reg'lar—specially getting up of a morning. I gets up in the dark by the light of the lamp in the court. When the snow is on the ground, there's no creases. I bears the cold—you must; so I puts my hands under my shawl, though it hurts 'em to take hold of the creases, especially when we takes 'em to the pump to wash 'em. No; I never see any children crying—it's no use.

"Sometimes I make a great deal of money. One day I took 1s. 6d., and the creases cost 6d.; but it isn't often I get such luck as that. I oftener makes 3d. or 4d. than 1s.; and then I'm at work, crying 'Creases, four bunches a penny, creases!' from six in the morning to about ten.

"I always give mother my money, she's so very good to me. She don't often beat me; but, when she do, she don't play with me. She's very poor, and goes out cleaning rooms sometimes, now she don't work at the fur. I ain't got no father, he's a father-in-law. No; mother ain't married again—he's a father-in-law. He grinds scissors, and he's very good to me. No; I don't mean by that that he says kind things to me, for he never hardly speaks. When I gets home, after selling creases, I stops at home. I put the room to rights: mother don't make me do it, I does it myself. I cleans the chairs, though there's only two to clean. I takes a tub and scrubbing-brush and flannel and scrubs the floor—that's what I do three or four time a week.

"I don't have no dinner. Mother gives me two slices of bread-and-butter and a cup of tea for breakfast, and then I go till tea, and has the same. We has meat of a Sunday, and of course, I should like to have it every day. Mother has just the same to eat as we has, but she takes more tea—three cups, sometimes. No; I never has no sweet-stuff; I never buy none—I don't like it. . . . I knows a good many games, but I don't play at 'em 'cos going out with creases tires me. On a Friday night, too, I goes to a Jew's house till eleven o'clock on Saturday night. All I has to do is to snuff the candles and poke the fire. You see they keep their Sabbath then, and they won't touch anything; so they gives me my wittals and 1½d., and I does it for 'em. I have a regular good lot to eat. Supper of Friday night, and tea after that, and fried fish of a Saturday morning, and meat for dinner, and tea, and supper, and I like it very well.

"Oh, yes: I've got some toys at home. I've a fire-place, and a box of toys, and a knife and fork, and two little chairs. The Jews gave 'em to me where I go to on a Friday, and that's why I said they was very kind to me. I never had no doll; but I misses little sister—she's only two years old. . . . I can't read or write, but I knows how many pennies goes to a shilling, why, twelve, of course, but I don't know how many ha'pence there is, though there's two to a penny. When I've bought 3d., of creases, I ties 'em up into as many little bundles as I can. They must look biggish, or the people won't buy them, some puffs them out as much as they'll go. All my money I earns I puts in a club and draws it out to buy clothes with. It's better than spending it in sweet-stuff, for them as has a living to earn. Besides it's like a child to care for sugar-sticks, and not like one who's got a living and vittals to earn. I ain't a child, and I shan't be a woman till I'm twenty, but I'm past eight, I am. I don't know nothing about what I earns during the year, I only know how many pennies goes to a shilling, and two ha'pence goes to a penny, and four fardens goes to a penny. I knows, too, how many fardens goes to tuppence—eight. That's as much as I wants to know for the markets."

Fever in Manchester

ELIZABETH CLEGHORN GASKELL

[FROM *Mary Barton*]

1848

John Barton was not far wrong in his idea that the Messrs. Carson would not be over-much grieved for the consequences of the fire in their mill. They were well insured; the machinery lacked the improvements of late years, and worked but poorly in comparison with that which might now be procured. Above all, trade was very slack; cottons could find no market, and goods lay packed and piled in many a warehouse. The mills were merely worked to keep the machinery, human and metal, in some kind of order and readiness for better times. So this was an excellent opportunity, Messrs. Carson thought, for re-fitting their factory with first-rate improvements, for which the insurance-money would amply pay. They were in no hurry about the business, however. The weekly drain of wages given for labour, useless in the present state of the market, was stopped. The partners had more leisure than they had known for years; and promised wives and daughters all manner of pleasant excursions, as soon as the weather should become more genial. It was a pleasant thing to be able to lounge over breakfast with a review or newspaper in hand; to have time for becoming acquainted with agreeable and accomplished daughters, on whose education no money had been spared, but whose fathers, shut up during a long day with calicoes and accounts, had so seldom had leisure to enjoy their daughters' talents. There were happy family evenings, now that the men of business had time for domestic enjoyments.

There is another side to the picture. There were homes over which Carsons' fire threw a deep, terrible gloom; the homes of those who would fain work, and no man gave unto them

From Chapter 6.

—the homes of those to whom leisure was a curse. There, the family music was hungry wails, when week after week passed by, and there was no work to be had, and consequently no wages to pay for the bread the children cried aloud for in their young impatience of suffering. There was no breakfast to lounge over; their lounge was taken in bed, to try and keep warmth in them that bitter March weather, and, by being quiet, to deaden the gnawing wolf within. Many a penny that would have gone little way enough in oatmeal or potatoes, bought opium to still the hungry little ones, and make them forget their uneasiness in heavy troubled sleep. It was mother's mercy. . . .

As the cold, bleak spring came on (spring, in name alone), and consequently as trade continued dead, other mills shortened hours, turned off hands, and finally stopped work altogether.

Barton worked short hours; Wilson, of course, being a hand in Carsons' factory, had no work at all. But his son, working at an engineer's, and a steady man, obtained wages enough to maintain all the family in a careful way. Still it preyed on Wilson's mind to be so long indebted to his son. He was out of spirits, and depressed. Barton was morose, and soured towards mankind as a body, and the rich in particular. One evening, when the clear light at six o'clock contrasted strangely with the Christmas cold, and when the bitter wind piped down every entry, and through every cranny, Barton sat brooding over his stinted fire, and listening for Mary's step, in unacknowledged trust that her presence would cheer him. The door was opened, and Wilson came breathless in.

"You've not got a bit o' money by you, Barton?" asked he.

"Not I; who has now, I'd like to know. Whatten you want it for?"

"I donnot want it for mysel', tho' we've none to spare. But don ye know Ben Davenport as worked at Carsons'? He's down wi' the fever, and ne'er a stick o' fire nor a cowd potato in the house."

"I han got no money, I tell ye," said Barton. Wilson looked disappointed. Barton tried not to be interested, but he could not help it in spite of his gruffness. He rose, and went to the cupboard (his wife's pride long ago). There lay the remains of his dinner, hastily put by ready for supper. Bread, and a slice of cold fat boiled bacon. He wrapped them in his handkerchief, put them in the crown of his hat, and said—"Come, let's be going."

"Going—art thou going to work this time o' day?"

"No, stupid, to be sure not. Going to see the chap thou spoke on."

So they put on their hats and set out. On the way Wilson said Davenport was a good fellow, though too much of the Methodee; that his children were too young to work, but not too young to be cold and hungry; that they had sunk lower and lower, and pawned thing after thing, and that they now lived in a cellar in Berry Street, off Store Street. Barton growled inarticulate words of no benevolent import to a large class of mankind, and so they went along till they arrived in Berry Street. It was unpaved: and down the middle a gutter forced its way, every now and then forming pools in the holes with which the street abounded. Never was the old Edinburgh cry of "Gardez l'eau!" more necessary than in this street. As they passed, women from their doors tossed household slops of *every* description into the gutter; they ran into the next pool, which overflowed and stagnated. Heaps of ashes were the stepping-stones, on which the passer-by, who cared in the least for cleanliness, took care not to put his foot. Our friends were not dainty, but even they picked their way, till they got to some steps leading down to a small area, where a person standing would have his head about one foot below the level of the street, and might at the same time, without the least motion of his body, touch the window of the cellar and the damp muddy wall right opposite. You went down one step even from the foul area into the cellar in which a family of human beings lived. It was very dark inside. The window-panes of many of them were broken and stuffed with rags, which was reason enough for the dusky light that pervaded the place even at mid-day. After the account I have given of the state of the street, no one can be surprised that on going into the cellar inhabited by Davenport, the smell was so fœtid as almost to knock the two men down. Quickly recovering themselves, as those inured to such things do, they began to penetrate the thick darkness of the place, and to see three or four little children rolling on the damp, nay wet brick floor, through which the stagnant, filthy moisture of the street oozed up; the fireplace was empty and black; the wife sat on her husband's lair, and cried in the dark loneliness.

"See, missis, I'm back again.—Hold your noise, children, and don't mither your mammy for bread; here's a chap as has got some for you."

In that dim light, which was darkness to strangers, they clustered round Barton, and tore from him the food he had brought with him. It was a large hunch of bread, but it vanished in an instant.

"We mun do summut for 'em," said he, to Wilson. "Ye stop here, and I'll be back in half-an-hour."

So he strode, and ran, and hurried home. He emptied into the ever-useful pocket-handkerchief the little meal remaining in the mug. Mary would have her tea at Miss Simmond's; her food for the day was safe. Then he went up-stairs for his better coat, and his one gay red-and-yellow silk pocket-hand-kerchief—his jewels, his plate, his valuables, these were. He went to the pawnshop; he pawned them for five shillings, he stopped not, nor stayed, till he was once more in London Road, within five minutes' walk of Berry Street—then he loitered in his gait, in order to discover the shops he wanted. He bought meat, and a loaf of bread, candles, chips, and from a little retail yard he purchased a couple of hundredweights of coal. Some money still remained—all destined for them, but he did not yet know how best to spend it. Food, light, and warmth, he had instantly seen were necessary; for luxuries he would wait. Wilson's eyes filled with tears when he saw Barton enter with his purchases. He understood it all, and longed to be once more in work that he might help in some of these material ways, without feeling that he was using his son's money. But though "silver and gold he had none," he gave heart-service, and love-works of far more value. Nor was

John Barton behind in these. "The fever" was (as it usually is in Manchester) of a low, putrid, typhoid kind; brought on by miserable living, filthy neighbourhood, and great depression of mind and body. It is virulent, malignant, and highly infectious. But the poor are fatalists with regard to infection; and well for them it is so, for in their crowded dwellings no invalid can be isolated. Wilson asked Barton if he should catch it, and was laughed at for his idea.

The two men, rough, tender nurses as they were, lighted the fire, which smoked and puffed into the room as if it did not know the way up the damp, unused chimney. The very smoke seemed purifying and healthy in the thick clammy air. The children clamoured again for bread; but this time Barton took a piece first to the poor, helpless, hopeless woman, who still sat by the side of her husband, listening to his anxious miserable mutterings. She took the bread, when it was put into her hand, and broke a bit but could not eat. She was past hunger. She fell down on the floor with a heavy unresisting bang. The men looked puzzled. "She's well-nigh clemmed," said Barton. "Folk do say one mustn't give clemmed people much to eat; but, bless us, she'll eat nought."

"I'll tell yo what I'll do," said Wilson. "I'll take these two big lads, as does nought but fight, home to my missis for to-night, and I'll get a jug o' tea. Them women always does best with tea and such-like slop."

So Barton was now left alone with a little child, crying (when it had done eating) for mammy; with a fainting, dead-like woman; and with the sick man, whose mutterings were rising up to screams and shrieks of agonized anxiety. He carried the woman to the fire, and chafed her hands. He looked round for something to raise her head. There was literally nothing but some loose bricks. However, those he got; and taking off his coat he covered them with it as well as he could. He pulled her feet to the fire, which now began to emit some faint heat. He looked round for water, but the poor woman had been too weak to drag herself out to the distant pump, and water there was none. He snatched the child, and ran up the area-steps to the room above, and borrowed their only sauce-pan with some water in it. Then he began, with the useful skill of a working man, to make some gruel; and when it was hastily made, he seized a battered iron table-spoon (kept when many other little things had been sold in a lot, in order to feed baby,) and with it he forced one or two drops between her clenched teeth. The mouth opened mechanically to receive more, and gradually she revived. She sat up and looked round; and recollecting all, fell down again in weak and passive despair. Her little child crawled to her, and wiped with its fingers the thick-coming tears which she now had strength to weep. It was now high time to attend to the man. He lay on straw, so damp and mouldy no dog would have chosen it in preference to flags: over it was a piece of sacking, coming next to his worn skeleton of a body; above him was mustered every article of clothing that could be spared by mother or children this bitter weather; and in addition to his own, these might have given as much warmth as one blanket, could they have been kept on him; but as he restlessly tossed to and fro, they fell off and left him shivering in spite of the burning heat of his skin. Every now and then he started up in his naked madness, looking like the prophet of woe in the fearful plague-picture; but he soon fell again in exhaustion, and Barton found he must be closely watched, lest in these falls he should injure himself against the hard brick floor. He was thankful when Wilson reappeared, carrying in both hands a jug of steaming tea, intended for the poor wife; but when the delirious husband saw drink, he snatched at it with animal instinct, with a selfishness he had never shown in health.

Then the two men consulted together. It seemed decided, without a word being spoken on the subject, that both should spend the night with the forlorn couple; that was settled. But could no doctor be had? In all probability, no; the next day an infirmary order must be begged, but meanwhile the only medical advice they could have must be from a druggist's. So Barton (being the moneyed man) set out to find a shop in London Road. . . .

He reached a druggist's shop, and entered. The druggist (whose smooth manners seemed to have been salved over with his own spermaceti) listened attentively to Barton's description of Davenport's illness; concluded it was typhus fever, very prevalent in that neighbourhood; and proceeded to make up a bottle of medicine, sweet spirit of nitre, or some such innocent potion, very good, for slight colds, but utterly powerless to stop, for an instant, the raging fever of the poor man it was intended to relieve. He recommended the same course they had previously determined to adopt, applying the next morning for an infirmary order; and Barton left the shop with comfortable faith in the physic given him; for men of his class, if they believe in physic at all, believe that every description is equally efficacious.

Meanwhile, Wilson had done what he could at Davenport's home. He had soothed and covered the man many a time: he had fed and hushed the little child, and spoken tenderly to the woman, who lay still in her weakness and her weariness. He had opened a door, but only for an instant; it led into a back cellar, with a grating instead of a window, down which dropped the moisture from pigsties, and worse abominations. It was not paved; the floor was one mass of bad-smelling mud. It had never been used, for there was not an article of furniture in it; nor could a human being, much less a pig, have lived there many days. Yet the "back apartment" made a difference in the rent. The Davenports paid threepence more for having two rooms. When he turned round again, he saw the woman suckling the child from her dry, withered breast.

"Surely the lad is weaned!" exclaimed he, in surprise. "Why, how old is he?"

"Going on two year," she faintly answered. "But, oh! it keeps him quiet when I've nought else to gi' him, and he'll get a bit of sleep lying there, if he's getten nought beside. We han done our best to gi' the childer food, howe'er we pinch ourselves."

"Han ye had no money fra' th' town?"

"No; my master is Buckinghamshire born; and he's feared the town would send him back to his parish, if he went to th' board; so we've just borne on in hope o' better times. But

I think they'll never come in my day," and the poor woman began her weak high-pitched cry again.

"Here, sup this drop o' gruel, and then try and get a bit o' sleep. John and I will watch by your master to-night."

"God's blessing be on you."

She finished the gruel, and fell into a deep sleep. Wilson covered her with his coat as well as he could, and tried to move lightly for fear of disturbing her; but there need have been no such dread, for her sleep was profound and heavy with exhaustion. Once only she roused to pull the coat round her little child.

And now Wilson's care, and Barton's to boot, was wanted to restrain the wild mad agony of the fevered man. He started up, he yelled, he seemed infuriated by overwhelming anxiety. He cursed and swore, which surprised Wilson, who knew his piety in health, and who did not know the unbridled tongue of delirium. At length he seemed exhausted, and fell asleep; and Barton and Wilson drew near the fire, and talked together in whispers. They sat on the floor, for chairs there were none; the sole table was an old tub turned upside down. They put out the candle and conversed by the flickering fire-light.

"Han yo known this chap long?" asked Barton.

"Better nor three year. He's worked wi' Carsons that long, and were always a steady, civil-spoken fellow, though, as I said afore, somewhat of a Methodee. I wish I'd getten a letter he'd sent his missis, a week or two agone, when he were on tramp for work. It did my heart good to read it; for, yo see, I were a bit grumbling mysel; it seemed hard to be spunging on Jem, and taking a' his flesh-meat money to buy bread for me and them as I ought to be keeping. But, yo know, though I can earn nought, I mun eat summit. Well, as I told ye, I were grumbling, when she (indicating the sleeping woman by a nod) brought me Ben's letter, for she could na' read hersel. It were as good as Bible-words; ne'er a word o' repining; a' about God being our father, and that we mun bear patiently whate'er he sends."

"Don ye think he's th' masters' father, too? I'd be loath to have 'em for brothers."

"Eh, John! donna talk so; sure there's many and many a master as good or better nor us."

"If you think so, tell me this. How comes it they're rich, and we're poor? I'd like to know that. Han they done as they'd be done for by us?"

But Wilson was no arguer; no speechifier, as he would have called it. So Barton, seeing he was likely to have it his own way, went on.

"You'll say (at least many a one does), they'n getten capital an' we'n getten none. I say, our labour's our capital, and we ought to draw interest on that. They get interest on their capital somehow a' this time, while ourn is lying idle, else how could they all live as they do? Besides, there's many on 'em has had nought to begin wi'; there's Carsons, and Duncombes, and Mengies, and many another, as comed into Manchester with clothes to their back, and that were all, and now they're worth their tens of thousands, a' getten out of our labour; why the very land as fetched but sixty pound twenty year agone is now worth six hundred, and that, too, is owing to our labour: but look at yo, and see me, and poor Davenport yonder; whatten better are we? They'n screwed us down to th' lowest peg, in order to make their great big fortunes, and build their great big houses, and we, why we're just clemming, many and many of us. Can you say there's nought wrong in this?"

"Well, Barton, I'll not gainsay ye. But Mr. Carson spoke to me after th' fire, and says he, 'I shall ha' to retrench, and be very careful in my expenditure during these bad times, I assure ye'; so yo see th' masters suffer too."

"Han they ever seen a child o' their'n die for want o' food?" asked Barton, in a low, deep voice.

"I donnot mean," continued he, "to say as I'm so badly off. I'd scorn to speak for mysel; but when I see such men as Davenport there dying away, for very clemming, I cannot stand it. I've but gotten Mary, and she keeps herself pretty much. I think we'll ha' to give up housekeeping; but that I donnot mind."

And in this kind of talk the night, the long heavy night of

watching, wore away. As far as they could judge, Davenport continued in the same state, although the symptoms varied occasionally. The wife slept on, only roused by the cry of her child now and then, which seemed to have power over her, when far louder noises failed to disturb her. The watchers agreed, that as soon as it was likely Mr. Carson would be up and visible, Wilson should go to his house, and beg for an infirmary order. At length the grey dawn penetrated even into the dark cellar; Davenport slept, and Barton was to remain there until Wilson's return; so, stepping out into the fresh air, brisk and reviving, even in that street of abominations, Wilson took his way to Mr. Carson's.

Wilson had about two miles to walk before he reached Mr. Carson's house, which was almost in the country. The streets were not yet bustling and busy. The shopmen were lazily taking down the shutters, although it was near eight o'clock; for the day was long enough for the purchases people made in that quarter of the town, while trade was so flat. One or two miserable-looking women were setting off on their day's begging expedition. But there were few people abroad. Mr. Carson's was a good house, and furnished with disregard to expense. But, in addition to lavish expenditure, there was much taste shown, and many articles chosen for their beauty and elegance adorned his rooms. As Wilson passed a window which a housemaid had thrown open, he saw pictures and gilding, at which he was tempted to stop and look; but then he thought it would not be respectful. So he hastened on to the kitchen door. The servants seemed very busy with preparations for breakfast; but good-naturedly, though hastily, told him to step in, and they could soon let Mr. Carson know he was there. So he was ushered into a kitchen hung round with glittering tins, where a roaring fire burnt merrily, and where numbers of utensils hung round, at whose nature and use Wilson amused himself by guessing. Meanwhile, the servants bustled to and fro; an outdoor man-servant came in for orders, and sat down near Wilson. The cook broiled steaks, and the kitchen-maid toasted bread, and boiled eggs.

The coffee steamed upon the fire, and altogether the odours were so mixed and appetising, that Wilson began to yearn for food to break his fast, which had lasted since dinner the day before. If the servants had known this, they would have willingly given him meat and bread in abundance; but they were like the rest of us, and not feeling hunger themselves, forgot it was possible another might. So Wilson's craving turned to sickness, while they chatted on, making the kitchen's free and keen remarks upon the parlour.

"How late you were last night, Thomas!"

"Yes, I was right weary of waiting; they told me to be at the rooms by twelve; and there I was. But it was two o'clock before they called me." . . .

A servant, semi-upper-housemaid, semi-lady's-maid, now came down with orders from her mistress.

"Thomas, you must ride to the fishmonger's, and say missis can't give above half-a-crown a pound for salmon for Tuesday; she's grumbling because trade's so bad. And she'll want the carriage at three to go to the lecture, Thomas; at the Royal Execution, you know."

"Ay, ay, I know."

"And you'd better all of you mind your P's and Q's, for she's very black this morning. She's got a bad headache. . . . Missis will have her breakfast up-stairs, cook, and the cold partridge as was left yesterday, and put plenty of cream in her coffee, and she thinks there's a roll left, and she would like it well buttered."

So saying, the maid left the kitchen to be ready to attend to the young ladies' bell when they chose to ring, after their late assembly the night before.

In the luxurious library, at the well-spread breakfast-table, sat the two Mr. Carsons, father and son. Both were reading—the father a newspaper, the son a review—while they lazily enjoyed their nicely prepared food. The father was a prepossessing-looking old man; perhaps self-indulgent you might guess. The son was strikingly handsome, and knew it. His dress was neat and well appointed, and his manners far more gentlemanly than his father's. He was the only son, and his sisters were proud of him; his father and mother were proud of him; he could not set up his judgment against theirs; he was proud of himself.

The door opened and in bounded Amy, the sweet youngest daughter of the house, a lovely girl of sixteen, fresh and glowing, and bright as a rosebud. She was too young to go to assemblies, at which her father rejoiced, for he had little Amy with her pretty jokes, and her bird-like songs, and her playful caresses all the evening to amuse him in his loneliness; and she was not too much tired like Sophy and Helen, to give him her sweet company at breakfast the next morning.

He submitted willingly while she blinded him with her hands, and kissed his rough red face all over. She took his newspaper away after a little pretended resistance, and would not allow her brother Harry to go on with his review.

"I'm the only lady this morning, papa, so you know you must make a great deal of me."

"My darling, I think you have your own way always, whether you're the only lady or not."

"Yes, papa, you're pretty good and obedient, I must say that; but I'm sorry to say Harry is very naughty, and does not do what I tell him; do you Harry?"

"I'm sure I don't know what you mean to accuse me of, Amy; I expected praise and not blame; for did not I get you that eau de Portugal from town, that you could not meet with at Hughes', you little ungrateful puss?"

"Did you? Oh, sweet Harry; you're as sweet as eau de Portugal yourself; you're almost as good as papa; but still you know you did go and forget to ask Bigland for that rose, that new rose they say he has got."

"No, Amy, I did not forget. I asked him, and he has got the Rose, *sans reproche;* but do you know, little Miss Extravagance, a very small one is half a guinea?"

"Oh, I don't mind. Papa will give it me, won't you, dear father? He knows his little daughter can't live without flowers and scents?"

Mr. Carson tried to refuse his darling, but she coaxed him

into acquiescence, saying she must have it, it was one of her necessaries. Life was not worth having without flowers. . . .

"If you please, sir," said a servant, entering the room, "here's one of the mill people wanting to see you; his name is Wilson, he says."

"I'll come to him directly; stay, tell him to come in here."

Amy danced off into the conservatory which opened out of the room, before the gaunt, pale, unwashed, unshaven weaver was ushered in. There he stood at the door, sleeking his hair with old country habit, and every now and then stealing a glance round at the splendour of the apartment.

"Well, Wilson, and what do you want to-day, man?"

"Please, sir, Davenport's ill of the fever, and I'm come to know if you've got an infirmary order for him?"

"Davenport—Davenport; who is the fellow? I don't know the name?"

"He's worked in your factory better nor three years, sir."

"Very likely; I don't pretend to know the names of the men I employ; that I leave to the overlooker. So he's ill, eh?"

"Ay, sir, he's very bad; we want to get him in at the Fever Wards."

"I doubt if I've an in-patient's order to spare at present; but I'll give you an out-patient's, and welcome."

So saying, he rose up, unlocked a drawer, pondered a minute, and then gave Wilson an out-patient's order to be presented the following Monday.

Monday! How many days there were before Monday!

Meanwhile, the younger Mr. Carson had ended his review, and began to listen to what was going on. He finished his breakfast, got up, and pulled five shillings out of his pocket, which he gave to Wilson as he passed him, for the "poor fellow." He went past quickly, and calling for his horse, mounted gaily, and rode away. He was anxious to be in time to have a look and a smile from lovely Mary Barton, as she went to Miss Simmonds'. But to-day he was to be disappointed.

Wilson left the house, not knowing whether to be pleased or grieved. It was long to Monday, but they had all spoken kindly to him, and who could tell if they might not remember this and do something before Monday. Besides, the cook, who, when she had had time to think, after breakfast was sent in, had noticed his paleness, had had meat and bread ready to put in his hand when he came out of the parlour; and a full stomach makes every one of us more hopeful.

When he reached Berry Street, he had persuaded himself he bore good news, and felt almost elated in his heart. But it fell when he opened the cellar door, and saw Barton and the wife both bending over the sick man's couch with awe-struck, saddened look.

"Come here," said Barton. "There's a change comed over him sin' yo left, is there not?"

Wilson looked. The flesh was sunk, the features prominent, bony, and rigid. The fearful clay-colour of death was over all. But the eyes were open and sensitive, though the films of the grave were setting upon them.

"He wakened fra' his sleep, as yo left him in, and began to mutter and moan; but he soon went off again, and we never knew he were awake till he called his wife, but now she's here he's gotten nought to say to her."

Most probably, as they all felt, he could not speak, for his strength was fast ebbing. They stood round him still and silent; even the wife checked her sobs, though her heart was like to break. She held her child to her breast, to try and keep him quiet. Their eyes were all fixed on the yet living one, whose moments of life were passing so rapidly away. At length he brought (with jerking convulsive effort) his two hands into the attitude of prayer. They saw his lips move, and bent to catch the words, which came in gasps, and not in tones.

"Oh, Lord God! I thank thee, that the hard struggle of living is over."

"Oh, Ben! Ben!" wailed forth his wife, "have you no thought for me? Oh, Ben! Ben! do say one word to help me through life."

He could not speak again. The trump of the archangel would set his tongue free; but not a word more would it utter till then. Yet he heard, he understood, and though sight failed, he moved his hand gropingly over the covering. They knew what he meant, and guided it to her head, bowed and hidden in her hands, when she had sunk in her woe. It rested there with a feeble pressure of endearment. The face grew beautiful, as the soul neared God. A peace beyond understanding came over it. The hand was a heavy stiff weight on the wife's head. No more grief or sorrow for him. They reverently laid out the corpse—Wilson fetching his only spare shirt to array it in. The wife still lay hidden in the clothes, in a stupor of agony. . . .

It was agreed the town must bury him; he had paid to a burial club as long as he could, but by a few week's omission, he had forfeited his claim to a sum of money now. . . .

So when the funeral day came, Mrs. Davenport was neatly arrayed in black, a satisfaction to her poor heart in the midst of her sorrow. Barton and Wilson both accompanied her, as she led her two elder boys, and followed the coffin. It was a simple walking funeral, with nothing to grate on the feelings of any; far more in accordance with its purpose, to my mind, than the gorgeous hearses, and nodding plumes, which form the grotesque funeral pomp of respectable people. There was no "rattling the bones over the stones" of the pauper's funeral. Decently and quietly was he followed to the grave by one determined to endure her woe meekly for his sake. The only mark of pauperism attendant on the burial concerned the living and joyous, far more than the dead, or the sorrowful. When they arrived in the churchyard, they halted before a raised and handsome tombstone; in reality a wooden mockery of stone respectabilities which adorned the burial-ground. It was easily raised in a very few minutes, and below was the grave in which the pauper bodies were piled until within a foot or two of the surface; when the soil was shovelled over, and stamped down, and the wooden cover went to do temporary duty over another hole. But little recked they of this who now gave up their dead.

Mrs. Pardiggle Visits the Brickmakers

CHARLES DICKENS

[FROM *Bleak House*]

1852-1853

I was glad when we came to the brickmaker's house; though it was one of a cluster of wretched hovels in a brick-field, with pigsties close to the broken windows, and miserable little gardens before the doors, growing nothing but stagnant pools. Here and there, an old tub was put to catch the droppings of rain-water from a roof, or they were banked up with mud into a little pond like a large dirt-pie. At the doors and windows, some men and women lounged or prowled about, and took little notice of us, except to laugh to one another, or to say something as we passed, about gentle-folks minding their own business, and not troubling their heads and muddying their shoes with coming to look after other people's.

Mrs. Pardiggle, leading the way with a great show of moral determination, and talking with much volubility about the untidy habits of the people (though I doubted if the best of us could have been tidy in such a place), conducted us into a cottage at the farthest corner, the ground-floor room of which we nearly filled. Besides ourselves, there were in this damp offensive room—a woman with a black eye, nursing a poor little gasping baby by the fire; a man, all stained with clay and mud, and looking very dissipated, lying at full length on the ground, smoking a pipe; a powerful young man, fastening a collar on a dog; and a bold girl, doing some kind of washing in very dirty water. They all looked up at us as we came in, and the woman seemed to turn her face towards the fire, as if to hide her bruised eye; nobody gave us any welcome.

"Well, my friends," said Mrs. Pardiggle; but her voice had

From Chapter 8.

not a friendly sound, I thought; it was much too business-like and systematic. "How do you do, all of you? I am here again. I told you, you couldn't tire me, you know. I am fond of hard work, and am true to my word."

"There an't," growled the man on the floor, whose head rested on his hand as he stared at us, "any more on you to come in, is there?"

"No, my friend," said Mrs. Pardiggle, seating herself on one stool, and knocking down another. "We are all here."

"Because I thought there warn't enough of you, perhaps?" said the man, with his pipe between his lips, as he looked round upon us.

The young man and the girl both laughed. Two friends of the young man whom we had attracted to the doorway, and who stood there with their hands in their pockets, echoed the laugh noisily.

"You can't tire me, good people," said Mrs. Pardiggle to these latter. "I enjoy hard work; and the harder you make mine, the better I like it."

"Then make it easy for her!" growled the man upon the floor. "I wants it done, and over. I wants a end of these liberties took with my place. I wants a end of being drawed like a badger. Now you're a-going to poll-pry and question according to custom—I know what you're a-going to be up to. Well! You haven't got no occasion to be up to it. I'll save you the trouble. Is my daughter a-washin? Yes, she *is* a-washin. Look at the water. Smell it! That's wot we drinks. How do you like it, and what do you think of gin, instead! An't my place dirty? Yes, it is dirty—it's nat'rally dirty, and it's nat'rally onwholesome; and we've had five dirty and on-wholesome children, as is all dead infants, and so much the better for them, and for us besides. Have I read the little book wot you left? No, I an't read the little book wot you left. There an't nobody here as knows how to read it; and if there wos, it wouldn't be suitable to me. It's a book fit for a babby, and I'm not a babby. If you was to leave me a doll, I shouldn't nuss it. How have I been conducting of myself? Why, I've been drunk for three days; and I'd a been drunk four, if I'd

a had the money. Don't I never mean for to go to church?
No, I don't never mean for to go to church. I shouldn't be
expected there, if I did; the beadle's too gen-teel for me. And
how did my wife get that black eye? Why, I giv' it her; and
if she says I didn't, she's a Lie!"

He had pulled his pipe out of his mouth to say all this, and
he now turned over on his other side, and smoked again.
Mrs. Pardiggle, who had been regarding him through her spectacles with a forcible composure, calculated, I could not help
thinking, to increase his antagonism, pulled out a good book,
as if it were a constable's staff, and took the whole family
into custody. I mean into religious custody, of course; but
she really did it, as if she were an inexorable moral Policeman
carrying them all off to a station-house.

Ada and I were very uncomfortable. We both felt intrusive
and out of place; and we both thought that Mrs. Pardiggle
would have got on infinitely better, if she had not had such a
mechanical way of taking possession of people. The children
sulked and stared; the family took no notice of us whatever,
except when the young man made the dog bark: which he
usually did when Mrs. Pardiggle was most emphatic. We both
felt painfully sensible that between us and these people there
was an iron barrier, which could not be removed by our new
friend. By who, or how, it could be removed, we did not
know; but we knew that. Even what she read and said, seemed
to us to be ill chosen for such auditors, if it had been imparted
ever so modestly and with ever so much tact. As to the little
book to which the man on the floor had referred, we acquired
a knowledge of it afterwards; and Mr. Jarndyce said he
doubted if Robinson Crusoe could have read it, though he
had had no other on his desolate island.

We were much relieved, under these circumstances, when
Mrs. Pardiggle left off. The man on the floor then turning
his head round again, said morosely, "Well! You've done,
have you?"

"For to-day, I have, my friend. But I am never fatigued.
I shall come to you again, in your regular order," returned
Mrs. Pardiggle, with demonstrative cheerfulness.

"So long as you goes now," said he, folding his arms and shutting his eyes with an oath, "you may do wot you like!"

Mrs. Pardiggle accordingly rose, and made a little vortex in the confined room from which the pipe itself very narrowly escaped. Taking one of her young family in each hand, and telling the others to follow closely, and expressing her hope that the brickmaker and all his house would be improved when she saw them next, she then proceeded to another cottage. I hope it is not unkind in me to say that she certainly did make, in this, as in everything else, a show that was not conciliatory, of doing charity by wholesale, and of dealing in it to a large extent.

She supposed that we were following her; but as soon as the space was left clear, we approached the woman sitting by the fire, to ask if the baby were ill.

She only looked at it as it lay on her lap. We had observed before, that when she looked at it she covered her discoloured eye with her hand, as though she wished to separate any association with noise and violence and ill-treatment, from the poor little child.

Ada, whose gentle heart was moved by its appearance, bent down to touch its little face. As she did so, I saw what happened and drew her back. The child died.

"O Esther!" cried Ada, sinking on her knees beside it. "Look here! O Esther, my love, the little thing! The suffering, quiet, pretty little thing! I am so sorry for it. I am so sorry for the mother. I never saw a sight so pitiful as this before! O baby, baby!". . .

Ada was so full of grief all the way home, and Richard, whom we found at home, was so distressed to see her in tears (though he said to me when she was not present, how beautiful it was too!) that we arranged to return at night with some little comforts, and repeat our visit at the brickmaker's house. We said as little as we could to Mr. Jarndyce, but the wind changed directly.

Cheap Clothes and Nasty

CHARLES KINGSLEY

[FROM *Cheap Clothes and Nasty*]

1850

You are always calling out for facts, and have a firm belief in salvation by statistics. Listen to a few.

The Metropolitan Commissioner of the *Morning Chronicle* called two meetings of the Working Tailors, one in Shadwell, and the other at the Hanover-Square Rooms, in order to ascertain their condition from their own lips. Both meetings were crowded. At the Hanover-Square Rooms there were more than one thousand men; they were altogether unanimous in their descriptions of the misery and slavery which they endured. It appears that there are two distinct tailor trades—the 'honourable' trade, now almost confined to the West End, and rapidly dying out there, and the 'dishonourable' trade of the show-shops and slop-shops—the plate-glass palaces, where gents—and, alas! those who would be indignant at that name—buy their cheap-and-nasty clothes. The two names are the tailors' own slang; slang is true and expressive enough, though, now and then. The honourable shops in the West End number only sixty; the dishonourable, four hundred and more; while at the East End the dishonourable trade has it all its own way. The honourable part of the trade is declining at the rate of one hundred and fifty journeymen per year; the dishonourable increasing at such a rate that, in twenty years, it will have absorbed the whole tailoring trade, which employs upwards of twenty-one thousand journeymen. At the honourable shops, the work is done, as it was universally thirty years ago, on the premises and at good wages. In the dishonourable trade, the work is taken home by the men, to be done at the very lowest possible prices, which decrease year by year, almost month by month. At the honourable shops, from 36s. to 24s. is paid for a piece of work for which the dishonourable shop pays from 22s. to 9s. But not to the workmen; happy is he if he really gets two-thirds, or half of that. For at the honourable shops, the master deals directly with his workmen; while at the dishonourable ones, the greater part of the work, if not the whole, is let out to contractors, or middle-men—'sweaters,' as their victims significantly call them—who, in their turn, let it out again, sometimes to the workmen, sometimes to fresh middlemen; so that out of the price paid for labour on each article, not only the workmen, but the sweater, and perhaps the sweater's sweater, and a third, and a fourth, and a fifth, have to draw their profit. And when the labour price has been already beaten down to the lowest possible, how much remains for the workmen after all these deductions, let the poor fellows themselves say!

One working tailor (at the Hanover-Square Rooms meeting) 'mentioned a number of shops, both at the east and west ends, whose work was all taken by sweaters; and several of these shops were under royal and noble patronage. There was one notorious sweater who kept his carriage. He was a Jew, and, of course, he gave a preference to his own sect. Thus, another Jew received it from him second hand and at a lower rate; then it went to a third—till it came to the unfortunate Christian at perhaps the eighth rate, and he performed the work at barely living prices; this same Jew required a deposit of 5l. in money before he would give out a single garment to be made. He need not describe the misery which this system entailed upon the workmen. It was well known; but it was almost impossible, except for those who had been at the two, to form an idea of the difference between the present meeting and one at the East-end, where all who attended worked for slop-shops and sweaters. The present was a highly respectable assembly; the other presented no other appearance but those of misery and degradation.'

Another says—'We have all worked in the honourable trade,

so we know the regular prices from our own personal experience. Taking the bad work with the good work, we might earn 11s. a-week upon an average. Sometimes we do earn as much as 15s.; but, to do this, we are obliged to take part of our work home to our wives and daughters. We are not always fully employed. We are nearly half our time idle. Hence, our earnings are, upon an average throughout the year, not more than 5s. 6d. a-week.' 'Very often I have made only 3s. 4d. in the week,' said one. 'That's common enough with us all, I can assure you,' said another. 'Last week my wages was 7s. 6d.,' declared one. 'I earned 6s. 4d.' exclaimed the second. 'My wages came to 9s. 2d. The week before I got 6s. 3d.' 'I made 7s. 9d,' and 'I 7s. or 8s., I can't exactly remember which.' 'This is what we term the best part of our winter season. The reason why we are so long idle is because more hands than are wanted are kept on the premises, so that in case of a press of work coming in, our employers can have it done immediately. Under the day-work system no master tailor had more men on the premises than he could keep continually going; but since the change to the piece-work system, masters made a practice of engaging double the quantity of hands that they have any need for, so that an order may be executed "at the shortest possible notice," if requisite. A man must not leave the premises when unemployed,—if he does, he loses his chance of work coming in. I have been there four days together, and had not a stitch of work to do.' 'Yes; that is common enough.' 'Ay, and then you're told if you complain, you can go, if you don't like it. I am sure twelve hands would do all they have done at home, and yet they keep forty of us. It's generally remarked, that however strong and healthy a man may be when he goes to work at that shop, in a month's time he'll be a complete shadow, and have almost all his clothes in pawn. By Sunday morning, he has no money at all left, and he has to subsist till the following Saturday upon about a pint of weak tea, and four slices of bread and butter per day ! ! !'

'Another of the reasons for the sweaters keeping more hands than they want is, the men generally have their meals with them. The more men they have with them the more breakfasts and teas they supply, and the more profit they make. The men usually have to pay 4d., and very often 5d. for their breakfast, and the same for their tea. The tea or breakfast is mostly a pint of tea or coffee, and three to four slices of bread and butter. *I worked for one sweater who almost starved the men; the smallest eater there would not have had enough if he had got three times as much. They had only three thin slices of bread and butter, not sufficient for a child, and the tea was both weak and bad. The whole meal could not have stood him in 2d. a head, and what made it worse was, that the men who worked there couldn't afford to have dinners, so that they were starved to the bone.* The sweater's men generally lodge where they work. A sweater usually keeps about six men. These occupy two small garrets; one room is called the kitchen, and the other the workshop; and here the whole of the six men, and the sweater, his wife, and family, live and sleep. One sweater *I worked with had four children and six men, and they, together with his wife, sister-in-law, and himself, all lived in two rooms, the largest of which was about eight feet by ten. We worked in the smallest room, and slept there as well—all six of us. There were two turn-up beds in it, and we slept three in a bed. There was no chimney, and, indeed, no ventilation whatever. I was near losing my life there—the foul air of so many people working all day in the place, and sleeping there at night, was quite suffocating. Almost all the men were consumptive, and I myself attended the dispensary for disease of the lungs. The room in which we all slept was not more than six feet square. We were all sick and weak, and loth to work.* Each of the six of us paid 2s. 6d. a-week for our lodging, or 15s. altogether, and I am sure such a room as we slept and worked in might be had for 1s. a-week; you can get a room with a fire-place for 1s. 6d. The usual sum that the men working for sweaters pay for their tea, breakfasts, and lodging is 6s. 6d. to 7s. a-week, and they seldom earn more money in the week. Occasionally at the week's end, they are in debt to the sweater. This is seldom for more than 6d. for the sweater will not give them victuals

if he has no work for them to do. Many who live and work
at the sweater's are married men, and are obliged to keep
their wives and children in lodgings by themselves. Some send
them to the workhouse, others to their friends in the country.
Besides the profit of the board and lodging, the sweater takes
6d. out of the price paid for every garment under 10s.; some
take 1s., and I do know of one who takes as much as 2s. This
man works for a large show-shop at the West End. The usual
profit of the sweater, over and above the board and lodging,
is 2s. out of every pound. Those who work for sweaters soon
lose their clothes, and are unable to seek for other work,
because they have not a coat to their back to go and seek
it in. *Last week, I worked with another man at a coat for one
of her Majesty's ministers, and my partner never broke his
fast while he was making his half of it.* The minister dealt
at a cheap West-end show-shop. All the workman had the
whole day-and-a-half he was making the coat was a little tea.
But sweaters' work is not so bad as government work after all.
At that, we cannot make more than 4s. or 5s. a-week altogether
—that is, counting the time we are running after it, of course.
*Government contract work is the worst of all, and the starved-
out and sweated-out tailor's last resource.* But still, government does not do the regular trade so much harm as the
cheap show and slop shops. These houses have ruined thousands. They have cut down the prices, so that men cannot
live at the work; and the masters who did and would pay
better wages, are reducing the workmen's pay every day. They
say they must either compete with the large show-shops or go
into the *Gazette.*'

Sweet competition! Heavenly maid!—Now-a-days hymned
alike by penny-a-liners and philosophers as the ground of all
society—the only real preserver of the earth! Why not of
Heaven, too? Perhaps there is competition among the angels,
and Gabriel and Raphael have won their rank by doing the
maximum of worship on the minimum of grace? We shall
know some day. In the meanwhile, 'these are thy works, thou
Parent of all good!' Man eating man, eaten by man, in every
variety of degree and method! Why does not some enthusiastic

political economist write an epic on 'The Consecration of Cannibalism?'

But if any one finds it pleasant to his soul to believe the poor journeymen's statements exaggerated, let him listen to one of the sweaters themselves:—

'I wish,' says he, 'that others did for the men as decently as I do. I know there are many who are living entirely upon them. Some employ as many as fourteen men. . . . The profits of the sweater, however, would be from 4*l*. to 5*l*. out of twelve men, working on his premises. The usual number of men working under each sweater is about six individuals: and the average rate of profit, about 2*l*. 10*s*., without the sweater doing any work himself. It is very often the case that a man working under a sweater is obliged to pawn his own coat to get any pocket-money that he may require. Over and over again the sweater makes out that he is in his debt from 1*s*. to 2*s*. at the end of the week, and when the man's coat is in pledge, he is compelled to remain imprisoned in the sweater's lodgings for months together. In some sweating places, there is an old coat kept called a "reliever," and this is borrowed by such men as have none of their own to go out in. There are very few of the sweaters' men who have a coat to their backs or a shoe to their feet to come out into the streets on Sunday. Down about Fullwood's-rents, Holborn, I am sure I would not give 6*d*. for the clothes that are on a dozen of them; and it is surprising to me, working and living together in such numbers and in such small close rooms, in narrow close back courts as they do, that they are not all swept off by some pestilence. I myself have seen half-a-dozen men at work in a room that was a little better than a bedstead long. It was as much as one could do to move between the wall and the bedstead when it was down. There were two bedsteads in this room, and they nearly filled the place when they were down. The ceiling was so low, that I couldn't stand upright in the room. There was no ventilation in the place. There was no fireplace, and only a small window. When the window was open, you could nearly touch the houses at the back, and if the room had not been at the top of the house, the men could not have seen at all in the place. The staircase was so narrow, steep, and dark, that it was difficult to grope your way to the top of the house—it was like going up a steeple. This is the usual kind of place in which the sweater's men are lodged. The reason why there are so many Irishmen working for the sweaters is, because they are seduced over to this country by the prospect of high wages and plenty of work. They are brought over by the Cork boats at 10*s*. a-head, and when they once get here, the prices they receive are so small, that they are unable to go back. In less than a week after they get here, their clothes are all pledged, and they are obliged to continue working under the sweaters.

'The extent to which this system of "street-kidnapping" is carried on is frightful. Young tailors, fresh from the country, are decoyed by the sweater's wives into their miserable dens, under extravagant promises of employment, to find themselves deceived, imprisoned, and starved, often unable to make their escape for months—perhaps years; and then only fleeing from one dungeon to another as abominable.'

In the meantime, the profits of the beasts of prey who live on these poor fellows—both masters and sweaters—seem as prodigious as their cruelty. . . .

Folks are getting somewhat tired of the old rodomontade that a slave is free the moment he sets foot on British soil! Stuff!—are these tailors free? Put any conceivable sense you will on the word, and then say—are they free? We have, thank God, emancipated the black slaves; it would seem a not inconsistent sequel to that act to set about emancipating these white ones. Oh! we forgot; there is an infinite difference between the two cases—the black slaves worked for our colonies; the white slaves work for *us*. But, indeed, if, as some preach, self-interest is the mainspring of all human action, it is difficult to see who will step forward to emancipate the said white slaves; for all classes seem to consider it equally their interest to keep them as they are; all classes, though by their own confession they are ashamed, are yet not afraid to profit by the system which keeps them down. . . .

But of course the men most interested in keeping up the

system are those who buy the clothes of these cheap shops. And who are they? Not merely the blackguard Gent—the butt of Albert Smith and Punch, who flaunts at the Casinos and Cremorne Gardens in vulgar finery wrung out of the souls and bodies of the poor; not merely the poor lawyer's clerk or reduced half-pay officer who has to struggle to look as respectable as his class commands him to look on a pittance often no larger than that of the day labourer—no, strange to say—and yet not strange, considering our modern eleventh commandment—'Buy cheap and sell dear,' the richest as well as the poorest imitate the example of King Ryence and the tanners of Meudon.[1] At a great show establishment—to take one instance out of many—the very one where, as we heard just now, 'however strong and healthy a man may be when he goes to work at that shop, in a month's time he will be a complete shadow, and have almost all his clothes in pawn'—

'We have also made garments for Sir —— ——, Sir —— ——, Alderman ——, Dr. ——, and Dr. ——. We make for several of the aristocracy. We cannot say whom, because the tickets frequently come to us as Lord —— and the Marquis of ——. This could not be a Jew's trick, because the buttons on the liveries had coronets upon them. And again, we know the house is patronized largely by the aristocracy, clergy and gentry, by the number of court-suits and liveries, surplices, regimentals, and ladies' riding-habits that we continually have to make up. *There are more clergymen among the customers than any other class, and often we have to work at home upon the Sunday at their clothes, in order to get a living.* The customers are mostly ashamed of dealing at this house, for the men who take the clothes to the customers' houses in the cart have directions to pull up at the corner of the street. We had a good proof of the dislike of gentlefolks to have it known that they dealt at that shop for their clothes, for when the trowsers buttons were stamped with the name of the firm,

---

[1] In Arthurian legend, Ryence, a king of Wales and Ireland, wore a coat made of the beards of knights he had overcome. During the French Revolution, skins of the victims of the guillotine were tanned at Meudon.—ED.

we used to have the garments returned, daily, to have other buttons put on them, and now the buttons are unstamped' ! ! !

We shall make no comment on this extract. It needs none. If these men know how their clothes are made, they are past contempt. Afraid of man, and not afraid of God! As if His eye could not see the cart laden with the plunder of the poor, because it stopped round the corner! If, on the other hand, they do *not* know these things, and doubtless the majority do not,—it is their sin that they do not know it. Woe to a society whose only apology to God and man is, 'Am I my brother's keeper?' Men ought to know the condition of those by whose labour they live. Had the question been the investment of a few pounds in a speculation, these gentlemen would have been careful enough about good security. Ought they to take no security when they invest their money in clothes, that they are not putting on their backs accursed garments, offered in sacrifice to devils, reeking with the sighs of the starving, tainted—yes, tainted, indeed, for it comes out now that diseases numberless are carried home in these same garments from the miserable abodes where they are made. Evidence to this effect was given in 1844; but Mammon was too busy to attend to it. These wretched creatures, when they have pawned their own clothes and bedding, will use as substitutes the very garments they are making. So Lord ——'s coat has been seen covering a group of children blotched with small-pox. The Rev. D —— finds himself suddenly unpresentable from a cutaneous disease, which it is not polite to mention on the south of Tweed, little dreaming that the shivering dirty being who made his coat has been sitting with his arms in the sleeves for warmth while he stitched at the tails. The charming Miss C —— is swept off by typhus or scarlatina, and her parents talk about 'God's heavy judgement and visitation'—had they tracked the girl's new riding-habit back to the stifling undrained hovel where it served as a blanket to the fever-stricken slop-worker, they would have seen *why* God had visited them, seen that his judgments are true judgments. . . .

But to us, almost the worst feature in the whole matter is, that the government are not merely parties to, but actually the originators of this system. The contract system, as a working tailor stated in the name of the rest, 'had been mainly instrumental in destroying the living wages of the working man. Now, the government were the sole originators of the system of contracts and of sweating. Forty years ago, there was nothing known of contracts, except government contracts; and at that period the contractors were confined to making slops for the navy, the army, and the West India slaves. It was never dreamt of then that such a system was to come into operation in the better classes of trade, till ultimately it was destructive of masters as well as men. The government having been the cause of the contract system, and consequently of the sweating system, he called upon them to abandon it. The sweating system had established the show-shops and the ticket system, both of which were countenanced by the government, till it had become a fashion to support them.

'Even the court assisted to keep the system in fashion, and the royal arms and royal warrants were now exhibited common enough by slop-sellers.

'Government said, its duty was to do justice. But was it consistent with justice to pay only 2s. 6d. for making navy jackets, which would be paid 10s. for by every "honourable" tradesman? Was it consistent with justice for the government to pay for Royal Marine clothing (private's coat and epaulettes) 1s. 9d.? Was it consistent with justice for the government to pay for making a pair of trowsers (four or five hours' work) only 2½d.? And yet, when a contractor, noted for paying just wages to those he employed, brought this under the consideration of the Admiralty, they declared they had nothing to do with it. . . .'

'The government,' says another tailor at the same meeting, 'had really been the means of reducing prices in the tailoring trade to so low a scale that no human being, whatever his industry, could live and be happy in his lot. The government were really responsible for the first introduction of female labour. He would clearly prove what he had stated. He would refer first to the army clothing. Our soldiers were comfortably clothed, as they had a right to be; but surely the men who made the clothing which was so comfortable, ought to be paid for their labour so as to be able to keep themselves comfortable and their families virtuous. But it was in evidence that the persons working upon army clothing could not, upon an average, earn more than 1*s.* a day. Another government department, the post-office, afforded a considerable amount of employment to tailors; but those who worked upon the post-office clothing earned, at the most, only 1*s.* 6*d.* a day. The police clothing was another considerable branch of tailoring; this, like the others, ought to be paid for at living prices; but the men at work at it could only earn 1*s.* 6*d.* a day, supposing them to work hard all the time, fourteen or fifteen hours. The Custom House clothing gave about the same prices. Now, all these sorts of work were performed by time workers, who, as a natural consequence of the wages they received, were the most miserable of human beings. Husband, wife, and family all worked at it; they just tried to breathe upon it; to live it never could be called. *Yet the same Government which paid such wretched wages, called upon the wretched people to be industrious, to be virtuous, and happy.* How was it possible, whatever their industry, to be virtuous and happy? The fact was, the men who, at the slack season, had been compelled to fall back upon these kinds of work, became so beggared and broken down by it, notwithstanding the assistance of their wives and families, that they were never able to rise out of it.'

And now comes the question—What is to be done with these poor tailors, to the number of between fifteen and twenty thousand? Their condition, as it stands, is simply one of ever-increasing darkness and despair. The system which is ruining them is daily spreading, deepening. While we write, fresh victims are being driven by penury into the slop-working trade, fresh depreciations of labour are taking place. . . . What can be done?

First—this can be done. That no man who calls himself

a Christian—no man who calls himself a man—shall ever disgrace himself by dealing at any show-shop or slop-shop. It is easy enough to know them. The ticketed garments, the impudent puffs, the trumpery decorations, proclaim them,—every one knows them at first sight. He who pretends not to do so is simply either a fool or a liar. Let no man enter them —they are the temples of Moloch—their thresholds are rank with human blood. God's curse is on them, and on those who, by supporting them, are partakers of their sins. Above all, let no clergyman deal at them. Poverty—and many clergymen are poor—doubly poor, because society often requires them to keep up the dress of gentlemen on the income of an artisan; because, too, the demands on their charity are quadruple those of any other class—yet poverty is no excuse. The thing is damnable—not Christianity only, but common humanity cries out against it. Woe to those who dare to outrage in private the principles which they preach in public! God is not mocked; and his curse will find out the priest at the altar, as well as the nobleman in his castle.

But it is so hard to deprive the public of the luxury of cheap clothes! Then let the public look out for some other means of procuring that priceless blessing. If that, on experiment, be found impossible—if the comfort of the few be for ever to be bought by the misery of the many—if civilization is to benefit every one except the producing class—then this world is truly the devil's world, and the sooner so ill-constructed and infernal a machine is destroyed by that personage, the better.

But let, secondly, a dozen, or fifty, or a hundred journeymen say to one another: 'It is competition that is ruining us, and competition is division, disunion, every man for himself, every man against his brother. The remedy must be in association, co-operation, self-sacrifice for the sake of one another. We can work together at the honourable tailor's workshop— we can work and live together in the sweater's den for the profit of our employers; why should we not work and live together in our own workshops, or our own homes, for our own profit?. . . Then we will open our common shop, and sell at as low a price as the cheapest of the show-shops. We *can* do this—by the abolition of sweaters' profits—by the using, as far as possible, of one set of fires, lights, rooms, kitchens, and wash-houses—above all, by being true and faithful to one another, as all partners should be. And, then, all that the master slop-sellers had better do, will be simply to vanish and become extinct.'

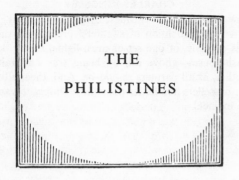

THE PHILISTINES

Dodson Protestantism

GEORGE ELIOT

[FROM *The Mill on the Floss*]

1860

It was at eleven o'clock the next morning that the aunts and uncles came to hold their consultation. The fire was lighted in the large parlour, and poor Mrs Tulliver, with a confused impression that it was a great occasion, like a funeral, un-bagged the bell-rope tassels, and unpinned the curtains, adjusting them in proper folds—looking round and shaking her head sadly at the polished tops and legs of the tables, which sister Pullet herself could not accuse of insufficient brightness.

Mr Deane was not coming—he was away on business; but Mrs Deane appeared punctually in that handsome new gig with the head to it, and the livery-servant driving it, which had thrown so clear a light on several traits in her character to some of her female friends in St Ogg's. Mr Deane had been advancing in the world as rapidly as Mr Tulliver had been going down in it; and in Mrs Deane's house the Dodson linen and plate were beginning to hold quite a subordinate

From Book III, Chapter 3.

position, as a mere supplement to the handsomer articles of the same kind, purchased in recent years: a change which had caused an occasional coolness in the sisterly intercourse between her and Mrs Glegg, who felt that Susan was getting "like the rest," and there would soon be little of the true Dodson spirit surviving except in herself, and, it might be hoped, in those nephews who supported the Dodson name on the family land, far away in the Wolds. People who live at a distance are naturally less faulty than those immediately under our own eyes; and it seems superfluous, when we consider the remote geographical position of the Ethiopians, and how very little the Greeks had to do with them, to inquire further why Homer calls them "blameless."

Mrs Deane was the first to arrive; and when she had taken her seat in the large parlour, Mrs Tulliver came down to her with her comely face a little distorted, nearly as it would have been if she had been crying: she was not a woman who could shed abundant tears, except in moments when the prospect of losing her furniture became unusually vivid, but she felt how unfitting it was to be quite calm under present circumstances.

"O sister, what a world this is!" she exclaimed as she entered; "what trouble, O dear!"

Mrs Deane was a thin-lipped woman, who made small well-considered speeches on peculiar occasions, repeating them afterwards to her husband, and asking him if she had not spoken very properly.

"Yes, sister," she said, deliberately, "this is a changing world, and we don't know to-day what may happen to-morrow. But it's right to be prepared for all things, and if trouble's sent, to remember as it isn't sent without a cause. I'm very sorry for you as a sister, and if the doctor orders jelly for Mr Tulliver, I hope you'll let me know: I'll send it willingly. For it is but right he should have proper attendance while he's ill."

"Thank you, Susan," said Mrs Tulliver, rather faintly, withdrawing her fat hand from her sister's thin one. "But there's been no talk o' jelly yet." Then after a moment's pause she added, "There's a dozen o' cut jelly-glasses up-stairs. . . . I shall never put jelly into 'em no more."

Her voice was rather agitated as she uttered the last words, but the sound of wheels diverted her thoughts. Mr and Mrs Glegg were come, and were almost immediately followed by Mr and Mrs Pullet.

Mrs Pullet entered crying, as a compendious mode, at all times, of expressing what were her views of life in general, and what, in brief, were the opinions she had concerning the particular case before her.

Mrs Glegg had on her fuzziest front, and garments which appeared to have had a recent resurrection from rather a creasy form of burial; a costume selected with the high moral purpose of instilling perfect humility into Bessy and her children.

"Mrs G., won't you come nearer the fire?" said her husband, unwilling to take the more comfortable seat without offering it to her.

"You see I've seated myself here, Mr Glegg," returned this superior woman; "*you* can roast yourself, if you like."

"Well," said Mr Glegg, seating himself good-humouredly, "and how's the poor man up-stairs?"

"Dr Turnbull thought him a deal better this morning," said Mrs Tulliver; "he took more notice, and spoke to me; but he's never known Tom yet—looks at the poor lad as if he was a stranger, though he said something once about Tom and the pony. The doctor says his memory's gone a long way back, and he doesn't know Tom because he's thinking of him when he was little. Eh dear, eh dear!"

"I doubt it's the water got on his brain," said aunt Pullet, turning round from adjusting her cap in a melancholy way at the pier-glass. "It's much if he ever gets up again; and if he does, he'll most like be childish, as Mr Carr was, poor man! They fed him with a spoon as if he'd been a babby for three year. He'd quite lost the use of his limbs, but then he'd got a Bath chair, and somebody to draw him; and that's what you won't have, I doubt, Bessy."

"Sister Pullet," said Mrs Glegg, severely, "if I understand right, we've come together this morning to advise and consult about what's to be done in this disgrace as has fallen upon the family, and not to talk o' people as don't belong to us. Mr Carr was none of our blood, nor noways connected with us, as I've ever heared."

"Sister Glegg," said Mrs Pullet, in a pleading tone, drawing on her her gloves again, and stroking the fingers in an agitated manner, "if you've got anything disrespectful to say o' Mr Carr, I do beg of you as you won't say it to me. *I* know what he was," she added, with a sigh; "his breath was short to that degree as you could hear him two rooms off."

"Sophy!" said Mrs Glegg, with indignant disgust, "you *do* talk o' people's complaints till it's quite undecent. But I say again, as I said before, I didn't come away from home to talk about acquaintance, whether they'd short breath or long. If we aren't come together for one to hear what the other 'ull do to save a sister and her children from the parish, *I* shall go back. *One* can't act without the other, I suppose; it isn't to be expected as *I* should do everything."

"Well, Jane," said Mrs Pullet, "I don't see as you've been so very forrard at doing. So far as I know, this is the first time as here you've been, since it's been known as the bailiff's in the house; and I was here yesterday, and looked at all Bessy's linen and things, and I told her I'd buy in the spotted table-cloths. I couldn't speak fairer; for as for the teapot as she doesn't want to go out o' the family, it stands to sense I can't do with two silver teapots, not if it *hadn't* a straight spout—but the spotted damask I was allays fond on."

"I wish it could be managed so as my teapot and chany and the best castors needn't be put up for sale," said poor Mrs Tulliver, beseechingly, "and the sugar-tongs, the first things ever I bought."

"But that can't be helped, you know," said Mr Glegg. "If one o' the family chooses to buy 'em in, they can, but one thing must be bid for as well as another."

"And it isn't to be looked for," said uncle Pullet, with unwonted independence of idea, "as your own family should pay more for things nor they'll fetch. They may go for an old song by auction."

"O dear, O dear," said Mrs Tulliver, "to think o' my chany being sold i' that way—and I bought it when I was married, just as you did yours, Jane and Sophy: and I know you didn't like mine, because o' the sprig, but I was fond of it; and there's never been a bit broke, for I've washed it myself—and there's the tulips on the cups, and the roses, as anybody might go and look at 'em for pleasure. You wouldn't like *your* chany to go for an old song and be broke to pieces, though yours has got no colour in it, Jane—it's all white and fluted, and didn't cost so much as mine. And there's the castors—sister Deane, I can't think but you'd like to have the castors, for I've heard you say they're pretty."

"Well, I've no objection to buy some of the best things," said Mrs Deane, rather loftily; "we can do with extra things in our house."

"Best things!" exclaimed Mrs Glegg with severity, which had gathered intensity from her long silence. "It drives me past patience to hear you all talking o' best things, and buying in this, that, and the other, such as silver and chany. You must bring your mind to your circumstances, Bessy, and not be thinking o' silver and chany; but whether you shall get so much as a flock bed to lie on, and a blanket to cover you, and a stool to sit on. You must remember, if you get 'em, it'll be because your friends have bought 'em for you, for you're dependent upon *them* for everything; for your husband lies there helpless, and hasn't got a penny i' the world to call his own. And it's for your own good I say this, for it's right you should feel what your state is, and what disgrace your husband's brought on your own family, as you've got to look to for everything—and be humble in your mind."

Mrs Glegg paused, for speaking with much energy for the good of others is naturally exhausting. Mrs Tulliver, always borne down by the family predominance of sister Jane, who had made her wear the yoke of a younger sister in very tender years, said pleadingly—

"I'm sure, sister, I've never asked anybody to do anything, only buy things as it 'ud be a pleasure to 'em to have, so as they mightn't go and be spoiled i' strange houses. I never asked anybody to buy the things in for me and my children; though there's the linen I spun, and I thought when Tom was born—I thought one o' the first things when he was lying i' the cradle, as all the things I'd bought wi' my own money, and been so careful of, 'ud go to him. But I've said nothing as I wanted my sisters to pay their money for me. What my husband has done for *his* sister's unknown, and we should ha' been better off this day if it hadn't been as he's lent money and never asked for it again."

"Come, come," said Mr Glegg, kindly, "don't let us make things too dark. What's done can't be undone. We shall make a shift among us to buy what's sufficient for you; though, as Mrs G. says, they must be useful, plain things. We mustn't be thinking o' what's unnecessary. A table, and a chair or two, and kitchen things, and a good bed, and suchlike. Why, I've seen the day when I shouldn't ha' known myself if I'd lain on sacking i'stead o' the floor. We get a deal o' useless things about us, only because we've got the money to spend."

"Mr Glegg," said Mrs G., "if you'll be kind enough to let me speak, i'stead o' taking the words out o' my mouth—I was going to say, Bessy, as it's fine talking for you to say as you've never asked us to buy anything for you; let me tell you, you *ought* to have asked us. Pray, how are you to be purvided for, if your own family don't help you? You must go to the parish, if they didn't. And you ought to know that, and keep it in mind, and ask us humble to do what we can for you, i'stead o' saying, and making a boast, as you've never asked us for anything."

"You talked o' the Mosses, and what Mr Tulliver's done for 'em," said uncle Pullet, who became unusually suggestive where advances of money were concerned. "Haven't *they* been anear you? They ought to do something, as well as other folks; and if he's lent 'em money, they ought to be made to pay it back."

"Yes, to be sure," said Mrs Deane; "I've been thinking so.

How is it Mr and Mrs Moss aren't here to meet us? It is but right they should do their share."

"O dear!" said Mrs Tulliver, "I never sent 'em word about Mr Tulliver, and they live so back'ard among the lanes at Basset, they niver hear anything only when Mr Moss comes to market. But I niver gave 'em a thought. I wonder Maggie didn't, though, for she was allays so fond of her aunt Moss."

"Why don't your children come in, Bessy?" said Mrs Pullet, at the mention of Maggie. "They should hear what their aunts and uncles have got to say: and Maggie—when it's me as have paid for half her schooling, she ought to think more of her aunt Pullet than of aunt Mosses. I may go off sudden when I get home to-day—there's no telling."

"If I'd had *my* way," said Mrs Glegg, "the children 'ud ha' been in the room from the first. It's time they knew who they've to look to, and it's right as *somebody* should talk to 'em, and let 'em know their condition i' life, and what they're come down to, and make 'em feel as they've got to suffer for their father's faults."

"Well, I'll go and fetch 'em, sister," said Mrs Tulliver, resignedly. She was quite crushed now, and thought of the treasures in the store-room with no other feeling than blank despair. . . .

[FROM Book IV, Chapter 1]

Journeying down the Rhone on a summer's day, you have perhaps felt the sunshine made dreary by those ruined villages which stud the banks in certain parts of its course, telling how the swift river once rose, like an angry, destroying god, sweeping down the feeble generations whose breath is in their nostrils, and making their dwellings a desolation. Strange contrast, you may have thought, between the effect produced on us by these dismal remnants of commonplace houses, which in their best days were but the sign of a sordid life, belonging in all its details to our own vulgar era; and the effect produced by those ruins on the castled Rhine, which have crumbled and mellowed into such harmony with the

green and rocky steeps, that they seem to have a natural fitness, like the mountain pine: nay, even in the day when they
were built they must have had this fitness, as if they had been
raised by an earth-born race, who had inherited from their
mighty parent a sublime instinct of form. And that was a
day of romance! If those robber barons were somewhat grim
and drunken ogres, they had a certain grandeur of the wild
beast in them—they were forest boars with tusks, tearing
and rending, not the ordinary domestic grunter; they represented the demon forces for ever in collision with beauty,
virtue, and the gentle uses of life; they made a fine contrast
in the picture with the wandering minstrel, the soft-lipped
princess, the pious recluse, and the timid Israelite. That was
a time of colour, when the sunlight fell on glancing steel and
floating banners; a time of adventure and fierce struggle—
nay, of living, religious art and religious enthusiasm; for were
not cathedrals built in those days, and did not great emperors
leave their Western palaces to die before the infidel strong-
holds in the sacred East? Therefore it is that these Rhine
castles thrill me with a sense of poetry: they belong to the
grand historic life of humanity, and raise up for me the vision
of an epoch. But these dead-tinted, hollow-eyed, angular
skeletons of villages on the Rhone oppress me with the feeling
that human life—very much of it—is a narrow, ugly, grovelling existence, which even calamity does not elevate, but
rather tends to exhibit in all its bare vulgarity of conception;
and I have a cruel conviction that the lives these ruins are
the traces of, were part of a gross sum of obscure vitality, that
will be swept into the same oblivion with the generations of
ants and beavers.

Perhaps something akin to this oppressive feeling may have
weighed upon you in watching this old-fashioned family life
on the banks of the Floss, which even sorrow hardly suffices
to lift above the level of the tragi-comic. It is a sordid life,
you say, this of the Tullivers and Dodsons—irradiated by no
sublime principles, no romantic visions, no active, self-re-
nouncing faith—moved by none of those wild, uncontrollable
passions which create the dark shadows of misery and crime

—without that primitive rough simplicity of wants, that hard submissive ill-paid toil, that childlike spelling-out of what nature has written, which gives its poetry to peasant life. Here, one has conventional worldly notions and habits without instruction and without polish—surely the most prosaic form of human life: proud respectability in a gig of unfashionable build: worldliness without side-dishes. Observing these people narrowly, even when the iron hand of misfortune has shaken them from their unquestioning hold on the world, one sees little trace of religion, still less of a distinctively Christian creed. Their belief in the Unseen, so far as it manifests itself at all seems to be rather of a pagan kind; their moral notions, though held with strong tenacity, seem to have no standard beyond hereditary custom. You could not live among such people; you are stifled for want of an outlet towards something beautiful, great, or noble; you are irritated with these dull men and women, as a kind of population out of keeping with the earth on which they live—with this rich plain where the great river flows for ever onward, and links the small pulse of the old English town with the beating of the world's mighty heart. A vigorous superstition, that lashes its gods or lashes its own back, seems to be more congruous with the mystery of the human lot, than the mental condition of these emmet-like Dodsons and Tullivers.

I share with you this sense of oppressive narrowness; but it is necessary that we should feel it, if we care to understand how it acted on the lives of Tom and Maggie—how it has acted on young natures in many generations, that in the onward tendency of human things have risen above the mental level of the generation before them, to which they have been nevertheless tied by the strongest fibres of their hearts. The suffering, whether of martyr or victim, which belongs to every historical advance of mankind, is represented in this way in every town, and by hundreds of obscure hearths; and we need not shrink from this comparison of small things with great; for does not science tell us that its highest striving is after the ascertainment of a unity which shall bind the smallest things with the greatest? In natural science, I have understood, there is nothing petty to the mind that has a large vision of relations, and to which every single object suggests a vast sum of conditions. It is surely the same with the observation of human life.

Certainly the religious and moral ideas of the Dodsons and Tullivers were of too specific a kind to be arrived at deductively, from the statement that they were part of the Protestant population of Great Britain. Their theory of life had its core of soundness, as all theories must have on which decent and prosperous families have been reared and have flourished; but it had the very slightest tincture of theology. If, in the maiden days of the Dodson sisters, their Bibles opened more easily at some part than others, it was because of dried tulip-petals, which had been distributed quite impartially, without preference for the historical, devotional, or doctrinal. Their religion was of a simple, semi-pagan kind, but there was no heresy in it—if heresy properly means choice—for they didn't know there was any other religion, except that of chapel-goers, which appeared to run in families, like asthma. How *should* they know? The vicar of their pleasant rural parish was not a controversialist, but a good hand at whist, and one who had a joke always ready for a blooming female parishioner. The religion of the Dodsons consisted in revering whatever was customary and respectable: it was necessary to be baptised, else one could not be buried in the churchyard, and to take the sacrament before death as a security against more dimly understood perils; but it was of equal necessity to have the proper pall-bearers and well-cured hams at one's funeral, and to leave an unimpeachable will. A Dodson would not be taxed with the omission of anything that was becoming, or that belonged to that eternal fitness of things which was plainly indicated in the practice of the most substantial parishioners, and in the family traditions—such as, obedience to parents, faithfulness to kindred, industry, rigid honesty, thrift, the thorough scouring of wooden and copper utensils, the hoarding of coins likely to disappear from the currency, the production of first-rate commodities for the market, and the general preference for whatever was home-made. The Dodsons were a very proud race, and their pride lay in the utter frustration of all desire to tax them with a breach of traditional duty or propriety. A wholesome pride in many respects, since it identified honour with perfect integrity, thoroughness of work, and faithfulness to admitted rules: and society owes some worthy qualities in many of her members to mothers of the Dodson class, who made their butter and their fromenty well, and would have felt disgraced to make it otherwise. To be honest and poor was never a Dodson motto, still less to seem rich though being poor; rather, the family badge was to be honest and rich; and not only rich, but richer than was supposed. To live respected, and have the proper bearers at your funeral, was an achievement of the ends of existence that would be entirely nullified if, on the reading of your will, you sank in the opinion of your fellow-men, either by turning out to be poorer than they expected, or by leaving your money in a capricious manner, without strict regard to degrees of kin. The right thing must always be done towards kindred. The right thing was to correct them severely, if they were other than a credit to the family, but still not to alienate from them the smallest rightful share in the family shoe-buckles and other property. A conspicuous quality in the Dodson character was its genuineness: its vices and virtues alike were phases of a proud, honest egoism, which had a hearty dislike to whatever made against its own credit and interest, and would be frankly hard of speech to inconvenient "kin," but would never forsake or ignore them—would not let them want bread, but only require them to eat it with bitter herbs.

The same sort of traditional belief ran in the Tulliver veins, but it was carried in richer blood, having elements of generous imprudence, warm affection, and hot-tempered rashness. Mr Tulliver's grandfather had been heard to say that he was descended from one Ralph Tulliver, a wonderfully clever fellow, who had ruined himself. It is likely enough that the clever Ralph was a high liver, rode spirited horses, and was very decidedly of his own opinion. On the other hand, nobody had ever heard of a Dodson who had ruined himself: it was not the way of that family.

If such were the views of life on which the Dodsons and

Tullivers had been reared in the praiseworthy past of Pitt and high prices, you will infer from what you already know concerning the state of society in St Oggs, that there had been no highly modifying influence to act on them in their maturer life. It was still possible, even in that later time of anti-Catholic preaching, for people to hold many pagan ideas, and believe themselves good church-people notwithstanding; so we need hardly feel any surprise at the fact that Mr Tulliver, though a regular church-goer, recorded his vindictiveness on the fly-leaf of his Bible. It was not that any harm could be said concerning the vicar of that charming rural parish to which Dorlcote Mill belonged: he was a man of excellent family, an irreproachable bachelor, of elegant pursuits—had taken honours, and held a fellowship. Mr Tulliver regarded him with dutiful respect, as he did everything else belonging to the church-service; but he considered that church was one thing and common-sense another, and he wanted nobody to tell *him* what common-sense was. Certain seeds which are required to find a nidus for themselves under unfavourable circumstances, have been supplied by nature with an apparatus of hooks, so that they will get a hold on very unreceptive surfaces. The spiritual seed which had been scattered over Mr Tulliver had apparently been destitute of any corresponding provision, and had slipped off to the winds again, from a total absence of hooks.

The Veneerings

CHARLES DICKENS

[FROM *Our Mutual Friend*]

1864-1865

Mr. and Mrs. Veneering were bran-new people in a bran-new house in a bran-new quarter of London. Everything about the Veneerings was spick and span new. All their furniture was new, all their friends were new, all their servants were new, their plate was new, their carriage was new, their harness was new, their horses were new, their pictures were new, they themselves were new, they were as newly married as was lawfully compatible with their having a bran-new baby, and if they had set up a great-grandfather, he would have come home in matting from the Pantechnicon, without a scratch upon him, French-polished to the crown of his head.

For, in the Veneering establishment, from the hall-chairs with the new coat of arms, to the grand pianoforte with the new action, and up-stairs again to the new fire-escape, all things were in a state of high varnish and polish. And what was observable in the furniture, was observable in the Veneerings—the surface smelt a little too much of the workshop and was a trifle sticky.

There was an innocent piece of dinner-furniture that went upon easy castors and was kept over a livery stable-yard in Duke Street, Saint James's, when not in use, to whom the Veneerings were a source of blind confusion. The name of this article was Twemlow. Being first cousin to Lord Snigsworth, he was a frequent requisition, and at many houses might be said to represent the dining-table in its normal state. Mr. and Mrs. Veneering, for example, arranging a dinner, habitually

From Chapter 2.

started with Twemlow, and then put leaves in him, or added guests to him. Sometimes, the table consisted of Twemlow and half-a-dozen leaves; sometimes, of Twemlow and a dozen leaves; sometimes, Twemlow was pulled out to his utmost extent of twenty leaves. Mr. and Mrs. Veneering on occasions of ceremony faced each other in the centre of the board, and thus the parallel still held; for, it always happened that the more Twemlow was pulled out, the further he found himself from the centre, and the nearer to the sideboard at one end of the room, or the window-curtains at the other.

But it was not this which steeped the feeble soul of Twemlow in confusion. This he was used to, and could take soundings of. The abyss to which he could find no bottom, and from which started forth the engrossing and ever-swelling difficulty of his life, was the insoluble question whether he was Veneering's oldest friend, or newest friend. To the excogitation of this problem, the harmless gentleman had devoted many anxious hours, both in his lodgings over the livery stable-yard, and in the cold gloom, favourable to meditation, of St. James's Square. Thus, Twemlow had first known Veneering at his club, where Veneering then knew nobody but the man who made them known to one another, who seemed to be the most intimate friend he had in the world, and whom he had known two days—the bond of union between their souls, the nefarious conduct of the committee respecting the cookery of a fillet of veal, having been accidentally cemented at that date. Immediately upon this, Twemlow received an invitation to dine with Veneering, and dined: the man being of the party. Immediately upon that, Twemlow received an invitation to dine with the man, and dined: Veneering being of the party. At the man's were a Member, an Engineer, a Payer-off of the National Debt, a Poem on Shakespeare, a Grievance, and a Public Office, who all seemed to be utter strangers to Veneering. And yet immediately after that, Twemlow received an invitation to dine at Veneering's, expressly to meet the Member, the Engineer, the Payer-off of the National Debt, the Poem on Shakespeare, the Grievance, and the Public Office, and, dining, discovered that all of them were the most intimate friends Veneering had in the world, and that the wives of all of them (who were all there) were the objects of Mrs. Veneering's most devoted affection and tender confidence.

Thus it had come about, that Mr. Twemlow had said to himself in his lodgings, with his hand to his forehead: "I must not think of this. This is enough to soften any man's brain"— and yet was always thinking of it, and could never form a conclusion.

This evening the Veneerings give a banquet. Eleven leaves in the Twemlow; fourteen in company all told. Four pigeon-breasted retainers in plain clothes stand in line in the hall. A fifth retainer, proceeding up the staircase with a mournful air— as who should say, "Here is another wretched creature come to dinner; such is life!"—announces, "Mis-ter Twemlow!"

Mrs. Veneering welcomes her sweet Mr. Twemlow. Mr. Veneering welcomes his dear Twemlow. Mrs. Veneering does not expect that Mr. Twemlow can in nature care much for such insipid things as babies, but so old a friend must please look at baby. "Ah! You will know the friend of your family better, Tootleums," says Mr. Veneering, nodding emotionally at that new article, "when you begin to take notice." He then begs to make his dear Twemlow known to his two friends, Mr. Boots and Mr. Brewer—and clearly has no distinct idea which is which.

But now a fearful circumstance occurs.

"Mis-ter and Mis-sis Podsnap!"

"My dear," says Mr. Veneering to Mrs. Veneering, with an air of much friendly interest, while the door stands open, "the Podsnaps."

A too, too smiling large man, with a fatal freshness on him, appearing with his wife, instantly deserts his wife and darts at Twemlow with:

"How do you do? So glad to know you. Charming house you have here. I hope we are not late. So glad of this opportunity, I am sure!"

When the first shock fell upon him, Twemlow twice skipped back in his neat little shoes and his neat little silk stockings of a bygone fashion, as if impelled to leap over a sofa behind him; but the large man closed with him and proved too strong.

"Let me," says the large man, trying to attract the attention of his wife in the distance, "have the pleasure of presenting Mrs. Podsnap to her host. She will be"—in his fatal freshness he seems to find perpetual verdure and eternal youth in the phrase—"she will be so glad of the opportunity, I am sure!"

In the meantime, Mrs. Podsnap, unable to originate a mistake on her own account, because Mrs. Veneering is the only other lady there, does her best in the way of handsomely supporting her husband's, by looking towards Mr. Twemlow with a plaintive countenance and remarking to Mrs. Veneering in a feeling manner, firstly, that she fears he has been rather bilious of late, and, secondly, that the baby is already very like him.

It is questionable whether any man quite relishes being mistaken for any other man; but Mr. Veneering having this very evening set up the shirt-front of the young Antinous (in new-worked cambric just come home), is not at all complimented by being supposed to be Twemlow, who is dry and weazen and some thirty years older. Mrs. Veneering equally resents the imputation of being the wife of Twemlow. As to Twemlow, he is so sensible of being a much better bred man than Veneering, that he considers the large man an offensive ass.

In this complicated dilemma, Mr. Veneering approaches the large man with extended hand, and smilingly assures that incorrigible personage that he is delighted to see him: who in his fatal freshness instantly replies:

"Thank you. I am ashamed to say that I cannot at this moment recall where we met, but I am so glad of this opportunity, I am sure!"

Then pouncing upon Twemlow, who holds back with all his feeble might, he is haling him off to present him, as Veneering, to Mrs. Podsnap, when the arrival of more guests unravels the mistake. Whereupon, having reshaken hands with Veneering as Veneering, he reshakes hands with Twemlow as Twemlow, and winds it all up to his own perfect satisfaction by saying to the last-named, "Ridiculous opportunity—but so glad of it, I am sure!"

Now, Twemlow having undergone this terrific experience, having likewise noted the fusion of Boots in Brewer and Brewer in Boots, and having further observed that of the remaining seven guests four discreet characters enter with wandering eyes and wholly decline to commit themselves as to which is Veneering, until Veneering has them in his grasp; —Twemlow having profited by these studies, finds his brain wholesomely hardening as he approaches the conclusion that he really is Veneering's oldest friend, when his brain softens again and all is lost, through his eyes encountering Veneering and the large man linked together as twin brothers in the back drawing-room near the conservatory door, and through his ears informing him in the tones of Mrs. Veneering that the same large man is to be baby's godfather.

"Dinner is on the table!"

Thus the melancholy retainer, as who should say, "Come down and be poisoned, ye unhappy children of men!"

Twemlow, having no lady assigned him, goes down in the rear, with his hand to his forehead. Boots and Brewer, thinking him indisposed, whisper, "Man faint. Had no lunch." But he is only stunned by the unvanquishable difficulty of his existence.

Revived by soup, Twemlow discourses mildly of the Court Circular with Boots and Brewer. Is appealed to, at the fish stage of the banquet, by Veneering, on the disputed question whether his cousin Lord Snigsworth is in or out of town? Gives it that his cousin is out of town. "At Snigsworthy Park?" Veneering inquires. "At Snigsworthy," Twemlow rejoins. Boots and Brewer regard this as a man to be cultivated; and Veneering is clear that he is a remunerative article. Meantime the retainer goes round, like a gloomy Analytical Chemist; always seeming to say, after "Chablis, sir?"—"You wouldn't if you knew what it's made of."

The great looking-glass above the sideboard reflects the table and the company. Reflects the new Veneering crest, in gold and eke in silver, frosted and also thawed, a camel of all work. The Herald's College found out a Crusading ancestor for Veneering who bore a camel on his shield (or might have done it if he had thought of it), and a caravan of camels take charge of the fruits and flowers and candles, and kneel down to be loaded with the salt. Reflects Veneering; forty, wavy-haired, dark, tending to corpulence, sly, mysterious, filmy—a kind of sufficiently well-looking veiled-prophet, not prophesying. Reflects Mrs. Veneering; fair, aquiline-nosed and fingered, not so much light hair as she might have, gorgeous in raiment and jewels, enthusiastic, propitiatory, conscious that a corner of her husband's veil is over herself. Reflects Podsnap; prosperously feeding, two little light-coloured wiry wings, one on either side of his else bald head, looking as like his hair-brushes as his hair, dissolving view of red beads on his forehead, large allowance of crumpled shirt-collar up behind. Reflects Mrs. Podsnap; fine woman for Professor Owen, quantity of bone, neck and nostrils like a rocking-horse, hard features, majestic head-dress in which Podsnap has hung golden offerings. Reflects Twemlow; grey, dry, polite, susceptible to east wind, First-Gentleman-in-Europe collar and cravat, cheeks drawn in as if he had made a great effort to retire into himself some years ago, and had got so far and had never got any farther. Reflects mature young lady; raven locks, and complexion that lights up well when well-powdered—as it is—carrying on considerably in the captivation of mature, young gentleman; with too much nose in his face, too much ginger in his whiskers, too much torso in his waistcoat, too much sparkle in his studs, his eyes, his buttons, his talk, and his teeth. Reflects charming old Lady Tippins on Veneering's right; with an immense obtuse drab oblong face, like a face in a tablespoon, and a dyed Long Walk up the top of her head, as a convenient public approach to the bunch of false hair behind, pleased to patronize Mrs. Veneering opposite, who is pleased to be patronized. Reflects a certain "Mortimer," another of Veneering's oldest friends; who never was in the house before, and appears not to want to come again, who sits disconsolate on Mrs. Veneering's left, and who was inveigled by Lady Tippins (a friend of his boyhood) to come to these people's and talk, and who won't talk. Reflects Eugene, friend of Mortimer; buried alive in the back of his chair, behind a shoulder—with a powder-epaulette on it—of the mature young lady, and gloomily resorting to the champagne chalice whenever proffered by the Analytical Chemist. Lastly, the looking-glass reflects Boots and Brewer, and two other stuffed Buffers interposed between the rest of the company and possible accidents.

The Veneering dinners are excellent dinners—or new people wouldn't come—and all goes well.

———◆◆◆———

Podsnappery

CHARLES DICKENS

[FROM *Our Mutual Friend*]

1864-1865

Mr. Podsnap was well to do, and stood very high in Mr. Podsnap's opinion. Beginning with a good inheritance, he had married a good inheritance, and had thriven exceedingly in the Marine Insurance way, and was quite satisfied. He never could make out why everybody was not quite satisfied, and he felt conscious that he set a brilliant social example in being particularly well satisfied with most things, and, above all other things, with himself.

Thus happily acquainted with his own merit and importance, Mr. Podsnap settled that whatever he put behind him he put out of existence. There was a dignified conclusive-

From Chapter 11.

ness—not to add a grand convenience—in this way of getting rid of disagreeables, which had done much towards establishing Mr. Podsnap in his lofty place in Mr. Podsnap's satisfaction. "I don't want to know about it; I don't choose to discuss it; I don't admit it!" Mr. Podsnap had even acquired a peculiar flourish of his right arm in often clearing the world of its most difficult problems, by sweeping them behind him (and consequently sheer away) with those words and a flushed face. For they affronted him.

Mr. Podsnap's world was not a very large world, morally; no, nor even geographically: seeing that although his business was sustained upon commerce with other countries, he considered other countries, with that important reservation, a mistake, and of their manners and customs would conclusively observe, "Not English!" when, PRESTO! with a flourish of the arm, and a flush of the face, they were swept away. Elsewise, the world got up at eight, shaved close at a quarter-past, breakfasted at nine, went to the City at ten, came home at half-past five, and dined at seven. Mr. Podsnap's notions of the Arts in their integrity might have been stated thus. Literature; large print, respectively descriptive of getting up at eight, shaving close at a quarter-past, breakfasting at nine, going to the City at ten, coming home at half-past five, and dining at seven. Painting and Sculpture; models and portraits representing Professors of getting up at eight, shaving close at a quarter-past, breakfasting at nine, going to the City at ten, coming home at half-past five, and dining at seven. Music; a respectable performance (without variations) on stringed and wind instruments, sedately expressive of getting up at eight, shaving close at a quarter-past, breakfasting at nine, going to the City at ten, coming home at half-past five, and dining at seven. Nothing else to be permitted to those same vagrants the Arts, on pain of excommunication. Nothing else To Be—anywhere!

As a so eminently respectable man, Mr. Podsnap was sensible of its being required of him to take Providence under his protection. Consequently he always knew exactly what Providence meant. Inferior and less respectable men might fall short of that mark, but Mr. Podsnap was always up to it. And it was very remarkable (and must have been very comfortable) that what Providence meant, was invariably what Mr. Podsnap meant.

These may be said to have been the articles of a faith and school which the present chapter takes the liberty of calling, after its representative man, Podsnappery. They were confined within close bounds, as Mr. Podsnap's own head was confined by his shirt-collar; and they were enunciated with a sounding pomp that smacked of the creaking of Mr. Podsnap's own boots.

There was a Miss Podsnap. And this young rocking-horse was being trained in her mother's art of prancing in a stately manner without ever getting on. But the high parental action was not yet imparted to her, and in truth she was but an under-sized damsel, with high shoulders, low spirits, chilled elbows, and a rasped surface of nose, who seemed to take occasional frosty peeps out of childhood into womanhood, and to shrink back again, overcome by her mother's head-dress and her father from head to foot—crushed by the mere dead-weight of Podsnappery.

A certain institution in Mr. Podsnap's mind which he called "the young person" may be considered to have been embodied in Miss Podsnap, his daughter. It was an inconvenient and exacting institution, as requiring everything in the universe to be filed down and fitted to it. The question about everything was, would it bring a blush into the cheek of the young person? And the inconvenience of the young person was that, according to Mr. Podsnap, she seemed always liable to burst into blushes when there was no need at all. There appeared to be no line of demarcation between the young person's excessive innocence, and another person's guiltiest knowledge. Take Mr. Podsnap's word for it, and the soberest tints of drab, white, lilac, and grey, were all flaming red to this troublesome Bull of a young person.

The Podsnaps lived in a shady angle adjoining Portman Square. They were a kind of people certain to dwell in the shade, wherever they dwelt. Miss Podsnap's life had been, from her first appearance on this planet, altogether of a shady order; for Mr. Podsnap's young person was likely to get little good out of association with other young persons, and had therefore been restricted to companionship with not very congenial older persons, and with massive furniture. Miss Podsnap's early views of life being principally derived from the reflections of it in her father's boots, and in the walnut and rosewood tables of the dim drawing-room, and in their swarthy giants of looking-glasses, were of a sombre cast; and it was not wonderful that now, when she was on most days solemnly tooled through the Park by the side of her mother in a great tall custard-coloured phaeton, she showed above the apron of that vehicle like a dejected young person sitting up in bed to take a startled look at things in general, and very strongly desiring to get her head under the counterpane again.

Said Mr. Podsnap to Mrs. Podsnap, "Georgiana is almost eighteen."

Said Mrs. Podsnap to Mr. Podsnap, assenting, "Almost eighteen."

Said Mr. Podsnap then to Mrs. Podsnap, "Really I think we should have some people on Georgiana's birthday."

Said Mrs. Podsnap then to Mr. Podsnap, "Which will enable us to clear off all those people who are due."

So it came to pass that Mr. and Mrs. Podsnap requested the honour of the company of seventeen friends of their souls at dinner; and that they substituted other friends of their souls for such of the seventeen original friends of their souls as deeply regretted that a prior engagement prevented their having the honour of dining with Mr. and Mrs. Podsnap, in pursuance of their kind invitation; and that Mrs. Podsnap said of all these inconsolable personages, as she checked them off with a pencil in her list, "Asked, at any rate, and got rid of"; and that they successfully disposed of a good many friends of their souls in this way, and felt their consciences much lightened.

There were still other friends of their souls who were not entitled to be asked to dinner, but had a claim to be invited to come and take a haunch of mutton vapour-bath at half-past nine. For the clearing off of these worthies, Mrs. Podsnap added a small and early evening to the dinner, and looked in at the music-shop to bespeak a well-conducted automaton to come and play quadrilles for a carpet dance.

Mr. and Mrs. Veneering, and Mr. and Mrs. Veneering's bran-new bride and bridegroom, were of the dinner company; but the Podsnap establishment had nothing else in common with the Veneerings. Mr. Podsnap could tolerate taste in a mush-room man who stood in need of that sort of thing, but was far above it himself. Hideous solidity was the characteristic of the Podsnap plate. Everything was made to look as heavy as it could, and to take up as much room as possible. Every-thing said boastfully, "Here you have as much of me in my ugliness as if I were only lead; but I am so many ounces of precious metal worth so much an ounce—wouldn't you like to melt me down?" A corpulent straggling epergne, blotched all over as if it had broken out in an eruption rather than been ornamented, delivered this address from an unsightly silver platform in the centre of the table. Four silver wine-coolers, each furnished with four staring heads, each head obtrusively carrying a big silver ring in each of its ears, con-veyed the sentiment up and down the table, and handed it on to the pot-bellied silver salt-cellars. All the big silver spoons and forks widened the mouths of the company expressly for the purpose of thrusting the sentiment down their throats with every morsel they ate. The majority of the guests were like the plate, and included several heavy articles weighing ever so much.

Millbank

BENJAMIN DISRAELI

[FROM *Coningsby; or, the New Generation*]

1844

In a green valley of Lancaster, contiguous to that district of factories on which we have already touched, a clear and powerful stream flows through a broad meadow land. Upon its margin, adorned, rather than shadowed, by some old elm-trees, for they are too distant to serve except for ornament, rises a vast deep red brick pile, which though formal and monotonous in its general character, is not without a certain beauty of proportion and an artist-like finish in its occasional masonry. The front, which is of great extent, and covered with many tiers of small windows, is flanked by two projecting wings in the same style, which form a large court, completed by a dwarf wall crowned with a light, and rather elegant railing; in the centre, the principal entrance, a lofty portal of bold and beautiful design, surmounted by a statue of Commerce.

This building, not without a degree of dignity, is what is technically, and not very felicitously, called a mill; always translated by the French in their accounts of our manufacturing riots, *moulin;* and which really was the principal factory of Oswald Millbank, the father of that youth whom, we trust, our readers have not quite forgotten.

At some little distance, and rather withdrawn from the principal stream, were two other smaller structures of the same style. About a quarter of a mile further on, appeared a village of not inconsiderable size, and remarkable from the neatness and even picturesque character of its architecture, and the gay gardens that surrounded it. On a sunny knoll in

From Book IV, Chapter 3.

the background rose a church, in the best style of Christian architecture, and near it was a clerical residence and a school-house of similar design. The village, too, could boast of another public building; an Institute where there were a library and a lecture-room; and a reading-hall, which any one might frequent at certain hours, and under reasonable regulations.

On the other side of the principal factory, but more remote, about half-a-mile up the valley, surrounded by beautiful mead-ows, and built on an agreeable and well-wooded elevation, was the mansion of the mill-owner; apparently a commodious and not inconsiderable dwelling-house, built in what is called a villa style, with a variety of gardens and conservatories. The atmosphere of this somewhat striking settlement was not dis-turbed and polluted by the dark vapour, which, to the shame of Manchester, still infests that great town, for Mr. Millbank, who liked nothing so much as an invention, unless it were an experiment, took care to consume his own smoke.

The sun was declining when Coningsby arrived at Millbank, and the gratification which he experienced on first beholding it, was not a little diminished, when, on inquiring at the village, he was informed that the hour was past for seeing the works. Determined not to relinquish his purpose without a struggle, he repaired to the principal mill, and entered the counting-house, which was situated in one of the wings of the building.

'Your pleasure, sir?' said one of three individuals sitting on high stools behind a high desk.

'I wish, if possible, to see the works.'

'Quite impossible, sir'; and the clerk, withdrawing his glance, continued his writing. 'No admission without an order, and no admission with an order after two o'clock.'

'I am very unfortunate,' said Coningsby.

'Sorry for it, sir. Give me ledger K. X., will you, Mr. Benson?'

'I think, Mr. Millbank would grant me permission,' said Coningsby.

'Very likely, sir; to-morrow. Mr. Millbank is there, sir, but very much engaged.' He pointed to an inner counting-house, and the glass doors permitted Coningsby to observe several individuals in close converse.

'Perhaps his son, Mr. Oswald Millbank, is here?' inquired Coningsby.

'Mr. Oswald is in Belgium,' said the clerk.

'Would you give a message to Mr. Millbank, and say a friend of his son's at Eton is here, and here only for a day, and wishes very much to see his works?'

'Can't possibly disturb Mr. Millbank now, sir; but, if you like to sit down, you can wait and see him yourself.'

Coningsby was content to sit down, but he grew very impatient at the end of a quarter of an hour. The ticking of the clock, the scratching of the pens of the three silent clerks, irritated him. At length, voices were heard, doors opened, and the clerk said, 'Mr. Millbank is coming, sir,' but nobody came; voices became hushed, doors were shut; again nothing was heard, save the ticking of the clock and the scratching of the pen.

At length there was a general stir, and they all did come forth, Mr. Millbank among them, a well-proportioned, comely man, with a fair face inclining to ruddiness, a quick, glancing, hazel eye, the whitest teeth, and short, curly, chestnut hair, here and there slightly tinged with grey. It was a visage of energy and decision.

He was about to pass through the counting-house with his companions, with whom his affairs were not concluded, when he observed Coningsby, who had risen.

'This gentleman wishes to see me?' he inquired of his clerk, who bowed assent.

'I shall be at your service, sir, the moment I have finished with these gentlemen.'

'The gentleman wishes to see the works, sir,' said the clerk.

'He can see the works at proper times,' said Mr. Millbank, somewhat pettishly; 'tell him the regulations'; and he was about to go.

'I beg your pardon, sir,' said Coningsby, coming forward,

and with an air of earnestness and grace that arrested the step of the manufacturer. 'I am aware of the regulations, but would beg to be permitted to infringe them.'

'It cannot be, sir,' said Mr. Millbank, moving.

'I thought, sir, being here only for a day, and as a friend of your son—'

Mr. Millbank stopped and said, 'Oh! a friend of Oswald's eh? What, at Eton?'

'Yes, sir, at Eton; and I had hoped perhaps to have found him here.'

'I am very much engaged, sir, at this moment,' said Mr. Millbank; 'I am sorry I cannot pay you any personal attention, but my clerk will show you everything. Mr. Benson, let this gentleman see everything'; and he withdrew.

'Be pleased to write your name here, sir,' said Mr. Benson, opening a book, and our friend wrote his name and the date of his visit to Millbank:

'HARRY CONINGSBY, SEPT. 2, 1836.'

Coningsby beheld in this great factory the last and the most refined inventions of mechanical genius. The building had been fitted up by a capitalist as anxious to raise a monument of the skill and power of his order, as to obtain a return for the great investment.

'It is the glory of Lancashire!' exclaimed the enthusiastic Mr. Benson.

The clerk spoke freely of his master, whom he evidently idolised, and his great achievements, and Coningsby encouraged him. He detailed to Coningsby the plans which Mr. Millbank had pursued, both for the moral and physical well-being of his people; how he had built churches, and schools, and institutes; houses and cottages on a new system of ventilation; how he had allotted gardens; established singing classes.

'Here is Mr. Millbank,' continued the clerk, as he and Coningsby, quitting the factory, re-entered the court.

Mr. Millbank was approaching the factory, and the moment that he observed them, he quickened his pace.

'Mr. Coningsby?' he said, when he reached them. His countenance was rather disturbed, and his voice a little trembled, and he looked on our friend with a glance scrutinising and serious. Coningsby bowed.

'I am sorry that you should have been received at this place with so little ceremony, sir,' said Mr. Millbank; 'but had your name been mentioned, you would have found it cherished here.' He nodded to the clerk, who disappeared.

Coningsby began to talk about the wonders of the factory, but Mr. Millbank recurred to other thoughts that were passing in his mind. He spoke of his son: he expressed a kind reproach that Coningsby should have thought of visiting this part of the world without giving them some notice of his intention, that he might have been their guest, that Oswald might have been there to receive him, that they might have made arrangements that he should see everything, and in the best manner; in short, that they might all have shown, however slightly, the deep sense of their obligations to him.

'My visit to Manchester, which led to this, was quite accidental,' said Coningsby. 'I am bound for the other division of the county, to pay a visit to my grandfather, Lord Monmouth; but an irresistible desire came over me during my journey to view this famous district of industry. It is some days since I ought to have found myself at Coningsby, and this is the reason why I am so pressed.'

A cloud passed over the countenance of Millbank as the name of Lord Monmouth was mentioned, but he said nothing. Turning towards Coningsby, with an air of kindness:

'At least,' said he, 'let not Oswald hear that you did not taste our salt. Pray dine with me to-day; there is yet an hour to dinner; and as you have seen the factory, suppose we stroll together through the village.'

[FROM Chapter 4]

The village clock struck five as Mr. Millbank and his guest entered the gardens of his mansion. Coningsby lingered a moment to admire the beauty and gay profusion of the flowers.

'Your situation,' said Coningsby, looking up the green and silent valley, 'is absolutely poetic.'

'I try sometimes to fancy,' said Mr. Millbank, with a rather fierce smile, 'that I am in the New World.'

They entered the house; a capacious and classic hall, at the end a staircase in the Italian fashion. As they approached it, the sweetest and the clearest voice exclaimed from above, 'Papa! Papa!' and instantly a young girl came bounding down the stairs, but suddenly seeing a stranger with her father she stopped upon the landing-place, and was evidently on the point of as rapidly retreating as she had advanced, when Mr. Millbank waved his hand to her and begged her to descend. She came down slowly; as she approached them her father said, 'A friend you have often heard of, Edith: this is Mr. Coningsby.'

She started; blushed very much; and then, with a trembling and uncertain gait, advanced, put forth her hand with a wild unstudied grace, and said in a tone of sensibility, 'How often have we all wished to see and to thank you!'

This daughter of his host was of tender years; apparently she could scarcely have counted sixteen summers. She was delicate and fragile, but as she raised her still blushing visage to her father's guest, Coningsby felt that he had never beheld a countenance of such striking and such peculiar beauty.

'My only daughter, Mr. Coningsby, Edith; a Saxon name, for she is the daughter of a Saxon.'

But the beauty of the countenance was not the beauty of the Saxons. It was a radiant face, one of those that seem to have been touched in their cradle by a sunbeam, and to have retained all their brilliancy and suffused and mantling lustre. One marks sometimes such faces, diaphanous with delicate splendour, in the southern regions of France. Her eye, too, was the rare eye of Aquitaine; soft and long, with lashes drooping over the cheek, dark as her clustering ringlets.

They entered the drawing-room.

'Mr. Coningsby,' said Millbank to his daughter, 'is in this part of the world only for a few hours, or I am sure he would become our guest. He has, however, promised to stay with us now and dine.'

'If Miss Millbank will pardon this dress,' said Coningsby, bowing an apology for his inevitable frock and boots; the maiden raised her eyes and bent her head.

The hour of dinner was at hand. Millbank offered to show Coningsby to his dressing-room. He was absent but a few minutes. When he returned he found Miss Millbank alone. He came somewhat suddenly into the room. She was playing with her dog, but ceased the moment she observed Coningsby.

Coningsby, who since his practice with Lady Everingham, flattered himself that he had advanced in small talk, and was not sorry that he had now an opportunity of proving his prowess, made some lively observations about pets and the breeds of lapdogs, but he was not fortunate in extracting a response or exciting repartee. He began then on the beauty of Millbank, which he would on no account have avoided seeing, and inquired when she had last heard of her brother. The young lady, apparently much distressed, was murmuring something about Antwerp, when the entrance of her father relieved her from her embarrassment.

Dinner being announced, Coningsby offered his arm to his fair companion, who took it with her eyes fixed on the ground.

'You are very fond, I see, of flowers,' said Coningsby, as they moved along; and the young lady said 'Yes.'

The dinner was plain, but perfect of its kind. The young hostess seemed to perform her office with a certain degree of desperate determination. She looked at a chicken and then at Coningsby, and murmured something which he understood. Sometimes she informed herself of his tastes or necessities in more detail, by the medium of her father, whom she treated as a sort of dragoman; in this way: 'Would not Mr. Coningsby, papa, take this or that, or do so and so?' Coningsby was always careful to reply in a direct manner, without the agency of the interpreter; but he did not advance. Even a petition for the great honour of taking a glass of sherry with her only induced the beautiful face to bow. And yet when she had first seen him, she had addressed him even with emotion. What could it be? He felt less confidence in his increased power of conversation. Why, Theresa Sydney was scarcely a year older than Miss Millbank, and though she did not certainly originate like Lady Everingham, he got on with her perfectly well.

Mr. Millbank did not seem to be conscious of his daughter's silence: at any rate, he attempted to compensate for it. He talked fluently and well; on all subjects his opinions seemed to be decided, and his language was precise. He was really interested in what Coningsby had seen, and what he had felt; and his sympathy divested his manner of the disagreeable effect that accompanies a tone inclined to be dictatorial. More than once Coningsby observed the silent daughter listening with extreme attention to the conversation of himself and her father.

The dessert was remarkable. Millbank was proud of his fruit. A bland expression of self-complacency spread over his features as he surveyed his grapes, his peaches, his figs.

'These grapes have gained a medal,' he told Coningsby. 'Those too are prize peaches. I have not yet been so successful with my figs. These however promise, and perhaps this year I may be more fortunate.'

'What would your brother and myself have given for such a dessert at Eton!' said Coningsby to Miss Millbank. . . .

The walls of the dining-room were covered with pictures of great merit, all of the modern English school. Mr. Millbank understood no other, he was wont to say! and he found that many of his friends who did, bought a great many pleasing pictures that were copies, and many originals that were very displeasing. He loved a fine free landscape by Lee, that gave him the broad plains, the green lanes, and running streams of his own land; a group of animals by Landseer, as full of speech and sentiment as if they were designed by Æsop; above all, he delighted in the household humour and homely pathos of Wilkie. And if a higher tone of imagination pleased him, he could gratify it without difficulty among his favourite masters. He possessed some specimens of Etty worthy of

Venice when it was alive; he could muse amid the twilight
ruins of ancient cities raised by the magic pencil of Danby,
or accompany a group of fair Neapolitans to a festival by the
genial aid of Uwins.

Captains of Industry

THOMAS CARLYLE

[FROM *Past and Present*]

1843

The Leaders of Industry, if Industry is ever to be led,
are virtually the Captains of the World; if there be no nobleness in them, there will never be an Aristocracy more. But let
the Captains of Industry consider: once again, are they born
of other clay than the old Captains of Slaughter; doomed for
ever to be not Chivalry, but a mere gold-plated *Doggery,*—
what the French well name *Canaille,* 'Doggery' with more or
less gold carrion at its disposal? Captains of Industry are the
true Fighters, henceforth recognisable as the only true ones:
Fighters against Chaos, Necessity and the Devils and Jötuns;
and lead on Mankind in that great, and alone true, and
universal warfare; the stars in their courses fighting for them,
and all Heaven and all Earth saying audibly, Well done! Let
the Captains of Industry retire into their own hearts, and ask
solemnly, If there is nothing but vulturous hunger for fine
wines, valet reputation and gilt carriages, discoverable there?
Of hearts made by the Almighty God I will not believe such
a thing. Deep-hidden under wretchedest god-forgetting Cants,
Epicurisms, Dead-Sea Apisms; forgotten as under foulest fat

From Book IV, Chapter 4.

Lethe mud and weeds, there is yet, in all hearts born into this God's-World, a spark of the God-like slumbering. Awake, O nightmare sleepers; awake, arise, or be for ever fallen! This is not playhouse poetry; it is sober fact. Our England, our world cannot live as it is. It will connect itself with a God again, or go down with nameless throes and fire-consummation to the Devils. Thou who feelest aught of such a God-like stirring in thee, any faintest intimation of it as through heavy-laden dreams, follow *it,* I conjure thee. Arise, save thyself, be one of those that save thy country.

Bucaniers, Chactaw Indians, whose supreme aim in fighting is that they may get the scalps, the money, that they may amass scalps and money; out of such came no Chivalry, and never will! Out of such came only gore and wreck, infernal rage and misery; desperation quenched in annihilation. Behold it, I bid thee, behold there, and consider! What is it that thou have a hundred thousand-pound bills laid up in thy strong-room, a hundred scalps hung up in thy wigwam? I value not them or thee. Thy scalps and thy thousand-pound bills are as yet nothing, if no nobleness from within irradiate them; if no Chivalry, in action, or in embryo ever struggling towards birth and action, be there.

Love of men cannot be bought by cash-payment; and without love, men cannot endure to be together. You cannot lead a Fighting World without having it regimented, chivalried: the thing, in a day, becomes impossible; all men in it, the highest at first, the very lowest at last, discern consciously, or by a noble instinct, this necessity. And can you any more continue to lead a Working World unregimented, anarchic? I answer, and the Heavens and Earth are now answering, No! The thing becomes not 'in a day' impossible; but in some two generations it does. Yes, when fathers and mothers, in Stockport hunger-cellars, begin to eat their children, and Irish widows have to prove their relationship by dying of typhus-fever; and amid Governing 'Corporations of the Best and Bravest,' busy to preserve their game by 'bushing,' dark millions of God's human creatures start up in mad Chartisms, impracticable Sacred-Months, and Manchester Insurrections;—and there is a virtual Industrial Aristocracy as yet only half-alive, spell-bound amid money-bags and ledgers; and an actual Idle Aristocracy seemingly near dead in somnolent delusions, in trespasses and double-barrels; 'sliding,' as on inclined-planes, which every new year they *soap* with new Hansard's-jargon under God's sky, and so are 'sliding' ever faster, towards a 'scale' and balance-scale whereon is written *Thou art found Wanting:*—in such days, after a generation or two, I say, it does become, even to the low and simple, very palpably impossible! No Working World, any more than a Fighting World, can be led on without a noble Chivalry of Work, and laws and fixed rules which follow out of that,—far nobler than any Chivalry of Fighting was. As an anarchic multitude on mere Supply-and-demand, it is becoming inevitable that we dwindle in horrid suicidal convulsion, and self-abrasion, frightful to the imagination, into *Chactaw* Workers. With wigwams and scalps,—with palaces and thousand-pound bills; with savagery, depopulation, chaotic desolation! Good Heavens, will not one French Revolution and Reign of Terror suffice us, but must there be two? There will be two if needed; there will be twenty if needed; there will be precisely as many as are needed. The Laws of Nature will have themselves fulfilled. That is a thing certain to me.

Your gallant battle-hosts and work-hosts, as the others did, will need to be made loyally yours; they must and will be regulated, methodically secured in their just share of conquest under you;—joined with you in veritable brotherhood, son-hood, by quite other and deeper ties than those of temporary day's wages! How would mere redcoated regiments, to say nothing of chivalries, fight for you, if you could discharge them on the evening of the battle, on payment of the stipulated shillings,—and they discharge you on the morning of it! Chelsea Hospitals, pensions, promotions, rigorous lasting covenant on the one side and on the other, are indispensable even for a hired fighter. The Feudal Baron, much more,—how could he subsist with mere temporary mercenaries round him, sixpence a day; ready to go over to the other side, if seven-pence were offered? He could not have subsisted;—and his noble instinct saved him from the necessity of even trying! The Feudal Baron had a Man's Soul in him; to which anarchy, mutiny, and the other fruits of temporary mercenaries, were intolerable: he had never been a Baron otherwise, but had continued a Chactaw and Bucanier. He felt it precious, and at last it became habitual, and his fruitful enlarged existence included it as a necessity, to have men round him who in heart loved him; whose life he watched over with rigour yet with love; who were prepared to give their life for him, if need came. It was beautiful; it was human! Man lives not otherwise, nor can live contented, anywhere or anywhen. Isolation is the sum-total of wretchedness to man. To be cut off, to be left solitary: to have a world alien, not your world; all a hostile camp for you; not a home at all, of hearts and faces who are yours, whose you are! It is the frightfulest enchantment; too truly a work of the Evil One. To have neither superior, nor inferior, nor equal, united manlike to you. Without father, without child, without brother. Man knows no sadder destiny. 'How is each of us,' exclaims Jean Paul, 'so lonely in the wide bosom of the All!' Encased each as in his transparent 'ice-palace'; our brother visible in his, making signals and gesticulations to us;—visible, but for ever unattainable: on his bosom we shall never rest, nor he on ours. It was not a God that did this; no!

Awake, ye noble Workers, warriors in the one true war: all this must be remedied. It is you who are already half-alive, whom I will welcome into life; whom I will conjure in God's name to shake off your enchanted sleep, and live wholly! Cease to count scalps, gold-purses; not in these lies your or our salvation. Even these, if you count only these, will not be left. Let bucaniering be put far from you; alter, speedily abrogate all laws of the bucaniers, if you would gain any victory that shall endure. Let God's justice, let pity, nobleness and manly valour, with more gold-purses or with fewer, testify themselves in this your brief Life-transit to all the Eternities, the Gods and Silences. It is to you I call; for ye are not dead, ye are already half-alive: there is in you a sleepless dauntless energy, the prime-matter of all nobleness in man. Honour to you in your kind. It is to you I call: ye know at least this, That the mandate of God to His creature man is: Work! The future Epic of the World rests not with those that are near dead, but with those that are alive, and those that are coming into life.

Look around you. Your world-hosts are all in mutiny, in confusion, destitution; on the eve of fiery wreck and madness! They will not march farther for you, on the sixpence a day and supply-and-demand principle: they will not; nor ought they, nor can they. Ye shall reduce them to order, begin reducing them. To order, to just subordination; noble loyalty in return for noble guidance. Their souls are driven nigh mad; let yours be sane and ever saner. Not as a bewildered bewildering mob; but as a firm regimented mass, with real captains over them, will these men march any more. All human interests, combined human endeavours, and social growths in this world, have, at a certain stage of their development, required organising: and Work, the grandest of human interests, does now require it.

God knows, the task will be hard: but no noble task was ever easy. This task will wear away your lives, and the lives of your sons and grandsons: but for what purpose, if not for tasks like this, were lives given to men? Ye shall cease to count your thousand-pound scalps, the noble of you shall cease! Nay, the very scalps, as I say, will not long be left if you count only these. Ye shall cease wholly to be barbarous vulturous Chactaws, and become noble European Nineteenth-Century Men. Ye shall know that Mammon, in never such gigs and flunky 'respectabilities,' is not the alone God; that of himself he is but a Devil, and even a Brute-god.

Difficult? Yes, it will be difficult. The short-fibre cotton; that too was difficult. The waste cotton-shrub, long useless, disobedient, as the thistle by the wayside,—have ye not conquered it; made it into beautiful bandana webs; white woven shirts for men; bright-tinted air-garments wherein flit goddesses? Ye have shivered mountains asunder, made the hard iron pliant to you as soft putty: the Forest-giants, Marsh-jötuns bear sheaves of golden grain; Aegir the Sea-demon

himself stretches his back for a sleek highway to you, and on
Firehorses and Windhorses ye career. Ye are most strong.
Thor red-bearded, with his blue sun-eyes, with his cheery
heart and strong thunder-hammer, he and you have prevailed.
Ye are most strong, ye Sons of the icy North, of the far
East,—far marching from your rugged Eastern Wildernesses,
hitherward from the grey Dawn of Time! Ye are Sons of the
Jötun-land; the land of Difficulties Conquered. Difficult? You
must try this thing. Once try it with the understanding that
it will and shall have to be done. Try it as ye try the paltrier
thing, making of money! I will bet on you once more, against
all Jötuns, Tailor-gods, Double-barrelled Law-wards, and
Denizens of Chaos whatsoever!

The Railway Mania

SAMUEL SMILES

[FROM *Life of George Stephenson*]

1857

The extension of railways had, up to the year 1844, been
effected principally by men of the commercial classes, interested in opening up improved communications between particular towns and districts. The first lines had been bold
experiments—many thought them exceedingly rash and un-
warranted; they had been reluctantly conceded by the legislature, and were carried out in the face of great opposition
and difficulties. At length the locomotive vindicated its power;
railways were recognized, by men of all classes, as works of

From Chapter 31.

great utility; and their vast social as well as commercial advantages forced themselves on the public recognition. What had been regarded as but doubtful speculations, and by many as certain failures, were now ascertained to be beneficial investments, the most successful of them paying from eight to ten per cent on the share capital expended.

The first railways were, on the whole, well managed. The best men that could be got were appointed to work them. It is true, mistakes were made, and accidents happened; but men did not become perfect because railways had been invented. The men who constructed, and the men who worked the lines, were selected from the general community, consisting of its usual proportion of honest, practical, and tolerably stupid persons. Had it been possible to create a class of perfect men, a sort of railway guardian-angels, directors would have been too glad to appoint them at good salaries. For with all the mistakes that may have been committed by directors, the jobbing of railway appointments, or the misuse of patronage in selecting the persons to work their lines, has not been charged against them. We have never yet seen a Railway Living advertised for sale; nor have railway situations of an important character been obtainable through "interest." From the first, directors chose the best men they could find for their purpose; and, on the whole, the system, considering the extent of its operations, worked satisfactorily, though admitted to be capable of considerable improvement.

The first boards of directors were composed of men of the highest character and integrity that could be found; and they almost invariably held a large stake in their respective undertakings, sufficient to give them a lively personal interest in their successful management. They were also men who had not taken up the business of railway direction as a trade, but who entered upon railway enterprise for its own sake, looking to its eventual success for an adequate return on their large investments.

The first shareholders were principally confined to the manufacturing districts,—the capitalists of the metropolis as yet holding aloof, and prophesying disaster to all concerned in railway projects. The stock exchange looked askance upon them, and it was with difficulty that respectable brokers could be found to do business in the shares. But when the lugubrious anticipations of the City men were found to be so completely falsified by the results, when, after the lapse of years, it was ascertained that railway traffic rapidly increased and dividends steadily improved, a change came over the spirit of the London capitalists: they then invested largely in railways, and the shares became a leading branch of business on the stock exchange. Speculation fairly set in; brokers prominently called the attention of investors to railway stock; and the prices of shares in the principal lines rose to nearly double their original value.

The national wealth soon poured into this new channel. A stimulus was given to the projection of further lines, the shares in the most favourite of which came out at a premium, and became the subject of immediate traffic on 'change. The premiums constituted their sole worth in the estimation of the speculators. As titles to a future profitable investment, the tens of thousands of shares created and issued in 1844 and 1845 were not in the slightest degree valued. What were they worth to hold for a time, and then to sell? what profit could be made by the venture?—that was the sole consideration.

A share-dealing spirit was thus evoked; and a reckless gambling for premiums set in, which completely changed the character and objects of railway enterprise. The public outside the stock exchange shortly became infected with the same spirit, and many people, utterly ignorant of railways, knowing and caring nothing about their great national uses, but hungering and thirsting after premiums, rushed eagerly into the vortex of speculation. They applied for allotments, and subscribed for shares in lines, of the engineering character or probable traffic of which they knew nothing. "Shares! shares!" became the general cry. The ultimate issue of the projects themselves was a matter of no moment. The multitude were bitten by the universal rage for acquiring sudden fortunes without the labour of earning them. Provided they could but obtain allotments which they could sell at a premium, and put the profit—often the only capital they possessed[1]—into their pockets, it was enough for them. The mania was not confined to the precincts of the stock exchange, but infected all ranks throughout the country. Share markets were established in the provincial towns, where people might play their stakes as on a roulette table. The game was open to all,—to the workman, who drew his accumulation of small earnings out of the savings' bank to try a venture in shares; to the widow and spinster of small means, who had up to that time blessed God that their lot had lain between poverty and riches, but were now seized by the infatuation of becoming suddenly rich; to the professional man, who, watching the success of others, at length scorned the moderate gains of his calling, and rushed into speculation. The madness spread everywhere. It embraced merchants and manufacturers, gentry and shop-keepers, clerks in public offices and loungers at the clubs. Noble lords were pointed at as "stags"; there were even clergymen who were characterized as "bulls"; and amiable ladies who had the reputation of "bears," in the share markets. The few quiet men who remained uninfluenced by the speculation of the time, were, in not a few cases, even reproached for doing injustice to their families, in declining to help themselves from the stores of wealth that were poured out all around.

Folly and knavery were, for a time, completely in the ascendant. The sharpers of society were let loose, and jobbers and schemers became more and more plentiful. They threw out railway schemes as mere lures to catch the unwary. They fed the mania with a constant succession of new projects. The railway papers became loaded with their advertisements. The post-office was scarcely able to distribute the multitude of prospectuses and circulars which they issued. For the time their popularity was immense. They rose like froth

---

[1]The Marquis of Clanricarde brought under the notice of the House of Lords in 1845, that one Charles Guernsey, the son of a charwoman, and a clerk in a broker's office at 12s. a week, had his name down as a subscriber for shares in the London and York line, for 52,000l. Doubtless, he had been made useful for the purpose by the brokers, his employers.

into the upper heights of society, and the flunky Fitz Plushe, by virtue of his supposed wealth, sat amongst peers and was idolized. . . .

Parliament, whose previous conduct in connection with railway legislation was so open to reprehension, interposed no check—attempted no remedy. On the contrary, it helped to intensify the evils arising from this unseemly state of things. Many of its members were themselves involved in the mania, and as much interested in its continuance as were the vulgar herd of money-grubbers. The railway prospectuses now issued—unlike the original Liverpool and Manchester, and London and Birmingham schemes—were headed by peers, baronets, landed proprietors, and strings of M.Ps. Thus, it was found in 1845, that not fewer than 157 members of Parliament were on the lists of new companies as subscribers for sums ranging from 291,000*l.* downwards! The projectors of new lines even came to boast of their parliamentary strength, and of the number of votes which they could command in "the House." The influence which landowners had formerly brought to bear upon Parliament in resisting railways when called for by the public necessities, was now employed to carry measures of a far different kind, originated by cupidity, knavery, and folly. But these gentlemen had discovered by this time that railways were as a golden mine to them. They sat at railway boards, sometimes selling to themselves their own land at their own price, and paying themselves with the money of the unfortunate shareholders. Others used the railway mania as a convenient and, to themselves, comparatively inexpensive mode of purchasing constituencies. It was strongly suspected that honourable members adopted what Yankee legislators call "log-rolling," that is, "You help me to roll my log, and I help you to roll yours." At all events, it is matter of fact, that, through parliamentary influence, many utterly ruinous branches and extensions projected during the mania, calculated only to benefit the inhabitants of a few miserable old boroughs accidentally omitted from schedule A, were authorized in the memorable sessions of 1844 and 1845.

This boundless speculation of course gave abundant employment to the engineers. They were found ready to attach their names to the most daring and foolish projects—railways through hills, across arms of the sea, over or under great rivers, spanning valleys at great heights or boring their way under the ground, across barren moors, along precipices, over bogs, and through miles of London streets. One line was projected direct from Leeds to Liverpool, which, if constructed, would involve a tunnel, or a deep rock-cutting through the hills, twenty miles long. No scheme was so mad that it did not find an engineer, so called, ready to indorse it, and give it currency. Many of these, even men of distinction, sold the use of their names to the projectors. A thousand guineas was the price charged by one gentleman for the use of his name; and fortunate were the solicitors considered who succeeded in bagging an engineer of reputation for their prospectus.

Mr. Stephenson was anxiously entreated to lend his name in this way; but he invariably refused. Had he been less scrupulous, he might, without any trouble, have thus earned an enormous income; but he had no desire to accumulate a fortune without labour and without honour. He himself never speculated in shares. . . .

Among the characters brought prominently into notice by the mania, was the Railway navvy. The navvy was now a great man. He had grown rich, was a landowner, a railway shareholder, sometimes even a member of parliament; but he was a navvy still. He had imported the characteristics of his class into his new social position. He was always strong, rough, and ready; but withal he was unscrupulous. If there was a stout piece of work to be done, none could carry it out with greater energy, or execute it in better style according to contract—provided he was watched. But the navvy contractor was greatly given to "scamping." He was up to all sorts of disreputable tricks of the trade. In building a tunnel, he would, if he could, use half-baked clay instead of bricks, and put in two courses instead of four. He would scamp the foundations of bridges, use rubble instead of stone sets, and

Canadian timber instead of Memel for his viaducts; but he was greatest of all, perhaps, in the "scamping" of ballast. He had therefore—especially the leviathan navvy—to be very closely watched; and this was generally entrusted to railway inspectors at comparatively small salaries. The consequences were such as might have been anticipated. More bad and dishonest work was executed on the railways constructed in any single year subsequent to the mania, than was to be found on all the Stephenson lines during the preceding twenty years.

—•◆•—

A Lucky Speculator

WILLIAM MAKEPEACE THACKERAY

[FROM "Jeames's Diary"]

"Considerable sensation has been excited in the upper and lower circles in the West End, by a startling piece of good fortune which has befallen James Plush, Esq., lately footman in a respected family in Berkeley Square.

"One day last week, Mr. James waited upon his master, who is a banker in the City; and after a little blushing and hesitation, said he had saved a little money in service, was anxious to retire, and to invest his savings to advantage.

"His master (we believe we may mention, without offending delicacy, the well-known name of Sir George Flimsy, of the house of Flimsy, Diddler, and Flash) smilingly asked Mr. James what was the amount of his savings, wondering considerably how, out of an income of thirty guineas—the main part of which he spent in bouquets, silk stockings, and perfumery—Mr. Plush could have managed to lay by anything.

"Mr. Plush, with some hesitation, said he had been *speculating in railroads,* and stated his winnings to have been thirty thousand pounds. He had commenced his speculations with twenty, borrowed from a fellow-servant. He had dated his letters from the house in Berkeley Square, and humbly begged pardon of his master for not having instructed the Railway Secretaries who answered his applications to apply at the area-bell.

"Sir George, who was at breakfast, instantly rose, and shook Mr. P. by the hand; Lady Flimsy begged him to be seated, and partake of the breakfast which he had laid on the table; and has subsequently invited him to her grand *déjeuner* at Richmond, where it was observed that Miss Emily Flimsy, her beautiful and accomplished seventh daughter, paid the lucky gentleman *marked attention.*

"We hear it stated that Mr. P. is of a very ancient family (Hugo de la Pluche came over with the Conqueror); and the new brougham which he has started bears the ancient coat of his race.

"He has taken apartments in the Albany, and is a director of thirty-three railroads. He proposes to stand for Parliament at the next general election on decidedly Conservative principles, which have always been the politics of his family.

"Report says, that even in his humble capacity Miss Emily Flimsy had remarked his high demeanour. Well, 'None but the brave,' say we, 'deserve the fair.' "—*Morning Paper.* . . .

"Railway Spec is going on phamusly. You should see how polite they har at my bankers now! Sir Paul Pump Aldgate, & Company. They bow me out of the bank parlor as if I was a Nybobb. Everybody says I'm worth half a millium. The number of lines they're putting me upon, is inkumseavable. I've put Fitzwarren, my man, upon several. Reginald Fitzwarren, Esquire, looks splendid in a perspectus; and the raskle owns that he has made two thowsnd.

"How the ladies, & men too, foller and flatter me! If I go into Lady Binsis hopra box, she makes room for me, who ever is there, and cries out, 'O do make room for that dear creature!' And she complyments me on my taste in musick, or my new Broom-oss, or the phansy of my weskit, and always ends by asking me for some shares. Old Lord Bareacres, as stiff as a poaker, as prowd as Loosyfer, as poor as Joab—even he condysends to be sivvle to the great De la Pluche, and begged me at Harthur's, lately, in his sollom pompus way, 'to faver him with five minutes' conversation.' I knew what was coming—application for shares—put him down on my private list. Wouldn't mind the Scrag End Junction passing through Bareacres—hoped I'd come down and shoot there.

"I gave the old humbugg a few shares out of my own pocket. 'There, old Pride,' says I, 'I like to see you down on your knees to a footman. There, old Pompossaty! Take fifty pound; I like to see you come cringing and begging for it.' Whenever I see him in a *very* public place, I take my change for my money. I digg him in the ribs, or slap his padded old shoulders. I call him, 'Bareacres, my old buck!' and I see him wince. It does my art good. . . ."

"Have this day kimpleated a little efair with my friend George, Earl Bareacres, which I trust will be to the advantidge both of self & that noble gent. Adjining the Bareacre proppaty is a small piece of land of about 100 acres, called Squallop Hill, igseeding advantageous for the cultivation of sheep. . . . I gave Bareacres £50 an acre for this land (the igsact premium of my St. Helena Shares)—a very handsom price for land which never yielded two shillings an acre; and very convenient to his Lordship I know, who had a bill coming due at his Bankers which he had given them. James de la Pluche, Esquire, is thus for the fust time a landed proprietor— or rayther, I should say, is about to reshume the rank & dignity in the country which his Hancestors so long occupied.". . .

"As for Squallop Hill, its not to be emadgind that I was going to give 5000 lb. for a bleak mounting like that, unless I had some ideer in vew. Ham I not a Director of the Grand Diddlesex? Don't Squallop lie amediately betwigst Old Bone House, Single Gloster, and Scrag End, through which cities our line passes? I will have 400,000 lb. for that mounting, or my name is not Jeames. I have arranged a little barging too for my friend the Erl. The line will pass through a hangle of Bareacre Park. He shall have a good compensation I promis you; and then I shall get back the 3000 I lent him. His banker's account, I fear, is in a horrid state." . . .

"When my boddy-suvnt came with my ot water in the mawning, the livid copse in the charnill was not payler than the gashly De la Pluche!

" 'Give me the Share-list, Mandeville,' I micanickly igsclaimed. I had not perused it for the past 3 days, my etention being engayged elseware. Hevns & huth!—what was it I red there? What was it that made me spring outabed as if sumbady had given me cold pig?—I red Rewin in that Sharelist—the Pannick was in full hoparation!"

"Shall I describe that kitastrafy with which hall Hengland is familliar? My & rifewses to cronnicle the misfortns which lassarated my bleeding art in Hoctober last. On the fust of Hawgust where was I? Director of twenty-three Companies; older of scrip hall at a primmium, and worth at least a quarter of a millium. On Lord Mare's day, my Saint Helenas quotid at 14 pm, were down at $\frac{1}{2}$ discount; my Central Ichaboes at $\frac{3}{8}$ discount; my Table Mounting & Hottentot Grand Trunk, no where; my Bathershins and Derrynane Beg, of which I'd bought 2000 for the account at 17 primmium, down to nix; my Juan Fernandez, my Great Central Oregons, prostrit. There was a momint when I thought I shouldn't be alive to write my own tail!"

(Here follow in Mr. Plush's MS. about twenty-four pages of railroad calculations, which we pretermit.)

"Those beests, Pump & Aldgate, once so cringing and umble, wrote me a threatnen letter because I overdrew my account three-and-sixpence: woodn't advance me five thousand on 25,000 worth of scrip; kep me waiting 2 hours when I asked to see the house; and then sent out Spout, the jewnior partner, saying they wouldn't discount my paper, and implawed me to clothes my account. I did: I paid the three-and-six balliance, and never sor 'em mor.

"The market fell daily. The Rewin grew wusser and wusser. Hagnies, Hagnies! It wasn't in the city aloan my misfortns came upon me. They beerded me in my own ome. The biddle who kips watch at the Halbany wodn keep misfortn out of my chambers; and Mrs. Twiddler, of Pall Mall, and Mr. Hunx, of Long Acre, put egsicution into my apartmince, and swep off every stick of my furniture. 'Wardrobe & furniture of a man of fashion.' What an adwertisement George Robins *did* make of it; and what a crowd was collected to laff at the prospick of my ruing! My chice plait; my seller of wine; my picturs—that of myself included (it was Maryhann, bless her! that bought it, unbeknown to me); all—all went to the ammer. That brootle Fitzwarren, my exvally, womb I met, fimilliarly slapt me on the sholder, and said, 'Jeames, my boy, you'd best go into suvvis aginn.'

"I *did* go into suvvis—the wust of all suvvices—I went into the Queen's Bench Prison, and lay there a misrabble captif for 6 mortial weeks. Misrabble shall I say? no, not misrabble altogether; there was sunlike in the dunjing of the pore prisner. I had visitors. A cart used to drive hup to the prizn gates of Saturdays; a washy-woman's cart, with a fat old lady in it, and a young one. Who was that young one? Everyone who has an art can gess, it was my blue-eyed blushing hangel of a Mary Hann! 'Shall we take him out in the linnen-basket, Grandmamma?' Mary Hann said. Bless her, she'd already learned to say grandmamma quite natral; but I didn't go out that way; I went out by the door a white-washed man. Ho, what a feast there was at Healing the day I came out! I'd thirteen shillings left when I'd bought the gold ring. I wasn't prowd. I turned the mangle for three weeks; and then Uncle Bill said, 'Well, there *is* some good in the feller'; and it was agreed that we should marry."

The Plush manuscript finishes here; it is many weeks since we saw the accomplished writer, and we have only just learned his fate. We are happy to state that it is a comfortable and almost a prosperous one. . . .

Lady Angelina Silvertop presented five hundred pounds to her faithful and affectionate servant, Mary Ann Hoggins, on her marriage with Mr. James Plush, to whom her Ladyship also made a handsome present—namely, the lease, good-will, and fixtures of the "Wheel of Fortune" public-house, near Shepherd's Market, Mayfair: a house greatly frequented by all the nobility's footmen, doing a genteel stroke of business in the neighbourhood, and where, as we have heard, the "Butlers' Club" is held.

Here Mr. Plush lives, happy in a blooming and interesting wife: reconciled to a middle sphere of life, as he was to a humbler and a higher one before. He has shaved off his whiskers, and accommodates himself to an apron with perfect good-humour. A gentleman connected with this establishment dined at the "Wheel of Fortune" the other day, and collected the above particulars. Mr. Plush blushed rather, as he brought in the first dish, and told his story very modestly over a pint of excellent port. He had only one thing in life to complain of, he said—that a witless version of his adventures had been produced at the Princess's Theatre, "without with your leaf or by your leaf," as he expressed it. "Has for the rest," the worthy fellow said, "I'm appy—praps betwixt you and me I'm in my proper spear. I enjy my glass of beer or port (with your elth & my suvvice to you, sir) quite as much as my clarrit in my prawsprus days. I've a good business, which is likely to be better. If a man can't be appy with such a wife as my Mary Hann, he's a beest: and when a christening takes place in our famly, will you give my complments to *Mr. Punch,* and ask him to be godfather."

Mr. Bounderby

CHARLES DICKENS

[FROM *Hard Times*]

1854

Not being Mrs. Grundy, who *was* Mr. Bounderby?

Why, Mr. Bounderby was as near being Mr. Gradgrind's bosom friend, as a man perfectly devoid of sentiment can approach that spiritual relationship towards another man perfectly devoid of sentiment. So near was Mr. Bounderby—or, if the reader prefer it, so far off.

He was a rich man; banker, merchant, manufacturer, and what not. A big, loud man, with a stare, and a metallic laugh. A man made out of a coarse material, which seemed to have been stretched to make so much of him. A man with a great puffed head and forehead, swelled veins in his temples, and such a strained skin to his face that it seemed to hold his eyes open, and lift his eyebrows up. A man with a pervading appearance on him of being inflated like a balloon, and ready to start. A man who could never sufficiently vaunt himself a self-made man. A man who was always proclaiming, through that brassy speaking-trumpet of a voice of his, his old ignorance and his old poverty. A man who was the Bully of humility.

A year or two younger than his eminently practical friend, Mr. Bounderby looked older; his seven or eight and forty might have had the seven or eight added to it again, without surprising anybody. He had not much hair. One might have fancied he had talked it off; and that what was left, all standing up in disorder, was in that condition from being constantly blown about by his windy boastfulness.

From Chapter 4.

In the formal drawing-room of Stone Lodge, standing on the hearthrug, warming himself before the fire, Mr. Bounderby delivered some observations to Mrs. Gradgrind on the circumstance of its being his birthday. He stood before the fire, partly because it was a cool spring afternoon, though the sun shone; partly because the shade of Stone Lodge was always haunted by the ghost of damp mortar; partly because he thus took up a commanding position, from which to subdue Mrs. Gradgrind.

"I hadn't a shoe to my foot. As to a stocking, I didn't know such a thing by name. I passed the day in a ditch, and the night in a pigsty. That's the way I spent my tenth birthday. Not that a ditch was new to me, for I was born in a ditch."

Mrs. Gradgrind, a little, thin, white, pink-eyed bundle of shawls, of surpassing feebleness, mental and bodily; who was always taking physic without any effect, and who, whenever she showed a symptom of coming to life, was invariably stunned by some weighty piece of fact tumbling on her; Mrs. Gradgrind hoped it was a dry ditch?

"No! As wet as a sop. A foot of water in it," said Mr. Bounderby.

"Enough to give a baby cold," Mrs. Gradgrind considered.

"Cold? I was born with inflammation of the lungs, and of everything else, I believe, that was capable of inflammation," returned Mr. Bounderby. "For years, ma'am, I was one of the most miserable little wretches ever seen. I was so sickly, that I was always moaning and groaning. I was so ragged and dirty, that you wouldn't have touched me with a pair of tongs."

Mrs. Gradgrind faintly looked at the tongs, as the most appropriate thing her imbecility could think of doing.

"How I fought through it, *I* don't know," said Bounderby. "I was determined, I suppose. I have been a determined character in later life, and I suppose I was then. Here I am, Mrs. Gradgrind, anyhow, and nobody to thank for my being here, but myself."

Mrs. Gradgrind meekly and weakly hoped that his mother—

"*My* mother? Bolted, ma'am!" said Bounderby.

Mrs. Gradgrind, stunned as usual, collapsed, and gave it up.

"My mother left me to my grandmother," said Bounderby; "and, according to the best of my remembrance, my grandmother was the wickedest and the worst old woman that ever lived. If I got a little pair of shoes by any chance, she would take 'em off and sell 'em for drink. Why, I have known that grandmother of mine lie in her bed and drink her four-teen glasses of liquor before breakfast!"

Mrs. Gradgrind, weekly smiling, and giving no other sign of vitality, looked (as she always did) like an indifferently executed transparency of a small female figure, without enough light behind it.

"She kept a chandler's shop," pursued Bounderby, "and kept me in an egg-box. That was the cot of *my* infancy; an old egg-box. As soon as I was big enough to run away, of course I ran away. Then I became a young vagabond; and instead of one old woman knocking me about and starving me, everybody of all ages knocked me about and starved me. They were right; they had no business to do anything else. I was a nuisance, an incumbrance, and a pest. I know that very well."

His pride in having at any time of his life achieved such a great social distinction as to be a nuisance, an incumbrance, and a pest, was only to be satisfied by three sonorous repetitions of the boast.

"I was to pull through it I suppose, Mrs. Gradgrind. Whether I was to do it or not, ma'am, I did it. I pulled through it, though nobody threw me out a rope. Vagabond, errand-boy, vagabond, labourer, porter, clerk, chief manager, small partner, Josiah Bounderby of Coketown. Those are the antecedents, and the culmination. Josiah Bounderby of Coketown learnt his letters from the outsides of the shops, Mrs. Gradgrind, and was first able to tell the time upon a dialplate, from studying the steeple clock of St. Giles's Church, London, under the direction of a drunken cripple, who was a convicted thief, and an incorrigible vagrant. Tell Josiah Bounderby of Coketown, of your district schools and your model schools, and your training schools, and your whole kettle-of-fish of schools; and Josiah Bounderby of Coketown, tells you plainly, all right, all correct—he hadn't such advantages—but let us have hard-headed, solid-fisted people—the education that made him won't do for everybody, he knows well—such and such his education was, however, and you may force him to swallow boiling fat, but you shall never force him to suppress the facts of his life."

Being heated when he arrived at this climax, Josiah Bounderby of Coketown stopped.

——•◆•——

Traffic

JOHN RUSKIN

[FROM *The Crown of Wild Olive*]

1864 [1873]

My good Yorkshire friends, you asked me down here among your hills that I might talk to you about this Exchange you are going to build; but, earnestly and seriously asking you to pardon me, I am going to do nothing of the kind. I cannot talk, or at least can say very little, about this same Exchange. I must talk of quite other things, though not willingly;—I could not deserve your pardon, if, when you invited me to speak on one subject, I *wilfully* spoke on another. But I cannot speak, to purpose, of anything about which I do not care; and most simply and sorrowfully I have to tell you, in the outset, that I do *not* care about this Exchange of yours.

If, however, when you sent me your invitation, I had answered, "I won't come, I don't care about the Exchange of

From Lecture 2.

Bradford," you would have been justly offended with me, not knowing the reason of so blunt a carelessness. So I have come down, hoping that you will patiently let me tell you why, on this, and many other such occasions, I now remain silent, when formerly I should have caught at the opportunity of speaking to a gracious audience.

In a word, then, I do not care about this Exchange—because *you* don't; and because you know perfectly well I cannot make you. Look at the essential conditions of the case, which you, as business men, know perfectly well, though perhaps you think I forget them. You are going to spend £30,000, which to you, collectively, is nothing; the buying a new coat is, as to the cost of it, a much more important matter of consideration to me, than building a new Exchange is to you. But you think you may as well have the right thing for your money. You know there are a great many odd styles of architecture about; you don't want to do anything ridiculous; you hear of me, among others, as a respectable architectural man-milliner; and you send for me, that I may tell you the leading fashion; and what is, in our shops, for the moment, the newest and sweetest thing in pinnacles.

Now, pardon me for telling you frankly, you cannot have good architecture merely by asking people's advice on occasion. All good architecture is the expression of national life and character; and it is produced by a prevalent and eager national taste, or desire for beauty. And I want you to think a little of the deep significance of this word "taste," for no statement of mine has been more earnestly or oftener controverted than that good taste is essentially a moral quality. "No," say many of my antagonists, "taste is one thing, morality is another. Tell us what is pretty: we shall be glad to know that; but we need no sermons—even were you able to preach them, which may be doubted."

Permit me, therefore, to fortify this old dogma of mine somewhat. Taste is not only a part and an index of morality;—it is the ONLY morality. The first, and last, and closest trial question to any living creature is, 'What do you like?' Tell me what you like, and I'll tell you what you are. Go out into the street, and ask the first man or woman you meet, what their "taste" is; and if they answer candidly, you know them, body and soul. "You, my friend in the rags, with the unsteady gait, what do *you* like?" "A pipe and a quartern of gin." I know you. "You, good woman, with the quick step and tidy bonnet, what do you like?" "A swept hearth, and a clean tea-table; and my husband opposite me, and a baby at my breast." Good, I know you also. "You, little girl with the golden hair and the soft eyes, what do you like?" "My canary, and a run among the wood hyacinths." "You, little boy with the dirty hands, and the low forehead, what do you like?" "A shy at the sparrows, and a game at pitch farthing." Good; we know them all now. What more need we ask?

"Nay," perhaps you answer; "we need rather to ask what these people and children do, than what they like. If they *do* right, it is no matter that they like what is wrong; and if they *do* wrong, it is no matter that they like what is right. Doing is the great thing; and it does not matter that the man likes drinking, so that he does not drink; nor that the little girl likes to be kind to her canary, if she will not learn her lessons; nor that the little boy likes throwing stones at the sparrows, if he goes to the Sunday school." Indeed, for a short time, and in a provisional sense, this is true. For if, resolutely, people do what is right, in time to come they like doing it. But they only are in a right moral state when they *have* come to like doing it; and as long as they don't like it, they are still in a vicious state. The man is not in health of body who is always thinking of the bottle in the cupboard, though he bravely bears his thirst; but the man who heartily enjoys water in the morning, and wine in the evening, each in its proper quantity and time. And the entire object of true education is to make people not merely *do* the right things, but *enjoy* the right things:—not merely industrious, but to love industry—not merely learned; but to love knowledge—not merely pure, but to love purity— not merely just, but to hunger and thirst after justice. . . .

As I was thinking over this, in walking up Fleet Street the other day, my eye caught the title of a book standing open in a bookseller's window. It was—"On the necessity of the diffusion of taste among all classes." "Ah," I thought to myself, "my classifying friend, when you have diffused your taste, where will your classes be? The man who likes what you like, belongs to the same class with you, I think. Inevitably so. You may put him to other work if you choose; but, by the condition you have brought him into, he will dislike the work as much as you would yourself. You get hold of a scavenger or a costermonger, who enjoyed the Newgate Calendar for literature, and 'Pop goes the Weasel' for music. You think you can make him like Dante and Beethoven? I wish you joy of your lessons; but if you do, you have made a gentleman of him—he won't like to go back to his coster-mongering."

And so completely and unexceptionally is this so, that, if I had time tonight, I could show you that a nation cannot be affected by any vice, or weakness, without expressing it, legibly, and for ever, either in bad art, or by want of art; and that there is no national virtue, small or great, which is not manifestly expressed in all the art which circumstances enable the people possessing that virtue to produce. Take, for instance, your great English virtue of enduring and patient courage. You have at present in England only one art of any consequence—that is, iron-working. You know thoroughly well how to cast and hammer iron. Now, do you think, in those masses of lava which you build volcanic cones to melt, and which you forge at the mouths of the Infernos you have created; do you think, on those iron plates, your courage and endurance are not written for ever,—not merely with an iron pen, but on iron parchment? And take also your great English vice—European vice—vice of all the world—vice of all other worlds that roll or shine in heaven, bearing with them yet the atmosphere of hell—the vice of jealousy, which brings competition into your commerce, treachery into your councils, and dishonour into your wars . . . do you think that this national shame and dastardliness of heart are not written as legibly on every rivet of your iron armour as the strength of the right hands that forged it? . . .

I notice that among all the new buildings which cover your once wild hills, churches and schools are mixed in due, that is to say, in large proportion, with your mills and mansions; and I notice also that the churches and schools are almost always Gothic, and the mansions and mills are never Gothic. May I ask the meaning of this? for, remember, it is peculiarly a modern phenomenon. When Gothic was invented, houses were Gothic as well as churches; and when the Italian style superseded the Gothic, churches were Italian as well as houses. . . . But now you live under one school of architecture, and worship under another. What do you mean by doing this? Am I to understand that you are thinking of changing your architecture back to Gothic; and that you treat your churches experimentally, because it does not matter what mistakes you make in a church? Or am I to understand that you consider Gothic a pre-eminently sacred and beautiful mode of building, which you think, like the fine frankincense, should be mixed for the tabernacle only, and reserved for your religious services? For if this be the feeling, though it may seem at first as if it were graceful and reverent, at the root of the matter, it signifies neither more nor less than that you have separated your religion from your life . . . .

"But what has all this to do with our Exchange?" you ask me, impatiently. My dear friends, it has just everything to do with it; on these inner and great questions depend all the outer and little ones; and if you have asked me down here to speak to you, because you had before been interested in anything I have written, you must know that all I have yet said about architecture was to show this . . . . And now, you ask me what style is best to build in, and how can I answer, knowing the meaning of the two styles, but by another question—do you mean to build as Christians or as Infidels? And still more—do you mean to build as honest Christians or as honest Infidels? as thoroughly and confessedly either one or the other? You don't like to be asked such rude questions. I cannot help it; they are of much more importance than this Exchange business; and if they can be at once answered, the Exchange business settles itself in a moment. . . .

I hope, now, that there is no risk of your misunderstanding me when I come to the gist of what I want to say tonight—when I repeat, that every great national architecture has been the result and exponent of a great national religion. You can't have bits of it here, bits there—you must have it everywhere or nowhere. It is not the monopoly of a clerical company—it is not the exponent of a theological dogma—it is not the hieroglyphic writing of an initiated priesthood; it is the manly language of a people inspired by resolute and common purpose, and rendering resolute and common fidelity to the legible laws of an undoubted God.

Now there have as yet been three distinct schools of European architecture. I say, European, because Asiatic and African architectures belong so entirely to other races and climates, that there is no question of them here; only, in passing, I will simply assure you that whatever is good or great in Egypt, and Syria, and India, is just as good or great for the same reasons as the buildings on our side of the Bosphorus. We Europeans, then, have had three great religions: the Greek, which was the worship of the God of Wisdom and Power; the Mediæval, which was the worship of the God of Judgment and Consolation; the Renaissance, which was the worship of the God of Pride and Beauty: these three we have had—they are past—and now, at last, we English have got a fourth religion, and a God of our own, about which I want to ask you. . . .

You know we are speaking always of the real, active, continual, national worship; that by which men act, while they live; not that which they talk of, when they die. Now, we have, indeed, a nominal religion, to which we pay tithes of property and sevenths of time; but we have also a practical and earnest religion, to which we devote nine-tenths of our property and six-sevenths of our time. And we dispute a great deal about the nominal religion: but we are all unanimous about this practical one; of which I think you will admit that the ruling goddess may be best generally described as the "Goddess of Getting-on," or "Britannia of the Market." The Athenians had an "Athena Agoraia," or Athena of the Mar-

ket; but she was a subordinate type of their goddess, while our
Britannia Agoraia is the principal type of ours. And all your
great architectural works are, of course, built to her. It is long
since you built a great cathedral; and how you would laugh
at me if I proposed building a cathedral on the top of one
of these hills of yours, to make it an Acropolis! But your railroad mounds, vaster than the walls of Babylon; your railroad
stations, vaster than the temple of Ephesus, and innumerable;
your chimneys, how much more mighty and costly than cathedral spires! your harbour-piers; your warehouses; your exchanges!—all these are built to your great Goddess of "Getting-on"; and she has formed, and will continue to form, your
architecture, as long as you worship her; and it is quite
vain to ask me to tell you how to build to *her;* you know far
better than I.

There might, indeed, on some theories, be a conceivably
good architecture for Exchanges—that is to say, if there were
any heroism in the fact or deed of exchange which might be
typically carved on the outside of your building. For, you
know, all beautiful architecture must be adorned with sculpture or painting; and for sculpture or painting, you must have
a subject. And hitherto it has been a received opinion among
the nations of the world that the only right subjects for either,
were *heroisms* of some sort. Even on his pots and his flagons,
the Greek put a Hercules slaying lions, or an Apollo slaying
serpents, or Bacchus slaying melancholy giants, and earth-born
despondencies. On his temples, the Greek put contests of
great warriors in founding states, or of gods with evil spirits.
On his houses and temples alike, the Christian put carvings
of angels conquering devils; or of hero-martyrs exchanging
this world for another; subject inappropriate, I think, to our
manner of exchange here. And the Master of Christians not
only left His followers without any orders as to the sculpture
of affairs of exchange on the outside of buildings, but gave
some strong evidence of His dislike of affairs of exchange
within them. And yet there might surely be a heroism in such
affairs; and all commerce become a kind of selling of doves,
not impious. The wonder has always been great to me, that

heroism has never been supposed to be in any wise consistent with the practice of supplying people with food, or clothes; but rather with that of quartering one's self upon them for food, and stripping them of their clothes. Spoiling of armour is an heroic deed in all ages; but the selling of clothes, old or new, has never taken any colour of magnanimity. Yet one does not see why feeding the hungry and clothing the naked should ever become base businesses, even when engaged in on a large scale. If one could contrive to attach the notion of conquest to them anyhow! so that, supposing there were anywhere an obstinate race, who refused to be comforted, one might take some pride in giving them compulsory comfort! and, as it were, *"occupying* a country" with one's gifts, instead of one's armies? If one could only consider it as much a victory to get a barren field sown, as to get an eared field stripped; and contend who should build villages, instead of who should "carry" them! Are not all forms of heroism conceivable in doing these serviceable deeds? You doubt who is strongest? It might be ascertained by push of spade, as well as push of sword. Who is wisest? There are witty things to be thought of in planning other business than campaigns. Who is bravest? There are always the elements to fight with, stronger than men; and nearly as merciless. The only absolutely and unapproachably heroic element in the soldier's work seems to be—that he is paid little for it—and regularly: while you traffickers, and exchangers, and others occupied in presumably benevolent business, like to be paid much for it—and by chance . . . .

If you chose to take the matter up on any such soldierly principle; to do your commerce, and your feeding of nations, for fixed salaries; and to be as particular about giving people the best food, and the best cloth, as soldiers are about giving them the best gunpowder, I could carve something for you on your exchange worth looking at. But I can only at present suggest decorating its frieze with pendant purses; and making its pillars broad at the base, for the sticking of bills. And in the innermost chambers of it there might be a statue of Britannia of the Market, who may have, perhaps advisably, a partridge for her crest, typical at once of her courage in fighting for noble ideas, and of her interest in game; and round its neck; the inscription in golden letters, "Perdix fovit quæ non peperit." Then, for her spear, she might have a weaver's beam; and on her shield, instead of St. George's Cross, the Milanese boar, semi-fleeced, with the town of Gennesaret proper, in the field; and the legend, "In the best market," and her corslet, of leather, folded over her heart in the shape of a purse, with thirty slits in it, for a piece of money to go in at, on each day of the month. And I doubt not but that people would come to see your exchange, and its goddess, with applause.

Nevertheless, I want to point out to you certain strange characters in this goddess of yours. She differs from the great Greek and Mediæval deities essentially in two things—first, as to the continuance of her presumed power; secondly, as to the extent of it.

1st as to the Continuance.

The Greek Goddess of Wisdom gave continual increase of wisdom, as the Christian Spirit of Comfort (or Comforter) continual increase of comfort. There was no question, with these, of any limit or cessation of function. But with your Agora Goddess, that is just the most important question. Getting on—but where to? Gathering together—but how much? Do you mean to gather always—never to spend? If so, I wish you joy of your goddess, for I am just as well off as you, without the trouble of worshipping her at all. But if you do not spend, somebody else will — somebody else must. And it is because of this (among many other such errors) that I have fearlessly declared your so-called science of Political Economy to be no science; because, namely, it has omitted the study of exactly the most important branch of the business—the study of *spending*. For spend you must, and as much as you make ultimately . . . . Well, what in the name of Plutus is it you want? Not gold, not greenbacks, not ciphers after a capital I? You will have to answer, after all, "No; we want, somehow or other, money's *worth*." Well, what is that? Let your Goddess of Getting-on discover it, and let her learn to stay therein.

2nd. But there is yet another question to be asked respecting this Goddess of Getting-on. The first was of the continuance of her power; the second is of its extent.

Pallas and the Madonna were supposed to be all the world's Pallas, and all the world's Madonna. They could teach all men, and they could comfort all men. But, look strictly into the nature of the power of your Goddess of Getting-on; and you will find she is the Goddess—not of everybody's getting on—but only of somebody's getting on. This is a vital, or rather deathful, distinction. Examine it in your own ideal of the state of national life which this Goddess is to evoke and maintain. . . .

Your ideal of human life then is, I think, that it should be passed in a pleasant undulating world, with iron and coal everywhere underneath it. On each pleasant bank of this world is to be a beautiful mansion, with two wings; and stables, and coach-houses; a moderately-sized park; a large garden and hot-houses; and pleasant carriage drives through the shrubberies. In this mansion are to live the favoured votaries of the Goddess; the English gentleman, with his gracious wife, and his beautiful family; always able to have the boudoir and the jewels for the wife, and the beautiful ball dresses for the daughters, and hunters for the sons, and a shooting in the Highlands for himself. At the bottom of the bank, is to be the mill; not less than a quarter of a mile long with one steam engine at each end, and two in the middle, and a chimney three hundred feet high. In this mill are to be in constant employment from eight hundred to a thousand workers, who never drink, never strike, always go to church on Sunday, and always express themselves in respectful language.

Is not that, broadly, and in the main features, the kind of thing you propose to yourselves? It is very pretty indeed, seen from above; not at all so pretty, seen from below. For, observe, while to one family this deity is indeed the Goddess of Getting-on, to a thousand families she is the Goddess of *not* Getting-on. "Nay," you say, "they have all their chance." Yes, so has every one in a lottery, but there must always be the same number of blanks. "Ah! but in a lottery it is not

skill and intelligence which take the lead, but blind chance."
What then! do you think the old practice, that "they should
take who have the power, and they should keep who can,"
is less iniquitous, when the power has become power of brains
instead of fist? and that, though we may not take advantage
of a child's or a woman's weakness, we may of a man's
foolishness? "Nay, but finally, work must be done, and some
one must be at the top, some one at the bottom." Granted,
my friends. Work must always be, and captains of work must
always be; and if you in the least remember the tone of any
of my writings, you must know that they are thought unfit for
this age, because they are always insisting on need of government, and speaking with scorn of liberty. But I beg you to
observe that there is a wide difference between being captains
or governors of work, and taking the profits of it. It does
not follow, because you are general of an army, that you are
to take all the treasure, or land, it wins (if it fight for treasure
or land); neither, because you are king of a nation, that you
are to consume all the profits of the nation's work. Real kings,
on the contrary, are known invariably by their doing quite
the reverse of this—by their taking the least possible quantity
of the nation's work for themselves. There is no test of real
kinghood so infallible as that. . . .

You will tell me I need not preach against these things,
for I cannot mend them. No, good friends, I cannot; but you
can, and you will; or something else can and will. Even good
things have no abiding power—and shall these evil things
persist in victorious evil? All history shows, on the contrary,
that to be the exact thing they never can do. Change *must*
come; but it is ours to determine whether change of growth,
or change of death. Shall the Parthenon be in ruins on its
rock, and Bolton priory in its meadow, but these mills of
yours be the consummation of the buildings of the earth, and
their wheels be as the wheels of eternity? Think you that
"men may come, and men may go," but—mills—go on for
ever? Not so; out of these, better or worse shall come; and it
is for you to choose which.

Sweetness and Light

MATTHEW ARNOLD

[FROM *Culture and Anarchy*]

1869

The disparagers of culture make its motive curiosity; sometimes, indeed, they make its motive mere exclusiveness and vanity. The culture which is supposed to plume itself on a smattering of Greek and Latin is a culture which is begotten by nothing so intellectual as curiosity; it is valued either out of sheer vanity and ignorance or else as an engine of social and class distinction, separating its holder, like a badge or title, from other people who have not got it. No serious man would call this *culture*, or attach any value to it, as culture, at all. To find the real ground for the very different estimate which serious people will set upon culture, we must find some motive for culture in the terms of which may lie a real ambiguity; and such a motive the word *curiosity* gives us.

I have before now pointed out that we English do not, like the foreigners, use this word in a good sense as well as in a bad sense. With us the word is always used in a somewhat disapproving sense. A liberal and intelligent eagerness about the things of the mind may be meant by a foreigner when he speaks of curiosity, but with us the word always conveys a certain notion of frivolous and unedifying activity. In the *Quarterly Review*, some little time ago, was an estimate of the celebrated French critic, M. Sainte-Beuve, and a very inadequate estimate it in my judgment was. And its inadequacy consisted chiefly in this: that in our English way it left out of sight the double sense really involved in the word *curiosity*, thinking enough was said to stamp M. Sainte-Beuve with

From Chapter 1.

blame if it was said that he was impelled in his operations
as a critic by curiosity, and omitting either to perceive that
M. Sainte-Beuve himself, and many other people with him,
would consider that this was praiseworthy and not blame-
worthy, or to point out why it ought really to be accounted
worthy of blame and not of praise. For as there is a curiosity
about intellectual matters which is futile, and merely a disease,
so there is certainly a curiosity,—a desire after the things
of the mind simply for their own sakes and for the pleasure
of seeing them as they are,—which is, in an intelligent being,
natural and laudable. Nay, and the very desire to see things
as they are implies a balance and regulation of mind which
is not often attained without fruitful effort, and which is the
very opposite of the blind and diseased impulse of mind
which is what we mean to blame when we blame curiosity.
Montesquieu says: "The first motive which ought to impel us
to study is the desire to augment the excellence of our nature,
and to render an intelligent being yet more intelligent." This
is the true ground to assign for the genuine scientific passion,
however manifested, and for culture, viewed simply as a fruit
of this passion; and it is a worthy ground, even though we let
the term *curiosity* stand to describe it.

But there is of culture another view, in which not solely
the scientific passion, the sheer desire to see things as they
are, natural and proper in an intelligent being, appears as
the ground of it. There is a view in which all the love of our
neighbour, the impulses towards action, help, and beneficence,
the desire for removing human error, clearing human confusion, and diminishing human misery, the noble aspiration to
leave the world better and happier than we found it,—motives
eminently such as are called social,—come in as part of the
grounds of culture, and the main and pre-eminent part. Culture is then properly described not as having its origin in
curiosity, but as having its origin in the love of perfection;
it is *a study of perfection*. It moves by the force, not merely
or primarily of the scientific passion for pure knowledge, but
also of the moral and social passion for doing good. As, in
the first view of it, we took for its worthy motto Montesquieu's

words: "To render an intelligent being yet more intelligent!" so, in the second view of it, there is no better motto which it can have than these words of Bishop Wilson: "To make reason and the will of God prevail!"

Only, whereas the passion for doing good is apt to be over-hasty in determining what reason and the will of God say, because its turn is for acting rather than thinking and it wants to be beginning to act; and whereas it is apt to take its own conceptions, which proceed from its own state of development and share in all the imperfections and immaturities of this, for a basis of action; what distinguishes culture is, that it is possessed by the scientific passion as well as by the passion of doing good; that it demands worthy notions of reason and the will of God, and does not readily suffer its own crude conceptions to substitute themselves for them. And knowing that no action or institution can be salutary and stable which is not based on reason and the will of God, it is not so bent on acting and instituting, even with the great aim of diminish-ing human error and misery ever before its thoughts, but that it can remember that acting and instituting are of little use, unless we know how and what we ought to act and to institute.

This culture is more interesting and more far-reaching than that other, which is founded solely on the scientific passion for knowing. But it needs times of faith and ardour, times when the intellectual horizon is opening and widening all round us, to flourish in . . . . The danger now is, not that people should obstinately refuse to allow anything but their old routine to pass for reason and the will of God, but either that they should allow some novelty or other to pass for these too easily, or else that they should under-rate the importance of them altogether, and think it enough to follow action for its own sake, without troubling themselves to make reason and the will of God prevail therein . . . .

The moment this view of culture is seized, the moment it is regarded not solely as the endeavour to see things as they are, to draw towards a knowledge of the universal order which seems to be intended and aimed at in the world, and which it is a man's happiness to go along with or his misery to go counter to,—to learn, in short, the will of God,—the moment, I say, culture is considered not merely as the endeavour to *see* and *learn* this, but as the endeavour, also, to make it *prevail,* the moral, social, and beneficent character of culture becomes manifest . . . .

And religion, the greatest and most important of the efforts by which the human race has manifested its impulse to perfect itself,—religion, that voice of the deepest human experience, —does not only enjoin and sanction the aim which is the great aim of culture, the aim of setting ourselves to ascertain what perfection is and to make it prevail; but also, in determining generally in what human perfection consists, religion comes to a conclusion identical with that which culture,— culture seeking the determination of this question through *all* the voices of human experience which have been heard upon it, of art, science, poetry, philosophy, history, as well as of religion, in order to give a greater fulness and certainty to its solution,—likewise reaches. Religion says: *The kingdom of God is within you;* and culture, in like manner, places human perfection in an *internal* condition, in the growth and predominance of our humanity proper, as distinguished from our animality. It places it in the ever-increasing efficacy and in the general harmonious expansion of those gifts of thought and feeling, which make the peculiar dignity, wealth, and happiness of human nature . . . . Not a having and a resting, but a growing and a becoming, is the character of perfection as culture conceives it; and here, too, it coincides with religion . . . .

Faith in machinery is, I said, our besetting danger; often in machinery most absurdly disproportioned to the end which this machinery, if it is to do any good at all, is to serve; but always in machinery, as if it had a value in and for itself. What is freedom but machinery? what is population but machinery? what is coal but machinery? what are railroads but machinery? what is wealth but machinery? what are, even, religious organisations but machinery? Now almost every voice in England is accustomed to speak of these things as if they were precious ends in themselves, and therefore had some of the characters of perfection indisputably joined to them. I have before now noticed Mr. Roebuck's stock argument for proving the greatness and happiness of England as she is, and for quite stopping the mouths of all gainsayers. Mr. Roebuck is never weary of reiterating this argument of his, so I do not know why I should be weary of noticing it. "May not every man in England say what he likes?"— Mr. Roebuck perpetually asks; and that, he thinks, is quite sufficient, and when every man may say what he likes, our aspirations ought to be satisfied. But the aspirations of culture, which is the study of perfection, are not satisfied, unless what men say, when they may say what they like, is worth saying,— has good in it, and more good than bad. In the same way the *Times,* replying to some foreign strictures on the dress, looks, and behaviour of the English abroad, urges that the English ideal is that every one should be free to do and to look just as he likes. But culture indefatigably tries, not to make what each raw person may like the rule by which he fashions himself; but to draw ever nearer to a sense of what is indeed beautiful, graceful, and becoming, and to get the raw person to like that. . . .

Wealth, again, that end to which our prodigious works for material advantage are directed,—the commonest of commonplaces tells us how men are always apt to regard wealth as a precious end in itself; and certainly they have never been so apt thus to regard it as they are in England at the present time. Never did people believe anything more firmly than nine Englishmen out of ten at the present day believe that our greatness and welfare are proved by our being so very rich. Now, the use of culture is that it helps us, by means of its spiritual standard of perfection, to regard wealth as but machinery, and not only to say as a matter of words that we regard wealth as but machinery, but really to perceive and feel that it is so. If it were not for this purging effect wrought upon our minds by culture, the whole world, the future as well as the present, would inevitably belong to the Philistines. The people who believe most that our greatness and welfare

are proved by our being very rich, and who most give their
lives and thoughts to becoming rich, are just the very people
whom we call Philistines. Culture says: "Consider these people,
then, their way of life, their habits, their manners, the very
tones of their voice; look at them attentively; observe the
literature they read, the things which give them pleasure, the
words which come forth out of their mouths, the thoughts
which make the furniture of their minds; would any amount
of wealth be worth having with the condition that one was
to become just like these people by having it?" And thus
culture begets a dissatisfaction which is of the highest possible
value in stemming the common tide of men's thoughts in a
wealthy and industrial community, and which saves the future,
as one may hope, from being vulgarised, even if it cannot
save the present.

Population, again, and bodily health and vigour, are things
which are nowhere treated in such an unintelligent, misleading,
exaggerated way as in England. Both are really machinery;
yet how many people all around us do we see rest in them and
fail to look beyond them! Why, one has heard people, fresh
from reading certain articles of the *Times* on the Registrar-
General's returns of marriages and births in this country, who
would talk of our large English families in quite a solemn
strain, as if they had something in itself beautiful, elevating,
and meritorious in them; as if the British Philistine would
have only to present himself before the Great Judge with his
twelve children, in order to be received among the sheep as a
matter of right!

But bodily health and vigour, it may be said, are not to
be classed with wealth and population as mere machinery;
they have a more real and essential value. . . . Every one with
anything like an adequate idea of human perfection has distinctly marked this subordination to higher and spiritual ends
of the cultivation of bodily vigour and activity. "Bodily exercise profiteth little; but godliness is profitable unto all things,"
says the author of the Epistle to Timothy. And the utilitarian
Franklin says just as explicitly:—"Eat and drink such an exact
quantity as suits the constitution of thy body, *in reference to*

the services of the mind." But the point of view of culture, keeping the mark of human perfection simply and broadly in view, and not assigning to this perfection, as religion or utilitarianism assigns to it, a special and limited character, this point of view, I say, of culture is best given by these words of Epictetus:—"It is a sign of ἀφυΐα," says he,—that is, of a nature not finely tempered,—"to give yourselves up to things which relate to the body; to make, for instance, a great fuss about exercise, a great fuss about eating, a great fuss about drinking, a great fuss about walking, a great fuss about riding. All these things ought to be done merely by the way: the formation of the spirit and character must be our real concern." This is admirable; and, indeed, the Greek word εὐφυΐα, a finely tempered nature, gives exactly the notion of perfection as culture brings us to conceive it: a harmonious perfection, a perfection in which the characters of beauty and intelligence are both present, which unites "the two noblest of things,"—as Swift, who of one of the two, at any rate, had himself all too little, most happily calls them in his *Battle of the Books,*—"the two noblest of things, *sweetness and light."* The εὐφυής, is the man who tends towards sweetness and light; the ἀφυής, on the other hand, is our Philistine. The immense spiritual significance of the Greeks is due to their having been inspired with this central and happy idea of the essential character of human perfection; and Mr. Bright's misconception of culture, as a smattering of Greek and Latin, comes itself, after all, from this wonderful significance of the Greeks having affected the very machinery of our education, and is in itself a kind of homage to it.

In thus making sweetness and light to be characters of perfection, culture is of like spirit with poetry, follows one law with poetry. Far more than on our freedom, our population, and our industrialism, many amongst us rely upon our religious organisations to save us. I have called religion a yet more important manifestation of human nature than poetry, because it has worked on a broader scale for perfection, and with greater masses of men. But the idea of beauty and of a human nature perfect on all its sides, which is the dominant idea of poetry, is a true and invaluable idea, though it has not yet had the success that the idea of conquering the obvious faults of our animality, and of a human nature perfect on the moral side,—which is the dominant idea of religion,— has been enabled to have; and it is destined, adding to itself the religious idea of a devout energy, to transform and govern the other.

The best art and poetry of the Greeks, in which religion and poetry are one, in which the idea of beauty and of a human nature perfect on all sides adds to itself a religious and devout energy, and works in the strength of that, is on this account of such surpassing interest and instructiveness for us, though it was,—as, having regard to the human race in general, and, indeed, having regard to the Greeks themselves, we must own,—a premature attempt, an attempt which for success needed the moral and religious fibre in humanity to be more braced and developed than it had yet been. But Greece did not err in having the idea of beauty, harmony, and complete human perfection, so present and paramount. It is impossible to have this idea too present and paramount; only, the moral fibre must be braced too. And we, because we have braced the moral fibre, are not on that account in the right way, if at the same time the idea of beauty, harmony, and complete human perfection, is wanting or misapprehended amongst us; and evidently it *is* wanting or misapprehended at present. And when we rely as we do on our religious organisations, which in themselves do not and cannot give us this idea, and think we have done enough if we make them spread and prevail, then, I say, we fall into our common fault of overvaluing machinery. . . .

The impulse of the English race towards moral development and self-conquest has nowhere so powerfully manifested itself as in Puritanism. Nowhere has Puritanism found so adequate an expression as in the religious organisation of the Independents. The modern Independents have a newspaper, the *Nonconformist*, written with great sincerity and ability. The motto, the standard, the profession of faith which this organ of theirs carries aloft, is: "The Dissidence of Dissent

and the Protestantism of the Protestant religion." There is
sweetness and light, and an ideal of complete harmonious
human perfection! One need not go to culture and poetry
to find language to judge it. Religion, with its instinct for
perfection, supplies language to judge it, language, too, which
is in our mouths every day. "Finally, be of one mind, united
in feeling," says St. Peter. There is an ideal which judges the
Puritan ideal: "The Dissidence of Dissent and the Protestantism of the Protestant religion!" And religious organisations like this are what people believe in, rest in, would give
their lives for! . . .

But men of culture and poetry, it will be said, are again
and again failing, and failing conspicuously, in the necessary
first stage to a harmonious perfection, in the subduing of the
great obvious faults of our animality, which it is the glory
of these religious organisations to have helped us to subdue.
True, they do often so fail. They have often been without
the virtues as well as the faults of the Puritan; it has been
one of their dangers that they so felt the Puritan's faults that
they too much neglected the practice of his virtues. I will
not, however, exculpate them at the Puritan's expense. They
have often failed in morality, and morality is indispensable.
And they have been punished for their failure, as the Puritan
has been rewarded for his performance. They have been
punished wherein they erred; but their ideal of beauty, of
sweetness and light, and a human nature complete on all its
sides, remains the true ideal of perfection still; just as the
Puritan's ideal of perfection remains narrow and inadequate,
although for what he did well he has been richly rewarded.
Notwithstanding the mighty results of the Pilgrim Fathers'
voyage, they and their standard of perfection are rightly
judged when we figure to ourselves Shakspeare or Virgil,—
souls in whom sweetness and light, and all that in human
nature is most humane, were eminent,—accompanying them on
their voyage, and think what intolerable company Shakspeare
and Virgil would have found them! In the same way let us
judge the religious organisations which we see all around
us. . . . Look at the life imaged in such a newspaper as the

Nonconformist,—a life of jealousy of the Establishment, disputes, tea-meetings, openings of chapels, sermons; and then think of it as an ideal of a human life completing itself on all sides, and aspiring with all its organs after sweetness, light, and perfection!

Another newspaper, representing, like the *Nonconformist,* one of the religious organisations of this country, was a short time ago giving an account of the crowd at Epsom on the Derby day, and of all the vice and hideousness which was to be seen in that crowd; and then the writer turned suddenly round upon Professor Huxley, and asked him how he proposed to cure all this vice and hideousness without religion. I confess I felt disposed to ask the asker this question: and how do you propose to cure it with such a religion as yours? How is the ideal of a life so unlovely, so unattractive, so incomplete, so narrow, so far removed from a true and satisfying ideal of human perfection, as is the life of your religious organisation as you yourself reflect it, to conquer and transform all this vice and hideousness? . . . And I say that the English reliance on our religious organisations and on their ideas of human perfection just as they stand, is like our reliance on freedom, on muscular Christianity, on population, on coal, on wealth,—mere belief in machinery, and unfruitful; and that it is wholesomely counteracted by culture, bent on seeing things as they are, and on drawing the human race onwards to a more complete, a harmonious perfection

Culture, however, shows its single-minded love of perfection, its desire simply to make reason and the will of God prevail, its freedom from fanaticism, by its attitude towards all this machinery, even while it insists that it *is* machinery. Fanatics, seeing the mischief men do themselves by their blind belief in some machinery or other,—whether it is wealth and industrialism, or whether it is the cultivation of bodily strength and activity, or whether it is a political organisation,—or whether it is a religious organisation,—oppose with might and main the tendency to this or that political and religious organisation, or to games and athletic exercises, or to wealth and industrialism, and try violently to stop it. But the flexibility which sweetness and light give, and which is one of the rewards of culture pursued in good faith, enables a man to see that a tendency may be necessary, and even, as a preparation for something in the future, salutary, and yet that the generations or individuals who obey this tendency are sacrificed to it, that they fall short of the hope of perfection by following it; and that its mischiefs are to be criticised, lest it should take too firm a hold and last after it has served its purpose. . . .

Oxford, the Oxford of the past, has many faults; and she has heavily paid for them in defeat, in isolation, in want of hold upon the modern world. Yet we in Oxford, brought up amidst the beauty and sweetness of that beautiful place, have not failed to seize one truth,—the truth that beauty and sweetness are essential characters of a complete human perfection. When I insist on this, I am all in the faith and tradition of Oxford. I say boldly that this our sentiment for beauty and sweetness, our sentiment against hideousness and rawness, has been at the bottom of our attachment to so many beaten causes, of our opposition to so many triumphant movements. And the sentiment is true, and has never been wholly defeated, and has shown its power even in its defeat. We have not won our political battles, we have not carried our main points, we have not stopped our adversaries' advance, we have not marched victoriously with the modern world; but we have told silently upon the mind of the country, we have prepared currents of feeling which sap our adversaries' position when it seems gained, we have kept up our own communications with the future. Look at the course of the great movement which shook Oxford to its centre some thirty years ago! It was directed, as any one who reads Dr. Newman's *Apology* may see, against what in one word may be called "Liberalism." Liberalism prevailed, it was the appointed force to do the work of the hour; it was necessary, it was inevitable that it should prevail. The Oxford movement was broken, it failed: our wrecks are scattered on every shore:—

Quæ regio in terris nostri non plena laboris?

But what was it, this liberalism, as Dr. Newman saw it, and as it really broke the Oxford movement? It was the great middle-class liberalism, which had for the cardinal points of its belief the Reform Bill of 1832, and local self-government, in politics; in the social sphere, free-trade, unrestricted competition, and the making of large industrial fortunes; in the religious sphere, the Dissidence of Dissent and the Protestantism of the Protestant religion. I do not say that other and more intelligent forces than this were not opposed to the Oxford movement: but this was the force which really beat it; this was the force which Dr. Newman felt himself fighting with; this was the force which till only the other day seemed to be the paramount force in this country, and to be in possession of the future; this was the force whose achievements fill Mr. Lowe with such inexpressible admiration, and whose rule he was so horror-struck to see threatened. And where is this great force of Philistinism now? It is thrust into the second rank, it is become a power of yesterday, it has lost the future. A new power has suddenly appeared, a power which it is impossible yet to judge fully, but which is certainly a wholly different force from middle-class liberalism; different in its cardinal points of belief, different in its tendencies in every sphere. It loves and admires neither the legislation of middle-class Parliaments, nor the local self-government of middle-class vestries, nor the unrestricted competition of middle-class industrialists, nor the dissidence of middle-class Dissent and the Protestantism of middle-class Protestant religion. I am not now praising this new force, or saying that its own ideals are better; all I say is, that they are wholly different. And who will estimate how much the currents of feeling created by Dr. Newman's movements, the keen desire for beauty and sweetness which it nourished, the deep aversion it manifested to the hardness and vulgarity of middle-class liberalism, the strong light it turned on the hideous and grotesque illusions of middle-class Protestantism,—who will estimate how much all these contributed to swell the tide of secret dissatisfaction which has mined the ground under self-confident liberalism of the last thirty years, and has prepared the way for its

sudden collapse and supersession? It is in this manner that
the sentiment of Oxford for beauty and sweetness conquers,
and in this manner long may it continue to conquer! . . .

Mr. Bright, who has a foot in both worlds, the world of
middle-class liberalism and the world of democracy, but who
brings most of his ideas from the world of middle-class liberalism in which he was bred, always inclines to inculcate that
faith in machinery to which, as we have seen, Englishmen
are so prone, and which has been the bane of middle-class
liberalism. He complains with a sorrowful indignation of
people who "appear to have no proper estimate of the value
of the franchise"; he leads his disciples to believe,—what the
Englishman is always too ready to believe,—that the having
a vote, like the having a large family, or a large business, or
large muscles, has in itself some edifying and perfecting effect
upon human nature. Or else he cries out to the democracy,—
"the men," as he calls them, "upon whose shoulders the
greatness of England rests,"—he cries out to them: "See what
you have done! I look over this country and see the cities
you have built, the railroads you have made, the manufactures you have produced, the cargoes which freight the ships
of the greatest mercantile navy the world has ever seen! I see
that you have converted by your labours what was once a
wilderness, these islands, into a fruitful garden; I know that
you have created this wealth, and are a nation whose name
is a word of power throughout all the world." Why, this is
just the very style of laudation with which Mr. Roebuck or
Mr. Lowe debauches the minds of the middle classes, and
makes such Philistines of them. It is the same fashion of
teaching a man to value himself not on what he *is*, not on his
progress in sweetness and light, but on the number of the
railroads he has constructed, or the bigness of the tabernacle
he has built. . . .

Other well-meaning friends of this new power are for leading it, not in the old ruts of middle-class Philistinism, but in
ways which are naturally alluring to the feet of democracy,
though in this country they are novel and untried ways. I may
call them the ways of Jacobinism. Violent indignation with

the past, abstract systems of renovation applied wholesale, a new doctrine drawn up in black and white for elaborating down to the very smallest details a rational society for the future,—these are the ways of Jacobinism. . . . A current in people's minds sets towards new ideas; people are dissatisfied with their old narrow stock of Philistine ideas, Anglo-Saxon ideas, or any other; and some man, some Bentham or Comte, who has the real merit of having early and strongly felt and helped the new current, but who brings plenty of narrowness and mistakes of his own into his feeling and help of it, is credited with being the author of the whole current, the fit person to be entrusted with its regulation and to guide the human race. . . .

The pursuit of perfection, then, is the pursuit of sweetness and light. He who works for sweetness and light, works to make reason and the will of God prevail. He who works for machinery, he who works for hatred, works only for confusion. Culture looks beyond machinery, culture hates hatred; culture has one great passion, the passion for sweetness and light. It has one even yet greater!—the passion for making them *prevail*. It is not satisfied till we *all* come to a perfect man; it knows that the sweetness and light of the few must be imperfect until the raw and unkindled masses of humanity are touched with sweetness and light. If I have not shrunk from saying that we must work for sweetness and light, so neither have I shrunk from saying that we must have a broad basis, must have sweetness and light for as many as possible. Again and again I have insisted how those are the happy moments of humanity, how those are the marking epochs of a people's life, how those are the flowering times for literature and art and all the creative power of genius, when there is a *national* glow of life and thought, when the whole of society is in the fullest measure permeated by thought, sensible to beauty, intelligent and alive. Only it must be *real* thought and *real* beauty; *real* sweetness and *real* light. Plenty of people will try to give the masses, as they call them, an intellectual food prepared and adapted in the way they think proper for the actual condition of the masses. The ordinary popular literature is an example of this way of working on the masses. Plenty of people will try to indoctrinate the masses with the set of ideas and judgments constituting the creed of their own profession or party. Our religious and political organisations give an example of this way of working on the masses. I condemn neither way; but culture works differently. It does not try to teach down to the level of inferior classes; it does not try to win them for this or that sect of its own, with ready-made judgments and watchwords. It seeks to do away with classes; to make the best that has been thought and known in the world current everywhere; to make all men live in an atmosphere of sweetness and light, where they may use ideas, as it uses them itself, freely,—nourished, and not bound by them.

This is the *social idea;* and the men of culture are the true apostles of equality. The great men of culture are those who have had a passion for diffusing, for making prevail, for carrying from one end of society to the other, the best knowledge, the best ideas of their time; who have laboured to divest knowledge of all that was harsh, uncouth, difficult, abstract, professional, exclusive; to humanise it, to make it efficient outside the clique of the cultivated and learned, yet still remaining the *best* knowledge and thought of the time, and a true source, therefore, of sweetness and light.

Barbarians, Philistines, Populace

MATTHEW ARNOLD

[FROM *Culture and Anarchy*]

1869- [1882]

The same desire for clearness, which has led me thus to
extend a little my first analysis of the three great classes of
English society, prompts me also to improve my nomenclature
for them a little, with a view to making it thereby more
manageable. It is awkward and tiresome to be always saying
the aristocratic class, the middle class, the working class. For
the middle class, for that great body which, as we know, "has
done all the great things that have been done in all departments," and which is to be conceived as moving between its
two cardinal points of our commercial member of Parliament
and our fanatical Protestant Dissenter,—for this class we have
a designation which now has become pretty well known, and
which we may as well still keep for them, the designation of
Philistines. What this term means I have so often explained
that I need not repeat it here. For the aristocratic class, conceived mainly as a body moving between the two cardinal
points of our chivalrous lord and our defiant baronet, we have
as yet got no special designation. Almost all my attention has
naturally been concentrated on my own class, the middle
class, with which I am in closest sympathy, and which has
been, besides, the great power of our day, and has had its
praises sung by all speakers and newspapers.

Still the aristocratic class is so important in itself, and the
weighty functions which Mr. Carlyle proposes at the present
critical time to commit to it, must add so much to its importance, that it seems neglectful, and a strong instance of that

From Chapter 3.

want of coherent philosophic method for which Mr. Frederic Harrison blames me, to leave the aristocratic class so much without notice and denomination. It may be thought that the characteristic which I have occasionally mentioned as proper to aristocracies,—their natural inaccessibility, as children of the established fact, to ideas,—points to our extending to this class also the designation of Philistines; the Philistine being, as is well known, the enemy of the children of light or servants of the idea. Nevertheless, there seems to be an inconvenience in thus giving one and the same designation to two very different classes; and besides, if we look into the thing closely, we shall find that the term Philistine conveys a sense which makes it more peculiarly appropriate to our middle class than to our aristocratic. For *Philistine* gives the notion of something particularly stiff-necked and perverse in the resistance to light and its children; and therein it specially suits our middle class, who not only do not pursue sweetness and light, but who even prefer to them that sort of machinery of business, chapels, tea-meetings, and addresses from Mr. Murphy, which makes up the dismal and illiberal life on which I have so often touched. But the aristocratic class has actually, as we have seen, in its well-known politeness, a kind of image or shadow of sweetness; and as for light, if it does not pursue light, it is not that it perversely cherishes some dismal and illiberal existence in preference to light, but it is lured off from following light by those mighty and eternal seducers of our race which weave for this class their most irresistible charms,— by worldly splendour, security, power, and pleasure. These seducers are exterior goods, but in a way they are goods; and he who is hindered by them from caring for light and ideas, is not so much doing what is perverse as what is too natural.

Keeping this in view, I have in my own mind often indulged myself with the fancy of employing, in order to designate our aristocratic class, the name of *The Barbarians*. The Barbarians, to whom we all owe so much, and who reinvigorated and renewed our worn-out Europe, had, as is well known, eminent merits; and in this country, where we are for the most part sprung from the Barbarians, we have never had the prejudice against them which prevails among the races of Latin origin. The Barbarians brought with them that staunch individualism, as the modern phrase is, and that passion for doing as one likes, for the assertion of personal liberty, which appears to Mr. Bright the central idea of English life, and of which we have, at any rate, a very rich supply. The stronghold and natural seat of this passion was in the nobles of whom our aristocratic class are the inheritors; and this class, accordingly, have signally manifested it, and have done much by their example to recommend it to the body of the nation, who already, indeed, had it in their blood. The Barbarians, again, had the passion for field-sports; and they have handed it on to our aristocratic class, who of this passion too, as of the passion for asserting one's personal liberty, are the great natural stronghold. The care of the Barbarians for the body, and for all manly exercises; the vigour, good looks, and fine complexion which they acquired and perpetuated in their families by these means,—all this may be observed still in our aristocratic class. The chivalry of the Barbarians, with its characteristics of high spirit, choice manners, and distinguished bearing,—what is this but the attractive commencement of the politeness of our aristocratic class? In some Barbarian noble, no doubt, one would have admired, if one could have been then alive to see it, the rudiments of our politest peer. Only, all this culture to call it by that name of the Barbarians was an exterior culture mainly. It consisted principally in outward gifts and graces, in looks, manners, accomplishments, prowess. The chief inward gifts which had part in it were the most exterior, so to speak, of inward gifts, those which come nearest to outward ones; they were courage, a high spirit, self-confidence. Far within, and unawakened, lay a whole range of powers of thought and feeling, to which these interesting productions of nature had, from the circumstances of their life, no access. Making allowances for the difference of the times, surely we can observe precisely the same thing now in our aristocratic class. In general its culture is exterior chiefly; all the exterior graces and accomplishments, and the more external of the inward virtues, seem to be principally its portion. It now, of course, cannot but be often in contact with those studies by which, from the world of thought and feeling, true culture teaches us to fetch sweetness and light; but its hold upon these very studies appears remarkably external, and unable to exert any deep power upon its spirit. Therefore the one insufficiency which we noted in the perfect mean of this class was an insufficiency of light. And owing to the same causes, does not a subtle criticism lead us to make even on the good looks and politeness of our aristocratic class, and of even the most fascinating half of that class, the feminine half, the one qualifying remark, that in these charming gifts there should perhaps be, for ideal perfection, a shade more *soul?*

I often, therefore, when I want to distinguish clearly the aristocratic class from the Philistines proper, or middle class, name the former, in my own mind, *the Barbarians*. And when I go through the country, and see this and that beautiful and imposing seat of theirs crowning the landscape, "There," I say to myself, "is a great fortified post of the Barbarians."

It is obvious that that part of the working class which, working diligently by the light of Mrs. Gooch's Golden Rule, looks forward to the happy day when it will sit on thrones with commercial members of Parliament and other middle-class potentates, to survey, as Mr. Bright beautifully says, "the cities it has built, the railroads it has made, the manufactures it has produced, the cargoes which freight the ships of the greatest mercantile navy the world has ever seen,"—it is obvious, I say, that this part of the working class is, or is in a fair way to be, one in spirit with the industrial middle class. It is notorious that our middle-class Liberals have long looked forward to this consummation, when the working class shall join forces with them, aid them heartily to carry forward their great works, go in a body to their tea-meetings, and, in short, enable them to bring about their millennium. That part of the working class, therefore, which does really seem to lend itself to these great aims, may, with propriety, be numbered by us among the Philistines. That part of it, again, which so much occupies the attention of philanthropists at present,—the part which gives all its energies to organising itself, through trades' unions and other means, so as to constitute, first, a great working-class power independent of the middle and aristocratic classes, and then, by dint of numbers, give the law to them and itself reign absolutely,—this lively and promising part must also, according to our definition, go with the Philistines; because it is its class and its class instinct which it seeks to affirm—its ordinary self, not its best self; and it is a machinery, an industrial machinery, and power and pre-eminence and other external goods, which fill its thoughts, and not an inward perfection. It is wholly occupied, according to Plato's subtle expression, with the things of itself and not its real self, with the things of the State and not the real State. But that vast portion, lastly, of the working class which, raw and half-developed, has long lain half-hidden amidst its poverty and squalor, and is now issuing from its hiding-place to assert an Englishman's heaven-born privilege of doing as he likes, and is beginning to perplex us by marching where it likes, meeting where it likes, bawling what it likes, breaking what it likes,—to this vast residuum we may with great propriety give the name of *Populace*.

Thus we have got three distinct terms, *Barbarians, Philistines, Populace,* to denote roughly the three great classes into which our society is divided; and though this humble attempt at a scientific nomenclature falls, no doubt, very far short in precision of what might be required from a writer equipped with a complete and coherent philosophy, yet, from a notoriously unsystematic and unpretending writer, it will, I trust, be accepted as sufficient. . . .

All of us, so far as we are Barbarians, Philistines, or Populace, imagine happiness to consist in doing what one's ordinary self likes. What one's ordinary self likes differs according to the class to which one belongs, and has its severer and its lighter side; always, however, remaining machinery, and nothing more. The graver self of the Barbarian likes honours and consideration; his more relaxed self, field-sports and pleasure. The graver self of one kind of Philistine likes fanaticism, business, and money-making; his more relaxed self, comfort and tea-meetings. Of another kind of Philistine, the graver self likes rattening; the relaxed self, deputations, or hearing Mr. Odger speak. The sterner self of the Populace likes bawling, hustling, and smashing; the lighter self, beer. But in each class there are born a certain number of natures with a curiosity about their best self, with a bent for seeing things as they are, for disentangling themselves from machinery, for simply concerning themselves with reason and the will of God, and doing their best to make these prevail;— for the pursuit, in a word, of perfection. . . . And this bent always tends to take them out of their class, and to make their distinguishing characteristic not their Barbarianism or their Philistinism, but their *humanity*.

PART
TWO

REFORM

PARLIAMENTARY REFORM

Representatives for London

THOMAS BABINGTON MACAULAY

[FROM a speech delivered in a committee of the House of Commons, 28 February 1832]

I have spoken so often on the question of Parliamentary Reform, that I am very unwilling to occupy the time of the Committee. But the importance of the amendment proposed by the noble Marquess [of Chandos], and the peculiar circumstances in which we are placed to-night, make me so anxious that I cannot remain silent.

In this debate, as in every other debate, our first object should be to ascertain on which side the burden of the proof lies. Now, it seems to me quite clear that the burden of the proof lies on those who support the amendment. I am entitled to take it for granted that it is right and wise to give representatives to some wealthy and populous places which have hitherto been unrepresented. To this extent, at least, we all, with scarcely an exception, now profess ourselves Reformers. There is, indeed, a great party which still objects

From *The Works of Lord Macaulay*, edited by Lady Trevelyan (London: 1866), Volume VIII, pages 79-85.

to the disfranchising even of the smallest borough. But all the most distinguished chiefs of that party have, here and elsewhere, admitted that the elective franchise ought to be given to some great towns which have risen into importance since our representative system took its present form. If this be so, on what ground can it be contended that these metropolitan districts ought not to be represented? Are they inferior in importance to the other places to which we are all prepared to give members? . . . Here, take what standard you will, the result will be the same. Take population: take the rental: take the number of ten pound houses: take the amount of the assessed taxes: take any test in short: take any number of tests, and combine those tests in any of the ingenious ways which men of science have suggested: multiply: divide: substract: add: try squares or cubes: try square roots or cube roots: you will never be able to find a pretext for excluding these districts from Schedule C. If, then, it be acknowledged that the franchise ought to be given to important places which are at present unrepresented, and if it be acknowledged that these districts are in importance not inferior to any place which is at present unrepresented, you are bound to give us strong reasons for withholding the franchise from these districts.

The honourable and learned gentleman [Sir E. Sudgen] has tried to give such reasons: and, in doing so, he has completely refuted the whole speech of the noble Marquess [of Chandos], with whom he means to divide. The truth is that the noble Marquess and the honourable and learned gentleman, though they agree in their votes, do not at all agree in their forebodings or in their ulterior intentions. The honourable and learned gentleman thinks it dangerous to increase the number of metropolitan voters. The noble Lord is perfectly willing to increase the number of metropolitan voters, and objects only to any increase in the number of metropolitan members. "Will you," says the honourable and learned gentleman, "be so rash, so insane, as to create constituent bodies of twenty or thirty thousand electors?" "Yes," says the noble Marquess, "and much more than that. I will create constituent bodies of forty

thousand, sixty thousand, a hundred thousand. I will add
Marylebone to Westminster. I will add Lambeth to South-
wark. I will add Finsbury and the Tower Hamlets to the
City." The noble Marquess, it is clear, is not afraid of the
excitement which may be produced by the polling of immense
multitudes. Of what then is he afraid? Simply of eight members: nay, of six members: for he is willing, he tells us, to
add two members to the two who already sit for Middlesex,
and who may be considered as metropolitan members. Are six
members, then, so formidable? I could mention a single peer
who now sends more than six members to the House. But,
says the noble Marquess, the members for the metropolitan
districts will be called to a strict account by their constituents:
they will be mere delegates: they will be forced to speak, not
their own sense, but the sense of the capital. I will answer for
it, Sir, that they will not be called to a stricter account than
those gentlemen who are nominated by some great proprietors
of boroughs. Is it not notorious that those who represent it
as in the highest degree pernicious and degrading that a public
man should be called to account by a great city which has
entrusted its dearest interests to his care, do nevertheless think
that he is bound by the most sacred ties of honour to vote
according to the wishes of his patron or to apply for the
Chiltern Hundreds? It is a bad thing, I fully admit, that a
Member of Parliament should be a mere delegate. But it is
not worse that he should be the delegate of a hundred thousand people than of one too powerful individual. . . . Is it
not perfectly notorious that many members voted, year after
year, against Catholic Emancipation, simply because they
knew that, if they voted otherwise, they would lose their seats?
No doubt this is an evil. . . . Construct your representative
system as you will, these men will always be sycophants. . . .

But, it is said, the power of this huge capital is even now
dangerously great; and will you increase that power? Now,
Sir, I am far from denying that the power of London is, in
some sense, dangerously great; but I altogether deny that
the danger will be increased by this bill. It has always been
found that a hundred thousand people congregated close to

the seat of government exercise a greater influence on public affairs than five hundred thousand dispersed over a remote province. But this influence is not proportioned to the number of representatives chosen by the capital. This influence is felt at present, though the greater part of the capital is unrepresented. This influence is felt in countries where there is no representative system at all. Indeed, this influence is nowhere so great as under despotic governments. I need not remind the Committee that the Cæsars, while ruling by the sword, while putting to death without a trial every senator, every magistrate, who incurred their displeasure, yet found it necessary to keep the populace of the imperial city in good humour by distributions of corn and shows of wild beasts. Every country, from Britain to Egypt, was squeezed for the means of filling the granaries and adorning the theatres of Rome. On more than one occasion, long after the Cortes of Castile had become a mere name, the rabble of Madrid assembled before the royal palace, forced their King, their absolute King, to appear in the balcony, and exacted from him a promise that he would dismiss an obnoxious minister. . . . If there is any country in the world where pure despotism exists, that country is Turkey; and yet there is no country in the world where the inhabitants of the capital are so much dreaded by the Government. The Sultan, who stands in awe of nothing else, stands in awe of the turbulent populace, which may, at any moment, besiege him in his Seraglio. As soon as Constantinople is up, everything is conceded. The unpopular edict is recalled. The unpopular vizier is beheaded. This sort of power has nothing to do with representation. It depends on physical force and on vicinity. You do not propose to take this sort of power away from London. Indeed, you cannot take it away. Nothing can take it away but an earthquake more terrible than that of Lisbon, or a fire more destructive than that of 1666. Law can do nothing against this description of power; for it is a power which is formidable only when law has ceased to exist. While the reign of law continues, eight votes in a House of six hundred and fifty-eight Members will hardly do much harm. When the reign of law is at an end, and the reign of violence commences, the importance of a million and a half of people, all collected within a walk of the Palace, of the Parliament House, of the Bank, of the Courts of Justice, will not be measured by eight or by eighty votes. See, then, what you are doing. That power which is not dangerous you refuse to London. That power which is dangerous you leave undiminished; nay, you make it more dangerous still. For by refusing to let eight or nine hundred thousand people express their opinions and wishes in a legal and constitutional way, you increase the risk of disaffection and of tumult. . . . Why is it that the population of unrepresented London, though physically far more powerful than the population of Madrid or of Constantinople, has been far more peaceable? Why have we never seen the inhabitants of the metropolis besiege St. James's, or force their way riotously into this House? Why, but because they have other means of giving vent to their feelings, because they enjoy the liberty of unlicensed printing, and the liberty of holding public meetings. Just as the people of unrepresented London are more orderly than the people of Constantinople and Madrid, so will the people of represented London be more orderly than the people of unrepresented London. . . .

Our country has been in serious danger; and why? Because a representative system, framed to suit the England of the thirteenth century, did not suit the England of the nineteenth century; because an old wall, the last relique of a departed city, retained the privileges of that city, while great towns, celebrated all over the world for wealth and intelligence, had no more share in the government than when they were still hamlets. The object of this bill is to correct those monstrous disproportions, and to bring the legal order of society into something like harmony with the natural order. . . . A great crisis may be followed by the complete restoration of health. But no constitution will bear perpetual tampering. If the noble Marquess's amendment should unhappily be carried, it is morally certain that the immense population of Finsbury, of Marylebone, of Lambeth, of the Tower Hamlets, will, importunately and clamorously, demand redress from the reformed Parliament. That Parliament, you tell us, will be much more democratically inclined than the Parliaments of past times. If so, how can you expect that it will resist the urgent demands of a million of people close to its door? These eight seats will be given. More than eight seats will be given. The whole question of Reform will be opened again; and the blame will rest on those who will, by mutilating this great law in an essential part, cause hundreds of thousands who now regard it as a boon to regard it as an outrage.

Sir, our word is pledged. Let us remember the solemn promise which we gave to the nation last October at a perilous conjuncture. That promise was that we would stand firmly by the principles and leading provisions of the Reform Bill. Our sincerity is now brought to the test. One of the leading provisions of the bill is in danger. The question is, not merely whether these districts shall be represented, but whether we will keep the faith which we plighted to our countrymen. Let us be firm . . . . We have the confidence of our country. We have justly earned it. For God's sake let us not throw it away. Other occasions may arise on which honest Reformers may fairly take different sides. But to-night he that is not with us is against us.

Passage of the First Reform Bill

[FROM *The Times,* 6 June 1832, page 5]

There never was, in the history of the world, an example so ennobling to the character of the English nation, or so encouraging to the hopes of every other, as this triumph of intellectual and moral power, achieved over gross stupidity and brutal force. A race of usurpers have been ousted from the field of their usurpation, and a great empire reconquered by its own people, without the shedding of one drop of blood, or the disturbance of any one *right* of person or property which the common consent of civilized men holds sacred.

The passing of the Reform Bill has been the victory of dispassionate opinion over interested prejudice,—of universal justice over glaring selfishness,—of principles which are eternal over rotten and obsolete institutions. What had not the borough faction on their side? The KING only excepted (and that not within these three weeks), the Court was theirs. The House of Lords was theirs. The army they imagined was their own. The clergy, the magistracy, the old functionaries in all the public departments, the patronage derived from the collection of 48,000,000*l*. sterling of revenue, and the distribution of 20,000,000*l*.—every thing was anti-reform. The roots of their dominion struck into fearful depths, or stretched beneath the surface to immeasurable distances, while its branches waved above our heads, and overlaid the land with darkness. What, then, was for the people? Truth, enthusiasm in a just cause, hatred of wrong, and contempt of danger. Many generous men were seen to make a sacrifice of personal influence, wealth, and power, to the public good. This gave the country confidence in a portion of its aristocracy, and re-acted kindly upon the sentiments of the latter class,—a concord and union of the rich and industrious orders, which have mainly saved England from convulsion. That mirror, too, which reflects faithfully whatever passes within the bosom of society,—that which, because it is a faithful mirror of whatever animates the individual mind, is likewise a powerful and invaluable organ for the excitement of general sympathy—the PRESS,— that which is stigmatized as the "base press," by those to whom base motives, and no others, are conceivable,—the Press devoted itself to the people.

The people, in their political unions, were denounced by the Tories, who, in the wickedness of their own hypocrisy, charged those unions with indifference to the reform for which they petitioned Parliament, and with a fanatical thirst for revolution, which they did not ask for, but had associated themselves expressly and solemnly to prevent. "The Political Unions," cried the Tories, "must be put down, that we may not be bullied into reform." "You cannot put us down," said the united Englishmen, "because we transgress no law, and interfere with no authority. You shall not, moreover, put us down; for is it not better that you should be bullied into reform, than that we should be bayonetted out of it?" For, indeed, the army was "to be let loose" upon the "Radicals,"—so were denominated all friends of good Government, law and liberty,—all who, in the wise and statesmanlike spirit of Lord GREY, were for repairing those dilapidations by which "Time, the innovator,"—"Time, the destroyer," marks the human origin of the noblest political institutions. Yes, the army was to be let loose upon us! Many a green or grizzled jackanapes about the clubs, and public offices, and in Bond-street, was heard to declaim on the "necessity of placing the 'Hero of Waterloo' at the head of affairs," when the "edge of the sword" would settle the question in a fortnight. We have our own doubts whether the "Hero of Waterloo" would have resorted to such means, but none at all as to his utter and signal discomfiture had he been hard-hearted or soft-headed enough to try them. But how did the people receive this disgusting language? Did it terrify them into Toryism?—or exasperate them to violence?—or involve them in any course unworthy of respectable and honest citizens? Certainly not. They shed no blood: they attacked not the person of any public enemy. They only joined the Political Unions by myriads,—attended meetings by 200,000 at a time,—discussed public questions with more eagerness and ability than ever,—and signed and presented fresh petitions to Parliament. The threatened assault on the unions disgracefully failed.

The press next had its turn. The "vile press"—the head and front of revolution—the "omnipotent press"—was menaced with a system of gagging which should amount at last to suffocation. How did the press behave under this extra-judicial and unbecoming bitterness? Was it terrified or laid prostrate? Or, on the other hand, was it provoked to unlawful or unseemly outrage? We suspect not. The reform press, comprehending 9-10ths of the metropolitan, and 19-20ths of the whole press of England, held the tenour of its way unshaken. It answered not the furious charges of Lord LYNDHURST by congenial abuse. It turned not to the right hand nor the left; but worked onward for and with reform. The people and the press are alive and unscathed, and, thank GOD! triumphant. The Reform Bill will, in a few hours, become the law of England, and the nation and its liberties, and the much calumniated organ of its sentiments—the PRESS, the impersonation of the enlightened mind of England,—are from this day forth secure.

In what form, or with what circumstance, the Royal assent may be given to this great measure for establishing on their only solid ground the rights and true interests of the British monarchy, is of little moment to the nation. But to him by whom, or in whose name, that fiat is to be affixed to the Reform Charter, it will be a question of incalculable price. After having in its difficulties, and through obstructions numberless, maintained the measure, and manfully cheered on and supported his Ministers in their course,—shall King WILLIAM now, when that course has led Lord GREY to victory, —now, when difficulties and obstructions are at an end,—now when the British nation can scarce restrain itself from rushing to the feet of a beloved and paternal Sovereign, embracing his knees, and all but worshipping him as a glorious benefactor,—will King WILLIAM now recede? turn aside from his affectionate and grateful subjects?—separate for ever his name from that noble record which bears upon its page no syllable that will not be immortal?—will he let posterity infer, that reform in 1832 was carried not under his auspices, but in spite of him, and that to make manifest a posthumous and stingless detestation of the most splendid act by which English history is adorned?

If the anti-reforming courtiers would dissuade HIS MAJESTY from showing himself on this occasion to his happy subjects, on the plea that some wretched slight or insult might be offered to him, well worthy is such a calumny of the foul source whence it springs, but little worthy of credit from a sovereign who ought by this time to know the nature of English feelings. Let King WILLIAM but see the honest exultation of hundreds of thousands of freemen at his graceful performance of this crowning act of a reign which has hitherto procured for him the blessings of all who have the happiness of living under his sceptre—he will then be qualified to judge of the dreadful sacrifice which evil counsellors would exact from him when they urge HIS MAJESTY to pass the Bill by commission.

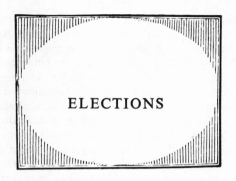

ELECTIONS

Polling in the Midlands, 1832

GEORGE ELIOT

[FROM *Felix Holt, the Radical*]

1866

At last the great epoch of the election for North Loamshire had arrived. The roads approaching Treby were early traversed by a larger number of vehicles, horsemen, and also foot-passengers, than were ever seen there at the annual fair. Treby was the polling-place for many voters whose faces were quite strange in the town; and if there were some strangers who did not come to poll, though they had business not unconnected with the election, they were not liable to be regarded with suspicion or especial curiosity. It was understood that no division of a county had ever been more thoroughly canvassed, and that there would be a hard run between Garstin and Transome. Mr Johnson's headquarters were at Duffield; but it was a maxim which he repeated after the great Putty, that a capable agent makes himself omnipresent; and quite apart from the express between him and Jermyn, Mr John Johnson's presence in the universe had potent effects on this December day at Treby Magna.

Chapter 31.

A slight drizzling rain which was observed by some Tories who looked out of their bedroom windows before six o'clock, made them hope that, after all, the day might pass off better than alarmists had expected. The rain was felt to be somehow on the side of quiet and Conservatism; but soon the breaking of the clouds and the mild gleams of a December sun brought back previous apprehensions. As there were already precedents for riot at a Reformed election, and as the Trebian district had had its confidence in the natural course of things somewhat shaken by a landed proprietor with an old name offering himself as a Radical candidate, the election had been looked forward to by many with a vague sense that it would be an occasion something like a fighting match, when bad characters would probably assemble, and there might be struggles and alarms for respectable men, which would make it expedient for them to take a little neat brandy as a precaution beforehand and a restorative afterwards. The tenants on the Transome estate were comparatively fearless: poor Mr Goffe, of Rabbit's End, considered that "one thing was as mauling as another," and that an election was no worse than the sheep-rot; while Mr Dibbs, taking the more cheerful view of a prosperous man, reflected that if the Radicals were dangerous, it was safer to be on their side. It was the voters for Debarry and Garstin who considered that they alone had the right to regard themselves as targets for evil-minded men; and Mr Crowder, if he could have got his ideas countenanced, would have recommended a muster of farm-servants with defensive pitchforks on the side of Church and King. But the bolder men were rather gratified by the prospect of being groaned at, so that they might face about and groan in return.

Mr Crow, the high constable of Treby, inwardly rehearsed a brief address to a riotous crowd in case it should be wanted, having been warned by the Rector that it was a primary duty on these occasions to keep a watch against provocation as well as violence. The Rector, with a brother magistrate who was on the spot, had thought it desirable to swear in some special constables, but the presence of loyal men not absolutely required for the polling was not looked at in the light of a provocation. The Benefit Clubs from various quarters made a show, some with the orange-coloured ribbons and streamers of the true Tory candidate, some with the mazarine of the Whig. The orange-coloured bands played "Auld Langsyne," and a louder mazarine band came across them with "Oh whistle and I will come to thee, my lad"—probably as the tune the most symbolical of Liberalism which their repertory would furnish. There was not a single club bearing the Radical blue: the Sproxton Club members wore the mazarine, and Mr Chubb wore so much of it that he looked (at a sufficient distance) like a very large gentianella. It was generally understood that "these brave fellows," representing the fine institution of Benefit Clubs, and holding aloft the motto, "Let brotherly love continue," were a civil force calculated to encourage voters of sound opinions and keep up their spirits. But a considerable number of unadorned heavy navvies, colliers, and stone-pit men, who used their freedom as British subjects to be present in Treby on this great occasion, looked like a possibly uncivil force whose politics were dubious until it was clearly seen for whom they cheered and for whom they groaned.

Thus the way up to the polling-booths was variously lined, and those who walked it, to whatever side they belonged, had the advantage of hearing from the opposite side what were the most marked defects or excesses in their personal appearance; for the Trebians of that day held, without being aware that they had Cicero's authority for it, that the bodily blemishes of an opponent were a legitimate ground for ridicule; but if the voter frustrated wit by being handsome, he was groaned at and satirised according to a formula, in which the adjective was Tory, Whig, or Radical, as the case might be, and the substantive a blank to be filled up after the taste of the speaker.

Some of the more timid had chosen to go through this ordeal as early as possible in the morning. One of the earliest was Mr Timothy Rose, the gentleman-farmer from Leek Malton. He had left home with some foreboding, having swathed his more vital parts in layers of flannel, and put on two greatcoats as a soft kind of armour. But reflecting with some trepidation that there were no resources for protecting his head, he once more wavered in his intention to vote; he once more observed to Mrs Rose that these were hard times when a man of independent property was expected to vote "willy-nilly"; but finally, coerced by the sense that he should be looked ill on "in these times" if he did not stand by the gentlemen round about, he set out in his gig, taking with him a powerful waggoner, whom he ordered to keep him in sight as he went to the polling-booth. It was hardly more than nine o'clock when Mr Rose, having thus come up to the level of his times, cheered himself with a little cherry-brandy at the Marquis, drove away in a much more courageous spirit, and got down at Mr Nolan's, just outside the town. The retired Londoner, he considered, was a man of experience, who would estimate properly the judicious course he had taken, and could make it known to others. Mr Nolan was superintending the removal of some shrubs in his garden.

"Well, Mr Nolan," said Rose, twinkling a self-complacent look over the red prominence of his cheeks, "have you been to give your vote yet?"

"No; all in good time. I shall go presently."

"Well, I wouldn't lose an hour, I wouldn't. I said to myself, if I've got to do gentlemen a favour, I'll do it at once. You see, I've got no landlord, Nolan—I'm in that position o' life that I can be independent."

"Just so, my dear sir," said the wiry-faced Nolan, pinching his under-lip between his thumb and finger, and giving one of those wonderful universal shrugs, by which he seemed to be recalling all his garments from a tendency to disperse themselves. "Come in and see Mrs Nolan?"

"No, no, thankye. Mrs Rose expects me back. But, as I was saying, I'm a independent man, and I consider it's not my part to show favour to one more than another, but to make things as even as I can. If I'd been a tenant to anybody, well, in course I must have voted for my landlord—that stands to sense. But I wish everybody well; and if one's returned to Parliament more than another, nobody can say it's my doing; for when you can vote for two, you can make things even. So I gave one to Debarry and one to Transome; and I wish Garstin no ill, but I can't help the odd number, and he hangs on to Debarry, they say."

"God bless me, sir," said Mr Nolan, coughing down a laugh, "don't you perceive that you might as well have stayed at home and not voted at all, unless you would rather send a Radical to Parliament than a sober Whig?"

"Well, I'm sorry you should have anything to say against what I've done, Nolan," said Mr Rose, rather crestfallen, though sustained by inward warmth. "I thought you'd agree with me, as you're a sensible man. But the most a independent man can do is to try and please all; and if he hasn't the luck—here's wishing I may do it another time," added Mr Rose, apparently confounding a toast with a salutation, for he put out his hand for a passing shake, and then stepped into his gig again.

At the time that Mr Timothy Rose left the town, the crowd in King Street and in the market-place, where the polling-booths stood, was fluctuating. Voters as yet were scanty, and brave fellows who had come from any distance this morning, or who had sat up late drinking the night before, required some reinforcement of their strength and spirits. Every public-house in Treby, not excepting the venerable and sombre Cross-Keys, was lively with changing and numerous company. Not, of course, that there was any treating: treating necessarily had stopped, from moral scruples, when once "the writs were out"; but there was drinking, which did equally well under any name.

Poor Tommy Trounsem, breakfasting here on Falstaff's pro-portion of bread, and something which, for gentility's sake, I will call sack, was more than usually victorious over the ills of life, and himself one of the heroes of the day. He had an immense light-blue cockade in his hat, and an amount of silver in a dirty little canvass bag which astonished himself. For some reason, at first inscrutable to him, he had been paid for his bill-sticking with great liberality at Mr Jermyn's office, in spite of his having been the victim of a trick by which he had once lost his own bills and pasted up Debarry's; but he soon saw that this was simply a recognition of his merit as "an old family kept out of its rights," and also of his peculiar share in an occasion when the family was to get into Parliament. Under these circumstances, it was due from him that he should show himself prominently where business was going forward, and give additional value by his presence to every vote for Transome. With this view he got a half-pint bottle filled with his peculiar kind of "sack," and hastened back to the market-place, feeling good-natured and patronising towards all political parties, and only so far partial as his family bound him to be.

But a disposition to concentrate at that extremity of King Street which issued in the market-place was not universal among the increasing crowd. Some of them seemed attracted towards another nucleus at the other extremity of King Street, near the Seven Stars. This was Garstin's chief house, where his committee sat, and it was also a point which must necessarily be passed by many voters entering the town on the eastern side. It seemed natural that the mazarine colours should be visible here, and that Pack, the tall "shepherd" of the Sproxton men, should be seen moving to and fro where there would be a frequent opportunity of cheering the voters for a gentleman who had the chief share in the Sproxton mines. But the side lanes and entries out of King Street were numerous enough to relieve any pressure if there was need to make way. The lanes had a distinguished reputation. Two of them had odours of brewing; one had a side entrance to Mr Tiliot's wine and spirit vaults; up another Mr Muscat's cheeses were frequently being unloaded; and even some of the entries had those cheerful suggestions of plentiful provision which were among the characteristics of Treby.

Between ten and eleven the voters came in more rapid succession, and the whole scene became spirited. Cheers, sarcasms, and oaths, which seemed to have a flavour of wit for many hearers, were beginning to be reinforced by more practical demonstrations, dubiously jocose. There was a disposition in the crowd to close and hem in the way for voters, either going or coming, until they had paid some kind of toll. It was difficult to see who set the example in the transition from words to deeds. Some thought it was due to Jacob Cuff, a Tory charity-man, who was a well-known ornament of the pothouse, and gave his mind much leisure for amusing devices; but questions of origination in stirring periods are notoriously hard to settle. It is by no means necessary in human things that there should be only one beginner. This, however, is certain—that Mr Chubb, who wished it to be noticed that he voted for Garstin solely, was one of the first to get rather more notice than he wished, and that he had his hat knocked off and crushed in the interest of Debarry by Tories opposed to coalition. On the other hand, some said it was at the same time that Mr Pink, the saddler, being stopped on his way and made to declare that he was going to vote for Debarry, got himself well chalked as to his coat, and pushed up an entry, where he remained the prisoner of terror combined with the want of any back outlet, and never gave his vote that day.

The second Tory joke was performed with much gusto. The majority of the Transome tenants came in a body from the Ram Inn, with Mr Banks the bailiff leading them. Poor Goffe was the last of them, and his worn melancholy look and forward-leaning gait gave the jocose Cuff the notion that the farmer was not what he called "compus." Mr Goffe was cut off from his companions and hemmed in; asked, by voices with hot breath close to his ear, how many horses he had, how many cows, how many fat pigs; then jostled from one to another, who made trumpets with their hands, and deafened him by telling him to vote for Debarry. In this way the melancholy Goffe was hustled on till he was at the polling-booth—filled with confused alarms, the immediate alarm being that of having to go back in still worse fashion than he had come. Arriving in this way after the other tenants had left, he astonished all hearers who knew him for a tenant of the Transomes by saying "Debarry," and was jostled back trembling amid shouts of laughter.

By stages of this kind the fun grew faster, and was in danger of getting rather serious. The Tories began to feel that

their jokes were returned by others of a heavier sort, and that
the main strength of the crowd was not on the side of sound
opinion, but might come to be on the side of sound cudgel-
ling and kicking. The navvies and pitmen in dishabille seemed
to be multiplying, and to be clearly not belonging to the party
of Order. The shops were freely resorted to for various forms
of playful missiles and weapons; and news came to the magistrates, watching from the large window of the Marquis, that
a gentleman coming in on horseback at the other end of the
street to vote for Garstin had had his horse turned round and
frightened into a headlong gallop out of it again.

Mr Crow and his subordinates, and all the special constables, felt that it was necessary to make some energetic effort,
or else every voter would be intimidated and the poll must
be adjourned. The Rector determined to get on horseback
and go amidst the crowd with the constables; and he sent a
message to Mr Lingon, who was at the Ram, calling on him
to do the same. "Sporting Jack" was sure the good fellows
meant no harm, but he was courageous enough to face any
bodily dangers, and rode out in his brown leggings and
coloured bandanna, speaking persuasively.

It was nearly twelve o'clock when this sally was made: the
constables and magistrates tried the most pacific measures,
and they seemed to succeed. There was a rapid thinning of
the crowd: the most boisterous disappeared, or seemed to do
so by becoming quiet; missiles ceased to fly, and a sufficient
way was cleared for voters along King Street. The magistrates
returned to their quarters, and the constables took convenient
posts of observation. Mr Wace, who was one of Debarry's
committee, had suggested to the Rector that it might be wise
to send for the military from Duffield, with orders that they
should station themselves at Hathercote, three miles off: there
was so much property in the town that it would be better
to make it secure against risks. But the Rector felt that this
was not the part of a moderate and wise magistrate, unless
the signs of riot recurred. He was a brave man, and fond
of thinking that his own authority sufficed for the maintenance
of the general good in Treby.

THE PEOPLE'S CHARTER

The Six Points

THOMAS BABINGTON MACAULAY

[FROM a speech delivered in the House of Commons,
3 May 1842]

The honourable member for Westminster [Mr. Leader] has
expressed a hope that the language of the petition will not
be subjected to severe criticism. If he means literary criticism,
I entirely agree with him. The style of this composition is
safe from any censure of mine; but the substance it is absolutely necessary that we should closely examine. What the
petitioners demand is this, that we do forthwith pass what is
called the People's Charter into a law without alteration,
diminution, or addition. This is the prayer in support of which
the honourable member for Finsbury would have us hear an
argument at the bar. Is it then reasonable to say, as some
gentlemen have said, that, in voting for the honourable member's motion, they mean to vote merely for an inquiry into
the causes of the public distress? If any gentleman thinks

From *The Works of Lord Macaulay*, edited by Lady Trevelyan (London:
1866), Volume VIII, pages 219-27.

that an inquiry into the causes of the public distress would be useful, let him move for such an inquiry. I will not oppose it. But this petition does not tell us to inquire. It tells us that we are not to inquire. It directs us to pass a certain law word for word, and to pass it without the smallest delay.

I shall, Sir, notwithstanding the request or command of the petitioners, venture to exercise my right of free speech on the subject of the People's Charter. There is, among the six points of the Charter, one for which I have voted. There is another of which I decidedly approve. There are others as to which, though I do not agree with the petitioners, I could go some way to meet them. In fact, there is only one of the six points on which I am diametrically opposed to them: but unfortunately that point happens to be infinitely the most important of the six. One of the six points is the ballot. I have voted for the ballot; and I have seen no reason to change my opinion on that subject. Another point is the abolition of the pecuniary qualification for members of this House. On that point I cordially agree with the petitioners. . . .

The Chartists demand annual parliaments. There, certainly, I differ from them: but I might, perhaps, be willing to consent to some compromise. I differ from them also as to the expediency of paying the representatives of the people, and of dividing the country into electoral districts. But I do not consider these matters as vital. The kingdom might, I acknowledge, be free, great, and happy, though the members of this House received salaries, and though the present boundaries of counties and boroughs were superseded by new lines of demarcation. These, Sir, are subordinate questions. I do not, of course, mean that they are not important. But they are subordinate when compared with that question which still remains to be considered. The essence of the Charter is universal suffrage. If you withhold that, it matters not very much what else you grant. If you grant that, it matters not at all what else you withhold. If you grant that, the country is lost.

I have no blind attachment to ancient usages. I altogether disclaim what has been nicknamed the doctrine of finality. I have said enough to-night to show that I do not consider the settlement made by the Reform Bill as one which can last for ever. I certainly do think that an extensive change in the polity of a nation must be attended with serious evils. Still those evils may be overbalanced by advantages: and I am perfectly ready, in every case, to weigh the evils against the advantages, and to judge as well as I can which scale preponderates. I am bound by no tie to oppose any reform which I think likely to promote the public good. I will go so far as to say that I do not quite agree with those who think that they have proved the People's Charter to be absurd when they have proved that it is incompatible with the existence of the throne and of the peerage. For though I am a faithful and loyal subject of Her Majesty, and though I sincerely wish to see the House of Lords powerful and respected, I cannot consider either monarchy or aristocracy as the ends of Government. They are only means. Nations have flourished without hereditary sovereigns or assemblies of nobles; and, though I should be very sorry to see England a republic, I do not doubt that she might, as a republic, enjoy prosperity, tranquillity, and high consideration. The dread and aversion with which I regard universal suffrage would be greatly diminished, if I could believe that the worst effect which it would produce would be to give us an elective first magistrate and a senate instead of a Queen and a House of Peers. My firm conviction is that, in our country, universal suffrage is incompatible, not with this or that form of government, but with all forms of government, and with everything for the sake of which forms of government exist; that it is incompatible with property, and that it is consequently incompatible with civilisation.

It is not necessary for me in this place to go through the arguments which prove beyond dispute that on the security of property civilisation depends; that, where property is insecure, no climate however delicious, no soil however fertile, no conveniences for trade and navigation, no natural endowments of body or of mind, can prevent a nation from sinking into barbarism; that where, on the other hand, men are protected in the enjoyment of what has been created by their industry and laid up by their self-denial, society will advance in arts and in wealth notwithstanding the sterility of the earth and the inclemency of the air, notwithstanding heavy taxes and destructive wars. . . .

If it be admitted that on the institution of property the wellbeing of society depends, it follows surely that it would be madness to give supreme power in the state to a class which would not be likely to respect that institution. And, if this be conceded, it seems to me to follow that it would be madness to grant the prayer of this petition. I entertain no hope that, if we place the government of the kingdom in the hands of the majority of the males of one and twenty told by the head, the institution of property will be respected. If I am asked why I entertain no such hope, I answer, because the hundreds of thousands of males of twenty-one who have signed this petition tell me to entertain no such hope; because they tell me that, if I trust them with power, the first use which they will make of it will be to plunder every man in the kingdom who has a good coat on his back and a good roof over his head. . . . In short, the petitioners ask you to give them power in order that they may not leave a man of a hundred a year in the realm.

I am far from wishing to throw any blame on the ignorant crowds which have flocked to the tables where this petition was exhibited. Nothing is more natural than that the labouring people should be deceived by the arts of such men as the author of this absurd and wicked composition. . . . Imagine a well meaning laborious mechanic fondly attached to his wife and children. Bad times come. He sees the wife whom he loves grow thinner and paler every day. His little ones cry for bread; and he has none to give them. Then come the professional agitators, the tempters, and tell him that there is enough and more than enough for everybody, and that he has too little only because landed gentlemen, fundholders, bankers, manufacturers, railway proprietors, shopkeepers, have too much. Is it strange that the poor man should be deluded, and should eagerly sign such a petition as this? The inequality with which wealth is distributed forces itself on everybody's notice. It is at once perceived by the eye.

The reasons which irrefragably prove this inequality to be necessary to the wellbeing of all classes are not equally obvious. Our honest working man has not received such an education as enables him to understand that the utmost distress that he has ever known is prosperity, when compared with the distress which he would have to endure if there were a single month of general anarchy and plunder. But you say, It is not the fault of the labourer that he is not well educated. Most true. It is not his fault. But, though he has no share in the fault, he will, if you are foolish enough to give him supreme power in the state, have a very large share of the punishment. You say that, if the Government had not culpably omitted to establish a good system of public instruction, the petitioners would have been fit for the elective franchise. But is that a reason for giving them the franchise when their own petition proves that they are not fit for it, when they give us fair notice that, if we let them have it, they will use it to our ruin and their own? It is not necessary now to inquire whether, with universal education, we could safely have universal suffrage. What we are asked to do is to give universal suffrage before there is universal education. Have I any unkind feeling towards these poor people? No more than I have to a sick friend who implores me to give him a glass of iced water which the physician has forbidden. No more than a humane collector in India has to those poor peasants who in a season of scarcity crowd round the granaries and beg with tears and piteous gestures that the doors may be opened and the rice distributed. I would not give the draught of water, because I know that it would be poison. I would not give up the keys of the granary, because I know that, by doing so, I should turn a scarcity into a famine. And in the same way I would not yield to the importunity of multitudes who, exasperated by suffering and blinded by ignorance, demand with wild vehemence the liberty to destroy themselves. . . .

It is supposed by many that our rulers possess, somewhere or other, an inexhaustible storehouse of all the necessaries and conveniences of life, and, from mere hardheartedness, refuse to distribute the contents of this magazine among the poor. We have all of us read speeches and tracts in which it seemed to be taken for granted that we who sit here have the power of working miracles, of sending a shower of manna on the West Riding, of striking the earth and furnishing all the towns of Lancashire with abundance of pure water, of feeding all the cottonspinners and weavers who are out of work with five loaves and two fishes. There is not a working man who has not heard harangues and read newspapers in which these follies are taught. And do you believe that as soon as you give the working men absolute and irresistible power they will forget all this? Yes, Sir, absolute and irresistible power. The Charter would give them no less. In every constituent body throughout the empire the working men will, if we grant the prayer of this petition, be an irresistible majority. In every constituent body capital will be placed at the feet of labour; knowledge will be borne down by ignorance; and is it possible to doubt what the result must be? . . . What could follow but one vast spoliation? One vast spoliation! That would be bad enough. That would be the greatest calamity that ever fell on our country. Yet would that a single vast spoliation were the worst! No, Sir; in the lowest deep there would be a lower deep. The first spoliation would not be the last. How could it? All the causes which had produced the first spoliation would still operate. They would operate more powerfully than before. The distress would be far greater than before. The fences which now protect property would all have been broken through, levelled, swept away. The new proprietors would have no title to show to anything that they held except recent robbery. With what face then could they complain of being robbed? What would be the end of these things? Our experience, God be praised, does not enable us to predict it with certainty. . . . The best event, the very best event, that I can anticipate,—and what must the state of things be, if an Englishman and a Whig calls such an event the very best?—the very best event, I say, that I can anticipate is that out of the confusion a strong military despotism may arise, and that the sword, firmly grasped by some rough hand, may give a sort of protection to the miserable wreck of all that immense prosperity and glory. But, as to the noble institutions under which our country has made such progress in liberty, in wealth, in knowledge, in arts, do not deceive yourselves into the belief that we should ever see them again. We should never see them again. We should not deserve to see them. All those nations which envy our greatness would insult our downfall, a downfall which would be all our own work; and the history of our calamities would be told thus: England had institutions which, though imperfect, yet contained within themselves the means of remedying every imperfection; those institutions her legislators wantonly and madly threw away; nor could they urge in their excuse even the wretched plea that they were deceived by false promises: for, in the very petition with the prayer of which they were weak enough to comply, they were told, in the plainest terms, that public ruin would be the effect of their compliance.

Thinking thus, Sir, I will oppose, with every faculty which God has given me, every motion which directly or indirectly tends to the granting of universal suffrage.

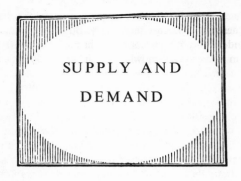

SUPPLY AND DEMAND

Working Aristocracy

THOMAS CARLYLE

[FROM *Past and Present*]

1843

A poor Working Mammonism getting itself 'strangled in the partridge-nets of an Unworking Dilettantism,' and bellowing dreadfully, and already black in the face, is surely a disastrous spectacle! But of a Midas-eared Mammonism, which indeed at bottom all pure Mammonisms are, what better can you expect? No better;—if not this, then something other equally disastrous, if not still more disastrous. Mammonisms, grown asinine, have to become human again, and rational; they have, on the whole, to cease to be Mammonisms, were it even on compulsion, and pressure of the hemp round their neck!—My friends of the Working Aristocracy, there are now a great many things which you also, in your extreme need, will have to consider.

The Continental people, it would seem, are exporting our machinery, beginning to spin cotton and manufacture for themselves, to cut us out of this market and then out of that'!

From Book III, Chapter 9.

Sad news indeed; but irremediable;—by no means the saddest news. The saddest news is, that we should find our National Existence, as I sometimes hear it said, depend on selling manufactured cotton at a farthing an ell cheaper than any other People. A most narrow stand for a great Nation to base itself on! A stand which, with all the Corn-Law Abrogations conceivable, I do not think will be capable of enduring.

My friends, suppose we quitted that stand; suppose we came honestly down from it, and said: 'This is our minimum of cotton-prices. We care not, for the present, to make cotton any cheaper. Do you, if it seem so blessed to you, make cotton cheaper. Fill your lungs with cotton-fuz, your hearts with copperas-fumes, with rage and mutiny; become ye the general gnomes of Europe, slaves of the lamp!'—I admire a Nation which fancies it will die if it do not undersell all other Nations, to the end of the world. Brothers, we will cease to *under*sell them; we will be content to *equal*-sell them; to be happy selling equally with them! I do not see the use of underselling them. Cotton-cloth is already two-pence a yard or lower; and yet bare backs were never more numerous among us. Let inventive men cease to spend their existence incessantly contriving how cotton can be made cheaper; and try to invent, a little, how cotton at its present cheapness could be somewhat justlier divided among us! Let inventive men consider, Whether the Secret of this Universe, and of Man's Life there, does, after all, as we rashly fancy it, consist in making money? There is One God, just, supreme, almighty: but is Mammon the name of him?—With a Hell which means 'Failing to make money,' I do not think there is any Heaven possible that would suit one well; nor so much as an Earth that can be habitable long! In brief, all this Mammon-Gospel, of Supply-and-demand, Competition, Laissez-faire, and Devil take the hindmost, begins to be one of the shabbiest Gospels ever preached; or altogether the shabbiest. Even with Dilettante partridge-nets, and at a horrible expenditure of pain, who shall regret to see the entirely transient, and at best somewhat despicable life strangled out of *it*? At the best, as we say, a somewhat despicable, unvenerable thing, this same 'Laissez-faire'; and now, at the *worst,* fast growing an altogether detestable one!

'But what is to be done with our manufacturing population, with our agricultural, with our ever-increasing population?' cry many.—Aye, what? Many things can be done with them, a hundred things, and a thousand things,—had we once got a soul, and begun to try. This one thing, of doing for them by 'underselling all people,' and filling our own bursten pockets and appetites by the road; and turning over all care for any 'population,' or human or divine consideration except cash only, to the winds, with a 'Laissez-faire' and the rest of it: this is evidently not the thing. Farthing cheaper per yard? No great Nation can stand on the apex of such a pyramid; screwing itself higher and higher; balancing itself on its great-toe! Can England not subsist without being *above* all people in working? England never deliberately purposed such a thing. If England work better than all people, it shall be well. England, like an honest worker, will work as well as she can; and hope the gods may allow her to live on that basis. Laissez-faire and much else being once well dead, how many 'impossibles' will become possible! they are impossible, as cotton-cloth at two-pence an ell was—till men set about making it. The inventive genius of great England will not for ever sit patient with mere wheels and pinions, bobbins, straps and billy-rollers whirring in the head of it. The inventive genius of England is not a Beaver's, or a Spinner's or Spider's genius: it is a *Man's* genius, I hope, with a God over him!

Supply-and-demand?—one begins to be weary of such work. Leave all to egoism, to ravenous greed of money, of pleasure, of applause:—it is the Gospel of Despair! Man *is* a Patent-Digester, then: only give him Free Trade, Free digesting-room; and each of us digest what he can come at, leaving the rest to Fate! My unhappy brethren of the Working Mammonism, my unhappier brethren of the Idle Dilettantism, no world was ever held together in that way for long. A world of mere Patent-Digesters will soon have nothing to digest: such worlds end, and by Law of Nature must end, in 'over-population'; in howling universal famine, 'impossibility,' and suicidal madness, as of endless dog-kennels run rabid. Supply-and-demand shall do its full part, and Free Trade shall be free as air;—thou of the shotbelts, see thou forbid it not, with those paltry, *worse* than Mammonism swindleries and Sliding-scales of thine, which are seen to be swindleries for all thy canting, which in times like ours are very scandalous to see! And Trade never so well freed, and all Tariffs settled or abolished, and Supply-and-demand in full operation,—let us all know that we have yet done nothing; that we have merely cleared the ground for doing.

Yes, were the Corn-Laws ended to-morrow, there is nothing yet ended; there is only room made for all manner of things beginning. The Corn-Laws gone, and Trade made free, it is as good as certain this paralysis of industry will pass away. We shall have another period of commercial enterprise, of victory and prosperity; during which, it is likely, much money will again be made, and all the people may, by the extant methods, still for a space of years, be kept alive and physically fed. The strangling band of Famine will be loosened from our necks; we shall have room again to breathe; time to bethink ourselves, to repent and consider! A precious and thrice-precious space of years; wherein to struggle as for life in reforming our foul ways; in alleviating, instructing, regulating our people; seeking, as for life, that something like spiritual food be imparted them, some real governance and guidance be provided them! It will be a priceless time. For our new period of paroxysm of commercial prosperity will and can, on the old methods of 'Competition and Devil take the hindmost,' prove but a paroxysm: a new paroxysm,—likely enough, if we do not use it better, to be our *last*. In this, of itself, is no salvation. If our Trade in twenty years, 'flourish-ing' as never Trade flourished, could double itself; yet then also, by the old Laissez-faire method, our Population is doubled: we shall be as we are, only twice as many of us, twice and ten times as unmanageable!

All this dire misery, therefore; all this of our poor Work-house Workmen, of our Chartisms, Trades-strikes, Corn-Laws,

Toryisms, and the general downbreak of Laissez-faire in these days,—may we not regard it as a voice from the dumb bosom of Nature, saying to us: 'Behold! Supply-and-demand is not the one Law of Nature; Cash-payment is not the sole nexus of man with man,—how far from it! Deep, far deeper than Supply-and-demand, are Laws, Obligations sacred as Man's Life itself: these also, if you will continue to do work, you shall now learn and obey. He that will learn them, behold Nature is on his side, he shall yet work and prosper with noble rewards. He that will not learn them, Nature is against him; he shall not be able to do work in Nature's empire,— not in hers. Perpetual mutiny, contention, hatred, isolation, execration shall wait on his footsteps, till all men discern that the thing which he attains, however golden it look or be, is not success, but the want of success.'

Supply-and-demand,—alas! For what noble work was there ever yet any audible 'demand' in that poor sense? The man of Macedonia, speaking in vision to an Apostle Paul, 'Come over and help us,' did not specify what rate of wages he would give! Or was the Christian Religion itself accomplished by Prize-Essays, Bridgewater Bequests, and a 'minimum of Four thousand five hundred a year'? No demand that I heard of was made then, audible in any Labour-market, Manchester Chamber of Commerce, or other the like emporium and hiring establishment; silent were all these from any whisper of such demand;—powerless were all these to 'supply' it, had the demand been in thunder and earthquake, with gold Eldorados and Mahometan Paradises for the reward. Ah me, into what waste latitudes, in this Time-Voyage, have we wandered; like adventurous Sindbads;—where the men go about as if by galvanism, with meaningless glaring eyes, and have no soul, but only a beaver-faculty and stomach! The haggard despair of Cotton-factory, Coal-mine operatives, Chandos Farm-labourers, in these days, is painful to behold; but not so painful, hideous to the inner sense, as that brutish god-forgetting Profit-and-Loss Philosophy and Life-theory, which we hear jangled on all hands of us, in senate-houses, spouting-clubs, leading-articles, pulpits and platforms, everywhere as

the Ultimate Gospel and candid Plain-English of Man's Life,
from the throats and pens and thoughts of all-but all men!—

Enlightened Philosophies, like Molière Doctors, will tell
you: 'Enthusiasms, Self-sacrifice, Heaven, Hell and such like:
yes, all that was true enough for old stupid times; all that
used to be true: but we have changed all that, *nous avons
changé tout cela!*' Well; if the heart be got round now into
the right side, and the liver to the left; if man have no heroism
in him deeper than the wish to eat, and in his soul there dwell
now no Infinite of Hope and Awe, and no divine Silence
can become imperative because it is not Sinai Thunder, and
no tie will bind if it be not that of Tyburn gallows-ropes,—
then verily you have changed all that; and for it, and for you,
and for me, behold the Abyss and nameless Annihilation is
ready. So scandalous a beggarly Universe deserves indeed
nothing else; I cannot say I would save it from Annihilation.
Vacuum, and the serene Blue, will be much handsomer; easier
too for all of us. I, for one, decline living as a Patent-Digester.
Patent-Digester, Spinning-Mule, Mayfair Clothes-Horse: many
thanks, but your Chaosships will have the goodness to excuse me!

[FROM Book III, Chapter 10]

Unhappily, my indomitable friend Plugson of Undershot
has, in a great degree, forgotten them;—as, alas, all the world
has; as, alas, our very Dukes and Soul-Overseers have, whose
special trade it was to remember them! Hence these tears.—
Plugson, who has indomitably spun Cotton merely to gain
thousands of pounds, I have to call as yet a Bucanier and
Chactaw; till there come something better, still more indomitable from him. His hundred Thousand-pound Notes, if there
be nothing other, are to me but as the hundred Scalps in
a Chactaw wigwam. The blind Plugson: he was a Captain of
Industry, born member of the Ultimate genuine Aristocracy
of this Universe, could he have known it! These thousand men
that span and toiled round him, they were a regiment whom
he had enlisted, man by man; to make war on a very genuine

enemy: Bareness of back, and disobedient Cotton-fibre, which will not, unless forced to it, consent to cover bare backs. Here is a most genuine enemy; over whom all creatures will wish him victory. He enlisted his thousand men; said to them, 'Come, brothers, let us have a dash at Cotton!' They follow with cheerful shout; they gain such a victory over Cotton as the Earth has to admire and clap hands at: but, alas, it is yet only of the Bucanier or Chactaw sort,—as good as no victory! Foolish Plugson of St. Dolly Undershot: does he hope to become illustrious by hanging up the scalps in his wigwam, the hundred thousands at his banker's, and saying, Behold my scalps? Why, Plugson, even thy own host is all in mutiny: Cotton is conquered; but the 'bare backs'—are worse covered than ever! Indomitable Plugson, thou must cease to be a Chactaw; thou and others; thou thyself, if no other!

LABOR LAWS

Women and Children in the Mines

HARRIET MARTINEAU

[FROM *History of England*]

1849

In 1842, Lord Ashley had brought forward a Bill on behalf of a set of people who really appeared to have been neglected by all mankind, and whose case, when exposed by Lord Ashley, startled Parliament and the country. People who move about above-ground, in the face of day, may exhibit their own case, and hope to have it considered by those who look on; but it now appeared that there was a class moving about underground, in the mines and coal-pits of England and Scotland, whose condition of suffering and brutalization exceeded all that had ever been known, or could be believed. A commission of inquiry, obtained by Lord Ashley, laid open a scene which shocked the whole country. Women were employed as beasts of burden; children were stunted and diseased, beaten, overworked, oppressed in every way; both women and children made to crawl on all-fours in the passages

From Book VI, Chapter 7.

of the pits, dragging carts by a chain passing from the waist between the legs; and all lived in an atmosphere of filth and profligacy which could hardly leave a thought or feeling untainted by vice. This was seen at once to be a special, as well as an extreme case; and a Bill for the relief of the women and children of the colliery population was passed with a rapidity which somewhat injured its quality. It was known that a strong opposition would be raised if the thing were not done at once. It was certain that a multitude of women and children would be thrown out of employment after the passage of the Bill; and not a few persons declared the commissioners' report to be full of exaggeration; and the great permanent objection remained, of the disastrous consequences of interfering with the labor-market. The great majority of the nation, however, felt that it was better to have a large burden thrown on the parishes for a time, than to let such abuses continue; that, making every allowance for exaggeration, the facts were horrible; and that, the labor-market being already interfered with by Factory Bills, this was not the point to stop at. So the Bill passed, with some amendments which Lord Ashley submitted to, rather than wait. By this Bill, women were excluded from mining and colliery labor altogether. Boys were not to be employed under the age of ten years; and the term of apprenticeship was limited. The Secretary of State was empowered to appoint inspectors of mines and collieries, to see that the provisions of the Bill were carried out. The new law took effect after nine months from its date. The operation has, from time to time, been reported as beneficial; and, though it has been found difficult to prevent women from getting down to work in the pits after the habits of a life had made other employment unsuitable or impossible to them, the pressure upon parish or other charity funds turned out to be less than had been anticipated. It was a great thing to have put a stop to the employment of women in toil wholly unsuited to their frame and their natural duties; and to have broken in upon a system of child-slavery which could never have existed so long in our country, if it had not been hidden in the chambers of the earth.

The Ten-Hours Bill

THOMAS BABINGTON MACAULAY

[FROM a speech delivered in the House of Commons,
22 May 1846]

The details of the bill, Sir, will be more conveniently and
more regularly discussed when we consider it in Committee.
Our business at present is with the principle: and the principle,
we are told by many gentlemen of great authority, is un-
sound. In their opinion, neither this bill, nor any other bill
regulating the hours of labour, can be defended. This, they
say, is one of those matters about which we ought not to
legislate at all: one of those matters which settle themselves
far better than any government can settle them. Now it is
most important that this point should be fully cleared up.
We certainly ought not to usurp functions which do not properly belong to us: but, on the other hand, we ought not to
abdicate functions which do properly belong to us. I hardly
know which is the greater pest to society, a paternal government, that is to say a prying, meddlesome government, which
intrudes itself into every part of human life, and which thinks
that it can do everything for everybody better than anybody
can do anything for himself; or a careless, lounging government, which suffers grievances, such as it could at once
remove, to grow and multiply, and which to all complaint
and remonstrance has only one answer: "We must let things
alone: we must let things take their course: we must let things
find their level." There is no more important problem in
politics than to ascertain the just mean between these two
most pernicious extremes, to draw correctly the line which
divides those cases in which it is the duty of the State to

From *The Works of Lord Macaulay*, edited by Lady Trevelyan
London: 1866), Volume VIII, pages 361-75.

interfere from those cases in which it is the duty of the State to abstain from interference. . . . Our statesmen cannot now be accused of being busybodies. But I am afraid that there is, even in some of the ablest and most upright among them, a tendency to the opposite fault. I will give an instance of what I mean. Fifteen years ago it became evident that railroads would soon, in every part of the kingdom, supersede to a great extent the old highways. The tracing of the new routes which were to join all the chief cities, ports, and naval arsenals of the island was a matter of the highest national importance. But unfortunately, those who should have acted for the nation refused to interfere. Consequently, numerous questions which were really public, questions which concerned the public convenience, the public prosperity, the public security, were treated as private questions. That the whole society was interested in having a good system of internal communication seemed to be forgotten. The speculator who wanted a large dividend on his shares, the landowner who wanted a large price for his acres, obtained a full hearing. But nobody applied to be heard on behalf of the community. The effects of that great error we feel, and we shall not soon cease to feel. Unless I am greatly mistaken, we are in danger of committing tonight an error of the same kind. The honourable Member for Montrose [Mr. Hume] and my honourable friend the Member for Sheffield [Mr. Ward] think that the question before us is merely a question between the old and the new theories of commerce. They cannot understand how any friend of free trade can wish the Legislature to interfere between the capitalist and the labourer. They say, "You do not make a law to settle the price of gloves, or the texture of gloves, or the length of credit which the glover shall give. You leave it to him to determine whether he will charge high or low prices, whether he will use strong or flimsy materials, whether he will trust or insist on ready money. You acknowledge that these are matters which he ought to be left to settle with his customers, and that we ought not to interfere. It is possible that he may manage his shop ill. But it is certain that we shall manage it ill. On the same grounds on which you leave the seller of gloves and the buyer of gloves to make their own contract, you ought to leave the seller of labour and the buyer of labour to make their own contract." . . .

Trade, considered merely as trade, considered merely with reference to the pecuniary interest of the contracting parties, can hardly be too free. But there is a great deal of trade which cannot be considered merely as trade, and which affects higher than pecuniary interests. And to say that Government never ought to regulate such trade is a monstrous proposition, a proposition at which Adam Smith would have stood aghast. We impose some restrictions on trade for purposes of police. Thus, we do not suffer everybody who has a cab and a horse to ply for passengers in the streets of London. We do not leave the fare to be determined by the supply and the demand. We do not permit a driver to extort a guinea for going half a mile on a rainy day when there is no other vehicle on the stand. We impose some restrictions on trade for the sake of revenue. Thus, we forbid a farmer to cultivate tobacco on his own ground. We impose some restrictions on trade for the sake of national defence. Thus, we compel a man who would rather be ploughing or weaving to go into the militia; and we fix the amount of pay which he shall receive without asking his consent. Nor is there in all this anything inconsistent with the soundest political economy. For the science of political economy teaches us only that we ought not on commercial grounds to interfere with the liberty of commerce; and we, in the cases which I have put, interfere with the liberty of commerce on higher than commercial grounds.

And now, Sir, to come closer to the case with which we have to deal, I say, first, that where the health of the community is concerned, it may be the duty of the State to interfere with the contracts of individuals . . . . We should have nothing to do with the contracts between you and your tenants, if those contracts affected only pecuniary interests. But higher than pecuniary interests are at stake. It concerns the commonwealth that the great body of the people should not live in a way which makes life wretched and short, which enfeebles the body and pollutes the mind. If, by living in

houses which resemble hogstyes, great numbers of our countrymen have contracted the tastes of hogs, if they have become
so familiar with filth and stench and contagion, that they
burrow without reluctance in holes which would turn the
stomach of any man of cleanly habits, that is only an additional proof that we have too long neglected our duties, and
an additional reason for our now performing them.

Secondly, I say that where the public morality is concerned
it may be the duty of the State to interfere with the contracts
of individuals. Take the traffic in licentious books and pictures. Will anybody deny that the State may, with propriety,
interdict that traffic? . . .

Will it be denied that the health of a large part of the rising
generation may be seriously affected by the contracts which
this bill is intended to regulate? Can any man who has read
the evidence which is before us, can any man who has ever
observed young people, can any man who remembers his own
sensations when he was young, doubt that twelve hours a day
of labour in a factory is too much for a lad of thirteen?

Or will it be denied that this is a question in which public
morality is concerned? Can any one doubt,—none, I am sure,
of my friends around me doubts,—that education is a matter
of the highest importance to the virtue and happiness of a
people? Now we know that there can be no education without
leisure. It is evident that, after deducting from the day twelve
hours for labour in a factory, and the additional hours necessary for exercise, refreshment, and repose, there will not
remain time enough for education. . . .

But, it is said, this bill, though it directly limits only the
labour of infants, will, by an indirect operation, limit also the
labour of adults. Now, Sir, though I am not prepared to vote
for a bill directly limiting the labour of adults, I will plainly
say that I do not think that the limitation of the labour of
adults would necessarily produce all those frightful consequences which we have heard predicted. You cheer me in
very triumphant tones, as if I had uttered some monstrous
paradox. Pray, does it not occur to any of you that the labour
of adults is now limited in this country? Are you not aware

that you are living in a society in which the labour of adults is limited to six days in seven? It is you, not I, who maintain a paradox opposed to the opinions and the practices of all nations and ages. . . . Is it not amusing to hear a gentleman pronounce with confidence that any legislation which limits the labour of adults must produce consequences fatal to society, without once reflecting that in the society in which he lives, and in every other society that exists, or ever has existed, there has been such legislation without any evil consequence? . . . The French Jacobins decreed that the Sunday should no longer be a day of rest; but they instituted another day of rest, the Decade. They swept away the holidays of the Roman Catholic Church; but they instituted another set of holidays, the Sansculottides, one sacred to Genius, one to Industry, one to Opinion, and so on. I say, therefore, that the practice of limiting by law the time of the labour of adults, is so far from being, as some gentlemen seem to think, an unheard of and monstrous practice, that it is a practice as universal as cookery, as the wearing of clothes, as the use of domestic animals. . . .

Now, is there a single argument in the whole Speech of my honourable friend the Member for Sheffield which does not tell just as strongly against the laws which enjoin the observance of the Sunday as against the bill on our table? Surely, if his reasoning is good for hours, it must be equally good for days. . . .

I hear men of eminent ability and knowledge lay down the proposition that a diminution of the time of labour must be followed by a diminution of the wages of labour, as a proposition universally true, as a proposition capable of being strictly demonstrated, as a proposition about which there can be no more doubt than about any theorem in Euclid. Sir, I deny the truth of the proposition; and for this plain reason. We have already, by law, greatly reduced the time of labour in factories. Thirty years ago, the late Sir Robert Peel told the House that it was a common practice to make children of eight years of age toil in mills fifteen hours a day. A law has since been made which prohibits persons under eighteen years of age from working in mills more than twelve hours a day. That law was opposed on exactly the same grounds on which the bill before us is opposed. Parliament was told, as it is told now, that with the time of labour the quantity of production would decrease, that with the quantity of production the wages would decrease, that our manufacturers would be unable to contend with foreign manufacturers, and that the condition of the labouring population instead of being made better by the interference of the Legislature would be made worse. Read over those debates; and you may imagine that you are reading the debate of this evening. Parliament disregarded these prophecies. The time of labour was limited. Have wages fallen? Has the cotton trade left Manchester for France or Germany? Has the condition of the working people become more miserable? Is it not universally acknowledged that the evils which were so confidently predicted have not come to pass? . . .

Of course, Sir, I do not mean to say that a man will not produce more in a week by working seven days than by working six days. But I very much doubt whether, at the end of a year, he will generally have produced more by working seven days a week than by working six days a week; and I firmly believe that, at the end of twenty years, he will have produced much less by working seven days a week than by working six days a week. In the same manner I do not deny that a factory child will produce more, in a single day, by working twelve hours than by working ten hours, and by working fifteen hours than by working twelve hours. But I do deny that a great society in which children work fifteen, or even twelve hours a day, will, in the lifetime of a generation, produce as much as if those children had worked less. If we consider man merely in a commercial point of view, if we consider him merely as a machine for the production of worsted and calico, let us not forget what a piece of mechanism he is, how fearfully and wonderfully made. We do not treat a fine horse or a sagacious dog exactly as we treat a spinning jenny. Nor will any slaveholder, who has sense enough to know his own interest, treat his human chattels exactly as he treats his horses and his dogs. And would you treat the free labourer of England like a mere wheel or pulley? Rely on it that intense labour, beginning too early in life, continued too long every day, stunting the growth of the body, stunting the growth of the mind, leaving no time for healthful exercise, leaving no time for intellectual culture, must impair all those high qualities which have made our country great. Your overworked boys will become a feeble and ignoble race of men, the parents of a more feeble and more ignoble progeny; nor will it be long before the deterioration of the labourer will injuriously affect those very interests to which his physical and moral energies have been sacrificed. On the other hand, a day of rest recurring in every week, two or three hours of leisure, exercise, innocent amusement or useful study, recurring every day, must improve the whole man, physically, morally, intellectually; and the improvement of the man will improve all that the man produces. . . . What is it, Sir, that makes the great difference between country and country? Not the exuberance of soil; not the mildness of climate; not mines, nor havens, nor rivers. . . . Look at North America. Two centuries ago the sites on which now arise mills, and hotels, and banks, and colleges, and churches, and the Senate Houses of flourishing commonwealths, were deserts abandoned to the panther and the bear. What has made the change? Was it the rich mould, or the redundant rivers? No: the prairies were as fertile, the Ohio and the Hudson were as broad and as full then as now. Was the improvement the effect of some great transfer of capital from the old world to the new? No: the emigrants generally carried out with them no more than a pittance; but they carried out the English heart, and head, and arm; and the English heart and head and arm turned the wilderness into cornfield and orchard, and the huge trees of the primeval forest into cities and fleets. Man, man is the great instrument that produces wealth. . . . Therefore it is that we are not poorer but richer, because we have, through many ages, rested from our labour one day in seven. That day is not lost. While industry is suspended, while the plough lies in the furrow, while the

Exchange is silent, while no smoke ascends from the factory, a process is going on quite as important to the wealth of nations as any process which is performed on more busy days. Man, the machine of machines, the machine compared with which all the contrivances of the Watts and the Arkwrights are worthless, is repairing and winding up, so that he returns to his labours on the Monday with clearer intellect, with livelier spirits, with renewed corporal vigour. Never will I believe that what makes a population stronger, and healthier, and wiser, and better, can ultimately make it poorer. You try to frighten us by telling us that, in some German factories, the young work seventeen hours in the twenty-four, that they work so hard that among thousands there is not one who grows to such a stature that he can be admitted into the army; and you ask whether, if we pass this bill, we can possibly hold our own against such competition as this? Sir, I laugh at the thought of such competition. If ever we are forced to yield the foremost place among commercial nations, we shall yield it, not to a race of degenerate dwarfs, but to some people pre-eminently vigorous in body and in mind.

Labor Laws and the Clergy

KARL MARX

[FROM the *New York Daily Tribune*, 15 March 1853]

The Parliamentary debates of the week offer but little of interest.... The industrial proletariat of England has renewed with double vigor its old campaign for the Ten-Hours Bill and against the *truck and shoppage system*. As the demands of this kind shall be brought before the House of

Commons, to which numerous petitions on the subject have already been presented, there will be an opportunity for me to dwell in a future letter on the cruel and infamous practices of the factory-despots, who are in the habit of making the press and the tribune resounding with their liberal rhetorics. For the present it may suffice to recall to memory that from 1802 there has been a continual strife on the part of the English working people for legislative interference with the duration of factory labor, until in 1847 the celebrated Ten-Hours Act of John Fielden was passed, whereby young persons and females were prohibited to work in any factory longer than ten hours a day. The liberal mill-lords speedily found out that under this act factories might be worked by shifts and relays. In 1849 an action of law was brought before the Court of Exchequer, and the Judge decided, that to work the relay or shift-system, with two sets of children, the adults working the whole space of time during which the machinery was running, was legal. It therefore became necessary to go to Parliament again, and in 1850 the relay and shift-system was condemned there, but the Ten-Hours Act was transformed into a Ten and a Half Hours act. Now, at this moment, the working-classes demand a restitution *in integrum* of the original Ten-Hours Bill: yet, in order to make it efficient, they add the demand of a restriction of the moving power of machinery.

Such is, in short, the exoteric history of the Ten-Hours Act. Its secret history was as follows: The landed Aristocracy having suffered a defeat from the bourgeoisie by the passing of the Reform bill of 1831, and being assailed in "their most sacred interests" by the cry of the manufacturers for free-trade and the abolition of the Corn Laws, resolved to resist the middle-class by espousing the cause and claims of the working men against their masters, and especially by rallying around their demands for the limitation of factory labor. So called philanthropic Lords were then at the head of all Ten-Hours meetings. Lord Ashley has even made a sort of "re-nommée" by his performances in this movement. The landed aristocracy having received a deadly blow by the actual aboli-tion of the Corn Laws in 1846, took their vengeance by forcing the Ten-Hours Bill of 1847 upon Parliament. But the industrial bourgeoisie recovered by judiciary authority, what they had lost by Parliamentary legislation. In 1850, the wrath of the Landlords had gradually subsided, and they made a compromise with the Mill lords, condemning the shift-system, but imposing, at the same time, as a penalty for the enforcement of the law, half an hour extra work *per diem* on the working-classes. At the present juncture, however, as they feel the approach of their final struggle with the men of the Manchester school, they are again trying to get hold of the short-time movement; but, not daring to come forward themselves, they endeavor to undermine the Cotton lords by directing the popular force against them through the medium of the *State Church Clergymen*. In what rude manner these holy men have taken the anti-industrial crusade into their hands, may be seen from the following few instances. . . .

The motive, that has so suddenly metamorphosed the gentlemen of the Established Church, into as many knight-errants of labor's rights, and so fervent knights too, has already been pointed out. They are not only laying in a stock of popularity for the rainy days of approaching Democracy, they are not only conscious, that the Established Church is essentially an aristocratic institution, which must either stand or fall with the landed Oligarchy—there is something more. The men of the Manchester School are Anti-State Church men, they are Dissenters, they are, above all, so highly enamored of the £13,000,000 annually abstracted from their pockets by the State-Church in England and Wales alone, that they are resolved to bring about a separation between those profane millions and the holy orders, the better to qualify the latter for heaven. The reverend gentlemen, therefore, are struggling *pro aris et focis*. The men of the Manchester School, however, may infer from this diversion, that they will be unable to abstract the political power from the hands of the Aristocracy, unless they consent, with whatever reluctance, to give the people also their full share in it.

On the Continent, hanging, shooting and transportation is the order of the day. But the executioners are themselves tangible and hangable beings, and their deeds are recorded in the conscience of the whole civilized world. At the same time there acts in England an invisible, intangible and silent despot, condemning individuals, in extreme cases, to the most cruel of deaths, and driving in its noiseless, every day working, whole races and whole classes of men from the soil of their forefathers, like the angel with the fiery sword who drove Adam from Paradise. In the latter form the work of the unseen social despot calls itself *forced emigration,* in the former it is called *starvation.*

Some further cases of starvation have occurred in London during the present month. I remember only that of Mary Ann Sandry, aged 43 years, who died in Coal-lane, Shadwell, London. Mr. Thomas Peene, the surgeon, assisting the Coroner's inquest, said the deceased died from starvation and exposure to the cold. The deceased was lying on a small heap of straw, without the slightest covering. The room was completely destitute of furniture, firing and food. Five young children were sitting on the bare flooring, crying from hunger and cold by the side of the mother's dead body.

On the working of *"forced emigration"* in my next.

KARL MARX.

LABOR UNIONS

Collective Bargaining

ELIZABETH CLEGHORN GASKELL

[FROM *Mary Barton*]

1848

The day arrived on which the masters were to have an interview with a deputation of the workpeople. The meeting was to take place in a public room, at an hotel; and there, about eleven o'clock, the mill-owners, who had received the foreign orders, began to collect.

Of course, the first subject, however full their minds might be of another, was the weather. Having done their duty by all the showers and sunshine which had occurred during the past week, they fell to talking about the business which brought them together. There might be about twenty gentlemen in the room, including some by courtesy, who were not immediately concerned in the settlement of the present question; but who, nevertheless, were sufficiently interested to attend. These were divided into little groups, who did not seem by any means unanimous. Some were for a slight concession, just a sugar-plum to quieten the naughty child, a

From Chapter 16.

sacrifice to peace and quietness. Some were steadily and vehemently opposed to the dangerous precedent of yielding one jot or one tittle to the outward force of a turn-out. It was teaching the workpeople how to become masters, said they. Did they want the wildest thing hereafter, they would know that the way to obtain their wishes would be to strike work. Besides, one or two of those present had only just returned from the New Bailey, where one of the turn-outs had been tried for a cruel assault on a poor north-country weaver, who had attempted to work at the low price. They were indignant, and justly so, at the merciless manner in which the poor fellow had been treated; and their indignation at wrong, took (as it often does) the extreme form of revenge. They felt as if, rather than yield to the body of men who were resorting to such cruel measures towards their fellow-workmen, they, the masters, would sooner relinquish all the benefits to be derived from the fulfilment of the commission, in order that the workmen might suffer keenly. They forgot that the strike was in this instance the consequence of want and need, suffered unjustly, as the endurers believed; for, however insane, and without ground of reason, such was their belief, and such was the cause of their violence. It is a great truth that you cannot extinguish violence by violence. You may put it down for a time; but while you are crowing over your imaginary success, see if it does not return with seven devils worse than its former self!

No one thought of treating the workmen as brethren and friends, and openly, clearly, as appealing to reasonable men, stating exactly and fully the circumstances which led the masters to think it was the wise policy of the time to make sacrifices themselves, and to hope for them from the operatives.

In going from group to group in the room, you caught such a medley of sentences as the following:

"Poor devils! they're near enough to starving, I'm afraid. Mrs. Aldred makes two cows' heads into soup every week, and people come many miles to fetch it; and if these times last, we must try and do more. But we must not be bullied into any thing!"

"A rise of a shilling or so won't make much difference, and they will go away thinking they've gained their point."

"That's the very thing I object to. They'll think so, and whenever they've a point to gain, no matter how unreasonable, they'll strike work."

"It really injures them more than us."

"I don't see how our interests can be separated."

"The d——d brute had thrown vitriol on the poor fellow's ankles, and you know what a bad part that is to heal. He had to stand still with the pain, and that left him at the mercy of the cruel wretch, who beat him about the head till you'd hardly have known he was a man. They doubt if he'll live."

"If it were only for that, I'll stand out against them, even if it is the cause of my ruin."

"Ay, I for one won't yield one farthing to the cruel brutes; they're more like wild beasts than human beings."

(Well, who might have made them different?)

"I say, Carson, just go and tell Duncombe of this fresh instance of their abominable conduct. He's wavering, but I think this will decide him."

The door was now opened, and the waiter announced that the men were below, and asked if it were the pleasure of the gentlemen that they should be shown up.

They assented, and rapidly took their places round the official table; looking, as like as they could, to the Roman senators who awaited the irruption of Brennus and his Gauls.

Tramp, tramp, came the heavy clogged feet up the stairs; and in a minute five wild, earnest-looking men, stood in the room. John Barton, from some mistake as to time, was not among them. Had they been larger boned men, you would have called them gaunt; as it was, they were little of stature, and their fustian clothes hung loosely upon their shrunk limbs. In choosing their delegates, too, the operatives had had more regard to their brains, and power of speech, than to their wardrobes; they might have read the opinions of that worthy Professor Teufelsdröckh, in *Sartor Resartus,* to judge from the dilapidated coats and trousers, which yet clothed men of parts and of power. It was long since many of them had known the luxury of a new article of dress; and air-gaps were to be seen in their garments. Some of the masters were rather affronted at such a ragged detachment coming between the wind and their nobility; but what cared they?

At the request of a gentleman hastily chosen to officiate as chairman, the leader of the delegates read, in a high-pitched, psalm-singing voice, a paper, containing the operatives' statement of the case at issue, their complaints, and their demands, which last were not remarkable for moderation.

He was then desired to withdraw for a few minutes, with his fellow-delegates, to another room, while the masters considered what should be their definite answer.

When the men had left the room, a whispered earnest consultation took place, every one re-urging his former arguments. The conceders carried the day, but only by a majority of one. The minority haughtily and audibly expressed their dissent from the measures to be adopted, even after the delegates re-entered the room; their words and looks did not pass unheeded by the quick-eyed operatives; their names were registered in bitter hearts.

The masters could not consent to the advance demanded by the workmen. They would agree to give one shilling per week more than they had previously offered. Were the delegates empowered to accept such offer?

They were empowered to accept or decline any offer made that day by the masters.

Then it might be as well for them to consult among themselves as to what should be their decision. They again withdrew.

It was not for long. They came back, and positively declined any compromise of their demands.

Then up sprang Mr. Henry Carson, the head and voice of the violent party among the masters, and addressing the chairman, even before the scowling operatives, he proposed some resolutions, which he, and those who agreed with him, had been concocting during this last absence of the deputation.

They were, firstly, withdrawing the proposal just made, and declaring all communication between the masters and that particular Trades' Union at an end; secondly, declaring that no master would employ any workman in future, unless he signed a declaration that he did not belong to any Trades' Union, and pledged himself not to assist or subscribe to any society, having for its object interference with the masters' powers; and, thirdly, that the masters should pledge themselves to protect and encourage all workmen willing to accept employment on those conditions, and at the rate of wages first offered. Considering that the men who now stood listening with lowering brows of defiance were all of them leading members of the Union, such resolutions were in themselves sufficiently provocative of animosity: but not content with simply stating them, Harry Carson went on to characterise the conduct of the workmen in no measured terms; every word he spoke rendering their looks more livid, their glaring eyes more fierce. One among them would have spoken, but checked himself in obedience to the stern glance and pressure on his arm, received from the leader. Mr. Carson sat down, and a friend instantly got up to second the motion. It was carried, but far from unanimously. The chairman announced it to the delegates (who had been once more turned out of the room for a division). They received it with deep brooding silence, but spake never a word, and left the room without even a bow.

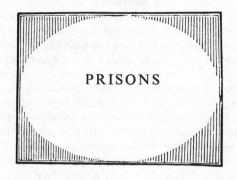

PRISONS

A Visit to Newgate

CHARLES DICKENS

[FROM *Sketches by Boz*]

1836

It is necessary to explain here, that the buildings in the prison, or in other words the different wards, form a square, of which the four sides abut respectively on the Old Bailey, the old College of Physicians (now forming a part of Newgate Market), the Sessions House, and Newgate Street. The intermediate space is divided into several paved yards, in which the prisoners take such air and exercise as can be had in such a place. These yards, with the exception of that in which prisoners under sentence of death are confined (of which we shall presently give a more detailed description), run parallel with Newgate Street, and consequently from the Old Bailey, as it were, to Newgate Market. The women's side is in the right wing of the prison nearest the Sessions House. As we were introduced into this part of the building first, we will adopt the same order and introduce our readers to it also.

From Scene 25.

Turning to the right, then, down the passage to which we
just now adverted, omitting any mention of intervening gates—
for if we noticed every gate that was unlocked for us to pass
through and locked again as soon as we had passed, we should
require a gate at every comma—we came to a door composed
of thick bars of wood, through which were discernible, passing
to and fro in a narrow yard, some twenty women: the majority
of whom, however, as soon as they were aware of the presence
of strangers, retreated to their wards. One side of this yard
is railed off at a considerable distance, and formed into a
kind of iron cage, about five feet ten inches in height, roofed
at the top, and defended in front by iron bars, from which
the friends of the female prisoners communicate with them.
In one corner of this singular-looking den, was a yellow,
haggard, decrepit old woman in a tattered gown that had
once been black, and the remains of an old straw bonnet,
with faded ribbon of the same hue, in earnest conversation
with a young girl—a prisoner, of course—of about two-and-
twenty. It is impossible to imagine a more poverty-stricken
object, or a creature so borne down in soul and body, by
excess of misery and destitution as the old woman. The girl
was a good-looking robust female, with a profusion of hair
streaming about in the wind—for she had no bonnet on—
and a man's silk pocket-handkerchief loosely thrown over a
most ample pair of shoulders. The old woman was talking
in that low, stifled tone of voice which tells so forcibly of
mental anguish; and every now and then burst into an irrepressible, sharp, abrupt cry of grief, the most distressing sound
that ears can hear. The girl was perfectly unmoved. Hardened
beyond all hope of redemption, she listened doggedly to her
mother's entreaties, whatever they were; and, beyond en-
quiring after "Jem," and eagerly catching at the few halfpence
her miserable parent had brought her, took no more apparent
interest in the conversation than the most unconcerned spectators. Heaven knows there were enough of them, in the
persons of the other prisoners in the yard, who were no more
concerned by what was passing before their eyes, and within
their hearing, than if they were blind and deaf. Why should

they be? Inside the prison and out such scenes were too
familiar to them to excite even a passing thought, unless of
ridicule or contempt for feelings which they had long since
forgotten.

A little farther on, a squalid-looking woman in a slovenly
thick-bordered cap, with her arms muffled in a large red
shawl, the fringed ends of which straggled nearly to the bottom
of a dirty white apron, was communicating some instructions
to *her* visitor—her daughter evidently. The girl was thinly
clad, and shaking with the cold. Some ordinary word of
recognition passed between her and her mother when she
appeared at the grating, but neither hope, condolence, regret,
nor affection was expressed on either side. The mother whispered her instructions, and the girl received them with her
pinched-up half-starved features twisted into an expression of
careful cunning. It was some scheme for the woman's defence
that she was disclosing, perhaps; and a sullen smile came over
the girl's face for an instant, as if she were pleased—not so
much at the probability of her mother's liberation, as at the
chance of her "getting off" in spite of her prosecutors. The
dialogue was soon concluded; and with the same careless indifference with which they had approached each other, the
mother turned towards the inner end of the yard, and the
girl to the gate at which she had entered. . . .

Two or three women were standing at different parts of
the grating, conversing with their friends, but a very large
proportion of the prisoners appeared to have no friends at
all, beyond such of their old companions as might happen to
be within the walls. So, passing hastily down the yard, and
pausing only for an instant to notice the little incidents we
have just recorded, we were conducted up a clean and well-
lighted flight of stone stairs to one of the wards. There are
several in this part of the building, but a description of one
is a description of the whole.

It was a spacious, bare, whitewashed apartment, lighted,
of course, by windows looking into the interior of the prison,
but far more light and airy than one could reasonably expect
to find in such a situation. There was a large fire with a deal

table before it, round which ten or a dozen women were seated on wooden forms at dinner. Along both sides of the room ran a shelf; below it, at regular intervals, a row of large hooks were fixed in the wall, on each of which was hung the sleeping-mat of a prisoner, her rug and blanket being folded up and placed on the shelf above. At night these mats are placed on the floor, each beneath the hook on which it hangs during the day; and the ward is thus made to answer the purposes both of a day-room and sleeping apartment. Over the fire-place was a large sheet of pasteboard, on which were displayed a variety of texts from Scripture, which were also scattered about the room in scraps about the size and shape of the copy-slips which are used in schools. On the table was a sufficient provision of a kind of stewed beef and brown bread, in pewter dishes, which are kept perfectly bright, and displayed on shelves in great order and regularity when they are not in use.

The women rose hastily, on our entrance, and retired in a hurried manner to either side of the fire-place. They were all cleanly—many of them decently—attired, and there was nothing peculiar, either in their appearance or demeanour. One or two resumed the needlework which they had probably laid aside at the commencement of their meal; others gazed at the visitors with listless curiosity; and a few retired behind their companions to the very end of the room, as if desirous to avoid even the casual observation of the strangers. Some old Irish women, both in this and other wards, to whom the thing was no novelty, appeared perfectly indifferent to our presence, and remained standing close to the seats from which they had just risen; but the general feeling among the females seemed to be one of uneasiness during the period of our stay among them, which was very brief. Not a word was uttered during the time of our remaining, unless, indeed, by the wardswoman in reply to some question which we put to the turnkey who accompanied us. In every ward on the female side, a wardswoman is appointed to preserve order, and a similar regulation is adopted among the males. The wardsmen and wardswomen are all prisoners, selected for good conduct.

They alone are allowed the privilege of sleeping on bedsteads; a small stump bedstead being placed in every ward for that purpose. On both sides of the gaol is a small receiving-room, to which prisoners are conducted on their first reception, and whence they cannot be removed until they have been examined by the surgeon of the prison.

Retracing our steps to the dismal passage in which we found ourselves at first (and which, by the bye, contains three or four dark cells for the accommodation of refractory prisoners), we were led through a narrow yard to the "school"—a portion of the prison set apart for boys under fourteen years of age. In a tolerable-sized room, in which were writing-materials and some copy-books, was the schoolmaster, with a couple of his pupils; the remainder having been fetched from an adjoining apartment, the whole were drawn up in line for our inspection. There were fourteen of them in all, some with shoes, some without; some in pinafores without jackets, others in jackets without pinafores, and one in scarce any thing at all. The whole number, without an exception we believe, had been committed for trial on charges of pocket-picking; and fourteen such terrible little faces we never beheld. There was not one redeeming feature among them—not a glance of honesty—not a wink expressive of any thing but the gallows and the hulks in the whole collection. As to any thing like shame or contrition, that was entirely out of the question. They were evidently quite gratified at being thought worth the trouble of looking at; their idea appeared to be, that we had come to see Newgate as a grand affair, and that they were an indispensable part of the show; and every boy as he "fell in" to the line, actually seemed as pleased and important as if he had done something excessively meritorious in getting there at all. We never looked upon a more disagreeable sight, because we never saw fourteen such hopeless creatures of neglect before.

On either side of the school-yard is a yard for men, in one of which—that towards Newgate Street—prisoners of the more respectable class are confined. Of the other, we have little description to offer, as the different wards necessarily partake of the same character. They are provided, like the wards on the women's side, with mats and rugs, which are disposed of in the same manner during the day; the only very striking difference between their appearance and that of the wards inhabited by the females is the utter absence of any employment. Huddled together on two opposite forms, by the fireside, sit twenty men perhaps,—here a boy in livery; there a man in a rough great-coat and top-boots; farther on, a desperate-looking fellow in his shirt sleeves, with an old Scotch cap upon his shaggy head; near him again, a tall ruffian, in a smock-frock; next to him a miserable being of distressed appearance, with his head resting on his hand,—all alike in one respect, all idle and listless: when they do leave the fire, sauntering moodily about, lounging in the window, or leaning against the wall, vacantly swinging their bodies to and fro. With the exception of a man reading an old newspaper, in two or three instances, this was the case in every ward we entered.

The only communication these men have with their friends, is through two close iron gratings, with an intermediate space of about a yard in width between the two, so that nothing can be handed across, nor can the prisoner have any communication by touch with the person who visits him. The married men have a separate grating at which to see their wives, but its construction is the same.

The prison chapel is situated at the back of the governor's house; the latter having no windows looking into the interior of the prison. Whether the associations connected with the place—the knowledge that here a portion of the burial service is, on some dreadful occasions, performed over the quick and not upon the dead—cast over it a still more gloomy and sombre air than art has imparted to it, we know not, but its appearance is very striking. There is something in a silent and deserted place of worship solemn and impressive at any time; and the very dissimilarity of this one from any we have been accustomed to only enhances the impression. The meanness of its appointments—the bare and scanty pulpit, with the paltry painted pillars on either side—the women's gallery with its great heavy curtain—the men's with its unpainted benches and dingy front—the tottering little table at the altar, with the commandments on the wall above it, scarcely legible through lack of paint, and dust and damp—so unlike the velvet and gilding, the marble and wood, of a modern church—are strange and striking. . . .

Leaving the chapel, descending to the passage so frequently alluded to, and crossing the yard before noticed as being allotted to prisoners of a more respectable description than the generality of men confined here, the visitor arrives at a thick iron gate of great size and strength. Having been admitted through it by the turnkey on duty, he turns sharp round to the left, and pauses before another gate; and having passed this last barrier, he stands in the most terrible part of this gloomy building—the condemned ward. . . .

In the first apartment into which we were conducted—which was at the top of a staircase, and immediately over the press-room—were five-and-twenty or thirty prisoners, all under sentence of death, awaiting the result of the recorder's report—men of all ages and appearances from a hardened old offender with swarthy face and grizzly beard of three days' growth, to a handsome boy, not fourteen years old, and of singularly youthful appearance even for that age, who had been condemned for burglary. There was nothing remarkable in the appearance of these prisoners. One or two decently dressed men were brooding with a dejected air over the fire; several little groups of two or three had been engaged in conversation at the upper end of the room or in the windows; and the remainder were crowded round a young man seated at a table, who appeared to be engaged in teaching the younger ones to write. The room was large, airy, and clean. There was very little anxiety or mental suffering depicted in the countenance of any of the men;—they had all been sentenced to death, it is true, and the recorder's report had not yet been made; but we question whether there was a man among them, notwithstanding, who did not *know* that although he had undergone the ceremony, it never was intended that his life should be sacrificed. On the table lay a Testament, but there were no tokens of its having been in recent use.

In the press-room below were three men, the nature of whose offence rendered it necessary to separate them, even from their companions in guilt. It is a long, sombre room, with two windows sunk into the stone wall, and here the wretched men are pinioned on the morning of their execution, before moving towards the scaffold. The fate of one of these prisoners was uncertain; some mitigatory circumstances having come to light since his trial, which had been humanely represented in the proper quarter. The other two had nothing to expect from the mercy of the crown; their doom was sealed; no plea could be urged in extenuation of their crime, and they well knew that for them there was no hope in this world. "The two short ones," the turnkey whispered, "were dead men."

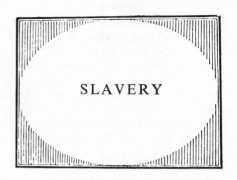

SLAVERY

Origins of the Slave Trade

WILLIAM EDWARD HARTPOLE LECKY

[FROM *A History of England in the Eighteenth Century*]

1878

Of all the many forms of suffering which man has inflicted upon man, with the exception of war, and, perhaps, of religious persecution, the slave trade has probably added most largely to the sum of human misery, and in the first half of the eighteenth century it occupied the very foremost place in English commerce. The first Englishman who took part in it appears to have been John Hawkins, who sailed in 1562 with three ships to Sierra Leone, where he secured, 'partly by the sworde and partly by other meanes,' some 300 negroes, whom he transported to Hispaniola. The enterprise proving succesful he made a much more considerable expedition in 1564 to the coast of Guinea, the English 'going every day on shore to take the inhabitants with burning and spoiling their towns,' and the achievement was so highly considered at home that he was knighted by Elizabeth, and selected for his crest a manacled negro. It is a slight fact, but full of a ghastly signi-

From Volume IV, Chapter 5.

ficance as illustrating the state of feeling prevailing at the time, that the ship in which Hawkins sailed on his second expedition to open the English slave trade was called 'The Jesus.' The traffic in human flesh speedily became popular. A monopoly of it was granted to the African Company, but it was invaded by numerous interlopers, and in 1698 the trade was thrown open to all British subjects. It is worthy of notice that while by the law of 1698 a certain percentage was exacted from other African cargoes for the maintenance of the forts along that coast, cargoes of negroes were especially exempted, for the Parliament of the Revolution desired above all things to encourage the trade. Nine years before, a convention had been made between England and Spain for supplying the Spanish West Indies with slaves from the island of Jamaica, and it has been computed that between 1680 and 1700 the English tore from Africa about 300,000 negroes, or about 15,000 every year.

The great period of the English slave trade had, however, not yet arrived. It was only in 1713 that it began to attain its full dimensions. One of the most important and most popular parts of the Treaty of Utrecht was the contract known as the Assiento, by which the British Government secured for its subjects during thirty years an absolute monopoly of the supply of slaves to the Spanish colonies. The traffic was regulated by a long and elaborate treaty, guarding among other things against any possible scandal to the Roman Catholic religion from the presence of heretical slave-traders, and it provided that in the thirty years from 1713 to 1743 the English should bring into the Spanish West Indies no less than 144,000 negroes, or 4,800 every year, that during the first twenty-five years of the contract they might import a still greater number on paying certain moderate duties, and that they might carry the slave trade into numerous Spanish ports from which it had hitherto been excluded. The monopoly of the trade was granted to the South Sea Company, and from this time its maintenance, and its extension both to the Spanish dominions and to her own colonies, became a central object of English policy. . . . A distinguished modern historian, after a careful comparison of the materials we possess, declares that in the century preceding the prohibition of the slave trade by the American Congress, in 1776, the number of negroes imported by the English alone, into the Spanish, French, and English colonies can, on the lowest computation, have been little less than three millions, and that we must add more than a quarter of a million, who perished on the voyage and whose bodies were thrown into the Atlantic.

These figures are in themselves sufficiently eloquent. No human imagination, indeed, can conceive, no pen can adequately portray, the misery they represent. Torn from the most distant parts of Africa, speaking no common language, connected by no tie except that of common misfortune, severed from every old association and from all they loved, and exchanging, in many cases, a life of unbounded freedom for a hopeless, abject, and crushing servitude, the wretched captives were carried across the waste of waters in ships so crowded and so unhealthy that, even under favourable circumstances, about twelve in every hundred usually died from the horrors of the passage. They had no knowledge, no rights, no protection against the caprices of irresponsible power. The immense disproportion of the sexes consigned them to the most brutal vice. Difference of colour and difference of religion led their masters to look upon them simply as beasts of burden, and the supply of slaves was too abundant to allow the motive of self-interest to be any considerable security for their good treatment. Often, indeed, it seemed the interest of the master rather to work them rapidly to death and then to replenish his stock. All Africa was convulsed by civil wars and infested with bands of native slave-dealers hunting down victims for the English trader, whose blasting influence, like some malignant providence, extended over mighty regions where the face of a white man was never seen.

It has been frequently stated that England is responsible for the introduction of negro slavery into British America; but this assertion will not stand the test of examination. The first cargo of negro slaves introduced into North America is said to have been conveyed by a Dutch vessel to Virginia in

1620. Slavery existed in New York and New Jersey when they were still Dutch; in Carolina, Maryland, and Pennsylvania when they were still subject to proprietary governments. Its encouragement only became an object of the colonial policy of England at the time of the Peace of Utrecht, but before that date it had been planted in every British colony in North America, had become eminently popular among the colonists, and had been sanctioned by many enactments issuing from colonial legislatures. . . .

A few isolated protests against slavery based on religious principles were heard, but they had no echo from the leading theologians. Jonathan Edwards, who occupied the first place among those born in America, left among other property, a negro boy. Berkeley had slaves when in Rhode Island, and appears to have felt no scruples on the subject, though he protested, with his usual humanity, against 'the irrational contempt of the blacks.' The article in the charter of Georgia forbidding slavery, being extremely unpopular among the colonists, was repealed in 1749; and it is melancholy to record that one of the most prominent and influential advocates of the introduction of slavery into the colony was George Whitefield. In Georgia there was an express stipulation for the religious instruction of the slaves; it is said that those in or about Savannah have always been noted in America for their piety, and the advantage of bringing negroes within the range of the Gospel teaching was a common argument in favour of the slave trade. The Protestants from Salzburg for a time had scruples, but they were reassured by a message from Germany: 'If you take slaves in faith,' it was said, 'and with intent of conducting them to Christ, the action will not be a sin but may prove a benediction.' In truth, however, but little zeal was shown in the work of conversion. Many who cordially approved of the slavery of pagans questioned whether it was right to hold Christians in bondage; there was a popular belief that baptism would invalidate the legal title of the master to his slave, and there was a strong and general fear lest any form of education should so brace the energies of the negro as to make him revolt against his lot. Of the extent to which this latter feeling was carried, one extraordinary instance of a later period may be given. The Society for the Propagation of the Gospel sent missionaries to convert the free negroes in Guinea, on the Gold Coast, and in Sierra Leone; but it was itself a large slave-owner, possessing numerous slaves on an estate in Barbadoes. In 1783 Bishop Porteus strongly urged upon the managers of the Society the duty of at least giving Christian instruction to these slaves; but, after a full discussion, the recommendation was absolutely declined.

In the American States slavery speedily gravitated to the South. The climate of the Southern provinces was eminently favourable to the negroes; and the crops, and especially the rice crop—which had been introduced into South Carolina from Madagascar in 1698—could hardly be cultivated by whites. In the Northern provinces the conditions were exactly reversed. We can scarcely have a better illustration of the controlling action of the physical on the moral world than is furnished by this fact. The conditions of climate which made the Northern provinces free States and the Southern provinces slave States established between them an intense social and moral repulsion, kindled mutual feelings of the bitterest hatred and contempt, and in our own day produced a war which threatened the whole future of American civilisation.

Abolition in the British Colonies

[FROM *The Times*, 14 May 1833]

On so complicated and embarrassing a subject as that of the abolition of colonial slavery,[1] it could not have been expected that any Government could have discovered the means of entirely reconciling extreme parties, by any device or project even of super-human wisdom or capacity. It was plainly impossible that there could be invented a middle term between the most direct contradictions,—between the spirit of the abolitionists, who demand an immediate manifesto of freedom for all our colonial slaves, and the West India planters, who insist upon maintaining their rights of property in these same slaves,—between those who regard the negroes as entitled to all the privileges of civil freedom, and those who consider them as human chattels, to be transferred by deed or gift from one proprietor to another,—to become the objects of a legacy, or to be disposed of by public auction for the debts of an estate.

While this contrariety existed between the demands of the abolitionists and the pretensions of the planters, it was equally impossible for any Administration to stand still, in a kind of neutral position, between their antagonist forces. The increasing voice of enlightened humanity—a growing respect for the rights of human nature—the diffusion of information on the barbarities of the colonial system—the new power of the pulpit, the hustings, and the press, in spreading knowledge on the state of the colonies—the repeated declarations of Parliament in promise of a speedy abolition of bondage—and the

[1]In 1833, the Great Emancipation Act was passed whereby, after August 1, 1834, all children under six years of age became free at once, field slaves were to serve their present masters as "apprenticed labourers" for seven years, and house slaves for five, and after that were to become free: these terms were shortened by subsequent enactment. Twenty million pounds were to be paid to the planters as compensation.—ED.

pledges taken by candidates at the last general election, must have convinced any Ministry that the abominations of the slave system could not be tolerated much longer. On the other hand, the planters, ever since the celebrated resolutions of Mr. CANNING in 1823, have appeared to make a merit of insulting the humane feelings and the legislative authority of the mother country,—have resisted the chief recommendations of the British Parliament for the mitigation of slavery,—have opposed all schemes for legal manumissions, at the instance of slaves prepared to purchase their freedom,—have refused the necessary time for relaxation from the labours of the cane-field and the mill,—have resisted the admission of slave evidence (where slave evidence was the only protection to the slave)—have opposed the moral education and religious instruction of their bondsmen,—have discouraged marriage,—and have continued the use of the cart-whip, even in its horrid laceration of women, not only as an instrument of vindictive punishment, but as a stimulus to ordinary labour. As if to give the finishing blow to any hope of amelioration from the planters, some of the colonies have absolutely placed themselves in open hostility to the KING'S Government,—have refused to admit a KING'S officer into their territory, as in the case of the Mauritius,—have denied the rights of the mother country to regulate their destiny,—and have insulted publicly the KING'S representative, as in the case of Jamaica. Is it possible to conceive that any government could hope to conciliate such opposite parties by a mutual compromise, or to stand long between them, like an isthmus, beaten by the waves of two furious seas?

But should not the very notoriety of these difficulties, and the irresistible acknowledgment of the necessity of some decisive measure, induce, if not the abolitionists and planters, at least all other persons, to concur in the adoption of some general principles, calculated to reconcile *as far as possible* such conflicting views and interests? The Ministers cannot be so bigoted to their own scheme as not to receive with favour every reasonable suggestion of improvement, come from what quarter it may; nor can they have a conceivable interest in ruining the colonists to please the abolitionists, or in postponing the hour of slave emancipation to gratify the planters, or, finally, in entailing an unnecessary burden upon the nation for the benefit of either or both.

They found it necessary to declare the liberation of 800,000 of our fellow subjects at present in bondage, at the almost unanimous call of the people of England, but though elevated by this act above the situation of mere chattels or brute animals, these coloured freemen are not released from that labour in which their masters ought only originally to have obtained a right. They are registered as "apprenticed labourers," and enter into a new engagement as such. They are not to be driven to the field, indeed, by the cart-whip of the driver, but they are to be punished for refusing to fulfil their contract with their masters, at the decision of the magistrate. But even this ameliorated state of things is not to be continued for ever. The "apprenticed labourer" would only be a slave under a different name, and working under a different authority, if his "apprenticeship" was to continue for ever; but provision is made in the act itself for his complete emancipation in the course of 12 years by the purchase of his freedom from the fruits of his own exertions. He will thus become accustomed to the management of his own affairs,—to the exchange of his labour for wages—and to the feeling of the benefits of industry, before he has been entirely released from the last fetters which his original bondage had imposed upon his race. His offspring will be instantly free, if he can maintain them in freedom; if not, they will become like himself, not slaves, liable to the lash of a driver, but servants, bound to reimburse the expenses of their infant maintenance by a subsequent contribution of their labour. They will, in fact, be in no worse condition than an English emigrant, who, for the price of his passage to one of our colonies, should engage to work a certain time for the person of capital who had aided in his transport and establishment. If the abolitionists are not satisfied with this arrangement, we entreat them to declare their objections to it without passion or violence, and they will, we are sure, receive a candid hearing. They must, at all events, allow that the great majority of the slave population having never been before accustomed to exercise any forethought as to their lot, or to provide for their future wants, having been naturally in the habit of regarding freedom as merely a release from toil, and having experienced the facility with which, in the course of one day of the week, they can produce all the scanty fare necessary for their subsistence, could not all at once become industrious labourers without the superintendance of the magistrate, or without passing through an intermediate state between the cart-whip of the driver and the emancipating wand of the lictor.

On the other hand, the West India planters, proprietors, and mortgagees, ought perpetually to keep before their minds that emancipation, by the refractory conduct of the colonists in resisting all improvement, had become with the Government not an act of choice, but of necessity, and that they can now only obtain a modification of its terms, and not a reversal of its substance. After the country has demanded, after the Ministry has granted, and after the Parliament has sanctioned a scheme of slave liberation, what could a handful of white masters, attorneys, or managers, do to resist the decree, which would show them instantly their weakness and isolation? What, for instance, in Jamaica, could 15,000 blustering or rebellious white colonists do against a slave population of 350,000, if the latter were supported in their claims by the power and authority of the mother country? Talk, indeed, of throwing themselves under the protection of the United States of America! The United States have too many slaves of their own, and would by no means add to the number by accepting so dangerous and unworthy a present.

But, in making such an observation, we do not wish to heap reproaches on the colonists, we only wish to sound the note of warning, and to invite the spirit of conciliation. Whatever suggestions may be made by the planters or their friends, short of an abandonment of the great principle of the measure, will be received with indulgence and examined with care; but let them not entertain the hope for a moment that *property in man* can any longer be permitted by law in any portion of the wide range of empire under the British sceptre, from "the rising to the setting sun." Let them reflect, that by agreeing to emancipation with a good grace, their compulsory slaves may become their willing servants; that they will have the cordial support of the British Government, assisted by a strong police and a zealous magistracy, to preserve order and to secure the performance of contracts; and that they may find in the promised pecuniary aid of the mother country more than they lose in the diminished labours of their negroes. Let them, at the same time, reflect on the total hopelessness of resistance, and never forget that St. Domingo saw its plantations in flames, and its white inhabitants massacred, simply because they entered into a contest at once with their slaves and with their mother country.

We have heard, as we have already hinted, and we believe it to be true, that the Government is willing to receive every reasonable suggestion for the improvement of their plan from any party whose interests it may affect, or whose feelings it may not satisfy. Let us, therefore, hope that no attempt will be made merely to embarrass their movements, or to misrepresent their objects—objects which ought to be considered by far too high and holy for the narrow spirit of faction.

First Sight of Slavery in 1834

HARRIET MARTINEAU

[FROM *Retrospect of Western Travel*]

1838

From the day of my entering the States till that of my leaving Philadelphia I had seen society basking in one bright sunshine of good-will. The sweet temper and kindly manners of the Americans are so striking to foreigners, that it is some time before the dazzled stranger perceives that, genuine as is all this good, evils as black as night exist along with it. I had been received with such hearty hospitality everywhere, and had lived among friends so conscientious in their regard for human rights, that, though I had heard of abolition riots, and had observed somewhat of the degradation of the blacks, my mind had not yet been really troubled about the enmity of the races. The time of awakening must come. It began just before I left Philadelphia.

I was calling on a lady whom I had heard speak with strong horror of the abolitionists (with whom I had then no acquaintance), and she turned round upon me with the question whether I would not prevent, if I could, the marriage of a white person with a person of colour. I saw at once the beginning of endless troubles in this inquiry, and was very sorry it had been made; but my determination had been adopted long before, never to evade the great question of colour; never to provoke it; but always to meet it plainly in whatever form it should be presented. I replied that I would never, under any circumstances, try to separate persons who really loved, believing such to be truly those whom God had joined; but I observed that the case she put was one not

From Volume I, pages 139-42, 218-19, 267-68.

likely to happen, as I believed the blacks were no more disposed to marry the whites than the whites to marry the blacks. "You are an amalgamationist!" cried she. I told her that the party term was new to me; but that she must give what name she pleased to the principle I had declared in answer to her question. This lady is an eminent religionist, and denunciations spread rapidly from her. . . .

The next day I first set foot in a slave state, arriving in the evening at Baltimore. I dreaded inexpressibly the first sight of a slave, and could not help speculating on the lot of every person of colour I saw from the windows the first few days. The servants in the house where I was were free blacks.

Before a week was over I perceived that all that is said in England of the hatred of the whites to the blacks in America is short of the truth. The slanders that I heard of the free blacks were too gross to injure my estimation of any but those who spoke them. In Baltimore the bodies of coloured people exclusively are taken for dissection, "because the whites do not like it, and the coloured people cannot resist." It is wonderful that the bodily structure can be (with the exception of the colouring of the skin) thus assumed to be the pattern of that of the whites; that the exquisite nervous system, the instrument of moral as well as physical pleasures and pains, can be nicely investigated, on the ground of its being analogous with that of the whites; that not only the mechanism, but the sensibilities of the degraded race should be argued from to those of the exalted order, and that men come from such a study with contempt for these brethren in their countenances, hatred in their hearts, and insult on their tongues. These students are the men who cannot say that the coloured people have not nerves that quiver under moral injury, nor a brain that is on fire with insult, nor pulses that throb under oppression. These are the men who should stay the hand of the rash and ignorant possessors of power, who crush the being of creatures, like themselves, "fearfully and wonderfully made." But to speak the right word, to hold out the helping hand, these searchers into man have not light nor strength. . . .

A lady from New-England, staying in Baltimore, was one day talking over slavery with me, her detestation of it being great, when I told her I dreaded seeing a slave. "You have seen one," said she. "You were waited on by a slave yesterday evening." She told me of a gentleman who let out and lent out his slaves to wait at gentlemen's houses, and that the tall handsome mulatto who handed the tea at a party the evening before was one of these. I was glad it was over for once; but I never lost the painful feeling caused to a stranger by inter-course with slaves. No familiarity with them, no mirth and contentment on their part, ever soothed the miserable restless-ness caused by the presence of a deeply-injured fellow-being. No wonder or ridicule on the spot avails anything to the stranger. He suffers, and must suffer from this, deeply and long, as surely as he is human and hates oppression. . . .

There is something inexpressibly disgusting in the sight of a slave woman in the field. I do not share in the horror of the Americans at the idea of women being employed in outdoor labour. It did not particularly gratify me to see the cows always milked by men (where there were no slaves); and the hay and harvest fields would have looked brighter in my eyes if women had been there to share the wholesome and cheerful toil. But a negro woman behind the plough presents a very different object from the English mother with her children in the turnip-field, or the Scotch lassie among the reapers. In her pre-eminently ugly costume, the long, scanty, dirty woollen garment, with the shabby large bonnet at the back of her head, the perspiration streaming down her dull face, the heavy tread of the splay foot, the slovenly air with which she guides her plough, a more hideous object cannot well be conceived, unless it be the same woman at home, in the negro quarter, as the cluster of slave dwellings is called.

You are now taken to the cotton-gin, the building to your left, where you are shown how the cotton, as picked from the pods, is drawn between cylinders so as to leave the seeds behind; and how it is afterward packed, by hard pressure, into bales. The neighbouring creek is dammed up to supply the water-wheel by which this gin is worked. You afterward see the cotton-seed laid in handfuls round the stalks of the young springing corn, and used in the cotton field as manure.

Meantime you attempt to talk with the slaves. You ask how old that very aged man is, or that boy; they will give you no intelligible answer. Slaves never know, or never will tell their ages, and this is the reason why the census presents such extraordinary reports on this point, declaring a great number to be above a hundred years old. If they have a kind master, they will boast to you of how much he gave for each of them, and what sums he has refused for them. If they have a hard master, they will tell you that they would have more to eat and be less flogged, but that massa is busy, and has no time to come down and see that they have enough to eat. Your hostess is well known on this plantation, and her kind face has been recognised from a distance; and already a negro woman has come to her with seven or eight eggs, for which she knows she shall receive a quarter dollar. You follow her to the negro quarter, where you see a tidy woman knitting, while the little children who are left in her charge are basking in the sun, or playing all kinds of antics in the road; little shining, plump, cleareyed children, whose mirth makes you sad when you look round upon their parents, and see what these bright creatures are to come to. You enter one of the dwellings, where everything seems to be of the same dusky hue: the crib against the wall, the walls themselves, and the floor, all look one yellow. More children are crouched round the wood fire, lying almost in the embers. You see a woman pressing up against the wall like an idiot, with her shoulder turned towards you, and her apron held up to her face. You ask what is the matter with her, and are told that she is shy. You see a woman rolling herself about in a crib, with her head tied up. You ask if she is ill, and are told that she has not a good temper; that she struck at a girl she was jealous of with an axe, and the weapon being taken from her, she threw herself into the well, and was nearly drowned before she was taken out, with her head much hurt.

The overseer has, meantime, been telling your host about the fever having been more or less severe last season, and how well off he shall think himself if he has no more than so many days' illness this summer: how the vegetation has suffered from the late frosts, pointing out how many of the oranges have been cut off, but that the great magnolia in the centre of the court is safe. You are then invited to see the house, learning by the way the extent and value of the estate you are visiting, and of the "force" upon it. You admire the lofty, cool rooms, with their green blinds, and the width of the piazzas on both sides the house, built to compensate for the want of shade from trees, which cannot be allowed near the dwelling for fear of moschetoes. You visit the ice-house, and find it pretty full, the last winter having been a severe one. You learn that, for three or four seasons after this icehouse was built, there was not a spike of ice in the state, and a cargo had to be imported from Massachusetts. . . .

I could never get out of the way of the horrors of slavery in this region [New Orleans]. Under one form or another, they met me in every house, in every street; everywhere but in the intelligence pages of newspapers, where I might read on in perfect security of exemption from the subject. In the advertising columns there were offers of reward for runaways, restored dead or alive; and notices of the capture of a fugitive with so many brands on his limbs and shoulders, and so many scars on his back. But from the other half of the newspaper, the existence of slavery could be discovered only by inference. What I saw elsewhere was, however, dreadful enough. In one house, the girl who waited on me with singular officiousness was so white, with blue eyes and light hair, that it never occurred to me that she could be a slave. Her mistress told me afterward that this girl of fourteen was such a depraved hussy that she must be sold. I exclaimed involuntarily, but was referred to the long heel in proof of the child's being of negro extraction. She had the long heel, sure enough. Her mistress told me that it is very wrong to plead in behalf of slavery that families are rarely separated; and gave me, as no unfair example of the dealings of masters, this girl's domestic history.

Slavery at Richmond in 1842

CHARLES DICKENS

[FROM a letter to John Forster]

At Washington again
Monday, March the Twenty-First [1842]

We had intended to go to Baltimore from Richmond, by a place called Norfolk: but one of the boats being under repair, I found we should probably be detained at this Norfolk two days. Therefore we came back here yesterday, by the road we had travelled before; lay here last night; and go on to Baltimore this afternoon, at four o'clock. It is a journey of only two hours and a half. Richmond is a prettily situated town; but, like other towns in slave districts (as the planters themselves admit), has an aspect of decay and gloom which to an unaccustomed eye is *most* distressing. In the black car (for they don't let them sit with the whites), on the railroad as we went there, were a mother and family whom the steamer was conveying away, to sell; retaining the man (the husband and father I mean) on his plantation. The children cried the whole way. Yesterday, on board the boat, a slave owner and two constables were our fellow-passengers. They were coming here in search of two negroes who had run away on the previous day. On the bridge at Richmond there is a notice

From *The Letters of Charles Dickens*, edited by W. Dexter (1938). Volume I, pages 409-10.

against fast driving over it, as it is rotten and crazy: penalty—
for whites, five dollars; for slaves, fifteen stripes. My heart
is lightened as if a great load had been taken from it, when
I think that we are turning our backs on this accursed and
detested system. I really don't think I could have borne it
any longer.

It is all very well to say "be silent on the subject." They
won't let you be silent. They *will* ask you what you think of
it; and *will* expatiate on slavery as if it were one of the greatest
blessings of mankind. "It's not," said a hard, bad-looking
fellow to me the other day, "it's not the interest of a man
to use his slaves ill. It's damned nonsense that you hear in
England."—I told him quietly that it was not a man's interest
to get drunk, or to steal, or to game, or to indulge in any
other vice, but he *did* indulge in it for all that. That cruelty,
and the abuse of irresponsible power, were two of the bad
passions of human nature, with the gratification of which,
considerations of interest or of ruin had nothing whatever to
do; and that, while every candid man must admit that even
a slave might be happy enough with a good master, all human
beings knew that bad masters, cruel masters, and masters
who disgraced the form they bore, were matters of experience
and history, whose existence was as undisputed as that of
slaves themselves. He was a little taken aback by this, and
asked me if I believed in the Bible. Yes, I said, but if any
man could prove to me that it sanctioned slavery, I would
place no further credence in it. "Well, then," he said, "by
God, sir, the niggers must be kept down, and the whites have
put down the coloured people wherever they have found them.'
"That's the whole question," said I. "Yes, and by God," says
he, "the British had better not stand out on that point when
Lord Ashburton comes over, for I never felt so warlike as
I do now,—and that's a fact."

I was obliged to accept a public supper in this Richmond,
and I saw plainly enough, there, that the hatred which these
Southern States bear to us as a nation has been fanned up
and revived again by this Creole business, and can scarcely
be exaggerated. . . .

Letters from Washington in 1853

WILLIAM MAKEPEACE THACKERAY

[FROM a letter to his mother]

Sunday, Feb 13 [1853].
Washington.

My dearest Mammy. . . . I feel as if my travels had only just begun—There was scarce any sensation of novelty until now when the slaves come on to the scene; and straightway the country assumes an aspect of the queerest interest: I don't know whether it is terror, pity or laughter that is predominant. They are not my men & brethren, these strange people with retreating foreheads, with great obtruding lips & jaws: with capacities for thought, pleasure, endurance quite different to mine. They are not suffering as you are impassioning yourself for their wrongs as you read Mrs Stowe they are grinning & joking in the sun; roaring with laughter as they stand about the streets in squads; very civil, kind & gentle, even winning in their manner when you accost them at gentlemen's houses, where they do all the service. But they don't seem to me to be the same as white men, any more than asses are the same animals as horses; I don't mean this disrespectfully, but simply that there is such a difference of colour, habits, conformation of brains, that we must acknowledge it, & can't by any rhetorical phrase get it over; Sambo is not my man & my brother; the very aspect of his face is grotesque & inferior. I can't help seeing & owning this; at the same time of course denying any white man's right to hold this fellow-creature in bondage & make goods & chattels of him & his issue; but

From *The Letters and Private Papers of William Makepeace Thackeray*, edited by Gordon N. Ray (4 volumes, 1945-1946), Volume III, pages 198-200, 228-29.

where the two races meet this weaker one must knock under; if it is to improve it must be on its own soil, away from the domineering whites; & who knows whether out of Liberia there mayn't go forth civilizers & improvers of the black race, in wh. case the sufferings of a small portion of their brethren during a few centuries under European task-masters, on this continent, will have worked for the ultimate good of the native community. It is certain that their Slavery at the very worst here has not been comparable to their degradation in their own country, where for uncounted time they have been bought, sold, murdered, tortured by their black tyrants more ruthlessly than (except by particular & occasional white villains) they ever have been treated here.

I have no doubt that all Mrs Stowe's individual instances of cruelty are only too true; that her case is not exaggerated at all, that even if the instances are occasional, she has a right to use them to prove it. But what the slaveholders retort against us is true too: the sum of unhappiness is as great among our wretched poor as it can be here; controversy has this good in it that it will pique black & white man-owners into generosity & I dare say better the labourer's condition in Dorsetshire as in Virginia.

An acquaintance tells me of an odd solution wh. may present itself of the Slave difficulty: & that comes from a queer quarter, no less than from China:—some gangs of Chinese labourers have been imported into Cuba, who do the field-work so well, are so healthy & orderly, & work at such a small price, that it is found that crops can be raised at a much less price than by the cumbrous & costly Slave machinery. A score or two of years hence, with the immense multiplication & rapidity of transport, (you'll settle the geography you know how profound I am about that) now only just beginning to be established; scores of thousands of Celestial immigrants may be working in the cotton & tobacco fields here & in the West Indies Islands. Then the African Slave will get his manumission quickly enough. As soon as the cheap substitute is found, depend on it the Planter, who stoutly pleads humanity now as one of the reasons why he can't liberate his people, will get rid of them quickly enough; & the price of the slave-goods will fall so that owners won't care to hold such an unprofitable & costly stock. . . .

[FROM a letter to Albany Fonblanque]

4 March [1853]

. . . The happiness of these niggers is quite a curiosity to witness. The little niggers are trotting and grinning about the streets, the women are fat and in good case, I wish you could see that waiter at our hotel with 5 gold medals in his shirt 2 gold chains and a gold ring. The African Church on a Sunday I am told is a perfect blaze of pea-green, crimson, ear-rings, lace collars, satin and velvet which the poor darkies wear. I don't mean to say that Slavery is right but that if you want to move your bowels with compassion for human unhappiness, that sort of aperient is to be found in such plenty at home, that it's a wonder people won't seek it there. I don't think it's of long duration though—unless perhaps in the cotton-growing countries where the whites can't live and the negroes can. Every person I have talked to here about it deplores it and owns that its the most costly domestic machinery ever devised. In a house where four servants would do with us (servants whom we can send about their business too, when they get ill and past work, like true philanthropists as we are) there must be a dozen blacks here, and the work is not well done. The hire of a house slave from his owner is 120 dollars—£25—besides of course his keep, clothing, etc. When he is old he must be kept well and kindly, and is—the little niggers wait upon the old effete niggers. The slave-servants working in the tobacco manufactories can lay up 100 dollars a year. The rule is kindness, the exception no doubt may be cruelty. The great plenty in this country ensures everyone enough to eat—and the people here entreat me to go on a plantation, to go about by myself, ask questions how and where I like and see if the black people are happy or not. This to be sure leaves the great question untouched that Slavery is a wrong. But if you could decree the Abolition to-morrow, by the Lord it would be the most awful curse and ruin to the black wh. Fate ever yet sent him. Of course we feel the cruelty of flogging and enslaving a negro— Of course they feel here the cruelty of starving an English labourer, or of driving an English child to a mine—Brother, Brother we are kin.

A Letter from Savannah in 1858

BARBARA LEIGH SMITH BODICHON

[FROM "Slavery in the South"]

1861

Savannah, 4th March [1858].—Here in this house the cow-hide is used to the back of my nice Clara, who works so hard. I was near going down to make an outcry, as Don Quixote would have done; but on second thoughts felt certain I should make matters worse, so I consoled Clara with full eyes, and wait my time to put in a word, if I can, to the mistress of this boarding house, who, by the by, is a Northern woman; and the Southerners all say they make the worst masters and mistresses; and next in honour come the French, because, when bad, the French have a prodigious capacity of wicked-ness. But the slaves in French households are generally treated more as the family and are taught more than by Americans. I find we have negroes in this house; they are "hired out" to the mistress; it is a bad look-out for slaves to be hired out to a boarding house.

Sunday, the 7th.—I have been to the Methodist Church. It is a pleasant-looking, white, Noah's ark kind of building, very large, very white, very cheerful, with windows all round.

From *English Woman's Journal*, 8 (December 1861), pages 261-66.

As I approached I heard singing. The minister, a slave and a very black negro, gave a good sermon on the Communion. In the evening I went to my Baptist Church close by, and heard another slave preach;—the regular minister, also a slave, whom I heard last Sunday, was not there. I asked a few questions about him of a very old man who seemed to be an authority. He said the minister could read and write and had studied. I asked how he could study if he worked all day? and was answered, "He studied at night. Of course he can't do as well as white men who have all their time, but he *worries and scuffles,* and so gets a little learning." I found the congregation as polite as usual, but the negroes are more reserved in their manners here than at New Orleans. They looked well and happy. I have talked to many, and cannot say they looked unhappy even when their circumstances would naturally have made them so. For instance, a woman told me to-day that she was the property of a gentleman in the country, who hires her out to a white washerwoman here in Savannah. Here she always stays unless she is going to have a child, and then she goes to the plantation, and stays till the child can toddle; then out to work again. She has had five children, but never sees them except under these circumstances. "Well," I said, "how do you get along?" "Oh, splendidly;—of course, I must get along. You see there ain't no other way:—splendidly." Sometimes, it is true, I meet faces which are tragedies to look on; but these are generally mulattoes.

12*th.*— . . . In the beautiful fir wood where I have been several times to paint, I have heard a pleasant voice singing hymns. Yesterday the singer appeared—a young negro girl, very slight and small, but she says eight years of age. She and her little sister of four or five sang to me negro songs and hymns; it seems more natural to negroes to sing than to talk. A boy came and joined them; and after some conversation I found he was much given to running away and was often whipped for it. The girl said she would never do anything so wicked. I was very much amused with these children and they were amused with me. "Never was anybody like you."

They were not sure whether I was Indian or not. They peeled off the inner bark of the fir, and chewed it like tobacco; but the girl said, "If master seed us do that he'd whip us, because it spoils the teeth." The boy was sent for to bring a cart and horse to his master directly, but he very coolly put it off, in a way that would have lost a boy his place in England. This fir wood is a lovely place to settle in, healthy and beautiful. I can hardly imagine any pleasanter country for emigrants to come to than the neighborhood of Savannah. I heard the stroke of the axe, and the trees falling at intervals, as I drew all day; and I understood the pleasure of cutting a square hole in the dense wood, building a house, and making a market garden, as this young man was doing with the certainty of making a good living.

March 13.— . . . I left our little Clara at Savannah with real sorrow; in two weeks I had seen a great deal of her and found her very intelligent and affectionate. She was so sorrowful at parting with me that she could not say one word, and put herself behind the door perfectly quiet. She told me she had no one in the world who cared for her. Her father was alive but she never saw him. Slave owners may say what they like, but families are separated: when they are not, it is an exception. What falsehoods I have read! Answers to Uncle Tom (which book is itself nowhere to be found) deluge the South in news-papers. It is always asserted that families are kept together, and that the reverse is a sad and rare occurrence. Why, every week hundreds from Virginia and Maryland are sold in New Orleans, and it is rarely that a family is sold altogether—father, mother, and children;—*never,* I was going to say; but it is sometimes the case. There is one slave dealer in New Orleans who does not sell slaves without consulting them as to their likes and dislikes: he asks them whether they will like such and such a master. This I heard on very good authority, but mentioned as a very curious and solitary instance. When I was talking as usual to these negro women on board the *Swan,* they said, "You must not speak loud; you must speak low, or you will get into trouble!" . . .

My feeling against the whites of the South is for their

wickedness in neglecting everything which might elevate the
African race. My anger is not only against the slave owners,
but against all in America who would exclude the dusky-
skinned from the lights of knowledge and the blessings of
freedom which all the white race here so abundantly enjoy.
We are both struck by the intelligence and general agreeable-
ness of the negroes and mulattoes. The race is not so low
in the human scale as I supposed before I came here. Probably the field hands are inferior. I take John Ormsted's
[Frederick Law Olmsted's] account as true, for I have not seen
much of plantation life. When I am in the country I paint,
and it is only in the towns I see the negroes. . . .

I do not know how others may feel, but I cannot come
amongst these people without the perception that every standard of right and wrong is unconsciously lost, and that they
are wretched in themselves and degraded by this one falsehood in the midst of which they dwell—to live in the belief
of a vital falsehood poisons all the springs of life.

The next morning the boat was moored close by a cotton
plantation and my friends the negroes knocked me up to go
and see how "the poor creatures work, like beasts, hundreds of
'em, and a white overseer." My husband went out into the
field and brought me a bunch of the cotton plant, and I sat
down after breakfast in the cabin to draw it. Mr C——, the
Californian gentleman, came and sat by me and said, "I wish
you, Madam, would write a book on America; you are more
candid and cool in your judgments than any English traveller
I have met. You will give a fair picture of slavery: it is no
evil; very far from it; quite a blessing to the African, &c."
And another gentleman chimed in, "I have lived all my life
in the slave states, and I assure you it is a good institution."
They both went on to say that families were very rarely
separated and begged me to write a fair view of the case.

I assured them I should not write a book on America, and
could say little about the actual condition of the slave. I could
only say that the principle of slavery was unjust, and that
every slave had a right to run away, &c. And I went into my
cabin and found Polly there, the black, real black woman,

whom I have mentioned to you before. I said to her, "Polly,
how many times have you been sold?" "Twice." "Have you
any children?" "I had three; God only knows where two of
them are—my master sold them. We lived in Kentucky;—
one, my darling, he sold South. She is in one of those fields
perhaps, picking with those poor creatures you saw. Oh dear!
mum, we poor creatures have need to believe in God; for if
God Almighty will not be good to us some day, why were
we born? When I hear of His delivering His people from
bondage, I know it means the poor African." Her voice was
so husky I could hardly understand her; but it seems her
master promised to keep *one* child, and then sold it without
telling her: and when she asked in agony, *"Where is my
child?"* the master said it was "hired out." But it never came
back. I found she was a member of a church I had visited
in Louisville. She said to me on parting, "Never forget me;
never forget what we suffer. Do all you can to alter it." A
free mulatto, a very intelligent man, told me some things too
horrible to write; he was a sort of upper waiter over all the
rest and much trusted by the captain. His master was his
father; he had bought himself of his own father. He told me
there was no career for free negroes;—no rights, no public
position.

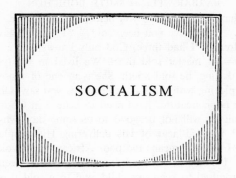

SOCIALISM

The Roots of Honour

JOHN RUSKIN

[FROM *"Unto This Last"*]

1860

Passing from these simple examples to the more complicated relations existing between a manufacturer and his
workmen, we are met first by certain curious difficulties,
resulting, apparently, from a harder and colder state of moral
elements. It is easy to imagine an enthusiastic affection existing among soldiers for the colonel. Not so easy to imagine
an enthusiastic affection among cotton-spinners for the proprietor of the mill. A body of men associated for purposes
of robbery (as a Highland clan in ancient times) shall be
animated by perfect affection, and every member of it be
ready to lay down his life for the life of his chief. But a
band of men associated for purposes of legal production and
accumulation is usually animated, it appears, by no such
emotions, and none of them are in any wise willing to give
his life for the life of his chief. Not only are we met by this
apparent anomaly, in moral matters, but by others connected

From Sections 12-16.

with it, in administration of system. For a servant or a soldier is engaged at a definite rate of wages, for a definite period; but a workman at a rate of wages variable according to the demand for labour, and with the risk of being at any time thrown out of his situation by chances of trade. Now, as, under these contingencies, no action of the affections can take place, but only an explosive action of *dis*affections, two points offer themselves for consideration in the matter.

The first—How far the rate of wages may be so regulated as not to vary with the demand for labour.

The second—How far it is possible that bodies of workmen may be engaged and maintained at such fixed rate of wages (whatever the state of trade may be), without enlarging or diminishing their number, so as to give them permanent interest in the establishment with which they are connected, like that of the domestic servants in an old family, or an *espirit de corps,* like that of the soldiers in a crack regiment.

The first question is, I say, how far it may be possible to fix the rate of wages, irrespectively of the demand for labour.

Perhaps one of the most curious facts in the history of human error is the denial by the common political economist of the possibility of thus regulating wages; while, for all the important, and much of the unimportant, labour, on the earth, wages are already so regulated.

We do not sell our prime-ministership by Dutch auction; nor, on the decease of a bishop, whatever may be the general advantages of simony, do we (yet) offer his diocese to the clergyman who will take the episcopacy at the lowest contract. We (with exquisite sagacity of political economy!) do indeed sell commissions; but not openly, generalships: sick, we do not inquire for a physician who takes less than a guinea; litigious, we never think of reducing six-and-eightpence to four-and-sixpence; caught in a shower, we do not canvass the cabmen, to find one who values his driving at less than sixpence a mile.

It is true that in all these cases there is, and in every conceivable case there must be, ultimate reference to the presumed difficulty of the work, or number of candidates for the office. If it were thought that the labour necessary to make a good physician would be gone through by a sufficient number of students with the prospect of only half-guinea fees, public consent would soon withdraw the unnecessary half-guinea. In this ultimate sense, the price of labour is indeed always regulated by the demand for it; but, so far as the practical and immediate administration of the matter is regarded, the best labour always has been, and is, as *all* labour ought to be, paid by an invariable standard.

"What!" the reader perhaps answers amazedly: "Pay good and bad workmen alike?"

Certainly. The difference between one prelate's sermons and his successor's—or between one physician's opinion and another's,—is far greater, as respects the qualities of mind involved, and far more important in result to you personally, than the difference between good and bad laying of bricks (though that is greater than most people suppose). Yet you pay with equal fee, contentedly, the good and bad workmen upon your soul, and the good and bad workmen upon your body; much more may you pay, contentedly, with equal fees, the good and bad workmen upon your house.

"Nay, but I choose my physician, and (?) my clergyman, thus indicating my sense of the quality of their work." By all means, also, choose your bricklayer; that is the proper reward of the good workman, to be "chosen." The natural and right system respecting all labour is, that it should be paid at a fixed rate, but the good workman employed, and the bad workman unemployed. The false, unnatural, and destructive system is when the bad workman is allowed to offer his work at half-price, and either take the place of the good, or force him by his competition to work for an inadequate sum.

This equality of wages, then, being the first object towards which we have to discover the directest available road, the second is, as above stated, that of maintaining constant numbers of workmen in employment, whatever may be the accidental demand for the article they produce.

I believe the sudden and extensive inequalities of demand, which necessarily arise in the mercantile operations of an active nation, constitute the only essential difficulty which has to be overcome in a just organization of labour.

The subject opens into too many branches to admit of being investigated in a paper of this kind; but the following general facts bearing on it may be noted.

The wages which enable any workman to live are necessarily higher, if his work is liable to intermission, than if it is assured and continuous; and however severe the struggle for work may become, the general law will always hold, that man must get more daily pay if, on the average, they can only calculate on work three days a week than they would require if they were sure of work six days a week. Supposing that a man cannot live on less than a shilling a day, his seven shillings he must get, either for three days' violent work, or six days' deliberate work. The tendency of all modern mercantile operations is to throw both wages and trade into the form of a lottery, and to make the workman's pay depend on intermittent exertion, and the principal's profit on dexterously used chance.

In what partial degree, I repeat, this may be necessary in consequence of the activities of modern trade, I do not here investigate; contenting myself with the fact that in its fatallest aspects it is assuredly unnecessary, and results merely from love of gambling on the part of the masters, and from ignorance and sensuality in the men. The masters cannot bear to let any opportunity of gain escape them, and frantically rush at every gap and breach in the walls of Fortune, raging to be rich, and affronting, with impatient covetousness, every risk of ruin, while the men prefer three days of violent labour, and three days of drunkenness, to six days of moderate work and wise rest. There is no way in which a principal, who really desires to help his workmen, may do it more effectually than by checking these disorderly habits both in himself and them; keeping his own business operations on a scale which will enable him to pursue them securely, not yielding to temptations of precarious gain; and at the same time, leading his workmen into regular habits of labour and life, either by inducing them rather to take low wages, in the form of a fixed salary, than high wages, subject to the chance of their being thrown out of work; or, if this be impossible, by discouraging the system of violent exertion for nominally high day wages, and leading the men to take lower pay for more regular labour.

In effecting any radical changes of this kind, doubtless there would be great inconvenience and loss incurred by all the originators of the movement. That which can be done with perfect convenience and without loss, is not always the thing that most needs to be done, or which we are most imperatively required to do.

Incentive in a Communist Society

WILLIAM MORRIS

[FROM *News from Nowhere*]

1891

"Now, this is what I want to ask you about—to wit, how you get people to work when there is no reward of labour, and especially how you get them to work strenuously?"

"No reward of labour?" said Hammond, gravely. "The reward of labour is *life*. Is that not enough?"

"But no reward for especially good work," quoth I.

"Plenty of reward," said he—"the reward of creation. The wages which God gets, as people might have said time agone. If you are going to ask to be paid for the pleasure of creation, which is what excellence in work means, the next thing we shall hear of will be a bill sent in for the begetting of children."

"Well, but," said I, "the man of the nineteenth century would say there is a natural desire towards the procreation of children, and a natural desire not to work."

From Chapter 15.

"Yes, yes," said he, "I know the ancient platitude,—wholly untrue; indeed, to us quite meaningless. Fourier, whom all men laughed at, understood the matter better."

"Why is it meaningless to you?" said I.

He said: "Because it implies that all work is suffering, and we are so far from thinking that, that, as you may have noticed, whereas we are not short of wealth, there is a kind of fear growing up amongst us that we shall one day be short of work. It is a pleasure which we are afraid of losing, not a pain."

"Yes," said I, "I have noticed that, and I was going to ask you about that also. But in the meantime, what do you positively mean to assert about the pleasurableness of work amongst you?"

"This, that *all* work is now pleasurable; either because of the hope of gain in honour and wealth with which the work is done, which causes pleasurable excitement, even when the actual work is not pleasant; or else because it has grown into a pleasurable *habit,* as in the case with what you may call mechanical work; and lastly (and most of our work is of this kind) because there is conscious sensuous pleasure in the work itself; it is done, that is, by artists."

"I see," said I. "Can you now tell me how you have come to this happy condition? For, to speak plainly, this change from the conditions of the older world seems to me far greater and more important than all the other changes you have told me about as to crime, politics, property, marriage.". . .

"Briefly," said he, "by the absence of artificial coercion, and the freedom for every man to do what he can do best, joined to the knowledge of what productions of labour we really wanted . . . .

"It is clear from all that we hear and read, that in the last age of civilisation men had got into a vicious circle in the matter of production of wares. They had reached a wonderful facility of production, and in order to make the most of that facility they had gradually created (or allowed to grow, rather) a most elaborate system of buying and selling, which has been called the World-Market; and that World-Market, once set a-going, forced them to go on making more and more of these wares, whether they needed them or not. So that while (of course) they could not free themselves from the toil of making real necessaries, they created in a never-ending series sham or artificial necessaries, which became, under the iron rule of the aforesaid World-Market, of equal importance to them with the real necessaries which supported life. By all this they burdened themselves with a prodigious mass of work merely for the sake of keeping their wretched system going."

"Yes—and then?" said I.

"Why, then, since they had forced themselves to stagger along under this horrible burden of unnecessary production, it became impossible for them to look upon labour and its results from any other point of view than one—to wit, the ceaseless endeavour to expend the least possible amount of labour on any article made, and yet at the same time to make as many articles as possible. To this 'cheapening of production,' as it was called, everything was sacrificed: the happiness of the workman at his work, nay, his most elementary comfort and bare health, his food, his clothes, his dwelling, his leisure, his amusement, his education—his life, in short—did not weigh a grain of sand in the balance against this dire necessity of 'cheap production' of things, a great part of which were not worth producing at all. Nay, we are told, and we must believe it, so overwhelming is the evidence, though many of our people scarcely *can* believe it, that even rich and powerful men, the masters of the poor devils aforesaid, submitted to live amidst sights and sounds and smells which it is in the very nature of man to abhor and flee from, in order that their riches might bolster up this supreme folly. The whole community, in fact, was cast into the jaws of this ravening monster, 'the cheap production' forced upon it by the World-Market."

"Dear me!" said I. "But what happened? Did not their cleverness and facility in production master this chaos of misery at last? Couldn't they catch up with the World-Market, and then set to work to devise means for relieving themselves from this fearful task of extra labour?"

He smiled bitterly. "Did they even try to?" said he. "I am not sure. You know that according to the old saw the beetle gets used to living in dung; and these people, whether they found the dung sweet or not, certainly lived in it."

His estimate of the life of the nineteenth century made me catch my breath a little; and I said feebly, "But the labour-saving machines?"

"Heyday!" quoth he. "What's that you are saying? the labour-saving machines? Yes, they were made to 'save labour' (or, to speak more plainly, the lives of men) on one piece of work in order that it might be expended—I will say wasted—on another, probably useless, piece of work. Friend, all their devices for cheapening labour simply resulted in increasing the burden of labour. The appetite of the World-Market grew with what it fed on: the countries within the ring of 'civilisation' (that is, organised misery) were glutted with the abortions of the market, and force and fraud were used unsparingly to 'open up' countries *outside* that pale. This process of 'opening up' is a strange one to those who have read the professions of the men of that period and do not understand their practice; and perhaps shows us at its worst the great vice of the nineteenth century, the use of hypocrisy and cant to evade the responsibility of vicarious ferocity. When the civilised World-Market coveted a country not yet in its clutches, some transparent pretext was found— the suppression of a slavery different from, and not so cruel as that of commerce; the pushing of a religion no longer believed in by its promoters; the 'rescue' of some desperado or homicidal madman whose misdeeds had got him into trouble amongst the natives of the 'barbarous' country—any stick, in short, which would beat the dog at all. Then some bold, unprincipled, ignorant adventurer was found (no difficult task in the days of competition), and he was bribed to 'create a market' by breaking up whatever traditional society there might be in the doomed country, and by destroying whatever

leisure or pleasure he found there. He forced wares on the
natives which they did not want, and took their natural products in 'exchange,' as this form of robbery was called, and
thereby he 'created new wants,' to supply which (that is,
to be allowed to live by their new masters) the hapless,
helpless people had to sell themselves into the slavery of
hopeless toil so that they might have something wherewith
to purchase the nullities of 'civilisation.' Ah," said the old
man pointing to the Museum, "I have read books and papers
in there, telling strange stories indeed of the dealings of
civilisation (or organised misery) with 'non-civilisation'; from
the time when the British Government deliberately sent blan-
kets infected with small-pox as choice gifts to inconvenient
tribes of Red-skins, to the time when Africa was infested by
a man named Stanley, who—"

"Excuse me," said I, "but as you know, time presses; and
I want to keep our question on the straightest line possible;
and I want at once to ask this about these wares made for
the World-Market—how about their quality; these people who
were so clever about making goods, I suppose they made
them well?"

"Quality!" said the old man crustily, for he was rather
peevish at being cut short in his story; "how could they
possibly attend to such trifles as the quality of the wares they
sold? The best of them were of a lowish average, the worst
were transparent make-shifts for the things asked for, which
nobody would have put up with if they could have got anything else. It was a current jest of the time that the wares were
made to sell and not to use; a jest which you, as coming from
another planet, may understand, but which our folk could
not." . . .

"And people put up with this?" said I.

"For a time," said he.

"And then?"

"And then the overturn," said the old man, smiling, "and
the nineteenth century saw itself as a man who has lost his
clothes whilst bathing, and has to walk naked through the
town."

"You are very bitter about that unlucky nineteenth century," said I.

"Naturally," said he, "since I know so much about it." . . .

"I think I do understand," said I: "but now, as it seems, you have reversed all this?"

"Pretty much so," said he. "The wares which we make are made because they are needed: men make for their neighbours' use as if they were making for themselves, not for a vague market of which they know nothing, and over which they have no control: as there is no buying and selling, it would be mere insanity to make goods on the chance of their being wanted; for there is no longer anyone who can be *compelled* to buy them. So that whatever is made is good, and thoroughly fit for its purpose. Nothing *can* be made except for genuine use; therefore no inferior goods are made. Moreover, as aforesaid, we have now found out what we want, so we make no more than we want; and as we are not driven to make a vast quantity of useless things, we have time and resources enough to consider our pleasure in making them. All work which would be irksome to do by hand is done by immensely improved machinery; and in all work which it is a pleasure to do by hand machinery is done without. There is no difficulty in finding work which suits the special turn of mind of everybody; so that no man is sacrificed to the wants of another. From time to time, when we have found out that some piece of work was too disagreeable or troublesome, we have given it up and done altogether without the thing produced by it. Now, surely you can see that under these circumstances all the work that we do is an exercise of the mind and body more or less pleasant to be done: so that instead of avoiding work everybody seeks it: and, since people have got defter in doing the work generation after generation, it has become so easy to do, that it seems as if there were less done, though probably more is produced. I suppose this explains that fear, which I hinted at just now, of a possible scarcity in work, which perhaps you have already noticed, and which is a feeling on the increase, and has been for a score of years."

"But do you think," said I, "that there is any fear of a work-famine amongst you?"

"No, I do not," said he, "and I will tell why; it is each man's business to make his own work pleasanter and pleasanter, which of course tends towards raising the standard of excellence, as no man enjoys turning out work which is not a credit to him, and also to greater deliberation in turning it out; and there is such a vast number of things which can be treated as works of art, that this alone gives employment to a host of deft people. Again, if art be inexhaustible, so is science also; and though it is no longer the only innocent occupation which is thought worth an intelligent man spending his time upon, as it once was, yet there are, and I suppose will be, many people who are excited by its conquest of difficulties, and care for it more than for anything else. Again, as more and more of pleasure is imported into work, I think we shall take up kinds of work which produce desirable wares, but which we gave up because we could not carry them on pleasantly. Moreover, I think that it is only in parts of Europe which are more advanced than the rest of the world that you will hear this talk of the fear of a work-famine. Those lands which were once the colonies of Great Britain, for instance, and especially America—that part of it, above all, which was once the United States—are now and will be for a long while a great resource to us. For these lands, and, I say, especially the northern parts of America, suffered so terribly from the full force of the last days of civilisation, and became such horrible places to live in, that they are now very backward in all that makes life pleasant. Indeed, one may say that for nearly a hundred years the people of the northern parts of America have been engaged in gradually making a dwelling-place out of a stinking dust heap; and there is still a great deal to do, especially as the country is so big."

"Well," said I, "I am exceedingly glad to think that you have such a prospect of happiness before you. . . ."

PART THREE

RELIGION

OMNE BONUM DESUPER   OPERA DEI MIRIFICA.

THE EVANGELICALS

Evangelicalism at Milby in 1830

GEORGE ELIOT

[FROM *Scenes of Clerical Life:* "Janet's Repentance"]

1857

The standard of morality at Milby, you perceive, was not inconveniently high in those good old times, and an ingenuous vice or two was what every man expected of his neighbour. Old Mr Crewe, the curate, for example, was allowed to enjoy his avarice in comfort, without fear of sarcastic parish demagogues; and his flock liked him all the better for having scraped together a large fortune out of his school and curacy, and the proceeds of the three thousand pounds he had with his little deaf wife. It was clear he must be a learned man, for he had once had a large private school in connection with the grammar-school, and had even numbered a young nobleman or two among his pupils. The fact that he read nothing at all now, and that his mind seemed absorbed in the commonest matters, was doubtless due to his having exhausted the resources of erudition earlier in life. It is true he was

From Chapter 2.

not spoken of in terms of high respect, and old Crewe's stingy housekeeping was a frequent subject of jesting; but this was a good old-fashioned characteristic in a parson who had been part of Milby life for half a century: it was like the dents and disfigurements in an old family tankard, which no one would like to part with for a smart new piece of plate fresh from Birmingham. The parishioners saw no reason at all why it should be desirable to venerate the parson or any one else: they were much more comfortable to look down a little on their fellow-creatures.

Even the Dissent in Milby was then of a lax and indifferent kind. The doctrine of adult baptism, struggling under a heavy load of debt, had let off half its chapel area as a ribbon-shop; and Methodism was only to be detected, as you detect curious larvæ, by diligent search in dirty corners. The Independents were the only Dissenters of whose existence Milby gentility was at all conscious, and it had a vague idea that the salient points of their creed were prayer without book, red brick, and hypocrisy. The Independent chapel, known as Salem, stood red and conspicuous in a broad street; more than one pew-holder kept a brass-bound gig; and Mr Jerome, a retired corn-factor, and the most eminent member of the congregation, was one of the richest men in the parish. But in spite of this apparent prosperity, together with the usual amount of extemporaneous preaching mitigated by furtive notes, Salem belied its name, and was not always the abode of peace. For some reason or other, it was unfortunate in the choice of its ministers. The Rev. Mr Horner, elected with brilliant hopes, was discovered to be given to tippling and quarrelling with his wife; the Rev. Mr Rose's doctrine was a little too "high," verging on Antinomianism; the Rev. Mr Stickney's gift as a preacher was found to be less striking on a more extended acquaintance; and the Rev. Mr Smith, a distinguished minister much sought after in the iron districts, with a talent for poetry, became objectionable from an inclination to exchange verses with the young ladies of his congregation. It was reasonably argued that such verses as Mr Smith's must take a long time for their composition, and the habit alluded to might intrench seriously on his pastoral duties. These reverend gentlemen, one and all, gave it as their opinion that the Salem church members were among the least enlightened of the Lord's people, and that Milby was a low place, where they would have found it a severe lot to have their lines fall for any long period; though to see the smart and crowded congregation assembled on occasion of the annual charity sermon, any one might have supposed that the minister of Salem had rather a brilliant position in the ranks of Dissent. Several Church families used to attend on that occasion, for Milby, in those uninstructed days, had not yet heard that the schismatic ministers of Salem were obviously typified by Korah, Dathan, and Abiram; and many Church people there were of opinion that Dissent might be a weakness, but, after all, had no great harm in it. These lax Episcopalians were, I believe, chiefly tradespeople, who held that, inasmuch as Congregationalism consumed candles, it ought to be supported, and accordingly made a point of presenting themselves at Salem for the afternoon charity sermon, with the expectation of being asked to hold a plate. Mr Pilgrim, too, was always there with his half-sovereign; for as there was no Dissenting doctor in Milby, Mr Pilgrim looked with great tolerance on all shades of religious opinion that did not include a belief in cures by miracle. . . .

Such as the place was, the people there were entirely contented with it. They fancied life must be but a dull affair for that large portion of mankind who were necessarily shut out from an acquaintance with Milby families, and that it must be an advantage to London and Liverpool that Milby gentlemen occasionally visited those places on business. But the inhabitants became more intensely conscious of the value they set upon all their advantages, when innovation made its appearance in the person of the Rev. Mr Tryan, the new curate, at the chapel-of-ease on Paddiford Common. It was soon notorious in Milby that Mr Tryan held peculiar opinions; that he preached extempore; that he was founding a religious lending library in his remote corner of the parish; that he expounded the Scriptures in cottages; and that his preaching was attracting the Dissenters, and filling the very aisles of his church. The rumour sprang up that Evangelicalism had invaded Milby parish—a murrain or blight all the more terrible, because its nature was but dimly conjectured. Perhaps Milby was one of the last spots to be reached by the wave of a new movement; and it was only now, when the tide was just on the turn, that the limpets there got a sprinkling. Mr Tryan was the first Evangelical clergyman who had risen above the Milby horizon: hitherto that obnoxious adjective had been unknown to the townspeople of any gentility; and there were even many Dissenters who considered "evangelical" simply a sort of baptismal name to the magazine which circulated among the congregation of Salem Chapel. But now, at length, the disease had been imported, when the parishioners were expecting it as little as the innocent Red Indians expected smallpox. As long as Mr Tryan's hearers were confined to Paddiford Common—which, by the by, was hardly recognisable as a common at all, but was a dismal district where you heard the rattle of the handloom, and breathed the smoke of coal-pits—the "canting parson" could be treated as a joke. Not so when a number of single ladies in the town appeared to be infected, and even one or two men of substantial property, with old Mr Landor, the banker, at their head, seemed to be "giving in" to the new movement—when Mr Tryan was known to be well received in several good houses, where he was in the habit of finishing the evening with exhortation and prayer. Evangelicalism was no longer a nuisance existing merely in by-corners, which any well-clad person could avoid; it was invading the very drawing-rooms, mingling itself with the comfortable fumes of port-wine and brandy, threatening to deaden with its murky breath all the splendour of the ostrich-feathers, and to stifle Milby ingenuousness, not pretending to be better than its neighbours, with a cloud of cant and lugubrious hypocrisy. The alarm reached its climax when it was reported that Mr Tryan was endeavouring to obtain authority from Mr Prendergast, the non-resident rector, to establish a Sunday evening lecture in the parish church, on the ground that old Mr Crewe did not preach the Gospel.

It now first appeared how surprisingly high a value Milby in general set on the ministrations of Mr Crewe; how convinced it was that Mr Crewe was the model of a parish priest, and his sermons the soundest and most edifying that had ever remained unheard by a church-going population. All allusions to his brown wig were suppressed, and by a rhetorical figure his name was associated with venerable grey hairs: the attempted intrusion of Mr Tryan was an insult to a man deep in years and learning; moreover, it was an insolent effort to thrust himself forward in a parish where he was clearly distasteful to the superior portion of its inhabitants. The town was divided into two zealous parties, the Tryanites and anti-Tryanites; and by the exertions of the eloquent Dempster, the anti-Tryanite virulence was soon developed into an organised opposition. A protest against the meditated evening lecture was framed by that orthodox attorney, and, after being numerously signed, was to be carried to Mr Prendergast by three delegates representing the intellect, morality, and wealth of Milby. The intellect, you perceive, was to be personified in Mr Dempster, the morality in Mr Budd, and the wealth in Mr Tomlinson; and the distinguished triad was to set out on its great mission, as we have seen, on the third day from that warm Saturday evening when the conversation recorded in the previous chapter took place in the bar of the Red Lion.

[FROM Chapter 10]

Meanwhile, the evening lecture drew larger and larger congregations; not perhaps attracting many from that select aristocractic circle in which the Lowmes and Pittmans were predominant, but winning the larger proportion of Mr Crewe's morning and afternoon hearers, and thinning Mr Stickney's evening audiences at Salem. Evangelicalism was making its way in Milby, and gradually diffusing its subtle odour into chambers that were bolted and barred against it. The movement, like all other religious "revivals," had a mixed effect. Religious ideas have the fate of melodies, which, once set afloat in the world, are taken up by all sorts of instruments, some of them woefully coarse, feeble, or out of tune, until people are in danger of crying out that the melody itself is detestable. It may be that some of Mr Tryan's hearers had gained a religious vocabulary rather than religious experience; that here and there a weaver's wife, who, a few months before, had been simply a silly slattern, was converted into that more complex nuisance, a silly and sanctimonious slattern; that the old Adam, with the pertinacity of middle age, continued to tell fibs behind the counter, notwithstanding the new Adam's addiction to Bible-reading and family prayer; that the children in the Paddiford Sunday-school had their memories crammed with phrases about the blood of cleansing, imputed righteousness, and justification by faith alone, which an experience lying principally in chuck-farthing, hop-scotch, parental slappings, and longings after unattainable lollypop, served rather to darken than to illustrate; and that at Milby, in those distant days, as in all other times and places where the mental atmosphere is changing, and men are inhaling the stimulus of new ideas, folly often mistook itself for wisdom, ignorance gave itself airs of knowledge, and selfishness, turning its eyes upward, called itself religion.

Nevertheless, Evangelicalism had brought into palpable existence and operation in Milby society that idea of duty, that recognition of something to be lived for beyond the mere satisfaction of self, which is to the moral life what the addition of a great central ganglion is to animal life. No man can begin to mould himself on a faith or an idea without rising to a higher order of experience: a principle of subordination of self-mastery, has been introduced into his nature; he is no longer a mere bundle of impressions, desires, and impulses. Whatever might be the weaknesses of the ladies who pruned the luxuriance of their lace and ribbons, cut out garments for the poor, distributed tracts, quoted Scripture, and defined the true Gospel, they had learned this—

that there was a divine work to be done in life, a rule of goodness higher than the opinion of their neighbours; and if the notion of a heaven in reserve for themselves was a little too prominent, yet the theory of fitness for that heaven consisted in purity of heart, in Christ-like compassion, in the subduing of selfish desires. They might give the name of piety to much that was only puritanic egoism; they might call many things sin that were not sin; but they had at least the feeling that sin was to be avoided and resisted, and colour-blindness, which may mistake drab for scarlet, is better than total blindness, which sees no distinction of colour at all. Miss Rebecca Linnet, in quiet attire, with a somewhat excessive solemnity of countenance, teaching at the Sunday-school, visiting the poor, and striving after a standard of purity and goodness, had surely more moral loveliness than in those flaunting peony-days, when she had no other model than the costumes of the heroines in the circulating library. Miss Eliza Pratt, listening in rapt attention to Mr Tryan's evening lecture, no doubt found evangelical channels for vanity and egoism; but she was clearly in moral advance of Miss Phipps giggling under her feathers at old Mr Crewe's peculiarities of enunciation. And even elderly fathers and mothers, with minds, like Mrs Linnet's, too tough to imbibe much doctrine, were the better for having their hearts inclined towards the new preacher as a messenger from God. They became ashamed, perhaps, of their evil tempers, ashamed of their worldliness, ashamed of their trivial, futile past. The first condition of human goodness is something to love; the second something to reverence. And this latter precious gift was brought to Milby by Mr Tryan and Evangelicalism.

Yes, the movement was good, though it had that mixture of folly and evil which often makes what is good an offence to feeble and fastidious minds, who want human actions and characters riddled through the sieve of their own ideas, before they can accord their sympathy or admiration. Such minds, I daresay, would have found Mr Tryan's character very much in need of that riddling process. The blessed work of helping the world forward, happily does not wait to be done by perfect men; and I should imagine that neither Luther nor John Bunyan, for example, would have satisfied the modern demand for an ideal hero, who believes nothing but what is true, feels nothing but what is exalted, and does nothing but what is graceful. The real heroes, of God's making, are quite different: they have their natural heritage of love and conscience which they drew in with their mother's milk; they know one or two of those deep spiritual truths which are only to be won by long wrestling with their own sins and their own sorrows; they have earned faith and strength so far as they have done genuine work; but the rest is dry barren theory, blank prejudice, vague hearsay. Their insight is blended with mere opinion; their sympathy is perhaps confined in narrow conduits of doctrine, instead of flowing forth with the freedom of a stream that blesses every weed in its course; obstinacy or self-assertion will often interfuse itself with their grandest impulses; and their very deeds of self-sacrifice are sometimes only the rebound of a passionate egoism. So it was with Mr Tryan: and any one looking at him with the bird's-eye glance of a critic might perhaps say that he made the mistake of identifying Christianity with a too narrow doctrinal system; that he saw God's work too exclusively in antagonism to the world, the flesh, and the devil; that his intellectual culture was too limited—and so on; making Mr Tryan the text for a wise discourse on the characteristics of the Evangelical school in his day.

A Word on the May-Meetings

[FROM *Punch*, 6 June 1846]

Punch is not popular in Exeter Hall. If he were to present himself upon the platform, as a practical philanthropist, pious ladies would faint, evangelical chairmen break out into unholy passions, and *Punch* would be hustled by indignant piety down the steps among the pickpockets, who are practising their vocation in the crowd outside.

He knows this, and deeply, sincerely regrets it. He has more sympathy with what goes on in May-meetings than Exeter Hall would be likely to give him credit for. . . .

Punch, it is true, teaches by laughter and wears motley. Exeter Hall dresses its charity in grave looks and black coats. But *Punch's* grin may cover thoughts as solemn as a drawn-down lip and a dead eye. His parti-coloured doublet has a heart under it as penetrable, as sympathetic, and as large as that which beats under the Rev. Jabez Blank's raven broadcloth, or Dr. Anonymous's sable cassock.

Punch has his peculiar theories of social improvements, like Exeter Hall, but his own strike him as the wider. He believes in the proverb, that "Charity begins at home," though it by no means ends there. Exeter Hall, on the contrary, seems to think that Charity begins abroad, and that it should keep its pockets buttoned till it crosses the line. *Punch* has no doubt that the heathen are in a horrible state of darkness and depravity. Exemplary missionaries assure him of the fact; and, moreover, that they have the greatest difficulty in convincing benighted but jolly Fejeeans that they are miserable sinners. But his eyes have taught him the existence of a deeper heathenism and a more benighted savageness lying round about us—the heathenism of untrained vice and the savageness of degraded civilisation.

Punch, Volume 10, page 259.

Suppose, besides its Pastoral Aid Societies and its Scripture Readers, Exeter Hall were to turn the stream of its benevolence—its millions of money, and its thousands of agents, for a year or two, through our own towns and hamlets; suppose the Bible Society were to sink its Foreign labours for a while, and to constitute itself a Society for the Education of the Poor—to multiply our Ragged Schools by ten thousand, and increase their efficiency and scope in the same ratio? What if the propagators of the Gospel were to look at home, and begin propagating the Gospel lessons of peace on earth and good-will towards men—to carry on, in short, the lessons of which their great Founder sowed the seeds and left the record?

What if some dozen of Societies, now ready to tear each other in pieces from sheer excess of Christian zeal, were to lump their activity and intentions into a great Metropolitan Social Improvement Union, to go on step by step with the Metropolitan Buildings' Improvement Commissioners? The latter pull down the hovels of the poor to build up houses for the respectable; why should not the proposed Society set to work to build up comfortable dwellings for the wretched who are thus displaced? What if, abandoning for a while their exclusive faith in tracts, they were to throw their energies into baths and wash-houses, and prepare the human vessel for receiving the purified contents they wish to pour into it?

The zealous for Christian education might combine to supersede those present unsatisfactory school-masters, the prison and the gallows. Saffron Hill and the Rookery lie nearer home than Caffraria and the Marquesas Islands. The missionaries to the savage and heathen districts of London would not have far to travel, and, short of cannibalism, would meet with every variety of evil habit to amend, and every degree of ignorance to enlighten. They would have abundance of discouragement, and enough of disappointment to satisfy the zeal of a St. Vincent, St. Paul, or a Henry Martyn. If not roasted at the stake, they would be roasted in slang, and the progress of their labours would be calculable by something more trustworthy than missionary letters, and marked by more cheering results than MASHEBOO'S giving up his taste for gold, or RAUPARAHU'S solemnly putting away eleven of his twelve wives. We throw out these hints to the May-meetings in the best spirit of co-operation, and remain, their brother in all good works, though they won't own him so,

PUNCH.

Mr. Brocklehurst's Catechism

CHARLOTTE BRONTE

[FROM *Jane Eyre, An Autobiography*]

1847

I feared to return to the nursery, and feared to go forward to the parlour; ten minutes I stood in agitated hesitation: the vehement ringing of the breakfast-room bell decided me; I *must* enter.

"Who could want me?" I asked inwardly, as with both hands I turned the stiff door-handle which, for a second or two, resisted my efforts. "What should I see besides aunt Reed in the apartment?—a man or a woman?" The handle turned, the door unclosed, and passing through and curtseying low, I looked up at—a black pillar!—such, at least, appeared to me, at first sight, the straight, narrow, sable-clad shape standing erect on the rug; the grim face at the top was like a carved mask, placed above the shaft by way of capital.

Mrs. Reed occupied her usual seat by the fireside: she made a signal to me to approach: I did so, and she introduced me to the stony stranger with the words: "This is the little girl respecting whom I applied to you."

From Chapter 4.

He, for it was a man, turned his head slowly towards where I stood, and having examined me with the two inquisitive-looking grey eyes which twinkled under a pair of bushy brows, said solemnly, and in a bass voice: "Her size is small: what is her age?"

"Ten years."

"So much?" was the doubtful answer; and he prolonged his scrutiny some minutes. Presently he addressed me:—

"Your name, little girl?"

"Jane Eyre, sir."

In uttering these words, I looked up: he seemed to me a tall gentleman; but then I was very little: his features were large, and they and all the lines of his frame were equally harsh and prim.

"Well, Jane Eyre, and are you a good child?"

Impossible to reply to this in the affirmative: my little world held a contrary opinion: I was silent. Mrs. Reed answered for me by an expressive shake of the head, adding soon, "Perhaps the less said on that subject the better, Mr. Brocklehurst."

"Sorry indeed to hear it! she and I must have some talk"; and bending from the perpendicular, he installed his person in the arm-chair, opposite Mrs. Reed's. "Come here," he said.

I stepped across the rug; he placed me square and straight before him. What a face he had, now that it was almost level with mine! what a great nose! and what a mouth! and what large prominent teeth!

"No sight so sad as that of a naughty child," he began, "especially a naughty little girl. Do you know where the wicked go after death?"

"They go to hell," was my ready and orthodox answer.

"And what is hell? Can you tell me that?"

"A pit full of fire."

"And should you like to fall into that pit, and to be burning there for ever?"

"No, sir."

"What must you do to avoid it?"

I deliberated a moment; my answer, when it did come, was objectionable: "I must keep in good health, and not die."

"How can you keep in good health? Children younger than you die daily. I buried a little child of five years old only a day or two since,—a good little child, whose soul is now in heaven. It is to be feared the same could not be said of you, were you to be called hence."

Not being in a condition to remove his doubts I only cast my eyes down on the two large feet planted on the rug, and sighed; wishing myself far enough away.

"I hope that sigh is from the heart, and that you repent of ever having been the occasion of discomfort to your excellent benefactress."

"Benefactress! benefactress!" said I inwardly: "they all call Mrs. Reed my benefactress; if so, a benefactress is a disagreeable thing."

"Do you say your prayers night and morning?" continued my interrogator.

"Yes, sir."

"Do you read your Bible?"

"Sometimes."

"With pleasure? Are you fond of it?"

"I like Revelations, and the book of Daniel, and Genesis and Samuel, and a little bit of Exodus, and some parts of Kings and Chronicles, and Job and Jonah."

"And the Psalms? I hope you like them?"

"No, sir."

"No? oh, shocking! I have a little boy, younger than you, who knows six Psalms by heart; and when you ask him which he would rather have, a gingerbread-nut to eat, or a verse of a Psalm to learn, he says: 'Oh! the verse of a Psalm! angels sing Psalms'; says he, 'I wish to be a little angel here below'; he then gets two nuts in recompense for his infant piety."

"Psalms are not interesting," I remarked.

"That proves you have a wicked heart; and you must pray to God to change it: to give you a new and clean one: to take away your heart of stone and give you a heart of flesh."

I was about to propound a question, touching the manner in which that operation of changing my heart was to be performed, when Mrs. Reed interposed, telling me to sit down; she then proceeded to carry on the conversation herself.

"Mr. Brocklehurst, I believe I intimated in the letter which I wrote to you three weeks ago, that this little girl has not quite the character and disposition I could wish: should you admit her into Lowood school, I should be glad if the superintendent and teachers were requested to keep a strict eye on her, and above all, to guard against her worst fault, a tendency to deceit. I mention this in your hearing, Jane, that you may not attempt to impose on Mr. Brocklehurst." . . .

"Deceit is, indeed, a sad fault in a child," said Mr. Brocklehurst; "it is akin to falsehood, and all liars will have their portion in the lake burning with fire and brimstone: she shall, however, be watched, Mrs. Reed; I will speak to Miss Temple and the teachers."

"I should wish her to be brought up in a manner suiting her prospects," continued my benefactress; "to be made useful, to be kept humble: as for the vacations, she will, with your permission, spend them always at Lowood."

"Your decisions are perfectly judicious, madam," returned Mr. Brocklehurst. "Humility is a Christian grace, and one peculiarly appropriate to the pupils of Lowood; I, therefore, direct that especial care shall be bestowed on its cultivation amongst them. I have studied how best to mortify in them the worldly sentiment of pride; and only the other day, I had a pleasing proof of my success. My second daughter, Augusta, went with her mama to visit the school, and on her return she exclaimed: 'Oh, dear papa, how quiet and plain all the girls at Lowood look; with their hair combed behind their ears, and their long pinafores, and those little holland pockets outside their frocks—they are almost like poor people's children! and,' said she, 'they looked at my dress and mama's, as if they had never seen a silk gown before.'"

"This is the state of things I quite approve," returned Mrs. Reed: "had I sought all England over, I could scarcely have found a system more exactly fitting a child like Jane Eyre. Consistency, my dear Mr. Brocklehurst; I advocate consistency in all things."

"Consistency, madam, is the first of Christian duties; and it has been observed in every arrangement connected with the establishment of Lowood: plain fare, simple attire, unsophisticated accommodations, hardy and active habits; such is the order of the day in the house and its inhabitants."

"Quite right, sir. I may then depend upon this child being received as a pupil at Lowood, and there being trained in conformity to her position and prospects?"

"Madam, you may: she shall be placed in that nursery of chosen plants—and I trust she will shew herself grateful for the inestimable privilege of her election."

"I will send her, then, as soon as possible, Mr. Brocklehurst; for, I assure you, I feel anxious to be relieved of a responsibility that was becoming too irksome."

"No doubt, no doubt, madam, and now I wish you good morning. I shall return to Brocklehurst-hall in the course of a week or two: my good friend, the Archdeacon, will not permit me to leave him sooner. I shall send Miss Temple notice that she is to expect a new girl, so that there will be no difficulty about receiving her. Good-bye."

"Good-bye, Mr. Brocklehurst; remember me to Mrs. and Miss Brocklehurst, and to Augusta and Theodore, and Master Broughton Brocklehurst."

"I will, madam. Little girl, here is a book entitled the 'Child's Guide'; read it with prayer, especially that part containing 'an account of the awfully sudden death of Martha G——, a naughty child addicted to falsehood and deceit.' "

With these words Mr. Brocklehurst put into my hand a thin pamphlet sewn in a cover, and having rung for his carriage, he departed.

The Sabbath Laws

CHARLES DICKENS

[FROM *Sunday under Three Heads*]

1836

The provisions of the bill introduced into the House of
Commons by Sir Andrew Agnew, and thrown out by that
House on the motion for the second reading, on the 18th of
May in the present year [1836], by a majority of 32, may very
fairly be taken as a test of the length to which the fanatics, of
which the honourable Baronet is the distinguished leader, are
prepared to go. . . .

The proposed enactments of the bill are briefly these:—
All work is prohibited on the Lord's Day, under heavy
penalties, increasing with every repetition of the offence. There
are penalties for keeping shops open—penalties for drunkenness—penalties for keeping open houses of entertainment—
penalties for being present at any public meeting or assembly
—penalties for letting carriages, and penalties for hiring them
—penalties for travelling in steamboats, and penalties for
taking passengers—penalties on vessels commencing their voyage on Sunday—penalties on the owners of cattle who suffer
them to be driven on the Lord's Day—penalties on constables
who refuse to act, and penalties for resisting them when they
do. In addition to these trifles, the constables are invested
with arbitrary, vexatious, and most extensive powers; and all
this in a bill which sets out with a hypocritical and canting
declaration that "nothing is more acceptable to God than the
true and sincere worship of Him according to His holy will,
and that it is the bounden duty of Parliament to promote the
observance of the Lord's Day, by protecting every class of

From Chapter 2.

society against being required to sacrifice their comfort, health,
religious privileges, and conscience, for the convenience, enjoyment, or supposed advantage of any other class on the Lord's
Day"! The idea of making a man truly moral through the
ministry of constables, and sincerely religious under the
influence of penalties, is worthy of the mind which could
form such a mass of monstrous absurdity as this bill is composed of. . . .

In the first place, it is by no means the worst characteristic
of this bill, that it is a bill of blunders: it is, from beginning
to end, a piece of deliberate cruelty, and crafty injustice. If
the rich composed the whole population of this country, not a
single comfort of one single man would be affected by it. It
is directed exclusively, and without the exception of a solitary instance, against the amusements and recreations of
the poor. . . . Menial servants, both male and female, are
specially exempted from the operation of the bill. "Menial
servants" are among the poor people. The bill has no regard
for them. The Baronet's dinner must be cooked on Sunday,
the Bishop's horses must be groomed, and the Peer's carriage
must be driven. So the menial servants are put utterly beyond
the pale of grace;—unless, indeed, they are to go to heaven
through the sanctity of their masters, and possibly they might
think even that rather an uncertain passport. . . .

With one exception, there are, perhaps, no clauses in the
whole bill so strongly illustrative of its partial operation, and
the intention of its framer, as those which relate to travelling
on Sunday. Penalties of ten, twenty, and thirty pounds, are
mercilessly imposed upon coach proprietors who shall run
their coaches on the Sabbath; one, two, and ten pounds upon
those who hire, or let to hire, horses and carriages upon the
Lord's Day, but not one syllable about those who have no
necessity to hire, because they have carriages and horses of
their own; not one word of a penalty on liveried coachmen
and footmen. The whole of the saintly venom is directed
against the hired cabriolet, the humble fly, or the rumbling
hackney-coach, which enables a man of the poorer class to
escape for a few hours from the smoke and dirt, in the midst

of which he has been confined throughout the week: while the escutcheoned carriage and the dashing cab may whirl their wealthy owners to Sunday feasts and private oratorios, setting constables, informers, and penalties at defiance . . . .

There is, in four words, a mock proviso, which affects to forbid travelling "with any animal" on the Lord's Day. This, however, is revoked, as relates to the rich man, by a subsequent provision. We have, then, a penalty of not less than fifty nor more than one hundred pounds, upon any person participating in the controul, or having the command, of any vessel which shall commence her voyage on the Lord's Day, should the wind prove favourable. The next time this bill is brought forward (which will no doubt be at an early period of the next session of Parliament) perhaps it will be better to amend this clause by declaring, that from and after the passing of the act, it shall be deemed unlawful for the wind to blow at all upon the Sabbath. It would remove a great deal of temptation from the owners and captains of vessels. . . .

Let us suppose such a bill as this to have actually passed both branches of the legislature; to have received the royal assent, and to have come into operation. Imagine its effect in a great city like London.

Sunday comes, and brings with it a day of general gloom and austerity. The man who has been toiling hard all the week has been looking towards the Sabbath, not as to a day of rest from labour, and healthy recreation, but as one of grievous tyranny and grinding oppression. The day which his Maker intended as a blessing, man has converted into a curse. Instead of being hailed by him as his period of relaxation, he finds it remarkable only as depriving him of every comfort and enjoyment. He has many children about him, all sent into the world at an early age, to struggle for a livelihood; one is kept in a warehouse all day, with an interval of rest too short to enable him to reach home, another walks four or five miles to his employment at the docks, a third earns a few shillings weekly, as an errand boy, or office messenger; and the employment of the man himself detains him at some distance from his home from morning till night. Sunday is the only day on which they could all meet together, and enjoy a homely meal in social comfort; and now they sit down to a cold and cheerless dinner; the pious guardians of the man's salvation having, in their regard for the welfare of his precious soul, shut up the bakers' shops. The fire blazes high in the kitchen chimney of these well-fed hypocrites, and the rich steams of the savoury dinner scent the air. What care they to be told that this class of men have neither a place to cook in—nor means to bear the expense, if they had?

Look into your churches—diminished congregations, and scanty attendance. People have grown sullen and obstinate, and are becoming disgusted with the faith which condemns them to such a day as this, once in every seven. And as you cannot make people religious by Act of Parliament, or force them to church by constables, they display their feeling by staying away.

Turn into the streets, and mark the rigid gloom that reigns over every thing around. The roads are empty, the fields are deserted, the houses of entertainment are closed. Groups of filthy and discontented-looking men are idling about at the street corners, or sleeping in the sun; but there are no decently dressed people of the poorer class, passing to and fro. Where should they walk to? It would take them an hour, at least, to get into the fields, and when they reached them, they could procure neither bit nor sup, without the informer and the penalty. Now and then, a carriage rolls smoothly on, or a well-mounted horseman, followed by a liveried attendant, canters by; but with these exceptions, all is as melancholy and quiet as if a pestilence had fallen on the city.

Bend your steps through the narrow and thickly inhabited streets, and observe the sallow faces of the men and women, who are lounging at the doors, or lolling from the windows. Regard well, the closeness of these crowded rooms, and the noisome exhalations that rise from the drains and kennels; and then laud the triumph of religion and morality which condemns people to drag their lives out in such stews as these, and makes it criminal for them to eat or drink in the fresh air, or under the clear sky.

Bishop Proudie's Chaplain, Mr. Slope

ANTHONY TROLLOPE

[FROM *Barchester Towers*]

1855

Of the Rev. Mr. Slope's parentage I am not able to say much. I have heard it asserted that he is lineally descended from that eminent physician who assisted at the birth of Mr. T. Shandy, and that in early years he added an "e" to his name, for the sake of euphony, as other great men have done before him. If this be so, I presume he was christened Obadiah, for that is his name, in commemoration of the conflict in which his ancestor so distinguished himself. All my researches on the subject have, however, failed in enabling me to fix the date on which the family changed its religion.

He had been a sizar at Cambridge, and had there conducted himself at any rate successfully, for in due process of time he was an M.A., having university pupils under his care. From thence he was transferred to London, and became preacher at a new district church built on the confines of Baker Street. He was in this position when congenial ideas on religious subjects recommended him to Mrs. Proudie, and the intercourse had become close and confidential....

His acquirements are not of the highest order; but such as they are they are completely under control, and he knows the use of them. He is gifted with a certain kind of pulpit eloquence, not likely indeed to be persuasive with men, but powerful with the softer sex. In his sermons he deals greatly in denunciations, excites the minds of his weaker hearers with a not unpleasant terror, and leaves an impression on their minds that all mankind are in a perilous state, and all woman-

From Chapter 4.

kind too, except those who attend regularly to the evening lectures in Baker Street. His looks and tones are extremely severe, so much so that one cannot but fancy that he regards the greater part of the world as being infinitely too bad for his care. As he walks through the streets, his very face denotes his horror of the world's wickedness; and there is always an anathema lurking in the corner of his eye.

In doctrine, he, like his patron, is tolerant of dissent, if so strict a mind can be called tolerant of anything. With Wesleyan-Methodists he has something in common, but his soul trembles in agony at the iniquities of the Puseyites. His aversion is carried to things outward as well as inward. His gall rises at a new church with a high pitched roof; a full-breasted black silk waistcoat is with him a symbol of Satan; and a profane jest-book would not, in his view more foully desecrate the church seat of a Christian, than a book of prayer printed with red letters and ornamented with a cross on the back. Most active clergymen have their hobby, and Sunday observances are his. Sunday, however, is a word which never pollutes his mouth—it is always "the Sabbath." The "desecration of the Sabbath," as he delights to call it, is to him meat and drink:—he thrives upon that as policemen do on the general evil habits of the community. It is the loved subject of all his evening discourses, the source of all his eloquence, the secrets of all his power over the female heart. To him the revelation of God appears only in that one law given for Jewish observance. . . . To him the New Testament is comparatively of little moment, for from it can he draw no fresh authority for that dominion which he loves to exercise over at least a seventh part of man's allotted time here below.

Mr. Slope is tall, and not ill made. His feet and hands are large, as has ever been the case with all his family, but he has a broad chest and wide shoulders to carry off these excrescences, and on the whole his figure is good. His countenance, however, is not specially prepossessing. His hair is lank, and of a dull pale reddish hue. It is always formed into three straight lumpy masses, each brushed with admirable precision, and cemented with much grease; two of them adhere closely to the sides of his face, and the other lies at right angles above them. He wears no whiskers, and is always punctiliously shaven. His face is nearly of the same colour as his hair, though perhaps a little redder: it is not unlike beef,—beef, however, one would say, of a bad quality. His forehead is capacious and high, but square and heavy, and unpleasantly shining. His mouth is large, though his lips are thin and bloodless; and his big, prominent, pale brown eyes inspire anything but confidence. His nose, however, is his redeeming feature: it is pronounced straight and well-formed; though I myself should have liked it better did it not possess a somewhat spongy, porous appearance, as though it had been cleverly formed out of a red coloured cork.

I never could endure to shake hands with Mr. Slope. A cold, clammy perspiration always exudes from him, the small drops are ever to be seen standing on his brow, and his friendly grasp is unpleasant.

Mrs. Proudie on Sabbath Travelling

ANTHONY TROLLOPE

[FROM *Barchester Towers*]

1855

Our friends found Dr. Proudie sitting on the old bishop's chair, looking very nice in his new apron; they found, too, Mr. Slope standing on the hearth-rug, persuasive and eager, just as the archdeacon used to stand; but on the sofa they also found Mrs. Proudie, an innovation for which a precedent

From Chapter 5.

might in vain be sought in all the annals of the Barchester bishopric!

There she was, however, and they could only make the best of her. . . .

"Do you reside in Barchester, Dr. Grantly?" asked the lady with her sweetest smile.

Dr. Grantly explained that he lived in his own parish of Plumstead Episcopi, a few miles out of the city. Whereupon the lady hoped that the distance was not too great for country visiting, as she would be so glad to make the acquaintance of Mrs. Grantly. She would take the earliest opportunity, after the arrival of her horses at Barchester; their horses were at present in London; their horses were not immediately coming down, as the bishop would be obliged, in a few days, to return to town. Dr. Grantly was no doubt aware that the bishop was at present much called upon by the "University Improvement Committee": indeed, the Committee could not well proceed without him, as their final report had now to be drawn up. The bishop had also to prepare a scheme for the "'Manu-facturing Towns Morning and Evening Sunday School Soci-ety," of which he was a patron, or president, or director, and therefore the horses would not come down to Barchester at present; but whenever the horses did come down, she would take the earliest opportunity of calling at Plumstead Episcopi, providing the distance was not too great for country visiting.

The archdeacon made his fifth bow: he had made one at each mention of the horses; and promised that Mrs. Grantly would do herself the honour of calling at the palace on an early day. Mrs. Proudie declared that she would be delighted: she hadn't liked to ask, not being quite sure whether Mrs. Grantly had horses; besides, the distance might have been, &c. &c.

Dr. Grantly again bowed, but said nothing. He could have bought every individual possession of the whole family of the Proudies, and have restored them as a gift, without much feeling the loss; and had kept a separate pair of horses for the exclusive use of his wife since the day of his marriage; whereas Mrs. Proudie had been hitherto jobbed about the streets of London at so much a month during the season; and at other times had managed to walk, or hire a smart fly from the livery stables.

"Are the arrangements with reference to the Sabbath-day schools generally pretty good in your archdeaconry?" asked Mr. Slope.

"Sabbath-day schools!" repeated the archdeacon with an affectation of surprise. "Upon my word, I can't tell; it depends mainly on the parson's wife and daughters. There is none at Plumstead."

This was almost a fib on the part of the Archdeacon, for Mrs. Grantly has a very nice school. To be sure it is not a Sunday school exclusively, and is not so designated; but that exemplary lady always attends there for an hour before church, and hears the children say their catechism, and sees that they are clean and tidy for church, with their hands washed, and their shoes tied; and Grisel and Florinda, her daughters, carry thither a basket of large buns, baked on the Saturday afternoon, and distribute them to all the children not especially under disgrace, which buns are carried home after church with considerable content, and eaten hot at tea, being then split and toasted. The children of Plumstead would indeed open their eyes if they heard their venerated pastor declare that there was no Sunday school in his parish.

Mr. Slope merely opened his wide eyes wider, and slightly shrugged his shoulders. He was not, however, prepared to give up his darling project.

"I fear there is a great deal of Sabbath travelling here," said he. "On looking at the 'Bradshaw,' I see that there are three trains in and three out every Sabbath. Could nothing be done to induce the company to withdraw them? Don't you think, Dr. Grantly, that a little energy might diminish the evil?"

"Not being a director, I really can't say. But if you can withdraw the passengers, the company I dare say will withdraw the trains," said the doctor. "It's merely a question of dividends."

"But surely, Dr. Grantly," said the lady, "surely we should

look at it differently. You and I, for instance, in our position: surely we should do all that we can to control so grievous a sin. Don't you think so, Mr. Harding?" and she turned to the precentor, who was sitting mute and unhappy.

Mr. Harding thought that all porters and stokers, guards, breaksmen, and pointsmen ought to have an opportunity of going to church, and he hoped that they all had.

"But surely, surely," continued Mrs. Proudie, "surely that is not enough. Surely that will not secure such an observance of the Sabbath as we are taught to conceive is not only expedient but indispensable; surely—"

Come what come might, Dr. Grantly was not to be forced into a dissertation on a point of doctrine with Mrs. Proudie, nor yet with Mr. Slope; so without much ceremony he turned his back upon the sofa, and began to hope that Dr. Proudie had found that the palace repairs had been such as to meet his wishes. . . .

Mrs. Proudie, though she had contrived to lend her assistance in recapitulating the palatial dilapidations, had not on that account given up her hold of Mr. Harding, nor ceased from her cross-examinations as to the iniquity of Sabbatical amusements. Over and over again had she thrown out her "Surely, surely," at Mr. Harding's devoted head, and ill had that gentlemen been able to parry the attack.

He had never before found himself subjected to such a nuisance. Ladies hitherto, when they had consulted him on religious subjects, had listened to what he might choose to say with some deference, and had differed, if they differed, in silence. But Mrs. Proudie interrogated him, and then lectured. "Neither thou, nor thy son, nor thy daughter, thy man servant, nor thy maid servant," said she, impressively, and more than once, as though Mr. Harding had forgotten the words. She shook her finger at him as she quoted the favourite law, as though menacing him with punishment; and then called upon him categorically to state whether he did not think that travelling on the Sabbath was an abomination and a desecration.

Mr. Harding had never been so hard pressed in his life.

He felt that he ought to rebuke the lady for presuming so to talk to a gentleman and a clergyman many years her senior; but he recoiled from the idea of scolding the bishop's wife, in the bishop's presence, on his first visit to the palace; moreover, to tell the truth, he was somewhat afraid of her. She, seeing him sit silent and absorbed, by no means refrained from the attack.

"I hope Mr. Harding," said she, shaking her head slowly and solemnly, "I hope you will not leave me to think that you approve of Sabbath travelling," and she looked a look of unutterable meaning into his eyes.

There was no standing this, for Mr. Slope was now looking at him, and so was the bishop, and so was the archdeacon, who had completed his adieux on that side of the room. Mr. Harding therefore got up also, and putting out his hand to Mrs. Proudie said: "If you will come to St. Cuthbert's some Sunday, I will preach you a sermon on that subject."

And so the archdeacon and the precentor took their departure, bowing low to the lady, shaking hands with the lord, and escaping from Mr. Slope in the best manner each could. Mr. Harding was again maltreated; but Dr. Grantly swore deeply in the bottom of his heart, that no earthly consideration should ever again induce him to touch the paw of that impure and filthy animal.

The Simeonites in 1858

SAMUEL BUTLER

[FROM *The Way of All Flesh*]

1903

Ernest returned to Cambridge for the May term of 1858, on the plea of reading for ordination, with which he was now face to face, and much nearer than he liked. Up to this time, though not religiously inclined, he had never doubted the truth of anything that had been told him about Christianity. He had never seen anyone who doubted, nor read anything that raised a suspicion in his mind as to the historical character of the miracles recorded in the Old and New Testaments.

It must be remembered that the year 1858 was the last of a term during which the peace of the Church of England was singularly unbroken. Between 1844, when *Vestiges of Creation* appeared, and 1859, when *Essays and Reviews* marked the commencement of that storm which raged until many years afterwards, there was not a single book published in England that caused serious commotion within the bosom of the Church. Perhaps Buckle's *History of Civilization* and Mill's *Liberty* were the most alarming, but they neither of them reached the substratum of the reading public, and Ernest and his friends were ignorant of their very existence. The Evangelical movement, with the exception to which I shall revert presently, had become almost a matter of ancient history. Tractarianism had subsided into a tenth day's wonder; it was at work, but it was not noisy. The *Vestiges* were forgotten before Ernest went up to Cambridge; the Catholic aggression scare had lost its terrors; Ritualism was still unknown by the general provincial public, and the Gorham

From Chapter 47.

and Hampden controversies were defunct some years since; Dissent was not spreading; the Crimean war was the one engrossing subject, to be followed by the Indian Mutiny and the Franco-Austrian war. These great events turned men's minds from speculative subjects, and there was no enemy to the faith which could arouse even a languid interest. At no time probably since the beginning of the century could an ordinary observer have detected less sign of coming disturbance than at that of which I am writing.

I need hardly say that the calm was only on the surface. Older men, who knew more than undergraduates were likely to do, must have seen that the wave of scepticism which had already broken over Germany was setting towards our own shores, nor was it long, indeed, before it reached them. Ernest had hardly been ordained before three works in quick succession arrested the attention even of those who paid least heed to theological controversy. I mean *Essays and Reviews,* Charles Darwin's *Origin of Species,* and Bishop Colenso's *Criticisms on the Pentateuch.*

This, however, is a digression; I must revert to the one phase of spiritual activity which had any life in it during the time Ernest was at Cambridge, that is to say, to the remains of the Evangelical awakening of more than a generation earlier, which was connected with the name of Simeon.

There were still a good many Simeonites, or as they were more briefly called "Sims," in Ernest's time. Every college contained some of them, but their headquarters were at Caius, whither they were attracted by Mr. Clayton who was at that time senior tutor, and among the sizars of St. John's.

Behind the then chapel of this last-named college, there was a "labyrinth" (this was the name it bore) of dingy, tumbledown rooms, tenanted exclusively by the poorest undergraduates, who were dependent upon sizarships and scholarships for the means of taking their degrees. To many, even at St. John's, the existence and whereabouts of the labyrinth in which the sizars chiefly lived was unknown; some men in Ernest's time, who had rooms in the first court, had never found their way through the sinuous passage which led to it.

In the labyrinth there dwelt men of all ages, from mere lads to grey-haired old men who had entered late in life. They were rarely seen except in hall or chapel or at lecture, where their manners of feeding, praying and studying, were considered alike objectionable; no one knew whence they came, whither they went, nor what they did, for they never showed at cricket or the boats; they were a gloomy, seedy-looking *confrérie*, who had as little to glory in in clothes and manners as in the flesh itself. . . . Unprepossessing then, in feature, gait and manners, unkempt and ill-dressed beyond what can be easily described, these poor fellows formed a class apart, whose thoughts and ways were not as the thoughts and ways of Ernest and his friends, and it was among them that Simeonism chiefly flourished.

Destined most of them for the Church (for in those days "holy orders" were seldom heard of), the Simeonites held themselves to have received a very loud call to the ministry, and were ready to pinch themselves for years so as to prepare for it by the necessary theological courses. To most of them the fact of becoming clergymen would be the *entrée* into a social position from which they were at present kept out by barriers they well knew to be impassable; ordination, therefore, opened fields for ambition which made it the central point in their thoughts, rather than as with Ernest, something which he supposed would have to be done some day, but about which, as about dying, he hoped there was no need to trouble himself as yet.

By way of preparing themselves more completely they would have meetings in one another's rooms for tea and prayer and other spiritual exercises. Placing themselves under the guidance of a few well-known tutors they would teach in Sunday Schools, and be instant, in season and out of season, in imparting spiritual instruction to all whom they could persuade to listen to them.

But the soil of the more prosperous undergraduates was not suitable for the seed they tried to sow. The small pieties with which they larded their discourse, if chance threw them into the company of one whom they considered worldly, caused nothing but aversion in the minds of those for whom they were intended. When they distributed tracts, dropping them by night into good men's letter boxes while they were asleep, their tracts got burnt, or met with even worse contumely; they were themselves also treated with the ridicule which they reflected proudly had been the lot of true followers of Christ in all ages. Often at their prayer meetings was the passage of St. Paul referred to in which he bids his Corinthian converts note concerning themselves that they were for the most part neither well-bred nor intellectual people. They reflected with pride that they too had nothing to be proud of in these respects, and like St. Paul, gloried in the fact that in the flesh they had not much to glory.

Ernest had several Johnian friends, and came thus to hear about the Simeonites and to see some of them, who were pointed out to him as they passed through the courts. They had a repellent attraction for him; he disliked them, but he could not bring himself to leave them alone. On one occasion he had gone so far as to parody one of the tracts they had sent round in the night, and to get a copy dropped into each of the leading Simeonites' boxes. The subject he had taken was "Personal Cleanliness." Cleanliness, he said, was next to godliness; he wished to know on which side it was to stand, and concluded by exhorting Simeonites to a freer use of the tub. I cannot commend my hero's humour in this matter; his tract was not brilliant, but I mention the fact as showing that at this time he was something of a Saul and took pleasure in persecuting the elect, not, as I have said, that he had any hankering after scepticism, but because, like the farmers in his father's village, though he would not stand seeing the Christian religion made light of, he was not going to see it taken seriously. Ernest's friends thought his dislike for Simeonites was due to his being the son of a clergyman who, it was known, bullied him; it is more likely, however, that it rose from an unconscious sympathy with them, which, as in St. Paul's case, in the end drew him into the ranks of those whom he had most despised and hated.

[FROM Chapter 49]

On his return to Cambridge in the May term of 1858, Ernest and a few other friends who were also intended for orders came to the conclusion that they must now take a more serious view of their position. They therefore attended chapel more regularly than hitherto, and held evening meetings of a somewhat furtive character, at which they would study the New Testament. . . .

I do not know how tidings of these furtive gatherings had reached the Simeonites, but they must have come round to them in some way, for they had not been continued many weeks before a circular was sent to each of the young men who attended them, informing them that the Rev. Gideon Hawke, a well-known London Evangelical preacher, whose sermons were then much talked of, was about to visit his young friend Badcock of St. John's, and would be glad to say a few words to any who might wish to hear them, in Badcock's rooms on a certain evening in May.

Badcock was one of the most notorious of all the Simeonites. Not only was he ugly, dirty, ill-dressed, bumptious, and in every way objectionable, but he was deformed and waddled when he walked. . . . It may be guessed, therefore, that the receipt of the circular had for a moment an almost paralysing effect on those to whom it was addressed, owing to the astonishment which it occasioned them. It certainly was a daring surprise, but like so many deformed people, Badcock was forward and hard to check; he was a pushing fellow to whom the present was just the opportunity he wanted for carrying war into the enemy's quarters.

Ernest and his friends consulted. Moved by the feeling that as they were now preparing to be clergymen they ought not to stand so stiffly on social dignity as heretofore, and also perhaps by the desire to have a good private view of a preacher who was then much upon the lips of men, they decided to accept the invitation. When the appointed time came they went with some confusion and self-abasement to the rooms of this man, on whom they had looked down hitherto as from an immeasurable height, and with whom nothing would have made them believe a few weeks earlier that they could ever come to be on speaking terms.

Mr. Hawke was a very different-looking person from Badcock. He was remarkably handsome, or rather would have been but for the thinness of his lips, and a look of too great firmness and inflexibility. His features were a good deal like those of Leonardo da Vinci; moreover he was kempt, looked in vigorous health, and was of a ruddy countenance. He was extremely courteous in his manner, and paid a good deal of attention to Badcock, of whom he seemed to think highly. Altogether our young friends were taken aback, and inclined to think smaller beer of themselves and larger of Badcock than was agreeable to the old Adam who was still alive within them. A few well-known "Sims" from St. John's and other colleges were present, but not enough to swamp the Ernest set, as for the sake of brevity, I will call them.

After a preliminary conversation in which there was nothing to offend, the business of the evening began by Mr. Hawke's standing up at one end of the table, and saying "Let us pray." The Ernest set did not like this, but they could not help themselves, so they knelt down and repeated the Lord's Prayer and a few others after Mr. Hawke, who delivered them remarkably well. Then, when all had sat down, Mr. Hawke addressed them, speaking without notes and taking for his text the words, "Saul, Saul, why persecutest thou me?" Whether owing to Mr. Hawke's manner, which was impressive, or to his well-known reputation for ability, or whether from the fact that each one of the Ernest set knew that he had been more or less a persecutor of the "Sims" and yet felt instinctively that the "Sims" were after all much more like the early Christians than he was himself—at any rate the text, familiar though it was, went home to the consciences of Ernest and his friends as it had never yet done. If Mr. Hawke had stopped here he would have almost said enough; as he scanned the faces turned towards him, and saw the impression he had made, he was perhaps minded to bring his sermon to an end before beginning it, but if so, he reconsidered himself and proceeded as follows. I give the sermon in full, for it is a typical one, and will explain a state of mind which in another generation or two will seem to stand sadly in need of explanation.

"My young friends," said Mr. Hawke, "I am persuaded there is not one of you here who doubts the existence of a Personal God. If there were, it is to him assuredly that I should first address myself. Should I be mistaken in my belief that all here assembled accept the existence of a God who is present amongst us though we see him not, and whose eye is upon our most secret thoughts, let me implore the doubter to confer with me in private before we part; I will then put before him considerations through which God has been mercifully pleased to reveal himself to me, so far as man can understand him, and which I have found bring peace to the minds of others who have doubted. . . .

"The next day but one after our Lord was buried, the tomb being still jealously guarded by enemies, an angel was seen descending from Heaven with glittering raiment and a countenance that shone like fire. This glorious being rolled away the stone from the grave, and our Lord himself came forth, risen from the dead.

"My young friends, this is no fanciful story like those of the ancient deities, but a matter of plain history as certain as that you and I are now here together. If there is one fact better vouched for than another in the whole range of certainties it is the Resurrection of Jesus Christ; nor is it less well assured that a few weeks after he had risen from the dead, our Lord was seen by many hundreds of men and women to rise amid a host of angels into the air upon a heavenward journey till the clouds covered him and concealed him from the sight of men.

"It may be said that the truth of these statements has been denied, but what, let me ask you, has become of the questioners? Where are they now? Do we see them or hear of them? Have they been able to hold what little ground they made during the supineness of the last century? Is there one of your fathers or mothers or friends who does not see through them? Is there a single teacher or preacher in this great University who has not examined what these men had to say, and found it naught? Did you ever meet one of them, or do you find any of their books securing the respectful attention of those competent to judge concerning them? I think not; and I think also you know as well as I do why it is that they have sunk back into the abyss from which they for a time emerged: it is because after the most careful and patient examination by the ablest and most judicial minds of many countries, their arguments were found so untenable that they themselves renounced them. They fled from the field routed, dismayed, and suing for peace; nor have they again come to the front in any civilized country.

"You know these things. Why, then, do I insist upon them? My dear young friends, your own consciousness will have made the answer to each one of you already; it is because, though you know so well that these things did verily and indeed happen, you know also that you have not realized them to yourselves as it was your duty to do, nor heeded their momentous, awful import.

"And now let me go further. You all know that you will one day come to die, or if not to die—for there are not wanting signs which make me hope that the Lord may come again, while some of us now present are alive—yet to be changed; for the trumpet shall sound, and the dead shall be raised incorruptible, for this corruption must put on incorruption, and this mortal put on immortality, and the saying shall be brought to pass that is written, 'Death is swallowed up in victory.'

"Do you, or do you not believe that you will one day stand before the Judgement Seat of Christ? Do you, or do you not believe that you will have to give an account for every idle word that you have ever spoken? Do you, or do you not believe that you are called to live, not according to the will of man, but according to the will of that Christ who came down from Heaven out of love for you, who suffered and died for you, who calls you to him, and yearns towards you that you may take heed even in this your day—but who, if you heed not, will also one day judge you, and with whom there is no variableness nor shadow of turning?

"My dear young friends, strait is the gate and narrow is the way which leadeth to Eternal Life, and few there be that find it. Few, few, few, for he who will not give up ALL for Christ's sake, has given up nothing.

"If you would live in the friendship of this world, if indeed you are not prepared to give up everything you most fondly cherish, should the Lord require it of you, then, I say, put the idea of Christ deliberately on one side at once. Spit upon him, buffet him, crucify him anew, do anything you like so long as you secure the friendship of this world while it is still in your power to do so; the pleasures of this brief life may not be worth paying for by the torments of eternity, but they are something while they last. If, on the other hand, you would live in the friendship of God, and be among the number of those for whom Christ has not died in vain; if, in a word, you value your eternal welfare, then give up the friendship of this world; of a surety you must make your choice between God and Mammon, for you cannot serve both.

"I put these considerations before you, if so homely a term may be pardoned, as a plain matter of business. There is nothing low or unworthy in this, as some lately have pretended, for all nature shows us that there is nothing more acceptable to God than an enlightened view of our own self-interest; never let any one delude you here; it is a simple question of fact; did certain things happen or did they not? If they did happen, is it reasonable to suppose that you will make yourselves and others more happy by one course of conduct or by another?

"And now let me ask you what answer you have made to this question hitherto? Whose friendship have you chosen? If, knowing what you know, you have not yet begun to act according to the immensity of the knowledge that is in you, then he who builds his house and lays up his treasure on the edge of a crater of molten lava is a sane, sensible person in comparison with yourselves. I say this as no figure of speech or bugbear with which to frighten you, but as an unvarnished unexaggerated statement which will be no more disputed by yourselves than by me."

And now Mr. Hawke, who up to this time had spoken with singular quietness, changed his manner to one of greater warmth and continued—

"Oh! my young friends turn, turn, turn, now while it is called to-day—now from this hour, from this instant; stay not even to gird up your loins; look not behind you for a second, but fly into the bosom of that Christ who is to be found of all who seek him, and from that fearful wrath of God which lieth in wait for those who know not the things belonging to their peace. For the Son of Man cometh as a thief in the night, and there is not one of us can tell but what this day his soul may be required of him. If there is even one here who has heeded me,"—and he let his eye fall for an instant upon almost all his hearers, but especially on the Ernest set—"I shall know that it was not for nothing that I felt the call of the Lord, and heard as I thought a voice by night that bade me come hither quickly, for there was a chosen vessel who had need of me."

Here Mr. Hawke ended rather abruptly; his earnest manner, striking countenance, and excellent delivery had produced an effect greater than the actual words I have given can convey to the reader; the virtue lay in the man more than in what he said; as for the last few mysterious words about his having heard a voice by night, their effect was magical; there was not one who did not look down to the ground, nor who in his heart did not half believe that he was the chosen vessel on whose especial behalf God had sent Mr. Hawke to Cambridge. Even if this were not so, each one of them felt that he was now for the first time in the actual presence of one who had had a direct communication from the Almighty, and they were thus suddenly brought a hundredfold nearer to the New Testament miracles. They were amazed, not to say scared, and as though by tacit consent they gathered together, thanked Mr. Hawke for his sermon, said good-night in a humble deferential manner to Badcock and the other Simeonites, and left the room together. They had heard nothing but what they had been hearing all their lives; how was it, then, that they were so dumbfounded by it? I suppose partly because they had lately begun to think more seriously, and were in a fit state to be impressed, partly from the greater directness with which each felt himself addressed, through the sermon being delivered in a room, and partly to the logical consistency, freedom from exaggeration, and profound air of conviction with which Mr. Hawke had spoken. His simplicity and obvious earnestness had impressed them even before he had alluded to his special mission, but this clenched everything, and the words "Lord, is it I?" were upon the hearts of each as they walked pensively home through moonlit courts and cloisters.

I do not know what passed among the Simeonites after the Ernest set had left them, but they would have been more than mortal if they had not been a good deal elated with the results of the evening. Why, one of Ernest's friends was in the University eleven, and he had actually been in Badcock's rooms and had slunk off on saying good-night as meekly as any of them. It was no small thing to have scored a success like this.

Ernest felt now that the turning point of his life had come. He would give up all for Christ—even his tobacco.

So he gathered together his pipes and pouches, and locked them up in his portmanteau under his bed where they should be out of sight, and as much out of mind as possible. He did not burn them, because someone might come in who wanted to smoke, and though he might abridge his own liberty, yet, as smoking was not a sin, there was no reason why he should be hard on other people.

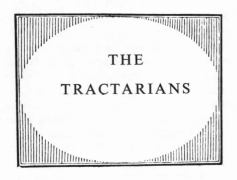

THE

TRACTARIANS

My Religious Opinions to the Year 1833

JOHN HENRY NEWMAN

[FROM *History of My Religious Opinions*]

1865

I was brought up from a child to take great delight in reading the Bible; but I had no formed religious convictions till I was fifteen. Of course I had a perfect knowledge of my Catechism.

After I was grown up, I put on paper my recollections of the thoughts and feelings on religious subjects, which I had at the time that I was a child and a boy,—such as had remained on my mind with sufficient prominence to make me then consider them worth recording. Out of these, written in the Long Vacation of 1820, and transcribed with additions in 1823, I select two, which are at once the most definite among them, and also have a bearing on my later convictions.

1. "I used to wish the Arabian Tales were true: my imagination ran on unknown influences, on magical powers, and talismans. . . . I thought life might be a dream, or I an

From Chapter 1.

Angel, and all this world a deception, my fellow-angels by a playful device concealing themselves from me, and deceiving me with the semblance of a material world."

Again: "Reading in the Spring of 1816 a sentence from [Dr. Watts's] 'Remnants of Time,' entitled 'the Saints unknown to the world,' to the effect, that 'there is nothing in their figure or countenance to distinguish them,' &c., &c., I supposed he spoke of Angels who lived in the world, as it were disguised."

2. The other remark is this: "I was very superstitious, and for some time previous to my conversion" [when I was fifteen] "used constantly to cross myself on going into the dark."

Of course I must have got this practice from some external source or other; but I can make no sort of conjecture whence; and certainly no one had ever spoken to me on the subject of the Catholic religion, which I only knew by name. The French master was an *émigré* Priest, but he was simply made a butt, as French masters too commonly were in that day, and spoke English very imperfectly. There was a Catholic family in the village, old maiden ladies we used to think; but I knew nothing about them. I have of late years heard that there were one or two Catholic boys in the school; but either we were carefully kept from knowing this, or the knowledge of it made simply no impression on our minds. My brother will bear witness how free the school was from Catholic ideas.

I had once been into Warwick Street Chapel, with my father, who, I believe, wanted to hear some piece of music; all that I bore away from it was the recollection of a pulpit and a preacher, and a boy swinging a censer.

When I was at Littlemore, I was looking over old copybooks of my school days, and I found among them my first Latin verse-book; and in the first page of it there was a device which almost took my breath away with surprise. I have the book before me now, and have just been showing it to others. I have written in the first page, in my school-boy hand, "John H. Newman, February 11th, 1811, Verse Book"; then follow my first Verses. Between "Verse" and "Book" I have drawn the figure of a solid cross upright, and next to it is, what may indeed be meant for a necklace, but what I cannot make out to be any thing else than a set of beads suspended, with a little cross attached. At this time I was not quite ten years old. I suppose I got these ideas from some romance, Mrs. Radcliffe's or Miss Porter's; or from some religious picture; but the strange thing is, how, among the thousand objects which meet a boy's eyes, these in particular should so have fixed themselves in my mind, that I made them thus practically my own. I am certain there was nothing in the churches I attended, or the prayer books I read, to suggest them. It must be recollected that Anglican churches and prayer books were not decorated in those days as I believe they are now.

When I was fourteen, I read Paine's Tracts against the Old Testament, and found pleasure in thinking of the objections which were contained in them. Also, I read some of Hume's Essays; and perhaps that on Miracles. So at least I gave my Father to understand; but perhaps it was a brag. Also, I recollect copying out some French verses, perhaps Voltaire's, in denial of the immortality of the soul, and saying to myself something like "How dreadful, but how plausible!"

When I was fifteen, (in the autumn of 1816) a great change of thought took place in me. I fell under the influences of a definite Creed, and received into my intellect impressions of dogma, which, through God's mercy, have never been effaced or obscured. Above and beyond the conversations and sermons of the excellent man, long dead, the Rev. Walter Mayers, of Pembroke College, Oxford, who was the human means of this beginning of divine faith in me, was the effect of the books which he put into my hands, all of the school of Calvin. One of the first books I read was a work of Romaine's; I neither recollect the title nor the contents, except one doctrine, which of course I do not include among those which I believe to have come from a divine source, viz. the doctrine of final perseverance. I received it at once, and believed that the inward conversion of which I was conscious, (and of which I still am more certain than that I have hands and feet,) would last into the next life, and that I was elected to eternal glory. I have no consciousness that this belief had any tendency whatever to lead me to be careless about pleasing God. I retained it till the age of twenty-one, when it gradually faded away; but I believe that it had some influence on my opinions, in the direction of those childish imaginations which I have already mentioned, viz. in isolating me from the objects which surrounded me, in confirming me in my mistrust of the reality of material phenomena, and making me rest in the thought of two and two only absolute and luminously self-evident beings, myself and my Creator;—for while I considered myself predestined to salvation, my mind did not dwell upon others, as fancying them simply passed over, not predestined to eternal death. I only thought of the mercy to myself.

The detestable doctrine last mentioned is simply denied and abjured, unless my memory strangely deceives me, by the writer who made a deeper impression on my mind than any other, and to whom (humanly speaking) I almost owe my soul,—Thomas Scott of Aston Sandford. I so admired and delighted in his writings, that, when I was an undergraduate, I thought of making a visit to his Parsonage, in order to see a man whom I so deeply revered. I hardly think I could have given up the idea of this expedition, even after I had taken my degree; for the news of his death in 1821 came upon me as a disappointment as well as a sorrow. I hung upon the lips of Daniel Wilson, afterwards Bishop of Calcutta, as in two sermons at St. John's Chapel he gave the history of Scott's life and death. I had been possessed of his "Force of Truth" and Essays from a boy; his Commentary I bought when I was an undergraduate.

What, I suppose, will strike any reader of Scott's history and writings, is his bold unworldliness and vigorous independence of mind. He followed truth wherever it led him, beginning with Unitarianism, and ending in a zealous faith in the Holy Trinity. It was he who first planted deep in my mind that fundamental truth of religion. With the assistance of Scott's Essays, and the admirable work of Jones of Nayland, I made a collection of Scripture texts in proof of the doctrine, with remarks (I think) of my own upon them, before I was sixteen; and a few months later I drew up a series of texts in support of each verse of the Athanasian Creed. These papers I have still.

Besides his unworldliness, what I also admired in Scott was his resolute opposition to Antinomianism, and the minutely practical character of his writings. They show him to be a true Englishman, and I deeply felt his influence; and for years I used almost as proverbs what I considered to be the scope and issue of his doctrine, "Holiness rather than peace," and "Growth the only evidence of life."

Calvinists make a sharp separation between the elect and the world; there is much in this that is cognate or parallel to the Catholic doctrine; but they go on to say, as I understand them, very differently from Catholicism,—that the converted and the unconverted can be discriminated by man, that the justified are conscious of their state of justification, and that the regenerate cannot fall away. Catholics on the other hand shade and soften the awful antagonism between good and evil, which is one of their dogmas, by holding that there are different degrees of justification, that there is a great difference in point of gravity between sin and sin, that there is the possibility and the danger of falling away, and that there is no certain knowledge given to any one that he is simply in a state of grace, and much less that he is to persevere to the end:—of the Calvinistic tenets the only one which took root in my mind was the fact of heaven and hell, divine favour and divine wrath, of the justified and the unjustified. The notion that the regenerate and the justified were one and the same, and that the regenerate, as such, had the gift of perseverance, remained with me not many years, as I have said already.

This main Catholic doctrine of the warfare between the city of God and the powers of darkness was also deeply impressed upon my mind by a work of a character very opposite to Calvinism, Law's "Serious Call."

From this time I have held with a full inward assent and belief the doctrine of eternal punishment, as delivered by our

Lord Himself, in as true a sense as I hold that of eternal happiness; though I have tried in various ways to make that truth less terrible to the imagination.

Now I come to two other works, which produced a deep impression on me in the same Autumn of 1816, when I was fifteen years old, each contrary to each, and planting in me the seeds of an intellectual inconsistency which disabled me for a long course of years. I read Joseph Milner's Church History, and was nothing short of enamoured of the long extracts from St. Augustine, St. Ambrose, and the other Fathers which I found there. I read them as being the religion of the primitive Christians: but simultaneously with Milner I read Newton on the Prophecies, and in consequence became most firmly convinced that the Pope was the Antichrist predicted by Daniel, St. Paul, and St. John. My imagination was stained by the effects of this doctrine up to the year 1843; it had been obliterated from my reason and judgment at an earlier date; but the thought remained upon me as a sort of false conscience. Hence came that conflict of mind, which so many have felt besides myself;—leading some men to make a compromise between two ideas, so inconsistent with each other,— driving others to beat out the one idea or the other from their minds,—and ending in my own case, after many years of intellectual unrest, in the gradual decay and extinction of one of them,—I do not say in its violent death, for why should I not have murdered it sooner, if I murdered it at all?

I am obliged to mention, though I do it with great reluctance, another deep imagination, which at this time, the autumn of 1816, took possession of me,—there can be no mistake about the fact; viz. that it would be the will of God that I should lead a single life. This anticipation, which has held its ground almost continuously ever since,—with the break of a month now and a month then, up to 1829, and, after that date, without any break at all,—was more or less connected in my mind with the notion, that my calling in life would require such a sacrifice as celibacy involved; as, for instance, missionary work among the heathen, to which I had a great drawing for some years. It also strengthened my feeling of separation from the visible world, of which I have spoken above. . . .

It was at about this date, I suppose, that I read Bishop Butler's "Analogy," the study of which has been to so many, as it was to me, an era in their religious opinions. Its inculcation of a visible Church, the oracle of truth and a pattern of sanctity, of the duties of external religion, and of the historical character of Revelation, are characteristics of this great work which strike the reader at once; for myself, if I may attempt to determine what I most gained from it, it lay in two points.... First, the very idea of an analogy between the separate works of God leads to the conclusion that the system which is of less importance is economically or sacramentally connected with the more momentous system, and of this conclusion the theory, to which I was inclined as a boy, viz. the unreality of material phenomena, is an ultimate resolution.... Secondly, Butler's doctrine that Probability is the guide of life, led me, at least under the teaching to which a few years later I was introduced, to the question of the logical cogency of Faith. . . . Thus to Butler I trace those two principles of my teaching, which have led to a charge against me both of fancifulness and of scepticism. . . .

During the first years of my residence at Oriel, though proud of my College, I was not quite at home there. . . . At that time indeed (from 1823) I had the intimacy of my dear and true friend Dr. Pusey, and could not fail to admire and revere a soul so devoted to the cause of religion, so full of good works, so faithful in his affections; but he left residence when I was getting to know him well. As to Dr. Whately himself, he was too much my superior to allow of my being at my ease with him; and to no one in Oxford at this time did I open my heart fully and familiarly. But things changed in 1826. At that time I became one of the Tutors of my College, and this gave me position; besides, I had written one or two Essays which had been well received. I began to be known. I preached my first University Sermon. Next year I was one of the Public Examiners for the B.A. degree. In 1828 I became Vicar of St. Mary's. It was to me like the feeling of spring weather after winter; and, if I may so speak, I came out of my shell; I remained out of it till 1841.

The two persons who knew me best at that time are still alive, beneficed clergymen, no longer my friends. They could tell better than any one else what I was in those years. From this time my tongue was, as it were, loosened, and I spoke spontaneously and without effort. One of the two, Mr. Rickards, said of me, I have been told, "Here is a fellow who, when he is silent, will never begin to speak; and when he once begins to speak, will never stop." It was at this time that I began to have influence, which steadily increased for a course of years. I gained upon my pupils, and was in particular intimate and affectionate with two of our probationer Fellows, Robert Isaac Wilberforce (afterwards Archdeacon) and Richard Hurrell Froude. Whately then, an acute man, perhaps saw around me the signs of an incipient party, of which I was not conscious myself. And thus we discern the first elements of that movement afterwards called Tractarian.

The true and primary author of it, however, as is usual with great motive-powers, was out of sight. Having carried off as a mere boy the highest honours of the University, he had turned from the admiration which haunted his steps, and sought for a better and holier satisfaction in pastoral work in the country. Need I say that I am speaking of John Keble? The first time that I was in a room with him was on occasion of my election to a fellowship at Oriel, when I was sent for into the Tower, to shake hands with the Provost and Fellows. How is that hour fixed in my memory after the changes of forty-two years, forty-two this very day on which I write! . . . I bore it till Keble took my hand, and then felt so abashed and unworthy of the honour done me, that I seemed desirous of quite sinking into the ground. . . . However, at the time when I was elected Fellow of Oriel he was not in residence, and he was shy of me for years in consequence of the marks which I bore upon me of the evangelical and liberal schools. At least so I have ever thought. Hurrell Froude brought us together about 1828: it is one of the sayings preserved in his "Remains,"—"Do you know the story of the murderer who had done one good thing in his life? Well; if I was ever asked what good deed I had ever done, I should say that I had brought Keble and Newman to understand each other."

The "Christian Year" made its appearance in 1827. It is not necessary, and scarcely becoming, to praise a book which has already become one of the classics of the language. When the general tone of religious literature was so nerveless and impotent, as it was at that time, Keble struck an original note and woke up in the hearts of thousands a new music, the music of a school, long unknown in England. Nor can I pretend to analyze, in my own instance, the effect of religious teaching so deep, so pure, so beautiful. I have never till now tried to do so; yet I think I am not wrong in saying, that the two main intellectual truths which it brought home to me, were the same two, which I had learned from Butler, though recast in the creative mind of my new master. The first of these was what may be called, in a large sense of the word, the Sacramental system; that is, the doctrine that material phenomena are both the types and the instruments of real things unseen,—a doctrine, which embraces in its fulness, not only what Anglicans, as well as Catholics, believe about Sacraments properly so called; but also the article of "the Communion of Saints"; and likewise the Mysteries of the faith. The connexion of this philosophy of religion with what is sometimes called "Berkeleyism" has been mentioned above; I knew little of Berkeley at this time except by name: nor have I ever studied him.

On the second intellectual principle which I gained from Mr. Keble, I could say a great deal; if this were the place for it. It runs through very much that I have written, and has gained for me many hard names. Butler teaches us that probability is the guide of life. The danger of this doctrine, in the case of many minds, is, its tendency to destroy in them absolute certainty, leading them to consider every conclusion as doubtful, and resolving truth into an opinion, which it is safe indeed to obey or to profess, but not possible to embrace with full internal assent. If this were to be allowed, then the celebrated saying, "O God, if there be a God, save my soul, if I have a soul!" would be the highest measure of devotion:—but who can really pray to a Being about whose existence he is seriously in doubt?

I consider that Mr. Keble met this difficulty by ascribing the firmness of assent which we give to religious doctrine, not to the probabilities which introduced it, but to the living power of faith and love which accepted it. . . . Thus the argument from Probability, in the matter of religion, became an argument from Personality, which in fact is one form of the argument from Authority. . . .

The main difference between my Essay on Miracles in 1826 and my Essay in 1842 is this: that in 1826 I considered that miracles were sharply divided into two classes, those which were to be received, and those which were to be rejected; whereas in 1842 I say that they were to be regarded according to their greater or less probability, which was in some cases sufficient to create certitude about them, in other cases only belief or opinion. . . .

Hurrell Froude was a pupil of Keble's, formed by him, and in turn reacting upon him. I knew him first in 1826, and was in the closest and most affectionate friendship with him from about 1829 till his death in 1836. He was a man of the highest gifts,—so truly many-sided, that it would be presumptuous in me to attempt to describe him, except under those aspects in which he came before me. Nor have I here to speak of the gentleness and tenderness of nature, the playfulness, the free elastic force and graceful versatility of mind, and the patient winning considerateness in discussion, which endeared him to those to whom he opened his heart; for I am all along engaged upon matters of belief and opinion, and am introducing others into my narrative, not for their own sake, or because I love and have loved them, so much as because, and so far as, they have influenced my theological views. In this respect then, I speak of Hurrell Froude,—in his intellectual aspect,—as a man of high genius, brimful and overflowing with ideas and views, in him original, which were too many and strong even for his bodily strength, and which crowded and jostled against each other in their effort after distinct shape and expression. And he had an intellect as critical and logical as it was speculative and bold. Dying prematurely, as he did, and in conflict and transition-state of opinion, his religious views never reached their ultimate conclusion, by the very reason of their multitude and their depth. His opinions arrested and influenced me, even when they did not gain my assent. He professed openly his admiration of the Church of Rome, and his hatred of the Reformers. He delighted in the notion of an hierarchical system, of sacerdotal power, and of full ecclesiastical liberty. He felt scorn of the maxim, "The Bible and the Bible only is the religion of Protestants"; and he gloried in accepting Tradition as a main instrument of religious teaching. He had a high severe idea of the intrinsic excellence of Virginity; and he considered the Blessed Virgin its great pattern. He delighted in thinking of the Saints; he had a vivid appreciation of the idea of sanctity, its possibility and its heights; and he was more than inclined to believe a large amount of miraculous interference as occurring in the early and middle ages. He embraced the principle of penance and mortification. He had a deep devotion to the Real Presence, in which he had a firm faith. He was powerfully drawn to the Medieval Church, but not to the Primitive.

He had a keen insight into abstract truth; but he was an Englishman to the backbone in his severe adherence to the real and the concrete. He had a most classical taste, and a genius for philosophy and art; and he was fond of historical inquiry, and the politics of religion. He had no turn for theology as such. He set no sufficient value on the writings of the Fathers, on the detail or development of doctrine, on the definite traditions of the Church viewed in their matter, on the teaching of the Ecumenical Councils, or on the controversies out of which they arose. He took an eager courageous view of things on the whole. I should say that his power of entering into the minds of others did not equal his other gifts; he could not believe, for instance, that I really held the Roman Church to be Antichristian. On many points he would not believe but that I agreed with him, when I did not. He seemed not to understand my difficulties. His were of a different kind, the contrariety between theory and fact. He was a high Tory of the Cavalier stamp, and was disgusted with the Toryism of the opponents of the Reform Bill. He was smitten with the love of the Theocratic Church; he went abroad and was shocked by the degeneracy which he thought he saw in the Catholics of Italy.

It is difficult to enumerate the precise additions to my theological creed which I derived from a friend to whom I owe so much. He taught me to look with admiration towards the Church of Rome, and in the same degree to dislike the Reformation. He fixed deep in me the idea of devotion to the Blessed Virgin, and he led me gradually to believe in the Real Presence. . . .

At this time I was disengaged from College duties, and my health had suffered from the labour involved in the composition of my Volume [*The Arians of the Fourth Century*]. It was ready for the Press in July, 1832, though not published till the end of 1833. I was easily persuaded to join Hurrell Froude and his Father, who were going to the south of Europe for the health of the former.

We set out in December, 1832. It was during this expedition that my Verses which are in the "Lyra Apostolica" were written;—a few indeed before it, but not more than one or two of them after it. Exchanging, as I was, definite Tutorial work, and the literary quiet and pleasant friendships of the last six years, for foreign countries and an unknown future, I naturally was led to think that some inward changes, as well as some larger course of action, were coming upon me. . . .

I went to various coasts of the Mediterranean; parted with my friends at Rome; went down for the second time to Sicily without companion, at the end of April; and got back to England by Palermo in the early part of July. The strangeness of foreign life threw me back into myself; I found pleasure in historical sites and beautiful scenes, not in men and manners. We kept clear of Catholics throughout our tour. I had a conversation with the Dean of Malta, a most pleasant man, lately dead; but it was about the Fathers, and the Library of the great church. I knew the Abbate Santini, at Rome, who did no more than copy for me the Gregorian tones. Froude and I made two calls upon Monsignore (now Cardinal) Wiseman at the Collegio Inglese, shortly before we left Rome. Once we heard him preach at a church in the Corso. I do not recollect being in a room with any other ecclesiastics, except a Priest at Castro-Giovanni in Sicily, who called on me when I was ill, and with whom I wished to hold a controversy. As to Church Services, we attended the Tenebræ, at the Sestine, for the sake of the Miserere; and that was all. My general feeling was, "All, save the spirit of man, is divine." I saw nothing but what was external; of the hidden life of Catholics I knew nothing. I was still more driven back into myself, and felt my isolation. England was in my thoughts solely, and the news from England came rarely and imperfectly. The Bill for the Suppression of the Irish Sees was in progress, and filled my mind. I had fierce thoughts against the Liberals.

It was the success of the Liberal cause which fretted me inwardly. I became fierce against its instruments and its manifestations. A French vessel was at Algiers; I would not even look at the tricolour. On my return, though forced to stop twenty-four hours at Paris, I kept indoors the whole time, and all that I saw of that beautiful city was what I saw from the Diligence. The Bishop of London had already sounded me as to my filling one of the Whitehall preacherships, which he had just then put on a new footing; but I was indignant at the line which he was taking, and from my Steamer I had sent home a letter declining the appointment by anticipation, should it be offered to me. At this time I was specially annoyed with Dr. Arnold, though it did not last into later years. Some one, I think, asked, in conversation at Rome, whether a certain interpretation of Scripture was Christian? it was answered that Dr. Arnold took it; I interposed, "But is *he* a Christian?". . .

When we took leave of Monsignore Wiseman, he had courteously expressed a wish that we might make a second visit to Rome; I said with great gravity, "We have a work to do in England." I went down at once to Sicily, and the presentiment grew stronger. I struck into the middle of the island, and fell ill of a fever at Leonforte. My servant thought that I was dying, and begged for my last directions. I gave them, as he wished; but I said, "I shall not die." I repeated, "I shall not die, for I have not sinned against light, I have not sinned against light." I never have been able quite to make out what I meant.

I got to Castro-Giovanni, and was laid up there for nearly three weeks. Towards the end of May I left for Palermo, taking three days for the journey. Before starting from my inn in the morning of May 26th or 27th, I sat down on my bed, and began to sob violently. My servant, who had acted as my nurse, asked what ailed me. I could only answer him, "I have a work to do in England."

I was aching to get home; yet for want of a vessel I was kept at Palermo for three weeks. I began to visit the Churches, and they calmed my impatience, though I did not attend any services. I knew nothing of the Presence of the Blessed Sacrament there. At last I got off in an orange boat, bound for Marseilles. Then it was that I wrote the lines, "Lead, kindly light," which have since become well known. We were becalmed a whole week in the Straits of Bonifacio. I was writing verses the whole time of my passage. At length I got to Marseilles, and set off for England. The fatigue of travelling was too much for me, and I was laid up for several days at Lyons. At last I got off again, and did not stop night or day, (except a compulsory delay at Paris), till I reached England, and my mother's house. My brother had arrived from Persia only a few hours before. This was on the Tuesday. The following Sunday, July 14th, Mr. Keble preached the Assize Sermon in the University Pulpit. It was published under the title of "National Apostasy." I have ever considered and kept the day, as the start of the religious movement of 1833.

Tract 90

JOHN HENRY NEWMAN

[FROM *Remarks on Certain Passages in the 39 Articles*]

1841

One remark may be made in conclusion. It may be objected that the tenor of the above explanations is anti-Protestant, whereas it is notorious that the Articles were drawn up by Protestants, and intended for the establishment of Protestantism; accordingly, that it is an evasion of their meaning to give them any other than a Protestant drift, possible as it may be to do so grammatically, or in each separate part.

But the answer is simple:—

1.   In the first place, it is a *duty* which we owe both to the Catholic Church and to our own, to take our reformed confessions in the most Catholic sense they will admit; we have no duties towards their framers. [Nor do we receive the Articles from their original framers, but from several successive convocations after their time; in the last instance, from that of 1662.]

2.   In giving the Articles a Catholic interpretation, we bring them into harmony with the Book of Common Prayer, an object of the most serious moment for those who have given their assent to both formularies.

3.   Whatever be the authority of the [Declaration] prefixed to the Articles, so far as it has any weight at all, it sanctions the mode of interpreting them above given. For its injoining the "literal and grammatical sense," relieves us from the necessity of making the known opinions of their framers, a comment upon their text; and its forbidding any person to "affix any *new* sense to any Article," was promulgated at a time

From the "Conclusion."

when the leading men of our Church were especially noted for those Catholic views which have been here advocated.

4. It may be remarked, moreover, that such an interpretation is in accordance with the well-known general leaning of Melanchthon, from whose writings our Articles are principally drawn, and whose Catholic tendencies gained for him that same reproach of popery, which has ever been so freely bestowed upon members of our own reformed Church. . . .

5. Further: the Articles are evidently framed on the principle of leaving open large questions, on which the controversy hinges. They state broadly extreme truths, and are silent about their adjustment. For instance, they say that all necessary faith must be proved from Scripture, but do not say *who* is to prove it. They say that the Church has authority in controversies, they do not say *what* authority. They say that it may enforce nothing beyond Scripture, but do not say *where* the remedy lies when it does. They say that works *before* grace *and* justification are worthless and worse, and that works *after* grace *and* justification are acceptable, but they do not speak at all of works *with* GOD'S aid, *before* justification. They say that men are lawfully called and sent to minister and preach, who are chosen and called by men who have public authority *given* them in the congregation to call and send; but they do not add *by whom* the authority is to be given. They say that Councils called *by princes* may err; they do not determine whether Councils called *in the name of* CHRIST will err.

6. The variety of doctrinal views contained in the Homilies, as above shown, views which cannot be brought under Protestantism itself, in its greatest comprehension of opinions, is an additional proof, considering the connexion of the Articles with the Homilies, that the Articles are not framed on the principle of excluding those who prefer the theology of the early ages to that of the Reformation; or rather let it be considered whether, considering both Homilies and Articles appeal to the Fathers and Catholic Antiquity, in interpreting them by these witnesses, we are not going to the very authority to which they profess to submit.

7. Lastly, their framers constructed them in such a way as best to comprehend those who did not go so far in Protestantism as themselves. Anglo-Catholics then are but the successors and representatives of those moderate reformers; and their case has been directly anticipated in the wording of the Articles. It follows that they are not perverting, they are using them, for an express purpose for which among others their authors framed them. The interpretation they take was intended to be admissible; though not that which their authors took themselves. Had it not been provided for, possibly the Articles never would have been accepted by our Church at all. If, then, their framers have gained their side of the compact in effecting the reception of the Articles, let Catholics have theirs too in retaining their own Catholic interpretation of them. . . .

The Protestant Confession was drawn up with the purpose of including Catholics; and Catholics now will not be excluded. What was an economy in the reformers, is a protection to us. What would have been a perplexity to us then, is a perplexity to Protestants now. We could not then have found fault with their words; they cannot now repudiate our meaning.

[J. H. N.]

OXFORD.
The Feast of the Conversion of St. Paul.
1841.

Newman's Preaching at St. Mary's

MATTHEW ARNOLD

[FROM "Emerson"]

1885

The name of Cardinal Newman is a great name to the imagination still; his genius and his style are still things of power. But he is over eighty years old; he is in the Oratory at Birmingham; he has adopted, for the doubts and difficulties which beset men's minds to-day, a solution which, to speak frankly, is impossible. Forty years ago he was in the very prime of life; he was close at hand to us at Oxford; he was preaching in St. Mary's pulpit every Sunday; he seemed about to transform and to renew what was for us the most national and natural institution in the world, the Church of England. Who could resist the charm of that spiritual apparition, gliding in the dim afternoon light through the aisles of St. Mary's, rising into the pulpit, and then, in the most entrancing of voices, breaking the silence with words and thoughts which were a religious music,—subtle, sweet, mournful? I seem to hear him still, saying: 'After the fever of life, after wearinesses and sicknesses, fightings and despondings, languor and fretfulness, struggling and succeeding; after all the changes and chances of this troubled, unhealthy state,—at length comes death, at length the white throne of God, at length the beatific vision.' Or, if we followed him back to his seclusion at Littlemore, that dreary village by the London road, and to the house of retreat and the church which he built there,—a mean house such as Paul might have lived in when he was tent-making at Ephesus, a church plain and thinly sown with worshippers,—who could resist him there either, welcoming back to the severe joys of church-fellowship, and of daily

From *Discourses in America* (1896), pages 139-42.

worship and prayer, the firstlings of a generation which had well-nigh forgotten them? Again I seem to hear him: 'The season is chill and dark, and the breath of the morning is damp, and worshippers are few; but all this befits those who are by their profession penitents and mourners, watchers and pilgrims. More dear to them that loneliness, more cheerful that severity, and more bright that gloom, than all those aids and appliances of luxury by which men nowadays attempt to make prayer less disagreeable to them. True faith does not covet comforts; they who realise that awful day, when they shall see Him face to face whose eyes are as a flame of fire, will as little bargain to pray pleasantly now as they will think of doing so then.'

Somewhere or other I have spoken of those 'last enchantments of the Middle Age' which Oxford sheds around us, and here they were!

THE LIBERALS

Rugby Chapel

ARTHUR PENRHYN STANLEY

[FROM *The Life and Correspondence of Thomas Arnold, D.D.*]

1884

If there is any one place at Rugby more than another which was especially the scene of Dr. Arnold's labours, both as a teacher and as a master, it is the School-chapel. Even its outward forms from "the very cross at the top of the building," on which he loved to dwell as a visible symbol of the Christian end of their education, to the vaults which he caused to be opened underneath for those who died in the school, must always be associated with his name. "I envy Winchester its antiquity," he said, "and am therefore anxious to do all that can be done to give us something of a venerable outside, if we have not the nobleness of old associations to help us.". . .

But of him especially it need hardly be said, that his chief interest in that place lay in the three hundred boys who, Sunday after Sunday, were collected, morning and after-noon, within its walls. . . . How lively is the recollection his scholars retain of the earnest attention with which, after the

From Volume I, pages 152-58.

service was over, he sat in his place looking at the boys as
they filed out one by one, in the orderly and silent arrangement which succeeded, in the latter part of his stay, to the
public calling over of their names in the chapel. How complete
was the image of his union of dignity and simplicity, of
manliness and devotion, as he performed the chapel service,
especially when at the communion table he would read or
rather repeat almost by heart the Gospel and Epistle of the
day, with the impressiveness of one who entered into it equally
with his whole spirit and also with his whole understanding.
How visible was the animation, with which by force of long
association he joined in the musical parts of the service, to
which he was by nature wholly indifferent, as in the chanting
of the Nicene Creed, which was adopted in accordance with
his conviction that creeds in public worship ought to be used
as triumphant hymns of thanksgiving; or still more in the
Te Deum, which he loved so dearly, and when his whole
countenance would be lit up at his favourite verse—"When
Thou hadst overcome the sharpness of death, Thou didst open
the kingdom of Heaven to all believers."

From his own interest in the service naturally flowed his
anxiety to impart it to his scholars; urging them in his later
sermons, or in his more private addresses, to join in the
responses, at times with such effect, that at least from all the
older part of the school the responses were very general. The
very course of the ecclesiastical year would often be associated
in their minds with their remembrance of the peculiar feeling,
with which they saw that he regarded the greater festivals,
and of the almost invariable connexion of his sermons. . . but
it must have been difficult for any one not to have been struck
by the triumphant exultation of his whole manner on the
recurrence of Easter Day. Lent was marked during his last
three years, by the putting up of boxes in the chapel and the
boarding-houses, to receive money for the poor, a practice
adopted not so much with the view of relieving any actual
want, as of affording the boys an opportunity for self-denial
and almsgiving.

He was anxious to secure the administration of the rite

of confirmation, if possible, once every two years; when the boys were prepared by himself and the other masters in their different boarding-houses, who each brought up his own division of pupils on the day of the ceremony. . . .

The Communion was celebrated four times a year. At first some of the Sixth Form boys alone were in the habit of attending; but he took pains to invite to it boys in all parts of the school, who had any serious thoughts, so that the number, out of two hundred and ninety or three hundred boys, was occasionally a hundred, and never less than seventy. To individual boys he rarely spoke on the subject, from the fear of its becoming a matter of form or favour; but in his sermons he dwelt upon it much, and would afterwards speak with deep emotion of the pleasure and hope which a larger attendance than usual would give him. It was impossible to hear these exhortations, or to see him administer it, without being struck by the strong and manifold interest, which it awakened in him; and at Rugby it was of course more than usually touching to him from its peculiar relation to the school. When he spoke of it in his sermons, it was evident that amongst all the feelings which it excited in himself, and which he wished to impart to others, none was so prominent as the sense that it was a communion not only with God, but with one another, and that the thoughts thus roused should act as a direct and especial counterpoise to that false communion and false companionship, which, as binding one another not to good but to evil, he believed to be the great source of mischief in the school at large. And when,—especially to the very young boys, who sometimes partook of the Communion,—he bent himself down with looks of fatherly tenderness, and glistening eyes and trembling voice, in the administration of the elements, it was felt, perhaps, more distinctly than at any other time, how great was the sympathy which he felt with the earliest advances to good in very individual boy.

That part of the Chapel service, however, which at least to the world at large, is most connected with him, as being the most frequent and most personal of his ministrations, was his preaching. Sermons had occasionally been preached by the head-master of this and other public schools to their scholars before his coming to Rugby; but (in some cases from the peculiar constitution or arrangement of the school) it has never before been considered an essential part of the head-master's office. The first half-year he confined himself to delivering short addresses, of about five minutes' length, to the boys of his own house. But from the second half-year he began to preach frequently; and from the autumn of 1831, when he took the chaplaincy, which had then become vacant, he preached almost every Sunday of the school year to the end of his life.

The Everlasting Yea

THOMAS CARLYLE

[FROM *Sartor Resartus*]

1836

'Temptations in the Wilderness!' exclaims Teufelsdröckh: 'Have we not all to be tried with such? Not so easily can the old Adam, lodged in us by birth, be dispossessed. Our Life is compassed round with Necessity; yet is the meaning of Life itself no other than Freedom, than Voluntary Force: thus have we a warfare; in the beginning, especially, a hard-fought battle. For the God-given mandate, *Work thou in Welldoing,* lies mysteriously written, in Promethean Prophetic Characters, in our hearts; and leaves us no rest, night or day, till it be deciphered and obeyed; till it burn forth, in our conduct, a visible, acted Gospel of Freedom. And as the clay-given mandate, *Eat thou and be filled,* at the same time persuasively proclaims itself through every nerve,—must not there be a

From Book II, Chapter 9.

confusion, a contest, before the better Influence can become
the upper?

'To me nothing seems more natural than that the Son of
Man, when such God-given mandate first prophetically stirs
within him, and the Clay must now be vanquished or vanquish,—should be carried of the spirit into grim Solitudes, and
there fronting the Tempter do grimmest battle with him; defi-
antly setting him at naught, till he yield and fly. Name it as we
choose: with or without visible Devil, whether in the natural
Desert of rocks and sands, or in the populous moral Desert
of selfishness and baseness,—to such Temptation are we all
called. Unhappy if we are not! Unhappy if we are but Half-
men, in whom that divine handwriting has never blazed forth,
all-subduing, in true sun-splendour; but quivers dubiously
amid meaner lights: or smoulders, in dull pain, in darkness,
under earthly vapours!—Our Wilderness is the wide World
in an Atheistic Century; our Forty Days are long years of
suffering and fasting: nevertheless, to these also comes an
end. Yes, to me also was given, if not Victory, yet the consciousness of Battle, and the resolve to persevere therein while
life or faculty is left. To me also, entangled in the enchanted
forests, demon-peopled, doleful of sight and of sound, it was
given, after weariest wanderings, to work out my way into the
higher sunlight slopes—of that Mountain which has no summit, or whose summit is in Heaven only!'. . .

So that, for Teufelsdröckh also, there has been a 'glorious
revolution': these mad shadow-hunting and shadow-hunted
Pilgrimings of his were but some purifying 'Temptation in
the Wilderness,' before his apostolic work (such as it was)
could begin; which Temptation is now happily over, and the
Devil once more worsted! Was 'that high moment in the
Rue de l'Enfer,' then, properly the turning-point of the battle;
when the Fiend said, *Worship me, or be torn in shreds;* and
was answered valiantly with an *Apage Satana?*—Singular
Teufelsdröckh, would thou hadst told thy singular story in
plain words! But it is fruitless to look there, in those Paper-
bags, for such. Nothing but innuendoes, figurative crotchets:
a typical Shadow, fitfully wavering, prophetico-satiric; no

clear logical Picture. 'How paint to the sensual eye,' asks he
once, 'what passes in the Holy-of-Holies of Man's Soul; in
what words, known to these profane times, speak even afar-
off of the unspeakable?' We ask in turn: Why perplex these
times, profane as they are, with needless obscurity, by omission and by commission? Not mystical only is our Professor,
but whimsical; and involves himself, now more than ever, in
eye-bewildering *chiaroscuro*. Successive glimpses, here faithfully imparted, our more gifted readers must endeavour to
combine for their own behoof.

He says: 'The hot Harmattan wind had raged itself out; its
howl went silent within me; and the long-deafened soul could
now hear. I paused in my wild wanderings; and sat me down
to wait, and consider; for it was as if the hour of change
drew nigh. I seemed to surrender, to renounce utterly, and
say: Fly, then, false shadows of Hope; I will chase you no
more, I will believe you no more. And ye too, haggard
spectres of Fear, I care not for you; ye too are all shadows
and a lie. Let me rest here: for I am way-weary and life-weary;
I will rest here, were it but to die: to die or to live is alike to
me; alike insignificant.'—And again: 'Here, then, as I lay in
that CENTRE OF INDIFFERENCE; cast, doubtless by benignant
upper Influence, into a healing sleep, the heavy dreams rolled
gradually away and I awoke to a new Heaven and a new
Earth. The first preliminary moral Act, Annihilation of Self
(*Selbst-tödtung*), had been happily accomplished; and my
mind's eyes were now unsealed, and its hands ungyved.'

Might we not also conjecture that the following passage
refers to his Locality, during this same 'healing sleep'; that
his Pilgrim-staff lies cast aside here, on 'the high table-land';
and indeed that the repose is already taking wholesome effect
on him? If it were not that the tone, in some parts, has more
of riancy, even of levity, than we could have expected! However, in Teufelsdröckh, there is always the strangest Dualism:
light dancing, with guitar-music, will be going on in the fore-
court, while by fits from within comes the faint whimpering
of woe and wail. We transcribe the piece entire.

'Beautiful it was to sit there, as in my skyey Tent, musing

and meditating; on the high table-land, in front of the Mountains; over me, as roof, the azure Dome, and around me, for
walls, four azure-flowing curtains,—namely, of the Four azure
Winds, on whose bottom-fringes also I have seen gilding.
And then to fancy the fair Castles that stood sheltered in
these Mountain hollows; with their green flower-lawns, and
white dames and damosels, lovely enough: or better still, the
straw-roofed Cottages, wherein stood many a Mother baking
bread, with her children round her:—all hidden and protect-
ingly folded-up in the valley-folds; yet there and alive, as sure
as if I beheld them. Or to see, as well as fancy, the nine
Towns and Villages, that lay round my mountain-seat, which,
in still weather, were wont to speak to me (by their steeple-
bells) with metal tongue; and, in almost all weather, proclaimed their vitality by repeated Smoke-clouds; whereon, as
on a culinary horologe, I might read the hour of the day. For
it was the smoke of cookery, as kind housewives at morning,
midday, eventide, were boiling their husbands' kettles; and
ever a blue pillar rose up into the air, successively or simultaneously, from each of the nine, saying, as plainly as smoke
could say: Such and such a meal is getting ready here. Not
uninteresting! For you have the whole Borough, with all its
love-makings and scandal-mongeries, contentions and content-
ments, as in miniature, and could cover it all with your hat.—
If, in my wide Wayfarings, I had learned to look into the
business of the World in its details, here perhaps was the place
for combining it into general propositions, and deducing inferences therefrom.

'Often also could I see the black Tempest marching in anger
through the Distance: round some Schreckhorn, as yet grim-
blue, would the eddying vapour gather, and there tumul-
tuously eddy, and flow down like a mad witch's hair; till,
after a space, it vanished, and, in the clear sunbeam, your
Schreckhorn stood smiling grim-white, for the vapour had
held snow. How thou fermentest and elaboratest, in thy great
fermenting-vat and laboratory of an Atmosphere, of a World,
O Nature!—Or what is Nature? Ha! why do I not name thee
GOD? Art not thou the "Living Garment of God"? O Heavens,

is it, in very deed, He, then, that ever speaks through thee; that lives and loves in thee, that lives and loves in me?

'Fore-shadows, call them rather fore-splendours, of that Truth, and Beginning of Truths, fell mysteriously over my soul. Sweeter than Dayspring to the Ship-wrecked in Nova Zembla; ah, like the mother's voice to her little child that strays bewildered, weeping, in unknown tumults; like soft streamings of celestial music to my too-exasperated heart, came that Evangel. The Universe is not dead and demoniacal, a charnel-house with spectres; but godlike, and my Father's!

'With other eyes, too, could I now look upon my fellow man: with an infinite Love, an infinite Pity. Poor, wandering, wayward man! Art thou not tried, and beaten with stripes, even as I am? Ever, whether thou bear the royal mantle or the beggar's gabardine, art thou not so weary, so heavy-laden; and thy Bed of Rest is but a Grave. O my Brother, my Brother, why cannot I shelter thee in my bosom, and wipe away all tears from thy eyes!—Truly, the din of many-voiced Life, which, in this solitude, with the mind's organ, I could hear, was no longer a maddening discord, but a melting one; like inarticulate cries, and sobbings of a dumb creature, which in the ear of Heaven are prayers. The poor Earth, with her poor joys, was now my needy Mother, not my cruel Stepdame; Man, with his so mad Wants and so mean Endeavours, had become the dearer to me; and even for his sufferings and his sins, I now first named him Brother. Thus was I standing in the porch of that "*Sanctuary of Sorrow*"; by strange, steep ways had I too been guided thither; and ere long its sacred gates would open, and the "*Divine Depth of Sorrow*" lie disclosed to me.'

The Professor says, he here first got eye on the Knot that had been strangling him, and straightway could unfasten it, and was free. 'A vain interminable controversy,' writes he, 'touching what is at present called Origin of Evil, or some such thing, arises in every soul, since the beginning of the world; and in every soul, that would pass from idle Suffering into actual Endeavouring, must first be put an end to. The most, in our time, have to go content with a simple, incomplete

enough Suppression of this controversy; to a few some Solution of it is indispensable. In every new era, too, such Solution
comes-out in different terms; and ever the Solution of the last
era has become obsolete, and is found unserviceable. For it is
man's nature to change his Dialect from century to century;
he cannot help it though he would. The authentic *Church-
Catechism* of our present century has not yet fallen into my
hands: meanwhile, for my own private behoof, I attempt to
elucidate the matter so. Man's Unhappiness, as I construe,
comes of his Greatness; it is because there is an Infinite in him,
which with all his cunning he cannot quite bury under the
Finite. Will the whole Finance Ministers and Upholsterers and
Confectioners of modern Europe undertake, in joint-stock
company, to make one Shoeblack HAPPY? They cannot accomplish it, above an hour or two: for the Shoeblack also has a
Soul quite other than his Stomach; and would require, if you
consider it, for his permanent satisfaction and saturation,
simply this allotment, no more, and no less: *God's infinite
Universe altogether to himself,* therein to enjoy infinitely, and
fill every wish as fast as it rose. Oceans of Hochheimer, a
Throat like that of Ophiuchus: speak not of them; to the infinite Shoeblack they are as nothing. No sooner is your ocean
filled, than he grumbles that it might have been of better vint-
age. Try him with half of a Universe, of an Omnipotence, he
sets to quarrelling with the proprietor of the other half, and
declares himself the most maltreated of men.—Always there
is a black spot in our sunshine: it is even, as I said, the
Shadow of Ourselves.

'But the whim we have of Happiness is somewhat thus.
By certain valuations, and averages, of our own striking, we
come upon some sort of average terrestrial lot; this we fancy
belongs to us by nature, and of indefeasible right. It is simple
payment of our wages, of our deserts; requires neither thanks
nor complaint; only such *overplus* as there may be do we
account Happiness; any *deficit* again is Misery. Now consider
that we have the valuation of our own deserts ourselves, and
what a fund of Self-conceit there is in each of us,—do you
wonder that the balance should so often dip the wrong way,

and many a Blockhead cry: See there, what a payment;
was ever worthy gentleman so used!—I tell thee, Blockhead,
it all comes of thy Vanity; of what thou *fanciest* those same
deserts of thine to be. Fancy that thou deservest to be hanged
(as is most likely), thou wilt feel it happiness to be only shot:
fancy that thou deservest to be hanged in a hair-halter, it will
be a luxury to die in hemp.

'So true is it, what I then said, that *the Fraction of Life
can be increased in value not so much by increasing your
Numerator as by lessening your Denominator*. Nay, unless my
Algebra deceive me, *Unity* itself divided by *Zero* will give
Infinity. Make thy claim of wages a zero then; thou hast the
world under thy feet. Well did the Wisest of our time write:
"It is only with Renunciation (*Entsagen*) that Life, properly
speaking, can be said to begin."

'I asked myself: What is this that, ever since earliest years,
thou hast been fretting and fuming, and lamenting and self-
tormenting, on account of? Say it in a word: is it not because
thou art not ‧HAPPY? Because the THOU (sweet gentleman)
is not sufficiently honoured, nourished, soft-bedded, and lovingly cared-for? Foolish soul! What Act of Legislature was
there that *thou* shouldst be Happy? A little while ago thou
hadst no right to *be* at all. What if thou wert born and predestined not to be Happy, but to be Unhappy! Art thou
nothing other than a Vulture, then, that fliest through the
Universe seeking after somewhat to *eat;* and shrieking dole-
fully because carrion enough is not given thee? Close thy
Byron; open thy *Goethe*.'

'*Es leuchtet mir ein*, I see a glimpse of it!' cries he elsewhere: 'there is in man a HIGHER than Love of Happiness: he
can do without Happiness, and instead thereof find Blessedness! Was it not to preach-forth this same HIGHER that sages
and martyrs, the Poet and the Priest, in all times, have spoken
and suffered; bearing testimony, through life and through
death, of the Godlike that is in Man, and how in the Godlike
only has he Strength and Freedom? Which God-inspired
Doctrine art thou also honoured to be taught; O Heavens!
and broken with manifold merciful Afflictions, even till thou

become contrite, and learn it! O, thank thy Destiny for these; thankfully bear what yet remain: thou hadst need of them; the Self in thee needed to be annihilated. By benignant fever-paroxysms is Life rooting out the deep-seated chronic Disease, and triumphs over Death. On the roaring billows of Time, thou art not engulfed, but borne aloft into the azure of Eternity. Love not Pleasure; love God. This is the EVERLASTING YEA, wherein all contradiction is solved: wherein whoso walks and works, it is well with him.'

And again: 'Small is it that thou canst trample the Earth with its injuries under thy feet, as old Greek Zeno trained thee: thou canst love the Earth while it injures thee, and even because it injures thee; for this a Greater than Zeno was needed, and he too was sent. Knowest thou that "*Worship of Sorrow*"? The Temple thereof, founded some eighteen centuries ago, now lies in ruins, overgrown with jungle, the habitation of doleful creatures: nevertheless, venture forward; in a low crypt, arched out of falling fragments, thou findest the Altar still there, and its sacred Lamp perennially burning.'

Without pretending to comment on which strange utterances, the Editor will only remark, that there lies beside them much of a still more questionable character; unsuited to the general apprehension; nay wherein he himself does not see his way. Nebulous disquisitions on Religion, yet not without bursts of splendour; on the 'perennial continuance of Inspiration'; on Prophecy; that there are 'true Priests, as well as Baal-Priests, in our own day': with more of the like sort. We select some fractions, by way of finish to this farrago.

'Cease, my much respected Herr von Voltaire,' thus apostrophises the Professor: 'shut thy sweet voice; for the task appointed thee seems finished. Sufficiently hast thou demonstrated this proposition, considerable or otherwise: That the Mythus of the Christian Religion looks not in the eighteenth century as it did in the eighth. Alas, were thy six-and-thirty quartos, and the six-and-thirty thousand other quartos and folios, and flying sheets or reams, printed before and since on the same subject, all needed to convince us of so little! But what next? Wilt thou help us to embody the divine Spirit of that Religion in a new Mythus, in a new vehicle and vesture, that our Souls, otherwise too like perishing, may live? What! thou hast no faculty in that kind? Only a torch for burning, no hammer for building? Take our thanks, then, and——thyself away.

'Meanwhile what are antiquated Mythuses to me? Or is the God present, felt in my own heart, a thing which Herr von Voltaire will dispute out of me; or dispute into me? To the *"Worship of Sorrow"* ascribe what origin and genesis thou pleasest, *has* not that Worship originated, and been generated; is it not *here*? Feel it in thy heart, and then say whether it is of God! This is Belief; all else is Opinion,—for which latter whoso will, let him worry and be worried.'

'Neither,' observes he elsewhere, 'shall ye tear-out one another's eyes, struggling over "Plenary Inspiration," and such-like: try rather to get a little even Partial Inspiration, each of you for himself. One BIBLE I know, of whose Plenary Inspiration doubt is not so much as possible; nay with my own eyes I saw the God's-Hand writing it: thereof all other Bibles are but Leaves,—say, in Picture-Writing to assist the weaker faculty. . . .

'But indeed Conviction, were it never so excellent, is worthless till it convert itself into Conduct. Nay properly Conviction is not possible till then; inasmuch as all Speculation is by nature endless, formless, a vortex amid vortices: only by a felt indubitable certainty of Experience does it find any centre to revolve round, and so fashion itself into a system. Most true is it, as a wise man teaches us, that "Doubt of any sort cannot be removed except by Action." On which ground, too, let him who gropes painfully in darkness or uncertain light, and prays vehemently that the dawn may ripen into day, lay this other precept well to heart, which to me was of invaluable service: *"Do the Duty which lies nearest thee,"* which thou knowest to be a Duty! Thy second Duty will already have become clearer. . . .

'I too could now say to myself: Be no longer a Chaos, but a World, or even Worldkin. Produce! Produce! Were it but the pitifullest infinitesimal fraction of a Product, produce it,

in God's name! 'Tis the utmost thou hast in thee: out with it,
then. Up, up! Whatsoever thy hand findeth to do, do it with
thy whole might. Work while it is called Today; for the Night
cometh, wherein no man can work.'

The Hero as Divinity

THOMAS CARLYLE

[FROM *On Heroes and Hero Worship*]

1841

We have undertaken to discourse here for a little on Great
Men, their manner of appearance in our world's business,
how they have shaped themselves in the world's history, what
ideas men formed of them, what work they did;—on Heroes,
namely, and on their reception and performance; what I
call Hero-worship and the Heroic in human affairs. Too
evidently this is a large topic; deserving quite other treatment
than we can expect to give it at present. A large topic; indeed,
an illimitable one; wide as Universal History itself. For, as
I take it, Universal History, the history of what man has
accomplished in this world, is at bottom the History of the
Great Men who have worked here. They were the leaders of
men, these great ones; the modellers, patterns, and in a wide
sense creators, of whatsoever the general mass of men contrived to do or to attain; all things that we see standing
accomplished in the world are properly the outer material
result, the practical realisation and embodiment, of Thoughts
that dwelt in the Great Men sent into the world: the soul of
the whole world's history, it may justly be considered, were

From Lecture 1.

the history of these. Too clearly it is a topic we shall do no justice to in this place!

One comfort is, that Great Men, taken up in any way, are profitable company. We cannot look, however imperfectly, upon a great man, without gaining something by him. He is the living light-fountain, which it is good and pleasant to be near. The light which enlightens, which has enlightened the darkness of the world; and this not as a kindled lamp only, but rather as a natural luminary shining by the gift of Heaven; a flowing light-fountain, as I say, of native original insight, of manhood and heroic nobleness;—in whose radiance all souls feel that it is well with them. . . .

It is well said, in every sense, that a man's religion is the chief fact with regard to him. A man's, or a nation of men's. By religion I do not mean here the church-creed which he professes, the articles of faith which he will sign and, in words or otherwise, assert; not this wholly, in many cases not this at all. We see men of all kinds of professed creeds attain to almost all degrees of worth or worthlessness under each or any of them. This is not what I call religion, this profession and assertion; which is often only a profession and assertion from the outworks of the man, from the mere argumentative region of him, if even so deep as that. But the thing a man does practically believe (and this is often enough *without* asserting it even to himself, much less to others); the thing a man does practically lay to heart, and know for certain, concerning his vital relations to this mysterious Universe, and his duty and destiny there, that is in all cases the primary thing for him, and creatively determines all the rest. That is his *religion;* or, it may be, his mere scepticism and *no-religion*: the manner it is in which he feels himself to be spiritually related to the Unseen World or No-World; and I say, if you tell me what that is, you tell me to a very great extent what the man is, what the kind of things he will do is. Of a man or of a nation we inquire, therefore, first of all, What religion they had? Was it Heathenism,—plurality of gods, mere sensuous representation of this Mystery of Life, and for chief recognised element therein Physical Force? Was it Christianism; faith in an Invisible, not as real only, but as the only reality; Time, through every meanest moment of it, resting on Eternity; Pagan empire of Force displaced by a nobler supremacy, that of Holiness? Was it Scepticism, uncertainty and inquiry whether there was an Unseen World, any Mystery of Life except a mad one;—doubt as to all this, or perhaps unbelief and flat denial? Answering of this question is giving us the soul of the history of the man or nation. The thoughts they had were the parents of the actions they did; their feelings were parents of their thoughts: it was the unseen and spiritual in them that determined the outward and actual;—their religion, as I say, was the great fact about them. In these Discourses, limited as we are, it will be good to direct our survey chiefly to that religious phasis of the matter. That once known well, all is known. We have chosen as the first Hero in our series, Odin the central figure of Scandinavian Paganism; an emblem to us of a most extensive province of things. Let us look for a little at the Hero as Divinity, the oldest primary form of Heroism.

Surely it seems a very strange-looking thing this Paganism; almost inconceivable to us in these days. A bewildering, inextricable jungle of delusions, confusions, falsehoods, and absurdities, covering the whole field of Life! A thing that fills us with astonishment, almost, if it were possible, with incredulity,—for truly it is not easy to understand that sane men could ever calmly, with their eyes open, believe and live by such a set of doctrines. That men should have worshipped their poor fellow-man as a God, and not him only, but stocks and stones, and all manner of animate and inanimate objects; and fashioned for themselves such a distracted chaos of hallucinations by way of Theory of the Universe: all this looks like an incredible fable. Nevertheless it is a clear fact that they did it. Such hideous inextricable jungle of misworships, misbeliefs, men, made as we are, did actually hold by, and live at home in. This is strange. Yes, we may pause in sorrow and silence over the depths of darkness that are in man; if we rejoice in the heights of purer vision he has attained to. Such things were and are in man; in all men; in us too.

Some speculators have a short way of accounting for the Pagan religion: mere quackery, priestcraft, and dupery, say they; no sane man ever did believe it,—merely contrived to persuade other men, not worthy of the name of sane, to believe it! It will be often our duty to protest against this sort of hypothesis about men's doings and history; and I here, on the very threshold, protest against it in reference to Paganism, and to all other *isms* by which man has ever for a length of time striven to walk in this world. They have all had a truth in them, or men would not have taken them up. Quackery and dupery do abound; in religions, above all in the more advanced decaying stages of religions, they have fearfully abounded: but quackery was never the originating influence in such things; it was not the health and life of such things, but their disease, the sure precursor of their being about to die! Let us never forget this. It seems to me a most mournful hypothesis, that of quackery giving birth to any faith even in savage men. Quackery gives birth to nothing; gives death to all things. We shall not see into the true heart of anything, if we look merely at the quackeries of it; if we do not reject the quackeries altogether; as mere diseases, corruptions, with which our and all men's sole duty is to have done with them, to sweep them out of our thoughts as out of our practice. Man everywhere is the born enemy of lies. I find Grand Lamaism itself to have a kind of truth in it. Read the candid, clear-sighted, rather sceptical Mr. Turner's *Account of his Embassy* to that country, and see. They have their belief, these poor Thibet people, that Providence sends down always an Incarnation of Himself into every generation. At bottom some belief in a kind of Pope! At bottom still better, belief that there is a *Greatest* Man; that *he* is discoverable; that, once discovered, we ought to treat him with an obedience which knows no bounds! This is the truth of Grand Lamaism; the 'discoverability' is the only error here. The Thibet priests have methods of their own of discovering what Man is Greatest, fit to be supreme over them. Bad methods: but are they so much worse than our methods,—of understanding him to be always the eldest-born of a certain genealogy? Alas, it is a difficult thing to find good methods for!—We shall begin to have a chance of understanding Paganism, when we first admit that to its followers it was, at one time, earnestly true. Let us consider it very certain that men did believe in Paganism; men with open eyes, sound senses, men made altogether like ourselves; that we, had we been there, should have believed in it. Ask now, What Paganism could have been?

Another theory, somewhat more respectable, attributes such things to Allegory. It was a play of poetic minds, say these theorists; a shadowing-forth, in allegorical fable, in personi-fication and visual form, of what such poetic minds had known and felt of this Universe. Which agrees, add they, with a primary law of human nature, still everywhere observably at work, though in less important things, That what a man feels intensely, he struggles to speak-out of him, to see repre-sented before him in visual shape, and as if with a kind of life and historical reality in it. Now doubtless there is such a law, and it is one of the deepest in human nature; neither need we doubt that it did operate fundamentally in this business. The hypothesis which ascribes Paganism wholly or mostly to this agency, I call a little more respectable; but I cannot yet call it the true hypothesis. Think, would *we* believe, and take with us as our life-guidance, an allegory, a poetic sport? Not sport but earnest is what we should require. It is a most earnest thing to be alive in this world; to die is not sport for a man. Man's life never was a sport to him; it was a stern reality, altogether a serious matter to be alive!

I find, therefore, that though these Allegory theorists are on the way towards truth in this matter, they have not reached it either. Pagan Religion is indeed an Allegory, a Symbol of what men felt and knew about the Universe; and all Religions are symbols of that, altering always as that alters: but it seems to me a radical perversion, and even *in*version, of the business, to put that forward as the origin and moving cause, when it was rather the result and termination. To get beautiful allegories, a perfect poetic symbol, was not the want of men; but to know what they were to believe about this Universe, what course they were to steer in it; what, in this mysterious Life of theirs, they had to hope and to fear, to do and to forbear doing. The *Pilgrim's Progress* is an Allegory, and a beautiful, just and serious one: but consider whether Bunyan's Allegory could have *preceded* the Faith it symbolises! The Faith had to be already there, standing believed by everybody;—of which the Allegory could *then* become a shadow; and, with all its seriousness, we may say a *sportful* shadow, a mere play of the Fancy, in comparison with that awful Fact and scientific certainty which it poetically strives to emblem. The Allegory is the product of the certainty, not the producer of it; not in Bunyan's nor in any other case. For Paganism, therefore, we have still to inquire, Whence came that scientific certainty, the parent of such a bewildered heap of allegories, errors and confusions?. How was it, what was it?

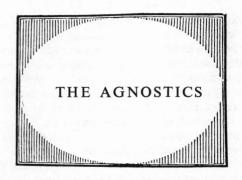

THE AGNOSTICS

The Higher Criticism

DAVID FRIEDRICH STRAUSS

[FROM *The Life of Jesus Critically Examined*]

1846

Having shown the possible existence of the mythical and the legendary in the gospels, both on extrinsic and intrinsic grounds, and defined their distinctive characteristics, it remains in conclusion to inquire how their actual presence may be recognized in individual cases?

The mythus presents two phases; in the first place it is not history; in the second it is fiction, the product of the particular mental tendency of a certain community. These two phases afford the one a negative, the other a positive criterion, by which the mythus is to be recognized.

I. *Negative.* That an account is not historical—that the matter related could not have taken place in the manner described is evident.

First. When the narration is irreconcileable with the known and universal laws which govern the course of events. . . .

Secondly. An account which shall be regarded as histori-

From Volume I, pages 87-95. Translated by George Eliot.

cally valid must neither be inconsistent with itself, nor in contradiction with other accounts. . . .

It may here be asked: is it to be regarded as a contradiction if one account is wholly silent respecting a circumstance mentioned by another? In itself, apart from all other considerations, the argumentum ex silentio is of no weight; but it is certainly to be accounted of moment when, at the same time, it may be shown that had the author known the circumstance he could not have failed to mention it, and also that he must have known it had it actually occurred.

II. *Positive.* The positive characters of legend and fiction are to be recognized sometimes in the form, sometimes in the substance of a narrative.

If the form be poetical, if the actors converse in hymns, and in a more diffuse and elevated strain than might be expected from their training and situations, such discourses, at all events, are not to be regarded as historical. The absence of these marks of the unhistorical do not however prove the historical validity of the narration, since the mythus often wears the most simple and apparently historical form: in which case the proof lies in the substance.

If the contents of a narrative strikingly accords with certain ideas existing and prevailing within the circle from which the narrative proceeded, which ideas themselves seem to be the product of preconceived opinions rather than of practical experience, it is more or less probable, according to circumstances, that such a narrative is of mythical origin. The knowledge of the fact, that the Jews were fond of representing their great men as the children of parents who had long been childless, cannot but make us doubtful of the historical truth of the statement that this was the case with John the Baptist; knowing also that the Jews saw predictions every where in the writings of their prophets and poets, and discovered types of the Messiah in all the lives of holy men recorded in their Scriptures; when we find details in the life of Jesus evidently sketched after the pattern of these prophecies and prototypes, we cannot but suspect that they are rather mythical than historical.

The more simple characteristics of the legend, and of additions by the author, after the observations of the former section, need no further elucidation.

Yet each of these tests, on the one hand, and each narrative on the other, considered apart, will rarely prove more than the possible or probable unhistorical character of the record. The concurrence of several such indications, is necessary to bring about a more definite result. The accounts of the visit of the Magi, and of the murder of the innocents at Bethlehem, harmonize remarkably with the Jewish Messianic notion, built upon the prophecy of Balaam, respecting the star which should come out of Jacob; and with the history of the sanguinary command of Pharaoh. Still this would not alone suffice to stamp the narratives as mythical. But we have also the corroborative facts that the described appearance of the star is contrary to the physical, the alleged conduct of Herod to the psychological laws; that Josephus, who gives in other respects so circumstantial an account of Herod, agrees with all other historical anthorities in being silent concerning the Bethlehem massacre; and that the visit of the Magi together with the flight into Egypt related in the one Gospel, and the presentation in the temple related in another Gospel, mutually exclude one another. Wherever, as in this instance, the several criteria of the mythical character concur, the result is certain, and certain in proportion to the accumulation of such grounds of evidence. . . .

In these last remarks we are, to a certain extent, anticipating the question which is, in conclusion, to be considered: viz., whether the mythical character is restricted to those features of the narrative, upon which such character is actually stamped; and whether a contradiction between two accounts invalidates one account only, or both? That is to say, what is the precise boundary line between the historical and the unhistorical?—the most difficult question in the whole province of criticism.

In the first place, when two narratives mutually exclude one another, one only is thereby proved to be unhistorical. If one be true the other must be false, but though the one be false the other may be true. Thus, in reference to the original residence of the parents of Jesus, we are justified in adopting the account of Luke which places it at Nazareth, to the exclusion of that of Matthew, which plainly supposes it to have been at Bethlehem; and, generally speaking, when we have to choose between two irreconcileable accounts, in selecting as historical that which is the least opposed to the laws of nature, and has the least correspondence with certain national or party opinions. But upon a more particular consideration it will appear that, since one account is false, it is possible that the other may be so likewise: the existence of a mythus respecting some certain point, shows that the imagination has been active in reference to that particular subject; (we need only refer to the genealogies); and the historical accuracy of either of two such accounts cannot be relied upon, unless substantiated by its agreement with some other well-authenticated testimony.

Concerning the different parts of one and the same narrative: it might be thought for example, that though the appearance of an angel, and his announcement to Mary that she should be the Mother of the Messiah, must certainly be regarded as unhistorical, still, that Mary should have indulged this hope before the birth of the child, is not in itself incredible. But what should have excited this hope in Mary's mind? It is at once apparent that that which is credible in itself is nevertheless unhistorical when it is so intimately connected with what is incredible that, if you discard the latter, you at the same time remove the basis on which the former rests. . . .

The following examples will serve to illustrate the mode of deciding in such cases. According to the narrative, as Mary entered the house and saluted her cousin Elizabeth, who was then pregnant, the babe leaped in her womb, she was filled with the Holy Ghost, and she immediately addressed Mary as the mother of the Messiah. This account bears indubitable marks of an unhistorical character. Yet, it is not, in itself, impossible that Mary should have paid a visit to her cousin, during which every thing went on quite naturally. The fact is, however, that there are psychological difficulties connected with this journey of the betrothed; and that the visit, and even the relationship of the two women, seem to have originated entirely in the wish to exhibit a connexion between the mother of John the Baptist, and the mother of the Messiah. Or when in the history of the transfiguration it is stated, that the men who appeared with Jesus on the Mount were Moses and Elias; and that the brilliancy which illuminated Jesus was supernatural; it might seem here also that, after deducting the marvellous, the presence of two men and a bright morning beam might be retained as the historical facts. But the legend was predisposed, by virtue of the current idea concerning the relation of the Messiah to these two prophets, not merely to make any two men (whose persons, object, and conduct, if they were not what the narrative represents them, remain in the highest degree mysterious) into Moses and Elias, but to create the whole occurrence; and in like manner not merely to conceive of some certain illumination as a supernatural effulgence (which, if a natural one, is much exaggerated and misrepresented), but to create it at once after the pattern of the brightness which illumined the face of Moses on Mount Sinai.

Hence is derived the following rule. Where not merely the particular nature and manner of an occurrence is critically suspicious, its external circumstances represented as miraculous and the like; but where likewise the essential substance and groundwork is either inconceivable in itself, or is in striking harmony with some Messianic idea of the Jews of that age, then not the particular alleged course and mode of the transaction only, but the entire occurrence must be regarded as unhistorical. Where on the contrary, the form only, and not the general contents of the narration, exhibits the characteristics of the unhistorical, it is at least possible to suppose a kernel of historical fact; although we can never confidently decide whether this kernel of fact actually exists, or in what it consists; unless, indeed, it be discoverable from other sources. In legendary narratives, or narratives embellished by the writer, it is less difficult,—by divesting them of all that betrays

itself as fictitious imagery, exaggeration, &c.—by endeavouring
to abstract from them every extraneous adjunct and to fill
up every hiatus—to succeed, proximately at least, in separating the historical groundwork.

The boundary line, however, between the historical and
the unhistorical, in records, in which as in our Gospels this
latter element is incorporated, will ever remain fluctuating
and unsusceptible of precise attainment. Least of all can it
be expected that the first comprehensive attempt to treat these
records from a critical point of view should be successful in
drawing a sharply defined line of demarcation. In the obscurity
which criticism has produced, by the extinction of all lights
hitherto held historical, the eye must accustom itself by
degrees to discriminate objects with precision; and at all
events the author of this work, wishes especially to guard
himself, in those places where he declares he knows not what
happened, from the imputation of asserting that he knows
that nothing happened.

<hr />

Is Genesis True?

JOHN WILLIAM COLENSO,
BISHOP OF NATAL

[FROM *A Critical Examination of the Pentateuch*]

1862

You will, of course, expect that, since I have had the charge
of this Diocese, I have been closely occupied in the study of
the Zulu tongue, and in translating the Scriptures into it.

From the Preface and Chapter 1.

Through the blessing of God, I have now translated the New Testament completely, and several parts of the Old, among the rest the books of Genesis and Exodus. In this work I have been aided by intelligent natives; and, having also published a Zulu Grammar and Dictionary, I have acquired sufficient knowledge of the language, to be able to have intimate communion with the native mind. . . .

Here, however, as I have said, amidst my work in this land, I have been brought face to face with the very questions which I then put by. While translating the story of the Flood, I have had a simple-minded, but intelligent, native,—one with the docility of a child, but the reasoning powers of mature age,—look up, and ask, 'Is all that true? Do you really believe that all this happened thus,—that all the beasts, and birds, and creeping things, upon the earth, large and small, from hot countries and cold, came thus by pairs, and entered into the ark with Noah? And did Noah gather food for them *all*, for the beasts and birds of prey, as well as the rest?' My heart answered in the words of the Prophet, 'Shall a man speak lies in the Name of the LORD?' Zech.xiii.3. I dared not do so. My own knowledge of some branches of science, of Geology in particular, had been much increased since I left England; and I now knew for certain, on geological grounds, a fact, of which I had only had misgivings before, viz. that a *Universal* Deluge, such as the Bible manifestly speaks of, could not possibly have taken place in the way described in the Book of Genesis, not to mention other difficulties which the story contains. . . . Of course, I am well aware that some have attempted to show that Noah's Deluge was only a *partial* one. But such attempts have ever seemed to me to be made in the very teeth of the Scripture statements, which are as plain and explicit as words can possibly be. Nor is anything really gained by supposing the Deluge to have been partial. For, as waters must find their own level on the Earth's surface, without a special miracle, of which the Bible says nothing, a Flood, which should begin by covering the top of Ararat, (if that were conceivable), or a much lower mountain, must necessarily become universal, and in due time sweep over the hills of Auvergne. Knowing this, I felt that I dared not, as a servant of the God of Truth, urge my brother man to believe that, which I did not myself believe, which I knew to be untrue, as a matter-of-fact, historical, narrative. I gave him, however, such a reply as satisfied him for the time, without throwing any discredit upon the general veracity of the Bible history.

But I was thus driven,—against my will at first, I may truly say,—to search more deeply into these questions; and I have since done so, to the best of my power, with the means at my disposal in this colony. And now I tremble at the result of my enquiries, rather, I should do so, were it not that I believe firmly in a God of Righteousness and Truth and Love, who both 'IS, and is a rewarder of them that diligently seek him.' . . .

The first five books of the Bible,—commonly called the Pentateuch (ἡ πεντατευχος βιβλος, Pentateuchus, sc. liber), or Book of Five Volumes,—are supposed by most English readers of the Bible to have been written by Moses, except the last chapter of Deuteronomy, which records the death of Moses, and which, of course, it is generally allowed, must have been added by another hand, perhaps that of Joshua. It is believed that Moses wrote under such special guidance and teaching of the Holy Spirit, that he was preserved from making any error in recording those matters, which came within his own cognisance, and was instructed also in respect of events, which took place before he was born,—before, indeed, there was a human being on the earth to take note of what was passing. He was in this way, it is supposed, enabled to write a true account of the Creation. And, though the accounts of the Fall and of the Flood, as well as of later events, which happened in the time of Abraham, Isaac, and Jacob, may have been handed down by tradition from one generation to another, and even, some of them, perhaps, written down in words, or represented in hieroglyphics, and Moses may, probably, have derived assistance from these sources also in the composition of his narrative, yet in all his statements, it is believed, he was under such constant control and superintendence of the Spirit of God, that he was kept from making any serious error, and certainly from writing anything altogether untrue. We may rely with undoubting confidence—such is the statement usually made—on the historical veracity, and infallible accuracy, of the Mosaic narrative in all its main particulars. . . .

But, among the many results of that remarkable activity in scientific enquiry of every kind, which, by God's own gift, distinguishes the present age, this also must be reckoned, that attention and labour are now being bestowed, more closely and earnestly than ever before, to search into the real foundations for such a belief as this. . . . The time is come, as I believe, in the Providence of God, when this question can no longer be put by,—when it must be resolutely faced, and the whole matter fully and freely examined, if we would be faithful servants of the God of Truth. . . .

The result of my enquiry is this, that I have arrived at the conviction,—as painful to myself at first, as it may be to my reader, though painful now no longer under the clear shining of the Light of Truth,—that the Pentateuch, as a whole, cannot possibly have been written by Moses, or by any one acquainted personally with the facts which it professes to describe, and, further, that the (so-called) Mosaic narrative, by whomsoever written, and though imparting to us, as I fully believe it does, revelations of the Divine Will and Character, cannot be regarded as *historically true*.

PART FOUR

EDUCATION

Ignorance of the Working Class

FRIEDRICH ENGELS

[FROM *The Condition of the Working-Class in England in 1844*]

1845

There is no compulsory education in England. In the factories, as we shall see, compulsory education exists only in name. During the parliamentary session of 1843 the Government proposed to enforce compulsory education for factory children. The factory owners resisted this proposal vigorously, although it was supported by the workers themselves. Large numbers of children work throughout the week in factories or at home and consequently have no time to attend school. There are evening institutes which are intended to serve the needs of such children and young workers, who are fully employed during the day-time. These institutes have very few scholars and those who do attend derive no profit from the instruction given. It is really too much to expect a young person who has been at work for twelve hours to go to school between 9 p.m. and 10 p.m. Most of those who do attend fall

Translated and edited by W. O. Henderson and W. H. Chaloner (New York: Macmillan, 1958); from pages 124-28.

asleep, as is proved by hundreds of statements by witnesses before the Children's Employment Commissioners. It is true that there are also Sunday schools in existence, but they are quite inadequately staffed and are of value only to pupils who have already learnt something in a day school. The interval between one Sunday and another is too long for an ignorant child to remember on the second attendance what he has learnt on the first a week before. On the basis of thousands of proofs contained in the statements of witnesses examined on behalf of the Children's Employment Commission, the Report of this Commission emphatically declares that the existing provision of day schools and Sunday schools is wholly inadequate for the present needs of the country.

This Report gives a picture of the abysmal ignorance of the English working classes which one might expect to find in such countries as Spain and Italy. What else is to be expected? The middle classes have little to hope and much to fear from the education of the workers. In an enormous budget of £55,000,000· a mere £40,000 is devoted to public education. If it were not for the fanaticism of the religious sects—which does at least as much harm as good—the amount of education available would be even less. The Anglicans have established their National schools and the various dissenting bodies have founded theirs, too, simply and solely in order to bring up children of their members in their particular faiths; and, if possible, now and again to filch the soul of some poor little child from a rival religious body. The result is that polemical discussions—the most sterile aspect of religion—dominate the school curriculum. The minds of the children are crammed with dogmas and theological principles which they do not understand. Consequently a narrow sectarianism and a fanatical bigotry are awakened in the children at as early an age as possible, to the serious neglect of any reasonable instruction in religion and morals. . . . The churches are still to this day quarrelling and so, for the time being, the working classes must remain steeped in ignorance.

The factory owners boast that the vast majority of the children in their employment have been taught to read, but the standard of reading is very inferior, as may be gathered from the reports of the Children's Employment Commission. Anyone who knows his alphabet claims to be able to read and with that the manufacturers are content. . . . The Sunday schools maintained by the Anglicans, the Quakers and, I believe, several other religious bodies, do not give any instruction in writing at all because 'this is too secular an occupation for Sunday.' A few examples may be given to illustrate the level of education of the English workers at the present day. They are taken from the Report of the Children's Employment Commission, which unfortunately does not include information concerning the true factory areas. . . .

In Wolverhampton Commissioner R. H. Horne found among others the following examples: A girl of eleven years who had attended both day and Sunday school, but had 'Never learnt of another world, nor of heaven, nor of another life. . . .' Another young person, 17 years of age, 'did not know how many two and two made, nor how many farthings there were in two-pence, even when the money was placed in his hand.' ' . . . You will find boys who have never heard of such a place as London, nor of Willenhall (which is only three miles distant, and in constant communication with Wolverhampton).' ' . . . Some [of the children] have never heard the name of Her Majesty, nor such names as Wellington, Nelson, Buonaparte, etc. But it is to be especially remarked, that among all those who had never even heard such names as St. Paul, Moses, Solomon, etc., there was a general knowledge of the character and course of life of Dick Turpin, the highwayman, and more particularly, of Jack Shepherd, the robber and prison-breaker.' A youth of 16 did not know 'how many twice two make,' nor 'how much money six farthings make, nor four farthings.' A youth of seventeen asserted that '10 farthings make 10 halfpence'; a third, sixteen years old, answered several very simple questions with the brief statement 'He be'nt no judge o' nothin'.'

These children, who are crammed with religious doctrines for four or five years at a stretch, know as little at the end as at the beginning. One child had 'attended a Sunday school

regularly for five years. . . .Does not know who Jesus Christ
was, but has heard the name of it. Never heard of the twelve
apostles. Never heard of Samson, nor of Moses, nor Aaron,
etc. Another had 'attended a Sunday school regularly nearly
six years. Knows who Jesus Christ was, he died on the cross
to shed his blood, to save our Saviour. Never heard of
St. Peter or St. Paul.' A third 'attended the Sunday schools
of different kinds about seven years; can read, only in the
thin books, easy words of one syllable; has heard of the
Apostles; does not know if St. Peter was one, nor if St. John
was one, unless it was St. John Wesley.' To the question
who Christ was, Horne received, among others, the following
answers: 'Yes, Adam,' 'He was an Apostle,' 'He was the
Saviour's Lord's Son,' and (from 'a young person 16 years
of age'): 'Jesus Christ was a king of London a long time ago.'
In Sheffield Commissioner J. C. Symons made the Sunday
school children read to him. The children could not tell
what they had been reading about, or what sort of people
apostles were. After he had put this question, 'to nearly every
one of the 16 in succession without a correct answer, a little
sharp-looking fellow cried out with great glee, "Please, Sir,
they were the lepers".' A similar state of affairs is reported
from the Potteries and from Lancashire.

Lowood: A Charity School

CHARLOTTE BRONTË

[FROM *Jane Eyre, An Autobiography*]

1847

I passed from compartment to compartment, from passage to passage, of a large and irregular building; till, emerging from the total and somewhat dreary silence pervading that portion of the house we had traversed, we came upon the hum of many voices and presently entered a wide, long room, with great deal tables, two at each end, on each of which burnt a pair of candles, and seated all round on benches, a congregation of girls of every age, from nine or ten to twenty. Seen by the dim lights of the dips, their number to me appeared countless, though not in reality exceeding eighty; they were uniformly dressed in brown stuff frocks of quaint fashion, and long holland pinafores. It was the hour of study; they were engaged in conning over their to-morrow's task, and the hum I had heard was the combined result of their whispered repetitions.

Miss Miller signed to me to sit on a bench near the door, then walking up to the top of the long room, she cried out,—

"Monitors, collect the lesson-books and put them away!"

Four tall girls arose from different tables, and going round, gathered the books and removed them. Miss Miller again gave the word of command,—

"Monitors, fetch the supper-trays!"

The tall girls went out and returned presently, each bearing a tray, with portions of something, I knew not what, arranged

From Chapter 5.

thereon, and a pitcher of water and mug in the middle of each tray. The portions were handed round; those who liked took a draught of the water, the mug being common to all. When it came to my turn, I drank, for I was thirsty, but did not touch the food, excitement and fatigue rendering me incapable of eating: I now saw, however, that it was a thin oaten cake, shared into fragments.

The meal over, prayers were read by Miss Miller, and the classes filed off, two and two, upstairs. Overpowered by this time with weariness, I scarcely noticed what sort of a place the bed-room was; except that, like the school-room, I saw it was very long. To-night I was to be Miss Miller's bed-fellow; she helped me to undress: when laid down I glanced at the long rows of beds, each of which was quickly filled with two occupants; in ten minutes the single light was extinguished; amid silence and complete darkness, I fell asleep.

The night passed rapidly: I was too tired even to dream: I only once awoke to hear the wind rave in furious gusts, and the rain fall in torrents, and to be sensible that Miss Miller had taken her place by my side. When I again unclosed my eyes, a loud bell was ringing: the girls were up and dressing; day had not yet begun to dawn, and a rushlight or two burnt in the room. I too rose reluctantly; it was bitter cold, and I dressed as well as I could for shivering, and washed when there was a basin at liberty, which did not occur soon, as there was but one basin to six girls, on the stands down the middle of the room. Again the bell rung: all formed in file, two and two, and in that order descended the stairs and entered the cold and dimly-lit school-room: here prayers were read by Miss Miller; afterwards she called out:—

"Form classes!"

A great tumult succeeded for some minutes, during which Miss Miller repeatedly exclaimed, "Silence!" and "Order!" When it subsided, I saw them all drawn up in four semicircles, before four chairs, placed at the four tables; all held books in their hands, and a great book, like a Bible, lay on each table, before the vacant seat. A pause of some seconds succeeded, filled up by the low, vague hum of numbers;

Miss Miller walked from class to class, hushing this indefinite sound.

A distant bell tinkled: immediately three ladies entered the room, each walked to a table and took her seat; Miss Miller assumed the fourth vacant chair, which was that nearest the door, and around which the smallest of the children were assembled: to this inferior class I was called, and placed at the bottom of it.

Business now began: the day's Collect was repeated, then certain texts of Scripture were said, and to these succeeded a protracted reading of chapters in the Bible, which lasted an hour. By the time that exercise was terminated, day had fully dawned. The indefatigable bell now sounded for the fourth time: the classes were marshalled and marched into another room to breakfast: how glad I was to behold a prospect of getting something to eat! I was now nearly sick from inanition, having taken so little the day before.

The refectory was a great, low-ceiled gloomy room; on two long tables smoked basins of something hot, which, however, to my dismay, sent forth an odour far from inviting. I saw a universal manifestation of discontent when the fumes of the repast met the nostrils of those destined to swallow it; from the van of the procession, the tall girls of the first class, rose the whispered words:—

"Disgusting! The porridge is burnt again!"

"Silence!" ejaculated a voice; not that of Miss Miller, but one of the upper teachers. . . . A long grace was said and a hymn sung; then a servant brought in some tea for the teachers, and the meal began.

Ravenous, and now very faint, I devoured a spoonful or two of my portion without thinking of its taste; but the first edge of hunger blunted, I perceived I had got in hand a nauseous mess: burnt porridge is almost as bad as rotten potatoes; famine itself soon sickens over it. The spoons were moved slowly: I saw each girl taste her food and try to swallow it; but in most cases the effort was soon relinquished. Breakfast was over, and none had breakfasted. Thanks being returned for what we had not got, and a second hymn chanted, the refectory was evacuated for the school-room. I was one of the last to go out, and in passing the tables, I saw one teacher take a basin of the porridge and taste it; she looked at the others; all their countenances expressed displeasure, and one of them, the stout one, whispered:—

"Abominable stuff! How shameful!"

A quarter of an hour passed before lessons again begun, during which the school-room was in a glorious tumult; for that space of time, it seemed to be permitted to talk loud and more freely, and they used their privilege. The whole conversation ran on the breakfast, which one and all abused roundly. . . .

A clock in the school-room struck nine; Miss Miller left her circle, and standing in the middle of the room, cried:—

"Silence! To your seats!"

Discipline prevailed: in five minutes the confused throng was resolved into order, and comparative silence quelled the Babel clamour of tongues. The upper-teachers now punctually resumed their posts: but still, all seemed to wait. Ranged on benches down the sides of the room, the eighty girls sat motionless and erect: a quaint assemblage they appeared, all with plain locks combed from their faces, not a curl visible; in brown dresses, made high and surrounded by a narrow tucker about the throat, with little pockets of holland (shaped something like a Highlander's purse) tied in front of their frocks, and destined to serve the purpose of a work-bag: all too wearing woollen stockings and country-made shoes fastened with brass buckles. Above twenty of those clad in this costume were full-grown girls, or rather young women: it suited them ill, and gave an air of oddity even to the prettiest. . . .

The superintendent of Lowood [Miss Temple], having taken her seat before a pair of globes placed on one of the tables, summoned the first class round her, and commenced giving a lesson in geography; the lower classes were called by the teachers: repetitions in history, grammar, etc., went on for an hour; writing and arithmetic succeeded, and music lessons were given by Miss Temple to some of the elder girls. The duration of each lesson was measured by the clock, which at last struck twelve. The superintendent rose:—

"I have a word to address to the pupils," said she.

The tumult of cessation from lessons was already breaking forth, but it sunk at her voice. She went on:—

"You had this morning a breakfast which you could not eat: you must be hungry:— I have ordered that a lunch of bread and cheese shall be served to all."

The teachers looked at her with a sort of surprise.

"It is to be done on my responsibility," she added, in an explanatory tone to them, and immediately afterwards left the room.

The bread and cheese was presently brought in and distributed, to the high delight and refreshment of the whole school. The order was now given "To the garden!" Each put on a coarse straw bonnet, with strings of coloured calico, and a cloak of grey frieze. I was similarly equipped, and, following the stream, I made my way into the open air.

The garden was a wide enclosure, surrounded with walls so high as to exclude every glimpse of prospect; a covered verandah ran down one side, and broad walks bordered a middle space divided into scores of little beds: these beds were assigned as gardens for the pupils to cultivate, and each bed had an owner. When full of flowers they would doubtless look pretty; but now, at the latter end of January, all was wintry blight and brown decay. I shuddered as I stood and looked round me: it was an inclement day for out-door exercise; not positively rainy, but darkened by a drizzling yellow fog; all underfoot was still soaking wet with the floods of yesterday. The stronger among the girls ran about and engaged in active games, but sundry pale and thin ones herded together for shelter and warmth in the verandah; and amongst these, as the dense mist penetrated to their shivering frames, I heard frequently the sound of a hollow cough. . . .

I looked round the convent-like garden, and then up at the house; a large building, half of which seemed grey and old, the other half quite new. The new part, containing the school-room and dormitory, was lit by mullioned and latticed windows, which gave it a church-like aspect; a stone tablet over the door bore this inscription:—

"Lowood Institution.—This portion was rebuilt A.D.——, by Naomi Brocklehurst, of Brocklehurst Hall, in this county." "Let your light so shine before men that they may see your good works, and glorify your Father which is in heaven."— St. Matt. v. 16.

I read these words over and over again: I felt that an explanation belonged to them, and was unable fully to penetrate their import. I was still pondering the signification of "Institution," and endeavouring to make out a connection between the first words and the verse of Scripture, when the sound of a cough close behind me, made me turn my head. I saw a girl sitting on a stone bench near; she was bent over a book, on the perusal of which she seemed intent. . . . I ventured to disturb her:—

"Can you tell me what the writing on that stone over the door means? What is Lowood Institution?"

"This house where you are come to live."

"And why do they call it Institution? Is it in any way different from other schools?"

"It is partly a charity-school: you and I, and all the rest of us, are charity-children. I suppose you are an orphan: are not either your father or your mother dead?"

"Both died before I can remember."

"Well, all the girls here have lost either one or both parents, and this is called an institution for educating orphans."

"Do we pay no money? Do they keep us for nothing?"

"We pay, or our friends pay, fifteen pounds a year for each."

"Then why do they call us charity-children?"

"Because fifteen pounds is not enough for board and teaching, and the deficiency is supplied by subscription."

"Who subscribes?"

"Different benevolent-minded ladies and gentlemen in this neighbourhood and in London."

"Who was Naomi Brocklehurst?"

"The lady who built the new part of this house as that

tablet records, and whose son overlooks and directs everything here."

"Why?"

"Because he is treasurer and manager of the establishment."

"Then this house does not belong to that tall lady who
wears a watch, and who said we were to have some bread
and cheese."

"To Miss Temple? Oh, no! I wish it did: she has to answer
to Mr. Brocklehurst for all she does. Mr. Brocklehurst buys
all our food and all our clothes."

"Does he live here?"

"No—two miles off, at a large hall."

"Is he a good man?"

"He is a clergyman, and is said to do a great deal of
good.". . .

"Have you been long here?"

"Two years."

"Are you an orphan?"

"My mother is dead."

"Are you happy here?"

"You ask rather too many questions. I have given you
answers enough for the present: now I want to read."

But at that moment the summons sounded for dinner: all
re-entered the house. The odour which now filled the refectory
was scarcely more appetizing than that which had regaled our
nostrils at breakfast: the dinner was served in two huge tin-
plated vessels, whence rose a strong steam redolent of rancid
fat. I found the mess to consist of indifferent potatoes and
strange shreds of rusty meat, mixed and cooked together. Of
this preparation a tolerably abundant plateful was apportioned
to each pupil. I ate what I could, and wondered within myself
whether every day's fare would be like this.

After dinner, we immediately adjourned to the school-
room: lessons recommenced, and were continued till five
o'clock . . . .

Soon after five P.M. we had another meal, consisting of
a small mug of coffee, and half a slice of brown bread. I
devoured my bread and drank my coffee with relish; but I

should have been glad of as much more—I was still hungry. Half an hour's recreation succeeded, then study; then the glass of water and the piece of oat-cake, prayers, and bed. Such was my first day at Lowood.

Dotheboys Hall: A Yorkshire School

CHARLES DICKENS

[FROM *Nicholas Nickleby*]

1838-1839

"EDUCATION.—At Mr. Wackford Squeers's Academy, Dotheboys Hall, at the delightful village of Dotheboys, near Greta Bridge in Yorkshire, Youth are boarded, clothed, booked, furnished with ,pocket-money, provided with all necessaries, instructed in all languages living and dead, mathematics, orthography, geometry, astronomy, trigonometry, the use of the globes, algebra, single stick (if required), writing, arithmetic, fortification, and every other branch of classical literature. Terms, twenty guineas per annum. No extras, no vacations, and diet unparalleled. Mr. Squeers is in town, and attends daily, from one till four, at the Saracen's Head, Snow Hill. N.B. An able assistant wanted. Annual salary £5. A Master of Arts would be preferred.'

"There!" said Ralph, folding the paper again. "Let him get that situation, and his fortune is made."

"But he is not a Master of Arts," said Mrs. Nickleby.

"That," replied Ralph, "that I think, can be got over."

"But the salary is so small, and it is such a long way off, uncle!" faltered Kate.

"Hush, Kate my dear," interposed Mrs. Nickleby; "your uncle must know best." . . .

From Chapter 3.

[FROM Chapter 8.]

Squeers, arming himself with his cane, led the way across a yard, to a door in the rear of the house.

"There," said the schoolmaster as they stepped in together; "this is our shop, Nickleby!"

It was such a crowded scene, and there were so many objects to attract attention, that, at first, Nicholas stared about him, really without seeing anything at all. By degrees, however, the place resolved itself into a bare and dirty room, with a couple of windows, whereof a tenth part might be of glass, the remainder being stopped up with old copybooks and paper. There were a couple of long old rickety desks, cut and notched, and inked, and damaged, in every possible way; two or three forms; a detached desk for Squeers; and another for his assistant. The ceiling was supported, like that of a barn, by cross beams and rafters; and the walls were so stained and discoloured, that it was impossible to tell whether they had ever been touched with paint or whitewash.

But the pupils—the young noblemen! How the last faint traces of hope, the remotest glimmering of any good to be derived from his efforts in this den, faded from the mind of Nicholas as he looked in dismay around! Pale and haggard faces, lank and bony figures, children with the countenances of old men, deformities with irons upon their limbs, boys of stunted growth, and others whose long meagre legs would hardly bear their stooping bodies, all crowded on the view together; there were the bleared eye, the hare-lip, the crooked foot, and every ugliness or distortion that told of unnatural aversion conceived by parents for their offspring, or of young lives which, from the earliest dawn of infancy, had been one horrible endurance of cruelty and neglect. There were little faces which should have been handsome, darkened with the scowl of sullen, dogged suffering; there was childhood with the light of its eye quenched, its beauty gone, and its help-lessness alone remaining; there were vicious-faced boys, brooding, with leaden eyes, like malefactors in a jail; and there were young creatures on whom the sins of their frail parents had descended, weeping even for the mercenary nurses they had known, and lonesome even in their loneliness. With every kindly sympathy and affection blasted in its birth, with every young and healthy feeling flogged and starved down, with every revengeful passion that can fester in swollen hearts, eating its evil way to their core in silence, what an incipient Hell was breeding there!...

"Now," said Squeers, giving the desk a great rap with his cane, which made half the little boys nearly jump out of their boots, "is that physicking over?"

"Just over," said Mrs. Squeers, choking the last boy in her hurry, and tapping the crown of his head with the wooden spoon to restore him. "Here, you Smike; take away now. Look sharp!"

Smike shuffled out with the basin, and Mrs. Squeers having called up a little boy with a curly head, and wiped her hands upon it, hurried out after him into a species of wash-house, where there was a small fire and a large kettle, together with a number of little wooden bowls which were arranged upon a board.

Into these bowls, Mrs. Squeers, assisted by the hungry servant, poured a brown composition, which looked like diluted pincushions without the covers, and was called porridge. A minute wedge of brown bread was inserted in each bowl, and when they had eat their porridge by means of the bread, the boys eat the bread itself, and had finished their breakfast; whereupon Mr. Squeers said, in a solemn voice, "For what we have received, may the Lord make us truly thankful!"—and went away to his own.

Nicholas distended his stomach with a bowl of porridge, for much the same reason which induces some savages to swallow earth—lest they should be inconveniently hungry when there is nothing to eat. Having further disposed of a slice of bread and butter, allotted to him in virtue of his office, he sat him-self down, to wait for school-time.

He could not but observe how silent and sad the boys all seemed to be. There was none of the noise and clamour of a school-room; none of its boisterous play, or hearty mirth. The children sat crouching and shivering together, and seemed to lack the spirit to move about. The only pupil who evinced the slightest tendency towards locomotion or playfulness, was Master Squeers, and as his chief amusement was to tread upon the other boys' toes in his new boots, his flow of spirits was rather disagreeable than otherwise.

After some half-hour's delay, Mr. Squeers reappeared, and the boys took their places and their books, of which latter commodity the average might be about one to eight learners. A few minutes having elapsed, during which Mr. Squeers looked very profound, as if he had a perfect apprehension of what was inside all the books, and could say every word of their contents by heart if he only chose to take the trouble, that gentleman called up the first class.

Obedient to this summons there ranged themselves in front of the schoolmaster's desk, half-a-dozen scarecrows, out at knees and elbows, one of whom placed a torn and filthy book beneath his learned eye.

"This is the first class in English spelling and philosophy, Nickleby," said Squeers, beckoning Nicholas to stand beside him. "We'll get up a Latin one, and hand that over to you. Now, then, where's the first boy?"

"Please, sir, he's cleaning the back parlour window," said the temporary head of the philosophical class.

"So he is, to be sure," rejoined Squeers. "We go upon the practical mode of teaching, Nickleby; the regular education system. C-l-e-a-n, clean, verb active, to make bright, to scour. W-i-n, win, d-e-r, der, winder, a casement. When the boy knows this out of book, he goes and does it. It's just the same principle as the use of the globes. Where's the second boy?"

"Please, sir, he's weeding the garden," replied a small voice.

"To be sure," said Squeers, by no means disconcerted. "So he is. B-o-t, bot, t-i-n, tin, bottin, n-e-y, ney, bottinney, noun substantive, a knowledge of plants. When he has learned that bottinney means a knowledge of plants, he goes and knows 'em. That's our system, Nickleby: what do you think of it?"

"It's a very useful one, at any rate," answered Nicholas significantly.

"I believe you," rejoined Squeers, not remarking the emphasis of his usher. "Third boy, what's a horse?"

"A beast, sir," replied the boy.

"So it is," said Squeers. "Ain't it, Nickleby?"

"I believe there is no doubt of that, sir," answered Nicholas.

"Of course there isn't," said Squeers. "A horse is a quadruped, and quadruped's Latin for beast, as every body that's gone through the grammar, knows, or else where's the use of having grammars at all?"

"Where, indeed!" said Nicholas abstractedly.

"As you're perfect in that," resumed Squeers, turning to the boy, "go and look after *my* horse, and rub him down well, or I'll rub you down. The rest of the class go and draw water up, till somebody tells you to leave off, for it's washing-day to-morrow, and they want the coppers filled."

So saying, he dismissed the first class to their experiments in practical philosophy, and eyed Nicholas with a look, half cunning and half doubtful, as if he were not altogether certain what he might think of him by this time.

"That's the way we do it, Nickleby," he said, after a long pause.

Dr. Blimber's Academy: Forcing

CHARLES DICKENS

[FROM *Dombey and Son*]

1846-1848

Whenever a young gentleman was taken in hand by Doctor Blimber, he might consider himself sure of a pretty tight squeeze. The Doctor only undertook the charge of ten young gentlemen, but he had, always ready, a supply of learning for a hundred, on the lowest estimate; and it was at once the business and delight of his life to gorge the unhappy ten with it.

In fact, Doctor Blimber's establishment was a great hot-house, in which there was a forcing apparatus incessantly at work. All the boys blew before their time. Mental green-peas were produced at Christmas, and intellectual asparagus all the year round. Mathematical gooseberries (very sour ones too) were common at untimely seasons, and from mere sprouts of bushes, under Doctor Blimber's cultivation. Every description of Greek and Latin vegetable was got off the driest twigs of boys under the frostiest circumstances. Nature was of no consequence at all. No matter what a young gentleman was intended to bear, Doctor Blimber made him bear to pattern, somehow or other.

This was all very pleasant and ingenious, but the system of forcing was attended with its usual disadvantages. There was not the right taste about the premature productions, and they didn't keep well. Moreover, one young gentleman, with a swollen nose and an excessively large head (the oldest of the ten who had "gone through" everything), suddenly left off blowing one day, and remained in the establishment a mere stalk. And people did say that the Doctor had rather over-

From Chapter. 11

done it with young Toots, and that when he began to have whiskers he left off having brains. . . . .

The Doctor was a portly gentleman in a suit of black, with strings at his knees, and stockings below them. He had a bald head, highly polished; a deep voice; and a chin so very double, that it was a wonder how he ever managed to shave into the creases. He had likewise a pair of little eyes that were always half shut up, and a mouth that was always half expanded into a grin, as if he had, that moment, posed a boy, and were waiting to convict him from his own lips. Insomuch, that when the Doctor put his right hand into the breast of his coat, and with his other hand behind him, and a scarcely perceptible wag of his head, made the commonest observation to a nervous stranger, it was like a sentiment from the sphynx, and settled his business.

The Doctor's was a mighty fine house, fronting the sea. Not a joyful style of house within, but quite the contrary. Sad-coloured curtains, whose proportions were spare and lean, hid themselves despondently behind the windows. The tables and chairs were put away in rows, like figures in a sum; fires were so rarely lighted in the rooms of ceremony, that they felt like wells, and a visitor represented the bucket; the dining-room seemed the last place in the world where any eating or drinking was likely to occur; there was no sound through all the house but the ticking of a great clock in the hall, which made itself audible in the very garrets; and sometimes a dull crying of young gentlemen at their lessons, like the murmurings of an assemblage of melancholy pigeons.

Miss Blimber, too, although a slim and graceful maid, did no soft violence to the gravity of the house. There was no light nonsense about Miss Blimber. She kept her hair short and crisp, and wore spectacles. She was dry and sandy with working in the graves of deceased languages. None of your live languages for Miss Blimber. They must be dead—stone dead—and then Miss Blimber dug them up like a Ghoul.

Mrs. Blimber, her mama, was not learned herself, but she pretended to be, and that did quite as well. She said at evening parties, that if she could have known Cicero, she thought she could have died contented. It was the steady joy of her life to see the Doctor's young gentlemen go out walking, unlike all other young gentlemen, in the largest possible shirt collars, and the stiffest possible cravats. It was so classical, she said.

As to Mr. Feeder, B.A., Doctor Blimber's assistant, he was a kind of human barrel-organ, with a little list of tunes at which he was continually working, over and over again, without any variation. He might have been fitted up with a change of barrels, perhaps, in early life, if his destiny had been favourable; but it had not been; and he had only one, with which, in a monotonous round, it was his occupation to bewilder the young ideas of Doctor Blimber's young gentlemen. The young gentlemen were prematurely full of carking anxieties. They knew no rest from the pursuit of stony-hearted verbs, savage noun-substantives, inflexible syntactic passages, and ghosts of exercises that appeared to them in their dreams. Under the forcing system, a young gentleman usually took leave of his spirits in three weeks. He had all the cares of the world on his head in three months. He conceived bitter sentiments against his parents or guardians, in four; he was an old misanthrope, in five; envied Quintius Curtius that blessed refuge in the earth, in six; and at the end of the first twelvemonth had arrived at the conclusion, from which he never afterwards departed, that all the fancies of the poets, and lessons of the sages, were a mere collection of words and grammar, and had no other meaning in the world.

But he went on, blow, blow, blowing, in the Doctor's hot-house, all the time; and the Doctor's glory and reputation were great, when he took his wintry growth home to his relations and friends. . . .

The Doctor was sitting in his portentous study, with a globe at each knee, books all round him, Homer over the door, and Minerva on the mantel-shelf. "And how do you, Sir," he said to Mr. Dombey, "and how is my little friend?" Grave as an organ was the Doctor's speech; and when he ceased, the great clock in the hall seemed (to Paul at least) to take him up, and to go on saying "how, is, my, lit, tle, friend, how, is, my, lit, tle, friend," over and over and over again. . . .

[FROM Chapter 12]

. . .They all went out for a walk before tea. Even Briggs (though he hadn't begun yet) partook of this dissipation; in the enjoyment of which he looked over the cliff two or three times darkly. Doctor Blimber accompanied them; and Paul had the honour of being taken in tow by the Doctor himself: a distinguished state of things, in which he looked very little and feeble.

Tea was served in a style no less polite than the dinner; and after tea, the young gentlemen rising and bowing as before, withdrew to fetch up the unfinished tasks of that day, or to get up the already looming tasks of to-morrow. In the meantime Mr. Feeder withdrew to his own room; and Paul sat in a corner wondering whether Florence was thinking of him, and what they were all about at Mrs. Pipchin's. . . .

At eight o'clock or so, the gong sounded again for prayers in the dining-room, where the butler afterwards presided over a side table, on which bread and cheese and beer were spread for such young gentlemen as desired to partake of those refreshments. The ceremonies concluded by the Doctor's saying, "Gentlemen, we will resume our studies at seven to-morrow"; and then, for the first time, Paul saw Cornelia Blimber's eye, and saw that it was upon him. When the Doctor had said these words, "Gentlemen, we will resume our studies at seven to-morrow," the pupils bowed again, and went to bed.

In the confidence of their own room up-stairs, Briggs said his head ached ready to split, and that he should wish himself dead if it wasn't for his mother, and a blackbird he had at home. Tozer didn't say much, but he sighed a good deal, and told Paul to look out, for his turn would come to-morrow. After uttering those prophetic words, he undressed himself moodily, and got into bed. Briggs was in his bed too, and Paul in his bed too, before the weak-eyed young man appeared to take away the candle, when he wished them good night and pleasant dreams. But his benevolent wishes were in vain, as far as Briggs and Tozer were concerned; for Paul, who lay awake for a long while, and often woke afterwards, found that Briggs was ridden by his lesson as a nightmare: and that Tozer, whose mind was affected in his sleep by similar causes, in a minor degree, talked unknown tongues, or scraps of Greek and Latin—it was all one to Paul—which, in the silence of night, had an inexpressibly wicked and guilty effect. . . .

"Now, Dombey," said Miss Blimber. "How have you got on with those books?"

They comprised a little English, and a deal of Latin— names of things, declensions of articles and substantives, exercises thereon, and preliminary rules—a trifle of orthography, a glance at ancient history, a wink or two at modern ditto, a few tables, two or three weights and measures, and a little general information. When poor Paul had spelt out number two, he found he had no idea of number one; fragments whereof afterwards obtruded themselves into number three, which slided into number four, which grafted itself on to number two. So that whether twenty Romuluses made a Remus, or hic hæc hoc was troy weight, or a verb always agreed with an ancient Briton, or three times four was Taurus a bull, were open questions with him.

"Oh, Dombey, Dombey!" said Miss Blimber, "this is very shocking. . . . You must take the books down, I suppose, Dombey, one by one, and perfect yourself in the day's instalment of subject A, before you turn at all to subject B. And now take away the top book, if you please, Dombey, and return when you are master of the theme."

Miss Blimber expressed her opinions on the subject of Paul's uninstructed state with a gloomy delight, as if she had expected this result, and were glad to find that they must be in constant communication. Paul withdrew with the top task, as he was told, and laboured away at it, down below: sometimes remembering every word of it, and sometimes forgetting it all, and everything else besides: until at last he ventured up-stairs again to repeat the lesson, when it was

nearly all driven out of his head before he began, by Miss
Blimber's shutting up the book, and saying "Go on, Dombey!"
a proceeding so suggestive of the knowledge inside of her,
that Paul looked upon the young lady with consternation,
as a kind of learned Guy Faux, or artificial Bogle, stuffed
full of scholastic straw.

He acquitted himself very well, nevertheless; and Miss
Blimber, commending him as giving promise of getting on
fast, immediately provided him with subject B; from which
he passed to C, and even D before dinner. It was hard work,
resuming his studies, soon after dinner; and he felt giddy
and confused and drowsy and dull. But all the other young
gentlemen had similar sensations, and were obliged to resume
their studies too, if there were any comfort in that. It was
a wonder that the great clock in the hall, instead of being
constant to its first inquiry, never said, "Gentlemen, we will
now resume our studies," for that phrase was often enough
repeated in its neighbourhood. The studies went round like
a mighty wheel, and the young gentlemen were always
stretched upon it.

A Clerical Tutor

GEORGE ELIOT

[FROM *The Mill on the Floss*]

1860

Mr Stelling set to work at his natural method of instilling
the Eton Grammar and Euclid into the mind of Tom Tulliver.
This, he considered, was the only basis of solid instruction:
all other means of education were mere charlatanism, and
could produce nothing better than smatterers. Fixed on this

From Book II, Chapter 1.

firm basis, a man might observe the display of various or special knowledge made by irregularly educated people with a pitying smile: all that sort of thing was very well, but it was impossible these people could form sound opinions. In holding this conviction Mr Stelling was not biassed, as some tutors have been, by the excessive accuracy or extent of his own scholarship; and as to his views about Euclid, no opinion could have been freer from personal partiality. Mr Stelling was very far from being led astray by enthusiasm, either religious or intellectual; on the other hand, he had no secret belief that everything was humbug. He thought religion was a very excellent thing, and Aristotle a great authority, and deaneries and prebends useful institutions, and Great Britain the providential bulwark of Protestantism, and faith in the unseen a great support to afflicted minds: he believed in all these things, as a Swiss hotel-keeper believes in the beauty of the scenery around him, and in the pleasure it gives to artistic visitors. And in the same way Mr Stelling believed in his method of education: he had no doubt that he was doing the very best thing for Mr Tulliver's boy. Of course, when the miller talked of "mapping" and "summing," in a vague and diffident manner, Mr Stelling had set his mind at rest by an assurance that he understood what was wanted; for how was it possible the good man could form any reasonable judgment about the matter? Mr Stelling's duty was to teach the lad in the only right way—indeed, he knew no other: he had not wasted his time in the acquirement of anything abnormal.

He very soon set down poor Tom as a thoroughly stupid lad; for though by hard labour he could get particular declensions into his brain, anything so abstract as the relation between cases and terminations could by no means get such a lodgment there as to enable him to recognise a chance genitive or dative. This struck Mr Stelling as something more than natural stupidity: he suspected obstinacy, or at any rate, indifference; and lectured Tom severely on his want of thorough application. "You feel no interest in what you're doing, sir," Mr Stelling would say, and the reproach was painfully true. Tom had never found any difficulty in discerning a pointer from a setter, when once he had been told the distinction, and his perceptive powers were not at all deficient. I fancy they were quite as strong as those of the Rev. Mr Stelling; for Tom could predict with accuracy what number of horses were cantering behind him, he could throw a stone right into the centre of a given ripple, he could guess to a fraction how many lengths of his stick it would take to reach across the playground, and could draw almost perfect squares on his slate without any measurement. But Mr Stelling took no note of these things: he only observed that Tom's faculties failed him before the abstractions hideously symbolised to him in the pages of the Eton Grammar, and that he was in a state bordering on idiocy with regard to the demonstration that two given triangles must be equal—though he could discern with great promptitude and certainty the fact that they *were* equal. Whence Mr Stelling concluded that Tom's brain, being peculiarly impervious to etymology and demonstrations, was peculiarly in need of being ploughed and harrowed by these patent implements: it was his favourite metaphor, that the classics and geometry constituted that culture of the mind which prepared it for the reception of any subsequent crop. . . .

Tom Tulliver, being abundant in no form of speech, did not use any metaphor to declare his views as to the nature of Latin: he never called it an instrument of torture; and it was not until he had got on some way in the next half-year, and in the Delectus, that he was advanced enough to call it a "bore" and "beastly stuff." At present, in relation to this demand that he should learn Latin declensions and conjugations, Tom was in a state of as blank unimaginativeness concerning the cause and tendency of his sufferings, as if he had been an innocent shrew-mouse imprisoned in the split trunk of an ash-tree in order to cure lameness in cattle. It is doubtless almost incredible to instructed minds of the present day that a boy of twelve, not belonging strictly to "the masses," who are now understood to have the monopoly of mental darkness, should have had no distinct idea how there came to be such a thing as Latin on this earth: yet so it was with Tom. It would have taken a long while to make conceivable to him that there ever existed a people who bought and sold sheep and oxen, and transacted the everyday affairs of life, through the medium of this language, and still longer to make him understand why he should be called upon to learn it, when its connection with those affairs had become entirely latent. So far as Tom had gained any acquaintance with the Romans at Mr Jacobs' academy, his knowledge was strictly correct, but it went no farther than the fact that they were "in the New Testament"; and Mr Stelling was not the man to enfeeble and emasculate his pupil's mind by simplifying and explaining, or to reduce the tonic effect of etymology by mixing it with smattering, extraneous information, such as is given to girls. . . .

Nothing but Facts

CHARLES DICKENS

[FROM *Hard Times*]

1854

"Now, what I want is, Facts, Teach these boys and girls nothing but Facts. Facts alone are wanted in life. Plant nothing else, and root out everything else. You can only form the minds of reasoning animals upon Facts: nothing else will ever be of any service to them. This is the principle on which I bring up my own children, and this is the principle on which I bring up these children. Stick to Facts, sir!"

From Chapter 1.

The scene was a plain, bare, monotonous vault of a school-room, and the speaker's square forefinger emphasised his observations by underscoring every sentence with a line on the schoolmaster's sleeve. The emphasis was helped by the speaker's square wall of a forehead, which had his eyebrows for its base, while his eyes found commodious cellarage in two dark caves, overshadowed by the wall. The emphasis was helped by the speaker's mouth, which was wide, thin, and hard set. The emphasis was helped by the speaker's voice, which was inflexible, dry, and dictatorial. The emphasis was helped by the speaker's hair, which bristled on the skirts of his bald head, a plantation of firs to keep the wind from its shining surface, all covered with knobs, like the crust of a plum pie, as if the head had scarcely warehouse-room for the hard facts stored inside. The speaker's obstinate carriage, square coat, square legs, square shoulders,—nay, his very neckcloth, trained to take him by the throat with an un-accommodating grasp, like a stubborn fact, as it was,—all helped the emphasis.

"In this life, we want nothing but Facts, sir; nothing but Facts!"

The speaker, and the schoolmaster, and the third grown person present, all backed a little, and swept with their eyes the inclined plane of little vessels then and there arranged in order, ready to have imperial gallons of facts poured into them until they were full to the brim.

[FROM Chapter 2]

Thomas Gradgrind, sir. A man of realities. A man of Facts and calculations. A man who proceeds upon the principle that two and two are four, and nothing over, and who is not to be talked into allowing for anything over. Thomas Gradgrind, sir—peremptorily Thomas—Thomas Gradgrind. With a rule and a pair of scales, and the multiplication table always in his pocket, sir, ready to weigh and measure any parcel of human nature, and tell you exactly what it comes to. It is a mere question of figures, a case of simple arithmetic. You might hope to get some other nonsensical belief into the head of George Gradgrind, or Augustus Gradgrind, or John Gradgrind, or Joseph Gradgrind (all suppositious, non-existent persons), but into the head of Thomas Gradgrind—no, sir!

In such terms Mr. Gradgrind always mentally introduced himself, whether to his private circle of acquaintance, or to the public in general. In such terms, no doubt, substituting the words "boys and girls," for "sir," Thomas Gradgrind now presented Thomas Gradgrind to the little pitchers before him, who were to be filled so full of facts.

Indeed, as he eagerly sparkled at them from the cellarage before mentioned, he seemed a kind of cannon loaded to the muzzle with facts, and prepared to blow them clean out of the regions of childhood at one discharge. He seemed a galvanising apparatus, too, charged with a grim mechanical substitute for the tender young imaginations that were to be stormed away.

"Girl number twenty," said Mr. Gradgrind, squarely pointing with his square forefinger, "I don't know that girl. Who is that girl?"

"Sissy Jupe, sir," explained number twenty, blushing, standing up, and curtseying.

"Sissy is not a name," said Mr. Gradgrind. "Don't call yourself Sissy. Call yourself Cecilia."

"It's father as calls me Sissy, sir," returned the young girl in a trembling voice, and with another curtsey.

"Then he has no business to do it," said Mr. Gradgrind. "Tell him he mustn't. Cecilia Jupe. Let me see. What is your father?"

"He belongs to the horse-riding, if you please, sir."

Mr. Gradgrind frowned, and waved off the objectionable calling with his hand.

"We don't want to know anything about that, here. You mustn't tell us about that, here. Your father breaks horses, don't he?"

"If you please, sir, when they can get any to break, they do break horses in the ring, sir."

"You mustn't tell us about the ring, here. Very well, then. Describe your father as a horsebreaker. He doctors sick horses, I dare say?"

"Oh yes, sir."

"Very well, then. He is a veterinary surgeon, a farrier, and horsebreaker. Give me your definition of a horse."

(Sissy Jupe thrown into the greatest alarm by this demand.)

"Girl number twenty unable to define a horse!" said Mr. Gradgrind, for the general behoof of all the little pitchers. "Girl number twenty possessed of no facts, in reference to one of the commonest of animals! Some boy's definition of a horse. Bitzer, yours."

The square finger, moving here and there, lighted suddenly on Bitzer, perhaps because he chanced to sit in the same ray of sunlight which, darting in at one of the bare windows of the intensely whitewashed room, irradiated Sissy. For, the boys and girls sat on the face of the inclined plane in two compact bodies, divided up the centre by a narrow interval; and Sissy, being at the corner of a row on the sunny side, came in for the beginning of a sunbeam, of which Bitzer, being at the corner of a row on the other side, a few rows in advance, caught the end. But, whereas the girl was so dark-eyed and dark-haired, that she seemed to receive a deeper and more lustrous colour from the sun when it shone upon her, the boy was so light-eyed and light-haired that the self-same rays appeared to draw out of him what little colour he ever possessed. His cold eyes would hardly have been eyes, but for the short ends of lashes which, by bringing them into immediate contrast with something paler than themselves, expressed their form. His short-cropped hair might have been a mere continuation of the sandy freckles on his forehead and face. His skin was so unwholesomely deficient in the natural tinge, that he looked as though, if he were cut, he would bleed white.

"Bitzer," said Thomas Gradgrind. "Your definition of a horse."

"Quadruped. Graminivorous. Forty teeth, namely twenty-four grinders, four eye-teeth, and twelve incisive. Sheds coat in the spring; in marshy countries, sheds hoofs, too. Hoofs hard, but requiring to be shod with iron. Age known by marks in mouth." Thus (and much more) Bitzer.

"Now girl number twenty," said Mr. Gradgrind. "You know what a horse is."

She curtseyed again, and would have blushed deeper, if she could have blushed deeper than she had blushed all this time. Bitzer, after rapidly blinking at Thomas Gradgrind with both eyes at once, and so catching the light upon his quivering ends of lashes that they looked like the antennæ of busy insects, put his knuckles to his freckled forehead, and sat down again.

The third gentleman now stepped forth. A mighty man at cutting and drying, he was; a government officer; in his way (and in most other people's too), a professed pugilist; always in training, always with a system to force down the general throat like a bolus, always to be heard of at the bar of his little Public-office, ready to fight all England. To continue in fistic phraseology, he had a genius for coming up to the scratch, wherever and whatever it was, and proving himself an ugly customer. He would go in and damage any subject whatever with his right, follow up with his left, stop, exchange, counter, bore his opponent (he always fought All England) to the ropes, and fall upon him neatly. He was certain to knock the wind out of common-sense, and render that unlucky adversary deaf to the call of time. And he had it in charge from high authority to bring about the great Public-office Millennium, when Commissioners should reign upon earth.

"Very well," said this gentleman, briskly smiling, and folding his arms. "That's a horse. Now, let me ask you girls and boys, Would you paper a room with representations of horses?"

After a pause, one half of the children cried in chorus, "Yes, sir!" Upon which the other half, seeing in the gentleman's face that Yes was wrong, cried out in chorus, "No, sir!"—as the custom is, in these examinations.

"Of course, no. Why wouldn't you?"

A pause. One corpulent slow boy, with a wheezy manner

of breathing, ventured the answer, Because he wouldn't paper a room at all, but would paint it.

"You *must* paper it," said the gentleman, rather warmly.

"You must paper it," said Thomas Gradgrind, "whether you like it or not. Don't tell *us* you wouldn't paper it. What do you mean, boy?"

"I'll explain to you, then," said the gentleman, after another and a dismal pause, "why you wouldn't paper a room with representations of horses. Do you ever see horses walking up and down the sides of rooms in reality—in fact? Do you?"

"Yes, sir!" from one half. "No, sir!" from the other.

"Of course, no," said the gentleman, with an indignant look at the wrong half. "Why, then, you are not to see anywhere, what you don't see in fact; you are not to have anywhere, what you don't have in fact. What is called Taste, is only another name for Fact."

Thomas Gradgrind nodded his approbation.

"This is a new principle, a discovery, a great discovery," said the gentleman. "Now, I'll try you again. Suppose you were going to carpet a room. Would you use a carpet having a representation of flowers upon it?"

There being a general conviction by this time that "No, sir!" was always the right answer to this gentleman, the chorus of No was very strong. Only a few feeble stragglers said Yes; among them Sissy Jupe.

"Girl number twenty," said the gentleman, smiling in the calm strength of knowledge.

Sissy blushed, and stood up.

"So you would carpet your room—or your husband's room, if you were a grown woman, and had a husband—with representations of flowers, would you," said the gentleman. "Why would you?"

"If you please, sir, I am very fond of flowers," returned the girl.

"And is that why you would put tables and chairs upon them, and have people walking over them with heavy boots?"

"It wouldn't hurt them, sir. They wouldn't crush and

wither, if you please, sir. They would be the pictures of what was very pretty and pleasant, and I would fancy—"

"Ay, ay, ay! But you mustn't fancy," cried the gentleman, quite elated by coming so happily to his point. "That's it! You are never to fancy."

"You are not, Cecilia Jupe," Thomas Gradgrind solemnly repeated, "to do anything of that kind."

"Fact, fact, fact!" said the gentleman. And "Fact, fact, fact!" repeated Thomas Gradgrind.

"You are to be in all things regulated and governed," said the gentleman, "by fact. We hope to have, before long, a board of fact, composed of commissioners of fact, who will force the people to be a people of fact, and of nothing but fact. You must discard the word Fancy altogether. You have nothing to do with it. You are not to have, in any object of use or ornament, what would be a contradiction in fact. You don't walk upon flowers in fact; you cannot be allowed to walk upon flowers in carpets. You don't find that foreign birds and butterflies come and perch upon your crockery; you cannot be permitted to paint foreign birds and butter-flies upon your crockery. You never meet with quadrupeds going up and down walls; you must not have quadrupeds represented upon walls. You must use," said the gentleman, "for all these purposes, combinations and modifications (in primary colours) of mathematical figures which are susceptible of proof and demonstration. This is the new discovery. This is fact. This is taste."

The girl curtseyed, and sat down. She was very young, and she looked as if she were frightened by the matter of fact prospect the world afforded.

"Now, if Mr. M'Choakumchild," said the gentleman, "will proceed to give his first lesson here, Mr. Gradgrind, I shall be happy, at your request, to observe his mode of procedure."

Mr. Gradgrind was much obliged. "Mr. M'Choakumchild, we only wait for you."

So, Mr. M'Choakumchild began in his best manner. He and some one hundred and forty other schoolmasters had been lately turned at the same time, in the same factory, on the same principles, like so many pianoforte legs. He had been put through an immense variety of paces, and had answered volumes of head-breaking questions. Orthography, etymology, syntax, and prosody, biography, astronomy, geography, and general cosmography, the sciences of compound proportion, algebra, land-surveying and levelling, vocal music, and drawing from models, were all at the ends of his ten chilled fingers. He had worked his stoney way into Her Majesty's most Honourable Privy Council's Schedule B, and had taken the bloom off the higher branches of mathematics and physical science, French, German, Latin, and Greek. He knew all about all the Water Sheds of all the world (whatever they are), and all the histories of all the peoples, and all the names of all the rivers and mountains, and all the productions, manners, and customs of all the countries, and all their boundaries and bearings on the two and thirty points of the compass. Ah, rather overdone, M'Choakumchild. If he had only learnt a little less, how infinitely better he might have taught much more! '

He went to work in this preparatory lesson, not unlike Morgiana in the Forty Thieves: looking into all the vessels ranged before him, one after another, to see what they contained. Say, good M'Choakumchild. When from thy boiling store thou shalt fill each jar brim full by and by, dost thou think that thou wilt always kill outright the robber Fancy lurking within—or sometimes only maim him and distort him?

Home Education

JOHN STUART MILL

[FROM *Autobiography*]

1873

I have no remembrance of the time when I began to learn Greek, I have been told that it was when I was three years old. My earliest recollection on the subject, is that of committing to memory what my father termed vocables, being lists of common Greek words, with their signification in English, which he wrote out for me on cards. Of grammar, until some years later, I learnt no more than the inflexions of the nouns and verbs, but, after a course of vocables, proceeded at once to translation; and I faintly remember going through Æsop's Fables, the first Greek book which I read. The Anabasis, which I remember better, was the second. I learnt no Latin until my eighth year. At that time I had read, under my father's tuition, a number of Greek prose authors, among whom I remember the whole of Herodotus, and of Xenophon's Cyropædia and Memorials of Socrates; some of the lives of the philosophers by Diogenes Laertius; part of Lucian, and Isocrates ad Demonicum and Ad Nicoclem. I also read, in 1813, the first six dialogues (in the common arrangement) of Plato, from the Euthyphron to the Theætetus inclusive: which last dialogue, I venture to think, would have been better omitted, as it was totally impossible I should understand it. But my father, in all his teaching, demanded of me not only the utmost that I could do, but much that I could by no possibility have done. What he was himself willing to undergo for the sake of my instruction, may be judged from the fact, that I went through the whole process of preparing

From Chapter 1.

my Greek lessons in the same room and at the same table at which he was writing: and as in those days Greek and English lexicons were not, and I could make no more use of a Greek and Latin lexicon than could be made without having yet begun to learn Latin, I was forced to have recourse to him for the meaning of every word which I did not know. This incessant interruption, he, one of the most impatient of men, submitted to, and wrote under that interruption several volumes of his History and all else that he had to write during those years.

The only thing besides Greek, that I learnt as a lesson in this part of my childhood, was arithmetic: this also my father taught me: it was the task of the evenings, and I well remember its disagreeableness. But the lessons were only a part of the daily instruction I received. Much of it consisted in the books I read by myself, and my father's discourses to me, chiefly during our walks. From 1810 to the end of 1813 we were living in Newington Green, then an almost rustic neighbourhood. My father's health required considerable and constant exercise, and he walked habitually before breakfast, generally in the green lanes towards Hornsey. In these walks I always accompanied him, and with my earliest recollections of green fields and wild flowers, is mingled that of the account I gave him daily of what I had read the day before. To the best of my remembrance, this was a voluntary rather than a prescribed exercise. I made notes on slips of paper while reading, and from these in the morning walks, I told the story to him; for the books were chiefly histories, of which I read in this manner a great number. . . . I felt a lively interest in Frederic of Prussia during his difficulties, and in Paoli, the Corsican patriot; but when I came to the American war, I took my part, like a child as I was (until set right by my father) on the wrong side, because it was called the English side. . . . Two books which I never wearied of reading were Anson's Voyages, so delightful to most young persons, and a collection (Hawkesworth's, I believe) of Voyages round the World, in four volumes, beginning with Drake and ending with Cook and Bougainville. Of children's books, any more than of playthings, I had scarcely any, except an occasional gift from a relation or acquaintance: among those I had, Robinson Crusoe was pre-eminent, and continued to delight me through all my boyhood. It was not part, however, of my father's system to exclude books of amusement, though he allowed them very sparingly. . . .

In my eighth year I commenced learning Latin, in conjunction with a younger sister, to whom I taught it as I went on, and who afterwards repeated the lessons to my father: and from this time, other sisters and brothers being successively added as pupils, a considerable part of my day's work consisted of this preparatory teaching. . . . I went in this manner through the Latin grammar, and a considerable part of Cornelius Nepos and Cæsar's Commentaries, but afterwards added to the superintendence of these lessons, much longer ones of my own.

In the same year in which I began Latin, I made my first commencement in the Greek poets with the Iliad. After I had made some progress in this, my father put Pope's translation into my hands. It was the first English verse I had cared to read, and it became one of the books in which for many years I most delighted: I think I must have read it from twenty to thirty times through. . . . Soon after this time I commenced Euclid, and somewhat later, Algebra, still under my father's tuition. . . .

During the same years I learnt elementary geometry and algebra thoroughly, the differential calculus, and other portions of the higher mathematics far from thoroughly: for my father, not having kept up this part of his early acquired knowledge, could not spare time to qualify himself for removing my difficulties, and left me to deal with them, with little other aid than that of books: while I was continually incurring his displeasure by my inability to solve difficult problems for which he did not see that I had not the necessary previous knowledge. . . .

Shakspeare my father had put into my hands, chiefly for the sake of the historical plays, from which, however, I went on to the others. My father never was a great admirer of

Shakspeare, the English idolatry of whom he used to attack with some severity. He cared little for any English poetry except Milton (for whom he had the highest admiration), Goldsmith, Burns, and Gray's Bard, which he preferred to his Elegy: perhaps I may add Cowper and Beattie. He had some value for Spenser, and I remember his reading to me (unlike his usual practice of making me read to him), the first book of the Fairie Queene; but I took little pleasure in it. The poetry of the present century he saw scarcely any merit in, and I hardly became acquainted with any of it till I was grown up to manhood, except the metrical romances of Walter Scott, which I read at his recommendation, and was intensely delighted with; as I always was with animated narrative. Dryden's Poems were among my father's books, and many of these he made me read, but I never cared for any of them except Alexander's Feast, which, as well as many of the songs in Walter Scott, I used to sing internally, to a music of my own: to some of the latter, indeed, I went so far as to compose airs, which I still remember. Cowper's short poems I read with some pleasure, but never got far into the longer ones; and nothing in the two volumes interested me like the prose account of his three hares. In my thirteenth year I met with Campbell's poems, among which Lochiel, Hohenlinden, The Exile of Erin, and some others, gave me sensations I had never before experienced from poetry. Here, too, I made nothing of the longer poems, except the striking opening of Gertrude of Wyoming, which long kept its place in my feelings as the perfection of pathos.

During this part of my childhood, one of my greatest amusements was experimental science; in the theoretical, however, not the practical sense of the word; not trying experiments— a kind of discipline which I have often regretted not having had—nor even seeing, but merely reading about them. I never remember being so wrapt up in any book, as I was in Joyce's Scientific Dialogues; and I was rather recalcitrant to my father's criticisms of the bad reasoning respecting the first principles of physics, which abounds in the early part of that work. I devoured treatises on Chemistry, especially that of my father's early friend and schoolfellow, Dr. Thomson, for years before I attended a lecture or saw an experiment.

From about the age of twelve, I entered into another and more advanced stage in my course of instruction; in which the main object was no longer the aids and appliances of thought, but the thoughts themselves. This commenced with Logic, in which I began at once with the Organon, and read it to the Analytics inclusive, but profited little by the Posterior Analytics, which belong to a branch of speculation I was not yet ripe for. Contemporaneously with the Organon, my father made me read the whole or parts of several of the Latin treatises on the scholastic logic; giving each day to him, in our walks, a minute account of what I had read, and answering his numerous and searching questions. After this, I went in a similar manner, through the "Computatio sive Logica" of Hobbes, a work of a much higher order of thought than the books of the school logicians, and which he estimated very highly; in my own opinion beyond its merits, great as these are. . . .

My own consciousness and experience ultimately led me to appreciate quite as highly as he did, the value of an early practical familiarity with the school logic. I know of nothing, in my education, to which I think myself more indebted for whatever capacity of thinking I have attained. The first intellectual operation in which I arrived at any proficiency, was dissecting a bad argument, and finding in what part the fallacy lay: and though whatever capacity of this sort I attained, was due to the fact that it was an intellectual exercise in which I was most perseveringly drilled by my father, yet it is also true that the school logic, and the mental habits acquired in studying it, were among the principal instruments of this drilling. I am persuaded that nothing, in modern education, tends so much, when properly used, to form exact thinkers, who attach a precise meaning to words and propositions, and are not imposed on by vague, loose, or ambiguous terms. The boasted influence of mathematical studies is nothing to it; for in mathematical processes, none of the real difficulties of correct ratiocination occur. . . .

During this time, the Latin and Greek books which I continued to read with my father were chiefly such as were worth studying, not for the language merely, but also for the thoughts. This included much of the orators, and especially Demosthenes, some of whose principal orations I read several times over, and wrote out, by way of exercise, a full analysis of them. . . . At this time I also read the whole of Tacitus, Juvenal, and Quintilian. The latter, owing to his obscure style and to the scholastic details of which many parts of his treatise are made up, is little read, and seldom sufficiently appreciated. His book is a kind of encyclopædia of the thoughts of the ancients on the whole field of education and culture; and I have retained through life many valuable ideas which I can distinctly trace to my reading of him, even at that early age. It was at this period that I read, for the first time, some of the most important dialogues of Plato, in particular the Gorgias, the Protagoras, and the Republic. There is no author to whom my father thought himself more indebted for his own mental culture, than Plato, or whom he more frequently recommended to young students. I can bear similar testimony in regard to myself. The Socratic method, of which the Platonic dialogues are the chief example, is unsurpassed as a discipline for correcting the errors, and clearing up the confusions incident to the *intellectus sibi permissus*, the understanding which has made up all its bundles of associations under the guidance of popular phraseology. . . .

In going through Plato and Demosthenes, since I could now read these authors, as far as the language was concerned, with perfect ease, I was not required to construe them sentence by sentence, but to read them aloud to my father, answering questions when asked: but the particular attention which he paid to elocution (in which his own excellence was remarkable) made this reading aloud to him a most painful task. Of all things which he required me to do, there was none which I did so constantly ill, or in which he so perpetually lost his temper with me. He had thought much on the principles of the art of reading, especially the most neglected part of it, the inflections of the voice, or *modulation* as writers on elocution call it (in contrast with *articulation* on the one side, and *expression* on the other), and had reduced it to rules, grounded on the logical analysis of a sentence. These rules he strongly impressed upon me, and took me severely to task for every violation of them; but I even then remarked (though I did not venture to make the remark to him) that though he reproached me when I read a sentence ill, and *told* me how I ought to have read it, he never, by reading it himself, *showed* me how it ought to be read. A defect running through his otherwise admirable modes of instruction, as it did through all his modes of thoughts, was that of trusting too much to the intelligibleness of the abstract, when not embodied in the concrete. . . .

A book which contributed largely to my education, in the best sense of the term, was my father's History of India. It was published in the beginning of 1818. During the year previous, while it was passing through the press, I used to read the proof sheets to him; or rather, I read the manuscript to him while he corrected the proofs. The number of new ideas which I received from this remarkable book, and the impulse and stimulus as well as guidance given to my thoughts by its criticisms and disquisitions on society and civilization in the Hindoo part, on institutions and the acts of governments in the English part, made my early familiarity with it eminently useful to my subsequent progress. . . .

This new employment of his time [in the East India Company] caused no relaxation in his attention to my education. It was this same year, 1819, that he took me through a complete course of political economy. His loved and intimate friend, Ricardo, had shortly before published the book which formed so great an epoch in political economy; a book which never would have been published or written, but for the entreaty and strong encouragement of my father. . . .

Though Ricardo's great work was already in print, no didactic treatise embodying its doctrines, in a manner fit for learners, had yet appeared. My father, therefore, commenced instructing me in the science by a sort of lectures, which he delivered to me in our walks. He expounded each day a portion of the subject, and I gave him next day a written account of it, which he made me rewrite over and over again until it was clear, precise, and tolerably complete. In this manner I went through the whole extent of the science. . . .

On Money, as the most intricate part of the subject, he made me read in the same manner Ricardo's admirable pamphlets, written during what was called the Bullion controversy; to these succeeded Adam Smith; and in this reading it was one of my father's main objects to make me apply to Smith's more superficial view of political economy, the superior lights of Ricardo, and detect what was fallacious in Smith's arguments, or erroneous in any of his conclusions. . . . I do not believe that any scientific teaching ever was more thorough, or better fitted for training the faculties, than the mode in which logic and political economy were taught to me by my father. Striving, even in an exaggerated degree, to call forth the activity of my faculties, by making me find out everything for myself, he gave his explanations not before, but after, I had felt the full force of the difficulties; and not only gave me an accurate knowledge of these two great subjects, as far as they were then understood, but made me a thinker on both. I thought for myself almost from the first, and occasionally thought differently from him, though for a long time only on minor points, and making his opinion the ultimate standard. At a later period I even occasionally convinced him, and altered his opinion on some points of detail: which I state to his honour, not my own. It at once exemplifies his perfect candour, and the real worth of his method of teaching.

At this point concluded what can properly be called my lessons: when I was about fourteen I left England for more than a year; and after my return, though my studies went on under my father's general direction, he was no longer my schoolmaster. . . .

In the course of instruction which I have partially retraced, the point most superficially apparent is the great effort to give, during the years of childhood an amount of knowledge in what are considered the higher branches of education, which is seldom acquired (if acquired at all) until the age of man-hood. The result of the experiment shows the ease with which this may be done, and places in a strong light the wretched waste of so many precious years as are spent in acquiring the modicum of Latin and Greek commonly taught to school-boys; a waste which has led so many educational reformers to entertain the ill-judged proposal of discarding these languages altogether from general education. If I had been by nature extremely quick of apprehension, or had possessed a very accurate and retentive memory, or were of a remarkably active and energetic character, the trial would not be con-clusive, but in all these natural gifts I am rather below than above par; what I could do, could assuredly be done by any boy or girl of average capacity and healthy physical consti-tution: and if I have accomplished anything, I owe it, among other fortunate circumstances, to the fact that through the early training bestowed on me by my father, I started, I may fairly say, with an advantage of a quarter of a century over my contemporaries. . . .

Mine, however, was not an education of cram. My father never permitted anything which I learnt to degenerate into a mere exercise of memory. He strove to make the under-standing not only go along with every step of the teaching, but, if possible, precede it. Anything which could be found out by thinking I never was told, until I had exhausted my efforts to find it out for myself. As far as I can trust my remembrance, I acquitted myself very lamely in this de-partment; my recollection of such matters is almost wholly of failures, hardly ever of success. It is true the failures were often in things in which success in so early a stage of my progress, was almost impossible. I remember at some time in my thirteenth year, on my happening to use the word idea, he asked me what an idea was; and expressed some dis-pleasure at my ineffectual efforts to define the word: I re-collect also his indignation at my using the common expression that something was true in theory but required correction in practice; and how, after making me vainly strive to define the word theory, he explained its meaning, and showed the fallacy of the vulgar form of speech which I had used; leaving me fully persuaded that in being unable to give a correct definition of Theory, and in speaking of it as something which might be at variance with practice, I had shown unparalleled ignorance. In this he seems, and perhaps was, very unreasonable; but I think, only in being angry at my failure. A pupil from whom nothing is ever demanded which he cannot do, never does all he can.

One of the evils most liable to attend on any sort of early proficiency, and which often fatally blights its promise, my father most anxiously guarded against. This was self-conceit. He kept me, with extreme vigilance, out of the way of hearing myself praised, or of being led to make self-flattering comparisons between myself and others. . . . I neither estimated myself highly nor lowly: I did not estimate myself at all. If I thought anything about myself, it was that I was rather backward in my studies, since I always found myself so, in comparison with what my father expected from me. . . .

It is evident that this, among many other of the purposes of my father's scheme of education, could not have been accomplished if he had not carefully kept me from having any great amount of intercourse with other boys. He was earnestly bent upon my escaping not only the corrupting influence which boys exercise over boys, but the contagion of vulgar modes of thought and feeling; and for this he was willing that I should pay the price of inferiority in the accomplishments which schoolboys in all countries chiefly cultivate. The deficiencies in my education were principally in the things which boys learn from being turned out to shift for themselves, and from being brought together in large numbers. From temperance and much walking, I grew up healthy and hardy, though not muscular; but I could do no feats of skill or physical strength, and knew none of the ordinary bodily exercises. It was not that play, or time for it, was refused me. Though no holidays were allowed, lest the habit of work should be broken, and a taste for idleness acquired, I had ample leisure in every day to amuse myself; but as I had no boy companions, and the animal need of physical activity was satisfied by walking, my amusements, which were mostly solitary, were in general, of a quiet, if not a bookish turn, and gave little stimulus to any other kind even of mental activity than that which was already called forth by my studies: I consequently remained long, and in a less degree have always remained, inexpert in anything requiring manual dexterity; my mind, as well as my hands, did its work very lamely when it was applied, or ought to have been applied, to the practical details which, as they are the chief interest of life to the majority of men, are also the things in which whatever mental capacity they have, chiefly shows itself. . . . The education which my father gave me, was in itself much more fitted for training me to *know* than to *do*. Not that he was unaware of my deficiencies; both as a boy and as a youth I was incessantly smarting under his severe admonitions on the subject. There was anything but insensibility or tolerance on his part towards such shortcomings: but, while he saved me from the demoralizing effects of school life, he made no effort to provide me with any sufficient substitute for its practicalizing influences. Whatever qualities he himself, probably, had acquired without difficulty or special training, he seems to have supposed that I ought to acquire as easily. He had not, I think, bestowed the same amount of thought and attention on this, as on most other branches of education; and here, as well in some other points of my tuition, he seems to have expected effects without causes.

Football at Rugby

THOMAS HUGHES

[FROM *Tom Brown's School Days*]

1857

"Hold the punt-about!" "To the goals!" are the cries, and all stray balls are impounded by the authorities, and the whole mass of boys moves up towards the two goals, dividing as they go into three bodies. That little band on the left, consisting of from fifteen to twenty boys, Tom amongst them, who are making for the goal under the School-house wall, are the School-house boys who are not to play-up, and have to stay in goal. The larger body moving to the island goal, are the school-boys in a like predicament. The great mass in the middle are the players-up, both sides mingled together; they are hanging their jackets, and all who mean real work, their hats, waistcoats, neck-handkerchiefs, and braces, on the railings round the small trees; and there they go by twos and threes up to their respective grounds. There is none of the colour and tastiness of get-up, you will perceive, which lends such a life to the present game at Rugby, making the dullest and worst fought match a pretty sight. Now each house has its own uniform of cap and jersey, of some lively colour: but at the time we are speaking of, plush caps have not yet come in, or uniforms of any sort, except the School-house white trousers, which are abominably cold to-day: let us get to work, bare-headed and girded with our plain leather straps—but we mean business, gentlemen.

And now that the two sides have fairly sundered, and each occupies its own ground, and we get a good look at them, what absurdity is this? You don't mean to say that those fifty

From Part I, Chapter 5.

or sixty boys in white trousers, many of them quite small, are going to play that huge mass opposite? Indeed I do, gentlemen; they're going to try at any rate, and won't make such a bad fight of it either, mark my word; for hasn't old Brooke won the toss, with his lucky halfpenny, and got choice of goals and kick-off? The new ball you may see lie there quite by itself, in the middle, pointing towards the school or island goal; in another minute it will be well on its way there. . . .

But now look, there is a slight move forward of the School-house wings; a shout of "Are you ready," and loud affirmative reply. Old Brooke takes half-a-dozen quick steps, and away goes the ball spinning towards the School goal; seventy yards before it touches ground, and at no point above twelve or fifteen feet high, a model kick-off; and the School-house cheer and rush on; the ball is returned, and they meet it and drive it back amongst the masses of the School already in motion. Then the two sides close, and you can see nothing for minutes but a swaying crowd of boys, at one point violently agitated. That is where the ball is, and there are the keen players to be met, and the glory and the hard-knocks to be got: you hear the dull thud thud of the ball, and the shouts of "Off your side," "Down with him," "Put him over," "Bravo." This is what we call a scrummage, gentlemen, and the first scrummage in a School-house match was no joke in the consulship of Plancus.

But see! it has broken, the ball is driven out on the School-house side, and a rush of the School carries it past the School-house players-up. "Look out in quarters," Brooke's and twenty other voices ring out; no need to call tho', the School-house captain of quarters has caught it on the bound, dodges the foremost School-boys, who are heading the rush, and sends it back with a good drop-kick well into the enemies' country. And then follows rush upon rush, and scrummage upon scrummage, the ball now driven through into the School-house quarters, and now into the School goal; for the School-house have not lost the advantage which the kick-off and a slight wind gave them at the outset, and are slightly "penning" their adversaries. . . .

Three-quarters of an hour are gone; first winds are failing, and weight and numbers beginning to tell. Yard by yard the School-house have been driven back, contesting every inch of ground. The bull-dogs are the colour of mother earth from shoulder to ancle, except young Brooke, who has a marvellous knack of keeping his legs. The School-house are being penned in their turn, and now the ball is behind their goal, under the Doctor's wall. The Doctor and some of his family are there looking on, and seem as anxious as any boy for the success of the School-house. We get a minute's breathing time before old Brooke kicks out, and he gives the word to play strongly for touch, by the three trees. Away goes the ball, and the bull-dogs after it, and in another minute there is shout of "In touch," "Our ball." Now's your time, old Brooke, while your men are still fresh. He stands with the ball in his hand, while the two sides form in deep lines opposite one another: he must strike it straight out between them. The lines are thickest close to him, but young Brooke and two or three of his men are shifting up further, where the opposite line is weak. Old Brooke strikes it out straight and strong, and it falls opposite his brother. Hurra! that rush has taken it right through the School line, and away past the three trees, far into their quarters, and young Brooke and the bull-dogs are close upon it. The School leaders rush back shouting. "Look out in goal," and strain every nerve to catch him, but they are after the fleetest foot in Rugby. There they go straight for the School goal-posts, quarters scattering before them. One after another the bull-dogs go down, but young Brooke holds on. "He is down," No! a long stagger, but the danger is past; that was the shock of Crew, the most dangerous of dodgers. And now he is close to the School goal, the ball not three yards before him. There is a hurried rush of the School fags to the spot, but no one throws himself on the ball, the only chance, and young Brooke has touched it right under the School goal-posts.

The School leaders come up furious, and administer toco to the wretched fags nearest at hand; they may well be angry, for it is all Lombard-street to a china orange that the School-house kick a goal with the ball touched in such a good place. Old Brooke of course will kick it out, but who shall catch and place it? Call Crab Jones. Here he comes, sauntering along with a straw in his mouth, the queerest, coolest fish in Rugby: if he were tumbled into the moon this minute, he would just pick himself up without taking his hands out of his pockets or turning a hair. But it is a moment when the boldest charger's heart beats quick. Old Brooke stands with the ball under his arm motioning the School back; he will not kick-out till they are all in goal, behind the posts; they are all edging forwards, inch by inch, to get nearer for the rush at Crab Jones, who stands there in front of old Brooke to catch the ball. If they can reach and destroy him before he catches, the danger is over; and with one and the same rush they will carry it right away to the School-house goal. Fond hope! it is kicked out and caught beautifully. Crab strikes his heel into the ground, to mark the spot where the ball was caught, beyond which the School line may not advance; but there they stand, five deep, ready to rush the moment the ball touches the ground. Take plenty of room! don't give the rush a chance of reaching you! place it true and steady! Trust Crab Jones—he has made a small hole with his heel for the ball to lie on, by which he is resting on one knee, with his eye on old Brooke. "Now!" Crab places the ball at the word, old Brooke kicks, and it rises slowly and truly as the School rush forward.

Then a moment's pause, while both sides look up at the spinning ball. There it flies, straight between the two posts, some five feet above the cross-bar, an unquestioned goal; and a shout of real genuine joy rings out from the School-house players-up, and a faint echo of it comes over the close from the goal-keepers under the Doctor's wall. A goal in the first hour—such a thing hasn't been done in the School-house match this five years.

"Over!" is the cry: the two sides change goals, and the School-house goal-keepers come threading their way across through the masses of the School; the most openly triumphant of them, amongst whom is Tom, a School-house boy of two hours' standing, getting their ears boxed in the transit. Tom indeed is excited beyond measure, and it is all the sixth-form boy, kindest and safest of goal-keepers, has been able to do, to keep him from rushing out whenever the ball has been near their goal. So he holds him by his side, and instructs him in the science of touching. . . .

The quarter to five has struck, and the play slackens for a minute before goal; but there is Crew, the artful dodger, driving the ball in behind our goal, on the island side, where our quarters are weakest. Is there no one to meet him? Yes! look at little East! the ball is just at equal distances between the two, and they rush together, the young man of seventeen and the boy of twelve, and kick it at the same moment. Crew passes on without a stagger; East is hurled forward by the shock, and plunges on his shoulder, as if he would bury himself in the ground; but the ball rises straight into the air, and falls behind Crew's back, while the "bravos" of the School-house attest the pluckiest charge of all that hard-fought day. Warner picks East up lame and half stunned, and he hobbles back into goal, conscious of having played the man.

And now the last minutes are come, and the School gather for their last rush every boy of the hundred and twenty who has a run left in him. Reckless of the defence of their own goal, on they come across the level big-side ground, the ball well down amongst them, straight for our goal, like the column of the old guard up the slope at Waterloo. All former charges have been child's play to this. Warner and Hedge have met them, but still on they come. The bull-dogs rush in for the last time; they are hurled over or carried back, striving hand, foot, and eyelids. Old Brooke comes sweeping round the skirts of the play, and turning short round, picks out the very heart of the scrummage, and plunges in. It wavers for a moment—he has the ball! No, it has passed him, and his voice rings out clear over the advancing tide, "Look out in goal." Crab Jones catches it for a moment; but before he can kick, the rush is upon him and passes over him; and he picks himself up behind them with his straw in his mouth, a little dirtier, but as cool as ever.

The ball rolls slowly in behind the School-house goal, not three yards in front of a dozen of the biggest School players-up.

There stand the School-house præpostor, safest of goal-keepers, and Tom Brown by his side, who has learned his trade by this time. Now is your time, Tom. The blood of all the Browns is up, and the two rush in together, and throw themselves on the ball, under the very feet of the advancing column; the præpostor on his hands and knees arching his back, and Tom all along on his face. Over them topple the leaders of the rush, shooting over the back of the præpostor, but falling flat on Tom, and knocking all the wind out of his small carcase. "Our ball," says the præpostor, rising with his prize, "but get up there, there's a little fellow under you." They are hauled and roll off him, and Tom is discovered a motionless body.

Old Brooke picks him up. "Stand back, give him air," he says; and then feeling his limbs, adds, "No bones broken. How do you feel, young'un?"

"Hah-hah," gasps Tom as his wind comes back, "pretty well thank you—all right."

"Who is he?" says Brooke. "Oh, it's Brown, he's a new boy; I know him," says East, coming up.

"Well, he is a plucky youngster, and will make a player," says Brooke.

And five o'clock strikes. "No side" is called, and the first day of the School-house match is over.

Friendship Tested

THOMAS HUGHES

[FROM *Tom Brown's School Days*]

1857

Tom, besides being very like East in many points of character, had largely developed in his composition the capacity for taking the weakest side. This is not putting it strongly enough; it was a necessity with him, he couldn't help it any more than he could eating or drinking. He could never play on the strongest side with any heart at foot-ball or cricket, and was sure to make friends with any boy who was unpopular, or down on his luck.

Now though East was not what is generally called unpopular, Tom felt more and more every day, as their characters developed, that he stood alone, and did not make friends among their contemporaries; and therefore sought him out. Tom was himself much more popular, for his power of detecting humbug was much less acute, and his instincts were much more sociable. He was at this period of his life, too, largely given to taking people for what they gave themselves out to be; but his singleness of heart, fearlessness, and honesty were just what East appreciated, and thus the two had been drawn into great intimacy.

This intimacy had not been interrupted by Tom's guardianship of Arthur.

East had often, as has been said, joined them in reading the Bible; but their discussions had almost always turned upon the characters of the men and women of whom they read, and not become personal to themselves. In fact, the two had shrunk from personal religious discussion, not knowing

From Part II, Chapter 7.

how it might end; and fearful of risking a friendship very dear to both, and which they felt somehow, without quite knowing why, would never be the same, but either tenfold stronger or sapped at its foundation, after such a communing together.

What a bother all this explaining is! I wish we could get on without it. But we can't. However, you'll all find, if you haven't found it out already, that a time comes in every human friendship, when you must go down into the depths of yourself, and lay bare what is there to your friend, and wait in fear for his answer. A few moments may do it; and, it may be (most likely will be, as you are English boys) that you never do it but once. But done it must be, if the friendship is to be worth the name. You must find what is there, at the very root and bottom of one another's hearts; and if you are at one there, nothing on earth can, or at least ought to sunder you.

East had remained lying down until Tom finished speaking, as if fearing to interrupt him; he now sat up at the table and leant his head on one hand, taking up a pencil with the other and working little holes with it in the table-cover. After a bit he looked up, stopped the pencil, and said, "Thank you very much, old fellow; there's no other boy in the house would have done it for me but you or Arthur. I can see well enough," he went on after a pause, "all the best big fellows look on me with suspicion; they think I'm a devil-may-care reckless young scamp—So I am—eleven hours out of twelve—but not the twelfth. Then all of our contemporaries worth knowing follow suit, of course; we're very good friends at games and all that, but not a soul of them but you and Arthur ever tried to break through the crust, and see whether there was anything at the bottom of me; and then the bad ones I won't stand, and they know that."

"Don't you think that's half fancy, Harry?"

"Not a bit of it," said East bitterly, pegging away with his pencil. "I see it all plain enough. Bless you, you think everybody's as straightforward and kind-hearted as you are."

"Well, but what's the reason of it? There must be a reason.

You can play all the games as well as any one, and sing the best song, and are the best company in the house. You fancy you're not liked, Harry. It's all fancy."

"I only wish it was, Tom. I know I could be popular enough with all the bad ones, but that I won't have, and the good ones won't have me."

"Why not?" persisted Tom; "you don't drink or swear, or get out at night; you never bully, or cheat at lessons. If you only showed you liked it, you'd have all the best fellows in the house running after you."

"Not I," said East. Then with an effort he went on, "I'll tell you what it is. I never stop the Sacrament. I can see from the Doctor downwards, how that tells against me."

"Yes, I've seen that," said Tom, "and I've been very sorry for it, and Arthur and I have talked about it. I've often thought of speaking to you, but it's so hard to begin on such subjects. I'm very glad you've opened it. Now, why don't you?"

"I've never been confirmed," said East.

"Not been confirmed!" said Tom, in astonishment. "I never thought of that. Why weren't you confirmed with the rest of us nearly three years ago? I always thought you'd been confirmed at home."

"No," answered East sorrowfully; "you see this was how it happened. Last Confirmation was soon after Arthur came, and you were so taken up with him, I hardly saw either of you. Well, when the Doctor sent round for us about it, I was living mostly with Green's set—you know the sort. They all went in—I daresay it was all right, and they got good by it; I don't want to judge them. Only all I could see of their reasons drove me just the other way. 'Twas, 'because the Doctor liked it'; 'no boy got on who didn't stay the Sacrament'; it was 'the correct thing,' in fact, like having a good hat to wear on Sundays. I couldn't stand it. I didn't feel that I wanted to lead a different life, I was very well content as I was, and I wasn't going to sham religious to curry favour with the Doctor, or any one else."

East stopped speaking, and pegged away more diligently

than ever with his pencil. Tom was ready to cry. He felt half sorry at first that he had been confirmed himself. He seemed to have deserted his earliest friend, to have left him by himself at his worst need for those long years. He got up and went and sat by East, and put his arm over his shoulder.

"Dear old boy," he said, "how careless and selfish I've been. But why didn't you come and talk to Arthur and me?"

"I wish to heaven I had," said East, "but I was a fool. It's too late talking of it now."

"Why too late? You want to be confirmed now, don't you?"

"I think so," said East. "I've thought about it a good deal: only often I fancy I must be changing, because I see it's to do me good here, just what stopped me last time. And then I go back again.". . .

"I say now," said Tom eagerly, "do you remember how we both hated Flashman?"

"Of course I do," said East; "I hate him still. What then?"

"Well, when I came to take the Sacrament, I had a great struggle about that. I tried to put him out of my head; and when I couldn't do that, I tried to think of him as evil, as something that the Lord who was loving me hated, and which I might hate too. But it wouldn't do. I broke down; I believe Christ himself broke me down; and when the Doctor gave me the bread and wine, and leant over me praying, I prayed for poor Flashman as if it had been you or Arthur."

East buried his face in his hands on the table. Tom could feel the table tremble. At last he looked up, "Thank you again, Tom," said he; "you don't know what you may have done for me to-night. I think I see now how the right sort of sympathy with poor devils is got at."

"And you'll stop the Sacrament next time, won't you?" said Tom.

"Can I, before I'm confirmed?"

"Go and ask the Doctor."

"I will."

That very night, after prayers, East followed the Doctor and the old Verger bearing the candle, up-stairs. Tom watched, and saw the Doctor turn round when he heard footsteps following him closer than usual, and say, "Hah, East! Do you want to speak to me, my man?"

"If you please, sir"; and the private door closed, and Tom went to his study in a state of great trouble of mind.

It was almost an hour before East came back; then he rushed in breathless.

"Well, it's all right," he shouted, seizing Tom by the hand. "I feel as if a ton weight were off my mind."

"Hurra," said Tom; "I knew it would be, but tell us all about it."

"Well, I just told him all about it. You can't think how kind and gentle he was, the great grim man, whom I've feared more than anybody on earth. When I stuck, he lifted me, just as if I'd been a little child. And he seemed to know all I'd felt, and to have gone through it all. And I burst out crying—more than I've done this five years, and he sat down by me, and stroked my head; and I went blundering on, and told him all; much worse things than I've told you. And he wasn't shocked a bit, and didn't snub me, or tell me I was a fool, and it was all nothing but pride or wickedness, tho' I dare say it was. And he didn't tell me not to follow out my thoughts, and he didn't give me any cut-and-dried explanation. But when I'd done he just talked a bit—I can hardly remember what he said, yet; but it seemed to spread round me like healing, and strength, and light; and to bear me up, and plant me on a rock, where I could hold my footing and fight for myself. I don't know what to do, I feel so happy. And it's all owing to you, dear old boy!" and he seized Tom's hand again.

"And you're to come to the Communion?" said Tom.

"Yes, and to be confirmed in the holidays."

Tom's delight was as great as his friend's. But he hadn't yet had out all his own talk, and was bent on improving the occasion: so he proceeded to propound Arthur's theory about not being sorry for his friends' deaths, which he had hitherto kept in the background, and by which he was much exercised; for he didn't feel it honest to take what pleased him and throw over the rest, and was trying vigorously to persuade himself that he should like all his best friends to die off-hand.

But East's powers of remaining serious were exhausted, and in five minutes he was saying the most ridiculous things he could think of, till Tom was almost getting angry again.

Despite of himself, however, he couldn't help laughing and giving it up, when East appealed to him with "Well, Tom, you ain't going to punch my head, I hope, because I insist upon being sorry when you got to earth?"

And so their talk finished for that time, and they tried to learn first lesson; with very poor success, as appeared next morning, when they were called up and narrowly escaped being floored, which ill-luck however did not sit heavily on either of their souls.

The True University

THOMAS CARLYLE

[FROM *On Heroes and Hero Worship:* "The Hero as Man of Letters"]

1841

Certainly the Art of Writing is the most miraculous of all things man has devised. Odin's *Runes* were the first form of the work of a Hero; *Books,* written words, are still miraculous *Runes,* the latest form! In Books lies the *soul* of the whole Past Time; the articulate audible voice of the Past, when the body and material substance of it has altogether vanished like a dream. Mighty fleets and armies, harbours and arsenals,

From Lecture 5.

vast cities, high-domed, many-engined,—they are precious, great: but what do they become? Agamemnon, the many Agamemnons, Pericleses, and their Greece; all is gone now to some ruined fragments, dumb mournful wrecks and blocks: but the Books of Greece! There Greece, to every thinker, still very literally lives; can be called-up again into life. No magic *Rune* is stranger than a Book. All that Mankind has done, thought, gained or been: it is lying as in magic preservation in the pages of Books. They are the chosen possession of men.

Do not Books still accomplish *miracles,* as *Runes* were fabled to do? They persuade men. Not the wretchedest circulating-library novel, which foolish girls thumb and con in remote villages, but will help to regulate the actual practical weddings and households of those foolish girls. So 'Celia' felt, so 'Clifford' acted: the foolish Theorem of Life, stamped into those young brains, comes out as a solid Practice one day. Consider whether any *Rune* in the wildest imagination of Mythologist ever did such wonders as, on the actual firm Earth, some Books have done! What built St. Paul's Cathedral? Look at the heart of the matter, it was that divine HEBREW Book,—the word partly of the man Moses, an outlaw tending his Midianitish herds, four thousand years ago, in the wildernesses of Sinai! It is the strangest of things, yet nothing is truer. With the art of Writing, of which Printing is a simple, an inevitable and comparatively insignificant corollary, the true reign of miracles for mankind commenced. It related, with a wondrous new contiguity and perpetual closeness, the Past and Distant with the Present in time and place; all times and all places with this our actual Here and Now. All things were altered for men; all modes of important work of men: teaching, preaching, governing, and all else.

To look at Teaching, for instance. Universities are a notable, respectable product of the modern ages. Their existence too is modified, to the very basis of it, by the existence of Books. Universities arose while there were yet no Books procurable; while a man, for a single Book, had to give an estate of land. That, in those circumstances, when a man had some knowledge to communicate, he should do it by gathering the learners round him, face to face, was a necessity for him. If you wanted to know what Abelard knew, you must go and listen to Abelard. Thousands, as many as thirty thousand, went to hear Abelard and that metaphysical theology of his. And now for any other teacher who had also something of his own to teach, there was a great convenience opened: so many thousands eager to learn were already assembled yonder; of all places the best place for him was that. For any third teacher it was better still; and grew ever the better, the more teachers there came. It only needed now that the King took notice of this new phenomenon; combined or agglomerated the various schools into one school; gave it edifices, privileges, encouragements, and named it *Universitas,* or School of all Sciences: the University of Paris, in its essential characters, was there. The model of all subsequent Universities; which down even to these days, for six centuries now, have gone on to found themselves. Such, I conceive, was the origin of Universities.

It is clear, however, that with this simple circumstance, facility of getting Books, the whole conditions of the business from top to bottom were changed. Once invent Printing, you metamorphosed all Universities, or superseded them! The teacher needed not now to gather men personally round him, that he might *speak* to them what he knew: print it in a Book, and all learners far and wide, for a trifle, had it each at his own fireside, much more effectually to learn it!— Doubtless there is still peculiar virtue in Speech; even writers of Books may still, in some circumstances, find it convenient to speak also,—witness our present meeting here! There is, one would say, and must ever remain while man has a tongue, a distinct province for Speech as well as for Writing and Printing. In regard to all things this must remain; to Universities among others. But the limits of the two have nowhere yet been pointed out, ascertained; much less put in practice: the University which would completely take-in that great new fact, of the existence of Printed Books, and stand on a clear footing for the Nineteenth Century as the Paris one did for the Thirteenth, has not yet come into existence If we think of it, all that a University, or final highest School can do for us, is still but what the first School began doing,—teach us to *read*. We learn to *read*, in various languages, in various sciences; we learn the alphabet and letters of all manner of Books. But the place where we are to get knowledge, even theoretic knowledge, is the Books themselves! It depends on what we read, after all manner of Professors have done their best for us. The true University of these days is a Collection of Books.

Knowledge Its Own End

JOHN HENRY NEWMAN

[FROM *The Idea of a University*]

1865

I have said that all branches of knowledge are connected together, because the subject-matter of knowledge is intimately united in itself, as being the acts and the work of the Creator. Hence it is that the Sciences, into which our knowledge may be said to be cast, have multiplied bearings one on another, and an internal sympathy, and admit, or rather demand, comparison and adjustment. They complete, correct, balance each other. This consideration, if well-founded, must be taken into account, not only as regards the attainment of truth, which is their common end, but as regards the influence which they exercise upon those whose education consists in the study of them. I have said already, that to give undue prominence to one is to be unjust to another; to neglect or

From Discourse 5.

supersede these is to divert those from their proper object. It is to unsettle the boundary lines between science and science, to disturb their action, to destroy the harmony which binds them together. Such a proceeding will have a corresponding effect when introduced into a place of education. There is no science but tells a different tale, when viewed as a portion of a whole, from what it is likely to suggest when taken by itself, without the safeguard, as I may call it, of others.

Let me make use of an illustration. In the combination of colours, very different effects are produced by a difference in their selection and juxtaposition; red, green, and white change their shades, according to the contrast to which they are submitted. And, in like manner, the drift and meaning of a branch of knowledge varies with the company in which it is introduced to the student. If his reading is confined simply to one subject, however such division of labour may favour the advancement of a particular pursuit, a point into which I do not here enter, certainly it has a tendency to contract his mind. If it is incorporated with others, it depends on those others as to the kind of influence which it exerts upon him. Thus the Classics, which in England are the means of refining the taste, have in France subserved the spread of revolutionary and deistical doctrines. In Metaphysics, again, Butler's *Analogy of Religion,* which has had so much to do with the conversion to the Catholic faith of members of the University of Oxford, appeared to Pitt and others, who had received a different training, to operate only in the direction of infidelity. And so again, Watson, Bishop of Llandaff, as I think he tells us in the narrative of his life, felt the science of Mathematics to indispose the mind to religious belief, while others see in its investigations the best parallel, and thereby defence, of the Christian Mysteries. In like manner, I suppose, Arcesilaus would not have handled logic as Aristotle, nor Aristotle have criticized poets as Plato; yet reasoning and poetry are subject to scientific rules.

It is a great point then to enlarge the range of studies which a University professes, even for the sake of the students;

and, though they cannot pursue every subject which is open to them, they will be the gainers by living among those and under those who represent the whole circle. This I conceive to be the advantage of a seat of universal learning, considered as a place of education. An assemblage of learned men, zealous for their own sciences, and rivals of each other, are brought, by familiar intercourse and for the sake of intellectual peace, to adjust together the claims and relations of their respective subjects of investigation. They learn to respect, to consult, to aid each other. Thus is created a pure and clear atmosphere of thought, which the student also breathes, though in his own case he only pursues a few sciences out of the multitude. He profits by an intellectual tradition, which is independent of particular teachers, which guides him in his choice of subjects, and duly interprets for him those which he chooses. He apprehends the great outlines of knowledge, the principles on which it rests, the scale of its parts, its lights and its shades, its great points and its little, as he otherwise cannot apprehend them. Hence it is that his education is called 'Liberal.' A habit of mind is formed which lasts through life, of which the attributes are, freedom, equitableness, calmness, moderation, and wisdom; or what in a former Discourse I have ventured to call a philosophical habit. This then I would assign as the special fruit of the education furnished at a University, as contrasted with other places of teaching or modes of teaching. This is the main purpose of a University in its treatment of its students.

And now the question is asked me, What is the *use* of it? and my answer will constitute the main subject of the Discourses which are to follow.

Cautious and practical thinkers, I say, will ask of me, what, after all, is the gain of this Philosophy, of which I make such account, and from which I promise so much. . . . I am asked what is the end of University Education, and of the Liberal or Philosophical Knowledge which I conceive it to impart: I answer, that what I have already said has been sufficient to show that it has a very tangible, real, and sufficient end, though the end cannot be divided from that knowledge itself. Knowledge is capable of being its own end. Such is the constitution of the human mind, that any kind of knowledge, if it be really such, is its own reward. And if this is true of all knowledge, it is true also of that special Philosophy, which I have made to consist in a comprehensive view of truth in all its branches, of the relations of science to science, of their mutual bearings, and their respective values. What the worth of such an acquirement is, compared with other objects which we seek,—wealth or power or honour or the conveniences and comforts of life, I do not profess here to discuss; but I would maintain, and mean to show, that it is an object, in its own nature so really and undeniably good, as to be the compensation of a great deal of thought in the compassing, and a great deal of trouble in the attaining. . . .

Hence it is that Cicero, in enumerating the various heads of mental excellence, lays down the pursuit of Knowledge for its own sake, as the first of them. 'This pertains most of all to human nature,' he says, 'for we are all of us drawn to the pursuit of Knowledge; in which to excel we consider excellent, whereas to mistake, to err, to be ignorant, to be deceived, is both an evil and a disgrace.' And he considers Knowledge the very first object to which we are attracted, after the supply of our physical wants. After the calls and duties of our animal existence, as they may be termed, as regards ourselves, our family, and our neighbours, follows, he tells us, 'the search after truth.' . . . The idea of benefiting society by means of 'the pursuit of science and knowledge,' did not enter at all into the motives which he would assign for their cultivation.

This was the ground of the opposition which the elder Cato made to the introduction of Greek Philosophy among his countrymen, when Carneades and his companions, on occasion of their embassy, were charming the Roman youth with their eloquent expositions of it. The fit representative of a practical people, Cato estimated everything by what it produced; whereas the Pursuit of Knowledge promised nothing beyond Knowledge itself. He despised that refinement or enlargement of mind of which he had no experience.

Things, which can bear to be cut off from everything else and yet persist in living, must have life in themselves; pursuits, which issue in nothing, and still maintain their ground for ages, which are regarded as admirable, though they have not as yet proved themselves to be useful, must have their sufficient end in themselves, whatever it turn out to be. And we are brought to the same conclusion by considering the force of the epithet, by which the knowledge under consideration is popularly designated. It is common to speak of *'liberal* knowledge,' of the *'liberal* arts and studies,' and of a *'liberal* education,' as the especial characteristic or property of a University and of a gentleman; what is really meant by the word? Now, first, in its grammatical sense it is opposed to *servile*; and by 'servile work' is understood, as our catechisms inform us, bodily labour, mechanical employment, and the like, in which the mind has little or no part. Parallel to such servile works are those arts, if they deserve the name, of which the poet speaks, which owe their origin and their method to hazard, not to skill; as, for instance, the practice and operations of an empiric. As far as this contrast may be considered as a guide into the meaning of the word, liberal education and liberal pursuits are exercises of mind, of reason, of reflection.

But we want something more for its explanation, for there are bodily exercises which are liberal, and mental exercises which are not so. For instance, in ancient times the practitioners in medicine were commonly slaves; yet it was an art as intellectual in its nature, in spite of the pretence, fraud, and quackery with which it might then, as now, be debased, as it was heavenly in its aim. And so in like manner, we contrast a liberal education with a commercial education or a professional; yet no one can deny that commerce and the professions afford scope for the highest and most diversified powers of mind. There is then a great variety of intellectual exercises, which are not technically called 'liberal'; on the other hand, I say, there are exercises of the body which do receive that appellation. Such, for instance, was the palæstra, in ancient times; such the Olympic games, in which strength and dexterity of body as well as of mind gained the prize. In Xenophon we read of the young Persian nobility being taught to ride on horseback and to speak the truth; both being among the accomplishments of a gentleman. War, too, however rough a profession, has ever been accounted liberal, unless in cases when it becomes heroic, which would introduce us to another subject.

Now comparing these instances together, we shall have no difficulty in determining the principle of this apparent variation in the application of the term which I am examining. Manly games, or games of skill, or military prowess, though bodily, are, it seems, accounted liberal; on the other hand, what is merely professional, though highly intellectual, nay, though liberal in comparison of trade and manual labour, is not simply called liberal, and mercantile occupations are not liberal at all. Why this distinction? because that alone is liberal knowledge, which stands on its own pretensions, which is independent of sequel, expects no complement, refuses to be *informed* (as it is called) by any end, or absorbed into any art, in order duly to present itself to our contemplation. The most ordinary pursuits have this specific character, if they are self-sufficient and complete; the highest lose it, when they minister to something beyond them. It is absurd to balance, in point of worth and importance, a treatise on reducing fractures with a game of cricket or a fox-chase; yet of the two the bodily exercise has that quality which we call 'liberal,' and the intellectual has not. And so of the learned professions altogether, considered merely as professions; although one of them be the most popularly beneficial, and another the most politically important, and the third the most intimately divine of all human pursuits, yet the very greatness of their end, the health of the body, or of the commonwealth, or of the soul, diminishes, not increases, their claim to the application 'liberal,' and that still more, if they are cut down to the strict exigencies of that end. If, for instance, Theology instead of being cultivated as a contemplation, be limited to the purposes of the pulpit or be represented by the catechism, it loses,—not its usefulness, not its divine character, not its meritoriousness, (rather it gains a claim upon these titles by such charitable condescension),—but it does lose the particular attribute which I am illustrating; just as a face worn by tears and fasting loses its beauty, or a labourer's hand loses its delicateness;—for Theology thus exercised is not simple knowledge, but rather is an art or a business making use of Theology. And thus it appears that even what is supernatural need not be liberal, nor need a hero be a gentleman, for the plain reason that one idea is not another idea. And in like manner the Baconian Philosophy, by using its physical sciences in the service of man, does thereby transfer them from the order of Liberal Pursuits to, I do not say the inferior, but the distinct class of the Useful. And, to take a different instance, hence again, as is evident, whenever personal gain is the motive, still more distinctive an effect has it upon the character of a given pursuit; thus racing, which was a liberal exercise in Greece, forfeits its rank in times like these, so far as it is made the occasion of gambling.

All that I have been now saying is summed up in a few characteristic words of the great Philosopher. 'Of possessions,' he says, 'those rather are useful, which bear fruit; those *liberal, which tend to enjoyment.* By fruitful, I mean, which yield revenue; by enjoyable, where *nothing accrues of consequence beyond the using.*'

Now bear with me, Gentlemen, if what I am about to say, has at first sight a fanciful appearance. Philosophy, then, or Science, is related to Knowledge in this way:—Knowledge is called by the name of Science or Philosophy, when it is acted upon, informed, or if I may use a strong figure, impregnated by Reason. Reason is the principle of that intrinsic fecundity of Knowledge, which, to those who possess it, is its especial value, and which dispenses with the necessity of their looking abroad for any end to rest upon external to itself. Knowledge, indeed, when thus exalted into a scientific form, is also power; not only is it excellent in itself, but whatever such excellence may be, it is something more, it has a result beyond itself. Doubtless; but that is a further consideration, with which I am not concerned. I only say that, prior to its being a power, it is a good; that it is, not only an instrument, but an end. I know well it may resolve itself into an art, and terminate in a mechanical process, and in tangible fruit; but it also may fall back upon that Reason which informs it, and resolve itself into Philosophy. In one case it is called Useful Knowledge, in the other Liberal. The same person may cultivate it in both ways at once; but this again is a matter foreign to my subject; here I do but say that there are two ways of using Knowledge, and in matter of fact those who use it in one way are not likely to use it in the other, or at least in a very limited measure. You see, then, here are two methods of Education; the end of the one is to be philosophical, of the other to be mechanical; the one rises towards general ideas, the other is exhausted upon what is particular and external. Let me not be thought to deny the necessity, or to decry the benefit, of such attention to what is particular and practical, as belongs to the useful or mechanical arts; life could not go on without them; we owe our daily welfare to them; their exercise is the duty of the many, and we owe to the many a debt of gratitude for fulfilling that duty. I only say that Knowledge, in proportion as it tends more and more to be particular, ceases to be Knowledge. It is a question whether Knowledge can in any proper sense be predicated of the brute creation; without pretending to metaphysical exactness of phraseology, which would be unsuitable to an occasion like this, I say, it seems to me improper to call that passive sensation, or perception of things, which brutes seem to possess, by the name of Knowledge. When I speak of Knowledge, I mean something intellectual, something which grasps what it perceives through the senses; something which takes a view of things; which sees more than the senses convey; which reasons upon what it sees, and while it sees; which invests it with an idea. It expresses itself, not in a mere enunciation, but by an enthymeme: it is of the nature of science from the first, and in this consists its dignity. The principle of real dignity in Knowledge, its worth, its desirableness, considered irrespectively of its results, is this germ within it of a scientific or a philosophical process. This is how it comes to be an end in itself; this is why it admits of being called Liberal. Not to know the relative disposition of things is the state of slaves or children; to have mapped out the Universe is the boast, or at least the ambition, of Philosophy.

Moreover, such knowledge is not a mere extrinsic or accidental advantage, which is ours to-day and another's to-morrow, which may be got up from a book, and easily forgotten again, which we can command or communicate at our pleasure, which we can borrow for the occasion, carry about in our hand, and take into the market; it is an acquired illumination, it is a habit, a personal possession, and an inward endowment. And this is the reason, why it is more correct, as well as more usual, to speak of a University as a place of education, than of instruction, though, when knowledge is concerned, instruction would at first sight have seemed the more appropriate word. We are instructed, for instance, in manual exercises, in the fine and useful arts, in trades, and in ways of business; for these are methods, which have little or no effect upon the mind itself, are contained in rules committed to memory, to tradition, or to use, and bear upon an end external to themselves. But education is a higher word; it implies an action upon our mental nature, and the formation of a character; it is something individual and permanent, and is commonly spoken of in connexion with religion and virtue. When, then, we speak of the communication of Knowledge as being Education, we thereby really imply that that Knowledge is a state or condition of mind; and since cultivation of mind is surely worth seeking for its own sake, we are thus brought once more to the conclusion, which the word 'Liberal' and the word 'Philosophy' have already suggested, that there is a Knowledge, which is desirable, though nothing come of it, as being of itself a treasure, and a sufficient remuneration of years of labour. . . .

Useful Knowledge then, I grant, has done its work; and Liberal Knowledge as certainly has not done its work,— that is, supposing, as the objectors assume, its direct end, like Religious Knowledge, is to make men better; but this, I will not for an instant allow, and, unless I allow it, those objectors have said nothing to the purpose. I admit, rather I maintain, what they have been urging, for I consider Knowledge to have its end in itself. For all its friends, or its enemies, may say, I insist upon it, that it is as real a mistake to burden it with virtue or religion as with the mechanical arts. Its direct business is not to steel the soul against temptation or to console it in affliction, any more than to set the loom in motion, or to direct the steam carriage; be it ever so much the means or the condition of both material and moral advancement, still, taken by and in itself, it as little mends our hearts as it improves our temporal circumstances. And if its eulogists claim for it such a power, they commit the very same kind of encroachment on a province not their own as the political economist who should maintain that his science educated him for casuistry or diplomacy. Knowledge is one thing, virtue is another; good sense is not conscience, refinement is not humility, nor is largeness and justness of view faith. Philosophy, however enlightened, however profound, gives no command over the passions, no influential motives, no vivifying principles. Liberal Education makes not the Christian, not the Catholic, but the gentleman. It is well to be a gentleman, it is well to have a cultivated intellect, a delicate taste, a candid, equitable, dispassionate mind, a noble and courteous bearing in the conduct of life;—these are the connatural qualities of a large knowledge; they are the objects of a University; I am advocating, I shall illustrate and insist upon them; but still, I repeat, they are no guarantee for sanctity or even for conscientiousness, they may attach to the man of the world, to the profligate, to the heartless,— pleasant, alas, and attractive as he shows when decked out in them. Taken by themselves, they do but seem to be what they are not; they look like virtue at a distance, but they are detected by close observers, and on the long run; and hence it is that they are popularly accused of pretence and hypocrisy, not, I repeat, from their own fault, but because their professors and their admirers persist in taking them for what they are not, and are officious in arrogating for them a praise to which they have no claim. Quarry the granite rock with razors, or moor the vessel with a thread of silk; then may you hope with such keen and delicate instruments as human knowledge and human reason to contend against those giants, the passion and the pride of man.

Surely we are not driven to theories of this kind, in order to vindicate the value and dignity of Liberal Knowledge. Surely the real grounds on which its pretensions rest are not so very subtle or abstruse, so very strange or improbable. Surely it is very intelligible to say, and that is what I say here, that Liberal Education, viewed in itself, is simply the cultivation of the intellect, as such, and its object is nothing more or less than intellectual excellence. Everything has its own perfection, be it higher or lower in the scale of things; and the perfection of one is not the perfection of another. Things animate, inanimate, visible, invisible, all are good in their kind, and have *best* of themselves, which is an object of pursuit. Why do you take such pains with your garden or your park? You see to your walks and turf and shrubberies; to your trees and drives; not as if you meant to make an orchard of the one, or corn or pasture land of the other, but because there is a special beauty in all that is goodly in wood, water, plain, and slope, brought all together by art into one shape, and grouped into one whole. Your cities are beautiful, your palaces, your public buildings, your territorial mansions, your churches; and their beauty leads to nothing beyond itself. There is a physical beauty and a moral: there is a beauty of person, there is a beauty of our moral being, which is natural virtue; and in like manner there is a beauty, there is a perfection, of the intellect. There is an ideal perfection in these various subject-matters, towards which individual instances are seen to rise, and which are the standards for all instances whatever. The Greek divinities and demigods, as the statuary has moulded them, with their symmetry of figure and their high forehead and their regular features, are the perfection of physical beauty. The heroes, of whom history tells, Alexander, or Cæsar, or Scipio, or Saladin, are the representatives of that magnanimity or self-mastery which is the greatness of human nature. Christianity too has its heroes, and in the supernatural order, and we call them Saints. The artist puts before him beauty of feature and form; the poet, beauty of mind; the preacher, the beauty of grace: then intellect too, I repeat, has its beauty, and it has those who aim at it. To open the mind, to correct it, to refine it, to enable it to know, and to digest, master, rule, and use its knowledge, to give it power over its own faculties, application, flexibility, method, critical exactness, sagacity, resource, address, eloquent expression, is an object as intelligible (for here we are inquiring, not what the object of a Liberal Education is worth, nor what use the Church makes of it, but what it is in itself), I say, an object as intelligible as the cultivation of virtue, while, at the same time, it is absolutely distinct from it.

This indeed is but a temporal object, and a transitory possession: but so are other things in themselves which we make much of and pursue. The moralist will tell us that man, in all his functions, is but a flower which blossoms and fades, except so far as a higher principle breathes upon him, and makes him and what he is immortal. Body and mind are carried on into an eternal state of being by the gifts of Divine Munificence; but at first they do but fail in a failing world; and if the powers of intellect decay, the powers of the body have decayed before them, and, as an Hospital or an Almshouse, though its end be ephemeral, may be sanctified to the service of religion, so surely may a University, even were it nothing more than I have as yet described it. We attain to heaven by using this world well, though it is to pass away; we perfect our nature, not by undoing it, but by adding to it what is more than nature, and directing it towards aims higher than its own.

A Definition of a Gentleman

JOHN HENRY NEWMAN

[FROM *The Idea of a University*]

1865

Such is the method, or the policy (so to call it), of the Church; but Philosophy looks at the matter from a very different point of view: what have Philosophers to do with the terror of judgment or the saving of the soul? Lord Shaftesbury calls the former a sort of "panic fear." Of the latter he scoffingly complains that "the saving of souls is now the heroic passion of exalted spirits." Of course he is at liberty, on his principles, to pick and choose out of Christianity what he will; he discards the theological, the mysterious, the spiritual; he makes selection of the morally or esthetically beautiful. . . .

This embellishment of the exterior is almost the beginning and the end of philosophical morality. This is why it aims at being modest rather than humble; this is how it can be proud at the very time that it is unassuming. To humility indeed it does not even aspire; humility is one of the most difficult of virtues both to attain and to ascertain. . . .

Pride, under such training, instead of running to waste in the education of the mind, is turned to account; it gets a new name; it is called self-respect; and ceases to be the disagreeable, uncompanionable quality which it is in itself. Though it be the motive principle of the soul, it seldom comes to view; and when it shows itself, then delicacy and gentleness are its attire, and good sense and sense of honour direct its motions. It is no longer a restless agent, without definite aim; it has a large field of exertion assigned to it, and it subserves

From Discourse 8.

those social interests which it would naturally trouble. It is directed into the channel of industry, frugality, honesty, and obedience; and it becomes the very staple of the religion and morality held in honour in a day like our own. It becomes the safeguard of chastity, the guarantee of veracity, in high and low; it is the very household god of society, as at present constituted, inspiring neatness and decency in the servant girl, propriety of carriage and refined manners in her mistress, uprightness, manliness, and generosity in the head of the family. It diffuses a light over town and country; it covers the soil with handsome edifices and smiling gardens; it tills the field, it stocks and embellishes the shop. It is the stimulating principle of providence on the one hand, and of free expenditure on the other; of an honourable ambition, and of elegant enjoyment. It breathes upon the face of the community, and the hollow sepulchre is forthwith beautiful to look upon.

Refined by the civilization which has brought it into activity, this self-respect infuses into the mind an intense horror of exposure, and a keen sensitiveness of notoriety and ridicule. It becomes the enemy of extravagances of any kind; it shrinks from what are called scenes; it has no mercy on the mock-heroic, on pretence or egotism, on verbosity in language, or what is called prosiness in conversation. It detests gross adulation; not that it tends at all to the eradication of the appetite to which the flatterer ministers, but it sees the absurdity of indulging it, it understands the annoyance thereby given to others, and if a tribute must be paid to the wealthy or the powerful, it demands greater subtlety and art in the preparation. Thus vanity is changed into a more dangerous self-conceit, as being checked in its natural eruption. It teaches men to suppress their feelings, and to control their tempers, and to mitigate both the severity and the tone of their judgments. As Lord Shaftesbury would desire, it prefers playful wit and satire in putting down what is objectionable, as a more refined and good-natured, as well as a more effectual method, than the expedient which is natural to uneducated minds. It is from this impatience of the tragic and the bombastic that it is now quietly but energetically opposing itself to the unchristian practice of duelling, which it brands as simply out of taste, and as the remnant of a barbarous age; and certainly it seems likely to effect what Religion has aimed at abolishing in vain.

Hence it is that it is almost a definition of a gentleman to say he is one who never inflicts pain. This description is both refined and, as far as it goes, accurate. He is mainly occupied in merely removing the obstacles which hinder the free and unembarrassed action of those about him; and he concurs with their movements rather than takes the initiative himself. His benefits may be considered as parallel to what are called comforts or conveniences in arrangements of a personal nature; like an easy chair or a good fire, which do their part in dispelling cold and fatigue, though nature provides both means of rest and animal heat without them. The true gentleman in like manner carefully avoids whatever may cause a jar or a jolt in the minds of those with whom he is cast;—all clashing of opinion, or collision of feeling, all restraint, or suspicion, or gloom, or resentment; his great concern being to make every one at their ease and at home. He has his eyes on all his company; he is tender towards the bashful, gentle towards the distant, and merciful towards the absurd; he can recollect to whom he is speaking, he guards against unseasonable allusions, or topics which may irritate; he is seldom prominent in conversation, and never wearisome. He makes light of favours while he does them, and seems to be receiving when he is conferring. He never speaks of himself except when compelled, never defends himself by a mere retort, he has no ears for slander or gossip, is scrupulous in imputing motives to those who interfere with him, and interprets every thing for the best. He is never mean or little in his disputes, never takes unfair advantage, never mistakes personalities or sharp sayings for arguments, or insinuates evil which he dare not say out. From a long-sighted prudence, he observes the maxim of the ancient sage, that we should ever conduct ourselves towards our enemy as if he were one day to be our friend. He has too much good sense to be affronted at insults, he is too well employed to remember injuries, and too indolent to bear malice. He is patient, forbearing, and resigned, on philosophical principles; he submits to pain, because it is inevitable, to bereavement, because it is irreparable, and to death, because it is his destiny. If he engages in controversy of any kind, his disciplined intellect preserves him from the blundering discourtesy of better, perhaps, but less educated minds; who, like blunt weapons, tear and hack instead of cutting clean, who mistake the point in argument, waste their strength on trifles, misconceive their adversary, and leave the question more involved than they find it. He may be right or wrong in his opinion, but he is too clear-headed to be unjust; he is as simple as he is forcible, and as brief as he is decisive. Nowhere shall we find greater candour, consideration, indulgence: he throws himself into the minds of his opponents, he accounts for their mistakes. He knows the weakness of human reason as well as its strength, its province and its limits. If he be an unbeliever, he will be too profound and large-minded to ridicule religion or to act against it; he is too wise to be a dogmatist or fanatic in his infidelity. He respects piety and devotion; he even supports institutions as venerable, beautiful, or useful, to which he does not assent; he honours the ministers of religion, and it contents him to decline its mysteries without assailing or denouncing them. He is a friend of religious toleration, and that, not only because his philosophy has taught him to look on all forms of faith with an impartial eye, but also from the gentleness and effeminacy of feeling, which is the attendant on civilization.

Not that he may not hold a religion too, in his own way, even when he is not a Christian. In that case, his religion is one of imagination and sentiment; it is the embodiment of those ideas of the sublime, majestic, and beautiful, without which there can be no large philosophy. Sometimes he acknowledges the being of God, sometimes he invests an unknown principle or quality with the attributes of perfection. And this deduction of his reason, or creation of his fancy, he makes the occasion

of such excellent thoughts, and the starting-point of so varied
and systematic a teaching, that he even seems like a disciple
of Christianity itself. From the very accuracy and steadiness
of his logical powers, he is able to see what sentiments are
consistent in those who hold any religious doctrine at all, and
he appears to others to feel and to hold a whole circle of
theological truths, which exist in his mind no otherwise than
as a number of deductions.

Such are some of the lineaments of the ethical character,
which the cultivated intellect will form, apart from religious
principle. They are seen within the pale of the Church and
without it, in holy men, and in profligate; they form the
beau-ideal of the world; they partly assist and partly distort
the development of the Catholic. They may subserve the
education of a St. Francis de Sales or a Cardinal Pole; they
may be the limits of the contemplation of a Shaftesbury or a
Gibbon. Basil and Julian were fellow-students at the schools
of Athens; and one became the Saint and Doctor of the
Church, the other her scoffing and relentless foe.

———◆◆◆———

Oxford, the Home of Lost Causes

MATTHEW ARNOLD

[FROM *Essays in Criticism. First Series*]

1865

No, we are all seekers still! seekers often make mistakes,
and I wish mine to redound to my own discredit only, and not
to touch Oxford. Beautiful city! so venerable, so lovely, so

From the Preface.

unravaged by the fierce intellectual life of our century, so serene!

There are our young barbarians, all at play!

And yet, steeped in sentiment as she lies, spreading her gardens to the moonlight, and whispering from her towers the last enchantments of the Middle Age, who will deny that Oxford, by her ineffable charm, keeps ever calling us nearer to the true goal of all of us, to the ideal, to perfection,—to beauty, in a word, which is only truth seen from another side?—nearer, perhaps, than all the science of Tübingen. Adorable dreamer, whose heart has been so romantic! who hast given thyself so prodigally, given thyself to sides and to heroes not mine, only never to the Philistines! home of lost causes, and forsaken beliefs, and unpopular names, and impossible loyalties! what example could ever so inspire us to keep down the Philistine in ourselves, what teacher could ever so save us from that bondage to which we are all prone, that bondage which Goethe, in his incomparable lines on the death of Schiller, makes it his friend's highest praise (and nobly did Schiller deserve the praise) to have left miles out of sight behind him;—the bondage of "*was uns alle bändigt*, DAS GEMEINE!" She will forgive me, even if I have unwittingly drawn upon her a shot or two aimed at her unworthy son; for she is generous, and the cause in which I fight is, after all, hers. Apparitions of a day, what is our puny warfare against the Philistines, compared with the warfare which this queen of romance has been waging against them for centuries, and will wage after we are gone?

A Liberal Education

THOMAS HENRY HUXLEY

[FROM "A Liberal Education; and Where to Find It"]

1868

The business which the South London Working Men's College has undertaken is a great work; indeed, I might say, that Education, with which that college proposes to grapple, is the greatest work of all those which lie ready to a man's hand just at present.

And, at length, this fact is becoming generally recognised. You cannot go anywhere without hearing a buzz of more or less confused and contradictory talk on this subject—nor can you fail to notice that, in one point at any rate, there is a very decided advance upon like discussions in former days. Nobody outside the agricultural interest now dares to say that education is a bad thing. If any representative of the once large and powerful party which, in former days, proclaimed this opinion still exists in a semi-fossil state, he keeps his thoughts to himself. In fact, there is a chorus of voices, almost distressing in their harmony, raised in favour of the doctrine that education is the great panacea for human troubles, and that, if the country is not shortly to go to the dogs, everybody must be educated.

The politicians tell us, "you must educate the masses because they are going to be masters." The clergy join in the cry for education, for they affirm that the people are drifting away from church and chapel into the broadest infidelity. The manufacturers and the capitalists swell the chorus lustily. They declare that ignorance makes bad workmen; that England will soon be unable to turn out cotton goods, or steam engines,

From *Macmillan's Magazine*, 17 (March 1868), pages 367-78.

cheaper than other people; and then, Ichabod, Ichabod! the glory will be departed from us. And a few voices are lifted up in favour of the doctrine that the masses should be educated because they are men and women with unlimited capacities of being, doing, and suffering, and that it is as true now, as ever it was, that the people perish for lack of knowledge. . . .

Compare the average artisan and the average country squire, and it may be doubted if you will find a pin to choose between the two in point of ignorance, class feeling, or prejudice. It is true that the ignorance is of a different sort— that the class feeling is in favour of a different class, and that the prejudice has a distinct flavour of wrong-headedness in each case—but it is questionable if the one is either a bit better, or a bit worse, than the other. The old protectionist theory is the doctrine of trades unions as applied by the squires, and the modern trades unionism is the doctrine of the squires applied by the artisans. Why should we be worse off under one regime than under the other?

Again, this sceptical minority asks the clergy to think whether it is really want of education which keeps the masses away from their ministrations—whether the most completely educated men are not as open to reproach on this score as the workmen; and whether, perchance, this may not indicate that it is not education which lies at the bottom of the matter?

Once more, these people, whom there is no pleasing, venture to doubt whether the glory which rests upon being able to undersell all the rest of the world is a very safe kind of glory— whether we may not purchase it too dear; especially if we allow education, which ought to be directed to the making of men, to be diverted into a process of manufacturing human tools, wonderfully adroit in the exercise of some technical industry, but good for nothing else.

And, finally, these people inquire whether it is the masses alone who need a reformed and improved education. They ask whether the richest of our public schools might not well be made to supply knowledge, as well as gentlemanly habits, a strong class feeling, and eminent proficiency in cricket. They seem to think that the noble foundations of our old universities are hardly fulfilling their functions in their present posture of half-clerical seminaries, half racecourses, where men are trained to win a senior wranglership, or a double-first, as horses are trained to win a cup, with as little reference to the needs of after-life in the case of the man as in that of the racer. And while as zealous for education as the rest, they affirm that if the education of the richer classes were such as to fit them to be the leaders and the governors of the poorer; and if the education of the poorer classes were such as to enable them to appreciate really wise guidance and good governance, the politicians need not fear mob-law, nor the clergy lament their want of flocks, nor the capitalists prognosticate the annihilation of the prosperity of the country.

Such is the diversity of opinion upon the why and the wherefore of education. And my readers will be prepared to expect that the practical recommendations which are put forward are not less discordant. There is a loud cry for compulsory education. We English, in spite of constant experience to the contrary, preserve a touching faith in the efficacy of acts of parliament; and I believe we should have compulsory education in the course of next session if there were the least probability that half a dozen leading statemen of different parties would agree what that education should be.

Some hold that education without theology is worse than none. Others maintain, quite as strongly, that education with theology is in the same predicament. But this is certain, that those who hold the first opinion can by no means agree what theology should be taught; and that those who maintain the second are in a small minority.

At any rate "make people learn to read, write, and cipher," say a great many; and the advice is undoubtedly sensible as far as it goes. But, as has happened to me in former days, those who, in despair of getting anything better, advocate this measure, are met with the objection that it is very like making a child practise the use of a knife, fork, and spoon, without giving it a particle of meat. I really don't know what reply is to be made to such an objection.

But it would be unprofitable to spend more time in disentangling, or rather in showing up the knots in the ravelled skeins of our neighbours. Much more to the purpose is it to ask if we possess any clue of our own which may guide us among these entanglements. And by way of a beginning, let us ask ourselves—What is education? Above all things, what is our ideal of a thoroughly liberal education?—of that education which, if we could begin life again, we would give ourselves—of that education which, if we could mould the fates to our own will, we would give our children. Well, I know not what may be my readers' conceptions upon this matter, but I will tell them mine, and I hope I shall find that our views are not very discrepant.

Suppose it were perfectly certain that the life and fortune of every one of us would, one day or other, depend upon his winning or losing a game of chess. Don't you think that we should all consider it to be a primary duty to learn at least the names and the moves of the pieces; to have a notion of a gambit, and a keen eye for all the means of giving and getting out of check? Do you not think that we should look with a disapprobation amounting to scorn upon the father who allowed his son, or the state which allowed its members, to grow up without knowing a pawn from a knight?

Yet, it is a very plain and elementary truth that the life, the fortune, and the happiness of every one of us, and, more or less, of those who are connected with us, do depend upon our knowing something of the rules of a game infinitely more difficult and complicated than chess. It is a game which has been played for untold ages, every man and woman of us being one of the two players in a game of his or her own. The chess-board is the world, the pieces are the phenomena of the universe, the rules of the game are what we call the laws of nature. The player on the other side is hidden from us. We know that his play is always fair, just, and patient. But also we know, to our cost, that he never overlooks a mistake, or makes the smallest allowance for ignorance. To the man who plays well the highest stakes are paid with that sort of overflowing generosity with which the strong shows delight in strength. And one who plays ill is checkmated—without haste, but without remorse. . . .

Well, what I mean by Education is learning the rules of this mighty game. In other words, education is the instruction of the intellect in the laws of nature, under which name I include not merely things and their forces, but men and their ways; and the fashioning of the affections and of the will into an earnest and loving desire to move in harmony with those laws. For me, education means neither more nor less than this. Anything which professes to call itself education must be tried by this standard, and if it fails to stand the test, I will not call it education, whatever may be the force of authority or of numbers upon the other side.

It is important to remember that, in strictness, there is no such thing as an uneducated man. Take an extreme case. Suppose that an adult man, in the full vigour of his faculties, could be suddenly placed in the world, as Adam is said to have been, and then left to do as he best might. How long would he be left uneducated? Not five minutes. Nature would begin to teach him through the eye, the ear, the touch, the properties of objects. Pain and pleasure would be at his elbow telling him to do this and avoid that; and by slow degrees the man would receive an education, which, if narrow, would be thorough, real, and adequate to his circumstances, though there would be no extras and very few accomplishments.

And if to this solitary man entered a second Adam, or, better still, an Eve, a new and greater world, that of social and moral phenomena would be revealed. Joys and woes, compared with which all others might seem but faint shadows, would spring from the new relations. Happiness and sorrow would take the place of the coarser monitors, pleasure and pain; but conduct would still be shaped by the observation of the natural consequences of actions; or, in other words, by the laws of the nature of man.

To every one of us, the world was once as fresh and new as to Adam. And then, long before we were susceptible of any other mode of instruction, nature took us in hand, and every minute of waking life brought its educational influence, shaping our actions into rough accordance with nature's laws, so that we might not be ended untimely by too gross disobedience. Nor should I speak of this process of education as past, for any one, be he as old as he may. For every man the world is as fresh as it was at the first day, and as full of untold novelties for him who has the eyes to see them. And nature is still continuing her patient education of us in that great university, the universe, of which we are all members—nature having no Test-Acts.

Those who take honours in nature's university, who learn the laws which govern men and things and obey them, are the really great and successful men in this world. The great mass of mankind are the "Poll," who pick up just enough to get through without much discredit. Those who won't learn at all are plucked; and then you can't come up again. Nature's pluck means extermination.

Thus the question of compulsory education is settled so far as nature is concerned. Her bill on that question was framed and passed long ago. But, like all compulsory legislation, that of nature is harsh and wasteful in its operation. Ignorance is visited as sharply as wilful disobedience—incapacity meets with the same punishment as crime. Nature's discipline is not even a word and a blow, and the blow first; but the blow without the word. It is left to you to find out why your ears are boxed.

The object of what we commonly call education—that education in which man intervenes and which I shall distinguish as artificial education—is to make good these defects in nature's methods; to prepare the child to receive nature's education, neither incapably nor ignorantly, nor with wilful disobedience; and to understand the preliminary symptoms of her displeasure without waiting for the box on the ear. In short, all artificial education ought to be an anticipation of natural education. And a liberal education is an artificial education—one which has not only prepared a man to escape the great evils of disobedience to natural laws, but has trained him to appreciate and to seize upon the rewards which nature scatters with as free a hand as her penalties.

That man, I think, has had a liberal education who has been so trained in youth that his body is the ready servant of his will, and does with ease and pleasure all the work that, as a mechanism, it is capable of; whose intellect is a clear, cold, logic engine, with all its parts of equal strength, and in smooth working order; ready, like a steam engine, to be turned to any kind of work, and spin the gossamers as well as forge the anchors of the mind; whose mind is stored with a knowledge of the great and fundamental truths of nature and of the laws of her operations; one who, no stunted ascetic, is full of life and fire, but whose passions are trained to come to heel by a vigorous will, the servant of a tender conscience; who has learned to love all beauty, whether of nature or of art, to hate all vileness, and to respect others as himself.

Such a one and no other, I conceive, has had a liberal education; for he is, as completely as a man can be, in harmony with nature. He will make the best of her, and she of him. They will get on together rarely; she as his ever beneficent mother; he as her mouthpiece, her conscious self, her minister and interpreter. . . .

But if the classics were taught as they might be taught— if boys and girls were instructed in Greek and Latin, not merely as languages, but as illustrations of philological science; if a vivid picture of life on the shores of the Mediterranean, two thousand years ago, were imprinted on the minds of scholars; if ancient history were taught, not as a weary series of feuds and fights, but traced to its causes in such men placed under such conditions; if, lastly, the study of the classical books were followed in such a manner as to impress boys with their beauties, and with the grand simplicity of their statement of the everlasting problems of human life, instead of with their verbal and grammatical peculiarities; I still think it as little proper that they should form the basis of a liberal education for our contemporaries, as I should think it fitting to make that sort of palæontology with which I am familiar the back-bone of modern education. . . .

But it will be said that I am forgetting the beauty, the

human interest which appertains to classical studies. To this I reply that it is only a very strong man who can appreciate the charms of a landscape as he is toiling up a steep hill, along a bad road. What with short-windedness, stones, ruts, and a pervading sense of the wisdom of rest and be thankful, most of us have little enough sense of the beautiful under these circumstances. The ordinary school-boy is precisely in this case. He finds Parnassus uncommonly steep, and there is no chance of his having much time or inclination to look about him till he gets to the top. And nine times out of ten he does not get to the top.

But if this be a fair picture of the results of classical teaching at its best—and I gather from those who have authority to speak on such matters that it is so—what is to be said of classical teaching at its worst, or in other words, of the classics of our ordinary middle-class schools? I will tell you. It means getting up endless forms and rules by heart. It means turning Latin and Greek into English, for the mere sake of being able to do it, and without the smallest regard to the worth, or worthlessness, of the author read. It means the learning of innumerable, not always decent, fables in such a shape that the meaning they once had is dried up into utter trash; and the only impression left upon a boy's mind is that the people who believed such things must have been the greatest idiots the world ever saw. And it means, finally, that after a dozen years spent at this kind of work, the sufferer shall be incompetent to interpret a passage in an author he has not already got up; that he shall loathe the sight of a Greek or Latin book; and that he shall never open, or think of, a classical writer again, until, wonderful to relate, he insists upon submitting his sons to the same process.

If I am justified in my conception of the ideal of a liberal education; and if what I have said about the existing educational institutions of the country is also true, it is clear that the two have no sort of relation to one another; that the best of our schools and the most complete of our university trainings give but a narrow, one-sided, and essentially illiberal education—while the worst give what is really next to no education at all. The South London Working-Men's College could not copy any of these institutions if it would. I am bold enough to express the conviction that it ought not if it could.

For what is wanted is the reality and not the mere name of a liberal education; and this college must steadily set before itself the ambition to be able to give that education sooner or later. At present we are but beginning, sharpening our educational tools, as it were, and, except a modicum of physical science, we are not able to offer much more than is to be found in an ordinary school.

Moral and social science—one of the greatest and most fruitful of our future classes, I hope—at present lacks only one thing in our programme, and that is a teacher. A considerable want, no doubt; but it must be recollected that it is much better to want a teacher than to want the desire to learn.

Further, we need what, for want of a better name, I must call Physical Geography. What I mean is that which the Germans call *Erdkunde*. It is a description of the earth, of its place and relation to other bodies; of its general structure, and of its great features—winds, tides, mountains, plains; of the chief forms of the vegetable and animal worlds, of the varieties of man. It is the peg upon which the greatest quantity of useful and entertaining information can be suspended.

Literature is not upon the College programme; but I hope some day to see it there. For literature is the greatest of all sources of refined pleasure, and one of the great uses of a liberal education is to enable us to enjoy that pleasure. There is scope enough for the purposes of liberal education in the study of the rich treasures of our own language alone. All that is needed is direction, and the cultivation of a refined taste by attention to sound criticism. But there is no reason why French and German should not be mastered sufficiently to read what is worth reading in those languages with pleasure and with profit.

And finally, by and by, we must have History; treated not as a succession of battles and dynasties; not as a series of biographies; not as evidence that Providence has always been on the side of either Whigs or Tories; but as the development of man in times past, and in other conditions than our own.

But, as it is one of the principles of our College to be self-supporting, the public must lead, and we must follow, in these matters. If my readers take to heart what I have said about liberal education, they will desire these things, and I doubt not we shall be able to supply them. But we must wait till the demand is made.

The Colleges of Unreason

SAMUEL BUTLER

[FROM *Erewhon; or Over the Range*]

1872

After supper Mr. Thims told me a good deal about the system of education which is here practised. I already knew a part of what I heard, but much was new to me, and I obtained a better idea of the Erewhonian position than I had done hitherto: nevertheless there were parts of the scheme of which I could not comprehend the fitness, although I fully admit that this inability was probably the result of my having been trained so very differently and to my being then much out of sorts.

The main feature in their system is the prominence which they give to a study which I can only translate by the word "hypothetics." They argue thus—that to teach a boy merely the nature of the things which exist in the world around him, and about which he will have to be conversant during his whole life, would be giving him but a narrow and shallow conception of the universe, which it is urged might contain all manner of things which are not now to be found therein. To open his eyes to these possibilities, and

From Chapter 21.

so to prepare him for all sorts of emergencies, is the object of this system of hypothetics. To imagine a set of utterly strange and impossible contingencies, and require the youths to give intelligent answers to the questions that arise therefrom, is reckoned the fittest conceivable way of preparing them for the actual conduct of their affairs in after life.

Thus they are taught what is called the hypothetical language for many of their best years—a language which was originally composed at a time when the country was in a very different state of civilization to what it is at present, a state which has long since disappeared and been superseded. Many valuable maxims and noble thoughts which were at one time concealed in it have become current in their modern literature, and have been translated over and over again into the language now spoken. Surely then it would seem enough that the study of the original language should be confined to the few whose instincts led them naturally to pursue it.

But the Erewhonians think differently; the store they set by this hypothetical language can hardly be believed; they will even give any one a maintenance for life if he attains a considerable proficiency in the study of it; nay, they will spend years in learning to translate some of their own good poetry into the hypothetical language—to do so with fluency being reckoned a distinguishing mark of a scholar and a gentleman. Heaven forbid that I should be flippant, but it appeared to me to be a wanton waste of good human energy that men should spend years and years in the perfection of so barren an exercise, when their own civilization presented problems by the hundred which cried aloud for solution and would have paid the solver handsomely; but people know their own affairs best. If the youths chose it for themselves I should have wondered less; but they do not choose it; they have it thrust upon them, and for the most part are disinclined towards it. I can only say that all I heard in defence of the system was insufficient to make me think very highly of its advantages.

The arguments in favour of the deliberate development of the unreasoning faculties were much more cogent. But here they depart from the principles on which they justify their study of hypothetics; for they base the importance which they assign to hypothetics upon the fact of their being a preparation for the extraordinary, while their study of Unreason rests upon its developing those faculties which are required for the daily conduct of affairs. Hence their professorships of Inconsistency and Evasion, in both of which studies the youths are examined before being allowed to proceed to their degree in hypothetics. The more earnest and conscientious students attain to a proficiency in these subjects which is quite surprising; there is hardly any inconsistency so glaring but they soon learn to defend it, or injunction so clear that they cannot find some pretext for disregarding it.

Life, they urge, would be intolerable if men were to be guided in all they did by reason and reason only. Reason betrays men into the drawing of hard and fast lines, and to the defining by language—language being like the sun, which rears and then scorches. Extremes are alone logical, but they are always absurd; the mean is illogical, but an illogical mean is better than the sheer absurdity of an extreme. There are no follies and no unreasonablenesses so great as those which can apparently be irrefragably defended by reason itself, and there is hardly an error into which men may not easily be led if they base their conduct upon reason only. . . .

[FROM Chapter 22]

When I talked about originality and genius to some gentlemen whom I met at a supper party given by Mr. Thims in my honour, and said that original thought ought to be encouraged, I had to eat my words at once. Their view evidently was that genius was like offences—needs must that it come, but woe unto that man through whom it comes. A man's business, they hold, is to think as his neighbours do, for Heaven help him if he thinks good what they count bad. And really it is hard to see how the Erewhonian theory differs from our own, for the word "idiot" only means a person who forms his opinions for himself.

The venerable Professor of Worldly Wisdom, a man verging on eighty but still hale, spoke to me very seriously on this subject in consequence of the few words that I had imprudently let fall in defence of genius. He was one of those who carried most weight in the university, and had the reputation of having done more perhaps than any other living man to suppress any kind of originality.

"It is not our business," he said, "to help students to think for themselves. Surely this is the very last thing which one who wishes them well should encourage them to do. Our duty is to ensure that they shall think as we do, or at any rate, as we hold it expedient to say we do." In some respects, however, he was thought to hold somewhat radical opinions, for he was President of the Society for the Suppression of Useless Knowledge, and for the Completer Obliteration of the Past.

As regards the tests that a youth must pass before he can get a degree, I found that they have no class lists, and discourage anything like competition among the students; this, indeed, they regard as self-seeking and unneighbourly. The examinations are conducted by way of papers written by the candidate on set subjects, some of which are known to him beforehand, while others are devised with a view of testing his general capacity and *savoir faire*.

My friend the Professor of Worldly Wisdom was the terror of the greater number of students; and, so far as I could judge, he very well might be, for he had taken his Professorship more seriously than any of the other Professors had done. I heard of his having plucked one poor fellow for want of sufficient vagueness in his saving clauses paper. Another was sent down for having written an article on a scientific subject without having made free enough use of the words "carefully," "patiently," and "earnestly." One man was refused a degree for being too often and too seriously in the right, while a few days before I came a whole batch had been plucked for insufficient distrust of printed matter.

About this there was just then rather a ferment, for it seems that the Professor had written an article in the leading university magazine, which was well known to be by him, and which abounded in all sorts of plausible blunders. He then set a paper which afforded the examinees an opportunity of repeating these blunders—which, believing the article to be by their own examiner, they of course did. The Professor plucked every single one of them, but his action was considered to have been not quite handsome.

I told them of Homer's noble line to the effect that a man should strive ever to be foremost and in all things to outvie his peers; but they said that no wonder the countries in which such a detestable maxim was held in admiration were always flying at one another's throats.

"Why," asked one Professor, "should a man want to be better than his neighbours? Let him be thankful if he is no worse."

I ventured feebly to say that I did not see how progress could be made in any art or science, or indeed in anything at all, without more or less self-seeking, and hence unamiability.

"Of course it cannot," said the Professor, "and therefore we object to progress."

———◆———

Science and Culture

THOMAS HENRY HUXLEY

[FROM *Science and Culture*]

1880

Sir Josiah Mason, without doubt most wisely, has left very large freedom of action to the trustees, to whom he proposes ultimately to commit the administration of the College, so that they may be able to adjust its arrangements in accordance with the changing conditions of the future. But, with respect

Science and Culture and Other Essays (New York: 1882), pages 12-30.

to three points, he has laid most explicit injunctions upon both administrators and teachers.

Party politics are forbidden to enter into the minds of either, so far as the work of the College is concerned; theology is as sternly banished from its precincts; and finally, it is especially declared that the College shall make no provision for "mere literary instruction and education." . . .

I am not acquainted with Sir Josiah Mason's reasons for the action which he has taken; but if, as I apprehend is the case, he refers to the ordinary classical course of our schools and universities by the name of "mere literary instruction and education," I venture to offer sundry reasons of my own in support of that action.

For I hold very strongly by two convictions—The first is, that neither the discipline nor the subject-matter of classical education is of such direct value to the student of physical science as to justify the expenditure of valuable time upon either; and the second is, that for the purpose of attaining real culture, an exclusively scientific education is at least as effectual as an exclusively literary education.

I need hardly point out to you that these opinions, especially the latter, are diametrically opposed to those of the great majority of educated Englishmen, influenced as they are by school and university traditions. In their belief, culture is obtainable only by a liberal education; and a liberal education is synonymous, not merely with education and instruction in literature, but in one particular form of literature, namely, that of Greek and Roman antiquity. They hold that the man who has learned Latin and Greek, however little, is educated; while he who is versed in other branches of knowledge, however deeply, is a more or less respectable specialist, not admissible into the cultured caste. The stamp of the educated man, the University degree, is not for him.

I am too well acquainted with the generous catholicity of spirit, the true sympathy with scientific thought, which pervades the writings of our chief apostle of culture to identify him with these opinions; and yet one may cull from one and another of those epistles to the Philistines, which so much delight all who do not answer to that name, sentences which lend them some support.

Mr. Arnold tells us that the meaning of culture is "to know the best that has been thought and said in the world." It is the criticism of life contained in literature. That criticism regards "Europe as being, for intellectual and spiritual purposes, one great confederation, bound to a joint action and working to a common result; and whose members have, for their common outfit, a knowledge of Greek, Roman, and Eastern antiquity, and of one another. Special, local, and temporary advantages being put out of account, that modern nation will in the intellectual and spiritual sphere make most progress, which most thoroughly carries out this programme. And what is that but saying that we too, all of us, as individuals, the more thoroughly we carry it out, shall make the more progress?"

We have here to deal with two distinct propositions. The first, that a criticism of life is the essence of culture; the second, that literature contains the materials which suffice for the construction of such a criticism.

I think that we must all assent to the first proposition. For culture certainly means something quite different from learning or technical skill. It implies the possession of an ideal, and the habit of critically estimating the value of things by comparison with a theoretic standard. Perfect culture should supply a complete theory of life, based upon a clear knowledge alike of its possibilities and of its limitations.

But we may agree to all this, and yet strongly dissent from the assumption that literature alone is competent to supply this knowledge. After having learnt all that Greek, Roman, and Eastern antiquity have thought and said, and all that modern literatures have to tell us, it is not self-evident that we have laid a sufficiently broad and deep foundation for that criticism of life which constitutes culture.

Indeed, to any one acquainted with the scope of physical science, it is not at all evident. Considering progress only in the "intellectual and spiritual sphere," I find myself wholly unable to admit that either nations or individuals will really advance, if their common outfit draws nothing from the stores of physical science. I should say that an army, without weapons of precision, and with no particular base of operations, might more hopefully enter upon a campaign on the Rhine, than a man, devoid of a knowledge of what physical science has done in the last century, upon a criticism of life. . . .

At that time [five or six hundred years ago], in fact, if any one desired knowledge beyond such as could be obtained by his own observation, or by common conversation, his first necessity was to learn the Latin language, inasmuch as all the higher knowledge of the western world was contained in works written in that language. Hence, Latin grammar, with logic and rhetoric, studied through Latin, were the fundamentals of education. With respect to the substance of the knowledge imparted through this channel, the Jewish and Christian Scriptures, as interpreted and supplemented by the Romish Church, were held to contain a complete and infallibly true body of information.

Theological dicta were, to the thinkers of those days, that which the axioms and definitions of Euclid are to the geometers of these. The business of the philosophers of the middle ages was to deduce from the data furnished by the theologians, conclusions in accordance with ecclesiastical decrees. They were allowed the high privilege of showing, by logical process, how and why that which the Church said was true, must be true. And if their demonstrations fell short of or exceeded this limit, the Church was maternally ready to check their aberrations, if need be, by the help of the secular arm.

Between the two, our ancestors were furnished with a compact and complete criticism of life. They were told how the world began, and how it would end; they learned that all material existence was but a base and insignificant blot upon the fair face of the spiritual world, and that nature was, to all intents and purposes, the playground of the devil; they learned that the earth is the centre of the visible universe, and that man is the cynosure of things terrestrial; and more especially is it inculcated that the course of nature had no fixed order, but that it could be, and constantly was, altered by the agency of innumerable spiritual beings, good and bad, according as they were moved by the deeds and prayers of men. The sum and substance of the whole doctrine was to produce the conviction that the only thing really worth knowing in this world was how to secure that place in a better which, under certain conditions, the Church promised.

Our ancestors had a living belief in this theory of life, and acted upon it in their dealings with education, as in all other matters. Culture meant saintliness—after the fashion of the saints of those days; the education that led to it was, of necessity, theological; and the way to theology lay through Latin.

That the study of nature—further than was requisite for the satisfaction of everyday wants—should have any bearing on human life was far from the thoughts of men thus trained. Indeed, as nature had been cursed for man's sake, it was an obvious conclusion that those who meddled with nature were likely to come into pretty close contact with Satan. And, if any born scientific investigator followed his instincts, he might safely reckon upon earning the reputation, and probably upon suffering the fate, of a sorcerer.

Had the western world been left to itself in Chinese isolation, there is no saying how long this state of things might have endured. But, happily, it was not left to itself. Even earlier than the thirteenth century, the development of Moorish civilisation in Spain and the great movement of the Crusades had introduced the leaven which, from that day to this, has never ceased to work. At first, through the intermediation of Arabic translations, afterwards, by the study of the originals, the western nations of Europe became acquainted with the writings of the ancient philosophers and poets, and, in time, with the whole of the vast literature of antiquity. . . .

I venture to think that the pretensions of our modern

Humanists to the possession of the monopoly of culture and
to the exclusive inheritance of the spirit of antiquity must be
abated, if not abandoned. But I should be very sorry that
anything I have said should be taken to imply a desire on my
part to depreciate the value of classical education, as it might
be and as it sometimes is. The native capacities of mankind
vary no less than their opportunities; and while culture is one,
the road by which one man may best reach it is widely
different from that which is most advantageous to another.
Again, while scientific education is yet inchoate and tentative,
classical education is thoroughly well organised upon the
practical experience of generations of teachers. So that, given
ample time for learning and destination for ordinary life, or
for a literary career, I do not think that a young Englishman
in search of culture can do better than follow the course
usually marked out for him, supplementing its deficiencies by
his own efforts.

But for those who mean to make science their serious
occupation; or who intend to follow the profession of medicine; or who have to enter early upon the business of life;
for all these, in my opinion, classical education is a mistake;
and it is for this reason that I am glad to see "mere literary
education and instruction" shut out from the curriculum of
Sir Josiah Mason's College, seeing that its inclusion would
probably lead to the introduction of the ordinary smattering
of Latin and Greek.

Nevertheless, I am the last person to question the importance of genuine literary education, or to suppose that
intellectual culture can be complete without it. An exclusively
scientific training will bring about a mental twist as surely
as an exclusively literary training. The value of the cargo does
not compensate for a ship's being out of trim; and I should
be very sorry to think that the Scientific College would turn
out none but lop-sided men.

There is no need, however, that such a catastrophe should
happen. Instruction in English, French, and German is provided, and thus the three greatest literatures of the modern
world are made accessible to the student. French and German,

and especially the latter language, are absolutely indispensable to those who desire full knowledge in any department of science. But even supposing that the knowledge of these languages acquired is not more than sufficient for purely scientific purposes, every Englishman has, in his native tongue, an almost perfect instrument of literary expression; and, in his own literature, models of every kind of literary excellence. If an Englishman cannot get literary culture out of his Bible, his Shakspeare, his Milton, neither, in my belief, will the profoundest study of Homer and Sophocles, Virgil and Horace, give it to him. . . .

If the Institution opened to-day fulfils the intention of its founder, the picked intelligences among all classes of the population of this district will pass through it. No child born in Birmingham, henceforward, if he have the capacity to profit by the opportunities offered to him, first in the primary and other schools, and afterwards in the Scientific College, need fail to obtain, not merely the instruction, but the culture most appropriate to the conditions of his life.

Within these walls, the future employer and the future artisan may sojourn together for a while, and carry, through all their lives, the stamp of the influences then brought to bear upon them. Hence, it is not beside the mark to remind you, that the prosperity of industry depends not merely upon the improvement of manufacturing processes, not merely upon the ennobling of the individual character, but upon a third condition, namely, a clear understanding of the conditions of social life on the part of both the capitalist and the operative, and their agreement upon common principles of social action. They must learn that social phenomena are as much the expression of natural laws as any others; that no social arrangements can be permanent unless they harmonise with the requirements of social statics and dynamics; and that, in the nature of things, there is an arbiter whose decisions execute themselves.

But this knowledge is only to be obtained by the application of the methods of investigation adopted in physical researches to the investigation of the phenomena of society.

Hence, I confess, I should like to see one addition made to the excellent scheme of education propounded for the College, in the shape of provision for the teaching of Sociology. For though we are all agreed that party politics are to have no place in the instruction of the College; yet in this country, practically governed as it is now by universal suffrage, every man who does his duty must exercise political functions. And, if the evils which are inseparable from the good of political liberty are to be checked, if the perpetual oscillation of nations between anarchy and despotism is to be replaced by the steady march of self-restraining freedom; it will be because men will gradually bring themselves to deal with political, as they now deal with scientific questions; to be as ashamed of undue haste and partisan prejudice in the one case as in the other; and to believe that the machinery of society is at least as delicate as that of a spinning-jenny, and as little likely to be improved by the meddling of those who have not taken the trouble to master the principles of its action.

◆●◆

Literature and Science

MATTHEW ARNOLD

[FROM *Discourses in America*]

1885

Practical people talk with a smile of Plato and of his absolute ideas; and it is impossible to deny that Plato's ideas do often seem unpractical and unpracticable, and especially when one views them in connexion with the life of a great work-a-day world like the United States. The necessary staple of the life of such a world Plato regards with disdain; handicraft and trade and the working professions he regards with disdain; but what becomes of the life of an industrial modern community

From pages 72-112.

if you take handicraft and trade and the working professions
out of it? . . .

Now education, many people go on to say, is still mainly
governed by the ideas of men like Plato, who lived when the
warrior caste and the priestly or philosophical class were
alone in honour, and the really useful part of the community
were slaves. It is an education fitted for persons of leisure in
such a community. This education passed from Greece and
Rome to the feudal communities of Europe, where also the
warrior caste and the priestly caste were alone held in honour,
and where the really useful and working part of the community, though not nominally slaves as in the pagan world, were
practically not much better off than slaves, and not more
seriously regarded. And how absurd it is, people end by
saying, to inflict this education upon an industrious modern
community, where very few indeed are persons of leisure,
and the mass to be considered has not leisure, but is bound,
for its own great good, and for the great good of the world
at large, to plain labour and to industrial pursuits, and the
education in question tends necessarily to make men dissatisfied with these pursuits and unfitted for them!

That is what is said. So far I must defend Plato, as to
plead that his view of education and studies is in the general,
as it seems to me, sound enough, and fitted for all sorts and
conditions of men, whatever their pursuits may be. 'An intelligent man,' says Plato, 'will prize those studies which result
in his soul getting soberness, righteousness, and wisdom, and
will less value the others.' I cannot consider *that* a bad description of the aim of education, and of the motives which
should govern us in the choice of studies, whether we are
preparing ourselves for a hereditary seat in the English House
of Lords or for the pork trade in Chicago.

Still I admit that Plato's world was not ours, that his scorn
of trade and handicraft is fantastic, that he had no conception
of a great industrial community such as that of the United
States, and that such a community must and will shape its
education to suit its own needs. If the usual education handed
down to it from the past does not suit it, it will certainly

before long drop this and try another. The usual education
in the past has been mainly literary. The question is whether
the studies which were long supposed to be the best for all
of us are practically the best now; whether others are not
better. The tyranny of the past, many think, weighs on us
injuriously in the predominance given to letters in education.
The question is raised whether, to meet the needs of our
modern life, the predominance ought not now to pass from
letters to science. . . .

Some of you may possibly remember a phrase of mine
which has been the object of a good deal of comment; an
observation to the effect that in our culture, the aim being
to know ourselves and the world, we have, as the means to
this end, *to know the best which has been thought and said
in the world.* A man of science, who is also an excellent writer
and the very prince of debaters, Professor Huxley, in a
discourse at the opening of Sir Josiah Mason's college at
Birmingham, laying hold of this phrase, expanded it by
quoting some more words of mine, which are these: 'The
civilised world is to be regarded as now being, for intellectual
and spiritual purposes, one great confederation, bound to a
joint action and working to a common result; and whose
members have for their proper outfit a knowledge of Greek,
Roman, and Eastern antiquity, and of one another. Special
local and temporary advantages being put out of account,
that modern nation will in the intellectual and spiritual sphere
make most progress, which most thoroughly carries out this
programme.'

Now on my phrase, thus enlarged, Professor Huxley remarks that when I speak of the above-mentioned knowledge
as enabling us to know ourselves and the world, I assert
literature to contain the materials which suffice for thus
making us know ourselves and the world. But it is not by any
means clear, says he, that after having learnt all which ancient
and modern literatures have to tell us, we have laid a sufficiently broad and deep foundation for that criticism of life,
that knowledge of ourselves and the world, which constitutes
culture. On the contrary, Professor Huxley declares that he

finds himself 'wholly unable to admit that either nations or individuals will really advance, if their outfit draws nothing from the stores of physical science. An army without weapons of precision, and with no particular base of operations, might more hopefully enter upon a campaign on the Rhine, than a man, devoid of a knowledge of what physical science has done in the last century, upon a criticism of life.'

This shows how needful it is for those who are to discuss any matter together, to have a common understanding as to the sense of the terms they employ,—how needful, and how difficult. What Professor Huxley says, implies just the reproach which is so often brought against the study of *belles lettres,* as they are called: that the study is an elegant one, but slight and ineffectual; a smattering of Greek and Latin and other ornamental things, of little use for any one whose object is to get at truth, and to be a practical man. . . .

Let us, I say, be agreed about the meaning of the terms we are using. I talk of knowing the best which has been thought and uttered in the world; Professor Huxley says this means knowing *literature.* Literature is a large word; it may mean everything written with letters or printed in a book. Euclid's *Elements* and Newton's *Principia* are thus literature. All knowledge that reaches us through books is literature. But by literature Professor Huxley means *belles lettres.* He means to make me say, that knowing the best which has been thought and said by the modern nations is knowing their *belles lettres* and no more. And this is no sufficient equipment, he argues, for a criticism of modern life. But as I do not mean, by knowing ancient Rome, knowing merely more or less of Latin *belles lettres,* and taking no account of Rome's military, and political, and legal, and administrative work in the world; and as, by knowing ancient Greece, I understand knowing her as the giver of Greek art, and the guide to a free and right use of reason and to scientific method, and the founder of our mathematics and physics and astronomy and biology,—I understand knowing her as all this, and not merely knowing certain Greek poems, and histories, and treatises, and speeches,—so as to the knowledge of modern nations also. By knowing modern nations, I mean not merely knowing their *belles lettres,* but knowing also what has been done by such men as Copernicus, Galileo, Newton, Darwin. . . .

There is, therefore, really no question between Professor Huxley and me as to whether knowing the great results of the modern scientific study of nature is not required as a part of our culture, as well as knowing the products of literature and art. But to follow the processes by which those results are reached, ought, say the friends of physical science, to be made the staple of education for the bulk of mankind. And here there does arise a question between those whom Professor Huxley calls with playful sarcasm 'the Levites of culture,' and those whom the poor humanist is sometimes apt to regard as its Nebuchadnezzars. . . .

Interesting, indeed, these results of science are, important they are, and we should all of us be acquainted with them. But what I now wish you to mark is, that we are still, when they are propounded to us and we receive them, we are still in the sphere of intellect and knowledge. And for the generality of men there will be found, I say, to arise, when they have duly taken in the proposition that their ancestor was 'a hairy quadruped furnished with a tail and pointed ears, probably arboreal in his habits,' there will be found to arise an invincible desire to relate this proposition to the sense in us for conduct, and to the sense in us for beauty. But this the men of science will not do for us, and will hardly even profess to do. They will give us other pieces of knowledge, other facts, about other animals and their ancestors, or about plants, or about stones, or about stars; and they may finally bring us to those great 'general conceptions of the universe, which are forced upon us all,' says Professor Huxley, 'by the progress of physical science.' But still it will be *knowledge* only which they give us; knowledge not put for us into relation with our sense for conduct, our sense for beauty, and touched with emotion by being so put; not thus put for us, and therefore, to the majority of mankind, after a certain while, unsatisfying, wearying. . . .

PART
FIVE

SCIENCE

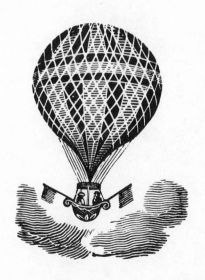

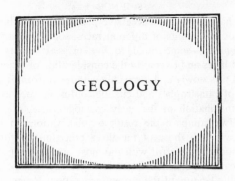

GEOLOGY

Man in the Geological Record

CHARLES LYELL

[FROM *The Principles of Geology. Being an Attempt to Explain the Former Changes of the Earth's Surface by Reference to Causes Now in Operation*]

1830-1833

No period could have been more fortunate for the discovery, in the immediate neighbourhood of Paris, of a rich store of well-preserved fossils, than the commencement of the present century; for at no former era had Natural History been cultivated with such enthusiasm in the French metropolis. The labours of Cuvier in comparative osteology, and of Lamarck in recent and fossil shells, had raised these departments of study to a rank of which they had never previously been deemed susceptible. Their investigations had eventually a powerful effect in dispelling the illusion which had long prevailed concerning the absence of analogy between the ancient and modern state of our planet. A close comparison of the recent and fossil species, and the inferences drawn in regard to their habits, accustomed the geologist to contemplate the

From the Introduction.

earth as having been at successive periods the dwelling-place of animals and plants of different races, some terrestrial, and others aquatic—some fitted to live in seas, others in the waters of lakes and rivers. By the consideration of these topics, the mind was slowly and insensibly withdrawn from imaginary pictures of catastrophes and chaotic confusion, such as haunted the imagination of the early cosmogonists. . . .

When we compare the result of observations in the last thirty years with those of the three preceding centuries, we cannot but look forward with the most sanguine expectations to the degree of excellence to which geology may be carried, even by the labours of the present generation. Never, perhaps, did any science, with the exception of astronomy, unfold, in an equally brief period, so many novel and unexpected truths, and overturn so many preconceived opinions. The senses had for ages declared the earth to be at rest, until the astronomer taught that it was carried through space with inconceivable rapidity. In like manner was the surface of the planet regarded as having remained unaltered since its creation, until the geologist proved that it had been the theatre of reiterated change, and was still the subject of slow but never-ending fluctuations. The discovery of other systems in the boundless regions of space was the triumph of astronomy: to trace the same system through various transformations—to behold it at successive eras adorned with different hills and valleys, lakes and seas, and peopled with new inhabitants, was the delightful meed of geological research. By the geometer were measured the regions of space, and the relative distances of the heavenly bodies;—by the geologist myriads of ages were reckoned, not by arithmetical computations, but by a train of physical events—a succession of phenomena in the animate and inanimate worlds—signs which convey to our minds more definite ideas than figures can do of the immensity of time. . . .

Introduction of man, to what extent a change in the system.—But setting aside the question of progressive development, another and a far more difficult one may arise out of the admission that man is comparatively of modern origin.

Is not the interference of the human species, it may be asked, such a deviation from the antecedent course of physical events, that the knowledge of such a fact tends to destroy all our confidence in the uniformity of the order of nature, both in regard to time past and future? If such an innovation could take place after the earth had been exclusively inhabited for thousands of ages by inferior animals, why should not other changes as extraordinary and unprecedented happen from time to time? If one new cause was permitted to supervene, differing in kind and energy from any before in operation, why may not others have come into action at different epochs? Or what security have we that they may not arise hereafter? And if such be the case, how can the experience of one period, even though we are acquainted with all the possible effects of the then existing causes, be a standard to which we can refer all natural phenomena of other periods?

Now these objections would be unanswerable, if adduced against one who was contending for the absolute uniformity throughout all time of the succession of sublunary events. . . . We have no reason to suppose, that when man first became master of a small part of the globe, a greater change took place in its physical condition than is now experienced when districts, never before inhabited, became successively occupied by new settlers. When a powerful European colony lands on the shores of Australia, and introduces at once those arts which it has required many centuries to mature; when it imports a multitude of plants and large animals from the opposite extremity of the earth, and begins rapidly to extirpate many of the indigenous species, a mightier revolution is effected in a brief period than the first entrance of a savage horde, or their continued occupation of the country for many centuries, can possibly be imagined to have produced. If there be no impropriety in assuming that the system is uniform when disturbances so unprecedented occur in certain localities, we can with much greater confidence apply the same language to those primeval ages when the aggregate number and power of the human race, or the rate of their advancement in civilisation, must be supposed to have been far inferior. . . .

The modifications in the system of which man is the instrument, do not, perhaps, constitute so great a deviation from previous analogy as we usually imagine; we often, for example, form an exaggerated estimate of the extent of our power in extirpating some of the inferior animals, and causing others to multiply; a power which is circumscribed within certain limits, and which, in all likelihood, is by no means exclusively exerted by our species. The growth of human population cannot take place without diminishing the numbers, or causing the entire destruction, of many animals. The larger carnivorous species give way before us, but other quadrupeds of smaller size, and innumerable birds, insects, and plants, which are inimical to our interests, increase in spite of us, some attacking our food, others our raiment and persons, and others interfering with our agricultural and horticultural labours. We behold the rich harvest which we have raised with the sweat of our brow devoured by myriads of insects, and are often as incapable of arresting their depredations, as of staying the shock of an earthquake, or the course of a stream of lava. . . .

We are often misled, when we institute such comparisons, by our knowledge of the wide distinction between the instincts of animals and reasoning power of man; and we are apt hastily to infer, that the effects of a rational and an irrational species, considered merely *as physical agents,* will differ almost as much as the faculties by which their actions are directed. . . .

If then an intelligent being, after observing the order of events for an indefinite series of ages, had witnessed at last so wonderful an innovation as this, to what extent would his belief in the regularity of the system be weakened?—would he cease to assume that there was permanency in the laws of nature?—would he no longer be guided in his speculations by the strictest rules of induction? To these questions it may be answered, that, had he previously presumed to dogmatize respecting the absolute uniformity of the order of nature, he would undoubtedly be checked by witnessing this new and unexpected event, and would form a more just estimate of the limited range of his knowledge, and the unbounded extent of the scheme of the universe. But he would soon perceive that no one of the fixed and constant laws of the animate or inanimate world was subverted by human agency, and that the modifications produced were on the occurrence of new and extraordinary circumstances, and those not of a physical but a moral nature. The deviation permitted would also appear to be as slight as was consistent with the accomplishment of the new moral end proposed, and to be in a great degree temporary in its nature, so that, whenever the power of the new agent was withheld, even for a brief period, a relapse would take place to the ancient state of things; the domesticated animal, for example, recovering in a few generations its wild instinct, and the garden-flower and fruit-tree reverting to the likeness of the parent stock.

Now, if it would be reasonable to draw such inferences with respect to the future, we cannot but apply the same rules of induction to the past. We have no right to anticipate any modifications in the results of existing causes in time to come, which are not conformable to analogy, unless they be produced by the progressive development of human power, or perhaps by some other new relations which may hereafter spring up between the moral and material worlds. In the same manner, when we speculate on the vicissitudes of the animate and inanimate creation in former ages, we ought not to look for any anomalous results, unless where man has interfered, or unless clear indications appear of some other moral source of temporary derangement. . . .

The uniformity of the plan being once assumed, events which have occurred at the most distant periods in the animate and inanimate world will be acknowledged to throw light on each other, and the deficiency of our information respecting some of the most obscure parts of the present creation will be removed. For as, by studying the external configuration of the existing land and its inhabitants, we may restore in imagination the appearance of the ancient continents which have passed away, so may we obtain from the deposits of ancient seas and lakes an insight into the nature of the sub-aqueous processes now in operation, and of many forms of organic life, which, though now existing, are veiled from sight. Rocks, also, produced by subterranean fire in former ages at great depths in the bowels of the earth, present us, when upraised by gradual movements, and exposed to the light of heaven, with an image of those changes which the deep seated volcano may now occasion in the nether regions. Thus, although we are mere sojourners on the surface of the planet, chained to a mere point in space, enduring but for a moment of time, the human mind is not only enabled to number worlds beyond the unassisted ken of mortal eye, but to trace the events of indefinite ages before the creation of our race, and is not even withheld from penetrating into the dark secrets of the ocean, or the interior of the solid globe; free, like the spirit which the poet described as animating the universe.

Terrasque, tractusque maris, cœlumque profundum.

—ire per omnes

[FROM Chapter 24]

That the greater part of the space now occupied by the European continent was sea when some of the secondary rocks were produced, must be inferred from the wide areas over which several of the marine groups are diffused; but we need not suppose that the quantity of land was less in those remote ages, but merely that its position was very different.

It has been shown that, immediately below the chalk and green-sand, a fluviatile formation, called the Wealden, occurs, which has been ascertained to extend from west to east about 200 English miles, and from northwest to southeast about 220 miles, the depth or total thickness of the beds, where greatest, being about 2000 feet. These phenomena clearly indicate that there was a constant supply in that region, for a long period, of a considerable body of fresh water, such as might be supposed to have drained a continent, or a large island, containing within it a lofty chain of mountains. . . .

If asked where the continent was placed from the ruins of

which the Wealden strata were derived, we might be almost tempted to speculate on the former existence of the Atlantis of Plato as true in geology, although fabulous as an historical event. We know that the present European lands have come into existence almost entirely since the deposition of the chalk; and the same period may have sufficed for the disappearance of a continent of equal magnitude, situated farther to the west.

But among the numerous fossils of the ancient delta of the Wealden no remains of mammalia have been detected; whereas we should naturally expect, on examining the deposits recently formed at the mouths of the Quorra, Indus, or Ganges, to find, not only the bones of birds and of amphibious and land reptiles, but also those of the hippopotamus, and other mammalia which frequent the banks of rivers. . . .

It is certainly a startling proposition to suppose, that a continent covered with vegetation, which had its forests of palms and tree-ferns, and its plants allied to the Dracæna and Cycas, which was inhabited by large saurians, and by birds, was, nevertheless, entirely devoid of land quadrupeds. . . .

On what grand laws in the animal physiology this remarkable phenomenon depends, cannot, in the present state of science, be explained; nor could we predict whether any apposite condition of the atmosphere in respect to heat, moisture, and other circumstances, would bring about a state of animal life which might be called the converse of that above described; a state of things in which large mammalia might abound, and reptiles disappear. We ought, however, to recollect, that a mean annual temperature like that now experienced at the equator, co-existing with the unequal days and nights of European latitudes, and with a distinct distribution of sea and land, would imply a climate to which we have now no parallel. Consequently, the type of animal and vegetable existence required for such a climate might deviate as widely from that now established in any part of the globe, as do the Flora and Fauna of our tropical differ from those of our arctic regions.

Concluding Remarks

In the history of the progress of geology, it has been stated that the opinion originally promulgated by Hutton, 'that the strata called *primitive* were mere altered sedimentary rocks,' was vehemently opposed for a time, on the ground of its supposed tendency to promote a belief in the past eternity of our planet. Before that period the absence of animal and vegetable remains in the so-called primitive strata had been appealed to, as proving that there had been an era when the planet was uninhabited by living beings, and when, as was also inferred, it was uninhabitable, and, therefore, probably in a nascent state.

The opposite doctrine, that the oldest visible strata might be the monuments of an antecedent period, when the animate world was already in existence, was declared to be equivalent to the assumption that there never was a beginning to the present order of things. The unfairness of this charge was clearly pointed out by Playfair, who observed, 'that it was one thing to declare that we had not yet discovered the traces of a beginning, and another to deny that the earth ever had a beginning.'

I regret, however, to find that the bearing of my arguments in the first book has been misunderstood in a similar manner; for I have been charged with endeavouring to establish the proposition, that 'the existing causes of change have operated with absolute uniformity from all eternity.'

It is the more necessary to notice this misrepresentation of my views, as it has proceeded from a friendly critic, whose theoretical opinions coincide in general with my own; but who has, in this instance, strangely misconceived the scope of the argument. With equal justice might an astronomer be accused of asserting that the works of creation extended throughout *infinite* space, because he refuses to take for granted that the remotest stars now seen in the heavens are on the utmost verge of the material universe. Every improvement of the telescope has brought thousands of new worlds into view; and it would, therefore, be rash and unphilosophical to imagine that we already survey the whole extent of the vast scheme, or that it will ever be brought within the sphere of human observation.

But no argument can be drawn from such premises in favour of the infinity of the space that has been filled with worlds; and if the material universe has any limits, it then follows that it must occupy a minute and infinitesimal point in infinite space.

So if, in tracing back the earth's history, we arrive at the monuments of events which may have happened millions of ages before our times, and if we still find no decided evidence of a commencement, yet the arguments from analogy in support of probability of a beginning remain unshaken; and if the past duration of the earth be finite, then the aggregate of geological epochs, however numerous, must constitute a mere moment of the past, a mere infinitesimal portion of eternity.

It has been argued, that, as the different states of the earth's surface, and the different species by which it has been inhabited, have all had their origin, and many of them their termination, so the entire series may have commenced at a certain period. It has also been urged, that, as we admit the creation of man to have occurred at a comparatively modern epoch—as we concede the astonishing fact of the first introduction of a moral and intellectual being—so also we may conceive the first creation of the planet itself.

I am far from denying the weight of this reasoning from analogy; but, although it may strengthen our conviction, that the present system of change has not gone on from eternity, it cannot warrant us in presuming that we shall be permitted to behold the signs of the earth's origin, or the evidences of the first introduction into it of organic beings. We aspire in vain to assign limits to the works of creation in *space*, whether we examine the starry heavens, or that world of minute animalcules which is revealed to us by the microscope. We are prepared, therefore, to find that in *time* also the confines of the universe lie beyond the reach of mortal ken. But in whatever direction we pursue our researches, whether in time or space, we discover everywhere the clear proofs of a Creative Intelligence, and of His foresight, wisdom, and power.

As geologists, we learn that it is not only the present condition of the globe which has been suited to the accommodation of myriads of living creatures, but that many former states also have been adapted to the organisation and habits of prior races of beings. The disposition of the seas, continents, and islands, and the climates, have varied; the species likewise have been changed; and yet they have all been so modelled, on types analogous to those of existing plants and animals, as to indicate throughout a perfect harmony of design and unity of purpose. To assume that the evidence of the beginning or end of so vast a scheme lies within the reach of our philosophical inquiries, or even of our speculations, appears to be inconsistent with a just estimate of the relations which subsist between the finite powers of man and the attributes of an Infinite and Eternal Being.

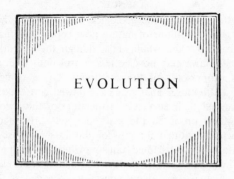

EVOLUTION

The Origin of the Animated Tribes

ROBERT CHAMBERS

[FROM *Vestiges of Creation*]

1844

Thus concludes the wondrous chapter of the earth's history which is told by geology. It takes up our globe at the period when its original incandescent state had nearly ceased; conducts it through what we have every reason to believe were vast, or at least very considerable, spaces of time, in the course of which many superficial changes took place, and vegetable and animal life was gradually developed; and drops it just at the point when man was apparently about to enter on the scene. The compilation of such a history, from materials of so extraordinary a character, and the powerful nature of the evidence which these materials afford, are calculated to excite our admiration, and the result must be allowed to exalt the dignity of science, as a product of man's industry and his reason.

If there is any thing more than another impressed on our

From 3rd edition (1845), pages 147-68.

minds by the course of the geological history, it is, that the same laws and conditions of nature now apparent to us have existed throughout the whole time, though the operation of some of these laws may now be less conspicuous than in the early ages, from some of the conditions having come to a settlement and a close. That seas have flowed and ebbed, and winds disturbed their surfaces, in the time of the secondary rocks, we have proof on the yet preserved surfaces of the sands which constituted margins of the seas in those days. Even the fall of wind-slanted rain is evidenced on the same tablets. The washing down of detached matter from elevated grounds, which we see rivers constantly engaged in at the present time, and which is daily shallowing the seas adjacent to their mouths, only proceeded on a greater scale in earlier epochs. The volcanic subterranean force, which we see belching forth lavas on the sides of mountains, and throwing up new elevations by land and sea, was only more powerfully operative in distant ages. To turn to organic nature, vegetation proceeded then exactly as now. The very alternations of the seasons has been read in unmistakable characters in sections of the trees of those days, precisely as it might be read in a section of a tree cut down yesterday. The system of prey amongst animals flourished throughout the whole of the pre-human period; and the adaptation of all plants and animals to their respective spheres of existence was as perfect in those early ages as it is still. . . .

Fossil history has no doubt still some obscure passages; and these have been partially adverted to in the preceding pages. Sea-weeds, it has been remarked, are not the lowest forms of aquatic vegetation; neither are the plants of the coal-measures the very lowest, though they are a low form, of land vegetation. But, it may be asked, could we expect to see confervæ, or land cryptogamia inferior to ferns, preserved in rocks? Is their organization such as to afford the least chance of their having been preserved? These blanks in the series are no more than blanks; and when a candid mind reflects on the nature of the missing forms, and further considers that those present are all in the order of their organic development, the whole phenomena appear exactly what might have been anticipated. . . .

It is scarcely less evident, from the geological record, that the progress of organic life has observed some correspondence with the progress of physical conditions on the surface. We do not know for certain that the sea, at the time when it supported radiated, molluscous, and articulated families, was incapable of supporting fishes; but causes for such a limitation are far from inconceivable. The huge saurians appear to have been precisely adapted to the low muddy coasts and sea margins of the time when they flourished. Marsupials appear at the time when the surface was generally in that flat, imperfectly variegated state in which we find Australia, the region where they now live in the greatest abundance, and one which has no higher native mammalian type. Finally, it was not till the land and sea had come into their present relations, and the former, in its principal continents, had acquired the irregularity of surface necessary for man, that man appeared. . . .

In examining the fossils of the lower marine creation, with a reference to the kind of rock in connexion with which they are found, it is observed that some strata are attended by a much greater abundance of both species and individuals than others. . . . Nor is it less remarkable how various species are withdrawn from the earth, when the proper conditions for their particular existence are changed. The trilobite, of which fifty species existed during the earlier formations, was extirpated before the secondary had commenced, and appeared no more. The ammonite is not found above the chalk. The species, and even genera of all the early radiata and mollusks were exchanged for others long ago. Not one species of any creature which flourished before the tertiary (Ehrenberg's infusoria excepted) now exists; and of the mammalia which arose during that series, many forms are altogether gone, while of others we have now only kindred species. Thus to find not only frequent additions to the previously existing forms, but frequent withdrawals of forms which had apparently become inappropriate—a constant shifting as well as advance—is a fact calculated very forcibly to arrest attention.

A candid consideration of all these circumstances can scarcely fail to introduce into our minds a somewhat different idea of organic creation from what has hitherto been generally entertained. That God created animated beings, as well as the terraqueous theatre of their being, is a fact so powerfully evidenced, and so universally received, that I at once take it for granted. But in the particulars of this so highly supported idea, we surely here see cause for some re-consideration. It may now be inquired,—In what way was the creation of animated beings effected? The ordinary notion may, I think, be described as this,—that the Almighty Author produced the progenitors of all existing species by some sort of personal or immediate exertion. But how does this notion comport with what we have seen of the gradual advance of species, from the humblest to the highest? How can we suppose an immediate exertion of this creative power at one time to produce zoophytes, another time to add a few marine mollusks, another to bring in one or two crustacea, again to produce crustaceous fishes, again perfect fishes, and so on to the end? This would surely be to take a very mean view of the Creative Power—to, in short, anthropomorphize it, or reduce it to some such character as that borne by the ordinary proceedings of mankind. And yet this would be unavoidable; for that the organic creation was thus progressive through a long space of time, rests on evidence which nothing can overturn or gainsay. Some other idea must then be come to with regard to *the mode* in which the Divine Author proceeded in the organic creation. Let us seek in the history of the earth's formation for a new suggestion on this point. We have seen powerful evidence, that the construction of this globe and its associates, and inferentially that of all the other globes of space, was the result, not of any immediate or personal exertion on the part of the Deity, but of natural laws which are expressions of his will. What is to hinder our supposing that the organic creation is also a result of natural laws, which are in like manner an expression of his will? More than this, the fact of the cosmical arrangements being an effect of natural law, is a powerful argument for the organic arrangements being so likewise, for how can we suppose that the august Being who brought all these countless worlds into form by the simple establishment of a natural principle flowing from his mind, was to interfere personally and specially on every occasion when a new shell-fish or reptile was to be ushered into existence on *one* of these worlds? Surely this idea is too ridiculous to be for a moment entertained. . . .

To a reasonable mind the Divine attributes must appear, not diminished or reduced in any way, by supposing a creation by law, but infinitely exalted. It is the narrowest of all views of the Deity, and characteristic of a humble class of intellects, to suppose him constantly acting in particular ways for particular occasions. It, for one thing, greatly detracts from his foresight, the most undeniable of all the attributes of Omnipotence. It lowers him towards the level of our own humble intellects. Much more worthy of him it surely is, to suppose that all things have been commissioned by him from the first, though neither is he absent from a particle of the current of natural affairs in one sense, seeing that the whole system is continually supported by his providence. Even in human affairs, if I may be allowed to adopt a familiar illustration, there is a constant progress from specific action for particular occasions, to arrangements which, once established, shall continue to answer for a great multitude of occasions. Such plans the enlightened readily form for themselves, and conceive as being adopted by all who have to attend to a multitude of affairs, while the ignorant suppose every act of the greatest public functionary to be the result of some special consideration and care on his part alone. Are we to suppose the Deity adopting plans which harmonize only with the modes of procedure of the less enlightened of our race? Those who would object to the hypothesis of a creation by the intervention of law, do not perhaps consider how powerful an argument in favour of the existence of God is lost by rejecting this doctrine. . . .

It may here be remarked that there is in our doctrine that

harmony in all the associated phenomena which generally marks great truths. First, it agrees, as we have seen, with the idea of planet-creation by natural law. Secondly, upon this supposition, all that geology tells us of the succession of species appears natural and intelligible. . . . It is also to be observed, that the thing to be accounted for is not merely the origination of organic being upon this little planet, third of a series which is but one of hundreds of thousands of series, the whole of which again form but one portion of an apparently infinite globe-peopled space, where all seems analogous. We have to suppose, that every one of these numberless globes is either a theatre of organic being, or in the way of becoming so. This is a conclusion which every addition to our knowledge makes only the more irresistible. Is it conceivable, as a fitting mode of exercise for creative intelligence, that it should be constantly moving from one sphere to another, to form and plant the various species which may be required in each situation at particular times? Is such an idea accordant with our general conception of the dignity, not to speak of the power, of the Great Author? Yet such is the notion which we must form, if we adhere to the doctrine of special exercise. Let us see, on the other hand, how the doctrine of a creation by law agrees with this expanded view of the organic world.

Unprepared as most men may be for such an announcement, there can be no doubt that we are able, in this limited sphere, to form some satisfactory conclusions as to the plants and animals of those other spheres which move at such immense distances from us. Suppose that the first persons of an early nation who made a ship and ventured to sea in it, observed, as they sailed along, a set of objects which they had never before seen—namely, a fleet of other ships—would they not have been justified in supposing that those ships were occupied, like their own, by human beings possessing hands to row and steer, eyes to watch the signs of the weather, intelligence to guide them from one place to another—in short, beings in all respects like themselves, or only shewing such differences as they knew to be producible by difference of climate and habits of life? Precisely in this manner we can speculate on the inhabitants of remote spheres. . . .

Assuming that organic beings are thus spread over all space, the idea of their having all come into existence by the operation of laws everywhere applicable, is only conformable to that principle, acknowledged to be so generally visible in the affairs of Providence, to have all done by the employment of the smallest possible amount of means. Thus, as one set of laws produced all orbs and their motions and geognostic arrangements, so one set of laws overspread them all with life. The whole productive or creative arrangements are therefore in perfect unity.

Special Creation or Modification?

HERBERT SPENCER

["The Development Hypothesis"]

1852

In a debate upon the development hypothesis, lately narrated to me by a friend, one of the disputants was described as arguing, that, as in all our experience we know of no such phenomenon as the transmutation of species, it is unphilosophical to assume that transmutation of species ever takes place. Had I been present, I think that, passing over his assertion, which is open to criticism, I should have replied that, as in all our experience we have never known a species *created*, it was, by his own showing, unphilosophical to assume that any species ever had been created.

From *Leader*, 3 (March 20, 1852), pages 280-81.

Those who cavalierly reject the theory of Lamarck and his followers, as not adequately supported by facts, seem quite to forget that their own theory is supported by no facts at all. Like the majority of men who are born to a given belief, they demand the most rigorous proof of any adverse doctrine, but assume that their own doctrine needs none. Here we find scattered over the globe vegetable and animal organisms numbering, of the one kind (according to Humboldt), some 320,000 species, and of the other, if we include insects, some *two millions* of species (see Carpenter); and if to these we add the numbers of animal and vegetable species that have become extinct (bearing in mind how geological records prove that, from the earliest appearance of life down to the present time, different species have been successively replacing each other, so that the world's Flora and Fauna have completely changed many times over), we may safely estimate the number of species that have existed, and are existing on the earth, at not less than ten millions. Well, which is the most rational theory about these ten millions of species? Is it most likely that there have been ten millions of special creations? or is it most likely that by continual modifications, due to change of circumstances, ten millions of varieties may have been produced, as varieties are being produced still? One of the two theories must be adopted. Which is most countenanced by facts?

Doubtless many will reply that they can more easily conceive ten millions of special creations to have taken place, than they can conceive that ten millions of varieties have been produced by the process of perpetual modification. All such, however, will find, on candid inquiry, that they are under an illusion. This is one of the many cases in which men do not really believe, but rather *believe they believe*. It is not that they can truly conceive ten millions of special creations to have taken place, but that they *think they can do so*. A little careful introspection will show them that they have never yet realized to themselves the creation of even *one* species. If they have formed a definite conception of the process, they will be able to answer such questions as—How is a new species constructed? and How does it make its appearance? Is it thrown down from the clouds? or must we hold to the notion that it struggles up out of the ground? Do its limbs and viscera rush together from all the points of the compass? or must we receive some such old Hebrew notion as, that God goes into a forest-cavern, and there takes clay and moulds a new creature? If they say that a new creature is produced in none of these modes, which are too absurd to be believed, then they are required to describe the mode in which a new creature *may* be produced—a mode which does *not* seem absurd; and such a mode they will find that they neither have conceived nor can conceive.

Should the believers in special creations consider it unfair thus to call upon them to describe how special creations take place, I reply, that this is far less than they demand from the supporters of the development hypothesis. They are merely asked to point out a *conceivable* mode; on the other hand, they ask, not simply for a *conceivable* mode, but for the *actual* mode. They do not say—Show us how this *may* take place; but they say—Show us how this *does* take place. So far from its being unreasonable to ask so much of them, it would be reasonable to ask not only for a possible mode of special creation, but for an ascertained mode; seeing that this is no greater a demand than they make upon their opponents.

And here we may perceive how much more defensible the new doctrine is than the old one. Even could the supporters of the development hypothesis merely show that the production of species by the process of modification is conceivable, they would be in a better position than their opponents. But they can do much more than this. They can show that the process of modification has effected and is effecting great changes in all organisms subject to modifying influences. Though, from the impossibility of getting at a sufficiency of facts, they are unable to trace the many phases through which any existing species has passed in arriving at its present form, or to identify the influences which caused the successive modifications, yet they can show that any existing species—animal or vegetable—when placed under conditions different from its previous ones, *immediately begins to undergo certain changes of structure fitting it for the new conditions*. They can show that in successive generations these changes continue until ultimately the new conditions become the natural ones. They can show that in cultivated plants, in domesticated animals, and in the several races of men, these changes have uniformly taken place. They can show that the degrees of difference so produced are often, as in dogs, greater than those on which distinctions of species are in other cases founded. They can show that it is a matter of dispute whether some of these modified forms *are* varieties or separate species. They can show, too, that the changes daily taking place in ourselves— the facility that attends long practice, and the loss of aptitude that begins when practice ceases—the strengthening of passions habitually gratified, and the weakening of those habitually curbed—the development of every faculty, bodily, moral, or intellectual, according to the use made of it—are all explicable on this same principle. And thus they can show that throughout all organic nature there *is* at work a modifying influence of the kind they assign as the cause of these specific differences—an influence which, though slow in its action, does, in time, if the circumstances demand it, produce marked changes—an influence which, to all appearance, would produce in the millions of years, and under the great varieties of conditions which geological records imply, any amount of change.

Which, then, is the most rational hypothesis; that of special creations which has neither a fact to support it nor is even definitely conceivable; or that of modification, which is not only definitely conceivable, but is countenanced by the habitudes of every existing organism?

That by any series of changes a zoophyte should ever become a mammal, seems to those who are not familiar with zoology, and who have not seen how clear becomes the relationship between the simplest and the most complex forms, when all intermediate forms are examined, a very grotesque notion. Habitually looking at things rather in their statical than in their dynamical aspect, they never realize the fact that, by small increments of modification, any amount of modification may in time be generated. That surprise which they feel on finding one whom they last saw as a boy, grown into a man, becomes incredulity when the degree of change is greater. Nevertheless, abundant instances are at hand of the mode in which we may pass to the most diverse forms by insensible gradations. Arguing the matter some time since with a learned professor, I illustrated my position thus:—You admit that there is no apparent relationship between a circle and an hyperbola. The one is a finite curve; the other is an infinite one. All parts of the one are alike; of the other no two parts are alike. The one incloses a space; the other will not inclose a space, though produced for ever. Yet opposite as are these curves in all their properties, they may be connected together by a series of intermediate curves, no one of which differs from the adjacent ones in any appreciable degree. Thus, if a cone be cut by a plane at right angles to its axis we get a circle. If, instead of being perfectly at right angles, the plane subtends with the axis an angle of $89° 59'$, we have an ellipse which no human eye, even when aided by an accurate pair of compasses can distinguish from a circle. Decreasing the angle minute by minute the ellipse becomes first perceptibly eccentric, then manifestly so, and by and by acquires so immensely elongated a form, as to bear no recognisable resemblance to a circle. By continuing this process the ellipse passes insensibly into a parabola; and ultimately, by still further diminishing the angle, into an hyperbola. Now here we have four different species of curve—circle, ellipse, parabola, and hyperbola—each having its peculiar properties, and its separate equation, and the first and last of which are quite opposite in nature, connected together as members of one series, all producible by a single process of insensible modification.

But the blindness of those who think it absurd to suppose that complex organic forms may have arisen by successive modifications out of simple ones, becomes astonishing when we remember that complex organic forms are daily being thus produced. A tree differs from a seed immeasurably in every respect—in bulk, in structure, in colour, in form, in specific gravity, in chemical composition; differs so greatly that no visible resemblance of any kind can be pointed out between them. Yet is the one changed in the course of a few years into the other—changed so gradually that at no moment can it be said—Now the seed ceases to be, and the tree exists. What can be more widely contrasted than a newly-born child and the small, semi-transparent, gelatinous spherule constituting the human ovum? The infant is so complex in structure that a cyclopædia is needed to describe its constituent parts. The germinal vesicle is so simple that a line will contain all that can be said of it. Nevertheless a few months suffices to develop the one out of the other, and that, too, by a series of modifications so small that were the embryo examined at successive minutes not even a microscope would disclose any sensible changes. That the uneducated and the ill-educated should think the hypothesis that all races of beings, man inclusive, may in process of time have been evolved from the simplest monad, a ludicrous one, is not to be wondered at. But from the physiologist, who knows that every individual being *is* so evolved,—who knows further, that in their earliest condition the germs of all plants and animals whatever are so similar, "that there is no appreciable distinction amongst them which would enable it to be determined whether a particular molecule is the germ of a conferva or of an oak, of a zoophyte or of a man"—for him to make a difficulty of the matter is inexcusable. Surely, if a single structureless cell may, when subjected to certain influences, become a man in the space of twenty years, there is nothing absurd in the hypothesis that under certain other influences, a cell may in the course of millions of years give origin to the human race. The two processes are generically the same, and differ only in length and complexity.

We have, indeed, in the part taken by many scientific men in this controversy of "Law *versus* Miracle," a good illustration of the tenacious vitality of superstitions. Ask one of our leading geologists or physiologists whether he believes in the Mosaic account of the creation, and he will take the question as next to an insult. Either he rejects the narrative entirely, or understands it in some vague non-natural sense. Yet one part of it he unconsciously adopts; and that, too, literally. For, whence has he got this notion of "special creations," which he thinks so reasonable, and fights for so vigorously? Evidently he can trace it back to no other source than this myth which he repudiates. He has not a single fact in nature to quote in proof of it; nor is he prepared with any chain of abstract reasoning by which it may be established. Catechise him, and he will be forced to confess that the notion was put into his mind in childhood as part of a story which he now thinks absurd. And why, after rejecting all the rest of this story, he should strenuously defend this last remnant of it as though he had received it on valid authority, he would be puzzled to say.

The Struggle for Existence

CHARLES DARWIN

[FROM *On the Origin of Species*]

1859

Nothing is easier than to admit in words the truth of the universal struggle for life, or more difficult—at least I have found it so—than constantly to bear this conclusion in mind. Yet unless it be thoroughly engrained in the mind, I am convinced that the whole economy of nature, with every fact on distribution, rarity, abundance, extinction, and variation, will be dimly seen or quite misunderstood. We behold the face of nature bright with gladness, we often see superabundance

From Chapter 3.

of food; we do not see, or we forget, that the birds which are idly singing round us mostly live on insects or seeds, and are thus constantly destroying life; or we forget how largely these songsters, or their eggs, or their nestlings, are destroyed by birds and beasts of prey; we do not always bear in mind, that though food may be now superabundant, it is not so at all seasons of each recurring year.

I should premise that I use the term Struggle for Existence in a large and metaphorical sense, including dependence of one being on another, and including (which is more important) not only the life of the individual, but success in leaving progeny. Two canine animals in a time of dearth, may be truly said to struggle with each other which shall get food and live. But a plant on the edge of a desert is said to struggle for life against the drought, though more properly it should be said to be dependent on the moisture. A plant which annually produces a thousand seeds, of which on an average only one comes to maturity, may be more truly said to struggle with the plants of the same and other kinds which already clothe the ground. . . . In these several senses, which pass into each other, I use for convenience sake the general term of struggle for existence.

A struggle for existence inevitably follows from the high rate at which all organic beings tend to increase. Every being, which during its natural lifetime produces several eggs or seeds, must suffer destruction during some period of its life, and during some season or occasional year, otherwise, on the principle of geometrical increase, its numbers would quickly become so inordinately great that no country could support the product. Hence, as more individuals are produced than can possibly survive, there must in every case be a struggle for existence, either one individual with another of the same species, or with the individuals of distinct species, or with the physical conditions of life. It is the doctrine of Malthus applied with manifold force to the whole animal and vegetable kingdoms; for in this case there can be no artificial increase of food, and no prudential restraint from marriage. Although some species may be now increasing, more or less rapidly, in numbers, all cannot do so, for the world would not hold them.

There is no exception to the rule that every organic being naturally increases at so high a rate, that if not destroyed, the earth would soon be covered by the progeny of a single pair. Even slow-breeding man has doubled in twenty-five years, and at this rate, in a few thousand years, there would literally not be standing room for his progeny. Linnæus has calculated that if an annual plant produced only two seeds—and there is no plant so unproductive as this—and their seedlings next year produced two, and so on, then in twenty years there would be a million plants. The elephant is reckoned to be the slowest breeder of all known animals, and I have taken some pains to estimate its probable minimum rate of natural increase: it will be under the mark to assume that it breeds when thirty years old, and goes on breeding till ninety years old, bringing forth three pair of young in this interval; if this be so, at the end of the fifth century there would be alive fifteen million elephants, descended from the first pair.

But we have better evidence on this subject than mere theoretical calculations, namely, the numerous recorded cases of the astonishingly rapid increase of various animals in a state of nature, when circumstances have been favourable to them during two or three following seasons. Still more striking is the evidence from our domestic animals of many kinds which have run wild in several parts of the world: if the statements of the rate of increase of slow-breeding cattle and horses in South-America, and latterly in Australia, had not been well authenticated, they would have been quite incredible. So it is with plants: cases could be given of introduced plants which have become common throughout whole islands in a period of less than ten years. . . . The obvious explanation is that the conditions of life have been very favourable, and that there has consequently been less destruction of the old and young, and that nearly all the young have been enabled to breed. In such cases the geometrical ratio of increase, the result of which never fails to be surprising, simply explains the extraordinarily rapid increase and wide diffusion of naturalised productions in their new homes. . . .

Many cases are on record showing how complex and unexpected are the checks and relations between organic beings, which have to struggle together in the same country. I will give only a single instance, which, though a simple one, has interested me. In Staffordshire, on the estate of a relation where I had ample means of investigation, there was a large and extremely barren heath, which had never been touched by the hand of man; but several hundred acres of exactly the same nature had been enclosed twenty-five years previously and planted with Scotch fir. The change in the native vegetation of the planted part of the heath was most remarkable, more than is generally seen in passing from one quite different soil to another: not only the proportional numbers of the heath-plants were wholly changed, but twelve species of plants (not counting grasses and carices) flourished in the plantations, which could not be found on the heath. The effect on the insects must have been still greater, for six insectivorous birds were very common in the plantations, which were not to be seen on the heath; and the heath was frequented by two or three distinct insectivorous birds. Here we see how potent has been the effect of the introduction of a single tree, nothing whatever else having been done, with the exception that the land had been enclosed, so that cattle could not enter. But how important an element enclosure is, I plainly saw near Farnham, in Surrey. Here there are extensive heaths, with a few clumps of old Scotch firs on the distant hill-tops: within the last ten years large spaces have been enclosed, and self-sown firs are now springing up in multitudes, so close together that all cannot live. When I ascertained that these young trees had not been sown or planted, I was so much surprised at their numbers that I went to several points of view, whence I could examine hundreds of acres of the unenclosed heath, and literally I could not see a single Scotch fir, except the old planted clumps. But on looking closely between the stems of the heath, I found a multitude of seedlings and little trees, which had been perpetually browsed down by the cattle. In one square yard, at a point some hundred yards distant from one of the old clumps, I counted thirty-two little trees; and one of them, judging from the rings of growth, had during twenty-six years tried to raise its head above the stems of the heath, and had failed. No wonder that, as soon as the land was enclosed, it became thickly clothed with vigorously growing young firs. Yet the heath was so extremely barren and so extensive that no one would ever have imagined that cattle would have so closely and effectually searched it for food.

Here we see that cattle absolutely determine the existence of the Scotch fir; but in several parts of the world insects determine the existence of cattle. Perhaps Paraguay offers the most curious instance of this; for here neither cattle nor horses nor dogs have ever run wild, though they swarm southward and northward in a feral state; and Azara and Rengger have shown that this is caused by the greater number in Paraguay of a certain fly, which lays its eggs in the navels of these animals when first born. The increase of these flies, numerous as they are, must be habitually checked by some means, probably by birds. Hence, if certain insectivorous birds (whose numbers are probably regulated by hawks or beasts of prey) were to increase in Paraguay, the flies would decrease —then cattle and horses would become feral, and this would certainly greatly alter (as indeed I have observed in parts of South America) the vegetation: this again would largely affect the insects; and this, as we just have seen in Staffordshire, the insectivorous birds, and so onwards in ever-increasing circles of complexity. We began this series by insectivorous birds, and we have ended with them. Not that in nature the relations can ever be as simple as this. Battle within battle must ever be recurring with varying success; and yet in the long-run the forces are so nicely balanced, that the face of nature remains uniform for long periods of time, though assuredly the merest trifle would often give the victory to one organic being over another. Nevertheless so profound is our ignorance and so high our presumption, that we marvel when we hear of the extinction of an organic being; and as we do not see the cause, we invoke cataclysms to desolate the world, or invent laws on the duration of the forms of life! . . .

[FROM Chapter 4]

The affinities of all the beings of the same class have sometimes been represented by a great tree. I believe this simile largely speaks the truth. The green and budding twigs may represent existing species; and those produced during each former year may represent the long succession of extinct species. At each period of growth all the growing twigs have tried to branch out on all sides, and to overtop and kill the surrounding twigs and branches, in the same manner as species and groups of species have tried to overmaster other species in the great battle for life. The limbs divided into great branches, and these into lesser and lesser branches, were themselves once, when the tree was small, budding twigs; and this connexion of the former and present buds by ramifying branches may well represent the classification of all extinct and living species in groups subordinate to groups. Of the many twigs which flourished when the tree was a mere bush, only two or three, now grown into great branches, yet survive and bear all the other branches; so with the species which lived during long-past geological periods, very few now have living and modified descendants. From the first growth of the tree, many a limb and branch has decayed and dropped off; and these lost branches of various sizes may represent those whole orders, families, and genera which have now no living representatives, and which are known to us only from having been found in a fossil state. As we here and there see a thin straggling branch springing from a fork low down in a tree, and which by some chance has been favoured and is still alive on its summit, so we occasionally see an animal like the Ornithorhynchus or Lepidosiren, which in some small degree connects by its affinities two large branches of life, and which has apparently been saved from fatal competition by having inhabited a protected station. As buds give rise by growth to fresh buds, and these, if vigorous, branch out and overtop on all sides many a feebler branch, so by generation I believe it has been with the great Tree of Life, which fills with its dead and broken branches the crust of the earth, and covers the surface with its ever branching and beautiful ramifications.

[FROM Chapter 14]

As each species tends by its geometrical ratio of reproduction to increase inordinately in number; and as the modified descendants of each species will be enabled to increase by so much the more as they become more diversified in habits and structure, so as to be enabled to seize on many and widely different places in the economy of nature, there will be a constant tendency in natural selection to preserve the most divergent offspring of any one species. Hence during a long-continued course of modification, the slight differences, characteristic of varieties of the same species, tend to be augmented into the greater differences characteristic of species of the same genus. New and improved varieties will inevitably supplant and exterminate the older, less improved and intermediate varieties; and thus species are rendered to a large extent defined and distinct objects. Dominant species belonging to the larger groups tend to give birth to new and dominant forms; so that each large group tends to become still larger, and at the same time more divergent in character. But as all groups cannot thus succeed in increasing in size, for the world would not hold them, the more dominant groups beat the less dominant. This tendency in the large groups to go on increasing in size and diverging in character, together with the almost inevitable contingency of much extinction, explains the arrangement of all the forms of life, in groups subordinate to groups, all within a few great classes, which we now see everywhere around us, and which has prevailed throughout all time. This grand fact of the grouping of all organic beings seems to me utterly inexplicable on the theory of creation.

As natural selection acts solely by accumulating slight,

successive, favourable variations, it can produce no great or sudden modification; it can act only by very short and slow steps. Hence the canon of "Natura non facit saltum," which every fresh addition to our knowledge tends to make more strictly correct, is on this theory simply intelligible. We can plainly see why nature is prodigal in variety, though niggard in innovation. But why this should be a law of nature if each species has been independently created, no man can explain. . . .

[FROM The Conclusion]

I have now recapitulated the chief facts and considerations which have thoroughly convinced me that species have changed, and are still slowly changing by the preservation and accumulation of successive slight favourable variations. Why, it may be asked, have all the most eminent living naturalists and geologists rejected this view of the mutability of species? It cannot be asserted that organic beings in a state of nature are subject to no variation; it cannot be proved that the amount of variation in the course of long ages is a limited quantity; no clear distinction has been, or can be, drawn between species and well-marked varieties. It cannot be maintained that species when intercrossed are invariably sterile, and varieties invariably fertile; or that sterility is a special endowment and sign of creation. The belief that species were immutable productions was almost unavoidable as long as the history of the world was thought to be of short duration; and now that we have acquired some idea of the lapse of time, we are too apt to assume, without proof, that the geological record is so perfect that it would have afforded us plain evidence of the mutation of species, if they had undergone mutation.

But the chief cause of our natural unwillingness to admit that one species has given birth to other and distinct species, is that we are always slow in admitting any great change of which we do not see the intermediate steps. The difficulty is the same as that felt by so many geologists, when Lyell first insisted that long lines of inland cliffs had been formed, and great valleys excavated, by the slow action of the coast-waves. The mind cannot possibly grasp the full meaning of the term of a hundred million years; it cannot add up and perceive the full effects of many slight variations, accumulated during an almost infinite number of generations.

Although I am fully convinced of the truth of the views given in this volume under the form of an abstract, I by no means expect to convince experienced naturalists whose minds are stocked with a multitude of facts all viewed, during a long course of years, from a point of view directly opposite to mine. It is so easy to hide our ignorance under such expressions as the "plan of creation," "unity of design," &c., and to think that we give an explanation when we only restate a fact. Any one whose disposition leads him to attach more weight to unexplained difficulties than to the explanation of a certain number of facts will certainly reject my theory. A few naturalists, endowed with much flexibility of mind, and who have already begun to doubt on the immutability of species, may be influenced by this volume; but I look with confidence to the future, to young and rising naturalists, who will be able to view both sides of the question with impartiality. Whoever is led to believe that species are mutable will do good service by conscientiously expressing his conviction; for only thus can the load of prejudice by which this subject is overwhelmed be removed. . . .

I believe that animals have descended from at most only four or five progenitors, and plants from an equal or lesser number. Analogy would lead me one step further, namely, to the belief that all animals and plants have descended from some one prototype. But analogy may be a deceitful guide. Nevertheless all living things have much in common, in their chemical composition, their germinal vesicles, their cellular structure, and their laws of growth and reproduction. We see this even in so trifling a circumstance as that the same poison often similarly affects plants and animals; or that the poison secreted by the gall-fly produces monstrous growths on the wild rose or oak-tree. Therefore I should infer from analogy that probably all the organic beings which have ever lived on this earth have descended from some one primordial form, into which life was first breathed. . . .

In the distant future I see open fields for far more important researches. Psychology will be based on a new foundation, that of the necessary acquirement of each mental power and capacity by gradation. Light will be thrown on the origin of man and his history.

Authors of the highest eminence seem to be fully satisfied with the view that each species has been independently created. To my mind it accords better with what we know of the laws impressed on matter by the Creator, that the production and extinction of the past and present inhabitants of the world should have been due to secondary causes, like those determining the birth and death of the individual. When I view all beings not as special creations, but as the lineal descendants of some few beings which lived long before the first bed of the Silurian system was deposited, they seem to me to become ennobled. Judging from the past, we may safely infer that not one living species will transmit its unaltered likeness to a distant futurity. And of the species now living very few will transmit progeny of any kind to a far distant futurity; for the manner in which all organic beings are grouped, shows that the greater number of species of each genus, and all the species of many genera, have left no descendants, but have become utterly extinct. We can so far take a prophetic glance into futurity as to foretell that it will be the common and widely-spread species, belonging to the larger and dominant groups, which will ultimately prevail and procreate new and dominant species. As all the living forms of life are the lineal descendants of those which lived long before the Silurian epoch, we may feel certain that the ordinary succession by generation has never once been broken, and that no cataclysm has desolated the whole world. Hence we may look with some confidence to a secure future of equally inappreciable length. And as natural selection works solely by and for the good of each being, all corporeal and mental endowments will tend to progress towards perfection.

It is interesting to contemplate an entangled bank, clothed with many plants of many kinds, with birds singing on the bushes, with various insects flitting about, and with worms crawling through the damp earth, and to reflect that these elaborately constructed forms, so different from each other, and dependent on each other in so complex a manner, have all been produced by laws acting around us. These laws, taken in the largest sense, being Growth with Reproduction; Inheritance which is almost implied by reproduction; Variability from the indirect and direct action of the external conditions of life, and from use and disuse; a Ratio of Increase so high as to lead to a Struggle for Life, and as a consequence to Natural Selection, entailing Divergence of Character and the Extinction of less-improved forms. Thus, from the war of nature, from famine and death, the most exalted object which we are capable of conceiving, namely, the production of the higher animals, directly follows. There is grandeur in this view of life, with its several powers, having been originally breathed into a few forms or into one; and that, whilst this planet has gone cycling on according to the fixed law of gravity, from so simple a beginning endless forms most beautiful and most wonderful have been, and are being, evolved.

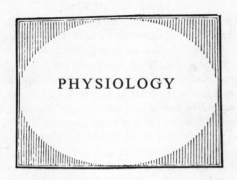

PHYSIOLOGY

Protoplasm, the Physical Basis of Life

THOMAS HENRY HUXLEY

[FROM "On the Physical Basis of Life"]

1869

In order to make the title of this discourse generally intelligible, I have translated the term "Protoplasm," which is the scientific name of the substance of which I am about to speak, by the words "the physical basis of life." I suppose that, to many, the idea that there is such a thing as a physical basis, or matter, of life may be novel—so widely spread is the conception of life as a something which works through matter, but is independent of it; and even those who are aware that matter and life are inseparably connected, may not be prepared for the conclusion plainly suggested by the phrase, *"the* physical basis or matter of life," that there is some one kind of matter which is common to all living beings, and that their endless diversities are bound together by a physical, as well as an ideal, unity. In fact, when first apprehended, such a doctrine as this appears almost shocking to common sense.

What, truly, can seem to be more obviously different from one another in faculty, in form, and in substance, than the

From *Fortnightly Review*, 5 (1 February 1869), pages 129-45.

various kinds of living beings? What community of faculty can there be between the brightly-coloured lichen, which so nearly resembles a mere mineral incrustation of the bare rock on which it grows, and the painter, to whom it is instinct with beauty, or the botanist, whom it feeds with knowledge?

Again, think of the microscopic fungus—a mere infinitesimal ovoid particle, which finds space and duration enough to multiply into countless millions in the body of a living fly; and then of the wealth of foliage, the luxuriance of flower and fruit, which lies between this bald sketch of a plant and the giant pine of California, towering to the dimensions of a cathedral spire, or the Indian fig, which covers acres with its profound shadow, and endures while nations and empires come and go around its vast circumference? Or, turning to the other half of the world of life, picture to yourselves the great Finner whale, hugest of beasts that live, or have lived, disporting his eighty or ninety feet of bone, muscle, and blubber, with easy roll, among waves in which the stoutest ship that ever left dockyard would founder hopelessly; and contrast him with the invisible animalcules—mere gelatinous specks, multitudes of which could, in fact, dance upon the point of a needle with the same ease as the angels of the schoolmen could, in imagination. With these images before your minds, you may well ask what community of form, or structure, is there between the animalcule and the whale; or between the fungus and the fig tree? And, *a fortiori*, between all four?

Finally, if we regard substance, or material composition, what hidden bond can connect the flower which a girl wears in her hair and the blood which courses through her youthful veins; or, what is there in common between the dense and resisting mass of the oak, or the strong fabric of the tortoise, and those broad disks of glassy jelly which may be seen pulsating through the waters of a calm sea, but which drain away to mere films in the hand which raises them out of their element?

Such objections as these must, I think, arise in the mind of every one who ponders, for the first time, upon the conception of a single physical basis of life underlying all the diversities of vital existence; but I propose to demonstrate to you that, notwithstanding these apparent difficulties, a threefold unity—namely, a unity of power, or faculty, a unity of form, and a unity of substantial composition—does pervade the whole living world. . . .

The spectacle afforded by the wonderful energies prisoned within the compass of the microscopic hair of a plant, which we commonly regard as a merely passive organism, is not easily forgotten by one who has watched its display, continued hour after hour, without pause or sign of weakening. The possible complexity of many other organic forms, seemingly as simple as the protoplasm of the nettle, dawns upon one; and the comparison of such a protoplasm to a body with an internal circulation, which has been put forward by an eminent physiologist, loses much of its startling character. Currents similar to those of the hairs of the nettle have been observed in a great multitude of very different plants, and weighty authorities have suggested that they probably occur, in more or less perfection, in all young vegetable cells. If such be the case, the wonderful noonday silence of a tropical forest is, after all, due only to the dulness of our hearing; and could our ears catch the murmur of these tiny Maelstroms, as they whirl in the innumerable myriads of living cells which constitute each tree, we should be stunned, as with the roar of a great city.

Among the lower plants, it is the rule rather than the exception, that contractility should be still more openly manifested at some periods of their existence. The protoplasm of *Algæ* and *Fungi* becomes, under many circumstances, partially, or completely, freed from its woody case, and exhibits movements of its whole mass, or is propelled by the contractility of one, or more, hair-like prolongations of its body, which are called vibratile cilia. And, so far as the conditions of the manifestation of the phenomena of contractility have yet been studied, they are the same for the plant as for the animal. Heat and electric shocks influence both, and in the same way, though it may be in different degrees. It is by no means my intention to suggest that there is no difference in faculty between the lowest plant and the highest, or between plants and animals. But the difference between the powers of the lowest plant, or animal, and those of the highest is one of degree, not of kind, and depends, as Milne-Edwards long ago so well pointed out, upon the extent to which the principle of the division of labour is carried out in the living economy. In the lowest organism all parts are competent to perform all functions, and one and the same portion of protoplasm may successively take on the function of feeding, moving, or reproducing apparatus. In the highest, on the contrary, a great number of parts combine to perform each function, each part doing its allotted share of the work with great accuracy and efficiency, but being useless for any other purpose.

On the other hand, notwithstanding all the fundamental resemblances which exist between the powers of the protoplasm in plants and in animals, they present a striking difference . . . in the fact that plants can manufacture fresh protoplasm out of mineral compounds, whereas animals are obliged to procure it ready-made, and hence, in the long run, depend upon plants. Upon what condition this difference in the powers of the two great divisions of the world of life depends nothing is at present known. . . .

Under these circumstances it may well be asked, how is one mass of non-nucleated protoplasm to be distinguished from another? why call one "plant" and the other "animal"?

The only reply is that, so far as form is concerned, plants and animals are not separable, and that, in many cases, it is a mere matter of convention whether we call a given organism an animal or a plant. . . .

Protoplasm, simple or nucleated, is the formal basis of all life. It is the clay of the potter: which, bake it and paint it as he will, remains clay, separated by artifice, and not by nature, from the commonest brick or sun-dried clod. . . .

Enough has, perhaps, been said to prove the existence of a general uniformity in the character of the protoplasm, or physical basis, of life, in whatever group of living beings it may be studied. But it will be understood that this general uniformity by no means excludes any amount of special modifications of the fundamental substance. The mineral, carbonate of lime, assumes an immense diversity of characters, though no one doubts that under all these Protean changes it is one and the same thing.

And now, what is the ultimate fate, and what the origin, of the matter of life? Is it, as some of the older naturalists supposed, diffused throughout the universe in molecules, which are indestructible and unchangeable in themselves; but, in endless transmigration, unite in innumerable permutations, into the diversified forms of life we know? Or, is the matter of life composed of ordinary matter, differing from it only in the manner in which its atoms are aggregated? Is it built up of ordinary matter, and again resolved into ordinary matter when its work is done?

Modern science does not hesitate a moment between these alternatives. Physiology writes over the portals of life—

Debemur morti nos nostraque,

with a profounder meaning than the Roman poet attached to that melancholy line. Under whatever disguise it takes refuge, whether fungus or oak, worm or man, the living protoplasm not only ultimately dies and is resolved into its mineral and lifeless constituents, but is always dying, and, strange as the paradox may sound, could not live unless it died. . . .

An animal cannot make protoplasm, but must take it ready-made from some other animal, or some plant—the animal's highest feat of constructive chemistry being to convert dead protoplasm into that living matter of life which is appropriate to itself.

Therefore, in seeking for the origin of protoplasm, we must eventually turn to the vegetable world. The fluid containing carbonic acid, water, and ammonia, which offers such a Barmecide feast to the animal, is a table richly spread to multitudes of plants; and, with a due supply of only such materials, many a plant will not only maintain itself in vigour, but grow and multiply until it has increased a million-fold, or a million million-fold, the quantity of protoplasm which it originally possessed; in this way building up the matter of life, to an indefinite extent, from the common matter of the universe. . . .

Thus the matter of life, so far as we know it (and we have no right to speculate on any other), breaks up, in consequence of that continual death which is the condition of its manifesting vitality, into carbonic acid, water, and ammonia, which certainly possess no properties but those of ordinary matter. And out of these same forms of ordinary matter, and from none which are simpler, the vegetable world builds up all the protoplasm which keeps the animal world agoing. Plants are the accumulators of the power which animals distribute and disperse.

But it will be observed, that the existence of the matter of life depends on the pre-existence of certain compounds, namely, carbonic acid, water, and ammonia. Withdraw any one of these three from the world and all vital phenomena come to an end. They are related to the protoplasm of the plant, as the protoplasm of the plant is to that of the animal. Carbon, hydrogen, oxygen, and nitrogen are all lifeless bodies. Of these, carbon and oxygen unite in certain proportions and under certain conditions, to give rise to carbonic acid; hydrogen and oxygen produce water; nitrogen and hydrogen give rise to ammonia. These new compounds, like the elementary bodies of which they are composed, are lifeless. But when they are brought together, under certain conditions they give rise to the still more complex body, protoplasm, and this protoplasm exhibits the phenomena of life.

I see no break in this series of steps in molecular complication, and I am unable to understand why the language which is applicable to any one term of the series may not be used to any of the others. We think fit to call different kinds of matter carbon, oxygen, hydrogen, and nitrogen, and to speak of the various powers and activities of these substances as the properties of the matter of which they are composed. . . .

What justification is there, then, for the assumption of the existence in the living matter of a something which has no representative or correlative in the not living matter which gave rise to it? . . . If the properties of water may be properly said to result from the nature and disposition of its component molecules, I can find no intelligible ground for refusing to say that the properties of protoplasm result from the nature and disposition of its molecules.

But I bid you beware that, in accepting these conclusions, you are placing your feet on the first rung of a ladder which, in most people's estimation, is the reverse of Jacob's, and leads to the antipodes of heaven. It may seem a small thing to admit that the dull vital actions of a fungus, or a foraminifer, are the properties of their protoplasm, and are the direct results of the nature of the matter of which they are composed. But if, as I have endeavoured to prove to you, their protoplasm is essentially identical with, and most readily converted into, that of any animal, I can discover no logical halting-place between the admission that such is the case, and the further concession that all vital action may, with equal propriety, be said to be the result of the molecular forces of the protoplasm which displays it. And if so, it must be true, in the same sense and to the same extent, that the thoughts to which I am now giving utterance, and your thoughts regarding them, are the expression of molecular changes in that matter of life which is the source of our other vital phenomena.

Past experience leads me to be tolerably certain that, when the propositions I have just placed before you are accessible to public comment and criticism, they will be condemned by many zealous persons, and perhaps by some few of the wise and thoughtful. I should not wonder if "gross and brutal materialism" were the mildest phrase applied to them in certain quarters. And most undoubtedly the terms of the propositions are distinctly materialistic. Nevertheless two things are certain: the one, that I hold the statements to be substantially true; the other, that I, individually, am no materialist, but, on the contrary, believe materialism to involve grave philosophical error. . . .

In itself it is of little moment whether we express the

phenomena of matter in terms of spirit; or the phenomena of spirit, in terms of matter; matter may be regarded as a form of thought, thought may be regarded as a property of matter—each statement has a certain relative truth. But with a view to the progress of science, the materialistic terminology is in every way to be preferred. For it connects thought with the other phenomena of the universe, and suggests inquiry into the nature of those physical conditions, or concomitants of thought, which are more or less accessible to us, and a knowledge of which may, in future, help us to exercise the same kind of control over the world of thought, as we already possess in respect of the material world; whereas, the alternative, or spiritualistic, terminology is utterly barren, and leads to nothing but obscurity and confusion of ideas.

Thus there can be little doubt that the further science advances the more extensively and consistently will all the phenomena of nature be represented by materialistic formulæ and symbols.

But the man of science, who, forgetting the limits of philosophical inquiry, slides from these formulæ and symbols into what is commonly understood by materialism, seems to me to place himself on a level with the mathematician, who should mistake the x's and y's, with which he works his problems, for real entities—and with this further disadvantage, as compared with the mathematician, that the blunders of the latter are of no practical consequence, while the errors of systematic materialism may paralyse the energies and destroy the beauty of a life.

THE GREAT EXHIBITION OF 1851

Prince Albert's Triumph

QUEEN VICTORIA

[FROM her Journal]

1851

May 1 [*1851*]. This day is one of the greatest and most glorious days of our lives, with which to my pride and joy, the name of my dearly beloved Albert is for ever associated! It is a day which makes my heart swell with thankfulness. We began the day with tenderest greetings and congratulations on the birth of our dear little Arthur. He was brought in at breakfast and looked beautiful with blue ribbon on his frock. Mama and Victor were there, as well as all the children and our dear guests. Our little gifts of toys were added to by ones from the Pce and Pcess [of Prussia].

The Park presented a wonderful spectacle, crowds streaming through it,—carriages and troops passing, quite like the Coronation, and for *me*, the same anxiety. The day was bright and all bustle and excitement. At ½ p. 11 the whole procession in 9 State carriages was set in motion. Vicky and

From *The Great Exhibition of 1851*, compiled by C. H. Gibbs—Smith (London: 1950), pages 16-18.

Bertie were in our carriage (the other children and Vivi did not go). Vicky was dressed in lace over white satin, with small wreath of pink wild roses in her hair, and looked very nice. Bertie was in full Highland dress. The Green Park and Hyde Park were one mass of densely crowded human beings, in the highest good humour and most enthusiastic. I never saw Hyde Park look as it did, being filled with crowds as far as the eye could reach. A little rain fell, just as we started, but before we neared the Crystal Palace, the sun shone and gleamed upon the gigantic edifice, upon which the flags of every nation were flying. We drove up Rotten Row and got out of our carriages at the entrance on that side. The glimpse, through the iron gates of the Transept, the waving palms and flowers, the myriads of people filling the galleries and seats around, together with the flourish of trumpets as we entered the building, gave a sensation I shall never forget, and I felt much moved. We went for a moment into a little room where we left our cloaks and found Mama and Mary. Outside, all the Princes were standing. In a few seconds we proceeded, Albert leading me, having Vicky at his hand and Bertie holding mine. The sight as we came to the centre where the steps and chair (on which I did *not* sit) was placed, facing the beautiful crystal fountain was magic and impressive. The tremendous cheering, the joy expressed in every face, the vastness of the building, with all its decoration and exhibits, the sound of the organ (with 200 instruments and 600 voices, which seemed nothing) and my beloved husband, the creator of this peace festival 'uniting the industry and art of all nations of the earth,' all this was indeed moving, and a day to live for ever. God bless my dearest Albert, and my dear Country, which has shown itself so great to-day. One felt so grateful to the great God, whose blessing seemed to pervade the whole undertaking. After the National Anthem had been sung, Albert left my side and at the head of the Commissioners,—a curious assemblage of political and distinguished men—read the Report to me, which is a long one, and I read a short answer. After this the Archbishop of Canterbury offered up a short and appropriate prayer, followed by the singing of Handel's Hallelujah Chorus, during which time the Chinese Mandarin came forward and made his obeisance. This concluded, the Procession of great length began, which was beautifully arranged, the prescribed order being exactly adhered to. The Nave was full of people, which had not been intended, and deafening cheers and waving of handkerchiefs continued the whole time of our long walk from one end of the building to the other. Every face was bright and smiling, and many had tears in their eyes. Many Frenchmen called out 'Vive la Reine.' One could, of course, see nothing but what was high up in the Nave, and nothing in the Courts. The organs were but little heard, but the Military Band at one end had a very fine effect, playing the march from *Athalie* as we passed along. The old Duke of Wellington and Ld. Anglesey walked arm in arm, which was a touching sight. I saw many acquaintances amongst those present. We returned to our place and Albert told Ld. Breadalbane to declare the Exhibition to be opened, which he did in a loud voice saying 'Her Majesty commands me to declare this Exhibition open,' when there was a flourish of trumpets, followed by immense cheering. We then made our bow and left.

All these Commissioners and the Executive Committee etc. who had worked so hard and to whom such immense praise is due, seemed truly happy, and no one more so than Paxton, who may feel justly proud. He rose from an ordinary gardener's boy! Everyone was astounded and delighted. The return was equally satisfactory, the crowd most enthusiastic, and perfect order kept. We reached the Palace at 20m. past 1 and went out on the balcony, being loudly cheered. The Pce and Pcess [of Prussia] were quite delighted and impressed. That *we* felt happy and thankful, I need not say, proud of all that had passed and of my beloved's success. I was more impressed by the scene I had witnessed than words can say. Dearest Albert's name is for ever immortalised, and the absurd reports of dangers of every kind and sort, put out by a set of people—the 'soi-disant' fashionables and the most violent protectionists,—are silenced. It is therefore doubly satisfactory that all should have gone off so well and without the slightest incident or mischief. Phipps and Col. Seymour spoke to me, with such pride and joy at my beloved one's success and vindication after so much opposition and such difficulties, which no one but he with his good temper, patience, firmness and energy could have achieved. Without these qualities, his high position alone could not have carried him through. Saw later in the evening good Stockmar after having had a little walk, and he rejoiced for and with me. There was but one voice of astonishment and admiration. The *Globe* had a beautiful article which touched me very much—I forgot to mention that I wore a dress of pink and silver, with a diamond ray diadem and little crown at the back with 2 feathers, all the rest of my jewels being diamonds. The Pcess [of Prussia] looked very handsome and was so kind and 'herzlich.' An interesting episode of the day was the visit of the good old Duke, on his 82nd birthday, to his little godson, our dear little boy. He came to us at 5, gave little Arthur a gold cup and toys, which he had chosen himself. Arthur gave him a nosegay. We all dined 'en Famille,' the children staying up a little longer, and then went to Covent Garden opera, where we saw the 2 finest acts of the *Huguenots*—given as beautifully as last year. Was rather tired, but we were both too happy and full of thankfulness for everything.

Punch Attends the Opening

WILLIAM MAKEPEACE THACKERAY

["What I Remarked at the Exhibition"]

1851

I remarked that the scene I witnessed was the grandest and most cheerful, the brightest and most splendid show that eyes had ever looked on since the creation of the world;—but as everybody remarked the same thing, this remark is not of much value.

I remarked, and with a feeling of shame, that I had long hesitated about paying three guineas—pooh-poohed—said I had seen the Queen and Prince before, and so forth, and felt now that to behold this spectacle, three guineas, or five guineas, or any sum of money (for I am a man of enormous wealth) would have been cheap; and I remarked how few of us know really what is good for us—have the courage of our situations, and what a number of chances in life we throw away. I would not part with the mere recollection of this scene for a small annuity; and calculate that, after paying my three guineas, I have the Exhibition before me, besides being largely and actually in pocket.

I remarked that a heavy packet of sandwiches which Jones begged me to carry, and which I pocketed in rather a supercilious and grumbling manner, became most pleasant friends and useful companions after we had been in our places two or three hours; and I thought to myself, that were I a lyric poet with a moral turn, I would remark how often in the hour of our need our humble friends are welcome and useful to us, like those dear sandwiches, which we pooh-poohed when we did not need them.

From *Punch*, Volume 20 (3 May 1851), page 189.

I remarked that when the Queen bowed and curtseyed, all the women about began to cry.

I remarked how eagerly the young Prince talked with his sister—how charmed everybody was to see those pretty young persons walking hand in hand with their father and mother, and how, in the midst of any magnificence you will, what touches us most is nature and human kindness, and what we love to witness most is love.

I remarked three Roman Catholic clergymen in the midst of the crowd, amusing themselves with an opera-glass.

I remarked to myself that it was remarkable that a priest should have an opera-glass.

I remarked that when the Archbishop of Canterbury was saying his prayer, the Roman Catholic clergymen seemed no more to care than I should if Mr. Longears was speaking in the House of Commons—and that they looked, stared, peered over people's shoulders, and used the opera-glass during the prayer.

I remarked that it would have been more decorous if, during *that* part of the day's proceedings, the reverend gentlemen had not used the opera-glass.

I remarked that I couldn't be paying much attention myself, else how should I have seen the reverend gentlemen?

I remarked my Lord Ivorystick and my Lord Ebonystick backing all the way round the immense building before the Queen; and I wondered to myself how long is *that* sort of business going to last? how long will freeborn men forsake the natural manner of walking, with which God endowed them, and continue to execute this strange and barbarous *pas*? I remarked that a Royal Chamberlain was no more made to walk backwards, than a Royal coachman to sit on the box and drive backwards. And having just been laughing at the kotoos of honest Lord Chopstick (the Chinese Ambassador with the pantomime face), most of us in our gallery remarked that the performance of Lord Ivorystick and Lord Ebonystick was not more reasonable than that of his Excellency Chopstick, and wished that part of the ceremony had been left out.

I remarked in the gold cage, to which the ladies would go the first thing, and in which the Koh-i-noor reposes, a shining thing like a lambent oyster, which I admired greatly, and took to be the famous jewel. But on a second visit I was told that that was not the jewel—that was only the case, and the real stone was that above, which I had taken to be an imitation in crystal.

I remarked on this, that there are many sham diamonds in this life which pass for real, and, *vice versa*, many real diamonds which go unvalued. This accounts for the non-success of those real mountains of light, my "Sonnets on Various Occasions."

I remarked that, if I were Queen of England, I would have a piece of this crystal set into my crown, and wear it as the most spendid jewel of the whole diadem—that I would.

And in fact I remarked altogether—GOD SAVE THE QUEEN!

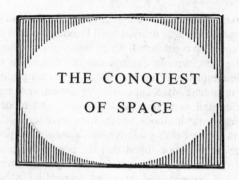

THE CONQUEST
OF SPACE

From Liverpool to Manchester in 1830

SAMUEL SMILES

[FROM *The Life of George Stephenson*]

1857

About the middle of 1829 the tunnel at Liverpool was finished; and being lit up with gas, it was publicly exhibited one day in each week. Many thousand persons visited the tunnel, at the charge of a shilling a head,—the fund thus raised being appropriated partly to the support of the families of labourers who had been injured upon the line, and partly in contributions to the Manchester and Liverpool infirmaries. Notwithstanding the immense quantity of rain that fell during the year, great progress had been made; and there seemed every probability that one line of road would be laid complete between the two towns by the 1st of January, 1830.

As promised by the engineer, a single line was ready by that day; and the "Rocket," with a carriage full of directors, engineers, and their friends, passed over the entire length of Chat Moss, and also along the greater part of the road between Liverpool and Manchester. The coal traffic had

From Chapter 24.

already been commenced at different parts of the railway; but the passenger traffic was delayed until locomotives and carrying stock could be constructed, which involved a considerable additional expenditure. In consequence of the wetness of the season, the completion of the works was somewhat postponed; but in the meantime Mr. Stephenson and his son were engaged in improving and perfecting the locomotive, and in devising new arrangements in those which were in course of construction in their workshops at Newcastle for the purposes of the railway. It was soon found that the performances of the "Rocket" on the day of competition were greatly within the scope of her powers; and at every succeeding effort she excelled her previous feats. Thus, in June, 1830, a trial trip was made between Liverpool and Manchester and back, on the occasion of the board meeting being held at the latter town. A great concourse of people assembled at both termini, and along the line, to witness the spectacle. The train consisted of two carriages filled with about forty persons, and seven wagons laden with stores—in all about thirty-nine tons. The "Rocket," light though it was as compared with modern engines, drew the train from Liverpool to Manchester in two hours and one minute, and performed the return journey in an hour and a half. The speed of the train over Chat Moss was at the rate of about twenty-seven miles an hour.

The public opening of the railway took place on the 15th of September, 1830. Eight locomotive engines had now been constructed by the Messrs. Stephenson, and placed upon the line. The whole of them had been repeatedly tried, and with success, weeks before. A high paling had been erected for miles along the deep cuttings near Liverpool, to keep off the pressure of the multitude, and prevent them from falling over in their eagerness to witness the opening ceremony. Constables and soldiers were there in numbers, to assist in keeping the railway clear. The completion of the work was justly regarded as a great national event, and was celebrated accordingly. The Duke of Wellington, then prime minister, Sir Robert Peel, secretary of state, Mr. Huskisson, one of the members for Liverpool, and an earnest supporter of the project from its commencement, were present, together with a large number of distinguished personages. The "Northumbrian" engine took the lead of the procession, and was followed by the other locomotives and their trains, which accommodated about 600 persons. Many thousands of spectators cheered them on their way,— through the deep ravine of Olive Mount; up the Sutton incline; over the Sankey viaduct, beneath which a multitude of persons had assembled,—carriages filling the narrow lanes, and barges crowding the river. The people gazed with wonder and admiration at the trains which sped along the line, far above their heads, at the rate of twenty-four miles an hour.

At Parkside, seventeen miles from Liverpool, the engines stopped to take in water. Here a deplorable accident occurred to one of the most distinguished of the illustrious visitors present which threw a deep shadow over the subsequent proceedings of the day. The "Northumbrian" engine, with the carriage containing the Duke of Wellington, was drawn up on one line, in order that the whole of the trains might pass in review before him and his party on the other. Mr. Huskisson had, unhappily, alighted from the carriage, and was landing on the opposite road, along which the "Rocket" engine was observed rapidly coming up. At this moment the Duke of Wellington, between whom and Mr. Huskisson some coolness had existed, made a sign of recognition, and held out his hand. A hurried but friendly grasp was given; and before it was loosened there was a general cry from the bystanders of "Get in, get in!" Flurried and confused, Mr. Huskisson endeavoured to get round the open door of the carriage, which projected over the opposite rail; but in so doing he was struck down by the "Rocket," and falling with his leg doubled across the rail, the limb was instantly crushed. His first words, on being raised, were, "I have met my death," which unhappily proved too true, for he expired that same evening in the neighbouring parsonage of Eccles. It was cited at the time as a remarkable fact, that the "Northumbrian" engine conveyed the wounded body of the unfortunate gentleman a distance of about fifteen miles in twenty-five minutes, or at the rate of thirty-six miles an hour. This incredible speed burst upon the world with the effect of a new and unlooked for phenomenon.

The lamentable accident threw a gloom over the rest of the day's proceedings. The Duke of Wellington and Sir Robert Peel expressed a wish that the procession should return to Liverpool. It was, however, represented to them that a vast concourse of people had assembled at Manchester to witness the arrival of the trains; that report would exaggerate the mischief if they did not complete the journey; and that a false panic on that day might seriously affect future railway travelling, and the value of the Company's property. The party consented accordingly to proceed to Manchester, but on the understanding that they should return as soon as possible, and refrain from further festivity.

The opening of the line was, however, accomplished. . . .

It is scarcely necessary that we should here speak of the commercial results of the Liverpool and Manchester Railway. Suffice it to say that its success was complete and decisive. The anticipations of its projectors were, however, in many respects at fault. They had based their calculations almost entirely on the heavy merchandise traffic—such as coal, cotton, and timber—relying little upon passengers; whereas the receipts derived from the conveyance of passengers far exceeded those derived from merchandise of all kinds, which, for a time, continued a subordinate branch of the traffic. In the evidence given before the committee of the House of Commons, the promoters stated their expectation of obtaining about one-half of the whole number of passengers that the coaches then running could take, which was from 400 to 500 a day. But the railway was scarcely opened before it carried on an average about 1200 passengers a day; and five years after the opening, it carried nearly half a million of persons yearly. In the first eighteen months, upwards of 700,000 persons, or about 1270 a day, were conveyed on the line without an accident. Formerly, the transit by coach had occupied four hours. The railway passenger trains performed the journey in an hour and a half on the average.

It was anticipated that the speed at which the locomotive could run upon the line would be about nine or ten miles an hour; but the wisest of the lawyers and the most experienced of the civil engineers did not believe this to be practicable, and they laughed outright at the idea of an engine running twenty miles in the hour. But very soon after the railway was opened for traffic, passengers were regularly carried the entire thirty miles between Liverpool and Manchester in little more than an hour. Two Edinburgh engineers, who went to report upon the railway, expressed their wonder at the travelling being smoother and easier than any they had hitherto experienced even on the smoothest turnpikes of Mr. Macadam. At the highest speed, of twenty-five miles an hour, they said, "we could observe the passengers, among whom were a good many ladies, talking to gentlemen with the utmost *sang froid.*" Such things were considered wonderful then. It was regarded as quite extraordinary that men should be enabled, by this remarkable invention, to proceed to Manchester in the morning, do a day's business there, and return to Liverpool the same night. So successful, indeed, was the passenger traffic, that it engrossed the whole of the Company's small stock of engines.

THE
THREAT OF THE
MACHINES

The Book of the Machines

SAMUEL BUTLER

[FROM *Erewhon; or Over the Range*]

1872

The writer commences: "There was a time when the earth was to all appearance utterly destitute both of animal and vegetable life, and when according to the opinion of our best philosophers it was simply a hot round ball with a crust gradually cooling. Now if a human being had existed while the earth was in this state and had been allowed to see it as though it were some other world with which he had no concern, and if at the same time he were entirely ignorant of all physical science, would he not have pronounced it impossible that creatures possessed of anything like consciousness should be evolved from the seeming cinder which he was beholding? Would he not have denied that it contained any potentiality of consciousness? Yet in the course of time consciousness came. Is it not possible then that there may be even yet new channels dug out for consciousness, though we can detect no signs of them at present?

From Chapter 23.

"Again. Consciousness, in anything like the present acceptation of the term, having been once a new thing—a thing, as far as we can see, subsequent even to an individual centre of action and to a reproductive system (which we see existing in plants without apparent consciousness)—why may not there arise some new phase of mind which shall be as different from all present known phases, as the mind of animals is from that of vegetables? . . .

"There is no security"—to quote his own words—"against the ultimate development of mechanical consciousness, in the fact of machines possessing little consciousness now. A mollusc has not much consciousness. Reflect upon the extraordinary advance which machines have made during the last few hundred years, and note how slowly the animal and vegetable kingdoms are advancing. The more highly organized machines are creatures not so much of yesterday, as of the last five minutes, so to speak, in comparison with past time. Assume for the sake of argument that conscious beings have existed for some twenty million years: see what strides machines have made in the last thousand! May not the world last twenty million years longer? If so, what will they not in the end become? Is it not safer to nip the mischief in the bud and to forbid them further progress?

"But who can say that the vapour engine has not a kind of consciousness? Where does consciousness begin, and where end? Who can draw the line? Who can draw any line? Is not everything interwoven with everything? Is not machinery linked with animal life in an infinite variety of ways? The shell of a hen's egg is made of a delicate white ware and is a machine as much as an egg-cup is: the shell is a device for holding the egg, as much as the egg-cup for holding the shell: both are phases of the same function; the hen makes the shell in her inside, but it is pure pottery. She makes her nest outside of herself for convenience' sake, but the nest is not more of a machine than the egg-shell is. A 'machine' is only a 'device.' . . .

"But it may be said that the plant is void of reason, because the growth of a plant is an involuntary growth. Given earth, air, and due temperature, the plant must grow: it is like a clock, which being once wound up will go till it is stopped or run down: it is like the wind blowing on the sails of a ship—the ship must go when the wind blows it. But can a healthy boy help growing if he have good meat and drink and clothing? can anything help going as long as it is wound up, or go on after it is run down? Is there not a winding up process everywhere?

"Even a potato in a dark cellar has a certain low cunning about him which serves him in excellent stead. He knows perfectly well what he wants and how to get it. He sees the light coming from the cellar window and sends his shoots crawling straight thereto: they will crawl along the floor and up the wall and out at the cellar window; if there be a little earth anywhere on the journey he will find it and use it for his own ends. . . .

"If it be urged that the action of the potato is chemical and mechanical only, and that it is due to the chemical and mechanical effects of light and heat, the answer would seem to lie in an inquiry whether every sensation is not chemical and mechanical in its operation? whether those things which we deem most purely spiritual are anything but disturbances of equilibrium in an infinite series of levers, beginning with those that are too small for microscopic detection, and going up to the human arm and the appliances which it makes use of? whether there be not a molecular action of thought, whence a dynamical theory of the passions shall be deducible? Whether strictly speaking we should not ask what kind of levers a man is made of rather than what is his temperament? How are they balanced? How much of such and such will it take to weigh them down so as to make him do so and so? . . .

"Either," he proceeds, "a great deal of action that has been called purely mechanical and unconscious must be admitted to contain more elements of consciousness than has been allowed hitherto (and in this case germs of consciousness will be found in many actions of the higher machines)—or (assuming the theory of evolution but at the same time denying the consciousness of vegetable and crystalline action) the race of man has descended from things which had no consciousness at all. In this case there is no *a priori* improbability in the descent of conscious (and more than conscious) machines from those which now exist, except that which is suggested by the apparent absence of anything like a reproductive system in the mechanical kingdom. This absence however is only apparent, as I shall presently show.

"Do not let me be misunderstood as living in fear of any actually existing machine; there is probably no known machine which is more than a prototype of future mechanical life. The present machines are to the future as the early Saurians to man. The largest of them will probably greatly diminish in size. Some of the lowest vertebrata attained a much greater bulk than has descended to their more highly organized living representatives, and in like manner a diminution in the size of machines has often attended their development and progress.

"Take the watch, for example; examine its beautiful structure; observe the intelligent play of the minute members which compose it: yet this little creature is but a development of the cumbrous clocks that preceded it; it is no deterioration from them. . . .

"But returning to the argument, I would repeat that I fear none of the existing machines; what I fear is the extraordinary rapidity with which they are becoming something very different to what they are at present. No class of beings have in any time past made so rapid a movement forward. Should not that movement be jealously watched, and checked while we can still check it? And is it not necessary for this end to destroy the more advanced of the machines which are in use at present, though it is admitted that they are in themselves harmless?

"As yet the machines receive their impressions through the agency of man's senses: one travelling machine calls to another in a shrill accent of alarm and the other instantly retires; but it is through the ears of the driver that the voice of the one has acted upon the other. Had there been no driver, the callee would have been deaf to the caller. There was a time when it must have seemed highly improbable that machines should learn to make their wants known by sound, even through the ears of man; may we not conceive, then, that a day will come when those ears will be no longer needed, and the hearing will be done by the delicacy of the machine's own construction?—when its language shall have been developed from the cry of animals to a speech as intricate as our own?

"It is possible that by that time children will learn the differential calculus—as they learn now to speak—from their mothers and nurses, or that they may talk in the hypothetical language, and work rule of three sums, as soon as they are born; but this is not probable; we cannot calculate on any corresponding advance in man's intellectual or physical powers which shall be a set-off against the far greater development which seems in store for the machines. Some people may say that man's moral influence will suffice to rule them; but I cannot think it will ever be safe to repose much trust in the moral sense of any machine.

"Again, might not the glory of the machines consist in their being without this same boasted gift of language? 'Silence,' it has been said by one writer, 'is a virtue which renders us agreeable to our fellow-creatures.' "

[FROM Chapter 24]

"But other questions come upon us. What is a man's eye but a machine for the little creature that sits behind in his brain to look through? A dead eye is nearly as good as a living one for some time after the man is dead. It is not the eye that cannot see, but the restless one that cannot see through it. Is it man's eyes, or is it the big seeing-engine which has revealed to us the existence of worlds beyond worlds into infinity? What has made man familiar with the scenery of the moon, the spots on the sun, or the geography of the planets? He is at the mercy of the seeing-engine for these things, and is powerless unless he tack it on to his own identity, and make it part and parcel of himself. Or, again, is it the eye, or the little see-engine which has shown us the existence of infinitely minute organisms which swarm unsuspected around us?

"And take man's vaunted power of calculation. Have we not engines which can do all manner of sums more quickly and correctly than we can? What prizeman in hypothetics at any of our Colleges of Unreason can compare with some of these machines in their own line? In fact, wherever precision is required man flies to the machine at once, as far preferable to himself. Our sum-engines never drop a figure, nor our looms a stitch; the machine is brisk and active, when the man is weary; it is clear-headed and collected, when the man is stupid and dull; it needs no slumber, when man must sleep or drop; ever at its post, ever ready for work, its alacrity never flags, its patience never gives in; its might is stronger than combined hundreds, and swifter than the flight of birds; it can burrow beneath the earth, and walk upon the largest rivers and sink not. This is the green tree; what then shall be done in the dry?

"Who shall say that a man does see or hear? He is such a hive and swarm of parasites that it is doubtful whether his body is not more theirs than his, and whether he is anything but another kind of ant-heap after all. May not man himself become a sort of parasite upon the machines? An affectionate machine-tickling aphid? . . .

"It can be answered that even though machines should hear never so well and speak never so wisely, they will still always do the one or the other for our advantage, not their own; that man will be the ruling spirit and the machine the servant; that as soon as a machine fails to discharge the service which man expects from it, it is doomed to extinction; that the machines stand to man simply in the relation of lower animals, the vapour-engine itself being only a more economical kind of horse; so that instead of being likely to be developed into a higher kind of life than man's, they owe their very existence and progress to their power of ministering to human wants, and must therefore both now and ever be man's inferiors.

"This is all very well. But the servant glides by imperceptible approaches into the master; and we have come to such a pass that, even now, man must suffer terribly on ceasing to benefit the machines. If all machines were to be annihilated at one moment, so that not a knife nor lever nor rag of clothing nor anything whatsoever were left to man but his bare body alone that he was born with, and if all knowledge of mechanical laws were taken from him so that he could make no more machines, and all machine-made food destroyed so that the race of man should be left as it were naked upon a desert island, we should become extinct in six weeks. A few miserable individuals might linger, but even these in a year or two would become worse than monkeys. Man's very soul is due to the machines; it is a machine-made thing: he thinks as he thinks, and feels as he feels, through the work that machines have wrought upon him, and their existence is quite as much a *sine qua non* for his, as his for theirs. This fact precludes us from proposing the complete annihilation of machinery, but surely it indicates that we should destroy as many of them as we can possibly dispense with, lest they should tyrannize over us even more completely.

"True, from a low materialistic point of view, it would seem that those thrive best who use machinery wherever its use is possible with profit; but this is the art of the machines— they serve that they may rule. They bear no malice towards man for destroying a whole race of them provided he creates a better instead; on the contrary, they reward him liberally for having hastened their development. It is for neglecting them that he incurs their wrath, or for using inferior machines, or for not making sufficient exertions to invent new ones, or for destroying them without replacing them; yet these are the very things we ought to do, and do quickly; for though our rebellion against their infant power will cause infinite suffering, what will not things come to, if that rebellion is delayed?

"They have preyed upon man's grovelling preference for his material over his spiritual interests, and have betrayed him into supplying that element of struggle and warfare without which no race can advance. The lower animals progress because they struggle with one another; the weaker die, the stronger breed and transmit their strength. The machines being of themselves unable to struggle, have got man to do their struggling for them: as long as he fulfils this function duly, all goes well with him—at least he thinks so; but the moment he fails to do his best for the advancement of machinery by encouraging the good and destroying the bad, he is left behind in the race of competition; and this means that he will be made uncomfortable in a variety of ways, and perhaps die.

"So that even now the machines will only serve on condition of being served, and that too upon their own terms; the moment their terms are not complied with, they jib, and either smash both themselves and all whom they can reach, or turn churlish and refuse to work at all. How many men at this hour are living in a state of bondage to the machines? How many spend their whole lives, from the cradle to the grave, in tending them by night and day? Is it not plain that the machines are gaining ground upon us, when we reflect on the increasing number of those who are bound down to them as slaves, and of those who devote their whole souls to the advancement of the mechanical kingdom?

"The vapour-engine must be fed with food and consume it by fire even as man consumes it; it supports its combustion by air as man supports it; it has a pulse and circulation as man has. It may be granted that man's body is as yet the more versatile of the two, but then man's body is an older thing; give the vapour-engine but half the time that man has had, give it also a continuance of our present infatuation, and what may it not ere long attain to? ... The comparison of similarities is endless: I only make it because some may say that since the vapour-engine is not likely to be improved in the main particulars, it is unlikely to be henceforward extensively modified at all. This is too good to be true: it will be modified and suited for an infinite variety of purposes, as much as man has been modified so as to exceed the brutes in skill.

"In the meantime the stoker is almost as much a cook for his engine as our own cooks for ourselves. Consider also the colliers and pitmen and coal merchants and coal trains, and the men who drive them, and the ships that carry coals—what an army of servants do the machines thus employ! Are there not probably more men engaged in tending machinery than in tending men? Do not machines eat as it were by mannery? Are we not ourselves creating our successors in the supremacy of the earth? daily adding to the beauty and delicacy of their organization, daily giving them greater skill and supplying more and more of that self-regulating, self-acting power which will be better than any intellect? . . .

"The main point, however, to be observed as affording cause for alarm is, that whereas animals were formerly the only stomachs of the machines, there are now many which have stomachs of their own, and consume their food themselves. This is a great step towards their becoming, if not animate, yet something so near akin to it, as not to differ more widely from our own life than animals do from vegetables. And though man should remain, in some respects, the higher creature, is not this in accordance with the practice of nature, which allows superiority in some things to animals which have, on the whole, been long surpassed? Has she not allowed the ant and the bee to retain superiority over man in the organization of their communities and social arrangements, the bird in traversing the air, the fish in swimming, the horse in strength and fleetness, and the dog in self-sacrifice?

"It is said by some with whom I have conversed upon this subject, that the machines can never be developed into animate or quasi-animate existences, inasmuch as they have no reproductive system, nor seem ever likely to possess one. If this be taken to mean that they cannot marry, and that we are never likely to see a fertile union between two vapour-engines with the young ones playing about the door of the shed, however greatly we might desire to do so, I will readily grant it. But the objection is not a very profound one. No one expects that all the features of the now existing organizations will be absolutely repeated in an entirely new class of life. The reproductive system of animals differs widely from that of plants, but both are reproductive systems. Has nature exhausted her phases of this power?

"Surely if a machine is able to reproduce another machine systematically, we may say that it has a reproductive system. What is a reproductive system, if it be not a system for reproduction? And how few of the machines are there which have not been produced systematically by other machines? But it is man that makes them do so. Yes; but is it not insects that make many of the plants reproductive, and would not whole families of plants die out if their fertilization was not effected by a class of agents utterly foreign to themselves? Does any one say that the red clover has no reproductive system because the humble bee (and the humble bee only) must aid and abet it before it can reproduce? No one. The humble bee is a part of the reproductive system of the clover. Each one of ourselves has sprung from minute animalcules whose entity was entirely distinct from our own, and which acted after their kind with no thought or heed of what we might think about it. These little creatures are part of our own reproductive system; then why not we part of that of the machines?

"But the machines which reproduce machinery do not reproduce machines after their own kind. A thimble may be made by machinery, but it was not made by, neither will it ever make, a thimble. Here, again, if we turn to nature we shall find abundance of analogies which will teach us that a reproductive system may be in full force without the thing produced being of the same kind as that which produced it. Very few creatures reproduce after their own kind; they reproduce something which has the potentiality of becoming that which their parents were. Thus the butterfly lays an egg, which egg can become a caterpillar, which caterpillar can become a chrysalis, which chrysalis can become a butterfly; and though I freely grant that the machines cannot be said to have more than the germ of a true reproductive system at present, have we not just seen that they have only recently obtained the germs of a mouth and stomach? And may not some stride be made in the direction of true reproduction which shall be as great as that which has been recently taken in the direction of true feeding? . . .

"We are misled by considering any complicated machine as a single thing; in truth it is a city or society, each member of which was bred truly after its kind. We see a machine as a whole, we call it by a name and individualize it; we look at our own limbs, and know that the combination forms an individual which springs from a single centre of reproductive action; we therefore assume that there can be no reproductive action which does not arise from a single centre; but this assumption is unscientific, and the bare fact that no vapour-engine was ever made entirely by another, or two others, of its own kind, is not sufficient to warrant us in saying that vapour-engines have no reproductive system. The truth is that each part of every vapour-engine is bred by its own special breeders, whose function it is to breed that part, and that only, while the combination of the parts into a whole forms another department of the mechanical reproductive system, which is at present exceedingly complex and difficult to see in its entirety.

"Complex now, but how much simpler and more intelligibly organized may it not become in another hundred thousand years? or in twenty thousand? For man at present believes that his interest lies in that direction; he spends an incalculable amount of labour and time and thought in making machines breed always better and better; he has already succeeded in effecting much that at one time appeared impossible, and there seem no limits to the results of accumulated improvements if they are allowed to descend with modification from generation to generation. It must always be remembered that man's body is what it is through having been moulded into its present shape by the chances and changes of many millions of years, but that his organization never advanced with anything like the rapidity with which that of the machines is advancing. This is the most alarming feature in the case, and I must be pardoned for insisting on it so frequently."

PART
SIX

HISTORY, THE ARTS,

AND LETTERS

Charlotte Corday

THOMAS CARLYLE

[FROM *The French Revolution*]

1837

In the leafy months of June and July [1793], several French Departments germinate a set of rebellious *paper*-leaves, named Proclamations, Resolutions, Journals, or Diurnals 'of the Union for Resistance to Oppression.' In particular, the Town of Caen, in Calvados, sees its paper-leaf of *Bulletin de Caen* suddenly bud, suddenly establish itself as Newspaper there; under the Editorship of Girondin National Representatives! . . .

What is more to the purpose, these Girondins have got a General in chief, one Wimpfen, formerly under Dumouriez; also a secondary questionable General Puisaye, and others; and are doing their best to raise a force for war. National Volunteers, whosoever is of right heart: gather in, ye National Volunteers, friends of Liberty; from our Calvados Townships, from the Eure, from Brittany, from far and near: forward to Paris, and extinguish Anarchy! Thus at Caen,

From Part III, Book V, Chapter 1.

in the early July days, there is a drumming and parading, a perorating and consulting: Staff and Army; Council; Club of *Carabots,* Anti-jacobin friends of Freedom, to denounce atrocious Marat. With all which, and the editing of *Bulletins,* a National Representative has his hands full.

At Caen it is most animated; and, as one hopes, more or less animated in the 'Seventy-two Departments that adhere to us.' And in a France begirt with Cimmerian invading Coalitions, and torn with an internal La Vendée, *this* is the conclusion we have arrived at: To put down Anarchy by Civil War! . . .

Against all which the Mountain and atrocious Marat must even make head as they can. They, anarchic Convention as they are, publish Decrees, expostulatory, explanatory, yet not without severity; they ray forth Commissioners, singly or in pairs, the olive-branch in one hand, yet the sword in the other. Commissioners come even to Caen; but without effect. Mathematical Romme, and Prieur named of the Côte d'Or, venturing thither, with their olive and sword, are packed into prison: there may Romme lie, under lock and key, 'for fifty days'; and meditate his New Calendar, if he please. Cimmeria, La Vendée, and Civil War! Never was Republic One and Indivisible at a lower ebb.—

Amid which dim ferment of Caen and the World, History specially notices one thing: in the lobby of the Mansion *de l' Intendance,* where busy Deputies are coming and going, a young Lady with an aged valet, taking grave graceful leave of Deputy Barbaroux. She is of stately Norman figure; in her twenty-fifth year; of beautiful still countenance: her name is Charlotte Corday, heretofore styled d'Armans, while Nobility still was. Barbaroux has given her a Note to Deputy Duperret,—him who once drew his sword in the effervescence. Apparently she will to Paris on some errand? 'She was a Republican before the Revolution, and never wanted energy.' A completeness, a decision is in this fair female Figure: 'by energy she means the spirit that will prompt one to sacrifice himself for his country.' What if she, this fair young Charlotte, had emerged from her secluded stillness, suddenly like a Star; cruel-lovely, with half-angelic, half-demonic splendour; to gleam for a moment, and in a moment be extinguished: to be held in memory, so bright complete was she, through long centuries!—Quitting Cimmerian Coalitions without, and the dim-simmering Twenty-five millions within, History will look fixedly at this one fair Apparition of a Charlotte Corday; will note whither Charlotte moves, how the little Life burns forth so radiant, then vanishes swallowed of the Night.

With Barbaroux's Note of Introduction, and slight stock of luggage, we see Charlotte on Tuesday the ninth of July, seated in the Caen Diligence, with a place for Paris. None takes farewell of her, wishes her Good-journey: her Father will find a line left, signifying that she is gone to England, that he must pardon her, and forget her. The drowsy Diligence lumbers along; amid drowsy talk of Politics, and praise of the Mountain; in which she mingles not: all night, all day, and again all night. On Thursday, not long before noon, we are at the bridge of Neuilly; here is Paris with her thousand black domes, the goal and purpose of thy journey! Arrived at the Inn de la Providence in the Rue des Vieux Augustins, Charlotte demands a room; hastens to bed; sleeps all afternoon and night, till the morrow morning.

On the morrow morning, she delivers her Note to Duperret. It relates to certain Family Papers which are in the Minister of the Interior's hand; which a Nun at Caen, an old Convent-friend of Charlotte's, has need of; which Duperret shall assist her in getting: this then was Charlotte's errand to Paris? She has finished this, in the course of Friday:—yet says nothing of returning. She has seen and silently investigated several things. The Convention, in bodily reality, she has seen; what the Mountain is like. The living physiognomy of Marat she could not see; he is sick at present, and confined to home.

About eight on the Saturday morning, she purchases a large sheath-knife in the Palais Royal; then straightway, in the Place des Victoires, takes a hackney-coach: "to the Rue

de l'Ecole de Médecine, No. 44." It is the residence of the
Citoyen Marat!—The Citoyen Marat is ill, and cannot be
seen; which seems to disappoint her much. Her business
is with Marat, then? Hapless beautiful Charlotte; hapless
squalid Marat! From Caen in the utmost West, from Neuchâtel
in the utmost East, they two are drawing nigh each other;
they two have, very strangely, business together.—Charlotte,
returning to her Inn, despatches a short Note to Marat;
signifying that she is from Caen, the seat of rebellion; that
she desires earnestly to see him, and 'will put it in his power
to do France a great service.' No answer. Charlotte writes
another Note, still more pressing: sets out with it by coach,
about seven in the evening, herself. Tired day-labourers have
again finished their Week; huge Paris is circling and simmer-
ing, manifold, according to its vague wont: this one fair
Figure has decision in it; drives straight,—towards a purpose.

It is yellow July evening, we say, the thirteenth of the
month; eve of the Bastille day,—when 'M. Marat,' four years
ago, in the crowd of the Pont Neuf, shrewdly required of
that Besenval Hussar-party, which had such friendly dispositions, "to dismount, and give up their arms, then"; and
became notable among Patriot men. Four years: what a
road he has travelled;—and sits now, about half-past seven
of the clock, stewing in slipper-bath; sore afflicted; ill of
Revolution Fever,—of what other malady this History had
rather not name. Excessively sick and worn, poor man: with
precisely elevenpence-halfpenny of ready money, in paper;
with slipper-bath; strong three-footed stool for writing on,
the while; and a squalid—Washerwoman, one may call her:
that is his civic establishment in Medical-School Street; thither
and not elsewhither has his road led him. Not to the reign
of Brotherhood and Perfect Felicity; yet surely on the way
towards that?—Hark, a rap again! A musical woman's-voice,
refusing to be rejected: it is the Citoyenne who would do
France a service. Marat, recognising from within, cries, Admit
her. Charlotte Corday is admitted.

Citoyen Marat, I am from Caen the seat of rebellion, and
wished to speak with you.—Be seated, *mon enfant*. Now

what are the Traitors doing at Caen? What Deputies are at Caen?—Charlotte names some Deputies. "Their heads shall fall within a fortnight," croaks the eager People's-Friend, clutching his tablets to write: *Barbaroux, Pétion,* writes he with bare shrunk arm, turning aside in the bath: *Pétion,* and *Louvet,* and—Charlotte has drawn her knife from the sheath; plunges it, with one sure stroke, into the writer's heart. *"À moi, chère amie,* Help, dear!" no more could the Death-choked say or shriek. The helpful Washerwoman running in, there is no Friend of the People, or Friend of the Washerwoman, left; but his life with a groan gushes out, indignant, to the shades below.

And so Marat People's-Friend is ended; the lone Stylites has got hurled down suddenly from his Pillar,—*whitherward* He that made him knows. Patriot Paris may sound triple and tenfold, in dole and wail; re-echoed by Patriot France; and the Convention, 'Chabot pale with terror declaring that they are to be all assassinated,' may decree him Pantheon Honours, Public Funeral, Mirabeau's dust making way for him; and Jacobin Societies, in lamentable oratory, summing up his character, parallel him to One, whom they think it honour to call 'the good Sansculotte,'—whom we name not here; also a Chapel may be made, for the urn that holds his Heart, in the Place du Carrousel; and new-born children be named Marat; and Lago-di-Como Hawkers bake mountains of stucco into unbeautiful Busts; and David paint his Picture, or Death-Scene; and such other Apotheosis take place as the human genius, in these circumstances, can devise: but Marat returns no more to the light of this Sun. One sole circumstance we have read with clear sympathy, in the old *Moniteur* Newspaper: how Marat's Brother comes from Neuchâtel to ask of the Convention, 'that the deceased Jean-Paul Marat's musket be given him.' For Marat too had a brother, and natural affections; and was wrapt once in swaddling-clothes, and slept safe in a cradle like the rest of us. Ye children of men!—A sister of his, they say, lives still to this day in Paris.

As for Charlotte Corday, her work is accomplished; the

recompense of it is near and sure. The *chère amie,* and neighbours of the house, flying at her, she 'overturns some movables,' entrenches herself till the gendarmes arrive; then quietly surrenders; goes quietly to the Abbaye Prison: she alone quiet, all Paris sounding, in wonder, in rage or admiration, round her. Duperret is put in arrest, on account of her; his Papers sealed,—which may lead to consequences. Fauchet, in like manner; though Fauchet had not so much as heard of her. Charlotte, confronted with these two Deputies, praises the grave firmness of Duperret, censures the dejection of Fauchet.

On Wednesday morning, the thronged Palais de Justice and Revolutionary Tribunal can see her face; beautiful and calm: she dates it 'fourth day of the Preparation of Peace.' A strange murmur ran through the Hall, at sight of her; you could not say of what character. Tinville has his indictments and tape-papers: the cutler of the Palais Royal will testify that he sold her the sheath-knife; "all these details are needless," interrupted Charlotte; "it is I that killed Marat." By whose instigation?—"By no one's." What tempted you, then? His crimes. "I killed one man," added she, raising her voice extremely (*extrêmement*), as they went on with their questions, "I killed one man to save a hundred thousand; a villain to save innocents; a savage wild-beast to give repose to my country. I was a Republican before the Revolution; I never wanted energy." There is therefore nothing to be said. The public gazes astonished: the hasty limners sketch her features, Charlotte not disapproving; the men of law proceed with their formalities. The doom is Death as a murderess. To her Advocate she gives thanks; in gentle phrase, in high-flown classical spirit. To the Priest they send her she gives thanks; but needs not any shriving, any ghostly or other aid from him.

On this same evening, therefore, about half-past seven o'clock, from the gate of the Conciergerie, to a City all on tiptoe, the fatal Cart issues: seated on it a fair young creature, sheeted in red smock of Murderess; so beautiful, serene, so full of life; journeying towards death,—alone amid the World.

Many take off their hats, saluting reverently; for what heart but must be touched? Others growl and howl. Adam Lux, of Mentz, declares that she is greater than Brutus; that it were beautiful to die with her: the head of this young man seems turned. At the Place de la Révolution, the countenance of Charlotte wears the same still smile. The executioners proceed to bind her feet; she resists, thinking it meant as an insult; on a word of explanation, she submits with cheerful apology. As the last act, all being now ready, they take the neckerchief from her neck: a blush of maidenly shame overspreads that fair face and neck; the cheeks were still tinged with it, when the executioner lifted the severed head, to shew it to the people. 'It is most true,' says Forster, 'that he struck the cheek insultingly; for I saw it with my eyes: the Police imprisoned him for it.'

In this manner have the Beautifullest and the Squalidest come in collision, and extinguished one another. Jean-Paul Marat and Marie-Anne Charlotte Corday both, suddenly, are no more. 'Day of the Preparation of Peace?' Alas, how were peace possible or preparable, while, for example, the hearts of lovely Maidens, in their convent-stillness, are dreaming not of Love-paradises, and the light of Life; but of Codrus'-sacrifices, and Death well-earned? That Twenty-five million hearts have got to such temper, this *is* the Anarchy; the soul of it lies in this: whereof not peace can be the embodyment! The death of Marat, whetting old animosities tenfold, will be worse than any life. O ye hapless Two, mutually extinctive, the Beautiful and the Squalid, sleep ye well,— in the Mother's bosom that bore you both!

This is the History of Charlotte Corday; most definite, most complete; angelic-demonic: like a Star! Adam Lux goes home, half-delirious; to pour forth his Apotheosis of her, in paper and print; to propose that she have a statue with this inscription, *Greater than Brutus*. Friends represent his danger; Lux is reckless; thinks it were beautiful to die with her.

The Stars and Stripes
By the Author of
"The Last of the Mulligans," "Pilot," etc.

WILLIAM MAKEPEACE THACKERAY

[FROM "Punch's Prize Novels"]

1847

The King of France was walking on the terrace of Versailles; the fairest, not only of Queens, but of women, hung fondly on the Royal arm; while the children of France were indulging in their infantile hilarity in the alleys of the magnificent garden of Le Nôtre (from which Niblo's garden has been copied, in our own Empire city of New York), and playing at leap-frog with their uncle, the Count of Provence; gaudy courtiers, emblazoned with orders, glittered in the groves, and murmured frivolous talk in the ears of high-bred beauty.

"Marie, my beloved," said the ruler of France, taking out his watch, " 'tis time that the Minister of America should be here."

"Your Majesty should know the time," replied Marie Antoinette archly, and in an Austrian accent; "is not my Royal Louis the first watchmaker in his empire?"

The King cast a pleased glance at his repeater, and kissed with courtly grace the fair hand of her who had made him the compliment. "My Lord Bishop of Autun," said he to Monsieur de Talleyrand Périgord, who followed the Royal pair, in his quality of Arch-chamberlain of the Empire, "I pray you look through the gardens, and tell his Excellency Doctor Franklin that the King waits." The Bishop ran off, with more than youthful agility, to seek the United States

From "Novels by Eminent Hands," *Punch*, Volume 13 (25 September 1847), pages 117-18.

WILLIAM MAKEPEACE THACKERAY 571

Minister. "These Republicans," he added confidentially, and with something of a supercilious look, "are but rude courtiers, methinks."

"Nay," interposed the lovely Antoinette, "rude courtiers, sire, they may be; but the world boasts not of more accomplished gentlemen. I have seen no grandee of Versailles that has the noble bearing of this American Envoy and his suite. They have the refinement of the Old World, with all the simple elegance of the New. Though they have perfect dignity of manner, they have an engaging modesty which I have never seen equalled by the best of the proud English nobles with whom they wage war. I am told they speak their very language with a grace which the haughty Islanders who oppress them never attained. They are independent, yet never insolent; elegant, yet always respectful; and brave, but not in the least boastful."

"What! savages and all, Marie?" exclaimed Louis, laughing, and chucking the lovely Queen playfully under the Royal chin. "But here comes Doctor Franklin, and your friend the Cacique with him." In fact, as the monarch spoke, the Minister of the United States made his appearance, followed by a gigantic warrior in the garb of his native woods.

Knowing his place as Minister of a sovereign State (yielding even then in dignity to none, as it surpasses all now in dignity, in valour, in honesty, in strength, and civilisation), the Doctor nodded to the Queen of France, but kept his hat on as he faced the French monarch, and did not cease whittling the cane he carried in his hand.

"I was waiting for you, sir," the King said peevishly, in spite of the alarmed pressure which the Queen gave his Royal arm.

"The business of the Republic, sire, must take precedence even of your Majesty's wishes," replied Doctor Franklin. "When I was a poor printer's boy and ran errands, no lad could be more punctual than poor Ben Franklin; but all other things must yield to the service of the United States of North America. I have done. What would you, sire?" and the intrepid republican eyed the monarch with a serene and easy dignity, which made the descendant of St. Louis feel ill at ease.

"I wished to—to say farewell to Tatua before his departure," said Louis XVI, looking rather awkward. "Approach, Tatua." And the gigantic Indian strode up, and stood undaunted before the first magistrate of the French nation: again the feeble monarch quailed before the terrible simplicity of the glance of the denizen of the primæval forests.

The redoubted chief of the Nose-ring Indians was decorated in his war-paint, and in his top-knot was a peacock's feather, which had been given him out of the head-dress of the beautiful Princess of Lamballe. His nose, from which hung the ornament from which his ferocious tribe took its designation, was painted a light-blue, a circle of green and orange was drawn round each eye, while serpentine stripes of black, white, and vermilion alternately were smeared on his forehead, and descended over his cheek-bones to his chin. His manly chest was similarly tatooed and painted, and round his brawny neck and arms hung innumerable bracelets and necklaces of human teeth, extracted (one only from each skull) from the jaws of those who had fallen by the terrible tomahawk at his girdle. His moccasins, and his blanket, which was draped on his arm and fell in picturesque folds to his feet, were fringed with tufts of hair—the black, the grey, the auburn, the golden ringlet of beauty, the red lock from the forehead of the Scottish or the Northern soldier, the snowy tress of extreme old age, the flaxen down of infancy—all were there, dreadful reminiscences of the Chief's triumphs in war. The warrior leaned on his enormous rifle, and faced the King.

"And it was with that carabine that you shot Wolfe in '57?" said Louis, eyeing the warrior and his weapon. "'Tis a clumsy lock, and methinks I could mend it," he added mentally.

"The Chief of the French pale-faces speaks truth," Tatua said. "Tatua was a boy when he went first on the war-path with Montcalm."

"And shot a Wolfe at the first fire!" said the King.

"The English are braves, though their faces are white," replied the Indian. "Tatua shot the raging Wolfe of the

English; but the other wolves caused the foxes to go to earth."
A smile played round Doctor Franklin's lips, as he whittled
his cane with more vigour than ever.

"I believe, your Excellency, Tatua has done good service
elsewhere than at Quebec," the King said, appealing to the
American Envoy: "at Bunker's Hill, at Brandywine, at York
Island? Now that Lafayette and my brave Frenchmen are
among you, your Excellency need have no fear but that the
war will finish quickly—yes, yes, it will finish quickly. They
will teach you discipline, and the way to conquer."

"King Louis of France," said the Envoy, clapping his hat
down over his head and putting his arms akimbo, "we have
learned that from the British to whom we are superior in
everything: and I'd have your Majesty to know that in the
art of whipping the world we have no need of any French
lessons. If your reglars jine General Washington, 'tis to larn
from *him* how Britishers are licked; for I'm blest if *yu* know
the way yet."

Tatua said, "Ugh," and gave a rattle with the butt of his
carabine, which made the timid monarch start; the eyes of
the lovely Antoinette flashed fire, but it played round the head
of the dauntless American Envoy harmless as the lightning
which he knew how to conjure away.

The King fumbled in his pocket, and pulled out a Cross
of the Order of the Bath. "Your Excellency wears no honour,"
the monarch said; "but Tatua, who is not a subject, only an
ally, of the United States, may. Noble Tatua, I appoint you
Knight Companion of my noble Order of the Bath. Wear this
cross upon your breast in memory of Louis of France"; and
the King held out the decoration to the Chief.

Up to that moment the Chief's countenance had been im-
passible. No look either of admiration or dislike had appeared
upon that grim and war-painted visage. But now, as Louis
spoke, Tatua's face assumed a glance of ineffable scorn, as,
bending his head, he took the bauble.

"I will give it to one of my squaws," he said. "The papooses
in my lodge will play with it. Come, Médicine, Tatua will go
and drink fire-water"; and shouldering his carabine, he turned

his broad back without ceremony upon the monarch and his train, and disappeared down one of the walks of the garden. Franklin found him when his own interview with the French Chief Magistrate was over; being attracted to the spot where the Chief was by the crack of his well-known rifle. He was laughing in his quiet way. He had shot the Colonel of the Swiss Guards through his cockade.

Three days afterwards, as the gallant frigate, the *Repudiator,* was sailing out of Brest Harbour, the gigantic form of an Indian might be seen standing on the binnacle in conversation with Commodore Bowie, the commander of the noble ship. It was Tatua, the Chief of the Nose-rings.

The Pre-Raphaelites

DAVID MASSON

[FROM "Pre-Raphaelitism in Art and Literature"]

1852

Some five years ago a few very young men then students in the Royal Academy, formed themselves into a kind of clique, with the intention of aiding and abetting each other while they prosecuted the study of Art in a new and somewhat peculiar manner. One of the most influential members of the clique, if not its actual founder, was William Holman Hunt, a young man who had already given proofs of his determination to be an artist by overcoming not a few difficulties that lay in his way; the other members were—Dante Gabriel Rossetti and William M. Rossetti, the sons of a well-known Italian professor, naturalized by a long residence in England; F. G. Stephens,

From *British Quarterly Review*, 16 (August 1852), pages 197-220.

J. Collinson, Thomas Woolner, and John Everett Millais. Of these seven, six were painters, and one, Mr. Woolner, a sculptor. Half in freak, half in earnest, they called themselves the Pre-Raphaelite Clique—a name which, from its reference to Italian art, we conclude that the Rossettis suggested. Afterwards, disliking the word 'clique,' they called themselves the 'Pre-Raphaelite Brotherhood,' or, more shortly, and to show that they were a good deal in fun all the while, the 'P. R. B's.' They were all young men of independent talent; and there was really nothing more of brotherhood about them than that they found themselves of a similar way of thinking in matters of art, and were, by choice, very much together both in the Academy and out of it. As was natural, they became known to the other students as the 'P. R. B.' set; and, as is very apt to happen in such cases, the name adopted in a moment of frolic has clung to them longer than some of them perhaps wished or expected. Of the original seven, however, one or two have either given up Art or fallen off from the brotherhood, while one or two others have been added in their places . . . .

So much for gossip; and now as to Pre-Raphaelitism itself. In its origin, we believe, Pre-Raphaelitism was a protest by the young artists whose names we have mentioned, against certain traditions in art which had come down with the double sanction of practice and teaching. Until very recently, the work which has served in England both as a text-book to the professional student of art, and as a compendium of information respecting art for the use of the general reader, has been 'Sir Joshua Reynolds's Discourses.' . . .

These maxims are certainly neither so clear in themselves, nor expressed with such a commanding appearance of intellectual authority, as to render assent inevitable. Accordingly, there have always been artists who have proceeded in a spirit contrary to that which they indicate. It was left for the Pre-Raphaelites, however, formally and openly to avow their denial of them, and to signalize the same by a peculiar style of practice.

The great principle which the Pre-Raphaelites took up

separately, and which became the bond of their union, was that they should go to Nature in all cases, and employ, as exactly as possible, her literal forms. If they were to paint a tree as part of a picture, then, instead of attempting to put down, according to Sir Joshua Reynolds's prescription, something that might stand as an ideal tree, the central form of a tree, the general conception of a beautiful tree derived from a previous collation of individual trees, their notion was that they should go to Nature for an actual tree, and paint *that*. So, also, if they were to paint a brick wall as part of the background of a picture, their notion was that they should not paint such a wall as they could put together mentally out of their past recollection of all the brick walls they had seen; but that they should take some actual brick wall and paint it exactly as it was, with all its seams, lichens, and weather-stains. So also, in painting the human figure, their notion was that they should not follow any conventional idea of corporeal beauty, but should take some actual man or woman, and reproduce his or her features with the smallest possible deviation consistent with the purpose of the picture. So also, in a historical picture, their notion was that there should be not be an effort, primarily at least, after what Sir Joshua calls the grand style, but the most faithful study of truth in detail, truth in costume, truth in the portraiture of the personages introduced, truth to all the contemporary circumstances of the action represented. Their notion, in painting a St. Paul, would have been, we believe, not to have idealized him, as Sir Joshua affirms that Raphael has done, but actually to have exhibited him as he was, a man in whom a great soul was shrined in a mean and contemptible body presence. And, in a similar manner, in painting Alexander, they would, we believe, have been resolutely attentive to the fact that he was a Greek of small stature.

This protest in favour of Naturalism or Realism, which constitutes the essence of the Pre-Raphaelite innovation in Art, is, it will be observed, almost exactly identical with that which constituted the Wordsworthian innovation in poetical literature. What Wordsworth affirmed was, that for nearly a century before his time, the persons calling themselves poets had, with a few exceptions, thought and written in a conventional manner, according to certain traditions of what poetry must be, neither looking directly to Nature for the objects of their descriptions, nor using such language as men use in real life. What he attempted, therefore, was to return to Nature, to take things as they actually are, to be rigidly true to fact both in the appearances of the external world, and in the moral circumstances which constitute human life, and while operating on this material with the imagination of a poet, to make use of natural and direct language. The Pre-Raphaelites apply the same theory to art. Until about the time of Raphael, they say, the painters of Europe, and those of Italy in particular, proceeded in the main on a true principle, faithfully copying what they found in Nature, and arriving at beauty and impressiveness through their implicit regard for truth; but since the time of Raphael, painters have for the most part held up Raphael between themselves and Nature; interposed, as it were, certain intellectual phantasms of ideal beauty between their eyes and the literal forms of God's world. Their own aim in Art, consequently, has been, to discard these intellectual phantasms, these generalized forms, which, by Sir Joshua Reynolds's advice, were to stand for ever by the painter's easel, teaching him what to accept and what to correct in Nature, and to go back to Nature herself with something of that docile and reverent spirit which characterized the early Italian masters.

It would be unjust to the Pre-Raphaelites, however, not to take note of the fact that this protest of theirs in favour of realism, was by no means a protest in favour of the Dutch kind of realism, and that no recent school of artists have been more disposed to vindicate the claims of painting to take rank as high imaginative or poetic art. Precisely as Wordsworth, by his demands for literal accuracy of delineation and for simple and direct language, did not depreciate the function of imagination in poetry, but rather exalted it and defined it more clearly, so the Pre-Raphaelites, while insisting on truthful observation and exact rendering as essential matters with the artist, recognised from the first, both in their theory and in their practice, that the greatness of an artist consists not in truthfulness of observation and exactness of rendering alone, but in the spirit manifested through these qualities, in the thought, purpose, or inner intention to which, in that artist's pictures, these qualities are made to minister. . . .

First of all, then, there was universally noted in the earlier works of the Pre-Raphaelites, a kind of contempt for all pre-established ideas of beauty. It even seemed as if, in their resolution to copy literally the forms of Nature, they took pleasure in seeking out such forms as would be called ugly or mean. Thus, instead of giving us figures with those fine conventional heads and regular oval faces and gracefully-formed hands and feet which we like to see in albums, they appeared to take delight in figures with heads phrenologically clumsy, faces strongly marked and irregular, and very pronounced ankles and knuckles. Their colouring, too, and especially their colouring of the human flesh, was not at all so pleasant as we had been accustomed to. In Mr. Millais's picture, for example, of the *Holy Family,* exhibited the year before last, the colouring of the faces, hands, and feet of the personages painted—and these the most sacred personages that an artist could paint—was altogether so peculiar that critics among his brother-artists declared that he must have had scrofulous subjects for his models. And so, in Mr. Hunt's *Jolly Shepherd,* in the present Exhibition, the complexions of the shepherd and shepherdess in which send away some ladies angry and others giggling. Are there no beautiful faces, or fingers, or feet in Nature, say the fair critics, that clever young men should paint things like those; or have the power young men been really so unfortunate in their life-series of feminine visions? . . . But what we desire specially to note at present is, that this tendency towards forms not conventionally agreeable, which has been found fault with in the Pre-Raphaelites, was natural, and even, to some extent, inevitable on their part; and was, in fact, a necessary consequence of their zeal in carrying out their favourite principle of attention to actual truth. Precisely as Wordsworth, in his resolution to break away from conventionalities in poetry, shocked his finical critics by selecting his subjects from among the pedlars, and waggoners, and tinkers of homely English life, and introducing into his verse donkeys and duffle-grey cloaks, and other things hardly before heard of in prose or rhyme; so the Pre-Raphaelites, bent on a similar innovation in Art, left, as it were, the beaten walk of traditional beauties to take a turn of exploration among Nature's less-favoured and more stunted things. Whether they have kept so well within bounds as Wordsworth did, or whether their practice in this respect will not in the end be seen even by themselves to have been a temporary exaggeration for a dogmatic purpose, is a question which we will not now wait to discuss.

Another peculiarity discernible in the works of the Pre-Raphaelites, and indeed inseparable from the very notion of Pre-Raphaelitism, is fondness for detail, and careful finish of the most minute objects. Instead of supposing that what the painters call breadth of effect is attainable only by a bold neglect of all except general arrangements and larger masses, the Pre-Raphaelites, from the very first, entertained the belief, that as broad effects in Nature are compatible with, and, in fact, produced by, infinite aggregations of detail, so they may be in Art. It is another point of similarity between Wordsworth and the Pre-Raphaelites, that this fondness for detail has manifested itself specially in their case, as in his, in extreme accuracy and minuteness in all matters pertaining to vegetation. The very essence of the Wordsworthian innovation in literature, considered in one of its aspects, consisted in this, that it tore men that were going to write poetry out of rooms and cities, and cast them on the green lap of Nature, forcing them to inhale the breath of the ploughed earth, and to know the leafage of the different forest trees, and to gaze in dank cool places at the pipy stalks, and into the coloured cups of weeds and wild flowers. Richness in botanical allusion is perhaps the one peculiarity that pre-eminently distinguishes the English poets after, from the English poets before, Wordsworth. There is, indeed, a closer attention throughout to all the appearances of Nature—the shapes and motions of the clouds, the forms of the hills and rocks, and the sounds and mystery of the seas and rivers; but, on the whole, one sees very clearly that Wordsworth's advice to be true to Nature has been interpreted, for the most part, as an advice to study vegetation. And so it is, in a great measure, with the Pre-Raphaelites. With them, also, vegetation seems to have become thus far synonymous with Nature, that it is chiefly by the extreme accuracy of their painting of trees, and grass, and water-lilies, and jonquils, and weeds, and mosses, that they have signalized their superior attentiveness to Nature's actual appearances. . . .

A third peculiarity of the Pre-Raphaelite painters, or at least of some of them, is a kind of studied quaintness of thought, most frequently bearing the character of archaism, or an attempt after the antique. Much of this, too, we believe, is resolvable into the desire to be literally true to Nature. One of the first results of such a desire, whether in art or literature, must always be a kind of baldness of thought and expression, a return to the most primitive style of thinking and speaking; a preference, so to speak, for words of one syllable. . . . On this point of the mediævalism of the Pre-Raphaelites as painters, Mr. Ruskin has the following passage:—

The current fallacy of society as well as of the press was, that the Pre-Raphaelites imitated the errors of early painters. . . . The Pre-Raphaelites imitate no pictures: they paint from Nature only. But they have opposed themselves, as a body, to that kind of teaching above described, which only began after Raphael's time; and they have opposed themselves as sternly to the entire feeling of the Renaissance schools,—a feeling compounded of indolence, infidelity, sensuality, and shallow pride. Therefore they have called themselves Pre-Raphaelite. If they adhere to their principles and paint Nature as it is around them, with the help of modern science—with the earnestness of the men of the thirteenth and fourteenth centuries, they will, as I said, found a new and noble school in England. If their sympathies with the early artists lead them into mediœvalism or

Romanism, they will of course come to nothing. But I believe there is no danger of this, at least for the strongest among them. There may be some weak ones, whom the Tractarian heresies may touch; but if so, they will drop off like decayed branches from a strong stem.

The authority of Mr. Ruskin is, of course, decisive as to the question whether there is anything like technical archaism in the Pre-Raphaelite painting,—any actual resemblance between the modern Pre-Raphaelite paintings and the paintings of the early Italian school as works of pictorial art. But that one of the characteristics of the Pre-Raphaelites as a body is sympathy with mediævalism of sentiment, we know to be a fact. Among other ways in which this has shown itself, is their tendency to that peculiar class of ecclesiastical subjects of which the early Christian artists were fond. . . .

As might be expected, Pre-Raphaelitism expresses itself far better on canvas than on paper. Yet, as all know, even the ablest of the Pre-Raphaelite painters have had a hard battle to fight. A year or two ago, their pictures, though praised by artists themselves for their technical skill, were the subjects of universal jesting and merriment. Visitors to the Exhibition, with the exception of a few of the more judicious, approached the Pre-Raphaelite pictures only to laugh and go away again. The critics of the press were, almost to a man, against them. As late as last year the notices of the Pre-Raphaelite pictures in the newspapers were, most of them, violent attacks. This year there is a complete change. The *Times,* indeed, attempted to renew the old cry, and to bring public ridicule once more down upon the 'opinionative youths' who had persisted, notwithstanding repeated warnings, in painting in their old manner. But even the *Times* was driven into silence; and the Pre-Raphaelite paintings of the present year, and especially those of Millais, have been more widely commented on, and more heartily praised than any others in the Exhibition. . . .
As the poets and the critics came round to Wordsworth, so, though scarcely yet on so large a scale, the artists and the critics seem to be coming round to the Pre-Raphaelites. That

the change has been so sudden, however, is owing, doubtless, in a considerable degree, to the generous intervention in behalf of the Pre-Raphaelites made by Mr. Ruskin last year. . . .

Mr. Hunt's single picture, marked No. 592 in the Catalogue, is entitled *The Hireling Shepherd,* and purports to be a free version of these lines in one of Shakespeare's snatches of ballad,—

> Sleepest thou or wakest thou, jolly shepherd?
>   Thy sheep be in the corn;
> And, for one blast of thy minikin mouth,
>   Thy sheep shall take no harm.

The suggestions of these lines are attended to in the picture, and perhaps there is an allusion also in the conception to the scriptural idea of a hireling shepherd; but, on the whole, the picture is a piece of broad rural reality, with none of the fantastic circumstance implied in the lines quoted, and with no attempt to bring out the scriptural allusion, if it exists, by deviating from what is English and modern. A brawny shepherd, in a brown jacket and corduroys, and as brawny a shepherdess, in a white smock and red petticoat, (too much like brother and sister, as we have heard it remarked,) are sitting among a clump of trees, separating a meadow from a field of ripe corn. They are idling away their time; and he has just caught a death's-head moth, which he is exhibiting to her, while she shrinks back, half in disgust, from the sight, though still curious enough to look at it intently. Meanwhile the sheep that they should have been attending to, are straggling about, and getting into mischief. Some are fighting; some are off to a distant part of the meadow; one is fairly up to the neck among the ripe corn, and several are following in the same direction. To make the mischief all the more patent, a lamb is lying quietly on the shepherdess's lap, munching one of the two green apples which the hussy has left there; green apples, as we understand, being certain death to lambs. All this is in the foreground of a fine breezy English landscape, on a pleasant summer's day; there are rich yellow fields in the distance, with rows of trees, and swallows are flying along the meadows. The picture is, in all respects, one of the best in the exhibition. Such corn, such sheep, such meadows, such rows of trees, and such cool grass and wild flowers to sit amidst, are not to be found in any painting that we know. The Pre-Raphaelitism of the artist in this picture shows itself, not only in the ordinary Pre-Raphaelite quality of minute truth of detail,—perhaps a little overdone, as in the introduction of the swallows in the act of flying,— but also in the audacity with which he has selected such a veritable pair of country labourers for the principal figures. There is certainly no attempt at poetry here; for a fellow more capable than the shepherd of drinking a great quantity of beer, or a more sunburnt slut than the shepherdess, we never saw in a picture. Mr. Hunt is clearly far more of a realist by constitution, and by resolute purpose, than Mr. Millais, and will probably continue for a longer period to paint pictures containing objects too harsh for the popular taste. He has something of the rigid reflective realism of Thackeray, without anything of Thackeray's bitter social humour; and as the man to whom this constituent of Pre-Raphaelitism was originally most native, it is natural that he should carry it farthest. . . .

Of Mr. Millais's three pictures, the chief are the *Ophelia* (No. 556), and the *Huguenot, on St. Bartholomew's Day, refusing to shield himself from danger by wearing the Roman-catholic badge* (No. 478). No pictures in the Exhibition have attracted so much attention as these. The death of Ophelia has been a favourite subject with artists, and with illustrators of Shakespeare; but we do not believe that the subject was ever treated before with any approach to the minuteness with which Millais has treated it in the present picture. The lines of Shakespeare describing the scene were, indeed, a sufficient temptation to any painter . . . . Mr. Millais, in his illustration of these lines, has given us such a pool as no other English painter could or would have painted. We believe he went into the country in search of an actual pool to suit the description; resided by it for some weeks, and painted from it morning and evening till the whole was finished. It is a deep, dark, silent, all but motionless pool, made by a brook in the dankest covert of a thick wood. The still living body of Ophelia has floated at full length down from the spot where she fell in, to a place where a huge pollarded trunk lies heavily athwart the stream, some of the multitudinous osiers which have sprouted from it dipping down among the ooze on one side, while the greater portion shoot upwards, and arch over with abundant leafage towards the water flags on the other. The hands are above the water; the face is crazy; the mouth is open as if still singing; and down the stream, and along the rich bridal dress which she wears, and which is completely under water, float the flowers which have escaped from her incapable hands. White blossoms on the branches above, and a robin perched on one of the branches, add a touch of quaint beauty to the weirdly aspect of the scene. Altogether the painting is a wonderful one, and it is with something of reluctance that we set down two critical observations that we have made upon it. The one is, that the artist seems to have been more faithful to the circumstantials of the actual brook which he selected as answering to Shakespeare's description, than to the text of the description itself. . . . The other observation we have to make is one in support of which we can allege nothing but our individual feeling and preconception. It is that the face of Ophelia, however admirable the expression depicted in such a face, is not the face of the real Ophelia of *Hamlet,* but a shade too fair in colour, and decidedly too marked and mature in form. . . .

The great purpose and effect of the Pre-Raphaelite movement in art has been to impress on artists the duty of being true to nature. But 'being true to nature' is a very vague phrase; and the advice contained in it can go but a very little way towards teaching an artist how he is to paint pictures. . . . In order to reconcile, therefore, the Pre-Raphaelite maxim of being true to nature with Goethe's famous maxim, so contrary in appearance, 'Art is called Art simply because it is *not* Nature,' it must be remembered that the true painting of natural objects is but the grammar or language of art, and that, as the greatness of a poem consists, not in the grammatical correctness of the language, but in the power and

beauty of the meaning, so the greatness of a painting depends
on what there is in it that the painter has added out of his
own mind. . . . Equally with the poet, the painter must take
his rank ultimately according to his power of invention—
according to that in his paintings which is, in the strict sense
of the word, *factitious*, or supplied out of his own heart and
mind, whether for the interpretation, or for the artistic combination into new and significant unions, of the appearances
of so-called Nature. The special merit of the Pre-Raphaelites
consists in this,—that they have treated as a mischievous
fallacy the notion that this power of artistic invention, this
painter's sway over Nature, is a thing to be taught in the
schools, and have called attention to the fact that what is
teachable in the art of painting, is the habit of patient observation and the power of correct imitation. If they have seemed
to insist upon this too much, it is not, we believe, because
they have undervalued invention, but because they truly
consider that the prerequisite to invention in painting is the
ability to paint.

Characteristics of Gothic Architecture

JOHN RUSKIN

[FROM *The Stones of Venice*]

1853

I believe, then, that the characteristic or moral elements of Gothic are the following, placed in the order of their importance:

1. Savageness.   2. Changefulness.   3. Naturalism.
4. Grotesqueness.   5. Rigidity.   6. Redundance....

1. SAVAGENESS. I am not sure when the word "Gothic" was first generically applied to the architecture of the North; but I presume that, whatever the date of its original usage, it was intended to imply reproach, and express the barbaric character of the nations among whom that architecture arose. It never implied that they were literally of Gothic lineage, far less that their architecture had been originally invented by the Goths themselves; but it did imply that they and their buildings together exhibited a degree of sternness and rudeness, which, in contradistinction to the character of Southern and Eastern nations, appeared like a perpetual reflection of the contrast between the Goth and the Roman in their first encounter. And when that fallen Roman, in the utmost impotence of his luxury, and insolence of his guilt, became the model for the imitation of civilized Europe, at the close of the so-called Dark Ages, the word Gothic became a term of unmitigated contempt, not unmixed with aversion. From that contempt, by the exertion of the antiquaries and architects of this century, Gothic architecture has been sufficiently vindicated; and perhaps some among us, in our admiration of the

magnificent science of its structure, and sacredness of its expression, might desire that the term of ancient reproach should be withdrawn, and some other, of more apparent honourableness, adopted in its place. There is no chance, as there is no need, of such a substitution. As far as the epithet was used scornfully, it was used falsely; but there is no reproach in the word, rightly understood; on the contrary, there is a profound truth, which the instinct of mankind almost unconsciously recognizes. It is true, greatly and deeply true, that the architecture of the North is rude and wild; but it is not true, that, for this reason, we are to condemn it, or despise. Far otherwise: I believe it is in this very character that it deserves our profoundest reverence.

The charts of the world which have been drawn up by modern science have thrown into a narrow space the expression of a vast amount of knowledge, but I have never yet seen any one pictorial enough to enable the spectator to imagine the kind of contrast in physical character which exists between Northern and Southern countries; . . . Let us watch him with reverence as he sets side by side the burning gems, and smooths with soft sculpture the jasper pillars, that are to reflect a ceaseless sunshine, and rise into a cloudless sky: but not with less reverence let us stand by him, when, with rough strength and hurried stroke, he smites an uncouth animation out of the rocks which he has torn from among the moss of the moorland, and heaves into the darkened air the pile of iron buttress and rugged wall, instinct with work of an imagination as wild and wayward as the northern sea; creations of ungainly shape and rigid limb, but full of wolfish life; fierce as the winds that beat, and changeful as the clouds that shade them.

There is, I repeat, no degradation, no reproach in this, but all dignity and honourableness: and we should err grievously in refusing either to recognize as an essential character of the existing architecture of the North, or to admit as a desirable character in that which it yet may be, this wildness of thought, and roughness of work; this look of mountain brotherhood between the cathedral and the Alp; this magnificence of sturdy power, put forth only the more energetically because the fine finger-touch was chilled away by the frosty wind, and the eye dimmed by the moor-mist, or blinded by the hail; this outspeaking of the strong spirit of men who may not gather redundant fruitage from the earth, nor bask in dreamy benignity of sunshine, but must break the rock for bread, and cleave the forest for fire, and show, even in what they did for their delight, some of the hard habits of the arm and heart that grew on them as they swung the axe or pressed the plough.

If, however, the savageness of Gothic architecture, merely as an expression of its origin among Northern nations, may be considered, in some sort, a noble character, it possesses a higher nobility still, when considered as an index, not of climate, but of religious principle. . . .

The Greek gave to the lower workman no subject which he could not perfectly execute. The Assyrian gave him subjects which he could only execute imperfectly, but fixed a legal standard for his imperfection. The workman was, in both systems, a slave.[1]

But in the mediæval, or especially Christian, system of ornament, this slavery is done away with altogether; Christianity having recognized, in small things as well as great, the individual value of every soul. But it not only recognizes its value; it confesses its imperfection, in only bestowing dignity upon the acknowledgment of unworthiness. That admission of lost power and fallen nature, which the Greek or Ninevite felt to be intensely painful, and, as far as might be, altogether refused, the Christian makes daily and hourly contemplating the fact of it without fear, as tending, in the end, to God's greater glory. Therefore, to every spirit which Christianity summons to her service, her exhortation is: Do what you can, and

[1]The third kind of ornament, the Renaissance, is that in which the inferior detail becomes principal, the executor of every minor portion being required to exhibit skill and possess knowledge as great as that which is possessed by the master of the design; and in the endeavour to endow him with this skill and knowledge, his own original power is overwhelmed, and the whole building becomes a wearisome exhibition of well-educated imbecility. . . .

confess frankly what you are unable to do; neither let your effort be shortened for fear of failure, nor your confession silenced for fear of shame. And it is, perhaps, the principal admirableness of the Gothic schools of architecture, that they thus receive the results of the labour of inferior minds; and out of fragments full of imperfection, and betraying that imperfection in every touch, indulgently raise up a stately and unaccusable whole.

But the modern English mind has this much in common with that of the Greek, that it intensely desires, in all things, the utmost completion or perfection compatible with their nature. This is a noble character in the abstract, but becomes ignoble when it causes us to forget the relative dignities of that nature itself, and to prefer the perfectness of the lower nature to the imperfection of the higher. . . . Now, in the make and nature of every man, however rude or simple, whom we employ in manual labour, there are some powers for better things: some tardy imagination, torpid capacity of emotion, tottering steps of thought, there are, even at the worst; and in most cases it is all our own fault that they *are* tardy or torpid. But they cannot be strengthened, unless we are content to take them in their feebleness, and unless we prize and honour them in their imperfection above the best and most perfect manual skill. And this is what we have to do with all our labourers; to look for the *thoughtful* part of them, and get that out of them, whatever we lose for it, whatever faults and errors we are obliged to take with it. For the best that is in them cannot manifest itself, but in company with much error. Understand this clearly: You can teach a man to draw a straight line, and to cut one; to strike a curved line, and to carve it; and to copy and carve any number of given lines or forms, with admirable speed and perfect precision; and you find his work perfect of its kind: but if you ask him to think about any of those forms, to consider if he cannot find any better in his own head, he stops; his execution becomes hesitating; he thinks, and ten to one he thinks wrong; ten to one he makes a mistake in the first touch he gives to his work as a thinking being. But you have made a man of him for all that. He was only a machine before, an animated tool.

And observe, you are put to stern choice in this matter. You must either make a tool of the creature, or a man of him. You cannot make both. Men were not intended to work with the accuracy of tools, to be precise and perfect in all their actions. If you will have that precision out of them, and make their fingers measure degrees like cog-wheels, and their arms strike curves like compasses, you must unhumanize them. . . .

And now, reader, look round this English room of yours, about which you have been proud so often, because the work of it was so good and strong, and the ornaments of it so finished. Examine again all those accurate mouldings, and perfect polishings, and unerring adjustments of the seasoned wood and tempered steel. Many a time you have exulted over them, and thought how great England was, because her slightest work was done so thoroughly. Alas! if read rightly, these perfectnesses are signs of a slavery in our England a thousand times more bitter and more degrading than that of the scourged African, or helot Greek. Men may be beaten, chained, tormented, yoked like cattle, slaughtered like summer flies, and yet remain in one sense, and the best sense, free. But to smother their souls within them, to blight and hew into rotting pollards the suckling branches of their human intelligence, to make the flesh and skin which, after the worm's work on it, is to see God, into leathern thongs to yoke machinery with,—this it is to be slave-masters indeed; and there might be more freedom in England, though her feudal lords' lightest words were worth men's lives, and though the blood of the vexed husbandman dropped in the furrows of her fields, than there is while the animation of her multitudes is sent like fuel to feed the factory smoke, and the strength of them is given daily to be wasted into the fineness of a web, or racked into the exactness of a line.

And, on the other hand, go forth again to gaze upon the old cathedral front, where you have smiled so often at the fantastic ignorance of the old sculptors: examine once more those ugly goblins, and formless monsters, and stern statues, anatomiless and rigid; but do not mock at them, for they are signs of the life and liberty of every workman who struck the stone; a freedom of thought, and rank in scale of being, such as no laws, no charters, no charities can secure; but which it must be the first aim of all Europe at this day to regain for her children.

Let me not be thought to speak wildly or extravagantly. It is verily this degradation of the operative into a machine, which, more than any other evil of the times, is leading the mass of the nations everywhere into vain, incoherent, destructive struggling for a freedom of which they cannot explain the nature to themselves. Their universal outcry against wealth, and against nobility, is not forced from them either by the pressure of famine, or the sting of mortified pride. These do much, and have done much in all ages; but the foundations of society were never yet shaken as they are at this day. It is not that men are ill fed, but that they have no pleasure in the work by which they make their bread, and therefore look to wealth as the only means of pleasure. It is not that men are pained by the scorn of the upper classes, but they cannot endure their own; for they feel that the kind of labour to which they are condemned is verily a degrading one, and makes them less than men. Never had the upper classes so much sympathy with the lower, or charity for them, as they have at this day, and yet never were they so much hated by them: for, of old, the separation between the noble and the poor was merely a wall built by law; now it is a veritable difference in level of standing, a precipice between upper and lower grounds in the field of humanity, and there is pestilential air at the bottom of it. I know not if a day is ever to come when the nature of right freedom will be understood, and when men will see that to obey another man, to labour for him, yield reverence to him or to his place, is not slavery. It is often the best kind of liberty,—liberty from care. . . .

We have much studied and much perfected, of late, the great civilized invention of the division of labour; only we give it a false name. It is not, truly speaking, the labour that is divided; but the men:—Divided into mere segments of men—broken into small fragments and crumbs of life; so that all the little piece of intelligence that is left in a man is not enough to make a pin, or a nail, but exhausts itself in making the point of a pin or the head of a nail. Now it is a good and desirable thing, truly, to make many pins in a day; but if we could only see with what crystal sand their points were polished,—sand of human soul, much to be magnified before it can be discerned for what it is,—we should think there might be some loss in it also. And the great cry that rises from all our manufacturing cities, louder than their furnace blast, is all in very deed for this,—that we manufacture everything there except men; we blanch cotton, and strengthen steel, and refine sugar, and shape pottery; but to brighten, to strengthen, to refine, or to form a single living spirit, never enters into our estimate of advantages. And all the evil to which that cry is urging our myriads can be met only in one way: not by teaching nor preaching, for to teach them is but to show them their misery, and to preach to them, if we do nothing more than preach, is to mock at it. It can be met only by a right understanding, on the part of all classes, of what kinds of labour are good for men, raising them, and making them happy; by a determined sacrifice of such convenience, or beauty, or cheapness as is to be got only by the degradation of the workman; and by equally determined demand for the products and results of healthy and ennobling labour.

And how, it will be asked, are these products to be recognized, and this demand to be regulated? Easily: by the observance of three broad and simple rules:

1. Never encourage the manufacture of any article not absolutely necessary, in the production of which *Invention* has no share.

2. Never demand an exact finish for its own sake, but only for some practical or noble end.

3. Never encourage imitation or copying of any kind, except for the sake of preserving record of great works. . . .

For instance. Glass beads are utterly unnecessary, and there is no design or thought employed in their manufacture. They are formed by first drawing out the glass into rods; these rods are chopped up into fragments of the size of beads by the human hand, and the fragments are then rounded in the furnace. The men who chop up the rods sit at their work all day, their hands vibrating with a perpetual and exquisitely timed palsy, and the beads dropping beneath their vibration like hail. Neither they, nor the men who draw out the rods or fuse the fragments, have the smallest occasion for the use of any single human faculty; and every young lady, therefore, who buys glass beads is engaged in the slave-trade, and in a much more cruel one than that which we have so long been endeavouring to put down.

But glass cups and vessels may become the subject of exquisite invention; and if in buying these we pay for the invention; that is to say for the beautiful form, or colour, or engraving, and not for mere finish of execution, we are doing good to humanity. . . .

So the rule is simple: Always look for invention first, and after that, for such execution as will help the invention, and as the inventor is capable of without painful effort, and *no more*. Above all, demand no refinement of execution where there is no thought, for that is slaves' work, unredeemed. Rather choose rough work than smooth work, so only that the practical purpose be answered, and never imagine there is reason to be proud of anything that may be accomplished by patience and sand-paper. . . .

Nay, but the reader interrupts me,—"If the workman can design beautifully, I would not have him kept at the furnace. Let him be taken away and made a gentleman, and have a studio, and design his glass there, and I will have it blown and cut for him by common workmen, and so I will have my design and my finish too."

All ideas of this kind are founded upon two mistaken suppositions: the first, that one man's thoughts can be, or ought to be, executed by another man's hands; the second, that manual labour is a degradation, when it is governed by intellect.

On a large scale, and in work determinable by line and

rule, it is indeed both possible and necessary that the thoughts of one man should be carried out by the labour of others; in this sense I have already defined the best architecture to be the expression of the mind of manhood by the hands of childhood. But on a smaller scale, and in a design which cannot be mathematically defined, one man's thought can never be expressed by another: and the difference between the spirit of touch of the man who is inventing, and of the man who is obeying directions, is often all the difference between a great and a common work of art. How wide the separation is between original and second-hand execution, I shall endeavour to show elsewhere; it is not so much to our purpose here as to make the other and more fatal error of despising manual labour when governed by intellect; for it is no less fatal an error to despise it when thus regulated by intellect, than to value it for its own sake. We are always in these days endeavouring to separate the two; we want one man to be always thinking, and another to be always working, and we call one a gentleman, and the other an operative; whereas the workman ought often to be thinking, and the thinker often to be working, and both should be gentlemen, in the best sense. As it is, we make both ungentle, the one envying, the other despising, his brother; and the mass of society is made up of morbid thinkers, and miserable workers. Now it is only by labour that thought can be made healthy, and only by thought that labour can be made happy, and the two cannot be separated with impunity. It would be well if all of us were good handicraftsmen in some kind, and the dishonour of manual labour done away with altogether; so that though there should still be a trenchant distinction of race between nobles and commoners, there should not, among the latter, be a trenchant distinction of employment, as between idle and working men, or between men of liberal and illiberal professions. All professions should be liberal, and there should be less pride felt in peculiarity of employment, and more in excellence of achievement. And yet more, in each several profession, no master should be too proud to do its hardest work. The painter should grind his own colours; the architect work in the mason's yard with his men; the master-manufacturer be himself a more skilful operative than any man in his mills; and the distinction between one man and another be only in experience and skill, and the authority and wealth which these must naturally and justly obtain.

I should be led far from the matter in hand, if I were to pursue this interesting subject. Enough, I trust, has been said to show the reader that the rudeness or imperfection which at first rendered the term "Gothic" one of reproach is indeed, when rightly understood, one of the most noble characters of Christian architecture, and not only a noble but an *essential* one. It seems a fantastic paradox, but it is nevertheless a most important truth, that no architecture can be truly noble which is *not* imperfect.

The Love of Clouds

JOHN RUSKIN

[FROM *Modern Painters:* "Of Modern Landscape"]

1856

We turn our eyes, therefore, as boldly and as quickly as may be, from these serene fields and skies of mediæval art, to the most characteristic examples of modern landscape. And, I believe, the first thing that will strike us, or that ought to strike us, is their *cloudiness*.

Out of perfect light and motionless air, we find ourselves on a sudden brought under sombre skies, and into drifting wind; and, with fickle sunbeams flashing in our face, or utterly drenched with sweep of rain, we are reduced to track the

From Volume III, Part IV, Chapter 16.

changes of the shadows on the grass, or watch the rents of twilight through angry cloud. And we find that whereas all the pleasure of the mediæval was in *stability, definiteness,* and *luminousness,* we are expected to rejoice in darkness, and triumph in mutability; to lay the foundation of happiness in things which momentarily change or fade; and to expect the utmost satisfaction and instruction from what it is impossible to arrest, and difficult to comprehend.

We find, however, together with this general delight in breeze and darkness, much attention to the real form of clouds, and careful drawing of effects of mist; so that the appearance of objects, as seen through it, becomes a subject of science with us; and the faithful representation of that appearance is made of primal importance, under the name of aerial perspective. The aspects of sunset and sunrise, with all their attendant phenomena of cloud and mist, are watchfully delineated; and in ordinary daylight landscape, the sky is considered of so much importance, that a principal mass of foliage, or a whole foreground, is unhesitatingly thrown into shade merely to bring out the form of a white cloud. So that, if a general and characteristic name were needed for modern landscape art, none better could be invented than "the service of clouds."

And this name would, unfortunately, be characteristic of our art in more ways than one. In the last chapter, I said that all the Greeks spoke kindly about the clouds, except Aristophanes; and he, I am sorry to say (since his report is so unfavourable), is the only Greek who had studied them attentively. He tells us, first, that they are "great goddesses to idle men"; then, that they are "mistresses of disputings, and logic, and monstrosities, and noisy chattering"; declares that whoso believes in their divinity must first disbelieve in Jupiter, and place supreme power in the hands of an unknown god "Whirlwind"; and, finally, he displays their influence over the mind of one of their disciples, in his sudden desire "to speak ingeniously concerning smoke."

There is, I fear, an infinite truth in this Aristophanic judgment applied to our modern cloud-worship. Assuredly, much of the love of mystery in our romances, our poetry, our art, and, above all, in our metaphysics, must come under that definition so long ago given by the great Greek, "speaking ingeniously concerning smoke." And much of the instinct, which, partially developed in painting, may be now seen throughout every mode of exertion of mind,—the easily encouraged doubt, easily excited curiosity, habitual agitation, and delight in the changing and the marvellous, as opposed to the old quiet serenity of social custom and religious faith,— is again deeply defined in those few words, the "dethroning of Jupiter," the "coronation of the whirlwind."

Nor of whirlwind merely, but also of darkness or ignorance respecting all stable facts. That darkening of the foreground to bring out the white cloud, is, in one aspect of it, a type of the subjection of all plain and positive fact, to what is uncertain and unintelligible. And, as we examine farther into the matter, we shall be struck by another great difference between the old and modern landscape, namely, that in the old no one ever thought of drawing anything but as well *as he could*. That might not be *well*, as we have seen in the case of rocks; but it was as well as he *could*, and always distinctly. Leaf, or stone, or animal, or man, it was equally drawn with care and clearness, and its essential characters shown. If it was an oak tree, the acorns were drawn; if a flint pebble, its veins were drawn; if an arm of the sea, its fish were drawn; if a group of figures, their faces and dresses were drawn— to the very last subtlety of expression and end of thread that could be got into the space, far off or near. But now our ingenuity is all "concerning smoke." Nothing is truly drawn but that; all else is vague, slight, imperfect; got with as little pains as possible. You examine your closest foreground, and find no leaves; your largest oak, and find no acorns; your human figure, and find a spot of red paint instead of a face; and in all this, again and again, the Aristophanic words come true, and the clouds seem to be "great goddesses to idle men."

The next thing that will strike us, after this love of clouds, is the love of liberty. Whereas the mediæval was always shutting himself into castles, and behind fosses, and drawing brickwork neatly, and beds of flowers primly, our painters delight in getting to the open fields and moors, abhor all hedges and moats; never paint anything but free-growing trees, and rivers gliding "at their own sweet will"; eschew formality down to the smallest detail; break and displace the brickwork which the mediæval would have carefully cemented; leave unpruned the thickets he would have delicately trimmed; and, carrying the love of liberty even to license, and the love of wildness even to ruin, take pleasure at last in every aspect of age and desolation which emancipates the objects of nature from the government of men;—on the castle wall displacing its tapestry with ivy, and spreading, through the garden, the bramble for the rose.

Connected with this love of liberty we find a singular manifestation of love of mountains, and see our painters traversing the wildest places of the globe in order to obtain subjects with craggy foregrounds and purple distances. Some few of them remain content with pollards and flat land; but these are always men of third-rate order; and the leading masters, while they do not reject the beauty of the low grounds, reserve their highest powers to paint Alpine peaks or Italian promontories. And it is eminently noticeable, also, that this pleasure in the mountains is never mingled with fear, or tempered by a spirit of meditation, as with the mediæval; but is always free and fearless, brightly exhilarating, and wholly unreflective; so that the painter feels that his mountain foreground may be more consistently animated by a sportsman than a hermit; and our modern society in general goes to the mountains, not to fast, but to feast, and leaves their glaciers covered with chicken-bones and egg-shells.

Connected with this want of any sense of solemnity in mountain scenery, is a general profanity of temper in regarding all the rest of nature; that is to say, a total absence of faith in the presence of any deity therein. Whereas the mediæval never painted a cloud, but with the purpose of placing an angel in it; and a Greek never entered a wood without expecting to meet a god in it; *we* should think the appearance of an angel in the cloud wholly unnatural, and should be seriously surprised by meeting a god anywhere. Our chief ideas about the wood are connected with poaching. We have no belief that the clouds contain more than so many inches of rain or hail, and from our ponds and ditches expect nothing more divine than ducks and watercresses.

Finally: connected with this profanity of temper is a strong tendency to deny the sacred element of colour, and make our boast in blackness. For though occasionally glaring or violent, modern colour is on the whole eminently sombre, tending continually to grey or brown, and by many of our best painters consistently falsified, with a confessed pride in what they call chaste or subdued tints: so that, whereas a mediæval paints his sky bright blue and his foreground bright green, gilds the towers of his castles, and clothes his figures with purple and white, we paint our sky grey, our foreground black, and our foliage brown, and think that enough is sacrificed to the sun in admitting the dangerous brightness of a scarlet cloak or a blue jacket.

These, I believe, are the principal points which would strike us instantly, if we were to be brought suddenly into an exhibition of modern landscapes out of a room filled with mediæval work. It is evident that there are both evil and good in this change: but how much evil, or how much good, we can only estimate by considering, as in the former divisions of our inquiry, what are the real roots of the habits of mind which have caused them.

At first, it is evident that the title "Dark Ages," given to the mediæval centuries, is, respecting art, wholly inapplicable. They were, on the contrary, the bright ages; ours are the dark ones. I do not mean metaphysically, but literally. They were the ages of gold; ours are the ages of umber. . . .

The profoundest reason of this darkness of heart is, I believe, our want of faith. There never yet was a generation of men (savage or civilized) who, taken as a body, so wofully fulfilled the words "having no hope, and without God in the world," as the present civilized European race. A Red Indian or Otaheitan savage has more sense of a divine existence round him, or government over him, than the plurality of refined Londoners and Parisians: and those among us who may in some sense be said to believe, are divided almost without exception into two broad classes, Romanist and Puritan; who, but for the interference of the unbelieving portions of society, would, either of them, reduce the other sect as speedily as possible to ashes; the Romanist having always done so whenever he could, from the beginning of their separation, and the Puritan at this time holding himself in complacent expectation of the destruction of Rome by volcanic fire. Such division as this between persons nominally of one religion, that is to say, believing in the same God, and the same Revelation, cannot but become a stumbling-block of the gravest kind to all thoughtful and far-sighted men,—a stumbling-block which they can only surmount under the most favourable circumstances of early education. Hence, nearly all our powerful men in this age of the world are unbelievers; the best of them in doubt and misery; the worst in reckless defiance; the plurality, in plodding hesitation, doing, as well as they can, what practical work lies ready to their hands. Most of our scientific men are in this last class: our popular authors either set themselves definitely against all religious form, pleading for simple truth and benevolence, (Thackeray, Dickens,) or give themselves up to bitter and fruitless statement of facts, (De Balzac,) or surface-painting, (Scott,) or careless blasphemy, sad or smiling, (Byron, Béranger). Our earnest poets and deepest thinkers are doubtful and indignant, (Tennyson, Carlyle); one or two, anchored, indeed, but anxious or weeping, (Wordsworth, Mrs. Browning); and of these two, the first is not so sure of his anchor, but that now and then it drags with him, even to make him cry out,—

> Great God, I had rather be
> A Pagan suckled in some creed outworn;
> So might I, standing on this pleasant lea,
> Have glimpses that would make me less forlorn.

In politics, religion is now a name; in art, a hypocrisy or affectation. Over German religious pictures the inscription,

"See how Pious I am," can be read at a glance by any clear-sighted person. Over French and English religious pictures the inscription, "See how Impious I am," is equally legible. All sincere and modest art is, among us, profane. . . .

There is, however, another, and a more innocent root of our delight in wild scenery.

All the Renaissance principles of art tended, as I have before often explained, to the setting Beauty above Truth, and seeking for it always at the expense of truth. And the proper punishment of such pursuit—the punishment which all the laws of the universe rendered inevitable—was, that those who thus pursued beauty should wholly lose sight of beauty. All the thinkers of the age, as we saw previously, declared that it did not exist. The age seconded their efforts, and banished beauty, so far as human effort could succeed in doing so, from the face of the earth, and the form of man. To powder the hair, to patch the cheek, to hoop the body, to buckle the foot, were all part and parcel of the same system which reduced streets to brick walls, and pictures to brown stains. One desert of Ugliness was extended before the eyes of mankind; and their pursuit of the beautiful, so recklessly continued, received unexpected consummation in high-heeled shoes and periwigs—Gower Street, and Gaspar Poussin.

Reaction from this state was inevitable, if any true life was left in the races of mankind; and, accordingly, though still forced, by rule and fashion, to the producing and wearing all that is ugly, men steal out, half-ashamed of themselves for doing so, to the fields and mountains; and, finding among these the colour, and liberty, and variety, and power, which are for ever grateful to them, delight in these to an extent never before known; rejoice in all the wildest shattering of the mountain side, as an opposition to Gower Street, gaze in a rapt manner at sunsets and sunrises, to see there the blue, and gold, and purple, which glow for them no longer on knight's armour or temple porch; and gather with care out of the fields, into their blotted herbaria, the flowers which the five orders of architecture have banished from their doors and casements.

The Pathetic Fallacy

JOHN RUSKIN

[FROM *Modern Painters*]

1856

Now, therefore, putting these tiresome and absurd words quite out of our way, we may go on at our ease to examine the point in question,—namely, the difference between the ordinary, proper, and true appearances of things to us; and the extraordinary, or false appearances, when we are under the influence of emotion, or contemplative fancy; false appearances, I say, as being entirely unconnected with any real power or character in the object, and only imputed to it by us.

For instance—

> The spendthrift crocus, bursting through the mould
> Naked and shivering, with his cup of gold.

This is very beautiful, and yet very untrue. The crocus is not a spendthrift, but a hardy plant; its yellow is not gold, but saffron. How is it that we enjoy so much the having it put into our heads that it is anything else than a plain crocus?

It is an important question. For, throughout our past reasonings about art, we have always found that nothing could be good or useful, or ultimately pleasurable, which was untrue. But here is something pleasurable in written poetry, which is nevertheless *un*true. And what is more, if we think over our favourite poetry, we shall find it full of this kind of fallacy, and that we like it all the more for being so.

From Volume III, Part IV, Chapter 12.

It will appear also, on consideration of the matter, that this fallacy is of two principal kinds. Either, as in this case of the crocus, it is the fallacy of wilful fancy, which involves no real expectation that it will be believed; or else it is a fallacy caused by an excited state of the feelings, making us, for the time, more or less irrational. Of the cheating of the fancy we shall have to speak presently; but in this chapter, I want to examine the nature of the other error, that which the mind admits when affected strongly by emotion. Thus, for instance, in *Alton Locke*,—

> They rowed her in across the rolling foam—
> The cruel, crawling foam.

The foam is not cruel, neither does it crawl. The state of mind which attributes to it these characters of a living creature is one in which the reason is unhinged by grief. All violent feelings have the same effect. They produce in us a falseness in all our impressions of external things, which I would generally characterize as the "pathetic fallacy."

Now we are in the habit of considering this fallacy as eminently a character of poetical description, and the temper of mind in which we allow it, as one eminently poetical, because passionate. But I believe, if we look well into the matter, that we shall find the greatest poets do not often admit this kind of falseness,—that it is only the second order of poets who much delight in it.[1]

Thus, when Dante describes the spirits falling from the bank of Acheron "as dead leaves flutter from a bough," he gives the most perfect image possible of their utter lightness, feebleness, passiveness, and scattering agony of despair, without, however, for an instant losing his own clear perception that *these* are souls, and *those* are leaves; he makes

[1] I admit two orders of poets, but no third; and by these two orders I mean the creative (Shakspeare, Homer, Dante), and Reflective or Perceptive (Wordsworth, Keats, Tennyson). But both of these must be *first*-rate in their range, though their range is different; and with poetry second-rate in *quality* no one ought to be allowed to trouble mankind.

no confusion of one with the other. But when Coleridge speaks of

> The one red leaf, the last of its clan,
> That dances as often as dance it can,

he has a morbid, that is to say, a so far false, idea about the leaf; he fancies a life in it, and will, which there are not; confuses its powerlessness with choice, its fading death with merriment, and the wind that shakes it with music. Here, however, there is some beauty, even in the morbid passage; but take an instance in Homer and Pope. Without the knowledge of Ulysses, Elpenor, his youngest follower, has fallen from an upper chamber in the Circean palace, and has been left dead, unmissed by his leader or companions, in the haste of their departure. They cross the sea to the Cimmerian land; and Ulysses summons the shades from Tartarus. The first which appears is that of the lost Elpenor. Ulysses, amazed, and in exactly the spirit of bitter and terrified lightness which is seen in Hamlet,[2] addresses the spirit with the simple, startled words :—

Elpenor! How camest thou under the shadowy darkness? Hast thou come faster on foot than I in my black ship?

Which Pope renders thus :—

> O, say, what angry power Elpenor led
> To glide in shades, and wander with the dead?
> How could thy soul, by realms and seas disjoined,
> Outfly the nimble sail, and leave the lagging wind?

I sincerely hope the reader finds no pleasure here, either in the nimbleness of the sail, or the laziness of the wind! And yet how is it that these conceits are so painful now, when they have been pleasant to us in the other instances?

For a very simple reason. They are not a *pathetic* fallacy at all, for they are put into the mouth of the wrong passion— a passion which never could possibly have spoken them—

[2]"Well said, old mole! canst work i' the ground so fast?"

agonized curiosity. Ulysses wants to know the facts of the matter; and the very last thing his mind could do at the moment would be to pause, or suggest in any wise what was *not* a fact. The delay in the first three lines, and conceit in the last, jar upon us instantly like the most frightful discord in music. No poet of true, imaginative power could possibly have written the passage.

Therefore we see that the spirit of truth must guide us in some sort, even in our enjoyment of fallacy. Coleridge's fallacy has no discord in it, but Pope's has set our teeth on edge. Without farther questioning, I will endeavour to state the main bearings of this matter.

The temperament which admits the pathetic fallacy, is, as I said above, that of a mind and body in some sort too weak to deal fully with what is before them or upon them; borne away, or over-clouded, or over-dazzled by emotion; and it is a more or less noble state, according to the force of the emotion which has induced it. For it is no credit to a man that he is not morbid or inaccurate in his perceptions, when he has no strength of feeling to warp them; and it is in general a sign of higher capacity and stand in the ranks of being, that the emotions should be strong enough to vanquish, partly, the intellect, and make it believe what they choose. But it is still a grander condition when the intellect also rises, till it is strong enough to assert its rule against, or together with, the utmost efforts of the passions; and the whole man stands in an iron glow, white hot, perhaps, but still strong, and in no wise evaporating; even if he melts, losing none of his weight.

So, then, we have the three ranks: the man who perceives rightly, because he does not feel, and to whom the primrose is very accurately the primrose, because he does not love it. Then, secondly, the man who perceives wrongly, because he feels, and to whom the primrose is anything else than a primrose: a star, or a sun, or a fairy's shield, or a forsaken maiden. And then, lastly, there is the man who perceives rightly in spite of his feelings, and to whom the primrose is for ever nothing else than itself—a little flower apprehended in the very plain and leafy fact of it, whatever and how many soever the associations and passions may be that crowd around it. And, in general, these three classes may be rated in comparative order, as the men who are not poets at all, and the poets of the second order, and the poets of the first; only however great a man may be, there are always some subjects which *ought* to throw him off his balance; some, by which his poor human capacity of thought should be conquered, and brought into the inaccurate and vague state of perception, so that the language of the highest inspiration becomes broken, obscure, and wild in metaphor, resembling that of the weaker man, overborne by weaker things.

And thus, in full, there are four classes: the men who feel nothing, and therefore see truly; the men who feel strongly, think weakly, and see untruly (second order of poets); the men who feel strongly, think strongly, and see truly (first order of poets); and the men who, strong as human creatures can be, are yet submitted to influences stronger than they, and see in a sort untruly, because what they see is inconceivably above them. This last is the usual condition of prophetic inspiration.

I separate these classes, in order that their character may be clearly understood; but of course they are united each to the other by imperceptible transitions, and the same mind, according to the influences to which it is subjected, passes at different times into the various states. Still, the difference between the great and less man is, on the whole, chiefly in this point of *alterability*. That is to say, the one knows too much, and perceives and feels too much of the past and future, and of all things beside and around that which immediately affects him, to be in any wise shaken by it. His mind is made up; his thoughts have an accustomed current; his ways are steadfast; it is not this or that new sight which will at once unbalance him. He is tender to impression at the surface, like a rock with deep moss upon it; but there is too much mass of him to be moved. The smaller man, with the same degree of sensibility, is at once carried off his feet; he wants to do something he did not want to do before; he views all the universe in a new light through his tears; he is gay or enthusiastic, melancholy or passionate, as things come and go to him. Therefore the high creative poet might even be thought, to a great extent, impassive (as shallow people think Dante stern), receiving indeed all feelings to the full, but having a great centre of reflection and knowledge in which he stands serene, and watches the feeling, as it were, from afar off.

Dante, in his most intense moods, has entire command of himself, and can look around calmly, at all moments, for the image or the word that will best tell what he sees to the upper or lower world. But Keats and Tennyson, and the poets of the second order, are generally themselves subdued by the feelings under which they write, or, at least, write as choosing to be so; and therefore admit certain expressions and modes of thought which are in some sort diseased or false.

Now so long as we see that the *feeling* is true, we pardon, or are even pleased by, the confessed fallacy of sight which it induces: we are pleased, for instance, with those lines of Kingsley's above quoted, not because they fallaciously describe foam, but because they faithfully describe sorrow. But the moment the mind of the speaker becomes cold, that moment every such expression becomes untrue, as being for ever untrue in the external facts. And there is no greater baseness in literature than the habit of using these metaphorical expressions in cool blood. An inspired writer, in full impetuosity of passion, may speak wisely and truly of "raging waves of the sea foaming out their own shame"; but it is only the basest writer who cannot speak of the sea without talking of "raging waves," "remorseless floods," "ravenous billows," etc.; and it is one of the signs of the highest power in a writer to check all such habits of thought, and to keep his eyes fixed firmly on the *pure fact,* out of which if any feeling comes to him or his reader, he knows it must be a true one. . . .

Realism

GEORGE ELIOT

[FROM "The Natural History of German Life"]

1856

How little the real characteristics of the working-classes are known to those who are outside them, how little their natural history has been studied, is sufficiently disclosed by our Art as well as by our political and social theories. Where, in our picture exhibitions, shall we find a group of true peasantry? What English artist even attempts to rival in truthfulness such studies of popular life as the pictures of Teniers or the ragged boys of Murillo? Even one of the greatest painters of the pre-eminently realistic school, while, in his picture of "The Hireling Shepherd" he gave us a landscape of marvellous truthfulness, placed a pair of peasants in the foreground who were not much more real than the idyllic swains and damsels of our chimney ornaments. . . . The notion that peasants are joyous, that the typical moment to represent a man in a smock-frock is when he is cracking a joke and showing a row of sound teeth, that cottage matrons are usually buxom, and village children necessarily rosy and merry, are prejudices difficult to dislodge from the artistic mind, which looks for its subjects into literature instead of life. The painter is still under the influence of idyllic literature, which has always expressed the imagination of the cultivated and town-bred, rather than the truth of rustic life. Idyllic ploughmen are jocund when they drive their team afield; idyllic shepherds make bashful love under hawthorn bushes; idyllic villagers dance in the chequered shade and refresh themselves, not immoderately, with spicy nut-brown ale. But no one who has seen much of actual ploughmen thinks them jocund; no

From *Westminster Review*, 66 (July 1856), pages 52-56.

one who is well acquainted with the English peasantry can pronounce them merry. The slow gaze, in which no sense of beauty beams, no humour twinkles,—the slow utterance, and the heavy slouching walk, remind one rather of that melancholy animal the camel, than of the sturdy country-man, with striped stockings, red waistcoat, and hat aside, who represents the traditional English peasant. Observe a company of haymakers. When you see them at a distance, tossing up the forkfuls of hay in the golden light, while the wagon creeps slowly with its increasing burthen over the meadow, and the bright green space which tells of work done gets larger and larger, you pronounce the scene 'smiling,' and you think these companions in labour must be as bright and cheerful as the picture to which they give animation. Approach nearer, and you will certainly find that haymaking time is a time for joking, especially if there are women among the labourers; but the coarse laugh that bursts out every now and then, and expresses the triumphant taunt, is as far as possible from your conception of idyllic merriment. That delicious effervescence of the mind which we call fun, has no equivalent for the northern peasant, except tipsy revelry; the only realm of fancy and imagination for the English clown exists at the bottom of the third quart pot.

The conventional countryman of the stage, who picks up pocket-books and never looks into them, and who is too simple even to know that honesty has its opposite, repre-sents the still lingering mistake, that an unintelligible dialect is a guarantee for ingenuousness, and that slouching shoulders indicate an upright disposition. It is quite true that a thresher is likely to be innocent of any adroit arithmetical cheating, but he is not the less likely to carry home his master's corn in his shoes and pocket; a reaper is not given to writing begging-letters, but he is quite capable of cajolling the dairy-maid into filling his small-beer bottle with ale. The selfish instincts are not subdued by the sight of buttercups, nor is integrity in the least established by that classic rural occu-pation, sheep-washing. To make men moral, something more is requisite than to turn them out to grass.

Opera peasants, whose unreality excites Mr. Ruskin's indignation, are surely too frank an idealization to be misleading; and since popular chorus is one of the most effective elements of the opera, we can hardly object to lyric rustics in elegant laced boddices and picturesque motley, unless we are prepared to advocate a chorus of colliers in their pit costume, or a ballet of char-women and stocking-weavers. But our social novels profess to represent the people as they are, and the unreality of their representations is a grave evil. The greatest benefit we owe to the artist, whether painter, poet, or novelist, is the extension of our sympathies. Appeals founded on generalizations and statistics require a sympathy ready-made, a moral sentiment already in activity; but a picture of human life such as a great artist can give, surprises even the trivial and the selfish into that attention to what is apart from themselves, which may be called the raw material of moral sentiment. When Scott takes us into Luckie Mucklebackit's cottage, or tells the story of 'The Two Drovers,'—when Wordsworth sings to us the reverie of 'Poor Susan,'—when Kingsley shows us Alton Locke gazing yearningly over the gate which leads from the highway into the first wood he ever saw,—when Hornung paints a group of chimney-sweepers,—more is done towards linking the higher classes with the lower, towards obliterating the vulgarity of exclusiveness, than by hundreds of sermons and philosophical dissertations. Art is the nearest thing to life; it is a mode of amplifying experience and extending our contact with our fellow-men beyond the bounds of our personal lot. All the more sacred is the task of the artist when he undertakes to paint the life of the People. Falsification here is far more pernicious than in the more artificial aspects of life. It is not so very serious that we should have false ideas about evanescent fashions—about the manners and conversation of beaux and duchesses; but it *is* serious that our sympathy with the perennial joys and struggles, the toil, the tragedy, and the humour in the life of our more heavily-laden fellow-men, should be perverted, and turned towards a false object instead of the true one.

This perversion is not the less fatal because the misrepresentation which gives rise to it has what the artist considers a moral end. The thing for mankind to know is, not what are the motives and influences which the moralist thinks *ought* to act on the labourer or the artisan, but what are the motives and influences which *do* act on him. We want to be taught to feel, not for the heroic artisan or the sentimental peasant, but for the peasant in all his coarse apathy, and the artisan in all his suspicious selfishness.

We have one great novelist who is gifted with the utmost power of rendering the external traits of our town population; and if he could give us their psychological character— their conceptions of life, and their emotions—with the same truth as their idiom and manners, his books would be the greatest contribution Art has ever made to the awakening of social sympathies. But while he can copy Mrs. Plornish's colloquial style with the delicate accuracy of a sun-picture, while there is the same startling inspiration in his description of the gestures and phrases of 'Boots,' as in the speeches of Shakspeare's mobs or numbskulls, he scarcely ever passes from the humorous and external to the emotional and tragic, without becoming as transcendent in his unreality as he was a moment before in his artistic truthfulness. But for the precious salt of his humour, which compels him to reproduce external traits that serve, in some degree, as a corrective to his frequently false psychology, his preternaturally virtuous poor children and artisans, his melodramatic boatmen and courtezans, would be as noxious as Eugène Sue's idealized proletaires in encouraging the miserable fallacy that high morality and refined sentiment can grow out of harsh social relations, ignorance, and want; or that the working-classes are in a condition to enter at once into a millennial state of *altruism,* wherein everyone is caring for everyone else, and no one for himself.

If we need a true conception of the popular character to guide our sympathies rightly, we need it equally to check our theories, and direct us in their application. The tendency created by the splendid conquests of modern generalization, to believe that all social questions are merged in economical science, and that the relations of men to their neighbours may be settled by algebraic equations,—the dream that the un-cultured classes are prepared for a condition which appeals principally to their moral sensibilities,—the aristocratic dilet-tantism which attempts to restore the 'good old times' by a sort of idyllic masquerading, and to grow feudal fidelity and veneration as we grow prize turnips, by an artificial system of culture,—none of these diverging mistakes can co-exist with a real knowledge of the People, with a thorough study of their habits, their ideas, their motives. The landholder, the clergy-man, the mill-owner, the mining-agent, have each an oppor-tunity for making precious observations on different sections of the working-classes, but unfortunately their experience is too often not registered at all, or its results are too scattered to be available as a source of information and stimulus to the public mind generally. If any man of sufficient moral and intellectual breadth, whose observations would not be vitiated by a foregone conclusion, or by a professional point of view, would devote himself to studying the natural history of our social classes, especially of the small shop-keepers, artisans, and peasantry,—the degree in which they are influenced by local conditions, their maxims and habits, the points of view from which they regard their religious teachers, and the degree in which they are influenced by religious doctrines, the inter-action of the various classes on each other, and what are the tendencies in their position towards disintegration or towards development,—and if, after all this study, he would give us the result of his observations in a book well nourished with specific facts, his work would be a valuable aid to the social and political reformer.

The Function of Criticism

MATTHEW ARNOLD

[FROM "The Function of Criticism at the Present Time"]

1865

The critical power is of lower rank than the creative. True;
but in assenting to this proposition, one or two things are to
be kept in mind. It is undeniable that the exercise of a creative
power, that a free creative activity, is the highest function of
man; it is proved to be so by man's finding in it his true
happiness. But it is undeniable, also, that men may have the
sense of exercising this free creative activity in other ways
than in producing great works of literature or art; if it were
not so; all but a very few men would be shut out from the
true happiness of all men. They may have it in well-doing,
they may have it in learning, they may have it even in
criticising. This is one thing to be kept in mind. Another is,
that the exercise of the creative power in the production of
great works of literature or art, however high this exercise of
it may rank, is not at all epochs and under all conditions
possible; and that therefore labour may be vainly spent in
attempting it, which might with more fruit be used in preparing for it, in rendering it possible. This creative power
works with elements, with materials; what if it has not those
materials, those elements, ready for its use? In that case it
must surely wait till they are ready. Now, in literature,—I
will limit myself to literature, for it is about literature that
the question arises,—the elements with which the creative
power works are ideas; the best ideas on every matter
which literature touches, current at the time. At any rate we
may lay it down as certain that in modern literature no

From *Essays in Criticism. First Series* (1865), Chapter 1.

manifestation of the creative power not working with these can be very important or fruitful. And I say *current* at the time, not merely accessible at the time; for creative literary genius does not principally show itself in discovering new ideas, that is rather the business of the philosopher. The grand work of literary genius is a work of synthesis and exposition, not of analysis and discovery; its gift lies in the faculty of being happily inspired by a certain intellectual and spiritual atmosphere, by a certain order of ideas, when it finds itself in them; of dealing divinely with these ideas, presenting them in the most effective and attractive combinations,—making beautiful works with them, in short. But it must have the atmosphere, it must find itself amidst the order of ideas, in order to work freely; and these it is not so easy to command. This is why great creative epochs in literature are so rare, this is why there is so much that is unsatisfactory in the productions of many men of real genius; because, for the creation of a master-work of literature two powers must concur, the power of the man and the power of the moment, and the man is not enough without the moment; the creative power has, for its happy exercise, appointed elements, and those elements are not in its own control.

Nay, they are more within the control of the critical power. It is the business of the critical power, as I said in the words already quoted, "in all branches of knowledge, theology, philosophy, history, art, science, to see the object as in itself it really is." Thus it tends, at last, to make an intellectual situation of which the creative power can profitably avail itself. It tends to establish an order of ideas, if not absolutely true, yet true by comparison with that which it displaces; to make the best ideas prevail. Presently these new ideas reach society, the touch of truth is the touch of life, and there is a stir and growth everywhere; out of this stir and growth come the creative epochs of literature. . . .

It has long seemed to me that the burst of creative activity in our literature, through the first quarter of this century, had about it in fact something premature; and that from this cause its productions are doomed, most of them, in spite of the

sanguine hopes which accompanied and do still accompany
them, to prove hardly more lasting than the productions of
far less splendid epochs. And this prematureness comes from
its having proceeded without having its proper data, without
sufficient materials to work with. In other words, the English
poetry of the first quarter of this century, with plenty of
energy, plenty of creative force, did not know enough. This
makes Byron so empty of matter, Shelley so incoherent,
Wordsworth even, profound as he is, yet so wanting in completeness and variety. Wordsworth cared little for books, and
disparaged Goethe. I admire Wordsworth, as he is, so much
that I cannot wish him different; and it is vain, no doubt, to
imagine such a man different from what he is, to suppose
that he *could* have been different. But surely the one thing
wanting to make Wordsworth an even greater poet than he
is,—his thought richer, and his influence of wider application,—was that he should have read more books, among
them, no doubt, those of that Goethe whom he disparaged
without reading him. . . .

The Englishman has been called a political animal, and
he values what is political and practical so much that ideas
easily become objects of dislike in his eyes, and thinkers
"miscreants," because ideas and thinkers have rashly meddled
with politics and practice. This would be all very well if the
dislike and neglect confined themselves to ideas transported
out of their own sphere, and meddling rashly with practice;
but they are inevitably extended to ideas as such, and to the
whole life of intelligence; practice is everything, a free play
of the mind is nothing. The notion of the free play of the
mind upon all subjects being a pleasure in itself, being an
object of desire, being an essential provider of elements without which a nation's spirit, whatever compensations it may
have for them, must, in the long run, die of inanition, hardly
enters into an Englishman's thoughts. It is noticeable that the
word *curiosity,* which in other languages is used in a good
sense, to mean, as a high and fine quality of man's nature,
just this disinterested love of a free play of the mind on all

subjects, for its own sake,—it is noticeable, I say, that this word has in our language no sense of the kind, no sense but a rather bad and disparaging one. But criticism, real criticism, is essentially the exercise of this very quality. It obeys an instinct prompting it to try to know the best that is known and thought in the world, irrespectively of practice, politics, and everything of the kind; and to value knowledge and thought as they approach this best, without the intrusion of any other considerations whatever. This is an instinct for which there is, I think, little original sympathy in the practical English nature, and what there was of it has undergone a long benumbing period of blight and suppression in the epoch of concentration which followed the French Revolution.

But epochs of concentration cannot well endure for ever; epochs of expansion, in the due course of things, follow them. Such an epoch of expansion seems to be opening in this country. In the first place all danger of a hostile forcible pressure of foreign ideas upon our practice has long disappeared; like the traveller in the fable, therefore, we begin to wear our cloak a little more loosely. Then, with a long peace, the ideas of Europe steal gradually and amicably in, and mingle, though in infinitesimally small quantities at a time, with our own notions. Then, too, in spite of all that is said about the absorbing and brutalising influence of our passionate material progress, it seems to me indisputable that this progress is likely, though not certain, to lead in the end to an apparition of intellectual life; and that man, after he has made himself perfectly comfortable and has now to determine what to do with himself next, may begin to remember that he has a mind, and that the mind may be made the source of great pleasure. I grant it is mainly the privilege of faith, at present, to discern this end to our railways, our business, and our fortune-making; but we shall see if, here as elsewhere, faith is not in the end the true prophet. Our ease, our travelling, and our unbounded liberty to hold just as hard and securely as we please to the practice to which our notions have given birth, all tend to beget an inclination to deal a little more freely with these notions themselves, to canvass

them a little, to penetrate a little into their real nature. Flutter-
ings of curiosity, in the foreign sense of the word, appear
amongst us, and it is in these that criticism must look to find
its account. Criticism first; a time of true creative activity,
perhaps,—which, as I have said, must inevitably be preceded
amongst us by a time of criticism,—hereafter, when criticism
has done its work.

It is of the last importance that English criticism should
clearly discern what rule for its course, in order to avail itself
of the field now opening to it, and to produce fruit for the
future, it ought to take. The rule may be summed up in one
word,—*disinterestedness*. And how is criticism to show disinterestedness? By keeping aloof from what is called "the
practical view of things"; by resolutely following the law of
its own nature, which is to be a free play of the mind on all
subjects which it touches. By steadily refusing to lend itself to
any of those ulterior, political, practical considerations about
ideas, which plenty of people will be sure to attach to them,
which perhaps ought often to be attached to them, which in this
country at any rate are certain to be attached to them quite
sufficiently, but which criticism has really nothing to do with.
Its business is, as I have said, simply to know the best that
is known and thought in the world, and by in its turn making
this known, to create a current of true and fresh ideas. Its
business is to do this with inflexible honesty, with due ability;
but its business is to do no more, and to leave alone all
questions of practical consequences and applications, questions
which will never fail to have due prominence given to them.
Else criticism, besides being really false to its own nature,
merely continues in the old rut which it has hitherto followed
in this country, and will certainly miss the chance now given
to it. For what is at present the bane of criticism in this
country? It is that practical considerations cling to it and
stifle it. It subserves interests not its own. Our organs of
criticism are organs of men and parties having practical ends
to serve, and with them those practical ends are the first thing
and the play of mind the second; so much play of mind as
is compatible with the prosecution of those practical ends

is all that is wanted. An organ like the *Revue des Deux Mondes,* having for its main function to understand and utter the best that is known and thought in the world, existing, it may be said, as just an organ for a free play of the mind, we have not. But we have the *Edinburgh Review,* existing as an organ of the old Whigs, and for as much play of the mind as may suit its being that; we have the *Quarterly Review,* existing as an organ of the Tories, and for as much play of mind as may suit its being that; we have the *British Quarterly Review,* existing as an organ of the political Dissenters, and for as much play of mind as may suit its being that; we have the *Times,* existing as an organ of the common, satisfied, well-to-do Englishman, and for as much play of mind as may suit its being that. And so on through all the various fractions, political and religious, of our society; every fraction has, as such, its organ of criticism, but the notion of combining all fractions in the common pleasure of a free disinterested play of mind meets with no favour. Directly this play of mind wants to have more scope, and to forget the pressure of practical considerations a little, it is checked, it is made to feel the chain. We saw this the other day in the extinction, so much to be regretted, of the *Home and Foreign Review.* Perhaps in no organ of criticism in this country was there so much knowledge, so much play of mind; but these could not save it. The *Dublin Review* subordinates play of mind to the practical business of English and Irish Catholicism, and lives. It must needs be that men should act in sects and parties, that each of these sects and parties should have its organ, and should make this organ subserve the interests of its action; but it would be well, too, that there should be a criticism, not the minister of these interests, not their enemy, but absolutely and entirely independent of them. No other criticism will ever attain any real authority or make any real way towards its end,—the creating a current of true and fresh ideas.

It is because criticism has so little kept in the pure intellectual sphere, has so little detached itself from practice, has been so directly polemical and controversial, that it has so ill accomplished, in this country, its best spiritual work;

which is to keep man from a self-satisfaction which is retarding and vulgarising, to lead him towards perfection, by making his mind dwell upon what is excellent in itself, and the absolute beauty and fitness of things. A polemical practical criticism makes men blind even to the ideal imperfection of their practice, makes them willingly assert its ideal perfection, in order the better to secure it against attack; and clearly this is narrowing and baneful for them. If they were reassured on the practical side, speculative considerations of ideal perfection they might be brought to entertain, and their spiritual horizon would thus gradually widen. Sir Charles Adderley says to the Warwickshire farmers:—

"Talk of the improvement of breed! Why, the race we ourselves represent, the men and women, the old Anglo-Saxon race, are the best breed in the whole world. . . . The absence of a too enervating climate, too unclouded skies, and a too luxurious nature, has produced so vigorous a race of people, and has rendered us so superior to all the world."

Mr. Roebuck says to the Sheffield cutlers:—

"I look around me and ask what is the state of England? Is not property safe? Is not every man able to say what he likes? Can you not walk from one end of England to the other in perfect security? I ask you whether, the world over or in past history, there is anything like it? Nothing. I pray that our unrivalled happiness may last."

Now obviously there is a peril for poor human nature in words and thoughts of such exuberant self-satisfaction, until we find ourselves safe in the streets of the Celestial City.

"Das wenige verschwindet leicht dem Blicke
  Der vorwärts sieht, wie viel noch übrig bleibt—"

says Goethe; "the little that is done seem nothing when we look forward and see how much we have yet to do." Clearly this is a better line of reflection for weak humanity, so long as it remains on this earthly field of labour and trial.

But neither Sir Charles Adderley nor Mr. Roebuck is by nature inaccessible to considerations of this sort. They only lose sight of them owing to the controversial life we all lead, and the practical form which all speculation takes with us. They have in view opponents whose aim is not ideal, but practical; and in their zeal to uphold their own practice against these innovators, they go so far as even to attribute to this practice an ideal perfection. Somebody has been wanting to introduce a six-pound franchise, or to abolish church-rates, or to collect agricultural statistics by force, or to diminish local self-government. How natural, in reply to such proposals, very likely improper or ill-timed, to go a little beyond the mark and to say stoutly, "Such a race of people as we stand, so superior to all the world! The old Anglo-Saxon race, the best breed in the whole world! I pray that our unrivalled happiness may last! I ask you whether, the world over or in past history, there is anything like it?" And so long as criticism answers this dithyramb by insisting that the old Anglo-Saxon race would be still more superior to all others if it had no church-rates, or that our unrivalled happiness would last yet longer with a six-pound franchise, so long will the strain, "The best breed in the whole world!" swell louder and louder, everything ideal and refining will be lost out of sight, and both the assailed and their critics will remain in a sphere, to say the truth, perfectly unvital, a sphere in which spiritual progression is impossible. But let criticism leave church-rates and the franchise alone, and in the most candid spirit, without a single lurking thought of practical innovation, confront with our dithyramb this paragraph on which I stumbled in a newspaper immediately after reading Mr. Roebuck:—

"A shocking child murder has just been committed at Nottingham. A girl named Wragg left the workhouse there on Saturday morning with her young illegitimate child. The child was soon afterwards found dead on Mapperly Hills, having been strangled. Wragg is in custody."

Nothing but that; but, in juxtaposition with the absolute eulogies of Sir Charles Adderley and Mr. Roebuck, how eloquent, how suggestive are those few lines! "Our old Anglo-Saxon breed, the best in the whole world!"—how much that is harsh and ill-favoured there is in this best! *Wragg!* If we

are to talk of ideal perfection, of "the best in the whole
world," has any one reflected what a touch of grossness in
our race, what an original shortcoming in the more delicate
spiritual perceptions, is shown by the natural growth amongst
us of such hideous names. Higginbottom, Stiggins, Bugg!
In Ionia and Attica they were luckier in this respect than
"the best race in the world"; by the Ilissus there was no
Wragg, poor thing! And "our unrivalled happiness";—what
an element of grimness, bareness, and hideousness mixes with
it and blurs it; the workhouse, the dismal Mapperly Hills,—
how dismal those who have seen them will remember;—the
gloom, the smoke, the cold, the strangled illegitimate child!
"I ask you whether, the world over or in past history, there
is anything like it?" Perhaps not, one is inclined to answer; but
at any rate, in that case, the world is very much to be pitied.
And the final touch,—short, bleak, and inhuman: *Wragg
is in custody*. The sex lost in the confusion of our unrivalled
happiness; or (shall I say?) the superfluous Christian name
lopped off by the straightforward vigour of our old Anglo-
Saxon breed! There is profit for the spirit in such contrasts
as this; criticism serves the cause of perfection by establishing
them. By eluding sterile conflict, by refusing to remain in the
sphere where alone narrow and relative conceptions have
any worth and validity, criticism may diminish its momentary
importance, but only in this way has it a chance of gaining
admittance for those wider and more perfect conceptions to
which all its duty is really owed. Mr. Roebuck will have a
poor opinion of an adversary who replies to his defiant songs
of triumph only by murmuring under his breath, *Wragg is
in custody*; but in no other way will these songs of triumph
be induced gradually to moderate themselves, to get rid of
what in them is excessive and offensive, and to fall into a
softer and truer key.

It will be said that it is a very subtle and indirect action
which I am thus prescribing for criticism, and that, by embracing in this manner the Indian virtue of detachment and
abandoning the sphere of practical life, it condemns itself
to a slow and obscure work. Slow and obscure it may be,

but it is the only proper work of criticism. The mass of mankind will never have any ardent zeal for seeing things as they are; very inadequate ideas will always satisfy them. On these inadequate ideas reposes, and must repose, the general practice of the world. That is as much as saying that whoever sets himself to see things as they are will find himself one of a very small circle; but it is only by this small circle resolutely doing its own work that adequate ideas will ever get current at all. The rush and roar of practical life will always have a dizzying and attracting effect upon the most collected spectator, and tend to draw him into its vortex; most of all will this be the case where that life is so powerful as it is in England. But it is only by remaining collected, and refusing to lend himself to the point of view of the practical man, that the critic can do the practical man any service; and it is only by the greatest sincerity in pursuing his own course, and by at last convincing even the practical man of his sincerity, that he can escape misunderstandings which perpetually threaten him. . . .

Do what he will, however, the critic will still remain exposed to frequent misunderstandings, and nowhere so much as in this country. For here people are particularly indisposed even to comprehend that without this free disinterested treatment of things, truth and the highest culture are out of the question. So immersed are they in practical life, so accustomed to take all their notions from this life and its processes, that they are apt to think that truth and culture themselves can be reached by the processes of this life, and that it is an impertinent singularity to think of reaching them in any other. "We are all *terræ filii*," cries their eloquent advocate; "all Philistines together. Away with the notion of proceeding by any other course than the course dear to the Philistines; let us have a social movement, let us organise and combine a party to pursue truth and new thought, let us call it *the liberal party*, and let us all stick to each other, and back each other up. Let us have no nonsense about independent criticism, and intellectual delicacy, and the few and the many. Don't let us trouble ourselves about foreign thought; we shall invent the whole thing for ourselves as we go along. If one of us speaks well, applaud him; if one of us speaks ill, applaud him too; we are all in the same movement, we are all liberals, we are all in pursuit of truth." In this way the pursuit of truth becomes really a social, practical, pleasurable affair, almost requiring a chairman, a secretary, and advertisements; with the excitement of an occasional scandal, with a little resistance to give the happy sense of difficulty overcome; but, in general, plenty of bustle and very little thought. To act is so easy, as Goethe says; to think is so hard! It is true that the critic has many temptations to go with the stream, to make one of the party of movement, one of these *terræ filii;* it seems ungracious to refuse to be a *terræ* filius, when so many excellent people are; but the critic's duty is to refuse, or, if resistance is vain, at least to cry with Obermann: *Périssons en résistant. . . .*

If I have insisted so much on the course which criticism must take where politics and religion are concerned, it is because, where these burning matters are in question, it is most likely to go astray. I have wished, above all, to insist on the attitude which criticism should adopt towards things in general; on its right tone and temper of mind. But then comes another question as to the subject-matter which literary criticism should most seek. Here, in general, its course is determined for it by the idea which is the law of its being; the idea of a disinterested endeavour to learn and propagate the best that is known and thought in the world, and thus to establish a current of fresh and true ideas. By the very nature of things, as England is not all the world, much of the best that is known and thought in the world cannot be of English growth, must be foreign; by the nature of things, again, it is just this that we are least likely to know, while English thought is streaming in upon us from all sides, and takes excellent care that we shall not be ignorant of its existence. The English critic of literature, therefore, must dwell much on foreign thought, and with particular heed on any part of it, which, while significant and fruitful in itself, is for any reason specially likely to escape him. Again, judging is often spoken of as the critic's one business, and so in some sense it is; but the judgment which almost insensibly forms itself in a fair and clear mind, along with fresh knowledge, is the valuable one; and thus knowledge, and ever fresh knowledge, must be the critic's great concern for himself. And it is by communicating fresh knowledge, and letting his own judgment pass along with it,—but insensibly, and in the second place, not the first, as a sort of companion and clue, not as an abstract lawgiver,—that the critic will generally do most good to his readers. Sometimes, no doubt, for the sake of establishing an author's place in literature, and his relation to a central standard (and if this is not done, how are we to get at our *best in the world*?) criticism may have to deal with a subject-matter so familiar that fresh knowledge is out of the question, and then it must be all judgment; an enunciation and detailed application of principles. Here the great safeguard is never to let oneself become abstract, always to retain an intimate and lively consciousness of the truth of what one is saying, and, the moment this fails us, to be sure that something is wrong. Still, under all circumstances, this mere judgment and application of principles is, in itself, not the most satisfactory work to the critic; like mathematics, it is tautological, and cannot well give us, like fresh learning, the sense of creative activity.

But stop, some one will say; all this talk is of no practical use to us whatever; this criticism of yours is not what we have in our minds when we speak of criticism; when we speak of critics and criticism, we mean critics and criticism of the current English literature of the day; when you offer to tell criticism its function, it is to this criticism that we expect you to address yourself. I am sorry for it, for I am afraid I must disappoint these expectations. I am bound by my own definition of criticism: *a disinterested endeavour to learn and propagate the best that is known and thought in the world*. How much of current English literature comes into this "best that is known and thought in the world"? Not very much, I fear; certainly less, at this moment, than of the current literature of France or Germany. Well, then, am I to alter my definition of criticism, in order to meet the requirements of a number of practising English critics, who, after all, are free in their choice of a business? That would be making criticism lend itself just to one of those alien practical considerations, which, I have said, are so fatal to it. One may say, indeed, to those who have to deal with the mass—so much better disregarded—of current English literature, that they may at all events endeavour, in dealing with this, to try it, so far as they can, by the standard of the best that is known and thought in the world; one may say, that to get anywhere near this standard, every critic should try and possess one great literature, at least, besides his own; and the more unlike his own, the better. But, after all, the criticism I am really concerned with,—the criticism which alone can much help us for the future, the criticism which, throughout Europe, is at the present day meant, when so much stress is laid on the importance of criticism and the critical spirit,—is a criticism which regards Europe as being, for intellectual and spiritual purposes, one great confederation, bound to a joint action and working to a common result; and whose members have, for their proper outfit, a knowledge of Greek, Roman, and Eastern antiquity, and of one another. Special, local, and temporary advantages being put out of account, that modern nation will in the intellectual and spiritual sphere make most progress, which most thoroughly carries out this programme. And what is that but saying that we too, all of us, as individuals, the more thoroughly we carry it out, shall make the more progress?

There is so much inviting us!—what are we to take? what will nourish us in growth towards perfection? That is the question which, with the immense field of life and of literature lying before him, the critic has to answer; for himself first, and afterwards for others. . . .

I conclude with what I said at the beginning: to have the sense of creative activity is the great happiness and the great proof of being alive, and it is not denied to criticism to have it; but then criticism must be sincere, simple, flexible, ardent, ever widening its knowledge. Then it may have, in no contemptible measure, a joyful sense of creative activity; a sense which a man of insight and conscience will prefer to what he might derive from a poor, starved, fragmentary, inadequate creation. And at some epochs no other creation is possible.

Still, in full measure, the sense of creative activity belongs only to genuine creation; in literature we must never forget that. But what true man of letters ever can forget it? It is no such common matter for a gifted nature to come into possession of a current of true and living ideas, and to produce amidst the inspiration of them, that we are likely to under-rate it. The epochs of Æschylus and Shakspeare make us feel their pre-eminence. In an epoch like those is, no doubt, the true life of literature; there is the promised land, towards which criticism can only beckon. That promised land it will not be ours to enter, and we shall die in the wilderness: but to have desired to enter it, to have saluted it from afar, is already, perhaps, the best distinction among contemporaries; it will certainly be the best title to esteem with posterity.

The Mona Lisa

WALTER PATER

[FROM *Studies in the History of the Renaissance* :
"Lionardo da Vinci"]

1873

'La Gioconda' is, in the truest sense, Lionardo's masterpiece, the revealing instance of his mode of thought and work. In suggestiveness, only the Melancholia of Dürer is comparable to it; and no crude symbolism disturbs the effect of its subdued and graceful mystery. We all know the face and hands

From Pages 116-19.

of the figure, set in its marble chair, in that cirque of fantastic
rocks, as in some faint light under sea. Perhaps of all ancient
pictures time has chilled it least. As often happens with works
in which invention seems to reach its limit, there is an element
in it given to, not invented by, the master. In that inestimable
folio of drawings, once in the possession of Vasari, were
certain designs by Verrocchio, faces of such impressive beauty
that Lionardo in his boyhood copied them many times. It is
hard not to connect with these designs of the elder by-past
master, as with its germinal principle, the unfathomable smile,
always with a touch of something sinister in it, which plays
over all Lionardo's work. Besides, the picture is a portrait.
From childhood we see this image defining itself on the
fabric of his dreams; and but for express historical testimony,
we might fancy that this was but his ideal lady, embodied
and beheld at last. What was the relationship of a living
Florentine to this creature of his thought? By what strange
affinities had she and the dream grown thus apart, yet so closely together? Present from the first, incorporeal in Lionardo's
thought, dimly traced in the designs of Verrocchio, she is
found present at last in Il Giocondo's house. That there is
much of mere portraiture in the picture is attested by the
legend that by artificial means, the presence of mimes and
flute-players, that subtle expression was protracted on the face.
Again, was it in four years and by renewed labour never
really completed, or in four months and as by stroke of magic,
that the image was projected?

The presence that thus so strangely rose beside the waters
is expressive of what in the ways of a thousand years man
had come to desire. Hers is the head upon which all 'the ends
of the world are come,' and the eyelids are a little weary. It
is a beauty wrought out from within upon the flesh, the
deposit, little cell by cell, of strange thoughts and fantastic
reveries and exquisite passions. Set it for a moment beside
one of those white Greek goddesses or beautiful women of
antiquity, and how would they be troubled by this beauty,
into which the soul with all its maladies has passed? All the
thoughts and experience of the world have etched and mould-

ed there in that which they have of power to refine and make
expressive the outward form, the animalism of Greece, the
lust of Rome, the reverie of the middle age with its spiritual
ambition and imaginative loves, the return of the Pagan
world, the sins of the Borgias. She is older than the rocks
among which she sits; like the vampire, she has been dead
many times, and learned the secrets of the grave; and has been
a diver in deep seas, and keeps their fallen day about her;
and trafficked for strange webs with Eastern merchants; and,
as Leda, was the mother of Helen of Troy, and, as Saint Anne,
the mother of Mary; and all this has been to her but as the
sound of lyres and flutes, and lives only in the delicacy with
which it has moulded the changing lineaments and tinged
the eyelids and the hands. The fancy of a perpetual life,
sweeping together ten thousand experiences, is an old one;
and modern thought has conceived the idea of humanity as
wrought upon by, and summing up in itself, all modes of
thought and life. Certainly Lady Lisa might stand as the
embodiment of the old fancy, the symbol of the modern idea.

Art for Art's Sake

WALTER PATER

[FROM *Studies in the History of the Renaissance*]

1873

To regard all things and principles of things as inconstant
modes or fashions has more and more become the tendency
of modern thought. Let us begin with that which is without—
our physical life. Fix upon it in one of its more exquisite

From the "Conclusion," Pages 207-13.

intervals, the moment, for instance, of delicious recoil from the flood of water in summer heat. What is the whole physical life in that moment but a combination of natural elements to which science gives their names? But these elements, phosphorous and lime and delicate fibres, are present not in the human body alone: we detect them in places most remote from it. Our physical life is a perpetual motion of them— the passage of the blood, the wasting and repairing of the lenses of the eye, the modification of the tissues of the brain by every ray of light and sound—processes which science reduces to simpler and more elementary forces. Like the elements of which we are composed, the action of these forces extends beyond us; it rusts iron and ripens corn. Far out on every side of us these elements are broadcast, driven by many forces; and birth and gesture and death and the springing of violets from the grave are but a few out of ten thousand resulting combinations. That clear perpetual outline of face and limb is but an image of ours under which we group them—a design in a web, the actual threads of which pass out beyond it. This at least of flame-like our life has, that it is but the concurrence, renewed from moment to moment, of forces parting sooner or later on their ways.

Or if we begin with the inward world of thought and feeling, the whirlpool is still more rapid, the flame more eager and devouring. There it is no longer the gradual darkening of the eye and fading of colour from the wall—the movement of the shore side, where the water flows down indeed, though in apparent rest,—but the race of the midstream, a drift of momentary acts of sight and passion and thought. At first sight experience seems to bury us under a flood of external objects, pressing upon us with a sharp importunate reality, calling us out of ourselves in a thousand forms of action. But when reflection begins to act upon those objects they are dissipated under its influence; the cohesive force is suspended like a trick of magic; each object is loosed into a group of impressions,—colour, odour, texture,—in the mind of the observer. And if we continue to dwell on this world, not of objects in the solidity with which language invests them, but of impressions unstable, flickering, inconsistent, which burn and are extinguished with our consciousness of them, it contracts still further; the whole scope of observation is dwarfed to the narrow chamber of the individual mind. Experience, already reduced to a swarm of impressions, is ringed round for each one of us by that thick wall of personality through which no real voice has ever pierced on its way to us, or from us to that which we can only conjecture to be without. Every one of those impressions is the impression of the individual in his isolation, each mind keeping as a solitary prisoner its own dream of a world.

Analysis goes a step further still, and tells us that those impressions of the individual to which, for each one of us, experience dwindles down, are in perpetual flight; that each of them is limited by time, and that as time is infinitely divisible, each of them is infinitely divisible also; all that is actual in it being a single moment, gone while we try to apprehend it, of which it may ever be more truly said that it has ceased to be than that it is. To such a tremulous wisp constantly reforming itself on the stream, to a single sharp impression, with a sense in it, a relic more or less fleeting, of such moments gone by, what is *real* in our life fines itself down. It is with the movement, the passage and dissolution of impressions, images, sensations, that analysis leaves off,— that continual vanishing away, that strange perpetual weaving and unweaving of ourselves.

Philosophiren, says Novalis, *ist dephlegmatisiren, vivifieiren.* The service of philosophy, and of religion and culture as well, to the human spirit, is to startle it into a sharp and eager observation. Every moment some form grows perfect in hand or face; some tone on the hills or sea is choicer than the rest; some mood of passion or insight or intellectual excitement is irresistibly real and attractive for us,—for that moment only. Not the fruit of experience, but experience itself is the end. A counted number of pulses only is given to us of a variegated, dramatic life. How may we see in them all that is to be seen in them by the finest senses? How can we pass most swiftly from point to point, and be present always at the focus where the greatest number of vital forces unite in their purest energy?

To burn always with this hard gem-like flame, to maintain this ecstasy, is success in life. Failure is to form habits; for habit is relative to a stereotyped world; meantime it is only the roughness of the eye that makes any two persons, things, situations, seem alike. While all melts under our feet, we may well catch at any exquisite passion, or any contribution to knowledge that seems, by a lifted horizon, to set the spirit free for a moment, or any stirring of the senses, strange dyes, strange flowers, and curious odours, or work of the artist's hands, or the face of one's friend. Not to discriminate every moment some passionate attitude in those about us, and in the brilliance of their gifts some tragic dividing of forces on their ways is, on this short day of frost and sun, to sleep before evening. With this sense of the splendour of our experience and of its awful brevity, gathering all we are into one desperate effort to see and touch, we shall hardly have time to make theories about the things we see and touch. What we have to do is to be for ever curiously testing new opinions and courting new impressions, never acquiescing in a facile orthodoxy of Comte or of Hegel, or of our own. Theories, religious or philosophical ideas, as points of view, instruments of criticism, may help us to gather up what might otherwise pass unregarded by us. *La philosophie, c'est la microscope de la pensée.* The theory, or idea, or system, which requires of us the sacrifice of any part of this experience, in consideration of some interest into which we cannot enter, or some abstract morality we have not identified with ourselves, or what is only conventional, has no real claim upon us.

One of the most beautiful places in the writings of Rousseau is that in the sixth book of the 'Confessions,' where he describes the awakening in him of the literary sense. An undefinable taint of death had always clung about him, and now in early manhood he believed himself stricken by mortal disease. He asked himself how he might make as much as possible of the interval that remained; and he was not biassed by anything in his previous life when he decided that it must be by intellectual excitement, which he found in the clear, fresh writings of Voltaire. Well, we are all *condamnés,* as Victor Hugo says: *les hommes sont tous condamnés à mort avec des sursis indéfinis*: we have an interval, and then our place knows us no more. Some spend this interval in listlessness, some in high passions, the wisest in art and song. For our one chance is in expanding that interval, in getting as many pulsations as possible into the given time. High passions give one this quickened sense of life, ecstasy and sorrow of love, political or religious enthusiasm, or the 'enthusiasm of humanity.' Only, be sure it is passion, that it does yield you this fruit of a quickened, multiplied consciousness. Of this wisdom, the poetic passion, the desire of beauty, the love of art for art's sake has most; for art comes to you professing frankly to give nothing but the highest quality to your moments as they pass, and simply for those moments' sake.

Style

WALTER PATER

[FROM "Style"]

1888

Since all progress of mind consists for the most part in differentiation, in the severance of an obscure complex into its parts or phases, it is surely the stupidest of losses to wear off the edge of achieved distinctions, and confuse things which right reason has put asunder—poetry and prose, for

From *Fortnightly Review*, 50 (December 1888), pages 728-42.

instance; or, to speak more exactly, the characteristic laws and excellences of prose and verse composition. On the other hand, those who have dwelt most emphatically on the distinction between prose and verse, prose and poetry, may sometimes have been tempted to limit the proper functions of prose too narrowly; which again is at least false economy, as being, in effect, the renunciation of a certain means or faculty, in a world where after all we must needs make the most of things. . . .

It might have been foreseen that, in the rotation of minds, the province of poetry in prose would find its assertor; and, a century after Dryden, amid very different intellectual needs, and with the need therefore of great modifications in literary form, the range of the poetic force in literature was effectively enlarged by Wordsworth. The true distinction between prose and poetry he regarded as the almost technical or accidental one of the absence or presence of metrical beauty, or say metrical restraint; and for him the opposition came to be between verse and prose of course (you can't scan Wordsworth's prose), but, as the essential dichotomy in this matter, between imaginative and unimaginative writing, parallel to De Quincey's distinction between "the literature of power and the literature of knowledge," in the former of which the composer gives us not fact, but his peculiar sense of fact, whether past or present, or prospective, it may be, as often in oratory.

Dismissing then, under sanction of Wordsworth, that harsher opposition of poetry to prose as savouring in fact of the arbitrary psychology of the last century, and with it the prejudice that there can be but one only beauty of prose style, I propose in this paper to point out certain qualities of all literature as a fine art, which, if they apply to the literature of fact, apply still more to the literature of the imaginative sense of fact, while they apply indifferently to verse and prose, so far as either is really imaginative—certain conditions of true art in both alike, which conditions may also contain in them the secret of the proper discrimination and guardianship of the peculiar excellences of either. . . .

Your historian, for instance, with absolutely truthful intention, amid the multitude of facts presented to him must needs select, and in selecting assert something of his own humour, something that comes not of the world without but of a vision within. . . . For just in proportion as the writer's aim, consciously or unconsciously, comes to be a transcript, not of the world, not of mere fact, but of his sense of it, he becomes an artist, his work *fine* art; and good art (as I hope ultimately to show) in proportion to the truth of his presentment of that sense; as in those humbler or plainer functions of literature also, truth—truth to bare fact there—is the essence of such artistic quality as they may have. Truth! there can be no merit, no craft at all, without that. And further, all beauty is in the long run only fineness of truth—expression—the finer accommodation of speech to that vision within. . . .

The literary artist is of necessity a scholar, and in what he proposes to do will have in mind, first of all, the scholar and the scholarly conscience. . . . Alive to the value of an atmosphere in which every term finds its utmost degree of expression, and with all the jealousy of a lover of words, he will resist a constant tendency on the part of the majority of those who use them to efface the distinctions of language, the facility of writers often reinforcing in this respect the work of the vulgar. He will feel the obligation not of the laws only but of those affinities, avoidances, those mere preferences of his language, which through the associations of literary history have become a part of its nature, prescribing the rejection of many a neology, many a license, many a gipsy phrase which might present itself as actually expressive. . . .

For meanwhile, braced only by those restraints, he is really vindicating his liberty in the making of a vocabulary, an entire system of composition, for himself, his own true manner; and when we speak of the manner of a true master we mean what is essential in his art. Pedantry being only the scholarship of *le cuistre* (we have no English equivalent) he is no pedant, and does but show his intelligence of the rules of language in his freedoms with it, addition or expansion, which

like the spontaneities of manner in a well-bred person will
still further illustrate good taste.—The right vocabulary!

That living authority which language needs lies, in truth,
in its scholars, who recognising always that every language
possesses a genius, a very fastidious genius, of its own, expand
at once and purify its very elements, which must needs change
along with the changing thoughts of living people. Ninety
years ago, for instance, great mental force, certainly, was
needed by Wordsworth, to break through the consecrated
poetic associations of a century, and speak the language that
was his, and was to become in a measure the language of
the next generation. But he did it with the tact of a scholar
also. English, for a quarter of a century past, has been assimi-
lating the phraseology of pictorial art; for half a century,
the phraseology of the great German metaphysical movement
of eighty years ago; in part also the language of mystical
theology: and none but pedants will regret a great consequent increase of its resources. For many years to come its
enterprise may well lie in the naturalisation of the vocabulary
of science, so only it be under the eye of a sensitive scholarship: in a liberal naturalisation of the ideas of science too,
for after all the chief stimulus of good style is to possess a
full, rich, complex matter to grapple with. The literary artist
therefore will be well aware of physical science; science too
attaining, in its turn, its true literary ideal. And then, as the
scholar is nothing without the historic sense, he will be apt
to restore not really obsolete or really worn-out words, but
the finer edge of words still in use:—ascertain, communicate,
discover—words like these it has been part of our "business"
to misuse. . . . Racy Saxon monosyllables, close to us as
touch and sight, he will intermix readily with those long,
savoursome, Latin words, rich in "second intention." In this
late day certainly, no critical process can be conducted reasonably without eclecticism. Of such eclecticism we have a justify-
ing example in one of the first poets of our time. How
illustrative of monosyllabic effect, of sonorous Latin, of the
phraseology of science, of metaphysic, of colloquialism even,

are the writings of Tennyson; yet with what a fine, fastidious scholarship throughout!

A scholar writing for the scholarly, he will of course leave something to the willing intelligence of his reader. . . . To really strenuous minds there is a pleasurable stimulus in the challenge for a continuous effort on their part, to be rewarded by securer and more intimate grasp of the author's sense. Self-restraint, a skilful economy of means—*ascêsis*—that too has a beauty of its own; and for the reader supposed there will be an æsthetic satisfaction in that frugal closeness of style which makes the most of a word, in the exaction from every sentence of a precise relief, in the just spacing out of word to thought—the logically filled space—connected always with the delightful sense of difficulty overcome. . . .

Here, then, with a view to the central need of a select few, those "men of a finer thread," who have formed and maintain the literary ideal—everything, every component element, will have undergone exact trial, and, above all, there will be no uncharacteristic or tarnished or vulgar decoration, permissible ornament being for the most part structural or necessary. . . . For to the grave reader words too are grave; and the ornamental word, the figure, the accessory form or colour or reference, is rarely content to die to thought precisely at the right moment, but will inevitably linger awhile, stirring a long "brain-wave" behind it of perhaps quite alien associations.

Just there, it may be, is the detrimental tendency of the sort of scholarly attentiveness I am recommending. But the true artist allows for it. He will remember that, as the very word ornament indicates what is in itself non-essential, so the "one beauty" of all literary style is of its very essence, and independent, in prose and verse alike, of all removable decoration; that it may exist in its fullest lustre, as in Flaubert's *Madame Bovary,* for instance, or in Stendhal's *Rouge et Noir,* in a composition utterly unadorned, with hardly a single suggestion of visibly beautiful things. . . . Surplusage! he will dread that, as the runner on his muscles. For in truth all art does but consist in the removal of surplusage, from the last finish of the gem-engraver blowing away the last particle of invisible dust, back to the earliest divination of the finished work to be, lying somewhere, according to Michelangelo's fancy, in the rough-hewn block of stone. . . .

An acute philosophical writer, the late Dean Mansel—a writer whose works illustrate the literary beauty there may be in closeness, and with obvious repression or economy of a fine rhetorical gift—wrote a book, of fascinating precision on a very obscure subject, to show that all the technical laws of logic are but means of securing, in each and all of its apprehensions, the unity, the strict identity with itself, of the apprehending mind. All the laws of good writing aim at a similar unity or identity of the mind in all the processes by which the word is associated to its import. The term is right, and has its essential beauty, when it becomes, in a manner, what it signifies, as with the names of simple sensations. To give the phrase, the sentence, the structural member, the entire composition, a song, or an essay, a similar unity with its subject and with itself:—style is in the right way when it tends towards that. All depends upon the original unity, the vital wholeness and identity, of the initiatory apprehension or view. So much is true of all art, which therefore requires always its logic, its comprehensive reason—insight, foresight, retrospect, in simultaneous action— true, most of all, of the literary art, as being of all the arts most closely cognate to the abstract intelligence. Such logical coherency may be evidenced not merely in the lines of composition as a whole, but in the choice of a single word, while it by no means interferes with, but may even prescribe, much variety, in the building of the sentence for instance, or in the manner, argumentative, descriptive, discursive, of this or that part or member of the entire design. The blithe, crisp sentence, decisive as a child's expression of its needs, may alternate with the long, contending, victoriously intricate sentence; the sentence, born with the integrity of a single word, relieving the sort of sentence in which, if you look closely, you can see much contrivance, much adjustment, to bring a highly qualified matter into compass at one view.

For the literary architecture, if it is to be rich and expressive, involves not only foresight of the end in the beginning, but also development or growth of design, in the process of execution, with many irregularities, surprises, and afterthoughts; the contingent as well as the necessary being subsumed under the unity of the whole. . . .

If all high things have their martyrs, Gustave Flaubert might perhaps rank as the martyr of literary style. . . . The one word for the one thing, the one thought, amid the multitude of words, terms, that might just do: there, was the problem of style!—the unique word, phrase, sentence, paragraph, essay, or song, absolutely proper to the single mental presentation or vision within. In that perfect justice, over and above the many contingent and removable beauties with which beautiful style may charm us, but which it can exist without, independent of them yet dexterously availing itself of them, omnipresent in good work, in function at every point, from single epithets to the rhythm of a whole book, lay the specific, indispensable, very intellectual beauty of literature, the possibility of which constitutes it a fine art. . . .

All the recognised flowers, the removable ornaments of literature (including harmony and ease in reading aloud, very carefully considered by him) counted, certainly; for these too are part of the actual value of what one says. But still, after all, with Flaubert the search, the unwearied research, was not for the smooth, or winsome, or forcible word, as such, as with false Ciceronians, but quite simply and honestly, for the word's adjustment to its meaning. The first condition of this must be, of course, to know yourself, to have ascertained your own sense exactly. Then, if we suppose an artist, he says to the reader, I want you to see precisely what I see. Into the mind sensitive to "form," a flood of random sounds, colours, incidents, is ever penetrating from the world without, to become, by sympathetic selection, a part of its very structure, and, in turn, the visible vesture and expression of that other world it sees so steadily within, nay, already with a partial conformity thereto, to be refined, enlarged, corrected, at a hundred points;

and it is just there, just at those doubtful points that the
function of style, as tact or taste, intervenes. The unique term
will come more quickly to one than another, at one time
than another, according also to the kind of matter in question.
Quickness and slowness, ease and closeness alike, have
nothing to do with the artistic character of the true word
found at last. As there is a charm of ease, so also a special
charm in the signs of discovery, of effort and contention
towards a due end, as so often with Flaubert himself—in
the style which has been pliant, as only obstinate, durable,
metal can be, to the inherent perplexities and recusancy of
a certain difficult thought. . . .

In the highest as in the lowliest literature, then, the one
indispensable beauty is, after all, truth:—truth to bare fact
here, as to a sense of fact there, diverted somewhat from men's
ordinary sense of it; truth here as accuracy, truth there as
expression, that finest and most intimate form of truth, the
vraie vérité. And what an eclectic principle this really is!
employing for its one sole purpose—that absolute accordance
of expression to idea—all other literary beauties and excellences whatever: how many kinds of style it covers, explains,
justifies, and at the same time safeguards! Scott's facility, Flaubert's deeply pondered evocation of "the phrase," are equally
good art. Say what you have to say, what you have a will
to say, in the simplest, the most direct and exact manner
possible, with no surplusage:—there, is the justification of the
sentence so fortunately born, "entire, smooth, and round,"
that it needs no punctuation, and also (there, is the point!)
of the most elaborate period, if it be right in its elaboration.
That is the office of ornament: it is also the purpose of
restraint in ornament. As the exponent of truth, that austerity
(the beauty, the function, of which in literature Flaubert
understood so well) becomes not the correctness or purism
of the mere scholar, but a security against the otiose, a
jealous exclusion of what does not really tell, in the pursuit
of relief, of life and vigour, in the portraiture of one's
sense. . . .

A relegation, you say, perhaps—a relegation of style to

the subjectivity, the mere caprice of the individual, which must soon transform it into mannerism. Not so! since there is, under the conditions supposed, for those elements of the man, for every lineament of the vision within, the one word, the one acceptable word, recognisable by the sensitive, by those "who have intelligence" in the matter, as absolutely as ever anything can be in the evanescent and delicate region of human language. The style, the manner, would be the man, not in his unreasoned and really uncharacteristic caprices, involuntary or affected, but in absolutely sincere apprehension of what is most real to him.

Degas

GEORGE MOORE

[FROM *Impressions and Opinions*]

1891

Degas was a pupil of Ingres, and any mention of this always pleases him, for he looks upon Ingres as the first star in the firmament of French art. And, indeed, Degas is the only one who ever reflected, even dimly, anything of the genius of the great master. The likeness to Ingres which some affect to see in Flandrin's work is entirely superficial, but in the *Semiramis Building the Walls of Babylon* and in the *Spartan Youths* there is a strange fair likeness to the master, mixed with another beauty, still latent, but ready for afflorescence, even as the beauty of the mother floats evanescent upon the face of the daughter hardly pubescent yet. But if Degas took from Ingres that method of drawing which may be defined

From pages 310-23.

as drawing by the character in contradistinction to that of drawing by the masses, he applied the method differently and developed it in a different direction. Degas bears the same relation to Ingres as Bret Harte does to Dickens. In Bret Harte and in Dickens the method is obviously the same when you go to its root, but the subject-matter is so different that the method is in all outward characteristics transformed, and no complaint of want of originality of treatment is for a moment tenable. So it is with Degas; at the root his drawing is as classical as Ingres', but by changing the subject-matter from antiquity to the boards of the opera-house, and taking curiosity for leading characteristic, he has created an art cognate and co-equal with Goncourt's, rising sometimes to the height of a page by Balzac. With marvellous perception he follows every curve and characteristic irregularity, writing the very soul of his model upon his canvas. He will paint portraits only of those whom he knows intimately, for it is part of his method only to paint his sitter in that environment which is habitual to her or him. With stagey curtains, balustrades, and conventional poses, he will have nothing to do. He will watch the sitter until he learns all her or his tricks of expression and movement, and then will reproduce all of them and with such exactitude and sympathetic insight that the very inner life of the man is laid bare. Mr. Whistler, whose short-sightedness allows him to see none of these beauties in nature, has declared that all such excellencies are literary and not pictorial, and the fact that he was born in Baltimore has led him to contradict all that the natural sciences have said on racial tendencies and hereditary faculties. But there are some who still believe that the *Ten O'clock* has not altogether overthrown science and history, and covered with ridicule all art that does not limit itself to a harmony in a couple of tints. And that Degas may render more fervidly all the characteristics that race, heredity, and mode of life have endowed his sitter with, he makes numerous drawings and paints from them; but he never paints direct from life. And as he sought new subject-matter, he sought for new means by which he might reproduce his subject in an original and novel manner.

At one time he renounced oil-painting entirely, and would only work in pastel or distemper. Then, again, it was water-colour painting, and sometimes in the same picture he would abandon one medium for another. There are examples extant of pictures begun in water-colour, continued in gouache, and afterwards completed in oils; and if the picture be examined carefully it will be found that the finishing hand has been given with pen and ink. Degas has worked upon his litho-graphs, introducing a number of new figures into the picture by means of pastel. He has done beautiful sculpture, but not content with taking a ballet-girl for subject, has declined to model the skirt, and had one made by the nearest milliner. In all dangerous ways and perilous straits he has sought to shipwreck his genius; genius knows no shipwreck, and triumphs in spite of obstacles. Not even Wagner has tested more thoroughly than Degas the invincibility of genius.

If led to speak on the marvellous personality of his art, Degas will say, 'It is strange, for I assure you no art was ever less spontaneous than mine. What I do is the result of reflection and study of the great masters; of inspiration, spon-taneity, temperament—temperament is the word—I know nothing. When people talk about temperament it always seems to me like the strong man in the fair, who straddles his legs and asks some one to step up on the palm of his hand.' Again, in reply to an assurance that he of all men now work-ing, whether with pen or pencil, is surest of the future, he will say, 'It is very difficult to be great as the old masters were great. In the great ages you were great or you did not exist at all, but in these days everything conspires to support the feeble.'

Artists will understand the almost superhuman genius it requires to take subject-matter that has never received artistic treatment before, and bring it at once within the sacred pale. Baudelaire was the only poet who ever did this; Degas is the only painter. Of all impossible things in this world to treat artistically the ballet-girl seemed the most impossible, but Degas accomplished that feat. He has done so many dancers and so often repeated himself that it is difficult to specify

any particular one. But one picture rises up in my mind—
perhaps it is the finest of all. It represents two girls practising
at the rail; one is straining forward lifting her leg into
torturous position—her back is turned, and the miraculous
drawing of that bent back! The other is seen in profile—
the pose is probably less arduous, and she stands, not un-
gracefully, her left leg thrown behind her, resting upon the
rail. The arrangement of the picture is most unacademical;
the figures are half-way up the canvas, and the great space
of bare floor is balanced by the watering-pot. This picture
is probably an early one. It was natural to begin with dancers
at rest; those wild flights of dancers—the première danseuse
springing amid the coryphées down to the footlights, her thin
arms raised, the vivid glare of the limelight revealing every
characteristic contour of face and neck—must have been a
later development. The philosophy of this art is in Degas'
own words, 'La danseuse n'est qu'un prétexte pour le dessin.'
Dancers fly out of the picture, a single leg crosses the foreground. The première danseuse stands on tiptoe, supported
by the coryphées, or she rests on one knee, the light upon
her bosom, her arms leaned back, the curtain all the while
falling. As he has done with the ballet, so he has done with
the race-course. A race-horse walks past a white post which
cuts his head in twain.

The violation of all the principles of composition is the
work of the first fool that chooses to make the caricature of
art his career, but, like Wagner, Degas is possessed of such
intuitive knowledge of the qualities inherent in the various
elements that nature presents that he is enabled, after having
disintegrated, to re-integrate them, and with surety of ever
finding a new and more elegant synthesis. After the dancers
came the washerwomen. It is one thing to paint washerwomen amid decorative shadows, as Teniers would have done,
and another thing to draw washerwomen yawning over the
ironing table in sharp outline upon a dark background. But
perhaps the most astonishing revolution of all was the introduction of the shop-window into art. Think of a large plate-
glass window, full of bonnets, a girl leaning forward to gather

one! Think of the monstrous and wholly unbearable thing any other painter would have contrived from such a subject; and then imagine a dim, strange picture, the subject of which is hardly at first clear; a strangely contrived composition, full of the dim, sweet, sad poetry of female work. For are not those bonnets the signs and symbols of long hours of weariness and dejection? and the woman that gathers them, iron-handed fashion has moulded and set her seal upon. See the fat woman trying on the bonnet before the pier-glass, the shop-women around her. How the lives of those poor women are epitomised and depicted in a gesture! Years of servility and obeisance to customers, all the life of the fashionable woman's shop is there. Degas says, 'Les artistes sont tellement pressés! et que nous faisons bien notre affaire avec les choses qu'ils ont oubliées.' ('Artists are always in such a hurry, and we find all that we want in what they have left behind.')

But perhaps the most astonishing of all Degas' innovations are his studies of the nude. The nude has become well-nigh incapable of artistic treatment. Even the more naïve are beginning to see that the well-known nymph exhibiting her beauty by the borders of a stream can be endured no longer. Let the artist strive as he will, he will not escape the conventional; he is running an impossible race. Broad harmonies of colour are hardly to be thought of; the gracious mystery of human emotion is out of all question—he must rely on whatever measure of elegant drawing he can include in his delineation of arms, neck, and thigh; and who in sheer beauty has a new word to say? Since Gainsborough and Ingres, all have failed to infuse new life into the worn-out theme. But cynicism was the great means of eloquence of the Middle Ages; and with cynicism Degas has again rendered the nude an artistic possibility. Three coarse women, middle-aged and deformed by toil, are perhaps the most wonderful. One sponges herself in a tin bath; another passes a rough night-dress over her lumpy shoulders, and the touching ugliness of this poor human creature goes straight to the heart. Then follows a long series conceived in the same spirit. A woman who has stepped out of a bath examines her arm. Degas says, 'La bête humaine qui s'occupe d'elle-même; une chatte qui se lèche.' Yes, it is the portrayal of the animal-life of the human being, the animal conscious of nothing but itself. 'Hitherto,' Degas says, as he shows his visitor three large peasant women plunging into a river, not to bathe, but to wash or cool themselves (one drags a dog in after her), 'the nude has always been represented in poses which presuppose an audience, but these women of mine are honest, simple folk, unconcerned by any other interests than those involved in their physical condition. Here is another; she is washing her feet. It is as if you looked through a key-hole.'

But the reader will probably be glad to hear of the pictures which the most completely represent the talent of the man. Degas might allow the word 'represent' to pass, he certainly would object to the word 'epitomise,' for, as we have seen, one of his æstheticisms is that the artist should not attempt any concentrated expression of his talent, but should persistently reiterate his thought twenty, fifty, yes, a hundred different views of the same phase of life. Speaking of Zola, who holds an exactly opposite theory, Degas says: 'il me fait l'effet d'un géant qui travaille le Bottin.' But no man's work is in exact accord with his theory, and the height and depth of Degas' talent is seen very well in the *Leçon de Danse,* in M. Faure's collection, and perhaps still better in the *Leçon de Danse* in M. Blanche's collection. In the latter picture a spiral staircase ascends through the room, cutting the picture at about two-thirds of its length. In the small space on the left, dancers are seen descending from the dressing-rooms, their legs and only their legs seen between the slender banisters. On the right, dancers advance in line, balancing themselves, their thin arms outstretched, the dancing-master standing high up in the picture by the furthest window. Through the cheap tawdry lace curtains a mean dusty daylight flows, neutralising the whiteness of the skirts and the brightness of the hose. It is the very atmosphere of the opera. The artificial life of the dancing-class on a dull afternoon. On the right, in the foreground, a group of dancers balances the composition. A dancer sits on a straw chair, her feet turned out, her shoulders covered by a green shawl; and by her, a little behind her, stands an old woman settling her daughter's sash. . . .

Another great portrait is Degas' portrait of Manet, but so entirely unlike is it to any other man's art that it would be vain to attempt any description of it. It shows Manet thrown on a white sofa in an attitude strangely habitual to him. Those who knew Manet well cannot look without pain upon this picture; it is something more than a likeness, it is as if you saw the man's ghost. Other portraits remind you of certain Spanish painters, the portrait of Mlle Malot for instance; and in his studies of the nude there is a frankness which seems borrowed from the earlier Italians. Degas' art is as he says himself based upon a profound knowledge of the great masters. He has understood them as none but a great painter could understand them, and according to the requirements of the subject in hand he has taken from them all something of their technique.

The following anecdote will give an idea of Degas' love of the great masters. In 1840, Degas set up his easel in the Louvre and spent a year copying Poussin's *Rape of the Sabines*. The copy is as fine as the original.

Degas now occupies the most enviable position an artist can attain. He is always the theme of conversation when artists meet, and if the highest honour is to obtain the admiration of your fellow-workers, that honour has been bestowed on Degas as it has been bestowed upon none other. His pictures are bought principally by artists, and when not by them by their immediate *entourage*. So it was before with Courbet, Millet, and Corot; and so all artists and connoisseurs believe it will be with Degas. Within the last few years his prices have gone up fifty per cent.; ten years hence they will have gone up a hundred per cent., and that is as certain as that the sun will rise to-morrow. That any work of his will be sold for twenty thousand pounds is not probable; the downcast eye full of bashful sentiment so popular with the uneducated does not exist in Degas; but it is certain that young artists of to-day value his work far higher than Millet's. He is, in truth, their god, and his influence is visible in a great deal of the work here and in France that strives to be most modern. But it must be admitted that the influence is a pernicious one. Some have calumniated Degas' art flagrantly and abominably, dragging his genius through every gutter, over every dunghill of low commonplace; others have tried to assimilate it honourably and reverentially, but without much success. True genius has no inheritors. Tennyson's parable of the gardener who once owned a unique flower, the like of which did not exist upon earth, until the wind carried the seeds far and wide, does not hold good in the instance of Degas. The winds, it is true, have carried the seeds into other gardens, but none have flourished except in native soil, and the best result the thieves have obtained is a scanty hybrid blossom, devoid alike of scent and hue.

The Critic as Artist

OSCAR WILDE

[FROM *Intentions*]

1891

Ernest. But what are the two supreme and highest arts?
Gilbert. Life and Literature, life and the perfect expression of life. The principles of the former, as laid down by the Greeks, we may not realize in an age so marred by false ideals as our own. The principles of the latter, as they laid them down, are, in many cases, so subtle that we can hardly understand them. Recognizing that the most perfect art is that which most fully mirrors man in all his infinite variety, they

From pages 111-211.

elaborated the criticism of language, considered in the light of the mere material of that art, to a point to which we, with our accentual system of reasonable or emotional emphasis, can barely if at all attain; studying, for instance, the metrical movements of a prose as scientifically as a modern musician studies harmony and counterpoint, and, I need hardly say, with much keener æsthetic instinct. In this they were right, as they were right in all things. Since the introduction of printing, and the fatal development of the habit of reading amongst the middle and lower classes of this country, there has been a tendency in literature to appeal more and more to the eye, and less and less to the ear which is really the sense which, from the standpoint of pure art, it should seek to please, and by whose canons of pleasure it should abide always. Even the work of Mr. Pater, who is, on the whole, the most perfect master of English prose now creating amongst us, is often far more like a piece of mosaic than a passage in music, and seems, here and there, to lack the true rhythmical life of words and the fine freedom and richness of effect that such rhythmical life produces. We, in fact, have made writing a definite mode of composition, and have treated it as a form of elaborate design. The Greeks, upon the other hand, regarded writing simply as a method of chronicling. Their test was always the spoken word in its musical and metrical relations. The voice was the medium, and the ear the critic. . . . Yes: writing has done much harm to writers. We must return to the voice. That must be our test, and perhaps then we shall be able to appreciate some of the subtleties of Greek art-criticism. . . .

Ernest. . . . I am quite ready to admit that I was wrong in what I said about the Greeks. They were, as you have pointed out, a nation of art-critics. I acknowledge it, and I feel a little sorry for them. For the creative faculty is higher than the critical. There is really no comparison between them.

Gilbert. The antithesis between them is entirely arbitrary. Without the critical faculty, there is no artistic creation at all, worthy of the name. You spoke a little while ago of that fine spirit of choice and delicate instinct of selection by which the artist realizes life for us, and gives to it a momentary perfection. Well, that spirit of choice, that subtle tact of omission, is really the critical faculty in one of its most characteristic moods, and no one who does not possess this critical faculty can create anything at all in art. Arnold's definition of literature as a criticism of life, was not very felicitous in form, but it showed how keenly he recognized the importance of the critical element in all creative work.

Ernest. I should have said that great artists worked unconsciously, that they were "wiser than they knew," as, I think, Emerson remarks somewhere.

Gilbert. It is really not so, Ernest. All fine imaginative work is self-conscious and deliberate. No poet sings because he must sing. At least, no great poet does. A great poet sings because he chooses to sing. It is so now, and it has always been so. We are sometimes apt to think that the voices that sounded at the dawn of poetry were simpler, fresher, and more natural than ours, and that the world which the early poets looked at, and through which they walked, had a kind of poetical quality of its own, and almost without changing could pass into song. . . . Our historical sense is at fault. Every century that produces poetry is, so far, an artificial century, and the work that seems to us to be the most natural and simple product of its time is always the result of the most self-conscious effort. Believe me, Ernest, there is no fine art without self-consciousness, and self-consciousness and the critical spirit are one. . . .

But, surely, Criticism is itself an art. And just as artistic creation implies the working of the critical faculty, and, indeed, without it cannot be said to exist at all, so Criticism is really creative in the highest sense of the word. Criticism is, in fact, both creative and independent.

Ernest. Independent?

Gilbert. Yes; independent. Criticism is no more to be judged by any low standard of imitation or resemblance than is the work of poet or sculptor. The critic occupies the same relation to the work of art that he criticises as the artist does to the visible world of form and colour, or the unseen world of passion and of thought. He does not even require for the perfection of his art the finest materials. Anything will serve his purpose. . . . To an artist so creative as the critic, what does subject-matter signify? No more and no less than it does to the novelist and the painter. Like them, he can find his motives everywhere. Treatment is the test. There is nothing that has not in it suggestion or challenge. . . . Nay, more, I would say that the highest Criticism, being the purest form of personal impression, is in its way more creative than creation, as it has least reference to any standard external to itself, and is, in fact, its own reason for existing, and, as the Greeks would put it, in itself, and to itself, an end. Certainly, it is never trammelled by any shackles of verisimilitude. No ignoble considerations of probability, that cowardly concession to the tedious repetitions of domestic or public life, affect it ever. One may appeal from fiction unto fact. But from the soul there is no appeal.

Ernest. From the soul?

Gilbert. Yes, from the soul. That is what the highest criticism really is, the record of one's own soul. It is more fascinating than history, as it is concerned simply with oneself. It is more delightful than philosophy, as its subject is concrete and not abstract, real and not vague. It is the only civilized form of autobiography, as it deals not with the events, but with the thoughts of one's life; not with life's physical accidents of deed or circumstance, but with the spiritual moods and imaginative passions of the mind. I am always amused by the silly vanity of those writers and artists of our day who seem to imagine that the primary function of the critic is to chatter about their second-rate work. The best that one can say of most modern creative art is that it is just a little less vulgar than reality, and so the critic, with his fine sense of distinction and sure instinct of delicate refinement, will prefer to look into the silver mirror or through the woven veil, and will turn his eyes away from the chaos and clamour of actual existence, though the mirror be tarnished and the veil be torn. His sole aim is to chronicle his own impressions. It is for him that pictures are painted, books written, and marble hewn into form. . . . For the highest Criticism deals with art not as expressive but as impressive purely.

Ernest. But is that really so?

Gilbert. Of course it is. Who cares whether Mr. Ruskin's views on Turner are sound or not? What does it matter? That mighty and majestic prose of his, so fervid and so fiery-coloured in its noble eloquence, so rich in its elaborate symphonic music, so sure and certain, at its best, in subtle choice of word and epithet, is at least as great a work of art as any of those wonderful sunsets that bleach or rot on their corrupted canvasses in England's Gallery; greater indeed, one is apt to think at times, not merely because its equal beauty is more enduring, but on account of the fuller variety of its appeal, soul speaking to soul in those long-cadenced lines, not through form and colour alone, though through these, indeed, completely and without loss, but with intellectual and emotional utterance, with lofty passion and with loftier thought, with imaginative insight, and with poetic aim; greater, I always think, even as Literature is the greater art. Who, again, cares whether Mr. Pater has put into the portrait of Monna Lisa something that Lionardo never dreamed of? . . .

Ernest. The highest Criticism, then, is more creative than creation, and the primary aim of the critic is to see the object as in itself it really is not; that is your theory, I believe?

Gilbert. Yes, that is my theory. To the critic the work of art is simply a suggestion for a new work of his own, that need not necessarily bear any obvious resemblance to the thing it criticises. The one characteristic of a beautiful form is that one can put into it whatever one wishes, and see in it whatever one chooses to see; and the Beauty, that gives to creation its universal and æsthetic element, makes the critic a creator in his turn, and whispers of a thousand different things which were not present in the mind of him who carved the statue or painted the panel or graved the gem.

It is sometimes said by those who understand neither the nature of the highest Criticism nor the charm of the highest Art, that the pictures that the critic loves most to write about are those that belong to the anecdotage of painting, and that deal with scenes taken out of literature or history. But this is not so. Indeed, pictures of this kind are far too intelligible. As a class, they rank with illustrations, and even considered from this point of view are failures, as they do not stir the imagination, but set definite bounds to it. . . . Most of our elderly English painters spend their wicked and wasted lives in poaching upon the domain of the poets, marring their motives by clumsy treatment, and striving to render, by visible form or colour, the marvel of what is invisible, the splendour of what is not seen. Their pictures are, as a natural conse-quence, insufferably tedious. They have degraded the visible arts into the obvious arts, and the one thing not worth looking at is the obvious. . . .

Ernest. The critic, then, considered as the interpreter, will give no less than he receives, and lend as much as he borrows?

Gilbert. He will be always showing us the work of art in some new relation to our age. He will always be reminding us that great works of art are living things—are, in fact, the only things that live. So much, indeed, will he feel this, that I am certain that, as civilization progresses and we become more highly organized, the elect spirits of each age, the critical and cultured spirits, will grow less and less interested in actual life, and *will seek to gain their impressions almost entirely from what Art has touched.* For Life is terribly deficient in form. Its catastrophes happen in the wrong way and to the wrong people. There is a grotesque horror about its comedies, and its tragedies seem to culminate in farce. One is always wounded when one approaches it. Things last either too long, or not long enough.

Ernest. Poor life! Poor human life! Are you not even touched by the tears that the Roman poet tells us are part of its essence?

Gilbert. Too quickly touched by them, I fear. For when one looks back upon the life that was so vivid in its emotional intensity, and filled with such fervent moments of ecstasy or of joy, it all seems to be a dream and an illusion. What are the unreal things, but the passions that once burned one like fire? What are the incredible things, but the things that one has faithfully believed? What are the improbable things? The things that one has done oneself. No, Ernest; life cheats us with shadows, like a puppet-master. We ask it for pleasure. It gives it to us, with bitterness and disappointment in its train. We come across some noble grief that we think will lend the purple dignity of tragedy to our days, but it passes away from us, and things less noble take its place, and on some grey windy dawn, or odorous eve of silence and of silver, we find ourselves looking with callous wonder, or dull heart of stone, at the tress of gold-flecked hair that we had once so wildly worshipped and so madly kissed.

Ernest. Life then is a failure?

Gilbert. From the artistic point of view, certainly. And the chief thing that makes life a failure from this artistic point of view is the thing that lends to life its sordid security, the fact that one can never repeat exactly the same emotion. How different it is in the world of Art! On a shelf of the bookcase behind you stands the *Divine Comedy,* and I know that, if I open it at a certain place, I shall be filled with a fierce hatred of some one who has never wronged me, or stirred by a great love for some one whom I shall never see. There is no mood or passion that Art cannot give us, and those of us who have discovered her secret can settle beforehand what our experiences are going to be. We can choose our day and select our hour. . . . Life! Life! Don't let us go to life for our fulfilment or our experience. It is a thing narrowed by circumstances, incoherent in its utterance, and without that fine correspondence of form and spirit which is the only thing that can satisfy the artistic and critical temperament. It makes us pay too high a price for its wares, and we purchase the meanest of its secrets at a cost that is monstrous and infinite.

Ernest. Must we go, then, to Art for everything?

Gilbert. For everything. Because Art does not hurt us. The tears that we shed at a play are a type of the exquisite sterile emotions that it is the function of Art to awaken. We weep, but we are not wounded. We grieve, but our grief is not bitter. In the actual life of man, sorrow, as Spinoza says somewhere, is a passage to a lesser perfection. But the sorrow with which Art fills us both purifies and initiates, if I may quote once more from the great art-critic of the Greeks. It is through Art, and through Art only, that we can realize our perfection; through Art, and through Art only, that we can shield ourselves from the sordid perils of actual existence. . . .

Ernest. Stop a moment. It seems to me that in everything that you have said there is something radically immoral.

Gilbert. All art is immoral.

Ernets. All art?

Gilbert. Yes. For emotion for the sake of emotion is the aim of art, and emotion for the sake of action is the aim of life, and of that practical organization of life that we call society. . . .

Ernest. We exist, then, to do nothing?

Gilbert. It is to do nothing that the elect exist. Action is limited and relative. Unlimited and absolute is the vision of him who sits at ease and watches, who walks in loneliness and dreams. But we who are born at the close of this wonderful age, are at once too cultured and too critical, too intellectually subtle and too curious of exquisite pleasures, to accept any speculations about life in exchange for life itself. . . . Metaphysics do not satisfy our temperaments, and religious ecstasy is out of date. . . . It is enough that our fathers believed. . . . No, Ernest, no. We cannot go back to the saint. There is far more to be learned from the sinner. We cannot go back to the philosopher, and the mystic leads us astray. Who, as Mr. Pater suggests somewhere, would exchange the curve of a single rose-leaf for that formless intangible Being which Plato rates so high? . . .

Ernest. Well, at least, the critic will be sincere.

Gilbert. A little sincerity is a dangerous thing, and a great deal of it is absolutely fatal. The true critic will, indeed, always be sincere in his devotion to the principle of beauty, but he will seek for beauty in every age and in each school, and will never suffer himself to be limited to any settled custom of thought, or stereotyped mode of looking at things. He will realize himself in many forms, and by a thousand different ways, and will ever be curious of new sensations and fresh points of view. Through constant change, and through constant change alone, he will find his true unity. He will not consent to be the slave of his own opinions. For what is mind but motion in the intellectual sphere? The essence of thought, as the essence of life, is growth. You must not be frightened by words, Ernest. What people call insincerity is simply a method by which we can multiply our personalities.

Ernest. I am afraid I have not been fortunate in my suggestions. . . .

Gilbert. Temperament is the primary requisite for the critic—a temperament exquisitely susceptible to beauty, and to the various impressions that beauty gives us. Under what conditions, and by what means, this temperament is engendered in race or individual, we will not discuss at present. It is sufficient to note that it exists, and that there is in us a beauty-sense, separate from the other senses and above them, separate from the reason and of nobler import, separate from the soul and of equal value—a sense that leads some to create, and others, the finer spirits as I think, to contemplate merely. But to be purified and made perfect, this sense requires some form of exquisite environment. Without this it starves, or is dulled. You remember that lovely passage in which Plato describes how a young Greek should be educated, and with what insistence he dwells upon the importance of surroundings, telling us how the lad is to be brought up in the midst of fair sights and sounds, so that the beauty of material things may prepare his soul for the reception of the beauty that is spiritual. . . . I need hardly say, Ernest, how far we in England have fallen short of this ideal, and I can imagine the smile that would illuminate the glossy face of the Philistine if one ventured to suggest to him that the true aim of education was the love of beauty, and that the methods by which education should work were the development of temperament, the cultivation of taste, and the creation of the critical spirit.

Yet, even for us, there is left some loveliness of environment..... All over England there is a Renaissance of the decorative Arts. Ugliness has had its day. Even in the houses of the rich there is taste, and the houses of those who are not rich have been made gracious and comely and sweet to live in. . . . By its deliberate rejection of Nature as the ideal of beauty, as well as of the imitative method of the ordinary painter, decorative art not merely prepares the soul for the reception of true imaginative work, but develops in it that sense of form which is the basis of creative no less than of critical achievement. For the real artist is he who proceeds, not from feeling to form, but from form to thought and passion. He does not first conceive an idea, and then say to himself, "I will put my idea into a complex metre of fourteen lines," but, realizing the beauty of the sonnet-scheme, he conceives certain modes of music and methods of rhyme, and the mere form suggests what is to fill it and make it intellectually and emotionally complete. From time to time the world cries out against some charming artistic poet, because, to use its hackneyed and silly phrase, he has "nothing to say." But if he had something to say, he would probably say it, and the result would be tedious. It is just because he has no new message, that he can do beautiful work. He gains his inspiration from form, and from form purely, as an artist should. A real passion would ruin him. Whatever actually occurs is spoiled for art. All bad poetry springs from genuine feeling. To be natural is to be obvious, and to be obvious is to be inartistic. . . . It is always with the best intentions that the worst work is done. . . .

Ernest. But what about technique? Surely each art has its separate technique?

Gilbert. Certainly: each art has its grammar and its materials. There is no mystery about either, and the incompetent can always be correct. But, while the laws upon which Art rests may be fixed and certain, to find their true realization they must be touched by the imagination into such beauty that they will seem an exception, each one of them. Technique is really personality. That is the reason why the artist cannot teach it, why the pupil cannot learn it, and why the æsthetic critic can understand it. To the great poet, there is only one method of music—his own. To the great painter, there is only one manner of painting—that which he himself employs. The æsthetic critic, and the æsthetic critic alone, can appreciate all forms and modes. It is to him that Art makes her appeal. . . . It is to criticism that the future belongs. The subject-matter at the disposal of creation becomes every day more limited in extent and variety. . . .

He who would stir us now by fiction must either give us an entirely new background, or reveal to us the soul of man in its innermost workings. The first is for the moment being done for us by Mr. Rudyard Kipling. As one turns over the pages of his *Plain Tales from the Hills,* one feels as if one were seated under a palm-tree reading life by superb flashes of vulgarity. The bright colours of the bazaars dazzle one's eyes. The jaded, second-rate Anglo-Indians are in exquisite incongruity with their surroundings. The mere lack of style in the story-teller gives an odd journalistic realism to what he tells us. From the point of view of literature Mr. Kipling is a genius who drops his aspirates. From the point of view of life, he is a reporter who knows vulgarity better than any one has ever known it. Dickens knew its clothes and its comedy. Mr. Kipling knows its essence and its seriousness. He is our first authority on the second-rate, and has seen marvellous things through key-holes, and his backgrounds are real works of art. As for the second condition, we have had Browning, and Meredith is with us. But there is still much to be done in the sphere of introspection. . . . The English mind is always in a rage. The intellect of the race is wasted in the sordid and stupid quarrels of second-rate politicians or third-rate theologians. It was reserved for a man of science to show us the supreme example of that "sweet reasonableness" of which Arnold spoke so wisely, and, alas! to so little effect. The author of the *Origin of Species* had, at any rate, the philosophic temper. . . . We are dominated by the fanatic, whose worst vice is his sincerity. Anything approaching to the free play of the mind is practically unknown amongst us. People cry out against the sinner, yet it is not the sinful, but the stupid, who are our shame. There is no sin except stupidity.

Ernest. Ah! what an antinomian you are!

Gilbert. The artistic critic, like the mystic, is an antinomian always. To be good, according to the vulgar standard of goodness, is obviously quite easy. It merely requires a certain amount of sordid terror, a certain lack of imaginative thought, and a certain low passion for middle-class respectability. Æsthetics are higher than ethics. They belong to a more spiritual sphere. To discern the beauty of a thing is the finest point to which we can arrive. Even a colour-sense is more important, in the development of the individual, than a sense of right and wrong. Æsthetics, in fact, are to Ethics in the sphere of conscious civilization, what, in the sphere of the external world, sexual is to natural selection. Ethics, like natural selection, make existence possible. Æsthetics, like sexual selection, make life lovely and wonderful, fill it with new forms, and give it progress, and variety and change. And when we reach the true culture that is our aim, we attain to that perfection of which the saints have dreamed, the perfection of those to whom sin is impossible, not because they make the renunciations of the ascetic, but because they can do everything they wish without hurt to the soul, and can wish for nothing that can do the soul harm, the soul being an entity so divine that it is able to transform into elements of a richer experience, or a finer susceptibility, or a newer mode of thought, acts or passions that with the common would be commonplace, or with the uneducated ignoble, or with the shameful vile. Is this dangerous? Yes; it is dangerous— all ideas, as I told you, are so. But the night wearies, and the light flickers in the lamp. . . .